IN LOVE AND DEATH

SPELLSTER AND THE HOUND — BOOK 2 —

ALDREA ALIEN

Thardrandian Publications

Cover design by MarosarArt
Map Design by renflowergrapx

ISBN: 978-1991157126
First Edition: March 2025

10 9 8 7 6 5 4 3 2 1

Dedicated to my elderly cats, 18-year-old Charlie & 15-year-old FizzyWhip, and our 12-year-old family dog, Jesse. All of whom passed across the rainbow bridge during the final year of writing this book.

You will be forever missed.

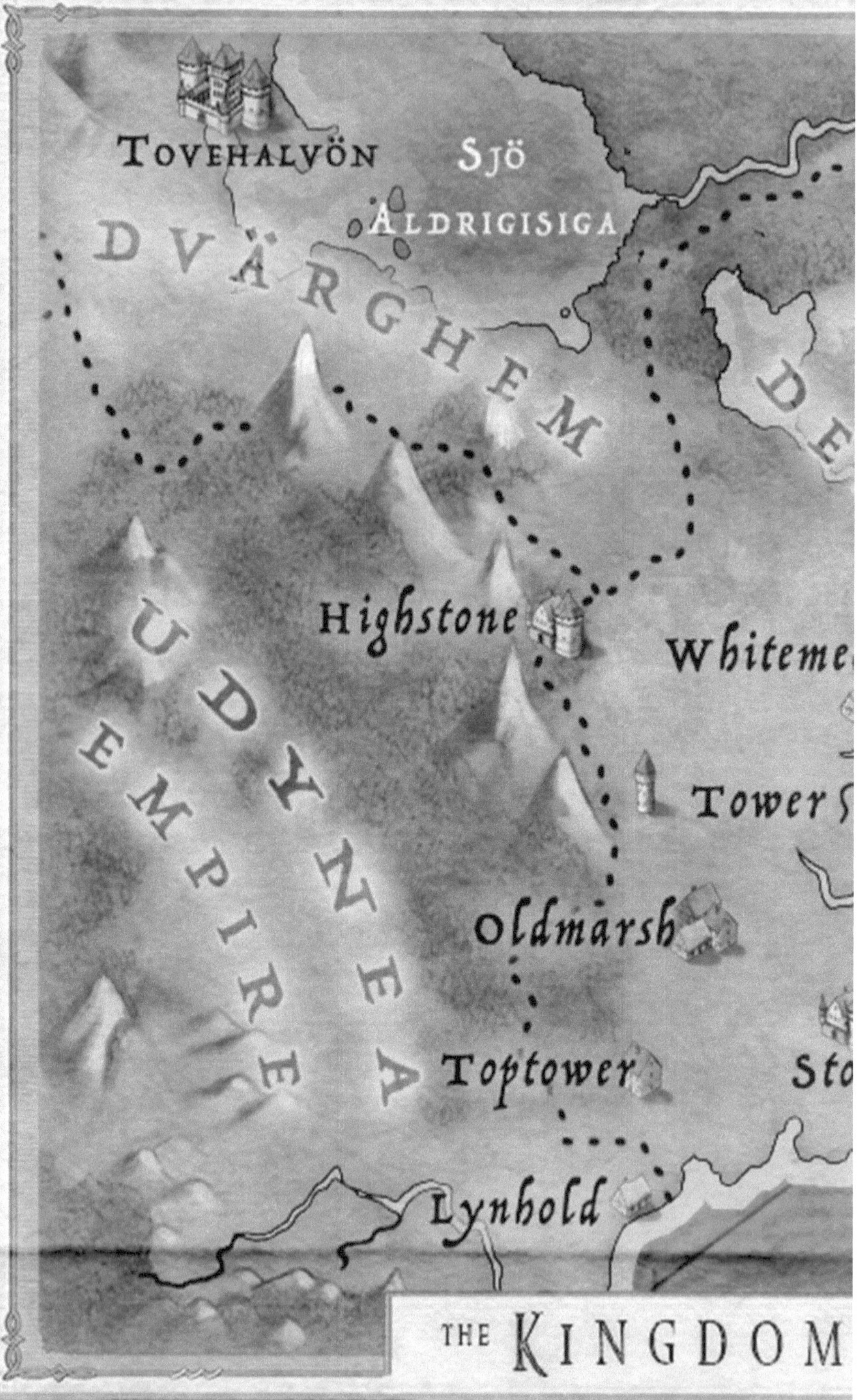

TOVEHALVÖN
SJÖ
ALDRIGISIGA
DVÄRGHEM
DE
Highstone
Whiteme
UDYNEA
EMPIRE
Tower
Oldmarsh
Toptower
Sto
Lynhold
THE KINGDOM

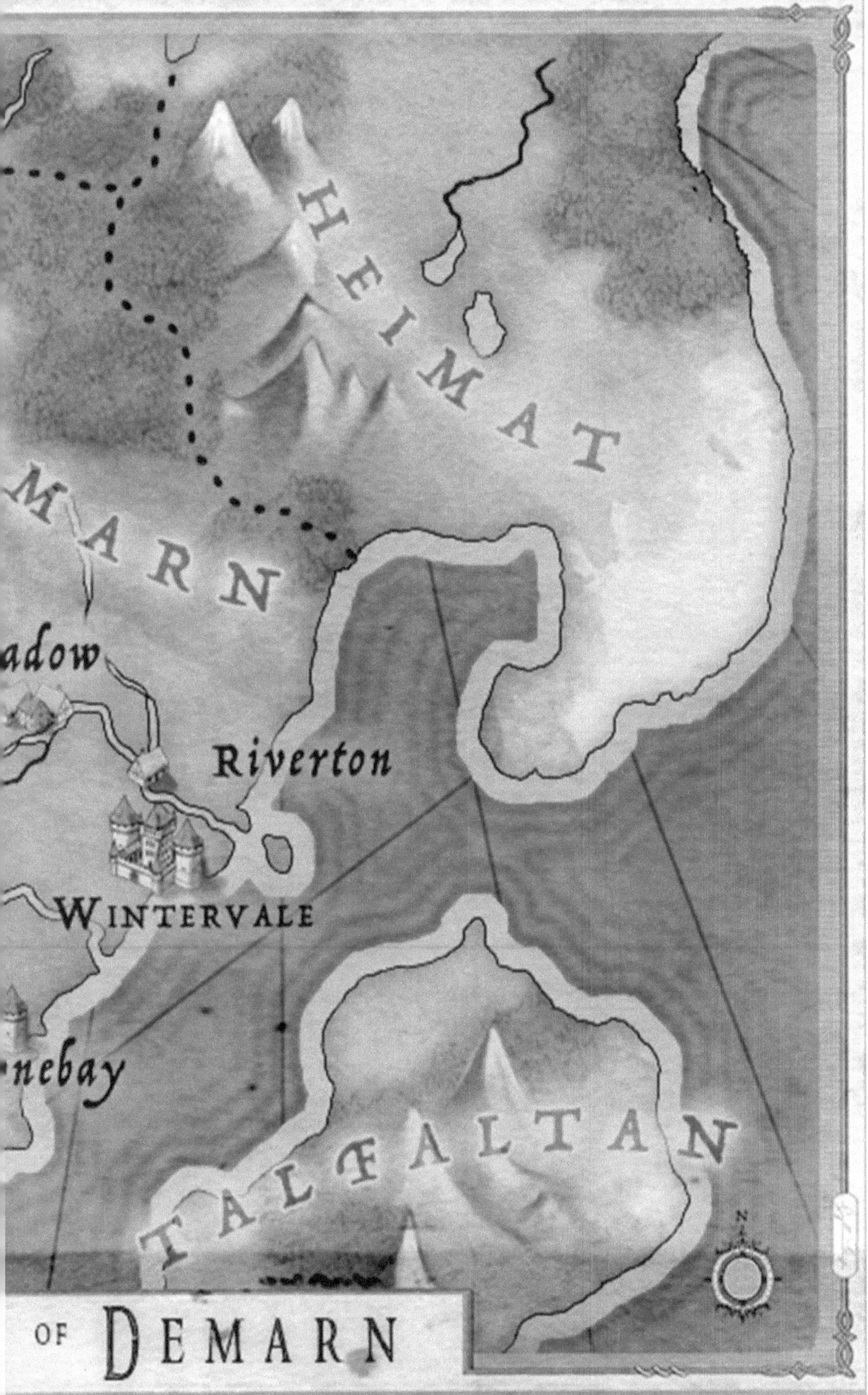

HEIMAT
MARN
adow
Riverton
WINTERVALE
nebay
TALFÆALTAN
OF DEMARN
N

PROLOGUE

The campsite was quiet, save for the odd rustle beneath the bushes and the faint coo of a distant owl. It wasn't enough to ease Tracker's mind. The enemy was out there, somewhere. Ahead of them, certainly, but they had no reliable way of knowing precisely how far.

It was for that very reason their group had abandoned the road. They hadn't gone too deep into the wilderness, but Talfaltaners were seafaring folk. Any foray they made into the forest would be noisy. Vastly more so than having them creeping up on their group camping on the roadside.

Content that the area was safe for the moment, Tracker headed back to the middle of camp. He would recheck the perimeter closer to the end of his time on watch, but he doubted the act would be more than one of formality before he handed the task over to the next in the roster.

He frowned out into the heavy darkness lurking beneath the trees. Perhaps he should let the spellster sleep on. Being able to fully relax during the time others guarded their camp was more of a luxury for himself, whereas Dylan had spent a great deal of energy the morning gone not only setting the spellster tower ablaze, but also in healing a stab wound that should've killed him.

The man rarely roused unless someone actually woke him. Far different to Tracker's own lightly sleeping state, brought on by years of travelling with only his horse for company.

Lullaby. A twinge of guilt tightened his chest, as it had done from the moment he had left the injured warhorse behind.

He had travelled far from Toptower since discovering Dylan in that border town. Every day thereafter had taken him further still from any chance of reuniting with his horse. They hadn't been separated this long before. Lullaby had to think himself abandoned by now. *I will find a way.* He just had to reach Whitemeadow first, to find a way to swallow the days stretching between him and that goal.

If we had a way to shorten the journey. That wasn't possible. The standard trip on horseback would see them taking a week to reach the city, but their circumstance was far from typical in any sense of the word. He was on foot with a distressed spellster in tow, a belligerent mercenary in the group, as well as potentially greater hostiles waiting ahead, and the possibility of other hounds being lured by the amount of magic Dylan used to set the spellster tower alight.

He took a steadying breath. Half of their concerns he had no control over. If his fellow hounds discovered them, then he would deal with it. Likewise, if they stumbled upon any flagging Talfaltaners, their only option would be to kill them. And whilst he could lament the absence of his horse for days, it wouldn't summon Lullaby all the way from Toptower.

They might've been able to keep the journey to Whitemeadow to a dozen days, providing the roads remained clear and everyone didn't dawdle, but that also wasn't feasible. As it was, the scent of approaching rain hung thickly in the air. Bad weather alone would slow them.

As for the hostile force they travelled with...

His thoughts swung to Authril. She had conversed with the others as though her suggestion to put Dylan down like a rabid beast was in the distant past rather than a mere day ago. Even Marin's cool responses didn't seem to faze her.

Informing Dylan that she had requested Tracker end the man because they couldn't leash him would definitely need to happen. *Not yet.* In truth, Tracker had hoped to wait until Whitemeadow, where they could also take a boat to distance themselves from Authril's toxic influence and, maybe, even convince the man that leaving Demarn entirely was the right thing. But Marin was right. Sooner would ensure whatever sway the warrior had over Dylan was shattered.

Keeping an eye on her was all he could do for now. Fortunately, Katarina had at least removed the woman from Dylan's side when it came to their sleeping arrangements. Tracker would've felt better if he had managed to convince the spellster to share his tent for the journey, but the suggestion had been met with such alarm from Dylan that he hadn't pushed the issue any further.

He slipped through the undergrowth edging the copse they had stumbled across in the fading daylight, halting as he spied another figure outside of the tents. It appeared he wasn't the only one still awake at this hour.

They sat by the fire, slowly poking the embers and feeding twigs into the meagre flames that stirred up.

"You should be asleep."

Their head turned Tracker's way. Dark eyes regarded him from a pale face framed by black, unkempt hair. The thrum of magic vibrated the air around him. Little more than formless whispers, there in a breath, then gone.

"Tried," Dylan murmured. "Can't."

Tracker nodded solemnly. The man had been through a lot long before returning to find his home had become the site of a massacre. He would've been worried about any spellster who didn't struggle to sleep so soon after witnessing such an aftermath. That Dylan was clearly a man who longed to help people, and blamed himself when he couldn't, only made it worse.

He settled next to the man, casually propping his arms on his upraised knees. He was certain the night would remain quiet, but it didn't hurt to keep a weapon or two close at hand. "Blanket or blade?"

Dylan's brow furrowed. "What?"

"It is a saying amongst the hounds. To put it simply, is your preference to be comforted or do you seek for me to provide a solution?" The latter often came via violent means, but he needn't be so literal when it came to what plagued the spellster.

The lines of confusion deepened upon the man's face. "I don't see how either one could help me. The only thing that really stopped my nightmares was when we..." His voice trailed off as he ducked his head, all expression vanishing behind a curtain of dark hair. "You know," he mumbled.

"Had sex?"

Dylan's head jerked towards the tent housing the three women. The gossamer sheen of a shield cloaked the man for an instant before fading back into his body.

Tracker doubted any one of the trio was awake at this hour, much less listening to their conversation. Marin had finished her portion of the watch some time ago and the hedgewitch had been before her. Whereas Authril would be getting what sleep she could until her turn near the end of the night.

"You still fear they will find out, yes?" Although Dylan hadn't voiced it, the man had expressed a clear discomfort towards the idea of others knowing about the night they shared in the tower.

Dylan didn't answer. His attention remained on the tent like a rabbit frozen in the middle of a clearing.

Tracker didn't understand the panic widening the spellster's eyes. The others had to know the man was an actively sexual being. Or maybe they didn't hear him with the warrior as clearly as Tracker. But the woman wasn't shy about making it known and Dylan was nowhere near as jittery when it came to *her* advances.

Was the man embarrassed to have engaged in such an act? He recalled Dylan admitting the tower *did* explain sex to them—a topic they clearly couldn't ignore when they'd all manner of people within their walls—whilst the overseers also stressed that it was discouraged. Surely, the tower had also taught them that any feelings they had regarding their attraction, or lack of, to another was a perfectly normal thing to occur.

The only logical conclusion Tracker could make of the truth behind the man's panic was linked to his own hound status. Whereas Authril was a mere mercenary, no matter how much she seemed to enjoy playing the role of Dylan's warden.

Looking at it from that point of view, he could admit that not wanting to divulge lying with a hound was understandable. They'd been used as bogeymen throughout the tower for far longer than either of them had been alive, a fact which often worked against their usual task of escorting newfound spellsters just as much as it aided in hunting down the rogue ones.

When it came down to it, Tracker supposed he would also baulk at confessing to anyone about being pleasured by the monsters of his nightmares.

Only when no one emerged from the tent did Dylan finally relax and seem to remember Tracker sat at his side. "Sorry. My nerves are a little..." He trailed off, grinning sheepishly as he rocked his hand.

"A *little* unsteady is quite the understatement, yes?" He shuffled closer, keeping his voice low and light. "I do not believe their opinion of you would change if they knew we had been intimate."

"Authril's would. She doesn't like how close you've been prior to... *then*, and you didn't exactly endear yourself to her at *The Gilded Lily*."

Tracker grunted. The feeling was very much mutual. Not that her abrasive manner wasn't anything he hadn't encountered before, especially amongst those who had seen battle, but her treatment of Dylan was inexcusable. "And the thought of her ill judgement bothers you." No matter how he tried to keep his true feelings contained, they hissed alongside the words.

By the way Dylan's brow creased with concerned bewilderment, the man had caught the thread of hostility in Tracker's voice.

Gritting his teeth, he breathed slowly until the urge to shed the woman's blood had waned. "Why? You are not beholden to her. To anyone." The warrior had outright said she didn't consider Dylan as a lover, that she harboured some twisted logic where having sex with the spellster supposedly kept him under her control.

And worse, it seemed to work. Not for the reason she believed, but because of Dylan's nature, that deep-rooted need to please those the man considered close to him.

Seeing her exploitation bearing fruit had him itching for his knives.

"I know," Dylan said. "But she has the same temper as... as—" The man stuttered into silence, staring into the fire. He stayed there for a time, his breathing growing increasingly laboured. The swell of his magic wavered with the same intensity, like a droplet not quite caught by the tide. "What I meant to say is she reminds me of..." His voice dissolved into a crackling sob.

Tracker laid a hand on Dylan's back, barely making contact at first, then rubbing in gentle circles as the touch wasn't rejected. Unbidden whispers of reassurance slipped between his lips. How much the man heard over his sobs was debatable, but it definitely helped still the erratic flares of magic.

Eventually, there was no sound save for the occasional sniff from the spellster and the scrape of Tracker's hand across the man's robe.

"This person she reminds you of," Tracker said, mindful of how Dylan's back stiffened beneath his fingertips. "You were close, yes?"

Dylan nodded. "Since we were children. A lot of us were. We..." His voice cracked. He scrubbed at his face with his sleeve. "Sorry, I—"

"No." Tracker shuffled on the spot to fully face the man. "Do not apologise for your grief." It hadn't even been a full day since they had left the tower. "No one expects you to put aside your mourning." For someone who had lost his home only yesterday, the man was holding himself together remarkably well.

"Authril does. She says I got over the army attack quickly enough, that this shouldn't be any different." He bowed his head, picking at the ragged ends of his robe. "That I'm a liability if I can't."

Heat suffused Tracker's body, his every muscle tightening with the call to attack. A liability? *Dylan?* He glared at the tent harbouring the woman in question. Authril hadn't uttered much in his presence, certainly not something so callous. A part of him wished she had, if only to give him cause to retaliate in the moment.

"You know what the worst thing is?" Dylan asked, continuing before Tracker could compose himself enough to give anything close to a reply. "She's right. I hadn't seen battle, not even a skirmish, before that ambush and look how well that went." He flung his arm in a southerly direction, as though the decimated grounds of the army encampment sat mere hours away, instead of weeks. "How am I supposed to help, to fight, anyone if I fall apart after every battle?"

"That is not true." They hadn't encountered much resistance during their journey to the tower, a few bandits that had underestimated their prey. Nothing serious. Dylan had handled each altercation well, despite using a meagre amount of his power. "Even if it was, the world needs more than warriors."

Dylan gave a derisive snort. "I was never a warrior. None of us were. I don't know why they trained us to think we could be when the army never saw us as anything more than weapons."

Tracker recalled similar words from his fellow hound, Fetcher. He wished he had believed her sooner. Wished there'd been something either of them could have done without their mistress knowing.

"And I was terrible at that, too." The spellster laughed, the sound carrying only heartache. "Weapons aren't supposed to feel, they're not meant to care that the soldier fighting alongside them fell trying to keep them alive." The campfire flared, spitting and sparking as though pig fat dripped onto the embers. "You don't see a sword getting weepy over the dead."

They are still meant to be cared for, though. Whether the weapon be of steel or magic, the army did a terrible job of looking after either. Nor did he believe the outcome would have changed.

"The perimeter is due to be checked again." Tracker unhurriedly got to his feet. He looked around the camp, marking the lack of change, before offering the spellster his hand. "Come, walk with me."

Dylan didn't move. Nor did he utter a sound. He just stared into the flames that grew bluer with heat.

"If anything, the cool air will aid in calming your feverish mind."

Slowly, the man's head tilted up at him. Those dark eyes reflected the firelight so perfectly that they looked molten. "You don't need me to help with checking anything."

"No," he agreed. "But I enjoy the company."

Dylan's gaze flicked towards the tents. He stood, slowly, as though his bones had forgotten how to move, a mirthless smile thinning his lips. "You're trying to get me away from them. In case I do something stupid."

"Not at all." He didn't believe the man would willingly bring any harm to others, but the state of his mind was tenuous and Tracker had come across a lot of accidental tragedies caused by such a combination of strong magic and high emotions. "I am simply trying to get you out of your own head." Between their impromptu intimacy last night, setting fire to the tower and their travelling, the man hadn't been given much space to calm his mind.

Linking their arms, Tracker casually guided Dylan away from the fire, noting how the flames shifted from a translucent blue to their original brassy hue the moment the man's full attention turned elsewhere.

They walked beneath the trees, Dylan wordlessly uncoupling their arms along the way. The spellster's head tipped back, his focus either on the canopy of leaves or the stars beyond, clearly having no desire to speak further.

As much as Tracker knew that talking would help the man vent some of his frustrations and guilt, he didn't want to push. Everything was still raw. He would, should it be required, if only to keep Dylan from suppressing his grief until he exploded.

The forest remained no less quiet than it had been during his last check. Cool air ghosted along his temples, absent of the smoke that had permeated much of their travels. The suggestion of it still clung to his clothes. Burning wood and parchment, overlaid by his jerkin's natural leather smell and the musk of a day's travel.

The owl that had made so much noise earlier had vanished. Tracker longed for its return, for any sound that would break up the slow crunch of their boots or the scrabbling of little feet scampering about the undergrowth at their passage.

He hoped the silence gave the spellster some measure of peace. There wasn't much else he could offer out here that didn't include distracting him with sex, and Dylan had already given his opinion on that option.

Eventually, Dylan exhaled in one drawn-out breath. The rigidity of his form relaxed, lowering his shoulders and returning the litheness to his stride. "I know it's your duty to look after my well-being, but you don't need to be so thorough. I can handle myself well enough."

He didn't doubt the spellster was less emotional under normal circumstances. That didn't mean Tracker was less inclined to offer his support. And not for the reason the man thought. "Duty," he mused aloud. If he was to follow hound law to the letter, the only state Dylan's head would be in was separate from his body. "Truthfully, I had considered us as travelling companions. Or maybe friends?"

"Friends?" Dylan echoed, finally lowering his face from the canopy to regard Tracker.

"Did you not say you were close to several people? I assumed that means you were allowed such relationships in the tower, yes?" They didn't foster the idea amongst the hounds, especially when it came to the uninitiated pups, but such bonds were inevitable.

The man nodded. He bit his lip, his chin wobbling.

"I apologise," Tracker murmured, bowing his head. He shouldn't have mentioned the tower. "It was not my intention to further upset you."

"I know." The admission was thick with unshed tears. He sniffed loudly, scrubbing at his face. "I can't stop thinking about it. How trapped everyone was. How terrified their last moments would have been. And I couldn't even find them. Not a damn trace!" Magic flickered briefly around the man. A gust of wind Tracker couldn't feel rustled the surrounding bushes, scattering the wildlife that hadn't already scurried off at their passing.

"Would it have helped if you had?"

"Yes," Dylan snapped. "No? I don't know." He whirled on his heel. The extra momentum stirred up another gust that neatly sliced a sapling in half. The man jumped back, his shield flickering to life. He eyed the damage as though never having witnessed his magic lash out unheeded before. "I-I didn't mean to—"

"Steady." Tracker reached towards the man's shoulder, stopping before his hand touched the barrier. He could pass through it easily enough, but the last thing Dylan needed was more pain.

It was for that reason he hadn't voiced any further speculations about the possibility of some having escaped. Having Dylan cling to the hope of his friends' surviving without solid evidence would be far crueller than letting the man mourn those deaths.

"I thought I knew my role in the world," Dylan confessed. "Thought I had survived the ambush because it was my fate to return home, but there's nothing left. No home. No friends. No life. So... why was I spared?"

Why? Tracker knew that question well. The memory of it lay cloaked in the gloom of the Pit, where a sallow flickering light danced upon broken and battered bodies. Even after all these years, he recalled how thickly the tang of human blood sat on his tongue. How the only sounds over his ragged breath were the moans of air escaping the dead, yet the stunned silence of the witnesses screamed the loudest, echoing in his mind for years after.

The knowledge that *he* should've been the one to die that day.

A surprising outcome. That was what their mistress had called his survival. Unexpected and problematic. She had him sent away. Officially, to be trained in seduction, but he knew it was to have little hopes like love and family literally screwed out of him.

He had learnt different lessons. Seduction, yes—difficult not to when it was a requirement to remain working in the brothel's upper tiers—but also compassion. They couldn't replace the family he had lost to Hunk's betrayal, but *The Gilded Lily* had offered a type of kinship. Without it, he wasn't certain he would've survived the first year.

And if he *had* died? What would it have altered? Which lives would've been saved or lost? The spellster protected by an entire mercenary company? The elven woman who had spent decades feeding on the nearby village? The countless young spellsters and would-be hounds he had aided in smuggling into Dvärghem?

And Dylan's fate?

He bumped the spellster's arm with a shoulder, hoping that gentle contact was enough to get the man's attention without startling him. "I am no priest, but if I remember my childhood teachings correctly, the gods do not control how our lives play out, they merely offer alternative paths. Everything else is our choice."

Dylan remained silent for some time. At first, Tracker thought he hadn't been heard, then the man spoke.

"My choices are responsible for my friends dying?"

"I did not say that. And this is the last time you will speak such a lie. No choice you could possibly make would have led to what happened. *That* blame lies squarely on another's shoulders." Who had made that decision was an answer Tracker didn't currently possess, but he was going to find out. And once he did, not a thing would stop him from dealing out the ultimate consequence. "As for why you were spared..." He inhaled, unthinkingly breathing in the scent of magic emanating from the man. The wisps of power might have died down, but that storm-cloud aroma remained a beacon, regardless. "I would say your strength played no small part there."

Dylan's face scrunched in confusion. "My strength? I could be the strongest spellster in the world and it wouldn't... I couldn't..." He ran a hand through his hair, further upsetting the already messy array. "I just feel..." His breath came out in one shuddering exhale. "I don't know what."

"Helpless? Hopeless?"

"Like no matter how hard I try, I'm utterly useless in keeping all the terrible things from happening."

Tracker laid a hand on Dylan's forearm. Even through the layers of his clothes, the man's shaking was palpable. "There was no way you could have predicted what happened. Not the ambush, not the army, not... any other outcome."

Dylan stared down at his hands. Unformed magic danced around his fingertips like a rolling fog. "I can't stop thinking I should've done more, should've *been* more, then maybe they'd be alive."

He drew the spellster into his arms, sensing the ghosts of pure magic crackle into something tangible as Dylan stiffened in his grasp, the flash briefer than a lightning strike.

With his ear pressed to the man's chest, he heard the spellster's heart thumping at a tempo that suggested Dylan had spent the day sprinting down the road rather than the steady pace they had taken through the forest. "I cannot tell you it will get better. That is not something anyone can judge for you. But I *am* here if you need me, in whatever capacity that may be." He didn't know if his presence alone would be enough to help, but he hoped so.

The man's heartbeat slowly calmed as Tracker talked. Dylan sagged into the embrace, his arms awkwardly wrapping around Tracker's shoulders, his cheek resting atop Tracker's head. Wetness seeped into his scalp. He ignored it and tightened his grip to match

Dylan's.

It was a while before the man unwound himself. He dried his face, giving a self-conscious little chuckle. "I really have to stop crying all over you."

"I do not mind."

Dylan ducked his head, the embarrassment behind his smile a little more familiar.

"But do me a favour and do not take our dear warrior's words to heart. She may try to bury it deep within, but she still grieves for her fallen company." Tracker had seen that look too many times to mistake the emotion behind it. "Until she acknowledges that pain, it will continue to fester. That you allow yourself to freely feel is likely what draws her scorn."

"I'll keep that in mind."

"Come." He gestured for the spellster to continue walking. "We have the rest of the perimeter to check."

"You mean this wasn't a ploy to get me alone and feel me up?" The light-hearted lilt in his voice and the grin he flashed—although wobbly on the edges, carried an echo of the playfulness he had displayed before reaching the tower—took the edge off the words.

Tracker answered the attempt at humour with a smile of his own. "Even if I somehow deemed the timing as appropriate, I would hardly need to bring you out here for such fun. I told you, I enjoy the company." He took up Dylan's hand, linking their fingers without a twitch of rejection. "But we have been gone a while. We should keep moving."

Their journey slipped back into silence, a lighter kind than when they'd begun. They circled the campsite until their path returned them to the tents. Nothing had changed beyond the fire having burnt itself out. That was to be expected.

Tracker's gaze drifted to his own tent. Given that he hadn't slept for more than a handful of hours beneath the canvas tonight, the time taken to pitch it seemed a waste. "I know you may not get any rest at all, but you should at least *attempt* sleep, yes? I will take your turn on watch tonight." Doing so wouldn't grant the man more than the scant two hours he would've spent alone out here, but there was nothing else to offer. Getting by on little sleep was practically a rite of passage for hounds.

He wouldn't bother with waking Authril, either. That way, he could keep an eye on both Dylan *and* the warrior. The last thing any of them needed was for the woman's callous words to incense the spellster.

Dylan made for his tent, pausing at the entrance. "Thank you. For letting me vent and..." One corner of his mouth lifted in a rueful smile. "It helped."

Tracker bowed his head in acknowledgement. "*Rest*, my dear man. It is a long way to Whitemeadow." By then, he would've found the words to sway Dylan into leaving Demarn.

It would be dangerous. He had known that from the moment he'd made his decision. It wouldn't be the first time he had helped spellsters escape Demarn, even if they'd been children.

Permitting a spellster to slip out of their grasp was against the hound creed. Getting caught helping one would see him put down. Dylan being an adult as well as the last known spellster alive only increased their chances of getting caught. Especially with the man still garbed in army attire.

Yet, he couldn't bring himself to stand by and let the alternative play out. After everything Dylan had been through—the violent unleashing that had left his throat scarred, the ambush on his scouting party and the decimation of the army, the destruction of his home and everyone he knew—ensuring the man didn't suffer further abuse had to be the right choice.

The *only* choice.

CHAPTER 1

The hearty scratching at his tent flap jolted Dylan from what his body had begrudgingly begun to accept was sleep. At first, he thought it was his turn to take over the night watch, but the gleam of light creeping through the tent was too much for a mere camp fire.

Morning had come.

He lay still, not sure if he'd the strength to haul himself out from beneath his cocoon of blankets. His gaze traversed the patchwork of leather stretched above him, following the outline of shadows created by the low sunlight shining through the trees.

Even though he had tried to follow Tracker's instructions, he didn't recall drifting off. He must have managed to at some point in order to be waking up. *How?* That was a mystery he wished he'd an answer to. Every time he had closed his eyes, images of the dead invaded the darkness. He had jerked out of that state so many times with his magic flickering around him, that he was surprised the tent still stood.

When it wasn't the horror of the tower, it was the hound. Those visions he hadn't minded as much, being less ghostly images and more a rehashing of the night they'd spent together. A night that had left him sleeping just as soundly as if he had never left home. Left him longing to have the man back in his arms, to bask in the companionable intimacy he hadn't really felt with Authril.

Surely, he didn't need the hound for *that*. Marin and Katarina were just as warm. They had sat with him easily enough, sympathetic where Authril had been dismissive. There'd been caution in their words, of course, but the softness came from a place of care rather than any fear of what he might do. Katarina had even tried to talk him through his grief as they pitched his tent last night.

None of them had been there to see him at his weakest, though. They hadn't been the ones to hold him without judgement as he bawled like a child fresh out of the nursery, hadn't made him feel safe enough to face his grief.

It had to be the unexpected tenderness behind the hound's touch that he craved so much. With all the conflicting emotions flooding his thoughts—the anger, the grief, the growing numbness—his mind had taken the ache of empathy and mistaken it for his attraction to the man.

Dylan hadn't realised he'd been missing that closeness until last night, when he had found himself lying alone, embraced only by his cold blankets.

It didn't help that the days he had slept alone throughout his life were minimal. In the tower, he had spent a large portion of his childhood sleeping in the dorm with a gaggle of other boys. After that, he'd gone a grand total of a few weeks before meeting the gangly, wary elven boy who had grown into his friend, Sulin.

Gods. He flung an arm over his face, unable to do more as fresh tears flowed. *I'm sorry, Su.* He should've been faster. Should've—

Should've what? Rushed to prevent a disaster he hadn't known about? The hound was right. There was no way any of them could've predicted what happened. It was a truth he unequivocally agreed with.

Knowing he'd been powerless to stop it did nothing to temper the guilt gnawing at his core.

"You arrogant prick!" Authril bellowed.

Dylan sat upright, his shield flickering for a brief moment. He stared warily at the tent entrance, waiting for the warrior to burst in and complain how his lack of movement was holding them back.

"What if you'd fallen asleep?" she continued to roar. "What if the people who attacked the tower were still near? We could've all died because of your arrogance."

Sluggishly, his mind realised he wasn't the target of her outrage.

He crept closer to the tent flap as the warrior raved on. Tracker had taken Dylan's watch to let him sleep, but he hadn't realised the hound would also choose to alleviate Authril of the duty, especially as they didn't seem to harbour any sort of camaraderie towards each other.

"We still live, yes?" Tracker said, his voice bordering on inaudible in comparison. "The camp is still in one piece?"

The tent entrance was shadowed by a person hunkered next to it. Definitely not either of the two elves. That left the hunter or the hedgewitch. He could think of no logical reason for either woman to be lingering there.

Dylan twitched a section of the flap to one side, crouching in the gap it gave him.

Marin's back faced him. The woman squatted with her hand on the hilt of her massive hunting knife as though expecting a fight.

Beyond her, the two elves stood in the centre of the camp. Authril glowered up at the man, her legs planted and her hand firmly grasping her sheathed sword. The hound's stance was far calmer, although no less ready to retaliate.

"You are not the leader here," Authril grated. "*I* am."

"If I may," Katarina interjected from her place seated by the fire. She hesitated as both elves turned their attention to her. "There might not be a tower, but that surely can't be enough to change how a King's Hound has jurisdiction over any spellster caught outside its walls?"

"That's only relevant when it involves those not in the army," Authril replied, once more making Tracker the full focus of her sour expression. "If anything, escorting Dylan makes him a glorified bodyguard."

"What you say about the army is true," the hound conceded with a shrug. "Wardens have been ranked above us for many years now. But we are not currently in the army and *you*, my dear warrior, are no warden."

Dylan sagged, the tent flap slithering back into place and obscuring the arguing duo. He hadn't fully accepted what awaited him at Wintervale, but the hound's words had brought the stark reality of it crashing down. He would be leashed, he knew that.

But to be placed under another warden?

With only one spellster available, whoever became his warden would undoubtedly be granted a lot of prestige. They'd be untouchable. Unaccountable for anything done to him beyond his own death. And if it wasn't someone he knew, someone he could trust...

The hollowness in his fellow spellster's eyes. The abuse heaped upon them. No beatings, nothing that would leave a mark and make those higher in command look twice, but forced into sexual acts they'd no say in performing. The utter glee in his warden's laughter as he bragged about past conquests, promising that Dylan would do his own share of servicing.

Liquid collected in the back of his mouth, burning his throat. He clapped his hands over his lips in an effort to keep himself from spewing the contents across his blankets. His innate healing rushed to mend the affected area, its constant soothing leaving a tingling patch. His breath fought for release, shuddering out his nose in burbling puffs.

The crude, shimmering shape of his shield enclosed him, muffling the arguing voices that continued outside.

He closed his eyes, blocking out the light. He was safe here. He'd a hound to watch over him, a hedgewitch that few people would risk, a concerned friend in Marin and...

Authril.

The warrior wouldn't allow anyone to use him like that. She had barely tolerated him being in the brothel, where he'd done nothing beyond looking. *And being almost kissed.* She'd spoken at great lengths regarding her opinion on Tracker's actions there.

If he was to be leashed, to have a warden overseeing his every move, he would vastly prefer it was her.

Certain the threat of vomiting had given up tormenting his gut, he wrapped his arms around his knees and squeezed until his breathing finally calmed. Only then did he let his shield dissipate.

The arguing had stopped. With the tension lingering in the air like the smoke clinging to his robes, he wasn't sure the silence was a good thing.

Dylan flung back the tent flap, the act startling Marin and drawing everyone's attention. He winced, an apology stuttering from his lips. He had forgotten her closeness to the tent.

She waved off his words with a good-natured smile.

"My dear spellster," Tracker said. "It is a pleasure to see you up and about. You look..." The man's piercing gaze ran over him. Could he somehow tell Dylan had used magic within the tent? Even something as simple as a shield? Did he wonder why? Suspect? *Know?* "...reasonably rested."

"Reasonably," he echoed despite feeling nothing of the sort.

Authril remained silent, but her stare remained unforgiving and distant. Her earlier sourness seemed to have etched itself into her face, even as she struggled to smooth her features and make her observation of him less noticeable. He'd seen such looks before, whenever the guardians thought someone was overstepping their freedoms.

Did she actually know what had happened between him and the hound? Had she heard Tracker's brazen mention of it last night? *No, not then.* Or at any other time, otherwise she would've been ranting about that, demanding she spend every second at Dylan's side.

Nowhere alone. Constantly watched. His movements scrutinised. Each social interaction judged for the hidden meaning. Every smile. Every look. *The punishment of the outed.* It taunted him, even out here. He couldn't run from it. Couldn't rest for one moment without the threat of its clawed fingers wrapping around his neck.

Concern moulded Tracker's brow. He took a step closer.

"I'm fine," he blurted.

The hound halted, albeit with visible reluctance. His lips pursed in disbelief, the usually unflattering expression oddly endearing. "As you say."

Marin laid a hand on Dylan's shoulder, squeezing slightly. She looked just as unconvinced as Tracker.

"Let's break camp and move on," Authril declared, stomping towards the tent she had shared with the other women.

The remaining trio shared a meaningful look that Dylan didn't understand. Then, Tracker shrugged and followed the example, prompting the other two women to do the same.

Dylan gathered his things and readied himself for their journey whilst everyone else moved through their tasks shrouded in awkward silence. Not even Authril insisted he do anything whilst the tents were swiftly dismantled and stowed, the fire doused and buried to ensure nothing whipped up an ember. Food was either shoved into packs or people's mouths.

By the time they were done, their mark on this little section of the forest was barely noticeable. Dylan couldn't understand why the rest were being so thorough now when they hadn't on their northward journey.

They forged their way back through the undergrowth, reaching the road at the same time a deafening rumble rolled across the ground. The source unmistakably coming from the direction of the tower.

The others turned at the sound. Both the hound and the warrior regarded the way with grim faces. Marin looked less stoic, but held her composure. It was the hedgewitch who clapped a hand over her mouth.

Steeling himself, he faced the sight.

He had looked back the once since leaving the tower to burn, just before they left the road yesterday evening. It had sat high above the treetops, tendrils of smoke drifting alongside the clouds.

Now, that same sky sat empty of its silhouette. Fresh smoke billowed up to fill the space, the unburnt supports from the upper levels having fallen into the fire he started. The shell of what had been all he'd known of the world for almost three decades finally succumbing to its fate as another of Demarn's ruins.

Dylan turned his back on it. He didn't need more horror to fuel his nightmares.

The day drifted on much the same as yesterday. Silence lingered over the group, what had been awkward quiet now tensing with each passing hour. Authril led the way, although there wasn't any chance of anyone getting lost with a solid route stretched before them.

He wished the road carried more than themselves to their destination, but they encountered not a soul. He had grown used to the bustle of others, the carts that trundled along, others on foot trudging just as earnestly as they, the few on horseback who looked down upon the rest. He supposed there wasn't much call for farmers or merchants out in the middle of nowhere.

That was where his home had stood. *Isolated*. He recognised that now. Remote in a way that people could forget the very spellsters who had once walked amongst them.

With no nearby civilisation, it could take days, maybe even weeks, for someone to stumble upon the tower ruins. Rumours of how it fell would race across the land, growing wilder with each retelling. How long until speculation turned into fact?

Until everything he'd known became a myth?

They paused at noon only long enough to divide food amongst themselves. The presence of food seemed to mellow the tension, at least as far as everyone but Authril was concerned.

As the afternoon drew closer to the end, they returned to the forest, seeking a place far enough from the road where they'd be hidden from any traveller. The others busied themselves in pitching tents and building a base for their campfire. It left little for him to do.

Dylan paced between two trees. His whole being vibrated, demanding he help with something. *Anything*. Yesterday, he had understood the hound's insistence that he couldn't have enough left in him to even light the campfire. He could've done the task. Fire was easy, but had accepted the time to rest.

He felt even better now. Not as rested as he should've been, but definitely strong enough to aid in setting up camp.

Convincing anyone to let him was a different matter. Where could he be of use when everyone else seemed content in winding down for the evening?

Marin was off somewhere out in the forest, having checked the strength of her traps whilst on the road. She wouldn't return until it was close to dark. Even if he had gone with her, he'd no knowledge of how to set a trap, never mind where.

The hedgewitch was busy leafing through the books he'd given her. Just looking at the tomes had his stomach twisting upon itself. He wasn't certain if he could face reading the pages. Authril sat next to her, getting the fire going and nodding along to whatever Katarina said, her expression one of resigned boredom.

Whereas Tracker…

The hound sat a short distance from the rest, reclining against a tree trunk. He had out one of his many daggers and was busy running a stone along the blade's edge.

Dylan watched that rhythmic sweep, a slow-burning thought coming to life. The man had offered to teach him sword fighting. Although he wasn't certain if it had been a jest or some strange attempt at flirting. It had been some time back, a few days before

Oldmarsh and *The Gilded Lily*. And their almost kiss.

Strange how it felt like that had happened years ago.

He strode towards the man. His mind hadn't stopped since last night, flicking through a multitude of other notions, the merits behind each one. Learning to handle a weapon beyond his natural abilities was the only one that made sense to act on. It would take weeks to reach Whitemeadow and several more to Wintervale, plenty of time to familiarise himself with the basics.

He had considered asking Authril, but her stance on him learning had never been positive. Changing her mind would be impossible. He would likely need to borrow a weapon from the hound anyway as the sword she swung about single-handedly with ease looked less manageable than Tracker's.

Without looking up, the hound's actions briefly halted at Dylan's approach before carrying on.

Dylan cleared his throat. "I want to take you up on your offer to train me. If it's still on the table," he quickly amended.

Tracker glanced up from the dagger, his hand unfaltering as he continued to sharpen the blade's edge. "You already know how to fight. I remember how you handled those bandits."

Dylan did, too. Even after trying to block out the memories.

The screams as his lightning hit. The death-spasms of their bodies. The charred remains left to rot, reminiscent of the countless dead they hadn't been able to bury at the army encampment.

"I don't know how to wield a weapon not of my own making. You recommended a sword." Or was a dagger better? He recalled the hound mentioning several methods. Did he have time to learn more than one?

That honey-coloured gaze ran over him. Frowning, the hound sheathed his dagger. "I believe I also suggested you would be suited to unarmed combat." His eyes narrowed. "Why the sudden interest? Blades are messy. Your magic is more precise than any sword could be."

Dylan rubbed his neck, focusing everywhere but the man's puzzled face. This was trickier than his mind had made it seem. "In the tower, you said most spellsters use magic before all else."

Tracker's nose wrinkled. "I said a lot of things then. Pay them no mind."

He sighed. If only it were that easy. "But you're right. We do. I want to fix that. Learn of a way to defend myself in such a situation where magic won't work."

"Like against a hound?" There was a humorous quirk to the man's lips now.

He shook his head. If the other hounds fought anything like Tracker, he had no chance of matching their skill. "They'll leash me once we reach Wintervale. I won't be able to use my magic unless given sanction." And all the vibrancy in the world would once again be diminished. All he could hope for was to be treated better as the last spellster in the army's possession. "If whatever destroyed the tower reaches the capital—"

Tracker held up his hand. "I understand. Correct me if I am wrong, but spellsters learning to fight without magic is not something the army allows."

Not according to Authril. "If you won't teach me to use a sword, I'll simply ask Marin how to wield a bow." He didn't know how readily available one would be to him compared to a sword, but he had witnessed the damage they did.

The hound tipped his head back and laughed. "If you think there is anything simple about archery, then you underestimate our dear hunter's prowess."

~ ~ ~

"What have I done?" Marin's voice rang out across the clearing.

Tracker twisted on the spot at the sound. He hadn't expected the hunter to return until the daylight was almost gone.

She stood at the clearing's edge, not far from them or the trail she had left their company via earlier. Her face remained oddly grim.

"Nothing wrong, I assure you," he replied, grinning to round off any edges to his good-natured jab. "Did you find nothing worth trapping?"

Rather than respond with a sarcastic comment of her own, she gestured for him to stand. "I need you to come with me. Now."

His brows shot up. Not since their first meeting had she been so curt with him. He glanced at Dylan, then the rest of the camp, before getting to his feet. "We will speak of this later, yes?" he asked of the man, a little relieved that he'd a reason not to answer now. Whatever Marin needed him for, it gave him time to mull over the consequences of a spellster knowing how to use a blade without the man standing over him.

Dylan frowned, a flush of disappointment colouring his cheeks like a slap. He nodded all the same and turned back to the others, leaving Tracker to wordlessly follow the hunter into the forest.

She offered no explanation. No warning of what might lie ahead. Her sole gesture was to ensure he stayed close and didn't dawdle.

Only when their camp was out of sight did she signal for him to halt.

He obeyed. He knew the woman well enough to admire her caution, but he couldn't tell if she was being overly so. She carried no hint of encountering anything dangerous, but concern vibrated through her every movement.

No sounds out of the ordinary reached him. Birds sang from the branches, unconcerned with their presence. A few fantailed varieties danced around them, peeping for them to keep moving and stir up more tiny morsels from the undergrowth. If he strained his hearing, he fancied there being a low hum in the distance.

Marin glanced over his shoulder, not acknowledging him until she was satisfied. Then, her sharp hazel gaze focused on him with the same intensity as a hawk. "How's he holding up?"

"About as well as can be expected. He wants me to train him in bladed weapons." He understood where the desire came from, the urge to regain control over something—anything—within his life.

Perhaps it would help.

Nodding almost absently, she scuffed her boot along the ground, leaving a line of dry soil amongst the leaf litter. "And have you told him? About Authril?"

"You mean what our dear warrior said in the tower? Not as yet." It was still too early. "But that cannot be why you brought me out here." Such a question could've easily been asked whilst changing their shifts on watch, when both Dylan and Authril were asleep. Insisting in front of the others that he vanish into the forest with her would bring questions upon their return.

Marin shook her head, her lips flattening into a grim line. "It's not. I need you to see something." She pushed on through the undergrowth. "This way."

He trailed behind her, the seriousness in her voice tweaking his curiosity. Clearly, she had found something that was of interest to them. That she didn't immediately inform him what it was suggested she wasn't entirely certain herself.

"It occurs to me," he said, aware that if their destination warranted silence, she would've told him. Questions about herself would turn her mind from Dylan and what had, or hadn't, been said to the man. "Whilst we all know a certain warrior's mind and much of her past." Some of it was to excess as the woman refused to keep quiet. "I have not heard of your opinion on recent matters. You do not appear to have the same reservations about magic as our dear warrior. Why is that?"

She paused for a moment to grin a little too broadly back at him. "Why do you want to know?"

Tracker shrugged. "It is always nice to have more than a passing acquaintance with travelling companions." If she didn't wish to speak of the past, he would push only to confirm the details she had already freely given. "You spoke of your home being burnt to the ground by Udyneans. Your village was on the border, yes?" Or what had once been the border. If the empire had succeeded in their invasion back when she was a child, then the land was well and truly under their control.

Her smile fell and her gaze drifted to the forest ahead. "Damn elven hearing," she muttered under her breath before speaking louder, "It was. Nothing extravagant or anything, just a hamlet south of Toptower and a little north of the Udynean border." She kicked a pinecone into the brush. "You won't find it on most maps nowadays."

"Lynhold. I remember hearing about it as a boy." The recollection was faint, mere mentions amongst older hounds whilst they oversaw the training young. Even without the empire trumping them so deftly, Udynea gnawed at Demarn's border like rats plundering a silo. Settlements too small to defend against magic became little more than rubble and a smudge in history. An isolated place like Lynhold would've had no chance.

"My grandfather used to say the place was doomed from the day they let the hounds drag away this pregnant elven woman."

"She would have carried a spellster child."

Marin shook her head. "It was years before I was born, but the way they spoke, I think *she* was the spellster."

"That is also possible." Places like Lynhold were rarely visited by the King's Hounds unless summoned. If the woman's magic was slight enough to go unnoticed by the average person, or even beneficial to the people, no one would've sought to be rid of her. "Still, you witnessed this destruction as a child and permitted a spellster into your home."

She laughed. "I gave shelter to the three drowned rats I found on my doorstep. Knew he was a spellster, of course. Those damn robes the army puts them in marked him as one from across a field. Looked pathetic enough that I didn't really think about what he might be capable of. Besides, without them, I wouldn't have known the Udyneans had destroyed the army." She fell silent for a few steps, likely thinking of just how much death would've been wrought for such an occurrence.

"You never saw the aftermath, yes?" It made her the only one of them who hadn't.

Marin shook her head. "Seeing something like that once in a lifetime is enough." She jerked a thumb back towards the camp. "They'd likely agree. In fact, if it wasn't for Authril's insistence about moving on, I think Kat and Dylan would've opted to stay a little longer."

And if they had, Tracker might have found them long before their encounter at Toptower, with perhaps a far more volatile outcome. "You believe she is the driving force behind their movements?" For all her talk of returning to Dvärghem, the hedgewitch seemed content to take her time. But that could easily be the woman's philosophy.

"Authril's brashness might have something to do with it."

Tracker grunted. Even though he had suggested the spellster stay close to him, he couldn't outright object to the current sleeping arrangements without causing some manner of friction.

He needed to separate Dylan from the group for long enough to tell the spellster of her true intentions behind her sexual advances or wait until she tried again and see if the man refused her of his own volition.

Both were a problem for another day.

"How far are we going?" Even as the question left his lips, the all-too-familiar buzz of flies reached his ears. The stench of decaying flesh assaulted his senses not long after. He covered his nose, his gaze darting Marin's way to see her grimness had returned. What had she found out here?

His thoughts flashed to the destroyed tower wall. Had some spellsters escaped after all? Only to be hunted and left to rot out in the wilderness?

Marin jerked her head, indicating they climb the ridge just ahead. "We're almost there. We're lucky the wind's changed since I found them. Smelt it long before now." She lifted a branch out of their path, the leaves creating a screen above her. "Reckon they've been there a few days."

Beyond her sat a natural ditch, the kind caused by a stream that had long since dried up. The remains of people filled the space, dumped with no effort to bury them, not even in a shallow grave.

Something had ravaged the bodies within, but what remained was bloated and discoloured. He'd put them as a few days older than the dead within the tower, although the fact these had succumbed to not only the elements but also wild animals, made judging just how many days before trickier.

"If I'm not mistaken," Marin said, having gone no further than the branch. "They're part of your pack."

"They are." The wildlife had done a good job of destroying individual features, but a few pieces of clothing were intact enough to be marked as the distinctive attire of the King's Hounds.

Tracker circled the ditch, looking for any clue as to how this had come to pass. The ground offered little, a few footprints that could've easily belonged to the dead and a handful of other markings muddied by hungry animals. No sign that the bodies had been slain here.

"I always thought hounds were impossible to kill." Marin had come forward a few steps, lingering just within sight.

"We die just as easily as any other being." Perhaps with even greater ease, seeing that the rest of the group had access to Dylan's healing, whereas a blade in the wrong place could end Tracker's life. A fact he had come to terms with long ago. Everything died in the end, he could only hope his was swift.

He bent to examine a single mark caused by a boot not too dissimilar to his own. The way it pressed into the ground, deeper nearer the fore, as though hefting something forwards. *A deliberate discarding of a body.* That put things in line with his first assessment of the site.

Investigating further from the ditch brought scuffs in the dirt, patches of broken foliage with dark smears of dried blood and a handful of other deep footprints. All signs that came from someone carelessly hauling a heavy load.

Returning to the ditch, he dared a fresh count of the bodies. *Eight heads.* Even accounting for the disarray of limbs caused, there weren't enough bodies to make that many people. Not anymore.

How had they all wound up dead? That so many had chosen to travel together was strange enough. And so close to the spellster tower. Had the mistress sent several of the pack to collect fresh victims for the army?

What sort of force had managed to overpower and slaughter eight fully trained hounds? The same one that had attacked the spellster tower? It was possible. Talfaltaners held almost the same distaste for hounds as they did towards spellsters.

But why go to the trouble of dumping the bodies here? He doubted anyone who came upon them on the roadside would've been able to warn the tower in time. Who did they hide this slaughter from?

The glint of a jewelled pommel caught his eye. He trod deeper into the ditch, picking his way through offal and dismembered limbs, to pluck the weapon from its sheath. The dagger sported a narrow blade, perfect for slipping between ribs. An intricate rope etching bound the hilt, with a generous dark blue stone gracing the top.

He knew the owner of this blade, had seen the man polishing it numerous times in his youth. *Whisper.* A gentle soul who had spent much of his life running the hound station in Oldmarsh.

The last he'd heard of the old hound's whereabouts had been directly from the man's lover. *Left months ago.* Answering the call for all of them to head for Wintervale, an order Tracker had directly refused.

How had Whisper ended up here?

"We should return to camp." Tracker cut the dagger's sheath free, nestling both it and the weapon beneath his belt. "Find another place whilst it is still light." He doubted the people responsible for this were close, nor did he think they were likely to put much distance between them and this place.

He was vastly more concerned about the animal tracks. They spoke of a few hefty pigs that were likely behind the missing body parts. He'd rather not wake to find such creatures stumbling through their camp in search of more exotic treats to gorge on. Any distance they gained from here would be an improvement to avoid that situation.

Marin didn't appear convinced about his choice, but she followed him back towards camp readily enough. "What do we tell the others?"

"That we found a pile of dead bodies. They do not need specifics." Not when he'd Dylan's safety to concern himself with. If the Talfaltaners were the ones responsible for those deaths alongside that of the spellsters, their little group would have to be extra vigilant in where they camped from now on.

Especially if they didn't want to wake up dead.

CHAPTER 2

Two days. That was how long they'd travelled with no further signs anyone else had recently trod the same road. Everything was quiet. *Idyllic.* Dylan could almost forget the destruction they'd left behind.

Yet, he couldn't shake the sight of Marin and Tracker emerging from the forest. The grim lines etching their faces. The talk of dead bodies. Their insistence on breaking camp and setting up elsewhere, never mind that it would leave half of them fumbling about in the twilight.

They hadn't spoken much about the incident since. When Dylan pressed the hound, the man confessed the bodies weren't from the tower. Whilst the knowledge crushed the dim hope Dylan had of people escaping the slaughter—for even if these people hadn't made it, knowing some had breached the outer wall meant others might've been more successful—it didn't answer where they'd come from.

There were few options. Given how many dead Talfaltaners had littered the tower grounds, he doubted they had taken the time to drag a few out into the forest. They could've been those critically wounded who had then passed away, but the placement seemed odd.

That left them being some poor souls who'd the misfortune of being in the wrong place.

It still left other questions. He might not be as worldly as the others, but he knew anyone claiming to be a merchant also had a wagon or two. And those he had encountered on their journey were always armed, be that themselves or their guards. They would've fought. And lost against insurmountable odds. Had they fled into the undergrowth, hoping to evade those who meant mortal harm? It clearly hadn't worked, but it suggested an explanation for the bodies' placement.

Yet, things still didn't quite add up. Tracker had spoken the truth about fighting with blades. It was messy. And messy left signs. If they had survived enough to avoid immediate death, then maybe not the dark marks that wouldn't fully seep into the compacted earth that was the road.

But what of their wagon? The road might've been hard under his boot and baked by the sun, but surely a carthorse or a laden wagon would be enough to make a more substantial impression of their passing. The road's surface showed not a single mark, be it foot, hoof or wheel.

At least, it hadn't until they crested a hill at noon.

He hadn't ever seen an armed force larger than a few people before leaving the tower. The army encampment had merely been a town of tents, its placement for generations moulding its surroundings, expanding slowly as the surrounding forest was culled to serve as fuel for the multiple fires.

What stood before them was vastly different. The trees lining the road had either been stripped of their branches or felled completely. Where the earth hadn't been trampled into a slurry by an onslaught of feet had instead been hacked open to make fire pits.

Marin knelt by one of them, her hand hovering over the broken ground before dipping deeper. The charred remains of a log jutted from that maw like a decaying tongue. She slapped her palm down onto the cracked charcoal surface, holding it there without a hint of harm. "This is days' cold."

"More than that," Tracker said. The hound crouched by a similar hole, this one cracked and split as though struck by lightning. The jagged edges obscured whatever the man saw within. "I would put all this at no earlier than a week."

"It just keeps going," Katarina yelled from her place halfway down the hill. She stood in the middle of the road, her gaze fixed eastward.

Dylan peered into the distance. From their spot atop the hill, he had witnessed the road on Whitemeadow winding on for miles. Even though he no longer had the same height advantage as the dwarf, that more than this patch of the roadside had suffered the same fate was obvious.

He squinted, trying to see even further. If he could just manage to make things clearer, then maybe he would spot those responsible for not only this chaos, but the destruction of his home.

No matter how hard he willed it, the view remained unchanged.

"I don't understand," the hedgewitch continued in a more sedate tone as she joined them at the base of the hill. "If they caused this much destruction all along the way, why are we only now coming across it? Why not sooner? Why did they stop at the base of *this* hill?"

"Siege tactics," Authril replied, shrugging. "No fire, no tents. Minimise all signs of precisely how big your horde is. It was one of Danny's favourite strategies." She rarely spoke of the mercenary company she'd been a part of before the army attack. Most times, it left her sullen, withdrawn and curt with everyone.

"Not an approach I would think Talfaltaners to know," Tracker pointed out. "There are few structures to besiege out in the ocean and their ships, although reputably fast, are not exactly built to promote stealth in their sailors."

Authril's shoulders lifted once more, this time, with an added air of indifference. The two elves hadn't argued since the other day, but she often responded to the hound's presence as though he was there only at her whim. "Clearly, I'm not as familiar with sea warfare as yourself."

The hound's brows lowered. "Warfare?" he echoed, the word practically a growl as it slipped between his clenched teeth. "If you had witnessed the aftermath of a merchant vessel against a Talfaltaner ship, you would not call it such. No more than you would claim the sea does battle with the shore."

"Are you saying they're a force of nature?" the warrior scoffed.

"I speak only of them striking with the same blunt inevitability. Not once have I heard of them exercising finesse. This tactic?" The man gestured to the stark difference between the top of the hill and their immediate surroundings. "I guarantee it was someone else's idea. Whose? I cannot be certain. But I suggest we be extra vigilant from here on out. There is no telling what lies ahead."

"There's no way around?" Katarina asked. She rummaged about in her many pouches, pulling out the old map she had claimed possession of back at the army encampment. "A farmer's road? Hunting trails?"

"Not this close to the tower," Tracker replied, the statement surprisingly backed up by an agreeing grunt from Authril, reluctant as it was. "No one lives this close. We will not even see farmland for several more days."

"Then we should stop wasting daylight and move on," Marin declared, taking the lead in marching down the road.

Having no other choice, the rest of them followed.

They continued until the afternoon had barely begun to wind down before abandoning the road to press further into the forest than they'd done the previous two evenings. With their surroundings looking as though they had never accommodated visitors so far from the roadside, it took a while to find somewhere that held enough space for everyone.

Dylan set about helping Katarina and Tracker clear the ground for their tents, whilst Marin disappeared into the forest to place her traps and find a stream to fill their water skins. He had offered to save her the trouble of the latter back when they'd first started travelling together. With the forest's natural dampness, condensing the morning dew that clung to the tents would leave them with more than enough.

Authril had opposed the act then, stating it was a frivolous use of his power. A valid concern at the time as he'd been worn out from not only the battle with the Udynean spellster, but also from combating exhaustion and a lack of proper nourishment. All things that he had recovered from. He would broach the subject tomorrow. No point offering after the deed was done and he'd never find Marin beforehand.

His gaze slid from unravelling his tent to where Authril knelt, hacking out a spot in the earth for the fire. Her efforts had produced little beyond a shallow pit. His magic could've done the task faster and deeper, with less strain on him. She knew that, had witnessed it when he dug a hole for Marin to bury the boar's innards, yet she didn't seek his help.

He put his back to the sight, knowing full well Authril wouldn't accept any assistance he offered, and returned to laying out his tent. Tracker, having already finished setting up his own shelter, currently aided Katarina with the enviable finesse of someone who'd spent their life travelling.

Dylan had spent years—decades—wondering what that was like. Night after night, he had wistfully watched the world beyond the tower, longing to walk this very road, to see the fields of Whitemeadow in bloom, to visit the cliffs at Wintervale and smell the sea air for the first time. And he would, in time.

He would've eagerly given up all those chances to return home with everything unchanged.

It wasn't long before the hound came to Dylan's side. The man didn't ask if his help in setting up the tent was required, merely took up a stone and started securing the opposite end. "All this would be a lot easier if we altered the sleeping arrangements," Tracker said in a matter-of-fact tone.

Dylan remained silent whilst tapping the last peg into place. He knew precisely what the man was getting at. He even agreed that, logically, having one less tent to worry about would lessen the strain of finding places to camp. It would likely decrease their chances of being found, too.

Yet the idea of sharing such an intimate space with the hound, of lying next to that warm, lithe form, the very air filled with the aroma of citrus and cinnamon whilst the faint purr in the man's breath thrummed through his body...

His final hit on the tent peg came down hard enough to crack the stone in his hand. The uneven edges bit into his palm, not enough to break skin, but his innate healing nevertheless rushed to the site to soothe the ache.

Shaking his hand to relieve the tingling such magic left behind, Dylan risked a glance at Tracker. Was elven hearing sensitive enough to hear a fist-sized rock break? Were his hound senses alerted to the small amount of magic?

If the man had noticed anything, he played the part of being oblivious well.

Dylan slowly exhaled. He had to stop these thoughts. *It was one night.* He'd spent plenty of nights with others. *Not as intensely.* Nor for as long and definitely not with that level of vulnerable intimacy.

He needed something else to distract him. But what? A scan of their camp showed little left he could assist in without also getting in the way. *Training, then.* The others were clearly doing their best to avoid any conflicts, but they also travelled in the same direction as the horde that took out the tower. Meeting those who meant them harm had to be inevitable. They needed to be ready.

And he needed to be capable of fending off an opponent without the use of his magic, be his inability due to lack of energy or even being leashed again.

His neck tingled at the memory of the cold metal wrapping around it, the iciness leeching into his mind, the world drained of any vibrancy. Sharper still was the recollection of pain, pinpricks of fire and lightning assaulting his flesh whenever he tried to use magic unsanctioned.

He'd gone into the original leashing blind. He understood that, now. He'd been so sure of what effect the collar would have on him, that it couldn't be any different to the isolation cells, just portable. And permanent.

Except it hadn't been. Not that time.

He ran his fingers across the smooth patch of skin at his throat. Whatever fault had allowed his magic to slip through, had saved him from a swift death, would be rectified by whoever was capable of leashing him at Wintervale.

Could he really go through it again? *I have to.* He was too dangerous to wander about unleashed. *Strong.* That was what the hound had called him. Strong enough to free himself, to leave him alive and unconscious, hidden from sight and presumed dead.

Just not enough to save any skin but his own.

Unruly. That was a more apt description of himself. Disorderly. Disobedient. Disruptive. Observations repeated by so many. The overseers who forced him to fight in the brawl or die because he had disobeyed. The sergeant who had sent him to the front line when he had only wanted to heal the wounded. The warden who had promised a short existence of abuse no matter how he followed orders.

"We are feeling poorly, yes?"

Dylan stiffened, the hound's words jerking him back into the present. Both them and the tent stood inside the sphere of his shield. The surface had hardened, shifting whorls of ice coating the outside. *I hadn't even noticed.* In its most basic form, a spellster's shield reacted on instinct, the desire to keep out what was likely to do a person harm. But he should've been aware.

"I..." He fought for speech, his tongue unable to form anything beyond a few garbled sounds. Even those scattered as he faced the man. Instead, he fumbled to dispel both the shield and the ice it had formed.

The whole time, Tracker continued to wordlessly watch him, those honey-coloured eyes boring deep. Concern drew his brows together. Was he reconsidering their journey? Their goal? His task as a hound?

Dylan didn't know what to say. He hadn't meant for his shield to form, but admitting that would mark him as unpredictable. Dangerous. To everyone around him.

"Am I right in thinking you would still like to learn swordsmanship?"

The man's question had Dylan's brows climbing to their highest. After being reminded how the army didn't allow spellsters to learn any other weapon beyond their magic, he hadn't bothered to speak with Authril about training. Tracker had brought up that very point and Dylan had assumed the man agreed, but he also hadn't said as such.

Wetting his lips, he searched for the right words that would leave him sounding adamant without seeming desperate.

"Does the silence mean no?"

"No. I mean, yes. That is—" He clapped a hand over his mouth, physically restraining himself before his babbling talked Tracker out of teaching him. "I want to learn," he finally managed. "I take that to mean you've changed your mind?"

"That would be difficult to do when I had not given you a solid response in the first place. I am open to teaching you, but not here. Not in front of them."

Dylan followed the hound's line of sight to where Authril eyed them over the beginnings of a fire. The bared length of her sword casually rested on the ground beside her. He had no doubts that she would object to him learning to use even the smallest blade in the hound's arsenal.

"Come." Tracker turned on his heel. "Let us see if we cannot find one of those smaller clearings."

He stared at the man, unable to even close his jaw, for a few breaths. "*Now?*" Why was the hound so keen to begin this? Granted,

Dylan felt stronger than the day he'd first asked, but he'd seen how much a sparring session could take out of a person. Surely, a meal and a little rest would be the way to go. "Weren't you advocating for me to rest not that long ago?" Was forcing him to train so soon after the day's travel some ploy to make him rethink the request?

Tracker peered over his shoulder, the gleam of those honey-coloured eyes just visible beneath the russet lashes. "You wish to learn to defend yourself without relying on magic before we reach Wintervale? You will start now." He smiled. "Do not worry, I promise to be gentle." With that, the man vanished behind a tree, leaving Dylan to follow.

They walked through the forest until reaching one of the clear patches they had encountered on their way in. Even to Dylan's inexperienced eye, the area was too small and uneven to hold three tents without hacking away a great deal of bush or felling one of the enormous trees. But it looked large enough for the basic sparring techniques he had witnessed the soldiers doing at the army encampment.

The hound circled the area, mumbling to himself and nodding. Occasionally, he would kick aside a cone or toss a heftier branch nearer the bushes. "This will do for today."

Dylan straightened. An odd, nervous bubble hit his stomach. He hadn't had anyone teach him something so completely foreign in years. "What's the first lesson?" He discreetly bounced on the balls of his feet, trying to expel some of the giddiness. A lot of it refused to be quelled so easily. "Stabbing?"

Tracker wrinkled his nose. "By the gods, no. We will begin with the basics." He unsheathed his sword and offered it, hilt first, towards Dylan. "Show me how you hold it."

"That's all?" Dylan took up the weapon, his fingers closing around the leather-wrapped hilt. The sword wasn't as heavy as he had presumed, perhaps the weight of a slinky mouser and just as likely to injure him if handled wrong.

He stared at the blade's fang-like point, not seeing the weapon at all. *The tower cats.* He hadn't seen a single one of them whilst they had walked the halls. They tended to skulk around where there was food or warmth, but even in the library, he'd seen no sign of them amongst the shelves.

"Dylan?" The hound's concern sat thickly in his voice. "Are you all right?"

He jerked his head up, the sword instantly dipping to graze the ground. "Did you see any cats back in the tower?"

Tracker shook his head, his gaze not leaving the sword. Did he regret handing the weapon over? "They likely fled during the attack."

"Are you sure? I thought you said Talfaltaners kill anything they believed was associated with a spellster." They had culled the messenger pigeons and those poor birds had done nothing but sit in their cages. Cats weren't seen as anything special about the tower, no more so than any mouser would be to a dense population, but he'd no idea how other realms saw the animals.

"They would never harm a cat. Such creatures are sacred to them."

That knowledge gave only a small measure of comfort. Being slaughtered by wicked people wasn't the only way they could've died. "I burnt the place to the ground." He stared off in the direction of the tower. With them days away and surrounded by tall trees, he wouldn't have seen his home even if it hadn't collapsed. "Do you think I—?"

"No." The gruff certainty in the man's voice had Dylan facing him once more. "Like I said, they would have fled into the surrounding forest." He frowned thoughtfully. "It is possible the Talfaltaners claimed some as their own in the name of rescuing them from evil, but the most you would have done is scorch a few rodents. The rest would have fled."

Out into the forest. Where there was no shelter, no people to offer up scraps of meat or a warm lap. *They're not pets.* Not the way those born outside the tower described them. The tower mousers were bred to hunt, to keep the rodent population from destroying the library and the food stocks. *They'll survive.* If what Tracker said was true, if the Talfaltaners had left the cats alone, let them run free into the forest, then they would live.

A piece of the tower would live.

Tracker eyed him as if expecting Dylan to burst into flame. "If you are not well, we can do this another time."

"No." He lifted the sword once more. "You promised to teach me." The sword refused to stop wobbling, the tip never quite swinging where he intended. Still, he tried to keep the length under his control. Gripping the hilt with both hands helped. "So, teach." He raised the weapon and struck the same pose he'd seen Authril do.

The hound circled him, humming. Those long fingers stroked his chin. His brows drew together, shading his eyes but failing to hide their intensity.

It was a side Dylan wasn't used to seeing from the man. It set his stomach bubbling anew.

At last, Tracker halted before him. "If I am to be entirely honest, I am uncertain I can make much of a swordsman from you in the time we have. Most start with some sense of form, even if it is a rather poor one. But with you..." The sentence trickled off into a groan.

"My form can't be *that* bad." He was a little unbalanced, certainly.

That came from a lack of experience in standing with his arms out. Fighting with magic lent itself to bursts of movement. The snap of a hand, the quick shift of a foot. Strength was measured in power, not muscle.

"Bad?" Tracker gave a low chuckle. "No, no. It would be better if it were merely bad. Atrocious is a far more fitting description."

He grimaced. Heat slowly slunk from where it had been pooling in his gut to his face. "Ouch."

"Perhaps you *would* be more suited to a dagger."

Dylan shook his head. He might be able to mimic the moves he'd seen from Marin during the rare times she used her hunting knife to spar with Authril, but a shorter blade would require closeness and a swiftness he hadn't the knack for.

"Very well. Although, I have not had to teach something quite as basic as *this* before."

"Basic?" he echoed. He had left any sort of offensive training behind with his adolescence, but surely his moves weren't *that* rusty.

"Most people have a certain understanding of at least how to hold a weapon so it will not fly off on the first strike." The hound kicked up a short branch, catching it in one hand. He stripped a few twigs off the end, trailing dried leaves as he continued to circle Dylan. "But I suppose a spellster child is unlikely to spend their spare time fighting with sticks."

Dylan frowned. Except for the evening, when they were bundled into their beds to sleep, he didn't recall having much in the way of time to spare during his childhood. Keeping young spellsters active and using their magic was considered the best way to ensure they were too exhausted to get into too much trouble at night.

Tracker gripped the thicker end of the stick like he would his sword, slashing it through the air. "The cities are always full of children scrapping as if they were warriors. It is not exactly the strict training hounds grow up with, but those children do manage to learn a little through trial-and-error." He pointed at Dylan with a flourish of the stick. "You, however, do not have such a luxury."

"I don't?" The journey to Wintervale would take some time at their current pace. Surely, he could become proficient in sword fighting within such a timeframe.

"No." Tracker tossed aside the stick. "Fortunately, you have me to teach you." The hound halted behind Dylan, those long fingers overlapping his own. "Your grip should be firm," he murmured, his cheek pressed to Dylan's bicep. "The last thing you desire is for your weapon to fly out of your grasp at the first strike. Nor do you want to squeeze too hard and tax yourself needlessly." The hand inched its way up Dylan's arm. "Your wrists must be sturdy, your arms solid but supple."

"Right." He could remember that. Fighting with fire or ice demanded a similar stance.

"As for *this*." The hound's other hand fell on Dylan's midsection. "You should endeavour to keep your core strong like the trunk of a tree. And your legs..." he whispered, his shin slipping between Dylan's. "They must be spread wider." Tucking his boot against Dylan's instep, he gently slid their feet further across the ground.

Dylan glanced over his shoulder at the hound. Having Tracker at his back whilst the fabric of his robe climbed up his leg had him feeling awfully exposed. "We *are* still talking about sword fighting?"

"That is what you wanted me to teach you, yes?" The man circled to stand before Dylan, withdrawing one of his daggers.

Dylan hadn't paid much attention to the array of weaponry the hound carried, but this particular dagger looked rather like a thin knife. Unlike the sword, the dagger's blade gleamed silver. It was quite a bit longer than the alchemist daggers he was used to seeing.

Tracker nodded at him. "Now we fight."

CHAPTER 3

"What?" Dylan blurted. "*Fight?*" It had to be a joke. A poor one. Except, Tracker looked far too serious, especially with having already fallen into the same prepared stance he'd seen the man use with Authril. "Y-you haven't taught me anything." No ways to attack, no blocking moves, nothing he'd seen the two elves do during their sparring.

The hound spread his hands wide. "You wanted me to teach you and my methods are very hands-on. If you learn quickly, then we may have time for you to focus on perfecting your technique, but for now..." He lunged at Dylan, his dagger coming up fast.

Dylan threw up his arms, a crude shield forming around him. The clash and jar of metal striking metal jolted him through to his teeth.

"Good," Tracker grunted. The smile he gave held a genuinely pleased edge. "Your reflexes are as I expected."

With his cheeks blazing at the praise, Dylan slowly let the barrier dissipate.

His gaze flicked to where dagger and sword had met. His brows twitched together, slight disapproval fighting to make their mark. "Do less blocking with the edge next time. I do not fancy fighting with dented weapons if we are attacked on the way to Whitemeadow."

Swinging Dylan's arm aside with a twirl of his wrist, the man attempted a second lunge.

This time, Dylan saw it coming soon enough to deflect the dagger's tip with a sweep of the sword's blade.

The hound faltered. Shock widened his eyes as if he had expected Dylan to do no better than the first attack. "Better." He straightened, idly twirling the dagger between his fingers. A grin parted his lips, his fangs gleaming. "But can you do it again?"

"I think so." It was a relatively simple movement. Although the sword's weight, small as it was, dragged at his arm. He briefly switched to the other hand, shaking and stretching the offended limb until his muscles didn't ache quite so much. He glanced up from the sword hilt to find his movements being tracked by the man.

"If you are finding it too much for one arm, you can always use two."

He had seen such warriors on the field. Their swords looked far beyond his capabilities. "Would I be able to lift a two-hander?"

Tracker tipped his head from side to side. "Fair point. If you are having difficulty with this blade, then probably not." He swung his arm at Dylan's middle, in a motion that would've gutted him had Dylan not blocked the attack and the man had truly been trying. "Do let me know if you start to tire. I would not wish to hurt you needlessly."

"I'll be fine." He stepped back as the hound switched his dagger to the other hand and made a lazy swipe for Dylan's legs.

"I would refrain from wandering too much, if I were you. Unless you wish to test your footwork?" The man slowly circled him, keeping out of Dylan's immediate reach. He strolled by one of the larger pine trees, dragging the tip of his dagger along the bark and causing bits to flake off. "Combat can be much like a dance. And I know how well you can do that on a flat surface, but the battlefield does not grant such luxuries."

Dylan eyed the ground around them. Although the area was littered with small rocks, humps of dirt, branches and the like, it held little in the way of major obstacles. "I'll manage."

Something cold and thin ran down the side of his neck, prickling his skin. The blunt edge of the man's dagger. How had the hound managed to move so quickly and quietly?

"I am certain you will," Tracker purred. "The question is, will you choose to follow or lead? You seem to do both rather well."

Dylan swung about, the sword arcing into a wide circle with him.

"Ha!" The man jumped beyond the blade's reach, a feral grin parting his lips. "Predictable." He eyed the spindly top of a low bush the sword had shaved in the strike. "The element of surprise is a vital tool. You must use it to your advantage if you want to keep your enemy on their toes."

Growling, Dylan swung again and again. It didn't matter how he struck, the man effortlessly leapt back every time.

"Come now, my dear spellster. Flailing your blade aimlessly will only tire you. Plan your strikes. See the moves in your mind."

A few muttered curses slipped out on a breath, the majority from languages he'd learnt over the years. *Plan my strikes?* Just what did the hound think he'd been doing this whole time?

Tracker laughed. He held a fist up to his hand, trying to make out he was coughing, but it was definitely a laugh. "Such language! Is that what they taught you in the tower?"

He snarled a little more, surprised to see the hound's brows twitch up. "You know the elven tongue?" There weren't many, even amongst his elven friends. Those who spoke the language had to learn from books or plead to be taught by the handful of inhabitants who'd learnt from the source, be that the elven nomads or the elves of Heimat. With them all confined to the tower, few bothered to learn more than the local tongue.

The hound shrugged. "I learnt a smattering here and there during my years in *The Gilded Lily*. Not enough to be terribly conversational outside of a bedchamber."

Heat brushed his cheeks at the thought of the man speaking the elven tongue with that thick, husky note Dylan had heard during their night in the tower. He cleared his throat, hoping his face wasn't as red as it felt. "I could teach you more." The language was a harsh one that hurt the back of his throat if he spoke it for long, but half that battle was in the guttural sounds. Something his native tongue didn't possess.

Tracker tilted his head to one side, puzzled.

Feeling his face grow even warmer under the hound's questioning look, Dylan continued, "Before I was sent to the army, I was one of the tower's main linguists. I was largely tasked with deciphering the text for suspected dwarven finds, but I've a reasonable grasp of the elven language."

"Thank you, but that is not necessary."

"Please, in exchange for teaching me to use this." He waggled the scimitar, realising his folly in the move when the hilt twisted in his grip and dropped the blade, point-first, into the dirt.

Tracker grimaced, his gaze falling along with the sword. He said nothing, but his thoughts towards the abuse of his weapon were plain.

With his cheeks blazing enough that they had to glow, Dylan hastened to retrieve the sword. He attempted to brush the dirt off the blade, stopping when it was clear his efforts merely smudged grime across the steel. "I know it's not much." Nor did he know how useful the language could be within Demarn's borders. As far as Dylan knew, the elven caravans didn't enter the kingdom and Heimat kept themselves isolated from the whole continent. "But it's the only thing I have of worth to give."

Sorrow took the hound's face. "That is not true." He spoke so softly, moved so slowly, that Dylan didn't notice the man had closed the distance between them until he was near enough to touch. "Nor should you judge your worth entirely on what you can offer people." He calmly adjusted Dylan's stance as he spoke. Little movements, from altering his grip on the hilt to the subtle shifting of a foot or arm. "I choose to teach you this form of combat for *your* benefit, not to have some hold over you."

The warmth in Dylan's face slithered down to nestle deep within his chest. He couldn't remember the last time someone taught him anything without an underlying motive. Even his linguistic teachings had stemmed from his guardian subtly turning his interests away from the training grounds. "Don't you want to learn the language of your ancestors?"

"I am content with the knowledge I have." He stepped back, looking over Dylan with the critical eye of an artist appraising his work. "If you are willing to try the offensive again..." Lifting his dagger in preparation to defend, he jerked his chin at the sword. "Begin."

Dylan tightened his grip on the sword hilt. The weapon sat balanced in his hands, ready to be wielded regardless of how prepared he felt. *See the moves in my mind.* He shifted his weight, uncertain where to make the first strike. The hound was sure to predict whatever he attempted.

He stepped to the man's left, bringing the sword up in a wide arc.

Tracker's arm came up, deflecting the weapon with a mere flick of his wrist. "I see we are growing more confident already. Good."

He ducked his head, concealing the smile that simply refused to be restrained. Something about the man's praise left him oddly warm. Was it the soft note of satisfaction in his voice? Not for himself, but for Dylan's ability.

"You're *training* him?"

At the sound of Authril's indignation, Dylan almost threw the sword into the nearby undergrowth. Only a last-second realisation kept his fingers from letting go, forcing him to fumble in an effort to control his swing.

Tracker also spun at the sound of the warrior's voice, his arm raised and the slim length of dark steel in the man's once-empty grasp.

Dylan frowned, unsure when the hound had drawn a throwing knife.

Authril stood amongst the foliage on the far side of the clearing, her feet planted and her arms akimbo. Those sea-green eyes flicked over Dylan, her inspection pausing at the sword dangling in his grasp, then settled back on Tracker.

"Training?" the hound echoed, lowering the weapon, but not sheathing it. "No. Clearly, I am taking the long route in undressing him whilst he holds my scimitar for me."

"After earlier, I thought you'd gone off to..." The sentence drifted off unfinished as her brows lowered further. "But *this*? Spellsters aren't allowed to touch normal weapons, much less use them."

"And you would be right, my dear woman," Tracker replied, his smile toothy. "They are not typically trained in such a manner. But given the possibility that someone is hunting them, someone who clearly means lethal harm, a little extra fighting knowledge is hardly a bad thing. Plus, it will aid in clearing his mind."

"Says you."

The man shrugged. "If you believe that to be so, but it was a common technique when I was a child. The elder hounds would have us train until we were ready to drop whenever we were hampered by emotions that left us vulnerable. Anger. Frustration. Grief. I am in the middle of determining whether he is capable of improving fast enough to make this worthwhile. Except..." He swung his attention back to Dylan, one brow lifting. His throwing knife had seemingly vanished, no doubt tucked away in some hidden sheath. "He appears to have stopped?"

Grimacing, Dylan gestured between the hound and the warrior with the sword's tip. "You two were talking." Even as the words escaped his lips, he realised the weakness of his excuse.

Tracker laughed. "My dear man, do you not know that proper sparring is always done under battlefield rules? When your opponent is distracted is precisely the time you *should* be attacking."

Dylan fiddled with the sword hilt, running his fingers over the designs etched into the pommel. His face blazed as if he were twelve again and back in the tower chapel. Only this time, it wasn't a simple matter of a breaking voice. "I know."

"Battlefield rules, huh?" Authril's echo of the hound's words was all the warning Dylan got before she unsheathed her sword and charged across the copse towards him.

He scrambled back, seeking shelter before realising there was none. His shield stuttering around him. The sword wavered in his grip. Did she expect him to retaliate against a proper attack? He'd only ever been a few battles and she had witnessed how he fought in all but one of them.

With every backwards step he took, Authril gained the ground twice as fast. A strange glee had taken her face, twisting her delicate features into something monstrous. She swiftly drew level with the hound's position. Any moment now and she'd be upon him, bearing that sword down with him incapable of stopping her without resorting to magic.

Dylan took another hurriedly retreating step.

His heel caught on an unforgiving section of ground, pitching him flat onto his backside in the grass. The impact sent a jarring twinge running from his rear right up his spine to rattle his teeth. His magic was quick to soothe the ache, even as he searched for the dropped sword to defend himself.

Swearing caught his attention. He rolled his head to one side to see Authril lying on the ground, clutching at her middle. She didn't appear to be bleeding.

Tracker stood over her, issuing a low growl that lifted Dylan's neck hairs. The man brandished a dagger, the edge showing no sign of having caused any injury. "You would advance on someone so new to the blade without warning?"

"You mean what you were doing more than just a few moments ago?" Authril managed between wheezing gasps. "The very thing you suggested *he* do?" Scoffing, she tilted her head to smirk at Dylan. "With a reaction like that, it'll take years for him to be a threat to anybody."

The hound barely took his gaze from her to glance Dylan's way. "Yes, he fell. Most entertaining." His lips flattened briefly before returning to their snarl as he faced Authril once more. "I cannot teach him if you are going to harass him and chuckle at his every misstep. Nor will he improve without proper guidance, as *I* was doing instead of lunging blindly. You recall your own training, yes?"

The amused curve of her lips quickly twisted in a sour pout. "I remember. Mine was on the streets. If you fell like that, you died. Few of us have the luxury of being taught fancy moves in some secluded little arena."

The hound's fingers flexed around the hilt of his dagger, then stilled as if he dismissed whatever thoughts running through his mind. "I will forgive you for speaking in ignorance, if only because you could never possibly know." He gestured at her, using the narrow blade like an admonishing finger. "But I will tell you this the once and you will listen closely. Understood?"

Authril nodded, her sea-green gaze fixed on the dagger.

"It is not uncommon for would-be hounds to *die* during their training. Our grounds are secluded, yes, but do not mistake such seclusion for being pampered."

"What *are* you trying to teach him, exactly?" Authril countered. "How to fall on his arse? The most painful way to lop off a limb?"

The hound thrust out his chin, amplifying his already unimpressed expression.

"Fine," she grumbled, clambering to her feet. A few tugs on her attire and a finger comb through her dishevelled hair seemed enough to have that woman regain her composure. "You want to tire out him, *and* yourself, by gambolling about like a pair of children playing war?" She gave a derisive snort. "Be my guest. Some of us have the brains to rest after a day's travel."

Muttering further words Dylan couldn't quite hear, she strode off back towards their camp with barely a pause at the tree line.

"Finally." The hound turned slowly, his attention more on Authril's departure. "I thought she would opt to stay and watch."

Dylan took a lazy swing at the man with the flat of the blade whilst he was still distracted, unsurprised when Tracker not only shifted his weight just enough that the sword would swing by without so much as a graze, but also deflected it with one of his daggers.

He grinned broadly over his shoulder at Dylan, wild pride lighting his eyes. "I see you are still eager to train further. May I suggest we—?"

"Tiring me out?" Dylan queried, echoing the man's previous explanation to Authril. Like he was a fussy child who refused to settle? "That's why you agreed to teach me?" It wouldn't work, not until he had also exhausted all that his magic could do. His innate healing did more than mend torn flesh or broken bones, it could also revitalise exhausted muscles.

"That is what *she* believes, yes."

"Should I consider myself fortunate you didn't offer a more intimate means to expend that energy?" The quip was out before he could stop it. He buried his face in his hand, peeking between his fingers only when the silence stretched for too long.

Tracker faced him with his arms crossed and his brows furrowed in confusion. "I do not see how that would aid you. It is rare for that sort of sparring to be of use in battle." One corner of his mouth lifted as he spoke, his amusement barely contained.

Groaning, Dylan retreated back to the safety behind his hand. What the hell was wrong with him?

"I hope our dear warrior's antic has not discouraged you. We can return to camp if you do not wish to continue."

Discouraged? Authril's attack had been unexpected and oddly predatory. He wordlessly adjusted his grip on the sword hilt. *Not too loose.* That was what had caused him to lose the weapon in the first place, he was sure of it.

He raised the sword into a prepared stance before trying a manoeuvre he'd seen the man use against Authril. His shoulder objected to the sudden request to swing the blade high over his back, but he brought it down easily enough, rotating the sword near his head before slashing at the man standing in front of him.

To where the hound *had* been.

Dylan spun, ready to strike again, and froze as a slight tingling of his magic pervaded the left side of his head. He touched his ear, feeling the slick coating of liquid. *Blood?* A swift check of his fingers confirmed the thought. "I didn't think it was that close," he mumbled.

"Do be careful," Tracker said. "That is not some simple training blade. It *will* remove bits of you as surely as it can from an opponent."

"So I see." How the hound could do the same action without harm was beyond Dylan. As an elf, Tracker had a far bigger target when it came to ear size and there didn't appear to be so much as a scratch on either of them.

"Are you badly injured?" Tracker stepped closer, rising on his toes as he reached up to examine the wound. His fingertips ghosted across Dylan's neck and earlobe.

Dylan shivered at the touch. All over, his hair prickled to attention.

"Fortunately for you, it seems to be intact." He stepped back, his face contorted in concern. "Perhaps we should stop? The light will fade soon and—"

Shaking his head in a very firm negative, Dylan tightened his grip on the sword hilt. "I can do more."

"Very well. But please do not attempt that move again until you have more than an evening of experience."

Dylan curtly bowed his head. His magic might've been able to mend the cut easily enough, but there were limits. He was in no hurry to risk removing the entirety of his ear. "Could we perhaps go slower? Maybe teach me how to stab?"

"I am not one for liking to do things slow, but if that is your wish..." Tracker bounced the dagger he wielded on his palm. "However, one does not typically do much stabbing with that type of blade."

Hefting the sword closer—to the strange sensation of comfort—Dylan examined the blade in detail. True, it held little resemblance to the weapon Authril used. Curved where hers was straight. The shape rather reminded him of the alchemist daggers. And, like those daggers, the sword was sharp along just the one edge. "You don't?"

Tracker frowned. "Well, no. It is a scimitar." He took hold of the sword and swung it around. As with all of the hound's weapons, it moved like a deadly extension of the man's arm. "It is designed to slash an opponent to pieces. You *can* stab with it, but only in certain situations." He sheathed the blade. "Perhaps it would be best to teach you with our dear warrior's sword. You are more likely to come across them on the field if the army will not let you have your own. For now..." He handed Dylan the long, knife-like dagger he'd been using to block each of Dylan's moves, whilst unsheathing a similar blade for himself. "Let us work on your footwork a little more, yes?"

They returned to the simpler, slower, motions of circling each other, feinting or lunging whenever there looked to be an opening. Tracker led him around the clearing, although not as fast as he'd seen the man do when training with Authril. The hound would veer around anything that might pose a threat to their safety, letting Dylan pick his way through the rest.

Nearer the trees, the land became less reliably flat. Their steps were slower, more mindful of their footing. Roots pushed up the dirt in irregular bumps, making for slippery and crumbling footing, and Dylan soon found himself spending more time staring at the ground than his opponent.

"Focus!" Tracker snapped. The man darted under the swing of Dylan's arm to tap him on the shoulder with the back of his unarmed hand.

Dylan jerked away from the unexpected touch. His foot slipped on a hump in the ground, leaving him flailing for a moment before regaining his balance. How was it that the hound didn't encounter the same issues? Tracker was even walking backwards for large portions. Was his hound training that in-depth? Was it some sort of elven sense that his friends had never mentioned?

The light was beginning to fade by the time their wandering had steered them from the edge of the clearing, where the ground was devoid of all but grass, into the middle and back.

Confident he wouldn't trip on anything out here, Dylan pressed the hound harder. Much to his surprise, Tracker gave ground.

After what had to be the eleventh time he'd effortlessly parried the man's attack, Dylan came to the conclusion that he was being toyed with. "Stop going easy on me," he growled.

Tracker scoffed. "You are the last person who should be complaining of how easy I am."

Tossing the dagger aside, Dylan lunged for the hound. His foot slid into a hollow as he collided bodily with the man, pitching him further forward. Pain lanced up his leg, a shard-like agony that began at his ankle. He tumbled to the ground, bringing Tracker down with him. Dust and bits of twig billowed around them.

"Sorry," Dylan ground out through clenched teeth. His ankle hummed with magic. He struggled to find his footing so he could relieve the hound of his weight, not that Tracker seemed overly concerned. "I didn't mean to—" The icy pain increased as he tried to stand, tearing a cry from his throat.

He managed to roll onto his back with an almighty thump. Grasping the offending ankle, he fumbled to remove his boot. His magic had the whole area throbbing, but even the smallest shift sent needles of fire up his leg.

Gritting his teeth, he persisted.

Tracker got to his knees, settling between Dylan's splayed feet. "That was quite the yelp." His gaze dropped to Dylan's ankle. His hand hovered above, hesitating in offering assistance. "How badly does it hurt?"

"Pretty bad," he admitted, the words barely slipping out on a whimper as his boot finally slid free. He fought to keep his breathing steady. If he relaxed for a moment, then the scream welling in his chest would escape.

The man's lips thinned with concern. "If it is broken—"

"It is." The pain was enough to tell him that. "I need to set it. Quickly." His innate healing wouldn't care about the bones being in the wrong place, it would simply build more to fill the cracks. If they didn't hurry, then the repair would need to be broken again.

Not asking any further questions, Tracker grabbed Dylan's ankle. Those long fingers that had done so many exquisite things to him now sent fresh waves of pain up his leg with their every tiny shift.

Dylan's jaw ached with how tightly he clenched it. His shield shimmered in and out of existence. Unbidden magic crackled around him in flares of sparks and gusts of heat. The former snapped and arced about Tracker as the hound continued to deftly manipulate the bones back into position. The grating of them only added to the pain his magic was fighting to quell.

Then, slowly, the pain began to subside. He might have mended broken bones before, but never one of his own. If he turned his attention to the injury, the sensation of his bones trying to knit back together was like a swarm of tiny, prickly ants crawling beneath his skin.

"You can let go," he said, rubbing at his cheeks to wipe away his tears.

Tracker's expression became one of disbelief. Unsurprising. Healing took years of studying and practice to become proficient enough to gain any talent. The hound had admitted to rarely coming across a spellster who knew such magic and had only witnessed Dylan use his abilities on flesh and organs. Bone might've been harder, but it still bent to his power.

The hound's gaze slid to the ankle he still held. His grip remained firm enough that Dylan doubted he could pull himself free. "It is a peculiar sensation, yes?"

Nodding, he managed a mumbled, "It'll be fine soon." Was his face getting warmer? Had to be the sun and the pain, coupled with the unexpected exertion of sparring. Clearing his throat, he added, "It's almost healed."

One of the hound's russet brows lifted in query. "And yet, you remain flushed." The intensity burning behind those honey-coloured eyes increased. "You are still in pain?"

Dylan shook his head, willing with all his might for the heat in his cheeks to fade. "You're holding my bare leg," he pointed out. One long-fingered hand had moved to neatly cup his calf, the warmth of the man's palm soaking through to the bone. The bastard had to be well aware of what his touch was doing.

Confusion twitched the hound's brows together. "And?"

"The last time you touched me there was when we... were intimate." The last two words came out in a breathless whisper, his tongue hesitant to speak any louder lest someone like Authril reappeared.

"I see." A haze of hurt fogged his eyes, dulling their typically rich honey colour. Tracker gently lowered Dylan's leg, the unfurling of his fingers a slow and measured movement. Their absence a keen void emblazoned on Dylan's skin. "You think of me as the kind of man who would impose his desires upon you."

"No." The hound had been direct, but he hadn't pushed Dylan. Offered to guide, perhaps, to distract. "In the tower..." His throat tightened, threatening to close entirely. "You helped me forget for a time that we were surrounded by the dead—and I'm grateful for that, truly—but it was..."

What?

Dylan raked at his hair. There was no point in pretending that night never happened. He certainly hadn't been able to so far.

So, what *had* it been? A bit of meaningless fun as Tracker had claimed? A mistake? No, he wouldn't go that far.

Tracker sat before him. Patient. Just as he'd been in the tower.

And come the morning after?

The hound had stated his willingness to hold himself responsible for their intimacy. He had even offered several excuses.

Dylan hadn't been able to accept any of them and he certainly couldn't bring himself to blame everything on Tracker. He hadn't exactly been an unwilling participant. He had agreed to the offer of sex, several times. Had even suggested the hound penetrate him.

But, in all... "It was ill-considered."

Something twitched across Tracker's face, there and gone too swiftly for Dylan to be certain the man's expression had changed at all. Had it been pity? Sorrow? Scorn? "You still feel guilty, yes? That we should not have engaged in such an act within those walls."

He did. What had he been thinking? *Rutting like an animal.* Worse than, really. Animals had the wherewithal to not do it surrounded by the dead.

Still, it wasn't the only thing that gnawed at him.

Tracker shuffled closer. "We are not there now. And we are alone."

"As far as you know." Anyone of the others could come upon them just as Authril had done. There was nothing to say she wasn't still out there, watching from the shadows as Tracker attempted to train him, waiting for them to give up and return.

"We *are* alone," the hound repeated. "Yet, you are afraid. Of what?"

He shook his head, his chest tightening. "Nothing."

The disbelief was back, alongside a concern that pulled the corners of the man's mouth down. "Your face when Authril announced herself spoke differently. You fear her."

"No, I was surprised." They were far enough from the camp that even those with elven hearing would have a difficult time making out anything if they yelled.

Tracker sighed. "Dylan." The firmness in his voice was back, along with the fluttering in Dylan's gut. "You think I have not seen fear before?"

"That's not comparable." Those who feared a King's Hound would've also been fleeing the threat of having their lives cut short. Many would already know their crimes demanded punishment. He was wary of Authril's temper, and could admit she was more than capable of making good on her threat to end him should he step out of line, but he had feared Tracker more upon their first meeting than he ever could the warrior.

"Even if she objects to you learning the blade—"

"It's not that." He wet his lips. "The thought of her knowing that we..." He couldn't even finish verbalising the thought without his stomach twisting.

It wasn't just her. Marin. Katarina. The mere idea that anyone knew he'd been with the hound robbed him of breath. The longer he let it fester in the forefront of his mind, the worse it became.

The hound's brows knitted together. "What difference do you believe it would make if she did?"

The difference? Her knowing would give her the leverage she sought to remove Tracker as the one in command of their group. Possibly even the full command of their travels. It would become just like the days before the hound found him. Her command. Her choices. Her decision over everything, including his very life. Just as the overseers had done.

There are no overseers. No tower to judge him. No guardians to expose him to. No threat of being ousted over a single night's decision, of having his every move shadowed, of being looked upon like a contagion.

Except...

Authril was clearly bent on becoming his warden, of reminding him precisely what his place was, be it the world or the army. Without her, another would be chosen as his warden once they reached Wintervale.

The one night he had spent with Tracker made him an indecisive in the tower's eyes. He didn't know if it was the same outside the walls. He couldn't risk Authril knowing, couldn't risk any of them knowing. He couldn't risk another claiming him as their warden. Couldn't risk what they might do. What they'd turn him into.

The blank faces. The lifeless eyes staring into nothing. The gentle sobs that echoed through the night, tearless cries that wouldn't stop.

The memory of the other leashed spellsters sunk its claws into his chest. His heart hammered in his ears, trying to escape the crushing tightness. He had mingled only briefly with those who had joined the army before him, but it had been enough. He couldn't risk becoming *that*. Nothing else mattered, if he could avoid—

"Dylan?"

He blinked to find Tracker before him, his head cradled by those long fingers.

The hound peered at him, his expression stark with concern. He didn't move save for the gentle sweep of a thumb across Dylan's cheek, the subtle roughness of the man's skin helping to ground him.

Dylan closed his eyes, leaning into the touch.

Tracker spoke, his voice soft and low as though Dylan was a spooked cat. He uttered the same words, or near similar ones, over and over, his lips barely parting. It took Dylan a moment to register just what the man said. "Steady now. You are safe, I swear. Just breathe slowly and concentrate on the sound of my voice."

The latter was simple enough. He could've spent years listening to the soft roll of the hound's accent. The way it purred along every word, sending a fluttering through his gut.

He opened his eyes and met that honey-coloured gaze, watching as the man's concern melted into relief. Dylan's focus dropped to the hound's lips. How easily he recalled their softness. Not only when they were upon his own. *So close.* He'd barely have to move. Would Tracker stop him? He doubted it.

No.

Dylan tilted back, keeping the hound from closing the distance with a hand on the man's chest. *Safe?* The tower might be gone, but he had stopped being a part of its walls before then. He was of the army and the threats imposed on the leashed still lingered. He wasn't *safe*.

He wasn't.

Tracker cleared his throat. "Clearly, this topic causes you a none-too-small measure of distress. I will not pry, but I am willing to listen if you ever find yourself able to speak further." The man stood and gathered up his weapons. "If your ankle is well enough to make the journey, we should return to the others before the light goes completely." He offered his hand, a warm smile stretching his lips. "I would not wish for you to take a third tumble."

Dylan grabbed the man's hand. He got to his feet with far less grace than the hound and, together, they strode off towards their camp.

CHAPTER 4

Dylan was having another nightmare.

These unwelcomed dreams came to the spellster so often that Tracker no longer needed to leave his tent to confirm just what the cause was. There was no mistaking the erratic rise and fall of unformed magic, how it scented the air like a brewing storm cloud. It held his focus even in the deepest of sleeps. He knew that only because of how many times he had awoken facing the spellster's tent and he'd never been a restless sleeper.

Stretching, Tracker waited to see if he needed to wake the man. It was already difficult at first to tell whether the spellster's sleep would require such assistance and, given how uncomfortable Dylan had been after their talk yesterday, Tracker would've preferred not to cause any further upset.

For the most part, the nightmares had been mercifully short and sporadic things. Some obviously startled the man awake, the resulting low pulse likewise jolting Tracker from his slumber. Other times, they left Dylan lying prone, his shield bulging the tent sides, threatening the seams.

The swelling power abruptly halted.

Tracker sat up, his senses locked onto the hum that was the dormant state of Dylan's magic. *He is awake.* And on the move. No doubt seeking the soothing touch of the cool night air.

Resuming his recline, he absently followed that wisp of barely restrained power as Dylan moved about the camp. The man's silhouette passed by Tracker's tent, the campfire warping the shadow across the canvas, giving the impression the spellster was headed for the entrance.

Perhaps he should go after Dylan, see if there was any assistance he could give to calm the man's mind. Or at least stop him from wandering too far from the camp. They'd come across no signs that the Talfaltaner horde had stragglers, but it wasn't wise to discount the possibility.

He had barely flung his blankets to one side when the tent flap parted.

Dylan crouched in the gap, clearly startled. "Sorry, I..." That dark gaze slid down Tracker's body, pausing for a moment at his waist, before snapping back up. "I didn't mean to wake you."

"Clearly you did. Otherwise, you would not be barging into my tent." Or was this a simple mistake? The clouds hung thick overhead, obscuring the moon's passage before it could rise. Had the man's mind been mired in such darkness that he had mistaken one tent for another in the firelight?

The spellster bowed his head. Was he ashamed? With the man's face in shadow, it was hard to determine. "I had another nightmare."

"I am aware." He settled in the middle of his bedding, crossing his legs. "You wish to talk about it, yes?"

Dylan shook his head. "I want the blanket." The request came softly. "That's the phrase, right? Blade or blanket?" Even in the darkness, Tracker felt the man's gaze peering at him through tangles of hair. "I can't sleep. I haven't been able to properly rest since..." His voice drifted off, the rasping of his breath swiftly taking its place.

Tracker remained silent, hoping the spellster would work through his thoughts without interruption.

"I keep seeing them." He clutched his head, fingers winding through his hair. The chaos of his magic flickered briefly into a shield. "It's just flashes, but they're there every time I close my eyes, waiting for me. I can't—"

"That is to be expected." Seeing that the man's mind would only continue running in circles, he couldn't keep himself from speaking any longer. "You have been through several traumatic experiences. I would be more concerned if they did *not* have an effect."

"*You* help lessen their hold, though. Not just in the tower, but out here. The forest..." he murmured, dazed and distant. "The camp... the clearing..."

"You asked for the blanket over the blade," Tracker gently reminded the man, seeking to bring Dylan back from the darkness as well as coax the truth from him. "Are you after platonic consoling or sex?" He wasn't sure just how late it was, but they could have only a short timeframe before Marin sought him to take his turn on watch.

Dylan shook himself. He stared at Tracker for some time, blinking rapidly, before the hint of a smile tweaked the corner of his mouth. "Reassurance would be nice. I already tried the other option." He bowed his head. "Authril insisted."

"She *what?*" He had hoped having her sleeping in a separate place would've been enough. Did he have to stand guard outside the spellster's tent to keep her from sneaking in like a lust-driven adolescent?

The man grimaced. "She came to me tonight, not long after you and Marin had gone to sleep. Said she could tire me out better than any amount of sword fighting you could teach me."

"I see." How he summoned the words without any heat in his voice was a miracle. *She came to him.* Initiated sex with Dylan after suggesting Tracker kill the man.

It only added to his distaste for the woman.

"I know you said that wasn't the reason you were teaching me," Dylan continued, the pale outline of his hands disappearing into darkness as he wrung his robe. "But it wouldn't actually work. I mean, tiring me out through physical activities. That is, it takes more effort than most. And it doesn't help with the nightmares."

Training his expression to remain neutral, Tracker gestured to the bedding. In this instance, what consoling the man sought could be served by a literal blanket. "Unless you find comfort in your current position, I would suggest coming closer." He patted the very ground he'd been sleeping upon only moments beforehand.

Dylan gave a sheepish smile before crawling inside. The tent flap flopped back into position the instant his backside was through, throwing the interior into deeper shadows that obscured the man's expression.

Tracker's eyes had adjusted to the dark by the time Dylan settled next to him, although finer details were still lost. The spellster's form was stiff, his face hidden by a curtain of dark hair.

Moving slowly, he closed the distance between them with a single arm around the shoulders, tipping the man sideways into an awkward hug. Dylan conceded to the act, laying his head on Tracker's shoulder. With his jaw resting against the spellster's temple, Tracker felt the rapid pulse. The poor man's heart had to be close to giving in. Was that even possible with the innate healing? He still wasn't sure of the limits to such magic.

Keeping Dylan's head tucked beneath his own also gave him a decent whiff of the warrior's scent. It drifted off the man like a brand. Perhaps Dylan was right, that she *did* know what had happened between them in the spellster tower and was seeking to assert her claim over him.

The very idea had Tracker itching for his knives, even as he struggled to keep the tension from taking over his body. A would-be warden, he had called her. A mantle she was far too eager to don.

One he wasn't about to let her step into.

Stroking Dylan's hair, Tracker softly hummed a tune he used around Lullaby whenever he'd the time to make a proper camp. The latter aided in soothing himself, whilst he hoped the former would help Dylan relax.

Sure enough, after a brief moment, the man melted into his grasp. He clutched at Tracker, seemingly unconcerned that his fingers dug into bare skin. A breath that sounded very much like a repressed sob interrupted Tracker's humming. Dampness trickled down his chest.

Tracker gently tipped back, seeking to coax the spellster into lying down. If he could convince Dylan to rest, to settle where he felt secure, then he might actually sleep for longer than a nap.

Dylan's head had barely touched the rolled up blanket Tracker was using for a pillow before he jerked upright again. "I-I can't stay here, the others..." The intake of his breath rasped in the stillness between them. "You'll want to rest further before Marin wakes you."

"Just for a moment, then," Tracker murmured. He drew Dylan into his arms, succeeding in pulling the man down onto the ground next to him with very little effort. Dylan lay flat on his back, but Tracker hardly expected the man to snuggle close to him.

He mimicked the pose and returned to humming the lullaby, falling silent when Dylan's breathing became shallow. He whispered the man's name, hoping whatever depth of sleep the spellster had fallen into was deep enough not to be immediately roused.

Sure enough, his gentle call got him little more than a faint snore.

"Truly so exhausted?" Tracker murmured, unable to restrain from stroking the man's glossy hair. He was sure they had travelled harder on the way to the tower. Perhaps he should leave the sword training until the man could get a decent night's rest. *Authril will love that.* Any excuse to exert her control.

He sneered up at the canvas roof of his tent. How much about wardens did she truly know? *Army tales, most likely.* The woman had been part of a mercenary company. They didn't typically get chosen for anything beyond the grunt work of dying first. And before joining Danny's Cutthroats? *A life of navigating Oldmarsh's slums.* Not many got out of there with their morals intact.

To think, they had once resided in the same city. He could've walked by her numerous times during his stint as one of *The Gilded Lily's* finest. Just another knobbly kneed, elven teenager amongst the crowd.

And equally strange how the company's name seemed familiar. Most tended to leave areas where hounds were required, lest they were commissioned to deal with the problem, but he had heard that name before. Was that the company he had escorted to the Udynean border all those years ago? He could've sworn there had been a Danny in the ranks.

No, her sensibilities over unleashed spellsters didn't fit. They certainly didn't align with the company he knew who had one as their second in command. Those mercenaries had been ferocious in protecting the man, too. Not like the woman he had encountered whilst hunting along Widow's Way. She had mindless drones who couldn't live without her.

Dylan abruptly shifted, rolling onto his side and flinging a leg over Tracker's thigh in the process, the bent knee perilously close to collecting his member.

Still, the man didn't wake.

"Settling in for the night, I see." Carefully adjusting the man's leg to keep himself from being kneed during any dream twitches, Tracker wriggled into a more favourable position, one that enabled him to wrap an arm around Dylan's slender form.

He closed his eyes, letting himself drift on the cusp of sleep. Surely, a little rest wouldn't hurt.

The blackness behind his lids faded in and out, the measured increments in line with the slap of bare feet pacing. Wynne. *Had to be. Zinnala's strides weren't as long.*

One-four pushed himself into a seated position, instantly regretting the act as his head throbbed. He felt along the back of his skull, seeking the spot where he faintly recalled something hard smacking him. The area was tacky. He hoped it was blood and not whatever filth covered the floor.

Opening his eyes only increased the pain. The darkness wasn't absolute—yellow light leaked beneath a single door—but it might as well have been. "Where are we?" A cell, clearly.

"Bound for oblivion if we cannot escape," Zinnala muttered. She knelt before the door, heedless to how her attempts at picking the lock were going nowhere.

He didn't bother offering his assistance. She'd always been the best amongst them. Any lock she touched practically fell apart beneath her deft fingers. If she couldn't free them, it was hopeless.

It had *been hopeless. He remembered that. Still tasted the blood of their betrayer in his mouth.*

One-four turned his attention to the shadowy figure of Wynne pacing the cell's meagre width. She stood stooped even though the ceiling seemed high enough, her arms empty, but bent before her as though she cradled something nevertheless.

Precious. He groped his way around the room on hands and knees, searching the dark for their child, knowing in his gut he would find nothing. Not here. This little cell hadn't been her fate.

The shadows shifted. Walls he could barely see no longer held them, just infinite blackness. And a single iron-bound door.

"You forgot," Zinnala said, her words reverberating into the void. She looked so small crouched against the door. Childlike. That was

what they had all been back then, children barely halfway through their second decade of life. All four of them.

What had he forgotten? Them? "Never." Their names were literally inked into his skin. Their deaths haunted his darkest days, stalked his dreams.

"The lesson!" Wynne stamped her foot against a ground he couldn't see. The limb twisted, snapping in two. Cuts and fractures rippled along her skin like a heat wave. Her battered form gaped at him, her jaw crushed. "You forgot the lesson!"

"No." He remembered precisely what their mistress had tried to impress on them, the price they had paid for disobedience. No attachments. No sympathy. Nothing that could be mistaken as closeness. Not for common folk. Not for the spellsters they hunted.

Not even for those of the pack.

The door swung inwards, sending Zinnala flying. Flickering light from the dungeon beyond outlined a figure he had once called to fondly. Six-one-eighteen-seventy. Better known amongst the would-be hounds as Hunk. Their lover. Their betrayer. Wynne and Zinnala's murderer.

He rushed at the man, the dagger in his hand bright and thirsty for blood. This time, he would win. This time, he would stop the deaths before they began. This time, he—

Six-one batted him aside with the sweep of his fist.

The world turned to slashes of red. The combined lifeblood of his lovers seeping across the Pit floor. The wetness coating his bare skin. The rivulet oozing from Six-one's punctured eye socket.

Through it all came an incessant grating. Like the rusty groan of hinges. Nails clawing at rock. A sliver of metal working endlessly at a lock it could never open in time. The rasp of lungs taking their final breath.

"Track?"

"Tracker?"

He lifted his head at the call, his mind still fogged in the memory of old. The darkness slowly lessened, as did the noise, changing from the harsh grate of rusted metal to the scrape of nails upon canvas, until he found himself staring at the shadowy interior of his tent.

"Are you awake?" Marin's voice cut through the silence, soft and sibilant with urgency.

His hand slid to where his dagger sat. His body refused to follow, pinned by the bulk of another. Long legs entwined with his own, a slender torso pressed close to his. The gentle hum of dormant magic hung in the air.

Dylan.

All at once, his grogginess fled. How long had he slept? Long enough for Marin's watch to be done, clearly. What time had Dylan come to him? After the hunter had taken over from Katarina? Before? Had he slumbered through the *whole* two hours? He should have stayed awake, not fallen to the comfort of another snuggled against him.

The scratching at the tent flap returned, followed by the low calling of his name.

Trying not to disturb Dylan—he had no idea how the spellster might react to waking with the knowledge of someone directly outside—Tracker extracted himself from the man's grasp and rolled closer to his gear.

The tent flap parted at the same moment. Marin's head slipped through the gap, freezing in place for a heartbeat before the woman vanished back into the night.

Shit! He hastened to don some semblance of clothing and join the hunter before she returned to her tent. Going directly against his better judgement, and his training, he forwent any actual upper armour for the ease of trousers, boots and his undershirt. He didn't even bother dressing himself in the latter before leaving the tent.

Marin waited just outside, her brows raised to their highest. She remained silent as he slipped on his undershirt before leaning in close. "How long has *that* been going on?"

Before his mind could think of a reasonable explanation behind why the spellster was in *his* tent, his tongue leapt straight for denial. "I have no idea what you are referring to, my dear woman."

Verbalising her disgust in one piggish grunt, she threw up her hands and turned on her heel. "You know very well what I'm talking about. Just how blind do elves think humans are? It's not all blackness once the sun goes down, you know."

"I am aware." He had learnt a great deal about the extent of human eyesight during games of seek-me in his childhood. But even if the form of another figure was the best she could make out, the options of who it could be were limited.

Muttering intelligibly, she halted near the campfire to gather her things. Several new traps, if he wasn't mistaken. Odd that the hunter had crafted so many and made no mention of needing them. He would have gladly helped.

Tracker idly followed her path, his gaze sliding over their surroundings. The trees crowded their little copse, leaving the moonlight to creep through the foliage. It was enough for him, enough for any elf. *Or dwarf.* Katarina had proven how good her night vision was many times during their travels. Humans were a different matter.

"So then…" Marin paused in stowing the last of her traps to stare unblinkingly his way. "You and him? Duelling beneath the sheets?"

"Duelling?" he repeated flatly. They hadn't really been under any sort of bedding, either. Perhaps it was fortunate that his dreams hadn't been the good kind.

"You know…" She straightened up from her crouched pose to thrust her hips forward, waggling them from side to side. "Crossing swords?"

"We were *not*." That wasn't to say he hadn't been tempted some nights. There was something about the coolness of Dylan's skin pressed against him, the way it contrasted with the man's feverish response to each touch, every glide of his fingers, every lick and nibble.

But it wasn't what Dylan needed right now. And if Tracker couldn't comfort the man without immediately choosing sex, then what differentiated his advances from Authril's?

The hum Marin gave sounded in no way convinced. "I know Authril's reasoning, twisted as it is, but yours? If you're attempting to see if her line of thinking holds any truth, then—"

"We were not having sex." The words hissed out as he fought to remain quiet and impress the truth upon Marin.

She fell silent, her expression still plainly stating her disbelief, but she at least seemed open to listening.

Tracker glanced at both occupied tents, waiting to see if his outburst had woken any of the others before continuing. "Our dear spellster has been having nightmares recently. Every night, in fact. You must have heard his cries." The sounds weren't as common as the flares of magic, but they were audible enough even for human hearing.

Her lips flattened on a sympathetic hum. She eyed his tent before shaking her head. "Sadly, I have. I'm not surprised. *I* can barely sleep after seeing what they did to those poor people." Her head snapped back around, one brow inquisitively raised. "But how does that explain him being in your tent?"

He settled beside the fire, throwing a chunk of wood into the flames. "A spellster experiencing nightmares is a vastly different thing than the bad dreams of other folk. When not using their magic, their power lies dormant but not absent, including whilst they sleep. As long as their dreaming remains neutral or good, the magic slumbers. But when the dreams are bad…"

He recalled the all-too-common sight of young spellsters being the demise of their families. The last had been a girl plagued by darkness, or so the village had said. All he'd had left to go by were the charred remains of the family huddled around her.

"Their power turns bad?" Marin supplied.

"Not *bad*." No more so than the frantic flails of a child's limbs whilst they slept. "But their magic can react to those dream terrors as though they were real." A spellster of Dylan's age and experience had to be aware. "I have woken him many times before he reached such a state. Not only over these past few days. This time, he came to me for comfort."

"And you what? Decided to snuggle with him?" Her eyes narrowed until even the firelight couldn't make them gleam. "I can't picture you as much of a cuddler."

"I am actually very good at it." He just rarely got the chance as most people who shared his bed were looking for more and rarely stayed after the deed was done. "As evidenced by our slumbering spellster."

"What's to stop him from having nightmares whilst you're on watch?"

"Nothing." No more so than when the man was in his arms. Neither himself nor his tent carried any instant solution. "But I am alert enough to rouse him before he becomes a danger." That she didn't know he'd done it before now was a testament to more skills than waking a sleeping spellster required.

"Since you're in a question-answering mood…" Marin waited until he inclined his head at her unasked permission to continue before whispering, "What's all this talk about wardens? I know they're used in the army, but why does Authril want to be one? What makes them so special?"

"They are meant to be soldiers who are trained in handling spellsters." The reality was far from it, at least according to Fetcher, but it must've been true in the beginning.

"Handling?" she echoed. "As in fighting against them?"

He shook his head. "Think more a pig hunter with his dogs." The comparison reminded him of Fetcher's usual rants, in the rare instances where he shared more than a hurried moment with his fellow hound, of why *they* couldn't take the place of the army's wardens. *Who better to mind a spellster than those trained to hunt them?* The answer had been simple. There were already too few hounds to do their current duty. Having some join the army, particularly a status that carried such high risks, would see the rest stretched too thin.

"Authril wants to become *that*? I know her mercenary company fell with the army, but…" She trailed off, exhaling in a blast big enough to disturb the closest flames.

"Our dear warrior believes herself to already be one." Worse, that Dylan might favour the woman for the task without considering he needn't pick up the mantle of army weapon at all.

Marin grunted. "I've noticed. But she hates magic. She's already threatened to kill him once, *before* we reached the tower."

"After he announced himself as unleashed by healing her arm without being ordered, yes? Our dear hedgewitch has informed me of this." It had been a foolish act for Dylan to make without warning, no matter that he meant the woman no harm. Having seen the aftermath of the army encampment, Tracker didn't blame Authril for such an outburst. The spellster was lucky her response hadn't been to slay him then and there. "Are you aware she entered his tent tonight?" Katarina might've been on watch during that time, but that only meant Marin would've been sharing the tent with the warrior. "Long enough to have sex?"

Marin wrinkled her nose. "I knew she'd left ours sometime during Kat's watch. Thought it was for other reasons." Her face scrunched further with the pucker of distaste. "You need to tell him what she said, what she asked you to do."

He shook his head. "It is too soon. He needs time to process his grief."

"Meanwhile, she does this."

Which was precisely why he had hoped to settle the man into his tent. No matter what Authril chose to believe about the army's wardens, she wouldn't dare the same tricks with him so close.

Just how many times had the warrior been sneaking into Dylan's tent? They were no more than a fistful of days from the tower and she'd been excluded from her prior sleeping spot since then. Had tonight been the first? Some spiteful act because Tracker had decided to train the spellster?

"He deserves to be told," Marin insisted.

"I agree. But we are not even a week from the site of his ruined home with at least another to go before we reach any type of civilisation." Not even farmer huts were found this close to the tower. As much as he loathed the warrior, he wasn't about to leave Authril to travel alone, especially when there could be worse than her out in the forest. "And someplace where we could reasonably go our separate ways is farther still."

"Separate? She's not likely to let you take Dylan anywhere without her."

He knew that. When they'd first started travelling together, Authril had barely let the man relieve himself alone. It was a wonder she had let the man wander Toptower unaccompanied. But if she was truly looking to take the position of a warden, then she certainly wouldn't let go of the only spellster left alive in Demarn.

"The longer we wait to tell him, the worse he's going to take the news."

Tracker had reached for the comfort of his sword hilt before realising that he had, in his haste to vacate the tent, forsaken carrying a weapon sturdier than his throwing knives. "Have you considered exactly how bad that reaction could be? What could happen? If he confronts our dear warrior in anger?" And Dylan likely would seek her out. He couldn't expect the man to accept such news on a single person's word. Providing he believed Tracker at all.

Marin scoffed. "He's not foolish enough to do that."

"If someone told you the woman you had lain with only started to, and continues to do so, in the belief that such an act would control you... would rational thought be the first thing that comes to you?" Even if, by some divine miracle, Dylan remained level-headed, it wasn't much of a leap to see how Authril could claim the man's questioning as an act of insubordination.

She frowned, but said nothing further.

"Perhaps *you* could help him."

"Me?"

"You lost your home." It wasn't the same situation, no more than the attack on the army encampment could compare, but it was closer in terms of loss. "You could speak with him. Aid him?"

She bit her lip. "That was a long time ago. I was just a child."

Tracker laid a hand on her shoulder. "I understand. I will not insist you dig through your trauma for the sake of another." Even under normal circumstances, it was a big ask for someone not trained to deal in such matters. "Only if you deem yourself prepared." The man needed someone on his side whose interest in him couldn't be explained away based on their position or personal wants.

The hunter was the only one amongst them who fit the description, who could offer the man a less biased view on matters. *And maybe Katarina.* He would've preferred not to drag her into this. When it came to Dylan's wellbeing, any interest from the hedgewitch was bound to come up against treaties, just as he had the hound creed.

Marin stood, her things bundled in her arms. "I'll think about it. Just try to keep her away from him in the meantime."

Tracker bowed his head in agreement. He fully intended to. "I cannot ask you for more." He watched her return to her tent, noticed the subtle stiffness before she vanished inside.

With luck, he hadn't just set a landslide in motion.

CHAPTER 5

Three.
That was how many times he had gone to Tracker's tent, seeking what seemed to be the only means of diminishing his nightmares. *Three nights.* All one after the other.

It worked. As much as he had chided himself for needing to cuddle up to another person like a frightened child to fight off the darkness in his mind, it worked remarkably well.

He didn't spend the whole time there, of course. He would venture over only after the first inkling of a bad dream to leave before it was Authril's turn on watch, often waking to find the hound had taken Dylan's turn as well as his own. It still left him with several hours of uninterrupted sleep.

Tonight could quite possibly be the first break in this new pattern. Finding an area big enough for three tents had been all but impossible. He couldn't see how they'd manage in their current spot without them being practically on top of each other.

But the daylight was fading fast beneath the trees and they'd no guarantee any further searching would offer a bigger spot before it got fully dark. None of them wanted to wander about at night.

But that wasn't his problem to solve. His job was to collect enough dry wood to get a fire going. He'd almost an armful, plenty to heat whatever food they had left from Marin's trapping, and an improvement on the meagre amounts he'd been able to forage over the past few days. Yesterday's haul had been so abysmal that the morning's meal had required his magic to keep the flames alight long enough to heat the leftover rabbit. Although, Authril had insisted on eating her serving cold.

Perhaps he should reconsider the idea of permanently sleeping within Tracker's tent. It wasn't as though he'd never seen the hound's reasoning as having merit. One less tent meant more than needing less space, it also meant needing less time, both in making and breaking camp. That ultimately meant more time on the road and a greater chance of catching up to the people responsible for the destruction of his home.

A horde that had slain hundreds of spellsters and their guardians. When he was one man, with a single warrior, an archer and a hound at his back. *And Katarina.* A hedgewitch who he couldn't endanger. He doubted the Talfaltaners would even pause before striking her down alongside the others. Did they even know about dwarves?

He shook his head and gathered another length of wood for the campfire before turning back. What chance did they even have of catching up? Their little group might travel faster than one of any great size, but they were already days behind before reaching the tower.

The rustle and crack of another making their way through the forest caught his ear.

Dylan stopped, the sound halting a few steps after.

The longer he stood there, the more his back itched with the prickly sensation of being watched. He peered into the foliage, trying to make out what it could be. One of the others? An animal? An enemy? He wasn't sure exactly what could be out here. Tracker insisted there couldn't be bandits, but they'd no proof of that either.

Without his less-than-delicate footsteps muffling his passage, far more familiar sounds reached him. Raised voices. Authril's unmistakably harsh tone and... *Tracker?* He'd never heard the man so angry before. Were they in danger? He strained to hear clearer, but got little.

He'd barely taken a step before spying a figure moving through the bushes directly ahead, the silhouette swiftly turning into Marin.

"There you are!" She grinned, the wide stretch of her mouth strangely disconnected from the rest of her features. "Didn't think you'd be too far away at this hour."

"Is everything all right?" He squinted in the direction the woman had come from, knowing he'd see little through the trees. Marin seemed calm enough, but he could've sworn he had heard some sort of scuffle at the end.

"Why wouldn't it be?" She wriggled her hand into the crook of his arm, slowly turning him in the opposite direction. "Actually, I require your help."

"*My* help?" He barely saw Marin unless they were travelling or eating. She spent every evening setting traps and each morning collecting her haul. Given the lateness of the day, he would've thought her done. "I can't imagine being good at any of the tasks you do."

"I can teach you that easily, but what I mean is that the sun's getting awfully low and I'm not entirely sure if I'll make it back before it gets too dark and..." She gestured vaguely. "You've the ability to make a big flaming ball of fire to light the way."

"You want me to play torch? Sure." He could illuminate their passage with something better than a fireball, too. Did she not know that? He only used his magic during their travels if pressed, whether by the elements or the brief bandit skirmish, and when it came to camping, it was merely for small necessary things. "Let me take this back to camp first, then—" He came to a halt as she grabbed his arm.

That oddly disembodied grin returned. "If you do that, then it'll be too late." She relinquished him of the wood, dumping it beside one of the bigger trees. "We'll get it on the way back, don't worry."

Marin continued to chatter as they walked, pointing out game trails, the traps she had already laid and what she hoped to have caught come the morning. He couldn't identify half of what she described. Not more than a couple of trails and absolutely none of the traps.

"You must have a good memory." He saw no other way for her to recall so many places.

Marin shrugged. "The trails are harder to see in the early light, but what they catch stands out easily enough."

"And the traps that fail?" With the number she laid out, they would've had enough game to feed thrice their company if each one caught its prey.

She shrugged, the action bobbing the bow on her back. She always kept her weapon strung and ready whilst they travelled, but it had originally been tucked inside her quiver. Since encountering the tower's ruin, she had attached it to her attire by way of hanging it off a simple nail bound to the bow's belly with a length of rope. "I do my best to memorise their placement," she begrudgingly admitted.

"If you've laid them out so thoroughly on this side of camp, then why—?"

"You know what I'd like to talk about? Tracker." She prodded his shoulder just hard enough to rouse his magic's innate healing.

"Why *him* exactly? Thinking of looking for a less cramped place to sleep?" Dylan's tent and the one the women shared were of similar size and left ample space for two, but a little on the cosy side with more.

Marin stuck out her tongue as if having tasted something bitter. "I'll admit he's not all that bad to look at." She gave a small huff of amusement. "And he definitely knows it. But even if I was that way inclined, I doubt his mind would be on *me* at all."

"Oh?" His throat constricted. The warning buzz of his shield threatening to form hummed along his skin. She didn't know about him and Tracker. She couldn't. "You think his mind is occupied with someone?"

She arched a brow at him. "Haven't you noticed the change? The difference in his demeanour?" Her lips twisted, briefly forming what he could've sworn was a sly smile. "Why, the way he used to look at you…" She whistled long and low. "I'm sure they outlawed those sorts of glances. If they haven't, they should consider it with him."

Dylan hunched his shoulders. "A-and how—" His tongue stumbled over the words. Nevertheless, he persisted with them. "How did he used to look at me?" He'd be lying if he claimed a lack of notice towards any change in the hound's behaviour, the way the man shadowed him, guiding him out of the hollows, ensuring he didn't sink into darkness.

He hadn't realised it didn't only happen when they were alone.

She gave a brief, considering hum. "It used to remind me of the feral cats around my hut. The way they'd toy with the birds if they weren't all that hungry, let them think they could get away. Then another would come along who was starving and they—" She snapped her fingers, causing a flock of fantailed birds to erupt out of a nearby bush and into the treetops where they chirped what were definitely curses. "That's what it was. He'd look at you like you were something to be devoured and he hadn't eaten in days."

He knew the looks she meant. Just the memory of them started an odd flutter in his stomach. "But it's no longer like that?" His tongue stuck to the roof of his mouth, as though afraid to ask for such clarification despite knowing the answer.

Did he want her to confirm it? If Marin had spotted a difference, then what of the others? What of Authril? What if the warrior connected the change to the tower? If she realised that Tracker and himself had been intimate?

The civility between them was already strained. He couldn't risk having them outright opposing each other.

Maybe it was a sign to stop going to Tracker's tent after every nightmare. Sleeping alone wasn't something he was used to, but if he couldn't manage a few bad dreams, then what was he doing heading back to the army?

He wouldn't even need an excuse as the man knew why Dylan came to him.

Marin shook her head. "I would say it changed drastically when we first entered the tower, but I think it might've softened before then." She shrugged, once again causing her bow to bob. "I don't know. It's only been a week since we left your home. My guess, he's trying to cut you a little slack."

"I don't need anyone's pity."

She slapped him on the back, jolting him forward a few lurching steps. "That's the spirit. Hey, maybe we'll come across the bastards who did it and give them a little taste of steel. Right between the eyes, I think." Marin draped her arm over his shoulder companionably once he had righted himself. "Did they ever tell you stories when you were younger?"

"Of course." When he lived in the collective dorms, one of the guardians would indulge them with a tale every night. "Although, I doubt they were anything like what you grew up hearing." Frowning, he peered at the woman.

Marin's good-natured smile had fallen. Her gaze drifted to the forest ahead. She listened intently to the others as they shared their pasts, but hardly ever spoke about herself beyond generalities.

"These stories you learnt," he said to fill the silence and take her mind off whatever thoughts that had darkened her eyes. "What did they entail?"

"You know." She pushed aside a thin, low-hanging branch in their path with perhaps a little more force than necessary given how alarmingly it creaked. "When the heroes of old gallivanted off on quests to avenge their people, they'd always manage to find help in the next village."

"I know of the ones you speak of." But not until he'd been old enough to start his own research into the world beyond the tower walls. "I'm no hero, though." If he'd learnt anything from those tales, it was that spellsters were always the villains. Evil, cackling and irredeemable beings. It might be true of those from the Udynea Empire, but he doubted the average man really cared where a spellster was from.

"That's what all the heroes say."

"And who does the hero wind up defeating in the end?"

"Well, it's typically some—" Her voice stopped as suddenly as a snuffed candle, leaving her mouth open in a silent exclamation.

"Precisely," Dylan mumbled, not at all liking the commiserating way she looked at him. The overseers had ensured every spellster in the tower knew precisely how the world viewed them. *Dangerous animals that must be contained or killed.*

He wasn't anything like the murdering bastards in the stories or the ones that harried the border. *He* was...

An utter terror to behold. That's what Tracker had said. And the hound had the right of it. He *was* dangerous. But so was any fool with a sword. *He* was the one less likely to cause undue injury.

They walked through the forest with little said between them beyond the hunter's occasional warning of a concealed rock or hollow.

Finally, Dylan couldn't wait for the camp to break the silence. "I assume you had a point beyond reminding me that spellsters are typically the bad guys in normal people's eyes." He could almost taste the bitterness the words left on his tongue. Pulling what he hoped was a warm smile, he asked, "What was it?"

Marin chewed on the corner of her lip, clearly considering. "Do you think we'd find anyone like that in Whitemeadow? Maybe you're right and the average person wouldn't risk themselves to avenge dead spellsters, but there were more than that in the tower, right? Only... the further we get from your home, the longer we leave it..." She sighed. "It's possible that the king might not care as much as Track believes."

"No." Even without the old stories, no one was going to stick their neck out to avenge the tower without the king being involved. "Maybe another hound," he amended. His gaze slid to her hip, remembering the reason Marin had dragged him deeper into the forest. "It occurs to me that I don't see any extra trapping equipment." She kept all her gear packed away during the day, in a more efficient parcel than Dylan could manage despite her teachings, but she always left with ropes hanging from her hip.

She sighed. "All right, you've caught me out. I actually placed them all earlier. I have ulterior motives for dragging you away from camp."

"The others are arguing again?"

"What? No. I mean, they were—and probably still are—when I left, but that's not the reason. I thought, since you're learning ways to stab things, would you like to try your hand at my bow?" She pointed at the thick trunk of a larger tree. "That'll be an easy enough goal."

"Now?"

Marin shrugged. "Why not?" She unslung her bow and offered it to him.

To look at, the bow seemed like such an easy weapon. Nock an arrow, pull back the bowstring, then release. Simple movements that didn't require any fancy footwork or reflexes faster than what he currently possessed. And the range would give him an advantage towards fleeing if necessary.

On the other hand... "You think I could even draw it?" The woman's attire hid much of her physique, but he'd seen how muscular Marin was and the weight she could lift with ease. Both exceeded what his body had to offer.

"Only one way to find out." She plucked an arrow from her quiver, motioning him to nock it.

Mimicking the act was simple enough. Marin had carved notches into the back end of each arrow, giving the bowstring a place to settle. Lining up his target also came with ease.

But the instant he attempted to draw the bowstring back, the weapon trembled in his grasp. Each slight twitch threatened to have the entire weapon fly out of his fingertips. The arrow tap-tapped a hurried staccato rhythm, further fraying his nerves.

Before he could even think to let the arrow fly, the end slipped out of his fingers and sent it tumbling to the grass at his feet.

Marin returned the arrow to him. Laughter danced in her eyes, miraculously absent as she offered the advice, "Keep your arms steady."

"I didn't drop it on purpose," he muttered. He hadn't realised the strength needed to draw a simple piece of string far enough for the arrow to actually leave the bow, let alone travel any distance. Both Marin and the archers he had witnessed in the army always made it look so easy.

Still, he didn't fight her as she adjusted the angle of his arms. He drew the bowstring back again until it sat not quite at the length of his arm. His muscles burned, his shoulders and back itching with the tingle of his magic constantly working to fix the ache. Pulling the bowstring back any further wasn't an option, not without his arms shaking right off his shoulders. Why hadn't she warned him about how much of his body archery demanded at one time?

Tracker had laughed when Dylan first suggested the hunter could teach him if the hound wouldn't, admonishing him that it wasn't simple. Dylan hadn't understood then what could be complicated about the act. Now he saw that, whilst the moves were simpler than sword fighting, the strength required was another thing entirely. And, no matter how hard he tried, he just couldn't draw the bowstring back as far as Marin could.

He released the arrow, grunting as the string snapped across his forearm. A heartbeat later, his innate healing had abandoned his aching shoulders to soothe the fresh sting. He paid it no mind—he'd suffered worse cavorting about the tower—his focus on the arrow.

Rather than fly true like Marin's examples, this attempt managed a glorious off-centre trajectory before cartwheeling to the ground.

"It's an improvement," she observed, still somehow keeping her tone free of amusement.

Grunting, Dylan absently rubbed at his forearm. It no longer hurt, but he understood why the hunter wore a bracer only on her left arm a little more now. His sleeve might've helped lessen this blow, but not by much. He couldn't imagine subjecting the same spot to the string's repetitive abuse.

Marin offered another arrow. "Let's try again."

After an hour of attempting to shoot a single arrow any farther than the first proper attempt, he was starting to regret having ever taken the woman up on her offer.

Dylan lowered the bow and turned to his tutor. "I'm getting worse at this, aren't I?" Every single arrow he loosed had barely made it more than a few feet.

Marin hummed. "Well, that depends if your aim is to kill your enemy or annoy them." Although he could see she was trying to remain calm, the note of her patience wearing thin had definitely grown stronger throughout his failures. "Even then, I think you'd be better served by running up and stabbing them in the eye."

He winced. Yes, even without the arrow's acrobatics, where the point had hit was far short of their agreed mark. Some were close enough that he could pick them out of the ground without taking a step. "That bad, huh?"

"Watch me again." She took the bow from him. "You need to draw back." The bow creaked as she showed him the action for what had to be the umpteenth time. "Keep your arms firm so the bow doesn't snap back in your face and…"

The arrow whizzed through the air, slamming into the tree they'd picked as a target. It already bore two arrows, both products of Marin's talent.

"I don't think I've the strength. I just can't seem to pull it back as far." He'd heard legends of spellsters increasing their physical capabilities via bolstering their muscles with magic, but no one in the tower seemed sure how to go about it. He had spent years trying to piece together all the old stories, hoping to glimpse a starting point, but the clearest parts were the warnings, the risk of tearing those very muscles or rupturing something. It never seemed worth it to try.

"I'm sure if you practised, maybe with a lighter bow…" Frowning down at her bow, Marin sighed. "I confess, as much fun as watching your scrawny self trying to wield this beauty has been… it wasn't really my reason for bringing you out here."

Dylan paused in collecting the nearby arrows. If she hadn't wanted him to aid in laying traps, nor for use as a walking torch—although, that would become a possibility if they didn't return to camp soon—and definitely not for archery lessons, then… "What *is* your reason?"

She drummed her fingertips on the bow's belly, making the entire weapon shiver. "I wanted to talk about Authril." The fading light was still strong enough to gleam beneath her lashes as she glanced up. "I've noticed she's been leaving the tent every night, outside of her turn to take over the watch and for longer than anyone needs to relieve themselves."

"You have?" He hadn't considered that any of the women would notice Authril's absence whenever she came to him, but he should have. Nor had he been aware of the warrior doing it so often. He hadn't been in his tent for very long the past two nights.

Marin nodded. "It doesn't take much thinking to realise where she's going."

He swallowed, forcing down the growing lump in his throat. "Oh," he managed. Had Marin also noticed *his* nightly movements? Had Authril? Was that the true reason behind her raised voice back at camp? Surely, she would've said something before now.

Holding up a placating hand, Marin continued, "I'm not going to get involved in what you two are doing at night. You're a grown man and I'm sure you can handle yourself there." She took a deep breath.

Dylan held his, waiting for whatever objection she clearly had.

"There's something you need to know. In the tower, before we agreed on spending the night there, Authril... she..." Marin scrunched her nose. "Well, I was going to say she suggested Track did it, but it honestly sounded more like an order."

"What was her suggestion?" He'd an inkling he already knew what Authril had demanded from the hound, but he asked anyway.

"That he should kill you."

Dylan nodded, her reply only confirming his suspicions. He didn't blame Authril. Their whole journey to his home had been to leash him. Without a tower, there was no way to do that and, with no collar to keep his magic bound, he was dangerous.

"Obviously," Marin continued, gesturing to his whole self as if to point out he was still in one piece. "Track refused and they wound up arguing."

Of course they did. Whilst the pair hadn't exactly been on good terms from the beginning, he had noticed the animosity they had for each other had grown since the tower. He simply hadn't realised why.

"That's also when we learnt her reasoning behind sharing your bed. The wardens, they..." Her cheeks puffed as she struggled with whatever she'd heard about them. "Apparently, they believed that having sex with their spellster charges kept them under their thrall."

His thoughts immediately turned to the warden in command of him. The man had both bragged about forcing himself upon his previous spellster charge and claimed the same fate was coming for Dylan, not from himself, of course, but from others with similar corrupted tastes. The laughing tone in which he spoke was not a sound he could ever banish from his mind.

He had no idea *that* was the reason the wardens gave to mask the truth of their sick acts.

Tracker had asked if Authril was forcing him. Had he known what the wardens did?

Had anyone known?

He doubted that. Who would even think to verify the truth, let alone dig enough to discover the reality? Those in the army who hadn't seen them as monsters, considered them as little more than tools. *A necessary bad to wipe out the evil.* So what if the wardens chose to have a little fun with them?

Dylan swallowed, trying to ignore how the back of his throat burned. "Authril said those exact words to you?" He had to be sure. There was a huge difference between the warrior guessing the reason behind the wardens' acts and knowing.

"Not to *me*, but I was there when Track and her started bickering. We all were," she swiftly added. "He practically laughed in her face."

"I see." That didn't answer his question of whether the hound had known about the wardens beforehand. And why hadn't Tracker brought it up? He'd been in the man's presence plenty of times. Surely one would've presented with an opportune moment.

Marin opened her mouth to speak, then bit her lip as she hesitated before mumbling, "I'm sorry."

"Don't be. I—" He settled between the roots of a tree, tucking his knees under his chin, before his legs gave way. "I need a moment to think." Flopping against the tree trunk at his back, he barely heard Marin's response. He watched her deliberately put some distance between them, choosing to use up the time by putting more arrows into their chosen target.

Her information about Authril wasn't surprising, but what was he meant to do with it? Confronting the warrior would do little beyond making her mad, maybe even enraged enough to demand his death or attempt taking his life herself. Either one would put Tracker on alert, but the latter would force the hound's hand and, if the two of them clashed, Dylan didn't doubt the man would win.

And if she chose to not become his warden?

He ran his fingers through his hair, tugging at the dishevelled clumps as though it would uproot the knowledge from his brain. He couldn't risk losing her.

He was no stranger to the idea of people using sex as a means of controlling another's actions. However, very few people in the tower engaged in any type of sexual intimacy with another without some level of interest and anyone actually using it to control wasn't looked upon favourably. For the most part, those who weaponised sex used it as blackmail. He had heard his fair share of people using it in other ways, but he hadn't ever been the target.

Perhaps if he explained the truth behind the wardens and how they treated the spellsters. If he swore to follow her word regardless...

He would still need to put himself between her and the hound. Her reasoning wasn't the cause of the hostility between them, but Tracker's animosity towards her certainly had increased after the tower. This whole time, Dylan had thought it because of the night they had shared, a night Tracker claimed was merely to distract him from their surroundings.

Had it been an attempt to test Authril's theory? *No.* The hound had admitted Dylan wasn't the first spellster he'd lain with. The man would've known her reasoning to be false. A small comfort.

What of the change in Tracker's mannerisms? The man's insistence on Dylan sharing his tent had to be because of Authril. It explained the waspish responses and cold nature towards the warrior, too.

It wasn't the first time she had suggested his life be the price they pay for safety. He understood her fear. Yet, he didn't think anyone gave much weight to her mutterings since their first encounter. If she wanted to be a warden, she would need a spellster. With the tower gone, with himself as the only spellster, only one would be allowed command of him. Authril knew that. Tracker knew.

The hound *knew...*

He knew and Dylan had told him she still snuck into his tent. The man had to have heard her sneaking around, too. Maybe Tracker had even caught her trying to enter Dylan's tent.

The raised voices. There'd been no mistaking Authril's tone. They had to be discussing—arguing about—him.

And here he was, getting distracted by Marin's offer of training with a weapon he clearly hadn't the strength for.

Shit! He flung his head back, instantly regretting the act as he smacked into the tree's rough bark. He clutched the site whilst his magic worked to heal his stupidity.

"Easy," Marin said, grinning as she holstered her bow and rejoined him. "You'll crack your skull open." She gave his shoulder a gentle squeeze, waiting until she'd his full attention before jerking her head in the direction of their camp. "We should probably head back. I did sort of waylay you before you'd delivered any wood, but maybe one of the others has gotten a fire started anyway."

His stomach rumbled at the faintest suggestion of food. Dylan nodded. Whilst distancing himself from the others had allowed him to calm down, he couldn't spend the night out here.

"Of course, I'll need to find the rest of my arrows. Someone—" She arched a meaningful brow at him. "—scattered his handful of tries all across the clearing. Found one, but there's still a handful missing. Not even counting those." She jerked a thumb at the ones jutting from the tree trunk.

Heat brushed his cheeks, dispelled by the evening breeze. He had forgotten how many arrows he'd tried to send anywhere near their target. Marin had a decent collection, but out here, losing even one could make a difference if they were attacked.

Dylan meandered through the clearing at the hunter's side, stopping every so often to gather an arrow as she made her way to the tree that had been his target to retrieve those she had loosed.

He barely heard the crack of another's footstep before a hand darted out of the shadows to grab Marin, slamming her face-first into the tree trunk. She staggered back, drawing her hunting knife to slash at her attacker, only to have the blade snatched from her grasp and tossed to one side.

His shield shimmered around him before he had finished turning to face the threat. Figures emerged from their cover. They came first in single file, then in pairs. Each one dressed in the same garb he'd seen on the dead Talfaltaners in the tower garden.

Ten men. Not exactly the biggest danger they had encountered, but not something he had faced alone.

They spoke amongst themselves in a quick, high tongue he didn't speak. One of them gestured to him with the point of his sword—a curved weapon, chunkier than Tracker's, but looking no less sharp.

The man continued to wave the sword as he ordered Dylan, pointing it between him and Marin.

"I don't understand what you're saying." He could guess and it certainly wasn't a call to heal the injuries they had inflicted. *Drop my shield.* His life for Marin's. Except, he recalled Tracker saying these people killed everyone who associated with spellsters.

Holding Marin by the hair, the leader dragged her before the shield to halt a few feet from the barrier's edge. With her face bathed in the shield's meagre light, she looked ghoulish. Her forehead was streaked with blood. More of it poured freely from her nose.

The leader snapped the same order, whacking the surface with his sword.

Dylan grimaced at the vibration it sent through his brain. He met the man's eyes. Dark like his own. And cold. Terribly, irrevocably, cold. Exactly the kind of eyes he expected to see from someone who could murder children.

Lightning crackled in his hands. In the low light, he caught the outline of others moving through the shadows. Their shifting about hindered his ability to gauge just how many lingered in the gloom, but there had to be at least twice his previous estimate. If he missed even one, if he failed to reach Marin before they could harm her...

The leader snarled something else, something brief and final. Shoving Marin to the ground, he pinned her there with a bare heel pressed to the base of her neck. He raised his sword high, issuing his previous order, before tensing to bring the blade down.

"Stop!" Dylan held up his hands in surrender, immediately

flattening his palms against the back of his head as the rest of the group closed in on him. It took all his willpower to resist further widening his shield, to not push them back.

Could he dare even the smallest fraction of his magic? Marin was close to the barrier's edge. Closer still and he could slip her through, then she'd be safe and he could deal with the Talfaltaners.

But with the leader practically standing on her, altering his shield to let her in would bring him, too. Him and the thick sword he currently rested in the small of her back.

Dylan gritted his teeth. He couldn't use his magic to fight his way out of this, but he'd nothing else at hand. No blade. No bow. Only a couple of Marin's arrows. Even if he had Nestria's skill at levitation, they wouldn't be enough.

They needed more people, needed something to even the odds. *He needed—*

Track.

Except, the hound was back at camp with the others. Dylan could shout until his throat gave out and they'd never hear a word.

The man could sense magic, though. He'd mentioned sensing when Dylan's magic was weakened from overuse, seemed to know when he used it up close. That didn't mean the man could sense him out here, but how else could he be so capable of finding spellsters? It had to mean he sent out some sort of alert with his magic.

He sent a tentative pulse through his shield. Satisfied that it didn't seem to alert the surrounding men, he did it again in rapid succession, blasting out a warning code his friends used as children to alert each other of approaching guardians. There was no guarantee someone else would recognise the signal, but the repetition should draw the hound's attention all the same.

Without help, his sacrifice might be all that kept Marin alive.

CHAPTER 6

Tracker hammered down the last of the pegs securing his tent. The space was indeed as tight as he had suspected, but it had been the best option and he doubted they'd come across anything better. At least with the tents so close together, he would hear if Authril intended to repeat her night-time visits.

He glanced up, taking in what other work needed to be done. Katarina looked to be nearly finished with erecting the tent the women shared, whereas Authril was already transferring Dylan's things into the third tent.

Bending down to gather his pack, Tracker paused upon spying the warrior throwing her gear in alongside Dylan's. "What are you doing?"

"Returning my stuff to where it belongs."

Sighing, he straightened to face her. Getting involved in an argument, especially against someone with as stubborn a streak as Authril, was the last thing he wanted to do after a day's travelling. "I gave you an order. As a mercenary, you are capable of following something so simple, yes?"

Anger darkened her face, turning the pale skin blotchy. "Your order is foolhardy. You're allowing a spellster to freely wander camp." She gestured in the direction Dylan had disappeared in the search of firewood. "And even beyond sight. What if he decides to just up and leave one night?"

"That is a serious accusation you are levelling at him." And one he doubted had any basis in truth. "Naturally, you have evidence to suggest such a move is plausible. Or an assumption based on past actions, perhaps?"

"I've been checking in on him in his tent whilst you sleep the night away. His bed is often empty."

"He was probably relieving himself in peace." The gods could attest that the warrior barely took her eyes off Dylan in the morning ever since the man had taken the opportunity of a nearby pond to bathe in relative isolation. Thankfully, Authril stopped short of tailing when it came to the spellster attending to his base needs.

"He could've been doing anything out there."

"I am certain he is only capable of two." Three if Tracker included more carnal desires, but the man didn't strike him as the type to casually jerk off behind a tree.

"And *you* have never once stirred during those moments."

He spread his hands. It wasn't entirely true, but he saw no need to become the man's second shadow. "What would have been your expectation there? Would you have preferred I held it for him whilst he urinated?"

The suggestion only increased the colour in her face. "What if he had fled?"

"Why would he run? And to where?" They were still a good week or so from the nearest farm. Dylan wasn't an idiot and had to know his limits when it came to survival beyond the comforts of a community like the tower.

She visibly floundered at the questions, muttering incoherently under her breath as she continued to pace. "How am I supposed to know his reasoning? He could've taken off on a whim, you wouldn't have known."

"I doubt Dylan is foolish enough to attempt leaving when we're in the middle of nowhere," Katarina said. "Even if he was, he couldn't possibly hide his trail from both Tracker's *and* Marin's expertise."

"Precisely." Tracker wouldn't even need to rely on his ability to sense the man's magic. Like now, where he felt the man wandering through the nearby trees in search of firewood.

He glanced in the direction he'd last seen Dylan venture forth, only now noticing the hunter had likewise vanished. He could've sworn she had returned not too long ago, yet only Katarina sat near the beginnings of their campfire. Had Marin gone in search of Dylan? Surely, the man was capable of gathering firewood without help.

Had she caught wind of danger? They hadn't come across anything suggesting others were out here, and any animal capable of seriously harming them would make enough noise for him to hear before duller human senses did. It had to be something benign, like one of her traps being sprung early or the call of nature.

"You better be listening to me." The shrillness of Authril's indignance cut through his musing.

"Why?" he replied. "You say nothing of interest."

His frankness seemed to catch her off guard as she spluttered and started to speak several times before abandoning the sentence to begin anew.

Tracker took the opportunity to return her gear to its rightful place alongside that of the other women's. For a person who never failed to let anyone within range know how dangerous an unleashed spellster was, she certainly was eager to remain close to Dylan.

"I don't know why you're so insistent about this," Authril finally managed. "You think I haven't seen *you* venturing into his tent? Don't try to tell me you were waking him for his watch or some other dribble. We both know you've been claiming his turn these past few days and you're in there for far too long."

"I have indeed been entering his tent." There was no point in denying something so innocent, regardless of how it looked. "Would you have me wake him from his nightmares, or would you prefer he burnt his tent to the ground?"

She crossed her arms and tipped her head back, peering at him with a gaze so narrow that he doubted she saw a thing past her lashes. "He wasn't having any nightmares when I was sharing his tent."

That statement was also doubtful. Dylan wasn't the type to thrash in his sleep, but he did talk—although yelling would be a far better description at times. "He also had not lost his home and everyone he knew there. How much do you think the psyche can cope with returning to supposed safety and finding it stripped to the bone?" All the nightmares were likely the man's mind working to make sense of it. Tracker's own thoughts did similar most nights, if not on the same emotional level.

"That just proves he shouldn't be sleeping alone."

"I am in agreement with that."

She halted, one leg still partially raised to take the next step. "You are?"

"It would be easier for me to keep an eye on him if he were to share my tent, yes?"

"That wasn't—"

"It would also eliminate the need for a third shelter, give us a smaller footprint for people to follow."

"You think someone is following us?" Katarina piped up.

"I have yet to see evidence, but there is also nothing to say it is not possible." Even if they weren't being directly targeted, a contingent of Talfaltaners could've ventured after anyone who might've escaped. "It is best if we stay vigilant on the matter."

"Stay vigilant," Authril mockingly echoed. "Is that what you're doing when you're gallivanting off into the forest to, of all things, *train* him? Teaching a spellster to fight with weapons?" She shook her head as if admonishing a child's actions. "Nothing good will come of it."

"I told you why I am doing that." Maybe it wasn't the full reason, but it wasn't an outright lie. Having Dylan focus on something so completely foreign to anything he'd been taught in the tower kept the spellster's mind from spiralling into depths Tracker wouldn't be able to retrieve him from.

"To wear him out?" She scoffed. "I've better methods. And the task of keeping him under control belongs to me."

Tracker gritted his teeth. She spoke as though Dylan was a lesser being. A toy. A *thing*. "If you do not watch that pretty mouth of yours, my dear warrior, it will have you winding up in a ditch. You have already done enough damage."

"And what damage are *you* doing?" she countered. "Not only to him, but the rest of us."

"You were here with our dear hedgewitch. Marin was not so far away that she wouldn't hear you yell. You were quite well protected. I do not see the problem."

"The *problem* is you believe yourself as the leader. I swallowed my opinion over your decision to head for Wintervale. I said nothing when you first decided to alter our sleeping arrangements. I was even prepared to let you escort us to the tower, but this has gone on long enough. Dylan belongs to the army. That means *you* don't have the authority to decide what happens to him."

"*I* am not the one strutting about pretending to be a warden. Nor am *I* the one who suggested we kill him." Even if he didn't agree with the latter stance, he understood her thinking there. But he couldn't fathom why she was so eager to return to the army, much less as a warden, unless she sought death via battle. If that were so, Tracker saw no merit in dragging Dylan into it.

The woman's pale skin darkened. Anger or embarrassment, it looked the same on her. "Can you blame me? Look at how he reacted to seeing his home attacked. Look at how he still reacts. Absolutely no emotion."

Around you *alone.* Had Dylan picked up on the subtle hostility vibrating off her?

"If he really was normal, don't you think he'd be a little more upset?"

"You think he is not?" Tracker growled. "If he is withdrawn, it is because he knows far better than *you* how much damage his magic can do running unchecked. I would even say he is aware of just how delicate his own mental state is. What *you* see as distant is him keeping himself contained to ensure you, and the others, stay safe."

Grunting her disgust, she gestured vaguely at their campsite. "All the more reason we should've done as I suggested. You really must be the most pathetic hound in the pack to let someone like him wind you around their finger."

Tracker slowly slid his tongue around the tip of a fang. It was the only way to keep his mind off his knives. "Be fortunate I am tolerant. A great deal of my fellow hounds would have left you and your mouth for dead long ago." He certainly couldn't imagine someone like Hunter enduring more than a few hours, but then, she was one of the more extreme examples of his fellow hounds.

"Then maybe they would've also done their duty the very moment they encountered an unleashed spellster."

"Do you listen to the words that come out of your mouth?" True, killing Dylan would have avoided everyone being stuck on their current mission. He could've still been in Toptower, nursing his injured horse in preparation for an altogether different journey. But as much as he silently chafed at the inconvenience and loathed some of the company, it wasn't worth the man's life. "I made my decision, trying to undermine it with your abuse of him will not—"

"Abuse?" she echoed, her voice straining as it tried to reach the higher notes. "You keep waving that excuse around when I'm treating him no differently to how the wardens treated their charges."

Just because that was how the wardens did things didn't mean it was right. "And degradation is also part of the warden process in keeping spellsters under control, yes?" The question was out before he could stop himself. They both knew she hadn't uttered any such words in his presence. That he was aware meant Dylan had mentioned it and the man wouldn't do so unprovoked.

"He's a grown man. If he—"

He held up his hand, stalling whatever else she'd been about to say. "I never said otherwise." The spellster's age didn't exclude him from being manipulated and he refused to stand by whilst that happened.

"You have no right sticking your nose into my managing of him. He is of the army. *I* am of the army."

"That may be, but until someone higher in the ranks appoints you as his warden, you are a common soldier. One who has experienced the loss of their entire way of living, yes, but also one who clearly lacks knowledge of what to do when it comes to helping someone who is grieving the loss of theirs." In that, he had to hope Marin's efforts would be far more fruitful aiding in Dylan's healing.

"And I suppose you're qualified there, too?" Smirking, she looked him over. "I'm beginning to think you aren't even a hound."

"Oh, really?" It wasn't the first time she had suggested he did things that weren't considered typical, but like most of the kingdom's citizens, she had no idea what their training actually dictated. And their creed forbade giving more than generalities. "Do tell me how I cannot possibly be who I am." Their mistress took a dim view of those outside of the pack donning the armour of a King's Hound and the lethal punishment for those found to be impersonating them was widely known.

"I'll admit, you look the part and you're... *decent* at fighting." She grimaced as if admitting he'd any skill at all, much less more than herself, physically pained her. "But your little brothel friend let slip how you spent years serving there. Everyone knows the King's Hounds are trained from childhood."

"*I* didn't," Katarina interjected. The hedgewitch no longer sat by the barely burning fire, but stood with the coiled energy of a person prepared to burst into action at the slightest provocation.

Tracker took a moment to unclench his fingers, surprised to find he had grabbed his sword hilt. As aggravating as the warrior was, and as satisfying as knocking that smug look off her face would be, fighting amongst themselves wouldn't help matters.

"You not knowing doesn't count," Authril said to the hedgewitch. "You're not a Demarner. You don't know the lore surrounding the King's Hounds. They're supposed to be mighty warriors who kill spellsters on sight."

"Only if they have done something to warrant such a death," he snapped. Few did, but the creed was clear about runaways: a spellster fleeing the tower could not be left alive to return lest they brought forbidden knowledge with them. "Dylan has done nothing to deserve such a fate. And I swear, the day you bring harm to him without reason will be your last." He didn't take pleasure in the more gruesome tasks a hound performed, but he could be persuaded when it came to the warrior.

Authril sneered at him. "Maybe you were a scrapper before you took up a different kind of swordplay, but the only way you could have that armour is if you killed a hound for it."

He lunged at the warrior, bearing her to the ground. They rolled across the dirt, lashing out at each other with bare fists before he pinned her beneath him. "Say it again!" he snarled, one hand unthinkingly going to her throat. "Call me an imposter one more time." He raised his other arm, ready to—

"Track!" The shock in Katarina's voice cut through his rage. Her hands were around his upraised arm, fighting to hold him back. "This isn't the way."

A glint of purple caught his eye. The alchemist's dagger sat in his grasp, the bare blade seeming to beg for blood. What had Dylan said about the weapon? That the smallest cut would never heal? The number of times he had brandished the dagger before spellsters fleeing the tower, the fear brought to life by a mere glimpse.

The way Authril stared back at him, unafraid, almost daring him to plunge it into her flesh. "It's true, isn't it?" she managed, her throat flexing under his grip as she fought for breath. "You've killed a hound."

The memory of Hunk, his lover—their betrayer—flashed across his vision. How that limp body had all but crushed the air from his lungs. The deep red of the blood oozing around the bone jutting from his eye, running freely from the chunk he'd bitten out of the man's shoulder.

"Once," he conceded, slowly loosening his grip on her throat. As much as he despised the warrior, yearned to end her hold over Dylan, Katarina was right. He gained nothing from attacking Authril. They needed her alive, for her blade if nothing else.

Triumph winked through the sea-green depths of her eyes like fish leaping across the waves. "I knew—"

"You know nothing!" Shoving her shoulder hard against the ground, he jerked out of Katarina's grasp and pushed himself to his feet in one movement. "You have a handful of tales—legends spoken by minstrels no less—to go by." Not a single one outside of the pack came close to the truth of their training, their abilities. They compared it to soldiers, to the knights of myth, as if one could simply *choose* to become a hound.

Authril sat up slowly. She rubbed at her throat. "What was it you said? Something about being tolerant? *You?* You're a flaming lunatic."

Snarling, Tracker once again aimed for the woman, his attack halted only by the hedgewitch and how swiftly she put herself between them. Only now did he notice Katarina held the *infitialis* dagger. She kept the weapon close to her chest rather than brandishing it, but he still had no idea when she relieved him of it. "I would appreciate you returning my blade to me." He extended his hand, halting as she twitched.

Once again, Dylan's warning of the blade's lethality jumped to the fore of his thoughts. The spellster hadn't specified if a hound could be damaged with the weapon beyond what a blade could normally do, but a dwarf had no such defences when it came to magic. "Carefully, if you please. The edge is... dangerous."

Katarina's gaze flicked to one side, clearly trying to see where the other woman sat in relation to them, but Authril had gotten to her feet and now paced the campsite, ranting and swearing. He caught snippets of the warrior's words.

"I do not mean to press, but—"

A burst of magic flooded his senses. Storm-cloud sweetness overrode the grassy aroma crushed into his jerkin and the metallic tang on his tongue. The tingle of distant, unformed lightning ran across his teeth and hummed along his skin.

Dylan.

He spun on the spot, his mind working furiously to explain the current situation without blurting information that could further upset Dylan or set Authril's ire upon the spellster.

Even the weakest of sentences fled as his gaze settled on where it expected to find the spellster, only to be greeted with nothing. He peered into the shadows shrouding the world beneath the trees to no avail. The man wasn't hiding. He didn't appear to be anywhere near.

"Are you listening?" the warrior demanded.

"No." He'd been aware of her movements and her voice, but it had been akin to someone conversing on the other side of a wall. Dylan's magic blazed strong enough that the man should've been standing right in front of them. At least it came from the same direction he had last seen both Dylan and the hunter.

But why the excess? Was it a beacon? Was the man in danger? Was Marin?

Authril spluttered a garbled mess of sounds before coming out with a shrill, "*What?*" Gathering some measure of composure, she continued, "I don't know what your—"

"Shut up!" he snapped back. Plucking his dagger from Katarina's hands, he strode towards the tree line. Whatever Dylan was attempting, finding the man would be a simple matter.

Authril followed on his heels. "You cannot just quiet me with a command. I refuse to be—" She fell silent as he levelled his dagger at her throat.

"Shush!" His attention returned to the spellster's magic before the woman's mouth could close. The pattern had changed. It no longer came in irregular bursts, but concentrated and repeating pulses as though the spellster was attempting to send a message. An alarm?

A call for help?

"Come with me," he commanded Authril. "Now."

"If you think I am wandering into the forest alone with you after you attacked—"

"Dylan is in trouble." Out here, there were few things that could threaten the spellster's life. It couldn't be hounds or the man would be dead already. That left bandits or Talfaltaners and only one of those was unlikely. If Marin was with the spellster as he assumed, then she could be in even greater danger.

He was not losing either companion. Not on his watch.

~ ~ ~

The Talfaltan leader had grown silent. Dylan might not have been able to understand a word of the man's tongue, but the disgust radiating from him was plain.

Nevertheless, he held the man's gaze. The rest of his focus remained devoted to keeping the low pulses—the call for aid—humming through the ground. It didn't stop the twisting, squirming worry wriggling through his gut. Or the buzz of his thoughts.

How long had he been stalling? How long could he keep it up? How long before help arrived?

Would it arrive? *Could* it? What if there were more Talfaltaners in the forest? What if they had attacked the camp? He had been acting on the presumption that the others were safe, but the reality was he didn't know how long Marin and himself had been followed.

How easily could the enemy have snuck up on a pair of battle-trained elves? Surely, between Authril and Tracker, there was little chance of the same ambushing tactic working with them. Or was that only a wishful thought? Some naive hope that he'd be saved, be it by Authril or Katarina or—

Track...

The hound would come for them, for him. He'd seen the man fight, knew how swiftly he reacted to a threat. Even if the camp was overrun by these monsters, it would take some doing to bring him down.

A whimper drew his attention to where Marin lay pinned beneath the leader's foot. The man's blade rested squarely on the small of her back. A dark stain seeped from beneath the point.

Reflexively, he took a step towards them. His shield warped and wavered, seeking to heed his desire to draw her into safety, to heal the damage before the man had a chance to inflict more.

The surrounding Talfaltaners stirred. Some crept closer, whilst others jabbed their weapons at him in warning. One dared to loose an arrow. The tip pierced a weak point in the barrier, halting in midair as the patch solidified around the shaft.

The leader remained unfazed. He barked an order at his men, halting the advance of all but two who assisted in dragging Marin further from Dylan's reach. The man growled his demand once again. The same words—always the same words—were just as indecipherable as the first time.

Dylan shook his head. "I don't understand you." He risked a glance in the direction of their camp, willing with all his might that help came soon. His gaze caught on the arrow still left hanging in the air by his shield. Having lost all momentum, it would drop the moment he let the barrier dissipate, unless he used it as a projectile. Manipulating objects in such a manner wasn't a talent he had much practice at, but if he could embed the arrow in the leader...

A scream of pain had him whipping his head around to the sight of

Marin with a sword firmly embedded in her back.

No! Rage tore through his throat in an unintelligible roar. Arcs of lightning snapped across the surface of his shield. He raised his hand, prepared to electrocute the leader on the spot.

The man pulled his sword free. Blood dripped from the blade as he raised the weapon high, his intention to behead Marin clear.

Dylan strode across the distance between them. Uneven ground and the forest underbrush bashed against his shield, but the surface was more a cage of crackling blue lightning rather than a solid entity. Singed earth and scorched foliage invaded his nostrils. He didn't care. They could all burn.

Arrows whizzed past his head, many of them charred or still on fire. He sent a blast of lightning in the direction of the archer without really aiming.

The barrage stopped.

Another Talfaltaner stood over Marin like a mouser guarding its kill. One of the men responsible for dragging her further from his grasp. The man raised his weapon as though he hadn't just witnessed his leader fall.

Dylan spread his fingers wide. Lightning bounced between the tips, growing stronger with every leap.

There was the glint of metal, and the man collapsed in a heap.

He didn't know how long he stared at the throwing knife jutting from the dead man's neck before registering it was there. *Track.* It was the only possible explanation. The hound had come for them. *Too late.*

He swivelled to spy Tracker bursting into the clearing with the other two women close at his heels.

The hound barely paused to take in the situation before rushing at his opponents. One fell without a chance to register the man was there. Tracker cut down another who'd enough wits to defend, sending the Talfaltaner's limb flying before opening the enemy's throat.

Behind the man, Authril slowed. She stared at Dylan, almost hesitant to come closer. Then the Talfaltaners were upon her, snapping her out of her trance.

A third man fell to the hound's blade, then Tracker was within the circumference of Dylan's lightning. The hound fell to his knees before fully stopping, sliding across the grass to halt at Marin's side, where he checked the woman for signs of life.

Or rather, the lack thereof.

Dylan barely felt the long fingers grabbing hold of his robe before he found himself level with the hound.

Tracker held him close with one hand, the other applying pressure to the wound in Marin's back. Blood seeped around his fingers. "Heal her!" he snarled, a feral sheen taking his eyes as his gaze slid elsewhere. "Let us deal with *them*."

She was still alive? He could've thought—

No. This wasn't a time for thinking.

He slammed his hand onto her back, mindlessly releasing his magic to seek out what the hound already knew. Marin was alive. Terribly wounded, but still alive.

His power immediately rushed to heal everything at once. The abrasions on her face, the broken cartilage and blood vessels in her nose. He fought against it, redirecting all his focus to the gaping wound in her back. None of the little injuries his magic worked on would matter if he didn't mend that first.

Delving deeper, he followed the path of destruction, surprised Tracker had felt a pulse at all with how weakly her heart pumped. The leader's blade had severed her spine, along with several of the tubes in her gut.

He hadn't ever been required to heal something so grave. Nor could he tell how much blood she had lost. *Too much.* There was little he could do about that beyond pouring more of his power into her.

Her body responded sluggishly to his command. Muscle and skin knitted back together. Her intestines writhed like worms, struggling against his command before slowly falling into place and fusing once more. The nerves and veins down her spine fought him as he sought to make them reattach. Pooling blood vacated the places it shouldn't be and returned to where it should.

Only when he was certain Marin's life was no longer at risk did he loosen his grasp on the healing process to finish mending the lesser injuries.

By the time he was done, the Talfaltaners lay dead around them. There were more than he remembered.

"Dylan!" Authril rushed for him as he faced the others, completely ignoring Marin's inert form. "Are you—?" Past her, he caught Tracker kneeling at the hunter's side, one hand on her back and the other checking her pulse. "Is Marin—?"

Sitting back, he waved her aside. Weariness fuzzed his vision and set a chill through his bones. Far more importantly... "She'll live." He had done his best, given it his all, yet had no idea if she would be able to use her legs. They would need her to wake before the side effects could be determined.

"Help our dear hedgewitch check none of our new acquaintances will be getting up," the hound ordered Authril.

Her gaze darkened slightly at the man's command, but she obeyed.

Tracker watched her leave, barely tilting his head to keep the woman in sight. "You did a good job healing her." When she was a fair distance from them, he laid a consoling hand on Dylan's arm. Marin's blood stained his fingers, just as it did Dylan's. "Are *you* all right?"

He shook his head. He wasn't hurt, but… "I froze," he confessed. "They just kept yelling the same thing. I couldn't understand a word." Amongst all the languages he had learnt, Talfaltanese hadn't been an option. Had they understood *him*? It seemed likely. "I should've done something to—"

"No." The hound's grip moved to Dylan's shoulder, those long fingers applying the faintest of pressures. "You took the best course of action. Had you dropped your shield, they would have killed you without hesitation." He jerked his chin at Marin. "Then finished the job with her."

He gnawed on the inside of his cheek, biting hard enough to draw blood. His magic tingled, repairing the damage. How he wished it worked as easily on the pain in his chest. *I wasn't too late*, he reminded himself. Not this time.

But almost.

Tracker offered his hand. "Come. You and Katarina should take our dear hunter back to camp. Authril and I will see what information our departed friends have to offer. If the gods favour us, they might have left behind something to help explain why they attacked the tower."

"I'll come with you." Gathering specific details on the people who had destroyed his home made sense. Grasping the hound's arm, Dylan got to his feet, wobbling slightly as his legs objected to holding his weight.

Judging by the critical slant to Tracker's lips, the man had noticed. "I think it would be better for you to recoup your strength. We will need you well-rested in case there are more lurking in the forest, yes?"

Knowing the hound spoke only to placate him and would continue to insist on rest the more Dylan argued, he bowed his head in agreement. With the enemy here dead, he'd already been denied the opportunity to repay their grisly deed.

But if he ever found himself with another chance, he would unleash everything he had. He couldn't allow them to get away with a single cut to those he travelled with. Not again.

If it meant putting his own life at risk, then so be it.

CHAPTER 7

Night had fallen by the time Tracker made it back to the group. Checking over the Talfaltaner bodies had revealed nothing they didn't already know from the spellster tower.

He had scoured the surrounding forest as far as he dared and found no sign of any other enemies lurking in the shadows. He also hadn't found any trace of where the Talfaltaners might've camped. That didn't bring him any comfort or convince him that there weren't more out there. At least, they seemed to have opted to remain hidden for now.

Pausing at the tree line, Tracker took in their little camp. Dylan and Katarina sat by the fire, the former seemingly engrossed in what seemed to be a piece of cloth whilst the latter leafed through the book Dylan had given her from the tower. There was a distinct absence of the warrior, but Authril had suggested checking further east to see if their ambushers had snuck around from that direction. That she hadn't returned at this time wasn't an indication of much.

His gaze slid over the tents, marking anew at how them being stationed so close together blocked sight of any advance from the north. They also shielded the forest from some of the firelight, but the other directions were exposed and the light travelled far beneath the trees. They would need to start digging pits if they wanted to continue eating hot meals.

Marin's traps. He had encountered one during his search, but he'd no idea how many the woman had lain out or where they could be. Whether she would be in any state to collect them come the morning was uncertain. Perhaps, when she was awake, he could—

Movement to his left drew his eye. Marin sat propped against a tree closest to the fire, draped in a blanket and quietly sipping from a steaming bowl that, no doubt, held the very concoction the hedgewitch had been in the middle of preparing before everything else happened. She watched in silence as the other two continued their chatter, pausing her observing only to drink.

He squatted next to the hunter, joining in her wordless

surveillance for a moment. "I am surprised to see you awake." Dylan had sworn the woman would need rest. Tracker had assumed that meant she would sleep, but she seemed comfortable enough, even if this was the quietest he'd ever seen her. "How are you feeling?"

"Tired." She chuckled wearily around her bowl, disturbing the thin coils of steam drifting up from her meal. "Seems like such a small thing to complain about." Lowering the bowl onto her lap, she slid one hand atop the blanket, tracing a line with her finger at the point where she'd been run through. "It's a strange sensation. Nothing like when he healed the cut on my leg."

"Due to the shock, I would say." The wound had been brutal and Marin had lost a lot of blood. If Dylan hadn't started the healing process when he did, it might've been a different story.

"You sound as though you've had a spellster heal you."

It wasn't a question. They all knew what his duty as a King's Hound required. He felt it deserved an answer nevertheless. "*That* would not be possible."

Her brows twitched, arching with the same curiosity that lit up her eyes.

"If you do not mind telling me..." He settled closer to the woman, letting her prop herself against his shoulder as he also leant back on the tree trunk. "What were you and our dear spellster doing out there that was such a distraction?"

Marin buried her face into her bowl. "Figured, since your attempt to train him with a sword wasn't going so well, I'd try to teach him archery."

Tracker smiled. The man's efforts would've been interesting to see. "And how did that go?"

Her snort almost saw her meal flying out of the bowl. "He's appalling. My bow's too much for him. My fault, really. Should've realised his scrawny frame's got no muscle. He needs something to help him build those up."

"I think you may find that a losing battle." Just as he'd never seen a terribly robust spellster, he rarely encountered ones who were physically strong unless they had little magic to rely on.

"A lighter bow could work."

Tracker grunted noncommittally. He had agreed to the man's request to train him to use a sword because the weapons would be common around the army grounds. Bows were less so. For Dylan to also require one of a certain draw weight would mean he'd need a bow made specifically for him. That in itself would garner attention. "Spellsters are forbidden to possess weapons." The exception being the alchemists and their daggers.

"Authril told me as much." He caught Marin's nose wrinkle before she hid her face behind the bowl once more. "Stupid rule," she mumbled into the dish.

He agreed with the hunter's assessment, but the army was unlikely to bend the rules. Not even to protect their last spellster charge.

"How did you know we were in trouble?"

"Dylan alerted me." The repeating pulse had been more than strong enough to sense. And unexpected. He hadn't realised the man had come to such a conclusion about hound abilities. He would need to speak to Dylan about that, in private. Stress that the man couldn't let on how he knew hounds were immune to direct magic in the presence of others. "I am surprised they managed to sneak up on you." Being human, Marin's hearing wouldn't be as sensitive as his own, but she was more vigilant than any guard he had met.

"What did those bastards want?" Marin asked around a mouthful of her meal. "Specifically, I mean. They kept making demands of him, but I couldn't understand a word of it."

"His life." Tracker jerked his head in Dylan's direction. "In exchange for that of his woman's."

Having been caught halfway through another mouthful, Marin momentarily choked. She thumped her chest whilst coughing, disturbing the blanket wrapped around her to reveal a bare shoulder and clavicle.

Tracker turned his attention to the fire, giving the woman time to fix her cover. "It makes sense to them. Talfaltaner women are considered part of the ship they are born on and just as precious." The way the Talfaltaner men he'd met on the Wintervale docks spoke of their women was almost pious. "They are the ones to plot the ship's courses, steer the city ships to places of good fishing or safe harbour."

"If they're so against magic, I'm surprised they don't try to claim their women use it."

He shrugged. "I have never asked, but I would say they see them as the average Demarner would the clergy." Not that there hadn't been a few members of the priesthood falsely accused of being spellsters, but such allegations were rare and generally had ulterior motives. "Like many in the kingdom, Talfaltaners believe magic can only harm. It would never occur to them that something like healing was a possibility, or the dozen other mundane tasks our dear friend uses it for."

"Like cleaning the blood out of clothes?" Marin added. "A shame magic can't also fix them."

That would explain the bursts of power he had felt whilst scouring the forest. He didn't understand why Dylan reached for magic when less extravagant means worked fine, but he supposed to someone so powerful, using the magical method was as simple as breathing. "I am surprised to find you are not attempting to mend your garments by firelight."

She gestured to the others with a jerk of her chin. "He insisted on doing that for me." Raising her voice, she continued, "As though saving my life wasn't enough after I was the one to drag him out there."

Dylan glanced up from his task. Now that Tracker's sight had adjusted to the fire's brightness, he realised just what the man had in his hand. More pieces of the woman's clothing lay strewn around him.

"I was unaware he knew how to sew." Or that there was much of a call for it in the spellster tower. In a place as big as Dylan's home, there would've been plenty of servants to do such tasks. Had it been part of some calming technique? A way to teach spellsters patience?

"Caught me off guard, too," Marin confessed. "But he patched his robe up well enough."

"Indeed." Tracker's gaze fell to the side of the man's robes where a section had clearly been burnt away and patched with completely different fabric. It had been that way when they'd met. Tracker could deduce the man had gained the hole whilst fighting with the Udynean spellsters. He merely hadn't considered Dylan would've been the one to repair it.

Dylan paused in his sewing, leaning forward enough to poke at the fire and stir whatever meal sat within the pot hanging above the flames. The meaty scent of stewing rabbit tweaked Tracker's nose, setting his stomach to grumbling.

Beside him, Marin snickered into her bowl. "Go and feed that beast, already."

"I believe I shall." He stood, dusting off the dirt from his trousers. "I will also endeavour to bring back the majority of your traps in the morning."

"That's not—" She ducked her head. The curve of her lips changed from pure mirth to warm gratitude. "I had already considered them lost. Thank you."

"My pleasure." He bowed extravagantly, garnering another chuckle from the woman. His offer wasn't entirely altruistic—they all benefited from supplementing the dry rations with fresh meat, but elves like Authril and himself required that little bit more—yet, having Marin rest whilst he collected the spoils of the night was a small thing.

Leaving the hunter to continue her respite in peace, he joined the others by the fire. Dylan acknowledged his presence with the bob of his head, his focus almost entirely on the shirt in his hands. He sewed with a measure of confidence Tracker rarely saw in the man, pausing only to tilt his work into the firelight.

Katarina sat on the other side, quietly humming as she continued to leaf through the book gained from the tower. If she knew he was there, she gave no indication.

Two unused bowls sat near the fire. Tracker ladled a decent helping of the stew into one, his mouth watering slightly as the scent continued to tease his nostrils. "Surely, my dear hedgewitch, you have the text memorised by now, yes?" They had been on the road for a week and she rarely wasn't studying the pages during their time at camp.

Her head jerked up, those hazel eyes wide as though she was a child caught stealing from a stall. A sheepish smile scrunched her face, warping the scar running across it. "Yes. But also no." She caressed the current page. "There are mentions of places I've never heard of, discoveries that seem to be glossed over as though I should know what they're talking about." She frowned into the book, softly muttering to herself.

Thinking it best to leave her be, Tracker tipped the bowl to his lips.

Authril came crashing out of the underbrush as the first mouthful of food touched Tracker's tongue. She took one look around their campsite, then plonked herself between him and Dylan, glowering at Tracker as though he had pricked her with the very needle the spellster used.

Dylan barely glanced at her before wordlessly returning to his task.

Tracker couldn't help but notice the man's subtle lean away from Authril, or the way Dylan disguised the motion as needing more light. Did that mean Marin had spoken to him about the woman's words during their stint in the spellster tower? He would need to ask her later. "Does your sour disposition mean you found no extra friends of ours lurking in the woods?" he enquired of the warrior.

"There was nothing," she curtly replied, her tone almost disappointed. Her gaze slid Marin's way and, as she bent closer to the spellster, her voice dropped to a whisper, "She's fine, right?"

Dylan continued his silence whilst tying off his work, searching the garment for the other hole.

Unperturbed, Authril grabbed a bowl and ladled the contents of the pot into it.

Only when the quiet had stretched out for too long did the spellster utter a soft, "She'll be tired for a few days. Food and rest will help her, but it's the body's common response. You would've felt a lesser version when I've healed you."

Tracker nodded at the explanation, more consumed in chewing the tough little pieces of rabbit in his meal. At least, he hoped it was rabbit. Damn thing had the consistency of leather. How had the others managed to digest this? To his knowledge, humans and dwarves had relatively blunt teeth. Had they left the meatier parts for Authril and himself?

"—can't affect him," Dylan said.

Knowing he was being spoken about, yet unsure of the full context behind the words, Tracker could only blankly stare at the man.

Authril gestured between them. "So you couldn't just... melt his pretty face off?"

Dylan shrugged. "I could try, but it wouldn't do much."

"*Pretty?*" The word flew out of his mouth, garnering the attention of all within the camp. With his cheeks growing hot, he continued, "All the words at hand and you use *that* to describe this face?" He indicated his head with a sharp wave of his hand. He had been called so many things during his years in *The Gilded Lily*, never that. "Not gorgeous or handsome?" He would've even settled for breathtaking. "But *pretty?*"

The last time someone had called him that, they'd been trying to kill him.

Katarina gasped. The book was slammed shut, all but forgotten as her gaze snapped up, fastening on him like a guard dog. "You're a Nulled One?"

Taken aback, Tracker jerked away from her. His fingers sought one of his throwing knives before he had considered just who his target would be.

His actions seemed to go unheeded as the hedgewitch pounded her fist into the palm of her other hand. "Of course! That's how you knew they were in trouble. You couldn't have heard them, otherwise Authril wouldn't have argued as long as she did. And diving through a lightning cage? I thought it was mere luck, but no. You knew it couldn't harm you." She rummaged through the pouch always hanging at the front of her belt, plucking a small writing pad, quill and ink from the depths. "It's obvious they would send Nulled Ones after rogue spellsters, but whenever we asked the tower for confirmation, we never got an answer that made sense."

Tracker watched the woman's writing hand, how the quill barely had time to leave enough ink for one word before she moved on to the next. His chest grew tighter the longer she wrote. "What are you doing?"

"Documenting," she curtly replied, not even glancing up. "The Coven has been trying for years to learn what Demarn did with her Nulled Ones. Is it the same for everyone within the King's Hounds? Is being a Nulled One a requirement? That must mean you know where they come from."

"I am not a null." He bristled at the very idea. He wasn't certain how many genders the dwarves believed there to be, but for the hedgewitch to speak the Demarn tongue, she had to be familiar with the idea of their belief. "I most definitely identify as a man."

The hedgewitch's brow furrowed with her confusion. Her lips pursed, poised to ask more questions, when understanding came to light in her eyes. "My apologies, I forgot you've a gender with a similar name. It's fascinating that the Demarn language came so close to the word, and yet chose to completely disregard it for—"

He had heard about the hedgewitches and their ingrained desire to record everything new they encountered. He hadn't thought it would encompass the truth behind his status as a hound. A truth that had been kept secret for generations. "This phrase has another meaning to you?" Hopefully, one that he wouldn't need to kill to maintain secrecy of. No one beyond their mistress and the pack was supposed to know the truth behind the hounds' abilities. He might have already broken that rule with Dylan, but he couldn't let it go much farther.

Katarina nodded. "It's what the Udyneans call them—although, they borrowed the term, like so many other things. Naturally, it was bastardised in their language. They're considered the property of their emperor as soon as their..." Her lips pressed together as she gave a thoughtful frown. "Well, I guess their *lack* of talent is identified."

"I was not aware there was another name for it." It wasn't as though he hadn't ever considered there would be hounds beyond Demarn's borders. As long as there were spellsters, hounds would be around. He had merely thought, given places like the Udynea Empire were controlled by spellsters, that any hound born there wouldn't live long.

"Oh, yes. It goes back as far as Domian, that's where the Nulled One terminology comes from. *Unus nullus* was the original wording. Of course, the Domians believed magic was innately tied to the soul and those who were unaffected by it were, in effect, lacking that part of themselves. They would train them as bodyguards, prestigious ones. Niholians still do this, although they call them... Well, it translates as Ghosts. They say it's because of their ability to walk through a conjured shield, but they've long been allies to the Udynea Empire. Each household head has at least one of them in their employ. I hear the current Tsarina—"

As much as Tracker tried to listen, his interest slowly drifted back to the quill and its wandering across the writing pad.

Dylan's chuckle neatly snapped him out of his trance. "I think you might've broken his brain."

He smiled, feeling a little sheepish about having let his mind wander. "No, it is fascinating. I just—"

"Wasn't expecting a full history lesson?" The spellster gave a knowing grin. "I learnt a long time ago to be prepared for a lengthy answer when asking a hedgewitch about the past. They collect information—from every culture they can, be it alive and thriving or very much dead—and are always eager to share it."

"I'm terribly sorry," Katarina said. "I know I can ramble something fierce. The Coven has been wondering where Demarn's Nulled Ones were for some time. We thought, because their abilities were unassuming and passive, that your people were more akin to the Tirglasians being unaware of their presence. But from what I can remember, whenever one of the hedgewitches queried the overseers, they would get quiet and usher our people out."

"The overseers were very protective of everyone in the tower," Dylan murmured.

"I just don't understand why they wouldn't tell us."

I do. And judging by the sober expression upon Dylan's face, the man was also aware of the reason. Just as the hounds were expected to keep the nature of their abilities quiet outside of the tower so, too, were the overseers within. They would've divulged little without a debate and risked even less on what they would've seen as a fruitless inquiry from any hedgewitch.

Offering up such knowledge would've brought more questions and trouble for the tower. For the hounds. For the kingdom.

"Say they had divulged such information," Tracker finally said. "Who would this hedgewitch then tell?"

Katarina gave him a puzzled frown. "The Coven, of course. Every piece of new information is placed before them to be catalogued."

"A catalogue," Tracker echoed. It was as he had suspected. "I see. And who has access to this place?"

The woman's frown spread to her wrinkled nose. "Everyone does. Knowledge is a right for all beings."

He knew several people who would disagree. "And in your great catalogue, which anyone can access and where you seem to also have a record of other Nulled One abilities, what does it say we are capable of?"

"Lots of things. The ability to withstand even the most powerful of magical attacks has been documented a half-dozen times, but—"

Tracker held up a hand, hoping to stall her sliding into another lecture. "*And* our weaknesses are also in there, yes?" He had too many injuries and not nearly enough bravado to think of himself as invincible.

She nodded.

"Udynea, you said? Niholia, Domian… These are places ruled by spellsters. Ghosts and Nulled Ones are bodyguards—"

"And assassins," Katarina added.

"That, too. But those… foreign hounds… they do not scour the land looking for new spellsters to cage." Tracker glanced at Dylan. The man stared straight ahead, his needlework lying forgotten in his lap as he clearly tried to mentally distance himself from the conversation. "The overseers were in control of the tower and their ruling was very explicit on what those under their care were to know."

Before Tracker could elaborate, Dylan spoke.

"The overseers taught us to fear hounds." His tone was soft, barely audible, as though afraid to speak. "The guardians, too. They said…" His fingers tightened on the cloth in his grasp. "They—"

"They used our presence as one would the bogeymen," Tracker interrupted. "Those in the tower were taught we would hunt them as soon as they stepped beyond the outer walls." It was partially true. "But they did not tell them what we are capable of, because a smart man would figure out a way around it once he turned his attention to the problem." He spread his hands wide. "Then, the crown has lost control of them and we hounds are left with but one recourse. It has happened in the past."

"It has?" Authril asked.

Tracker turned his full attention to the warrior. She'd been so quiet that he thought she had already sought her bed.

"The tower was wiped out before?" she pressed. "What we saw has happened in the past?"

"*Once.* Yes. But that was a long time ago." Because they had learnt the truth behind the hound's abilities. Even then, their history lessons spoke only of the hounds culling the spellsters. Not their guardians, not the overseers, certainly not the people living relatively normal lives within the outer wall.

The more he thought about the slaughter they'd found in the tower, the more he compared it to the past culling, the less sense it made. Talfaltaners were clearly involved. There'd been too many of their people strewn over the tower grounds for it to not have been a deliberate attack.

Yet, they wouldn't have known the tower layout. They hadn't the ability to corral the spellsters so skilfully. They would've left bodies inside the tower, just as they'd done outside. Someone had helped them. Perhaps even the same person responsible for the execution of the hounds Marin had discovered in the forest.

His gaze slid back to the pad page lying bare to the sky. "I suppose it matters less now. The crown is unlikely to rebuild the tower as it was."

"But they *will* make a new tower?" Dylan asked, the tone of his voice one of hope and sorrow.

"Of course they—" The placating confirmation stilled on his tongue. If the crown *did* choose to rebuild, it would likely only be to ensure they'd a steady supply of hounds, as the pack would wither without being able to monitor spellster births as they'd done within the tower. Centuries of hound tradition would become lost, just as the tower's knowledge was gone. "I cannot say." Whilst a tower built for the sole purpose of producing more hounds would certainly be a step down.

The crown opting for no tower would be far worse.

CHAPTER 8

Dylan couldn't sleep. After two nights, he would've settled for something resembling it. But, no matter how long he laid there with his eyes closed, the best he got was a softening of his senses. Never had he felt this restless.

Was it the after-effect of healing Marin? Except for the woman he had saved during the brawl that saw him out here, he hadn't ever successfully dealt with an injury as severe as the one Marin had taken. But this was the third night since the attack that almost took the hunter's life. There'd been no other attacks on them since then and barely any reason for him to use his magic. He hadn't pushed himself to the brink, but even if he had, two full days was adequate enough to recoup what he had lost.

Huffing into the stillness of his tent, he rolled onto his side and tucked the blankets tight to him. Magic thrummed through his body, his innate healing smoothing the effects of his exhaustion. It did little to still his mind.

It wasn't the nightmares, as much as they continued to plague him once he found sleep. Tracker's words refused to stop echoing through his mind, stirring more and more questions.

Rebuild the tower.

Dylan had seen the doubt darkening the man's honey-coloured eyes when he asked about it. Had the hound wondered if the place was worth rebuilding? Maybe the tower hadn't been perfect, but the alternative had always been unthinkable.

Who would dare form another? And how? Without the overseers and guardians to pass knowledge on, the method for teaching spellsters to control their magic would start from scratch. Everything would. Generations would pass before the building alone would be at the same level. It would take centuries for the infrastructure to match.

What would they do with the spellsters they found in the meantime? Demarn would always have spellsters. It only took a single parent to make one. That parent could easily be an alchemist who had evaded the King's Hounds.

And if they were found out?

The whole purpose behind the hounds was to bring spellsters to the tower where they'd been safe for centuries. Dylan doubted they'd stop scouring the kingdom for spellsters just because there was no place to put them in.

Without a tower, the hounds would have only the option of culling. Instead of spellsters being hunted for escaping the tower or harming others, it would be for just existing.

He recalled the tales of those brought to the tower. Some, like his friend Sulin, saw the hounds' discovery of them as a rescue and were thankful for it. Others, typically those found as adults, harboured resentment.

The far greater response had been terror.

Tracker had been right when he likened the King's Hounds to the bogeyman. Whilst the truth behind their abilities might have been kept secret, their status as efficient spellster hunters was well-known throughout the kingdom. But whether those same spellsters who'd been escorted to the tower had been resentful or grateful, they'd known themselves to be safe, providing they didn't run.

To know a hound's presence meant death? Dylan had no doubts that an inexperienced spellster would lash out in their fight to live. People would get hurt. Fear of magic would increase. Demarn would become like the distant Obuzan realm and the neighbouring Talfaltan Island. A land he wasn't sure he wanted to help protect.

And there was nothing he could do to change either his fate or that of the kingdom.

A wisp of cool night air drifted into the tent. He had scrunched himself further beneath the blankets before realising the breeze was due to the flap being opened. Someone was entering his tent, yet the hour was too early for his turn on watch.

He sat up to find a figure filling the entrance. Backlit by the moonlight, the points of their ears were the only discernible feature. *Track?*

"I thought you might come." It wouldn't be the first time Tracker had checked on Dylan when he was restless. The hound probably felt the surges of magic caused by his emotional state, even if they were contained within. Just as his guardian had taught him to.

The figure inched closer, letting the tent flap fall behind them. "What sort of warden would I be if I didn't attend to you?" Authril asked.

Dylan drew himself tighter together, tucking his legs before him, drawing the blankets around him. He hadn't been alone with the warrior since learning she had suggested Tracker kill him back at the tower. With her before him, he couldn't help but wonder just how much of the affection she showed was real. A little? None? He didn't feel capable enough to judge it anymore.

Slowly, he allowed a small globe of light to form in his hand. "What do you really want?" He heard nothing outside that suggested danger.

In the growing light, the wariness with which she eyed the globe sat starkly upon her face. "I already told you. I'm here to see to your needs."

"Because that's what wardens do? Why do you want to be one?" Someone in the army had to be there to give him commands. He wouldn't dispute the fact. He just didn't know the reasoning behind Authril wanting that position.

Her eyes rolled upwards before she seemed to catch herself and mould her features into a far more pleasant expression. "Are we really doing this now?" She crept closer, extending one hand towards him. "We could be doing something far more interesting."

He tilted away from her as far as he could without falling onto his back. It put less distance between them than he would've liked. "It's a simple question. I have no choice in returning to the army, but you—"

"You think *I* do?" Scoffing, she settled at his feet. "Everything I had died with my company. Fighting the Udyneans? Avenging my fallen brethren? That's my purpose now."

"And being a warden plays into it because...?"

"It'll get me up front." Cold madness flickered in her eyes. "Nice and close." She shuffled across the blankets. "And I'm the perfect choice. I've seen what magic is truly capable of, how destructive it can be. I know your abilities, how you wield your power. I know how—"

"To use me?" he finished, an uneasy weight forming in his chest.

Authril grinned. "Exactly!"

Like a stone dropped into water, the leadenness in his chest sank into the depths of his stomach. *A weapon.* That was how the army had viewed him. His cheek still tingled at the reminder. Authril had travelled with him from the beginning. They had shared a tent, and more, for over a month.

Yet, she still considered him as a thing to be pointed at the enemy.

"You don't have to do this, you know."

She frowned at him, bewilderment twitching across her face.

"Coming here to have sex with me," he clarified. "Whatever the wardens told you, that wasn't what kept their charges docile." From the outside, it might've looked like a similar act, but it was the violence that stemmed from it which did the job.

Her eyes narrowed until there wasn't a hint of their sea-green colour. "Who told you? The hound?"

He shook his head. If what Marin had said was true, that the two elves had almost come to blows over Authril's suggestion, then he understood why the warrior would immediately jump to such a conclusion. "Who told me doesn't matter. What does is that you don't have to mimic what the wardens did. I will follow your lead. Fight as you command without you having to debase yourself."

Authril slunk closer in what he guessed was meant to be a seductive crawl, settling onto his lap. Having witnessed a vastly superior move from Tracker, he now recognised the lack of sincerity in the act. "Without question?" she purred into his ear.

Dylan remained silent, his gaze having drifted to the tent flap. Wasn't it enough that he was prepared to return to the army? *To be leashed.* To fight a war against a foe that had already destroyed their best?

"That's what I thought." Entwining her fingers into his hair, she mashed their lips together.

Caught off guard, his light globe sputtered and winked out, throwing the tent into darkness.

Authril didn't seem to notice or care. She continued to smother him in kisses, leaving him very little space to speak or even breathe.

He sought to at least push her back with a firm shove against her chest. His palms connected with bare breasts. When had she started removing clothes? "Stop," he managed to mumble against her mouth. He hadn't the same agreement with her as he did with the hound, but it shouldn't matter.

Authril did little to heed his command. If anything, she pressed more insistently against him, tipping him onto his back. But that was often her way. Unrelenting. Greedy. It was familiar, much like those he had lain with in the tower.

And was very much unlike another.

Sure, the hound might've mercilessly teased him, but no more so than Dylan's friends had. He might flirt as easily as breathing, but when it came to sex, he hadn't gone any further until Dylan showed interest, had asked every step of the way and checked in on him in the spaces between.

He blamed the man's kisses. They were warm, welcoming and soft. Something he found himself craving more and more of.

Nothing like these cold, needy pecks that left no room for his own wants. Authril took and used. He had been fine with their simple arrangement at the beginning, but now? Knowing what he knew of her motives?

It wasn't...

"*Enough*," Dylan growled. Using his shield in one brief burst, he pushed Authril off his lap. He kept his hand raised between them in the off chance that she still wouldn't heed his words. "I said, *stop*. I don't feel like doing this tonight." Or likely any other.

She sat back. Without his light globe, the firelight streaming through the tent flap barely lit the tent interior. It was enough for him to see she was indeed half-naked. Her eyes glittered as an errant wind fluttered the tent flap and allowed the brief illumination of her face. The disappointment he had been expecting, and perhaps even a touch of annoyance... but anger?

Dylan quietly gathered his cloak, wrapping it over his undertunic. "I need some fresh air. You should return to your own bed." He exited the tent before she could attempt to get in another word.

The cold night nipped at his face the second he was outside. Dylan rubbed his arms, not prepared to sacrifice a scrap of magic to heat the air when the campfire still burned so brightly. Burrowing himself into his cloak, he strode over to the only source of heat.

Tracker sat near the fire, his back propped against the log they'd dragged to the fireside earlier to use as a seat. The man had taken the first watch, claiming he would still be awake tending to his weaponry, regardless. Although he would throw the occasional bit of wood into the flames, he seemed more engrossed in running a stone over the vast array of throwing knives spread out on the ground beside him.

Dylan closed the distance between them softly and slowly. His presence would've been marked the moment he exited the tent, but there was something about seeing the knives arranged in neat lines next to the man that demanded caution.

The hound waited until Dylan had halted just on the other side of the log before speaking. "Should you not be sleeping? Or rather, still entertaining a certain red-haired beauty?"

He knew the man meant Authril. Just as he knew the hound was aware she was currently in Dylan's tent. He had likely heard much of their conversion, too.

Nevertheless, his gaze flicked to Tracker's russet braid and how, in the firelight, it almost glowed. "I can't sleep," he confessed. "And I didn't feel like taking the other option."

Tracker hummed as he continued tending to the knives' edge, the sound carrying an unmistakably cheeky note. "Well, I cannot be of assistance at the moment, seeing that I am on watch, but if you are willing to wait a few hours, we could retire to my tent and—"

"No."

His firm denial had the hound's head snapping around, shock lifting his brows.

With his face growing far warmer than the fire could be to blame, Dylan continued, "I'd just prefer to sleep alone tonight." There were so many conflicting thoughts buzzing through his mind that it felt like a hive had taken up residence. Lying with anyone—whether that meant sleep or sex—was likely best left until he figured out precisely who he'd preferred to be doing either act with.

Tracker shrugged. "As you like. Seeing that sound sleep is clearly beyond your grasp at the moment... would you be amenable to talking?"

Dylan settled on the log, practically bending himself double to keep close to the fire and see the hound's face. "About what, exactly?"

"Anything you feel comfortable discussing. The tower, the army camp... whatever you wish. I would not even mind if it is something as absurd as your preferred nightcap."

He sucked on his teeth. Talking would give Authril time to dress and leave without causing a scene. "And why does my selection of topics not include *your* past?"

Tracker snorted and sheathed one of his knives, the weapon seemingly vanishing into the man's attire the instant he released the hilt. "My life is not something you want to hear about for too long. One can talk about torture only so many times before it grows boring."

"Why did they torture you in the first place?" Surely, if hounds were so rare compared to spellsters, those who trained them would've wanted to ensure all the young ones survived.

"It is supposed to make us strong." The man thumped his chest. "Harden our hearts to the pleas of spellsters who would prefer to live beyond the tower's confines. A weak hound is of no use to the crown and if you are of no use..." Shrugging, he returned to his blades.

You get put down. Dylan bit his lip as the thought surfaced unbidden. What else was denied to them with such hardening? "I don't know where I'd start." A lot of the things he could think of were far heavier than he wished to discuss so late. The absurd would have to do. "Blackberry cider."

Tracker glanced up. Even that small movement set the firelight twinkling through his earrings. His brow twitched. "Hmm?"

"You mentioned something about my preferred nightcap?"

The hound laughed. "So I did. A pity we have none. Unless our dear hunter is holding out on us. I was not even aware you could make cider from blackberries."

Dylan smiled, remembering the first time Sulin snuck one of his concoctions into their quarters. The aroma alone could've been enough to tan leather and the taste had been little better, but it got them drunk enough not to care about either fault. "You'd be surprised what you can make alcohol from."

"And where did *you* sample such a thing?"

"Home. The alchemists are very good at making something alcoholic. Sulin can make…" The words stalled. The firelight blurred, individual flames becoming one shimmering mass of amber.

Can. He didn't want to think about what had become of his friend. Any of them, even his guardian. A part of him hoped they'd escaped, but he knew the chances were slim. None, if they'd been in the tower itself.

He dashed the tears with a few quick swipes of his fingers. "I suppose he can't make much of anything now."

Tracker joined him atop the log, the knives abandoned as the hound laid a hand on Dylan's back. "My apologies," he breathed. "The memories must still be quite painful."

They were. He clung to them nevertheless. Letting himself forget almost felt like letting them die again. He would hold on to everything he could remember, keep them safe and alive until it was time for him to face the Seven Sisters.

How long did spellsters live serving the army? A year? A few months? Brawls like the one that had sent him to the front line happened annually, but it wasn't unheard of for there to be more in a year.

Movement from his tent drew his attention. Authril emerged from the entrance, dressed and definitely in a sour mood. She glowered at the hound, the firelight reflecting balefully in her eyes, but said nothing.

"Did we not have fun, my dear woman?" Tracker cheerily blurted the moment she had straightened to her full height. "Did I not warn you he might be less than receptive to your wiles?"

Muttering under her breath—too quiet for Dylan to make out, but definitely still loud enough for the hound, judging by the sharpness of the man's grin—Authril stalked back to the tent she shared with the other women.

Tracker watched her departure in silence, waiting even longer before asking in a whisper, "Marin informed you of what had been said, yes? Before we decided to bunk in the tower?"

He nodded. "I didn't know Authril had suggested I die rather than remain unleashed all the way to Wintervale." He understood the warrior's concerns. He *was* dangerous. "I already figured she had ulterior motives in sleeping with me, though."

The hound tore his gaze away from the tent to face him. "And it does not bother you?"

"Sex is—" He closed his eyes and took a deep, shuddering breath. "It *was* risky in the tower, but it was looked upon as a commodity. Using it the way she has been is—was—common."

The hound shuffled closer. A hand slid across the distance between them. The man's little finger—the digit as long as Dylan's ring finger—gingerly linked with his. "I know it likely hurts for you to remember those you have lost, but trust me, holding everything in will only let the pain burrow deeper into your soul."

"That almost sounds like you speak from experience."

Tracker shrugged. "A hound's life sometimes demands a sacrifice. But I would like to hear more about the tower, if you do not mind." Those honey-coloured eyes, seeming redder than usual in the firelight, stared up at him in warm, open invitation.

"I'm not sure I can."

"It will hurt at first, but you will find the memories flow sweeter if you try." His other hand alighted on Dylan's thigh, comfortably consoling rather than seeking anything further. "Tell me of your time there. Anything. What you studied. Your friends, if you have the strength to speak of them. Spellsters have individual guardians, yes?"

He nodded. Although, surely, a hound whose job it was to escort spellsters knew that. "I was assigned to Tricia at the moment of my birth." And she'd spent almost three decades raising him, only for him to abandon her advice and bound after the first chance to risk his life. "She was..."

"Like a mother to you, I would think."

"Yes." He would often call her such in a teasing manner, but he'd known no other carer. She'd been there for so many of his firsts, encouraging, soothing... protecting. Right up until their last moment together.

It had been years since he thought about his childhood, but he still recalled the times when he had grown bored going over the bare bones of literacy alongside others his age. How he would seek her out, craving nothing more than to snuggle into her arms as she read from texts that were supposed to be beyond a young child's understanding.

He could've done with that embrace right now.

"It isn't like that amongst the hounds?" he asked before the man could bring up another painful memory. "Do you raise your own?" He couldn't imagine any of them lingering at the main base to raise children.

Tracker flapped his hand as though to bat the notion aside. The grin stretching his face seemed oddly unnatural. "Not even remotely." The hand that had alighted on Dylan's leg shifted, helping to brace the man as he tipped back on the log. "The pack lives and trains in the old dungeons beneath the castle, but before then, we grow up in small groups scattered around the capital. Those rearing us would ensure we were healthy, but nothing more. Everything else is left to the trainers."

Who would physically beat and torture their charges, when they weren't doing only the gods' knew what else to them.

Tracker rocked forward. "It must have been hard leaving your guardian behind."

Not at first. But after seeing what had become of the tower...

His throat grew tight, as did his chest, leaving little space for petty things like air. His heart thundered. He stared at the spot, sure he would witness the organ burst from its constricting cage at any second.

Tricia was dead. His guardian was gone. There was no possible way she could've escaped.

And it was his fault.

He should've tried harder to be a better charge. He should've fled the tower when she had given him the chance. The guards wouldn't have been able to stop him. Only a hound could have. There might've been one in the tower at the time, but she'd been entrusted with guarding the leashed one.

He could've made it. Could've at least gotten his guardian far from the tower's destruction before another hound had neutralised him.

"She tried to stop me from competing," he said, the words dull even to his own ears. If only he had listened, thrown the brawl, maybe things would've been different.

"Competing?" the hound echoed, frowning. "For what?"

"To leave. Only the strongest are permitted to join the king's army." Laughter bubbled through his lips. "The overseers would tell us it's an honour." Had they known what really happened? *Quite likely*. And still, they sent more spellsters into the army's grasp.

Tracker's nose wrinkled as if he'd caught the whiff of something odorous. "Of course, they would say that," he muttered. "Is everyone made to compete?"

Dylan shook his head. "Just those deemed suitable. They start testing us once we reach adolescence." By then, only those who hadn't been raised in the tower needed any instruction on the basics. "See who can handle a fight and who would be better off in other pursuits."

The hound's lips parted in silent comprehension. "And you, naturally, were amongst the suitable."

"No." A bit of a mixed blessing, that. If he had been leashed earlier, then maybe he'd be suffering the same fate as the others in the attack. Death or slavery. "Not for some time, at least. My guardian? She—" His throat closed as he recalled the way she was towed from his side during her escape attempt. How she had tried to get him to forfeit. "Well, before the overseers placed me in the brawl, she had them believing I wasn't strong enough."

"A powerful man such as yourself? I am impressed she held up the ruse for so long."

Dylan rolled his eyes. The man had called him such many times, but he'd taken it as flattery. He wasn't in the mood for such sweet talk. "I'm not that strong."

Tracker laughed. "Did they also teach you modesty in your tower? You cannot lie to me on this. The raw power that flows off you eclipses everything like ink in water."

"It does?" This was the first time he had heard any precise mention of how his magic felt to the hound.

"I have never encountered a soul who could come close to the power you hold. Back in Toptower, I felt you approaching hours before we met. That brief burst near the gates?" He whistled low. "And yet, actually finding you?" He waggled a finger. "*That* was more like trying to locate the source of heat in a hot pool."

He had thought Tracker could only sense his magic when it was in use. Was he suggesting it was constant? Did that mean another hound would be able to sense him even if he didn't wield a flicker of his power?

"You use so little of your magic, I thought you must have realised this." Tracker's brows lowered, bewilderment clouding his gaze. "The way you move... react... you have *some* experience in fighting. You sparred with others in your arenas, yes? Surely, they did not send spellsters into battle who have not at least trained before."

"I used to spar against friends." There hadn't been many who could hold their own against him. Nestria, mostly, although she never truly put her heart into an actual spar when it came to attacking. "It was always easier to test defences with someone trustworthy." Henrie's terrible shield work would never have been a match against a proper opponent, but he'd been quick and his habit of vanishing from sight allowed Dylan to try out other methods of detection.

"Let me guess, you used your friendship as an excuse to hold back."

Dylan grunted his agreement, remembering the times in his youth when he had fought against others and sent his opponent to the healers with a simple burst of power. Fast followed by their wariness whenever he stepped onto the training grounds.

Yet, he recalled a few had managed to bring their fights to a stalemate. Then a handful more. He had thought his years of study and the lack of training had made him weak.

When had limiting himself become second nature?

And for Tracker to catch it so easily. Was it part of his hound abilities? Whilst he had pieced together the possibility of hounds sensing a spellster's power, he hadn't considered much beyond the idea. "What's it like to sense magic?"

Tracker sat in silence for a while, staring into the fire. "It is... a scent. A song. Colour drifting on the wind. The shape of a thought. And it is also none of those things."

"I don't understand."

"How could you? How does one explain sight to those who cannot see? The beauty of a symphony to those who cannot hear? The fragrance of a flower to those unable to smell?" He hummed thoughtfully, throwing more fuel on the fire. "Imagine walking down the street and smelling a family's dinner cooking on the stove. Faint, mixed with other scents, but distinct. When magic is used, it is like standing before the pot and your ability to smell anything else is gone."

"Was that what it was like when you found me?"

"*You?*" The hound grinned, the full length of his fangs gleaming in the flickering light. "If you wanted specifics, you should have said." He closed his eyes and breathed deeply, as though inhaling an undetectable scent.

The fire crackled. A spark burst from the wood with a pop, falling back into the flames. He wasn't sure how long the hound expected him to wait, but they had all night.

"Your magic is..." He opened his eyes, his brows still knitted together. "The closest I can compare is to a brewing storm cloud coming into shore. It leaves a ghostly charge in the air of..." The honey-coloured gaze ran over him, lingering a little too long on Dylan's torso. "...anticipation. Inexorable power waiting to be unleashed. This close? I can feel it rolling in your core like a thunderhead, heeding your every emotion. When in use, it is like lightning flashing across the sky. Chaotically fierce. Utterly breathtaking."

Dylan slowly sucked in a breath. He'd had people try to flatter him with pretty words about his looks or his skills. Never had a single person spoken that way about his magic. His whole body tingled as though Tracker had just caressed his soul.

He wasn't entirely sure the hound hadn't.

It didn't help that Tracker was still looking at him as though he might ravish him right there at any given second.

"And you..." His voice squeaked, forcing him to clear his throat as his face blazed hotter than the fire before them. "You can always sense it?"

"Always," the man murmured. "The more sensitive of us can even identify a spellster when they are still in the womb." He fell quiet, his gaze drifting to the fire.

Dylan mimicked the man. He had known they tested newborns for magical abilities for some time and, through Tracker, had learnt that those born of spellsters who didn't respond to the usual tests were sent to become hounds. He didn't realise the formation of those abilities could be detected before birth.

Abruptly shaking himself, Tracker picked up one of the knives and returned to his original task of running his whetstone along the blade. "Others are harder to pinpoint," he continued, talking faster as though doing so would distance himself from his previous words. "What we sense depends largely on the spellster's strength. You must have noticed the differences when living in the tower."

Other than the obvious variation between normal spellsters and alchemists? "In the training grounds, sure." That was the only place it mattered. Anyone who dared to use their magic to harm another was sent to solitary. Although, sometimes, they weren't seen again. "The tower divided us by tasks, not strength, and that was only during the day. At night, we were free to socialise until curfew."

"Curfew?" Tracker blurted. There was the faintest hint of repressed laughter hiding in the word. "Even for those all grown up? Did your guardians also tuck you in at night?"

Dylan chuckled. "They didn't go that far, no. Just guards on the lower levels. We were supposedly trustworthy enough to follow the rules without supervision. Most times."

"So, an enterprising young man could venture forth if he thought the journey worth it. Or was the tower harder to sneak about than I am imagining? You spoke of sex being risky. Your guardians patrolled the halls, yes?"

"At times," he admitted. "More so in the children's dorms. For the adults, it was mostly only when they already had suspicions." Was that why his guardian had been wandering the halls on that fateful night he caught the overseers' attention? So much happened then that he hadn't really considered why she'd been there in the first place.

To think, had the night gone the way he had hoped, she could've caught him doing more than strolling through the halls after curfew...

Would it have made a difference? He would've spent some time in solitary. And after?

Endless observation.

He tilted closer to the fire. It did nothing to thaw the chill settling into his gut. His guardian couldn't have known. But she'd found him easily enough. Which meant someone had alerted her of his whereabouts. Who? Why? Yes, he had upset Kaprina, but she couldn't possibly have been petty enough to—

"Dylan?" Tracker's smooth lilt slowly crept into his thoughts. "If you wish to stop talking about your home, we can."

He knew that, but if he stopped talking, then his mind was only going to run in circles. Worst still if he also returned to his tent. He just needed to take his mind off home for a bit. "How about you tell me about yours instead?" If he was baring his past to the man, it was only fair that the hound shared some of his.

CHAPTER 9

The hound sat back with a slightly amused quirk to the corner of his mouth. "You wish me to bore you with tales of training and punishment?" He spoke so casually, as though violence and pain were natural things to have throughout childhood.

"Then, how about you tell me what Wintervale's like." Most of what he knew about the place came via dry recountings in history books. There'd been the odd spellster snaffled up from the capital, but their recollection was like looking through the eyes of children who had spent much of their time hiding from the King's Hounds. "You said they housed you across the city. You must've seen a lot of it."

"When I was older, yes. But they only allowed us a short time to roam, generally after attending the monthly temple service. Training or tutoring consumed much of our days. I imagine it was the same for you."

Dylan nodded. "Once my magic fully manifested." Before then, his studies had been basic and communal. He still recalled sitting before a guardian, alongside a bunch of similarly aged children, chanting some rhyme that was meant to help their young minds retain information. The words for many of them were beyond his grasp, little more than fragments, but the melodies stuck.

Those memories had been formed on the same level in the tower where they'd found the first pile of little bodies. Where the hound had seduced him and they'd rutted like a pair of mindless animals.

Saliva pooled in the back of his mouth. He swallowed hard, but it didn't help. His stomach bubbled, the dinner he had consumed hours ago threatening to reverse the journey it had taken down his throat. He forced it back, along with the memory.

Whilst his thoughts regarding the hound's actions on that night were jumbled, he didn't regret the distraction it had offered. He *did* wish the imagery came with a more pleasing background.

"Honing my magic at a young age was a necessity," he rasped.

"Naturally." By the way the hound eyed him, the hoarseness in his voice had definitely been noticed. "I have witnessed the outcome of a spellster who has not learnt control many times." His gaze dropped, his mouth narrowing as though he chewed on something sour. "It is never a pleasant sight."

"You must've seen the worst of us a lot." Especially when hunting down rogue spellsters.

"Yes." The word was soft and quiet, almost sorrowful. Yet, it carried a weight that chilled Dylan faster than any breeze.

"It happened rarely back home. There'd be flare-ups." Often amongst the young who'd been escorted by the King's Hounds. They were generally the ones who suffered the kind of deep nightmares that magic reacted to. "Nothing destructive." Maybe that was because of the tower's construction. Tracker had mentioned the children's dormitory being crafted from some sort of stone that absorbed magic.

"I imagine they coddled you, too. Reduce the chance of tantrums or other upsets." There was no bitterness in his voice. No malice. He might as well have said the stars were out. "Our minders were less delicate with us. They expected us to be tough, even before they started feeding us poison."

Dylan jerked back. "*What?*"

"You wanted me to speak of my time in Wintervale. I assume you wish to know more than my sexual exploits. I could stick to them if that is your preference. They are far more pleasant. Why, there was this one woman who—"

"They *poisoned* you? I thought hounds were assets for the king?" Why was it even necessary for them to have such immunity? Did their mistress expect them to be set upon by spellsters with poisoned weapons? Or perhaps the ability to buy assassins? Both options seemed equally ludicrous.

"Do not take it the wrong way. It was nowhere near as gruesome as much of our training. They had me begin ingesting such substances when I reached my fifth year. They started small, you see, and our minder always had the antidote close at hand should we prove unable to handle the current dosage." He leant back, stretching his legs before the fire. "By the time I was old enough to be tested for a ranking amongst the hounds, I was immune to seventeen types of poison."

"And when did you become a full hound?"

"My eighteenth year."

"That's..." Dylan had spent a large chunk of his younger years training against the target blocks before he was remotely ready to face an opponent. To be considered as fully trained to hunt down unpredictable people with magic? "...so young."

The hound hummed thoughtfully. "Not really, no. Most of us are granted the title in our mid-teens. I should have become one much earlier, but they had me spend several more years being retrained because…” He fell silent. A distant, and rather haunted, look dulled his eyes.

“Because?” Dylan gently prompted. *Retrained?* Did he mean being beaten? Tortured?

Tracker rubbed at his right arm, his mind seemingly elsewhere. “I did something foolish. It cost the lives of several would-be hounds, including one our mistress favoured. Naturally, such a transgression cannot go unpunished. In time, my mistake was forgiven and I took the formal test to become part of the pack.”

They sat with the hushed breath of the forest surrounding them. The fire slowly turned to embers, glowing red and hot. With the moon concealed by thick clouds, his black-leather-clad companion became little more than shadows and the occasional gleam of an eye.

Dylan carefully placed another piece of wood onto the fire, watching it smoulder, then burst into flame before daring to speak. “We don’t need to talk about it,” he offered.

The hound smiled. The expression, although readily given, made no impact on his eyes. “The concern is appreciated, but not needed. It was a long time ago.”

“Was that how you ended up working in a brothel?” It didn’t make sense otherwise, especially if Tracker had truly grown up in Wintervale. Getting to Oldmarsh would’ve taken weeks, even on horseback. Such a journey was something he doubted Tracker’s mistress would’ve allowed casually.

“Ah.” A solemn smile curved the man’s lips. “Forgive me, but that is a heavier topic than I am willing to discuss tonight.”

“Fair enough.” There was so much Dylan wanted to ask, but he could hardly push the man when *he* was uncomfortable discussing his past. “But you never actually told me what Wintervale’s like.”

“I have not been near the capital for almost fifteen years.”

“How much could realistically change in that time?”

“A lot.” The hound fed another branch to the flames and sighed. “Before we are considered suitable to become hounds, the uninitiated were divvied up according to species and bits. We saw the others only during training or temple prayers.”

“Bits?”

“You know…” He gestured vaguely at his groin. “There are never enough pups to divide them by gender. The minders preferred to keep us segregated in such a manner. Male from female, elven from human. Curiosity leads to familiarity, which leads to closeness.” His gaze slid over Dylan. “Or so they say.”

Dylan reflexively swallowed. He’d been sitting in front of the fire for far too long to blame the flames for the sudden warmth in his cheeks.

"Naturally, I was housed with the rest of the elven males." He held up a warning finger. "Do not go imagining our quarters were at all like your spacious dormitories. Picture this instead..." He spread his hands as though sizing up an area for sketching. "Eleven children, from babies all the way to young teenagers, all crammed into a room barely twice the size of what an adult spellster has to themselves. Many of us shared beds or even cribs to keep warm in the winter. The noise..." The sombre smile returned. "I can no longer count the times we started the day with a baby wailing."

In the tower, babies and toddlers were a rare sight outside of the nursery. The only times he caught even a glimpse of one as an adult had been when they were brought in from beyond the tower walls. However, he did have vague memories of being woken by the cries of younger children when sharing the larger dormitories. He couldn't imagine sharing a smaller room with them.

There was one fundamental thing Tracker had gotten wrong about the tower when it came to sleeping arrangements. "We didn't have those rooms to ourselves." A few possibly did, but with space in the tower being limited, those people would've been exceptions. "I shared my sleeping quarters with Sulin." Not in the beginning. And he recalled resenting his friend when they first met. That had been the very day they shuffled the alchemist into what Dylan had just become used to thinking of as his personal space, the first he'd ever had since infancy.

It hadn't crossed his mind that the gangly, barely adolescent boy with long kinky hair would become one of his closest friends.

Tracker's brows rose. "An alchemist was your roommate?"

He bobbed his head in agreement, surprised that Tracker remembered. He'd only mentioned his friend the once and had barely alluded to his alchemist status. He hadn't realised the hound had been paying that much attention to what he said.

"So, not only do they allow you all to mingle, but they actually permitted an alchemist to bunk with one of the tower's strongest?"

Permitted? "Putting him in a room all on his own was the only alternative at the time and they don't like doing that to incomers. He came to the tower quite late. Originated from Stonebay, I believe." Even after years of knowing each other, his friend still wouldn't speak much about his home city. Dylan had learnt more about *infitialis* from Sulin than he'd ever heard of anything beyond the walls.

"So it was just the two of you sharing sleeping accommodations? For how long?"

"Since I was nearing thirteen." Plenty long enough to form a brotherly bond. "Not that the first few months weren't a little awkward." Back then, Dylan hadn't long realised that playing with certain parts of his body could be pleasurable. Coupled with puberty, the wet dreams and waking up hard...

It had taken a while before he could look Sulin in the eye, never mind hold a conversation, without getting flustered.

"By the way you speak of him, you chose to spend a good deal of that time in your roommate's company." A smirk tweaked the hound's lips. "I take it he was an attractive man."

"I..." Everyone agreed that most elves were pleasing to the eye. But Dylan recalled the multitude of times he had caught his gaze lingering on Sulin's lips whilst his friend spoke, wondering how the alchemist's split tongue would feel in his mouth, as well as on other places. "I guess so. What does that matter?"

Tracker leant closer, his head cocked to one side. "They left two teenage boys all alone and neither of you ever tried to—?"

"No." Despite the occasional fluttering thought in his teens, he never dared attempt anything. Even if he'd had the courage and the urge, Sulin wouldn't have been receptive to such an advance. "Just because two people share a room doesn't mean they have to be involved that way." And, whilst some spellsters did indeed sleep with their roommate, any attempt could've seen him outed just as easily.

"I am aware. But you truly never considered? Surely there must have been at least one such encounter. A brief one? Even an innocent kiss? Perhaps when you were drunk on cider?"

He shook his head. He definitely hadn't tried anything whilst sober and if he'd ever attempted such with Sulin after drinking, he would've known come the next morning. "My friend was rather wary of men who enjoy the company of other men. And I doubt he would have relished the thought of sharing the room with me if he thought I had any ideas of sleeping in his bed." Besides, he'd had Nestria. And she definitely would've objected to sharing him with men.

All traces of mirth slowly drained from the hound. "That is not a typical reaction. Something happened to make him so guarded, yes?"

Dylan shrugged. He didn't know his friend's reasons—there were just some things you didn't ask of those who'd been brought to the tower. He would wonder from time to time, especially when someone enraged the alchemist. Perhaps things in Stonebay hadn't been as rosy as Sulin's scant mentions made them seem.

There was the faint scrape of wood as the hound shuffled along the log, then a spray of embers as Tracker chucked another piece into the fire. The wood caught, throwing flickering shadows across them.

The hound cleared his throat. "Is that why you still do it?" he asked, the words barely above a whisper. "This hiding from others? You lived a lie, denied a part of yourself, all to keep a friend comfortable around you?"

Dylan shook his head. The reasons behind it were far more complicated than that. He didn't even know where to start explaining how indecisives were treated in the tower.

Worry wrinkled the man's forehead. "You must realise that burying the truth will do you no good. Nothing gnaws as deeply into the soul as denial."

"I know, it's just been... a *lot*." It hadn't even been a fortnight since leaving what had become of his home. His mind, his emotions, could barely keep up. That they might still be hunted by the very people responsible for the tower's slaughter... "I don't think I've space for a definitive thought right now. Especially not about sex."

"It likely does not help that you are perhaps raised a little less sheltered in such an aspect than most."

"I'm not *that* sheltered." Not when it came to sex. The guardians might've punished those caught in the act, but they *did* teach them about it. The bare minimum, granted. He'd learnt more under the healers' guidance. "It's not like I'm some celibate Tirglasian priest."

"That much was clear, thank you. If I had thought you entirely without experience, I would not have pursued you." He tipped his head back, exposing his throat to the firelight. "Truth be told, if you had not told me, I would not have marked you as *never* having been with a man."

Dylan eyed the hound. Had there been a hint of a question in those words? "Do you think I would lie about that? Besides, there really was only one thing you could've shown me that I hadn't already done." And he had walked in on enough people to have a fair understanding of how it worked.

Tracker hummed, tilting his head to one side in an obvious attempt to shield his face. There was a definite cheeky note to the vocalisation. "I can think of a few more. Whether you would be willing to try them is an altogether different matter." He rocked back to eye Dylan, one brow raised to its highest. "Does this mean you are ready to admit an attraction to men?"

"I wouldn't go that far." The very thought of letting such a confession loose had his chest tightening.

"Let us start with something simple, then. If I wanted to kiss you, would you want it?"

Biting his lip, he found himself unable to look the man in the eye. "We've gone a lot further than kissing."

"Was that the question?" The hound's broad grin took the edge off the intensity in his voice. "Did I ask if we had gone further than kissing or did I ask if you would want me to kiss you again?"

Dylan chuckled, despite the knots forming in his stomach. "I wouldn't object," he admitted. "But I also wouldn't exactly consider kissing as an entirely sexual act." A mouth was a mouth, no matter where it was placed. What was one more pair when he had kissed plenty of lips?

Although, he supposed the same could be said for hands, and he definitely minded where they roamed.

Tracker propped his chin on a raised fist. His cheek plumped in a lopsided smile that creased his eyes. "Truly?"

"You mean you think of it that way?"

The man's shoulders shook briefly with the silent mirth that danced in his eyes. "No, you are right. It is not sexual all the time. It depends entirely on the kiss." His voice grew husky. That honey-coloured gaze flicked down, then back up. "And the kisser." He pressed closer, their shoulders touching. "How about if I wanted to go further, would you object to that?"

"I—" Try as he might, words rather failed him. The hound sat so temptingly close, the heat radiating from his body just perceptible from the fire as it seeped through Dylan's clothes. It would take little effort on his part to eliminate the remaining distance. "Um..." He had already risked one of their companions witnessing him kissing the man in the past. Doing it again would only increase the chances of being spotted. "I..."

"Yes?" Tracker breathed, the word caressing Dylan's neck.

Would he object? That was a good question. One the answer to had been quite simple not that long ago.

He stared into the fire, trying to find the right way to explain what he felt. *Did* he prefer men and had only been fooling himself all these years? *Was* he indecisive? "To be honest, I'm not sure anymore." That had to mean he was the latter. Surely. The lack of making a choice was the whole basis of being indecisive, wasn't it?

His friend, Harriet, still considered herself as such and she had chosen. *Henrie above everyone.* That was what she always said. It was less about the gender and more about the person. Someone they considered worthy enough to risk everything for.

Never had he found anyone who sparked anything close to what she described.

Dylan wet his lips. "I... should go," he managed, struggling to clear the squeak from his throat. "Back to my tent. To rest."

The curve of the hound's mouth softened. "Are you entirely certain that is the preferred destination? It is a cool night and my tent is bound to keep you so much warmer."

Tracker's question gave him pause. Surely, the man had no idea what thoughts were tumbling through his mind right now. "Aren't you meant to be on watch? We can't endanger the others like that."

"We?" His lashes fluttered in a display of innocence. "I never suggested *we* do anything. I meant only that my blankets are far thicker and would shield you from the cold. However, since you brought it up, I am certain a quick tumble is unlikely to harm our chances of being attacked."

"I should sleep."

"That would be the wisest course." He laid a hand on Dylan's chest, his fingers curling into the fabric. "Before you go…" The hound tugged them closer and their lips brushed together, soft and indolent, something that had little chance of being caught by the others.

Before he could consider his actions, Dylan grabbed the hound's jerkin, the leather and metal digging into his hands. It took no effort to draw Tracker against him. He deepened the kiss, seeking to tease the hound as much as the man clearly enjoyed doing to him.

The reasoning behind his intentions vanished the instant Tracker reciprocated with a moan.

Dylan swallowed the sound, the thrill of knowing he'd been responsible for it tingling along his skin. Thrusting his tongue into the hound's mouth, he swirled against the man's in search of more delicious noises, his actions swiftly rewarded.

The soft jingle of a buckle loosening caught his ear. The hound's palm slid up Dylan's thigh, then his side. Those long fingers grasped at Dylan's clothes, seeking a way beneath the skirts. One tug almost pulled him onto the man's lap before he thumped back onto the log.

The realisation that they still sat before the fire ran its icy finger down his spine.

Dylan pushed against the hound, relinquishing their kiss. It took a great deal more effort than he cared to admit.

Tracker stared up at him, almost dazed. His chest heaved. Confusion moulded his features and Dylan swore he caught the flicker of panic flash in the hound's eyes. Only the gods knew what the man was thinking.

With his face burning, Dylan shuffled down the log. His new seat wasn't out of immediate arm's reach, but it was better than nothing. "I should get some rest before my watch."

Realising his words had been met with silence, he threw a branch onto the dimming flames in the hope of better seeing the hound's face.

It seemed to shake Tracker out of whatever trance he'd been in. "Rest?" he murmured as he buckled his belt. Odd that the man had been able to undo it and keep a firm grip on Dylan's clothes. "Yes, you should do that. Lack of sleep could lead to a lapse of judgement. I would not wish for you to do something you might regret."

Nodding slowly, Dylan had barely left the fireside before the hound spoke again.

"If I may make an observation? I would say you not objecting to being kissed by a man is somewhat of an understatement, yes?"

Dylan opened his mouth, the familiar tang of denial on his tongue.

Not a word came out. They both knew he'd been a hairsbreadth from undressing the man right out in the open. *What the hell is wrong with me?* No matter how hard he tried to ignore it, the hound stirred something in him that hadn't been roused for a very long time.

He should've considered himself fortunate that at least none of the women had materialised from their tent. His heart likely would've given out if someone had *seen* him being so reckless.

"We can talk further tomorrow night, if you desire." There was a note of something on the hound's final words. A question? A promise? "Sleep well, my dear man, and pleasant dreams."

He shook his head, laughing softly to himself as he made for his tent. There was no possible way he could sleep now. Not with his heart pounding like it was or the way his stomach refused to unknot.

If the man hadn't been tied up with the watch...

He pushed the thought aside. Perhaps he should've allowed Authril to have her way with him. It might've been enough to get the hound out of his head.

Was that what he wanted? To forget the night he had spent with Tracker? The questions rattled about his mind. The answer danced just on the edge of thought, not quite bold enough to be said.

Dylan idly scratched the side of his neck. "Don't spend the whole night on watch. I might need you to rescue me from danger again." He had meant enemies like the Talfaltaners, but now the words hung in the air between them, he realised it carried other meanings. Like how the hound's mere presence had sent Authril scampering.

Tracker's answering laugh warmed more than Dylan's face. "Your concern for my wellbeing is noted. Goodnight."

However long he had been outside talking with the hound, his bedding was well and truly cold. Wrapping himself up in the blankets, he carefully wound a wisp of hot air between them and him, remembering how the man had described him using magic. *A beacon.*

Was Tracker currently feeling this small amount right now? Did it truly blanket the man's senses? Perhaps pull at the memory of their night together?

Dylan closed his eyes. It did little to still his mind. Thoughts drifted in the darkness, hazed by dreams and memories. A mouth that fellated him to leg-weakening satisfaction, yet offered the softest kisses. Caresses that anchored him to reality, but also set his soul to singing from the heavens. And a voice that teased and praised and soothed.

Somewhere along the way, his hand had crept into his

smallclothes to fist his length. He stroked himself as his mind turned to the memory of Tracker dancing with that heavy sword, well aware that the man sat just outside. Even more aware that he didn't have to rely on the ghosts of memories to reach the edge.

If he only sought it.

He increased the speed with which he worked himself, pumping hard until he reached completion, his panting filling up the silence. Spent, he laid still, his ears straining to make out if he'd been heard.

The night's quiet greeted him, just as uninterested and chill as the air.

Shuddering, he cleaned himself up as best he could before once more curling up beneath his blankets. He closed his eyes and desperately sought the unfeeling darkness waiting for him at the end of his dreams. A place where he could sink into oblivion and be free.

CHAPTER 10

Dylan landed on his back, the air rushing out of his lungs. He fought to regain his breath, his chest aching, his magic humming in search of the source to no avail. The body currently straddling his stomach, much of their weight pressing on Dylan's chest, didn't make breathing any easier.

Slowly, his vision shifted, blurs of colour returning to actual shapes. His gaze flicked from the tree branches directly above to Tracker's disapproving face.

"What did I do wrong this time?" he managed to wheeze. This had to be the third time this evening the man had thrown him to the ground. If he was getting any better at this unarmed combat, he couldn't see it.

The hound shook his head. "It would be far quicker for me to tell you what you did *not* get wrong." He sat back with a sigh. The action relieved Dylan's chest of the constricting weight, but it also meant the man now fully straddled his hips. "Perhaps it is best to call it a day. We will go over the basics tomorrow. *Again.*"

"No. I—" He struggled to prop himself up on his elbows. Just a few tussles and his arms already felt jellified. "I can do more now." After his lack of improvement when it came to fighting with a blade—of any length—and his dismal attempt at archery, he had to get *this* right.

"If you insist." Tracker stood and offered his hand to assist Dylan to his feet. "You need to remember what I told you. This should be easy. You have the advantage of height and greater reach over me. I should not be able to get so close."

"Height and reach maybe," Authril said, the woman's musical laughter tinting the words, "but not the strength to go with it." She sat on the edge of the tents, watching them with her head tipped to one side, clearly finished with her nightly task of checking over her armour. "I'm a little confused what you're trying to teach him here," she added to Tracker. "Apart from how to land on his back."

"I am attempting to have him learn unarmed combat, dear

woman." The hound continued to stare at Dylan as if trying to solve a blacksmith's puzzle, the tilt of his head barely acknowledging he even spoke to the warrior.

She shook her head. "Still? I told you before you're wasting your time. It'll be of no use to him on the battlefield once he's leashed."

Dylan suppressed a shudder at the mention of having the *infitialis* collar once more wrapped around his neck. The scar at his throat seemed to burn at the mere mention. Taking several deep breaths helped to centre his mind. *For the tower.* The souls taken there deserved to be avenged. If he needed to be leashed in order to do that...

Well, what was a leashing when compared to the fate those back home had suffered?

"He'll be skewered by the first person with a blade," Authril continued.

Something altogether bitter flickered in Tracker's eyes. "That may be so, but I did not have the battlefield in mind for these particular moves."

Dylan frowned. The man had admitted to being close friends with Fetcher. Did that mean he knew precisely how most spellsters were used in the army? Of what people like the sergeant did to them?

Was learning Authril lying with Dylan had been an attempt to replicate what the wardens had done the reason why the man reacted so strongly? How *he* might've wound up being used had the Udynean army not ambushed his scouting party?

He doubted any amount of unarmed combat training would keep him safe in that department once he was leashed again. All he could hope for was a sympathetic warden.

Authril's gaze had grown sharp and cold, like a sea-green icicle waiting for the unsuspecting to walk beneath it. She had become increasingly argumentative towards Tracker since the tower, but her hostility had begun after the hound attempted to kiss Dylan back in Oldmarsh.

He'd no idea how she would react at learning they had done far more.

"I'm surprised you're not trying to teach him magic fighting techniques," she said.

Chuckling, the hound at last turned to acknowledge her fully, quirking a russet brow in her direction. "You would also have me teach a bird how to fly, yes?"

She rolled her eyes. "You've fought spellsters before, haven't you? Killed them? Everyone knows that's what proper hounds do."

That Tracker seemed to take this snub in stride definitely irked her. How the pair hadn't already come to blows, Dylan didn't couldn't imagine. Back in the tower, such animosity would've seen them battling it out on the training grounds. "Your point?"

"You must have come across techniques that they never taught in the tower."

"You speak of the forbidden." His grin widened, gaining that toothy sharpness it so often did these days. Just like there was always a certain hard edge lurking beneath his demeanour when Authril spoke with him for long. "You wish for him to learn things that could see him executed?"

Dylan froze. He knew of a few abilities that the guardians discouraged—levitation being the most common—but couldn't imagine anything dangerous enough that the army would rather kill him than point him towards the enemy.

Who even was their enemy? Katarina had stressed how their war with the Udynea Empire was more a skirmish against a trio of bickering border lords, that their emperor sought peace and likely didn't know the true extent of the fighting. Dylan wasn't sure if she thought such news would help, but it only served to make the little he'd done feel insignificant. They'd been fighting Udynea for generations, had lost so much and so many.

"Well," Authril said, "You'll have to do better than this sorry display if he's to improve before we reach Wintervale."

Tracker's single raised brow lifted higher. "Do you wish to teach him yourself, my dear warrior?" He gave the woman another excessively toothy smile. "Or perhaps join in as a partner? It is difficult to show what he is doing wrong on my own."

She wrinkled her nose as if smelling something distasteful. "As though I'm going to let you throw me to the ground again."

Again? In all the times Dylan had witnessed them sparring, not once had the hound borne Authril to the ground. Had they been fighting? When? He barely left sight of one or the other and never for long.

"No," Authril snapped. "And that's your answer to both questions."

Tracker scoffed. "Come now, surely a battle-hardened warrior such as yourself understands the application of hand-to-hand combat." He examined her, wickedness twisting his lips. "Unless, of course, you are denying the chance of him learning for different reasons? Perhaps as a way to hide the truth about yourself? Do we not know *how* to fight in such a manner? You only have to say so. There is nothing shameful about only being able to take on an opponent with a good few feet of steel in your hand."

Rage boiled across her face, the pale skin between her freckles deepening into a ruddy hue the longer the hound spoke. In one swift move, she leapt to her feet and waved Dylan out of the way.

He swiftly scurried over to Katarina, who stood not too far from where the warrior had been sitting, her attention intent on the two elves.

Dylan slowed as he caught the familiar quirk of the hedgewitch's lips. The scraps of conversation they'd had several weeks ago—when the two elves first started sparring—came to mind. "More strutting?" he asked, halting at her side. He quite enjoyed the show, if he was honest with himself. Why wouldn't he? Tracker was a handsome man with a fit physique, one that happened to be capable of bending in a lot of interesting ways.

Even without it, watching the pair certainly promised to be interesting.

Katarina smiled and, shaking her head, pressed one finger to her lips before pointing at the small space they'd cleared for tonight's lesson.

"I hope you are watching, my dear spellster," Tracker said. "I am doing this for your benefit, after all."

Dylan inclined his head and settled on the ground in a pose that he hoped showed his eagerness to learn this peculiar method of fighting. He recalled once hearing some of the younger guardians being pulled up for roughhousing, but it hadn't sounded at all as efficient as Tracker claimed.

Satisfied he was indeed the camp's entire focus, Tracker turned back to his opponent as he continued to speak to Dylan. "Now then, this is what *you* have been doing." He nodded at Authril to attack him.

The woman wasted no time in responding to the hound's command. She rushed at her opponent. There was a flurry of grappling limbs and, try as he might to make sense of their moves, all Dylan saw clearly was the feral grin plastered across Authril's face as she threw Tracker to the ground.

The hound grunted as he hit the dirt, although a smirk soon twisted his lips when Authril straddled his waist the same way as the man had done with Dylan. "Well now, dear woman," Tracker purred, a hint of mischievousness whispering through the words. "I had no idea you felt this way about me. It has been some time since we were so close."

Authril glared down at him, her teeth bared. "You let me win," she snarled.

"Nonsense," the man drawled. "Why would I do that when I am in the middle of showing our dear spellster precisely where he is rubbish at defending himself?"

Dylan's gaze locked onto what the woman already knew. The hound had taken their current position as the perfect opportunity to latch his fingers onto Authril's backside.

His stomach twisted at the sight, bitterly tying itself into knots.

What did Tracker mean some time since? The two elves rarely shared space by the campfire, avoiding it completely if they could. When they sparred, the hound made a display of how easy it was to keep his distance. Never had Dylan seen the pair of them this close.

Why would they even need to be? What was Tracker implying? That they were intimate? Surely not. Authril had made her opinions of the hound in that regard plain.

The longer he sat there stewing over the possibilities, the very thought of the two elves sleeping with each other, the more his stomach rolled.

He breathed deep, trying to tamp down the broiling nausea. Was he actually getting worked up over seeing the two of them in close quarters with each other? What was he? Jealous that he wasn't in Tracker's place?

That he wasn't in Authril's?

That was almost as troubling a thought. But then, his refusal of sex in regards to one elf hadn't shaken Dylan's desire for the other, however much he tried to curb it. And, whilst he had remained firm on keeping himself from venturing into the hound's tent for the past two nights—the act allowing nightmares, and more, to plague his sleep—Tracker had to be aware Dylan hadn't lain with the warrior during that time.

Authril sat back. "Get your hands off me before I remove them. Permanently."

Laughing, Tracker tightened his grasp and threw the warrior over his shoulder.

A surprised squeak left Authril's lips, followed by a stream of profanity as she tumbled across the ground to land flat on her back.

"Such language," the hound chided. He twisted his head towards Dylan and the joking on his face melted into seriousness. "Did you see where I went wrong?"

"I..." Dylan slowly unclenched his fist, praying the action hadn't been noticed. He wasn't jealous. He was concerned that the hound was going to get himself in trouble if he pushed the warrior. Who could be certain of the winner in such a dust-up? "I think so," he managed. "Yes."

"Really? First time? Are you certain?" One side of his mouth hitched upwards as he arched a brow towards Authril, who hadn't moved from her stance. "I am willing to go again."

Dylan nodded. "I'm sure." Even if he wasn't, admitting so would mean watching them grapple with each other. He'd rather not whilst he wasn't entirely sure who that bitter knot in his stomach was for.

The fact it was there at all unnerved him.

"As you like." With a roll of his hips, Tracker sprang off the ground and onto his feet.

There was a brief flail of limbs as Authril also sought to right herself. She got as far as being on all fours before scrambling across the clearing to reach her sword, rage warping her face. Only when she'd a firm grasp on the hilt did she finally make a move towards standing.

Tracker watched the display with clear indifference. "If you can identify the problem so easily, dear man, then perhaps you will learn how to do it correctly faster than I thought." He waited until Authril was once more on her feet before asking her, "Are you ready to defend yourself?"

She rolled her shoulders, giving an almost absent brush to her dirt and grass-covered arm. The whole time, her razor-sharp glare refused to waver from the hound. Nor had she relinquished her hold on the sword.

If Tracker noticed, he wasn't concerned. "Now then, *this* is what you should be doing." He nodded at Authril.

She fell into a crouch similar to the one Tracker had affected in the first attack.

The hound hedged around her, his eyes narrowing. He feinted a few times, smirking as she twitched in preparation for the closing lunge that didn't come. Each time, Dylan saw how her stance was off. She would twist, bringing her left shoulder forward in a move he had witnessed whenever the pair sparred. But there was no sword to block and she wielded no shield.

When Tracker finally made contact with her, it was over far quicker than the first time. The man grasped her sword arm with a speed akin to a swooping bird. His foot lashed out, hooking behind her leg and setting her off balance.

Authril let out a high-pitched gasp, clearly not expecting the hound to be so fast, before her back hit the ground. She tried to respond by pulling him down with her, but Tracker had already released her arms and now knelt over her, one knee pressed to her middle and his fist aimed at her face.

She flinched, throwing up her arms to protect her head as though she expected the hound to land the blow.

Tracker made no further move towards her. He merely grinned, his breath coming through his teeth in great gasps. From this distance, it almost seemed like the man enjoyed her small measure of discomfort.

"Well, shit."

Dylan jumped at Marin's voice. The flicker of a shield wrapped around him and dissipated in the time it took to breathe. He wasn't certain how long the hunter had been standing at the hedgewitch's shoulder, but by the frown, he could guess it wasn't long.

"Didn't expect to see him taking her for a tumble," the woman continued. "Hell, didn't think anyone was capable of putting her onto her arse."

"It's not the first time he's thrown her to the ground," Katarina said, earning her the hound's full attention.

"Indeed, my dear hedgewitch. However, that was not my desired result." He spread his arms wide, staring down at Authril, who remained curled up beneath him. "Whatever happened to defending yourself, my dear warrior?" The grin twisted, growing suggestive. "Or perhaps you wished to get closer again? I am certain that could be arranged without needing to be so rough with each other."

"Oh, get off." Authril hooked her arm around his waist, pushing the man to one side so Tracker had no choice but to roll onto the ground. "If you want to show him, then maybe *you* should be the one defending."

The hound sprang to his feet. "Very well. If you wish to go for another tumble, I am game."

Shaking her head, Authril stepped back. "Do you ever stop?"

Tracker's lips curled slightly. "Only when asked, dear woman. But if you insist on being the aggressor, then by all means." He waved at her to come forward.

Authril obeyed, attacking with a similar outcome to their last encounter. Dylan followed the movements, seeing the precise moment Tracker used the woman's speed and weight against her. It looked far easier than when he'd been attempting the move. But then, his weight had been off and—

Marin settled next to him with a grunt. "I thought he was supposed to be teaching you, not throwing her around."

"They're meant to be showing him where he's going wrong," Katarina replied. She arched a brow in his direction. "Although, I think there is a degree of strutting on Tracker's part."

The other woman gave a contemptuous snort. "Pretty sure that man can't put on a pair of trousers without showing off."

Dylan swung about, prepared to inform the woman that Tracker most certainly could do that, when he caught the little smirk fighting to be made known on the hunter's lips. A faint surge of heat hit his face. There was no chance she knew what had transpired between him and the hound in the tower.

Or had she caught their kiss by the fire two nights ago?

"Stop it," he hissed.

Those already large, light brown eyes widened in mock innocence.

"I was just talking to Kat." Marin jerked a thumb at the hedgewitch as if he'd somehow forgotten the woman was there.

"I know, it's just I—" He took a deep breath. *No chance.* But if he wasn't careful, then he'd be the one blurting secrets. *Then everyone would know.* His chest tightened at the mere thought of explaining, because there would undoubtedly be questions. Tracker might not mind divulging, but he certainly wasn't ready for any kind of scrutiny. "I'm trying to focus."

"Well, I certainly hope you have been," Tracker said. He had planted himself squarely in the centre of their little clearing, his fist firmly on his hips. "And perhaps our dear hunter would like to volunteer as your new partner?"

"But Authril was—" He turned towards the woman in question to see her stalking back towards the low-burning fire, muttering under her breath.

"Our dear warrior has had enough of being manhandled this evening. Come. Both of you." He waved them closer. "Let us see what, exactly, you have picked up from watching."

Marin glared at the hound in silence for some time before sighing. "Where do you want me?"

"Right here, if you please." He gestured to the ground at his feet. "You will play the aggressor and I will direct Dylan's movements."

Shrugging, she discarded the outer layer of her attire and joined them. "Not sure what makes you think I'd be any good at wrestling."

"With that physique?" Tracker countered. "How could you not be?"

She rolled her eyes, but there was a hint of a pleased smile tweaking the corners of her mouth. "I'm not exactly out there tackling rabbits."

"No, but I am willing to bet you visited Toptower more than you let on." Tracker took up position behind Dylan, making minute adjustments to his posture. "And you do not appear the type to shirk from a good brawl if given the right reason."

Marin's smile warped into a feral grin. "Pricks who had it coming don't get my sympathy."

"I would never suggest otherwise, my dear woman." He clapped his hands onto Dylan's hips. "Ready?"

"Yes?"

"*Yes?*" Tracker echoed. "Was that a question?" He clicked his tongue disapprovingly. "You simply must be more confident in yourself."

Dylan caught the man's gesture for Marin to approach. He barely noticed the woman step within reach before her hands were on him and his feet were kicked out from under him.

He landed hard, his shoulder hitting the ground first, the joint tingling with healing magic before he could finish tumbling.

"Again," Tracker ordered, hauling Dylan to his feet. "Do not go stiff when she grabs you."

Marin stuck out her tongue and mockingly gagged. "Yes, please, keep your stiffness away from my personage."

Chuckling, Dylan couldn't resist quipping back with, "I'll try not to make it too hard for you."

His response garnered a deep laugh from her, which only made him join in.

"Come on, you two," Tracker growled, the words lacking their full heat as the hound clearly stifled a snicker. "That is enough."

"*You* started it," Marin pointed out, wiping tears from her eyes. "Talking about his stiffness."

"I merely meant he would fare better if he kept himself loose whilst maintaining attention on his opponent."

"Why didn't you say so?" Marin replied. "We can do loose." She wriggled her arms and body, snapping her fingers to the beat of a song he didn't recognise and swaying as though she were boneless.

Dylan mimicked her, the snap of his fingers a fraction of a second behind hers.

"*Marin.*" Tracker's voice carried such annoyance that Dylan couldn't help looking over his shoulder. The man stood with his face firmly in the palm of his hand. "Stop fooling around. I am trying to train him."

The woman scoffed, but didn't halt her dancing. "Lighten up a little. You've had him out here for ages, letting everybody throw him to the ground every which way. Didn't you ever used to just get a little silly in the middle of your hound training?"

"No." The hound dropped his hand and fixed her with a stern look. "Our trainers would whip us for slacking off."

Marin froze mid-pose, remaining silent for a few breaths before flashing a lopsided grin. "Kinky."

One side of Tracker's mouth briefly twitched into a smile. "Get on with it before we lose the daylight completely. And *you...*" He turned his glare on Dylan. "Pay attention to *her* movements, not mine."

With his whole face burning, he circled Marin once more. The hound remained at his back, directing with a touch or a word. Each time, he struggled to keep his focus on Marin, even with her exaggerating her actions. She had to be. He definitely wasn't *that* good at discerning the twitch of a foot or the shifting balance that foretold her direction.

He hit the ground more than a handful of times, until he finally managed to set her off balance enough to return the favour.

"Again," Tracker demanded as Marin picked herself up off the ground.

Marin held up a hand, brushing leaves and grass off her backside with the other. "Actually, I think that's me for the day. I'll be happy to help tomorrow, but I've had enough."

"You're just saying that because you're afraid I'll win again," Dylan teased. He bounced on the balls of his feet, waiting for her to lunge at him. "Which I definitely will."

The hound peered at him, doubt creasing his brow. "If you are so confident of your abilities, perhaps you would like to attempt opposing me?"

"There you go." Marin gave Dylan a hearty slap on his back as she made her way back to where she had left the outer layers of her attire, causing him to stumble forward or fall on his face.

Dylan pointed a warning finger at Marin. "Not one word." She'd been bad enough with her not-at-all-helpful quips whenever he tried the other forms of fighting. He didn't need further distractions when facing the hound.

Marin flapped her hand. "I'll leave you two to keep at it. I've got my own tasks to get on with, anyway." She gathered up her discarded clothes, then lifted a trio of dead rabbits off the ground, shaking them as they dangled from their hind legs. "These won't skin themselves." Grinning, she jerked a thumb at where Authril and the hedgewitch sat near the fire. "If I can get Kat and sulky-britches to help me, we might even be able to have them tonight."

"That would be nice," Tracker said wistfully. "I have worked up quite the appetite." Between the two elves and the way they devoured any and all meat the hunter caught, the rest would be lucky to share a single rabbit.

Saluting, Marin strode off towards the fire, getting the attention of the other women as she neared.

Dylan waited until she had joined the others and wasn't at all focused on him before once more stepping up to Tracker. Whether or not she was close by, she would definitely have something to say if his next tussle wound up with him on his arse again. "You won't be as rough with me as you were with Authril, right? And not as quick?"

The man raised a brow at him and Dylan bit the inside of his lip to keep himself from blabbering further. So far, the hound had been accommodatingly slow during their lessons. Not particularly tender when it came to unarmed combat, but he seemed to be trying. "The people we come across will not be gentle with you."

"I'm not an idiot," Dylan mumbled. Anyone who attacked their group, and continued to do so whilst he slung magic at them, was hardly going to quibble at being rough. And once he reached Wintervale and was leashed again? They wouldn't exactly coddle him there, either.

"But you want a little reassurance that I am not going to slam you into the ground, yes?" Tracker placed his hands over his heart. "I promise, we will start slow. No one learns the basics flat on their back, after all. Is that good enough for you?"

He nodded his agreement and planted himself as he'd seen Tracker do. "I'm ready."

The hound wasted no time in talk. He came at Dylan, markedly slower than he'd done with Authril, but still at enough speed to be taken seriously.

Knowing where to do what had been easy with the hound's guidance. Doing so without it was a little more difficult, especially when Tracker was so close. Was it *there* that he was meant to attempt to lunge? Or—

Dylan reached out to grab the man, only to wind up tumbling.

He found himself following the trail of the clouds across the darkening sky for a few breaths before his mind registered being flipped onto his back once more.

"Still too hesitant," Tracker gently chided, his head coming into view as he bent over Dylan. He shook his head and his heavy braid slithered over his shoulder, slapping the side of Dylan's face.

He mutely glared up at the man. Had the hound done that on purpose?

Tracker grinned. "I would apologise, but you probably needed that." He straightened and offered a helping hand to bring Dylan to his feet. "You must be more forceful in your actions. I am not so easy to break."

"No," he agreed as he grasped the man's outstretched hand and hauled himself upright. "I seem to remember you mentioning that some time back."

Tracker's brows shot up. "I do not recall—"

Dylan drew the man closer. "I believe you said," he whispered into the hound's ear. "And I quote, you're not *some delicate flower*." The final few words passed his lips in a rough approximation of the man's accent. He had meant to tease. Anything to shake off some of the fluttering churning in his gut that seemed to spring to life whenever they were close.

He didn't expect the soft hitch in the man's breath.

Tracker cleared his throat. "Ah, *that*." He stepped back, a faint dark tinge briefly tinting his cheeks. "Yes, I do seem to remember saying that. Slightly different situation, yes?" He cocked his head. "Unless you would prefer to..."

"No," Dylan shot back, casting a glance at the campfire. The women still seemed involved in whatever it was they did around the flames. Although, they surely couldn't still be preparing the rabbits. "Like you said, we've only so much daylight left. I want to, at least, get the basics down before nightfall."

Giving a low chuckle, Tracker examined him, his gaze slow and with some measure of heat. "You did not lose often in your duels back in the tower, did you?"

"I don't see what that has to do with now." He had become adept at fighting with magic years before many of his peers. And he'd been stronger. Why wouldn't he win his duels against them? Or was the hound implying something else?

"No?" The little smirk he gave had the heat in his eyes jumping to Dylan's cheeks. "Very well, we will continue training, if that is your desire. But do keep in mind what I said. You must be sure in your actions. Do not be afraid that you will hurt me."

I don't mind a little pain, his treacherous thoughts echoed Tracker's words, said to him the first time they were intimate. Dylan rolled his tongue around his mouth to keep from sniggering or blurting the phrase.

He was well aware of needing to focus. But the way those long fingers wrapped around his limbs, each move strong, confident and graceful. It tightened his chest and churned his gut. His every breath came fast and ragged.

In a very short time, he was on his back again.

Tracker rested his head on Dylan's shoulder, his laughter shaking them. "You are going to need a *lot* of practice to get good at this." Giving a resigned sigh, he propped himself up in preparation to once again get to his feet.

Dylan held his breath, hoping the hound wouldn't notice the growing interest happening in his groin. He hadn't exactly intended on it, but Tracker often wound up straddling his waist and the friction, coupled with the hound's delicious heat, rather did the rest.

"I would suggest that we—" The soft twitch of surprise took the man's face for a moment. Tracker arched a brow at him, one side of his mouth lifting along with it. "Why, Dylan," he breathed. "Out in the open? Getting bolder, I see."

Heat flooded his face. Of course Tracker would notice. How could he expect the man not to when he was practically sitting on Dylan's pelvis?

"My dear man," Tracker murmured. "There is no need to be embarrassed." He got to his feet, allowing Dylan to sit up and draw his knees closer. "It is a common occurrence during such training, I swear."

Dylan chewed on the inside of his cheek. That didn't really stop the heat from slinking down his neck. How was he going to make it to the tents without anyone else noticing his current predicament?

"If you require help alleviating the situation, I am certain you would find willing assistance if asked."

"Actually." Dylan's focus slid to the man's mouth. He had experienced those lips wrapped around him the once, but the sensation wasn't one he could easily forget.

Tracker's lips fitting so snugly around his girth, forming the perfect seal. The silken motion of them gliding up and down his length. The pressure of the hound's tongue massaging the underside, guiding the head. The tightness of the man's throat as he swallowed every drop.

Hugging his knees tighter to his chest, Dylan pointedly fixed his gaze on the ground. The memory only served to increase the urgency in his loins. "Never mind," he mumbled, sure his heart would leap from his throat if he spoke any louder.

Two days. That was how long he had managed without succumbing to the walking temptation that was the hound's very presence. And all it had taken to bring him back to the idea of sleeping with the man was an accidental brush. Whilst they were supposed to be training, no less.

That still didn't mean he was about to let the hound, or anyone, blatantly have their way with him out in public.

Tracker's lips flattened. "If you would prefer to not enlist aid, then may I suggest heading that way?" He jerked his head at the nearby tree line. "It should be private enough for you to regain your composure."

Dylan eyed the undergrowth. He had rummaged through the area in search of firewood not too long ago. "You expect me to..." He took a deep breath as a fresh surge of heat flooded his cheeks. "...stroke one out in the bushes?"

The hound tipped his head to one side. A blast of laughter puffed out his nose. "That was not quite what I meant. Walking for a bit is generally enough to douse such heat, but if you believe yourself in need of more direct measures..." He tapped on his lips as if considering his options. A wicked grin took the man's face as he bent over Dylan. "I could make it quick?"

His heart increased its hammering. His stomach had knotted itself into a tangle that he wasn't sure would ever unwind. "I think I can handle this on my own." Walking? Would being alone be enough? His thoughts seemed to do plenty without any help.

"As you say." He toyed with the buckle of his vambrace as though his armour was far more interesting than their current topic. "Do not worry about the others finding out. I shall keep them entertained until you return. If they query your whereabouts, you are merely relieving yourself."

With a brief nod of gratitude, Dylan wasted little time in making for the bushes. If this truly was a common occurrence then, with the hound teaching him, he would need to find a better way to get this sort of reaction under control.

And fast.

CHAPTER 11

True to Tracker's word, walking through the forest with the gentle breeze cooling his feverish skin had been enough to douse his ardour without having to resort to jerking off in the bushes. With the sun's glow fading from the sky, he picked his way back to their camp, confident no further incidents would arise.

Marin had gotten the rabbits cooked by the time night had fully settled in. As he had expected, the two elves laid claim to one each, leaving the latter to be divided amongst the three of them alongside a broth that he hoped was more nourishing than the bland taste suggested.

He picked at his portion of rabbit, quietly mulling over the day's lesson whilst the others chatted. His mind refused to settle on anything beyond how quickly he had grown hard beneath the hound. If unarmed combat with Tracker elicited such a reaction, then perhaps he should consider one of the women as his sparring partner.

Which one would be better? Authril might've had more experience when it came to fighting, but she wasn't exactly gentle. He rubbed at his shoulder, digging his fingers into where the joint had met the ground with force several times. The aches were gone, his magic healing the battered flesh almost as soon as they were bruised, but the memory remained.

"Are you well?" Katarina asked, laying a hand on his knee. "I saw you land hard several times, but I thought healing magic would fix aching muscles."

Dylan glanced up from his meal. He had settled between Marin and the hedgewitch in the hopes that keeping the hound on the other side of the fire would still any growing fervour in his veins. "Healing?" he echoed. "Yes, it does. I just…" He stretched, almost knocking over his bowl, and feigned a yawn. "I guess I'm a little overtired."

"Yes?" Tracker managed around a mouthful of food. Chasing it down with a swing from his water skin, he continued, "Perhaps we should slow our pace. We have been pushing hard during our travels and none of us will do well defending another attack if we are exhausted." He fixed Authril with a stern look before the woman could do more than open her mouth.

The warrior wordlessly nodded her agreement.

Dylan bobbed his head along with her, absently rubbing his thigh in an effort to ignore how his length twitched against his smallclothes. He had only just managed to collect himself enough that a casual glance the hound's way didn't have certain parts getting ideas. Now he was reacting to the mere sound of the man's voice? Even watching Tracker devour an entire rabbit—especially the way his fangs effortlessly sliced chunks out of the flesh—wasn't enough to douse the heat steadily pooling in his gut.

Shovelling down the last few mouthfuls of dinner, he fled to his tent almost before the food had the chance to settle in his stomach. If he was ever going to unwind enough to sleep, he was going to have to deal with his needs manually.

Not that anything he did fully did the job these days. He wasn't a stranger to the act—even in the tower, no one could fault him for fulfilling his own desires—but he always wound up in the same panting mess, his heart racing and his body humming, but nowhere near sated.

His hands could never replicate the hound's long fingers or the man's skill. He wasn't sure how Tracker knew, but if Dylan had been a musical instrument, then he hit all the right notes.

And, however much he tried to avoid the thought, he so desperately wanted to experience that harmonious act again.

Just sleep. He closed his eyes, seeking to sink into his dreams. That was all he needed. A simple night of rest would settle the heat raging through his veins.

Outside the tent, he caught Marin's raucous laughter, the sound almost drowning out Tracker's deeper chuckle. The hound spoke further, an incomprehensible murmur that still stirred less-than-quiet thoughts.

Dylan scrunched himself into a tighter ball, throwing his blanket over his face in the hopes that it would also muffle his ability to hear. The darkness behind his eyes taunted him.

Sleep. The others would soon seek their beds or begin their time on watch. He just needed to be still until then, when the silence and the day's exertion would eventually drag him into a dreamless slumber.

Images flickered to life in the depths of his mind. He shrank from them, unsure if he wanted to risk dreaming. The nightmares hadn't vanished completely, not when he was alone, but at least they didn't lie in wait every time. New ones had joined them since the Talfaltaner attack. Being too exhausted to dream at all usually worked to keep the worst at bay.

Yet, in the spaces between visions of the tower's destruction and the army's decimation, Tracker's image prowled his mind. Lurid scenes that saw him jolting awake, breathless and sweating for a whole other reason. They'd only gotten worse since he had stopped seeking solace for his nightmares from the hound.

The single pop of the campfire jerked him awake. He rolled onto his back, holding his breath with his magic at the ready lest the sound was something sinister, but the world beyond his tent remained quiet.

How long had he slept? Clearly, he had managed some. Was it worth readying himself for his turn on watch? Dare he try to return to his dreams? They hadn't been unpleasant, just very singular.

The fluid movement of the hound as he danced, his many tattoos bidding him to follow them downwards to the glistening bronze erection. The honey-coloured gaze that sent coils of heat deep into Dylan's core with a mere look. The subtle smirk inviting him to join in.

And his dream self always did. Eagerly accepting the scorching touches that branded their desire upon Dylan's flesh with every caress, permitting the man to stoke an inner furnace he had never dared let anyone ignite.

His memories weren't much better, full of the man's touch, of the sounds he made, of the closeness they'd shared just sitting there. And there'd been that kiss just the other night. The one Tracker had clearly meant as a gentle tease that had ended with Dylan practically undressing the man.

Huffing, he rolled onto his side. That night in the tower had been a mistake. He wasn't an indecisive. He liked women, had slept with dozens. Yes, he had enjoyed the man's affections. The teasing, the kissing…

The sensation of the hound emptying into him…

He shook himself. None of that meant anything because he wasn't into men that way. Sure, he had admired a few—more than a few—in the past, from afar, but that didn't mean anything. Admiration didn't automatically translate into sexual desire. *Except—*

Except for when it had.

Dylan sat up, running a hand through his hair. He could blame Tracker all he wanted, but the truth was the man hadn't done much after that night beyond exist and maybe tease him a little. The hound had remained serious in his tutoring. *Mostly.* There was some truth to Marin's observation of how the hound couldn't seem to do anything without showing off. Like he'd done fighting Authril.

The memory of the man's hands upon the warrior's backside set off a different fire in his gut, one that simmered and stewed, chasing away all thoughts of sleep. How could he with that image running through his mind?

Sitting alone in the dark, he was willing to admit the root of that bitterness. He knew Tracker had no interest in the woman, but that wasn't the issue. Dylan had wanted to be in Authril's place. Wanted to feel the man's long fingers grasping *his* backside. Wanted that hard body beneath him.

All these muddled feelings might've been his to work through, but he didn't think he could do that alone. The hound was right about how keeping his feelings bottled up was only going to gnaw at him. In the tower, he would've talked to those he was closest with. Confided in the few indecisives he knew and trusted. Out here? He'd no access to any of it.

He had to do something. *Before* he exploded.

His gaze slid to the tent flap. He didn't know how late it was. Obviously well before his turn on watch, but early enough that either Marin or Katarina could be out there. The hound's tent lay a short distance away and Tracker slept just as alone as he did. Dylan had taken the trip there multiple times. It would be a simple thing to seek out the man and...

What? Proposition him? Tell him how vividly he danced naked through his dreams?

Explain that the reason he pushed back was due to him being terrified of a threat that might not even exist anymore?

Snarling, he fisted his hair. This shouldn't be so difficult. He had made similar advances to plenty of women in the tower. Had even been rejected by more than he wanted to count. Why did the right words elude him now? Because Tracker was a man? Because the hound was someone he shouldn't...

He bit the inside of his cheek, using the pain and the hum of his innate healing to ground himself. Even if he found the words, he knew that just being in the man's presence would turn him into an unintelligible, blushing mess.

The way he looks at you... Marin's words skittered through his thoughts. If Tracker's mannerisms around him had truly changed to the point that the hunter had noticed, then perhaps the hound's feelings on their night in the tower had also altered. After all, Tracker still pursued him. Still clearly wanted him.

And it wasn't all heat. There were the gentle embraces in the dark after nightmares had driven Dylan into the man's arms, caresses that sought to soothe. Their first soft kiss by the fire that whispered *more, more,* if only he would say yes. The way he remained companionably nearby, that honey-coloured gaze always finding him.

Just the thought twisted him up inside and set his face to blazing.

He laid a hand on his chest, sensing the thrum of his magic over his heart hammering against his ribcage. *An incoming storm.* No one had spoken about him like that before.

Was he being courted? The idea was, admittedly, a little thrilling. No one ever had before. He'd been flattered, flirted with, even pursued on the odd occasion, but never wooed.

Did he want that? From the hound? From... anyone?

There was only one way to know for sure. It couldn't wait. Tracker was to take the third watch, and he the watch after that. *Then Authril.* If he *was* to do this tonight, then it would have to be now, whilst one of the others was still on guard.

Rallying his courage, he slunk out into the night.

The tents were pitched close together, yet creeping across the space between them seemed to take far longer than it ever had. No matter the carefulness of how he trod, his every bare footstep seemed to fall in his ears like thunder.

But at last, he was at the entrance to the hound's smaller tent. He paused, his hand brushing the flap, equal parts unsure and keen.

He slipped into the tent, slowly lest he startled the man.

Inside, Tracker slept on, seemingly oblivious to his company for the first time since he had started sneaking in here. Perhaps he should let the man be and seek an alternative method to rid himself of these thoughts. *And that's worked so well thus far.*

Knowing he'd get no sleep otherwise, he knelt next to the man and laid a hand upon the blanket-covered shoulder. "Tr—"

The hound sat up before Dylan could twitch. The flash of metal in the gloom was all the warning he had of a blade at his throat.

Dylan froze, scarcely daring to breathe. The dagger's edge lay against his skin, not exerting quite enough pressure to cut. Even in the low light, the blade's purple sheen was unmistakable. *What did you expect?* he chided. They'd been attacked only a handful of days ago.

"Dylan?" His name left the hound's lips in a soft tone, deliciously husky with sleep. The blade withdrew. Now that his eyes had adjusted to the dimness, Dylan caught the man frowning in bewilderment. "It is a little early to be having nightmares, yes? You cannot have slept for long."

"I'm not sure I have at all." Maybe in bits here and there. He felt along his throat, seeking any sign that he'd been nicked and finding nothing. "I... I couldn't and..." His voice faltered as he became aware of the words spilling out his mouth. *By the gods.* Was that truly the best excuse he could come up with? Taking a deep breath, he pressed on. "And the nightmares aren't as bad every night. I can manage most times."

"I am sorry to hear they still plague you." The dagger was returned to its sheath, which Dylan now saw lay just on the edge of the man's blankets. "Come." He gestured for Dylan to join him. "You are welcome to sleep at my side if it will help."

He shuffled closer, laying his hand on the hound's chest, stilling Tracker and drawing confidence from the warmth radiating off the bare skin in the same move. "I'm not here for that sort of comfort." Clearing his throat, he continued, "I'm having other dreams." His face blazed as the confession slipped between his lips. "The erotic kind," he whispered.

Even though Dylan couldn't see the man's face well in the dim light, he felt the hound's gaze sliding over him. "And the subject of these dreams?"

"You," he confirmed, knowing the hound had damn well already reached that conclusion. "Dancing, like you did in *The Gilded Lily*. Only..." The heat in his cheeks grew. "...naked."

Even in the gloom, the crescent of Tracker's grin gleamed. "My, my," he purred, a definite snicker in his voice. "That is quite the expensive taste you have. Getting me to dance in private would cost a pretty amount back in the day."

"Whatever the number, I'm sure you'd still get it." Both the patrons and the workers at the brothel had been practically salivating over the hound's dancing. "If you were to change professions, I mean."

"There is only one way to stop being a hound and that does not leave much room for taking up an alternative vocation."

No, he supposed not.

"So, you are having dreams of myself and you are telling me because...?" Anticipation and self-satisfaction slathered the question in equal measure. He already knew the answer, but also just as clearly waited for Dylan to say it.

Sucking at his teeth, Dylan sat back on his heels. Was Tracker getting off on drawing every piece of information out of him? "I can't stop thinking about what happened between us in the tower." The confession rushed through his lips.

He certainly hadn't gone looking for sex back then, much less with the hound, but Tracker had offered himself as a distraction and had definitely lived up to that claim. That they both agreed it hadn't been the best time or place was a moot point now.

"How I... enjoyed it," Dylan added. Even with the hound's gentle teasing, it felt oddly freeing saying the words out loud, especially to the being of his desires. Like a band around his throat had been loosened. "And I wanted to know..." He fell silent, the pounding in his chest chasing out his mustered courage.

Tracker sat before him. Quiet. Patient. Still a bit smug, but accepting.

In the stillness, Dylan carefully regrouped his thoughts alongside his nerve. "I hadn't ever fully considered lying with a man before you and… we did so much." More than he'd ever done in a single moment with anyone.

The hound grunted his agreement. Was that a note of regret in the sound? Or just his fears toying with him?

Steeling himself, he continued, "I want to do it again, to know if that night was just a fluke or—"

"Or whether you truly enjoy being with men?" Tracker finished. He slowly removed Dylan's hand from his chest. "The fact you dream of it—and I am flattered, make no mistake, that you consider me as a safe harbour to do a little experimenting with."

"I didn't—" Dylan wrinkled his nose. "It wasn't meant to sound like that." It sounded terrible put that way.

Tracker gave a low chuckle. "Wanting to experiment is not something to be ashamed about. Many things require an attempt before being certain, sometimes more than once." He tipped his head to one side. "Or did you think it would upset me? It is not the first time my body has been used in such a manner."

"Please, don't say *used*." It only made him feel worse, like he was imposing himself upon the man, seeing Tracker only as an outlet for his own pleasure with no regard for the hound's preference.

Like Authril had been doing with him.

Yet Tracker didn't seem averse. The shoulders of his shadowy bulk lifted. "I *did* offer myself should you wish to engage in more sex. Why would I be upset that you are asking? But, surely, your dreaming was enough of an answer, yes?"

Is it? It didn't feel like it was, not when he awoke craving the man's touch. "These past few nights aren't the first time I've dreamt of you. Of *us*." He scrunched his hands into his undertunic. "Before the tower… before we kissed…" The fabric twisted in his grasp. "It got worse after *The Gilded Lily*." The amount of times he had woken hard, whether the hound was nearby or within another tent and—

He swallowed, desperately trying to moisten his tongue. "A part of me wanted to back then, but…" He'd been too cowardly to admit it to himself, much less the person fuelling those desires. "I thought our time in the tower would be enough." He hung his head. "I was wrong." Just like a single kiss hadn't satisfied his yearning, that night had been but a drop of rain against a parched land.

"Dylan." His name came softly from the hound's lips, brimming with such a mixture of emotion—sorrow, compassion and, yes, a rasping measure of lust—that Dylan wished he could see more than shadowy impressions of the man's face.

Tracker said not a single word further as he breached the space between them to cup one side of Dylan's jaw.

Dylan leant into the touch, closing his eyes as he lost himself to the gentle sweep of the man's thumb caressing his cheek.

He didn't know how long they sat there before Tracker spoke again.

"Permit me to ask one question." The man waited only long enough for Dylan's assenting hum before continuing. "What exactly is it that you wish of me?"

He wordlessly drew the man closer, claiming Tracker's mouth, trying to impress the fullness of his desires upon the hound. He'd been hesitant last time, touching Tracker sparingly, letting his curiosity be led by the man's experience. They hadn't the same luxury here.

Dylan palmed the man's length through his smallclothes, rubbing until the soft linen was damp and the hound was moaning into Dylan's mouth. He greedily swallowed the sound, hungry for every note.

Tracker wriggled his way out from beneath him, to recline on his side upon the blankets. "All right," he chuckled, his voice heavy with need. "I think you might tie yourself in knots if you try any harder. *But...*" There was a wary edge to the word. His long fingers travelled up from Dylan's hip, the pressure hovering close to tickling. "You understand it will not be the same as last time, yes?"

"I know."

"And, if it is to be now, it cannot be everything." He propped himself up on one arm, his free hand trailing down Dylan's chest. "Is there any particular way you wish for me to take you?"

He shook his head. Anything the hound did would be sufficient.

"Oh?" Tracker smirked and shuffled onto his knees. His hand slid past Dylan's groin, drawing the undertunic's hem higher. "And here I thought your dreams had left you with a lot of ideas." There was a pause, then the gentle caress of Dylan's exceedingly evident erection through his smallclothes.

Dylan shivered. His eyelids fluttered in their effort to shut and remain open at the same time. Not that he could see anything at this angle beyond impressions and shadows.

"It seems you have worked yourself into quite the state." The sound of Tracker's voice caressed his mind almost as much as those teasing fingers stroked him. "Allow me to relieve you of your confinement." It took very little effort on Dylan's part—some fidgeting here, a brief lifting there—for Tracker to divest him of his smallclothes. "Hello again." The words were followed by a soft gust of the man's breath across Dylan's length.

"Track…" he moaned, the desperate need to convey his desire overriding his lesser wish to remain silent.

Slender fingers encircled Dylan's length, softly stroking, a thumb sliding up and over the tip. The hound lowered his head and the heat of his breath washed over him an instant before the swirling of the man's tongue.

A groan rumbled from deep within his chest. Dylan bit his lip in an effort to muffle the sound. His hips strained to lift, held in place by the gentle pressure of the hound's fingers. The tickling passage of Tracker's unlaboured breath whistling through his nose heated far more than mere skin.

Tracker continued at an indolent pace until the slightly cold tip of his nose pressed against Dylan's body. He swallowed, the contraction of his throat tightening around the shaft.

Despite himself, Dylan bucked. Another groan broke free of his lips, louder than the first. He frantically stifled it with a hand, biting down hard on his fist to keep quiet.

The hound's actions were swiftly followed by suction as he pulled his head up, his tongue twirling in languid strokes near the end, before sliding back down.

Dylan's hand found its way into the man's hair. Tracker kept him neatly balanced, just enough to leave him softly moaning without pushing him over the edge. He wasn't certain how long the man planned to continue this state of comfortable delight, but a part of him wouldn't have minded if it never ended.

In too short a time, Tracker released him with a hushed pop.

Dylan reached out, seeking the man lest he tried to leave it at that, but the hound merely bent over him. Their lips brushed together. Slow. Measured.

With the hound atop him, the unmistakable hardness Dylan had worked to life rubbed against his own. Both damp, his via the hound's ministrations and Tracker's through natural means, enough so that it remained palpable through his smallclothes.

Tracker shifted, his weight lifting ever so slightly. The soft linen of the man's undergarments dragged across Dylan's skin, then was gone, leaving nothing between them but the night air.

Those long fingers cradled Dylan's shaft, supporting and stroking as the hound's warm, slippery length glided along the underside of his own. Tracker's hips moved in tandem with his hand, one sliding up as the other slid down.

Dylan's own hips sought to join in, his every little thrust hampered by the hound's glorious weight. Even without the buzz of his magic, the act drew groans and gasps of pleasure from his throat. He didn't think he could quell them if he tried.

And why would he want to? Tracker was clearly responding to the sounds, his hips steadily increasing their speed. Coupled with the ragged blast of his breath upon Dylan's throat, the hound had to be nearing the same glorious end as he. It lingered just on the horizon, growing closer with every silken glide.

Tracker suddenly clapped a hand across Dylan's mouth, his long fingers pressing against Dylan's lips, sealing them. His hips slowed, then stopped.

Reflexively holding his breath, Dylan squirmed against the hound as he struggled to figure out what had caused the man to halt his heavenly motion with them so close to the edge.

Tracker shuffled up to rest his chin atop Dylan's shoulder. "You cannot be so loud," he whispered, the words warming more than Dylan's ear. "Otherwise, the others will hear you. Or..." A small, amused exhalation danced in the air between them. Even in the dark, Dylan could picture the hound's teasing smile. "Is that what you *want?*"

He closed his eyes, trying not to think how they were only separated from the outside world by a piece of canvas. Vastly different to when they'd a whole section of the tower to themselves. "No," Dylan said, his lips sliding against the man's fingers. Being caught in this position wasn't exactly what he'd had in mind when he entered the tent. "But we *do* have a time limit." He'd no idea how long anyone had been on watch, but Marin would come here at the end of hers.

"I had no idea you were so eager to be done with this," the man murmured as he rocked his hips ever so slightly, the teasing sweep of his erection against Dylan's causing his body to lift as it followed the source of pleasure. "I promise, you will be more than satisfied before we run the risk of interruption. But you must be *quiet.*"

"I can do that." Whoring himself around the tower had been all the education he required when it came to muffling certain, telltale noises as needed.

The hound's soft laughter brushed across his skin. "Not as far as I have seen." Even so, he removed his hand, those same fingers slowly sliding down Dylan's chest to dig into the undertunic. He didn't move much else, certainly didn't return to the hectic thrusting he'd been doing moments before. He seemed more than satisfied in trailing tiny kisses along Dylan's earlobe and jaw.

Dylan rocked his head to one side. He gnawed on his bottom lip and fought to control the growing need bubbling inside him. This would've been fine if he had already climaxed and was waiting until they could perform a second time, but neither of them had gotten that far.

Was Tracker planning on teasing him for the remainder of the night?

The passage of kisses ventured down, turning into the slightly less delicate graze of teeth along the scarred skin at his throat. He unexpectedly quivered. Everything that could stand up, did. A groan slipped free of his lips, swiftly silenced by the hound's tongue.

He broke the kiss, pushing Tracker back far enough that the man couldn't continue, yet keeping a firm grip on him lest he left completely. "I've changed my mind," he managed, his mouth abruptly dry. "About what I want."

Although it wasn't a definite call to stop, Tracker did all the same. He sat back, his face hidden in shadow. "And that would be?"

Only here, with Tracker so deliciously close, could he give voice to the images that danced the most in his mind. His face warmed at the reminder, banishing the night chill from his extremities. He hoped even elven night vision couldn't tell the difference in the gloom. "To feel you inside me."

The hound gave a soft huff, the sound straddling relief and mirth. "Roll over, then," he breathed.

Dylan obeyed, perhaps a little too enthusiastically judging by the man's snicker. Lying flat on his stomach, he closed his eyes and listened to the hound rummaging through his pack. Should he take off his undertunic? *Might as well.* Even with the intermittent chilly breeze drifting under the canvas walls, it was already warm in the tent and would only grow hotter.

Swiftly shedding his last piece of clothing, he resumed his position on the blankets, resting his head on his arms. His body continued buzzing with anticipation, but a strange calm flooded his senses. Never had he faced the idea of sex without his every muscle, his every nerve, on edge.

Behind him, the rummaging stopped, replaced by the hurried rustle of discarded cloth, and then Tracker was back at his side. "Are you sure you want to do this?"

Dylan nodded and hummed his affirmation. He had come here fully intending to have sex with the man who dominated his dreams. He wasn't leaving for anything less.

The hound's warm hands travelled down his spine, massaging all the way. They halted at his rump, kneading the flesh like clay. A thumb slid between his cheeks and Dylan shuddered, the fire in his gut roaring to life. After last time, he felt reasonably certain that he was ready for whatever the man decided to do with him.

Tracker's fingers slid lower still, their passage leaving a tingling trail along Dylan's skin. "Remember," the man rasped as he gently encouraged Dylan's thighs to part. "Stopping me only takes a word."

Dylan's lips twisted into a manic grin. Even after witnessing how quickly he could heal grave wounds, the man seemed intent on taking the same precautions as before.

The muffled squeak of a cork reached his ears, giving him barely enough time to prepare for the cool touch of oil drizzling between his buttocks. A finger pressed against him and his hips gave an involuntary jerk upwards. But, rather than seeking a way in, the fingertip ran over his skin in small, light circles.

Dylan clamped a hand over his mouth, swallowing the unbidden whine of protest. He arched and writhed, seeking a way to put Tracker where he wanted him.

Chuckling, the man obliged. Like last time, he started slow, always managing to hit the right spot. Dylan's hips rocked in time to the movement, deepening each thrust and rubbing his length along the blankets.

The hiss of the hound's name danced on the tip of his tongue. Biting the inside of his lip helped, barely. His fingers tightened their hold on the blankets. He fought the desire to remove his other hand, even as his breath whistled frantically through his nose. That barrier was all that kept him from moaning aloud.

Dylan wasn't certain how long they remained like this or when a second finger joined in, but their sudden cessation as he began the climb towards the edge drew him back into the realisation that they didn't have all night.

"Ready?" Need, thick and hot, dripped from Tracker's voice.

The sound shuddered up his spine. *Now* and *there* and *please* bounced around his brain, all of them clamouring to be heard amongst the demand for more. "Yes," he managed. He craved the man's touch like he'd never wanted anything before. That frightening certainty delved deep into his mind, taking control of his body, thrusting himself backwards, seeking.

Tracker held his hips in place, gently guiding even as he slipped inside Dylan.

That little interwoven ball of pain and pleasure suffused his body, forcing all the breath from his lungs. Gasping, Dylan lowered his hands. It was either that or risk passing out. He swallowed great, open-mouthed gulps of air before burying his face into the blankets. They still clung to the man's glorious hot scent.

When he felt somewhat in control again, he braced himself on his forearms and resumed pushing against the hound, encouraging Tracker deeper to the sound of the man's hushed groan.

Long fingers dug into Dylan's flesh a split second before, snarling, the hound pressed Dylan's shoulders into the blankets, deftly reclaiming control over the leisurely speed with which they coupled. "Patience," Tracker breathed, the command coming through gritted teeth.

A shiver shimmied its way up Dylan's spine and back down to pulse in his groin. A frustrated, and embarrassingly needy, whine tightened his throat. "Please," he whispered against the blanket. He ached to lose himself to the man's actions, to know of nothing beyond right here and now. *Please.*

Tracker's grip tightened, bordering on painful. The half of him that was already buried in Dylan definitely twitched. A low warning hiss vibrated off the man. The rest of him slid in far faster, their hips connecting roughly to the accompaniment of Tracker's ragged, pleasure-soak growl.

The frantic pace Tracker had set earlier returned, his movements growing that little bit faster with every thrust until the man was all but slamming himself in. Each thrust also inched them up the blanket and ever closer to the tent wall. The slap of their bodies seemed loud in the otherwise carefully maintained silence, as was the man's hoarse breath. How were they not being heard?

Dylan bit the blanket, cramming as much of the fabric into his mouth as he could to keep himself from adding to the noises. Every movement rubbed him against the coarse fabric of the blankets, further warming the burning coil of lust searing a path through his gut.

It pulled a moan from him. Then another. Each one tightened his throat in ever-increasing volume.

A hand clamped over Dylan's mouth, the pressure of it arching his back until his spine connected with Tracker's chest. The heat rolling off the man's skin burrowed into his flesh. The hound didn't stop, didn't make any attempt to pull out, but his pace slowed significantly.

Dylan rolled his eyes, trying to see more than canvas and shadows. With Tracker's weight keeping him firmly pinned against the ground, the friction of the blankets was no longer sufficient. He tried to move, barely managing to lift his hips enough to get a hand beneath him.

Tracker grasped his wrist and withdrew it before he could do anything further. "Not yet," he growled, the words low and growing huskier with every breath. "I have plans for that."

The hound lifted off Dylan's back. Cool air coiled between them. He withdrew further, taking the remainder of the heat and pleasure with him. "On your back."

Dylan obeyed the gruff command. Anything to get back what he'd lost.

He barely registered the hound's arms sliding beneath his legs before he was dragged across the bedding and onto Tracker's lap in one smooth, breath-stealing movement.

"I would suggest keeping your hands free," Tracker said, bending over him as he moved himself into place. "You are going to need them to keep yourself quiet."

"I don't need my hands for that," Dylan said, stifling a slight moan as the hound effortlessly slid back inside. His breath rasped. Closing his eyes helped. A little. He bit his lip, determined to prove the man wrong.

Tracker's lips twisted in their dance down his chest, taking on a wicked tilt. "We will see," he murmured. He paused his descent of open-mouthed kisses, his tongue gliding along Dylan's skin. He groaned, the vibration shuddering through Dylan's stomach, his hips thrusting ever so slightly.

Softly echoing the sound, Dylan sought the man's head with shaking fingers, digging them into the thick hair. He tried desperately to keep his breathing steady. Not an easy feat with the fire merrily burning away in his core.

Tracker's head dipped lower still. The moist warmth of the man's breath bathed Dylan's length. Then the delicate brush of lips graced the tip.

Dylan stilled, his abrupt inhalation burning in his lungs. *He can't be.*

Yet, with his fingers still entwined in the man's hair, it was difficult to deny exactly where Tracker's head sat.

His eyes snapped open. Even in the gloom, he spied the man bent over, his head very much in the region of Dylan's groin. *By the gods...* He knew elves were flexible, but didn't think such a thing was possible. Yet the proof was currently upon him. And in him.

The unmistakable wet pressure of a tongue lavished the underside of his shaft, halting only to swirl around the tip. The hound's lips closed around his girth, taking in more and more as his head bobbed.

Flopping back onto the bedding, Dylan groaned to the accompaniment of the hound's wicked chuckle. The sound vibrated through the man's throat, softly constricting around Dylan's length and stoking the inferno blazing away in his gut.

His free hand clapped over his mouth, the fingers digging into his cheeks. He didn't know how Tracker had managed this feat of being inside him whilst also having those sinful lips around him, but if the hound kept this up, there was no chance that he could be quiet.

Tracker's head moved in tandem with his hips, drawing up at every thrust, then down as his hips withdrew. Slowly and haphazardly at first, then faster as he found a rhythm.

As much as Dylan tried to remain mindful of where they were and who might hear, thinking of anything beyond the hound's movement became impossible. He lay panting and groaning under Tracker's touch, desiring nothing more than to lose himself in this splendid act, regardless if anyone heard or not. Each subtle puff and moan from Tracker only added to his desire. His hips shifted, control all but gone. He moved against the hound, deepening each thrust.

Tracker's already firm grip on his hips tightened, keeping Dylan where he wanted. A warning growled through his throat.

Dylan's hips bucked of their own accord. His voice cracked in his effort to contain the cry bubbling up from his chest. His head swam, white rimmed his vision. By the gods, was he going to pass out before—?

He tumbled over the edge in a swirl of twinkling specks, the hound's name leaving his lips in a hoarse gasp.

Tracker's hips stilled. A soft groan vibrated through the man's throat. He still clutched Dylan, holding tight and continuing to suck, consuming every last drop.

Only once Dylan was completely spent did the hound release his hold, his tongue languidly sliding along the underside of Dylan's length, clearly savouring the departure from his mouth.

Tracker crawled up the bedding, stretching out atop Dylan, the weight and warmth a welcome addition to the euphoria still quaking through his veins. He kissed along Dylan's neck, making his way up the side to the base of his ear. "Was that what you were after?" he whispered, the hoarse note in his voice almost enough to send Dylan spiralling back over the edge on its own.

"You arse," he managed between heavy breaths. No, it hadn't been what he had come here for. It had been far more than he had hoped, had ever dreamed. "Be quiet, you said? Then you go and pull *that*?" He was going to wind up with fresh dreams of the man, of that he was certain.

The hound chuckled. "I have a few more tricks to show you, if you are interested in further experimentation. Not tonight, obviously. And it would depend on whether this was another ill-considered foray for you."

Groaning, Dylan clapped a hand over his face. *Gods*. He really had said that, hadn't he? "I'd rather hoped you'd forgotten about that," he mumbled.

"That? You mean how adamant you were on this not being repeated? *That* that?" He laughed again. This time there was definitely a smug edge to the husky richness heating his ear. "How could I forget?" The hound's tongue flicked across Dylan's earlobe.

Dylan bit his lip. His hips shifted involuntarily, rubbing his softening erection against the man's thigh. He tried repositioning himself to no avail. His legs, having long since lost the strength to hold themselves up, seemed more than content to remain sprawled on either side of the man's.

They lay in silence for a time, basking in their mutual release. Tracker softly nuzzled his neck whilst Dylan idly rubbed small circles up and down the man's back.

Tracker's breath grew shallow and Dylan slowly became aware of the hound's low purring. *We like that, do we?* Perhaps there were a few tricks Tracker would enjoy beyond sex. He chuckled to himself and, pressing his lips against the man's forehead, deepened the pressure of his fingers.

The purring increased. It vibrated through his chest, soothing. Coupled with the man's warmth, he found his eyelids growing heavier. What harm would there be in sleeping for a little while? He had done so many times before.

His eyes slid shut. He shouldn't, really. What he *should* do was dress, return to his bed and rest until Tracker woke him to take the penultimate watch.

He had almost drifted off to sleep when Tracker shook him fully awake. When had the hound moved?

Dylan sat up, rubbing at his eyes before taking in the whole scene. And just when had the man pulled on his smallclothes?

"Marin will be here soon," Tracker said as he bundled Dylan's undertunic into his arms. "If you would prefer to not have her barging in and seeing you as is, then it would be best if you dressed now."

The thought of the woman finding him here at all, much less naked, had Dylan hauling his clothing on and shuffling out the tent flap.

The night hadn't changed. The stars were still out, the moon was still high enough to illuminate the clearing, the wind shook the trees no differently.

And the air seemed far colder without the hound pressed against him.

He wobbled his way back to his tent, his stomach heavy and his feet objecting to every misplaced step.

The outline of a person moving on the outskirts of their little camp caught his attention, briefly halting him before panic took command of his legs. He ducked around the end of his tent.

The figure slowly became the familiar form of the hunter. Marin crouched by the fire, little more than faintly glowing embers now, and gave it a few experimental pokes. A tendril of flame crackled up, licking at the stick she held. When the wood was burning again, she stood and made for the hound's tent.

Dylan inched his way to his tent flap, careful not to place a foot wrong. Leaves and twigs seemed to be everywhere he stood, crackling at an alarming volume. By the gods, he'd always thought the forest floor was meant to be soft, covered in moss and the like. That's what the stories all made it out to be.

Marin paused. Her head silently jerked his way. Her fingers twitched, straying towards the quiver at her hip, then dropping as she seemed to deem him as non-threatening. And perhaps inedible.

Heat flooded his face like a wayward adolescent caught out of his quarters at night. Had she seen him? She had definitely heard him. Even if she chose not to openly acknowledge it. So, she must know it was him.

Did she also know where he had come from? *No.* There were others reasons he could be awake at this hour that had nothing to do with the hound.

He slipped into the tent before she could notice anything further.

Inside, the only thing greeting him was the chill of his blankets. He burrowed into them, warming himself faster than mere body heat could do with a subtle tweak of the surrounding air. It wasn't the same. His blankets lacked the hound's scent and the firmness of his embrace.

Dylan lay there, staring at the tent as it shuddered under the light breeze, the play of moonlight through the trees making it seem like the branches swayed far more than they did.

"I enjoy sleeping with more than one gender," he whispered into the night.

He held his breath, waiting for something—anything—to happen. For the world to collapse. For someone to drag him off into the darkness. For the gods to bring down their wrath upon him.

Tears pricked his eyes as the night's stillness remained. His chest ached with blissful, constricting relief. A chuckle that sounded exactly like a sob escaped his lips. He had been terrified of being labelled as indecisive for years, and the world didn't care.

Rolling onto his side, he curled into a ball. Whether his desire for genders beyond women extended to others or just the hound was a matter he had no wish to explore. It didn't change one important truth.

He *was* an indecisive. With everything that entailed.

And all it had taken to figure it out was for him to take advantage of Tracker's good nature. No different from what the army had done to him. What Authril had been doing.

What those in the tower expected indecisives like him to do.

CHAPTER 12

Tracker sighed as he collapsed onto the ground near their fire. With his eyes closed, he shuffled a little closer to the meagre warmth radiating from the newly lit flames. Tucking an arm beneath his head gained him a measure of comfort from the hard earth, enough that he could contentedly let the remainder of the afternoon quietly slip into the evening.

The day's travel hadn't come easily. They had crested a hill to find trees blocking the road. If it hadn't been for Dylan's efforts in clearing the way, they would've been forced to forge a path through the thick bush, likely stalling any attempts to reach Whitemeadow by a day or two.

But no, Dylan had marched along the trees, pacing out the road's width before methodically slashing at the trunks, taking each tree apart in huge slices and leaving a section big enough for a cart to squeeze through. The man had also tried to move the pieces he had cut, but his efforts to carve a path had left him exhausted.

It was the first time he had seen Dylan put more than a fraction of his power into a task that didn't involve healing. The buzz of his magic lingered in the air hours after the rest of them had finished rolling the segments of tree to one side. Humming. Electrifying. *Dangerous.*

I should have suggested caution. After the Talfaltaner ambush, treating any abnormality in their path as a trap seemed the wiser option. Yes, it would've meant a longer journey. Perhaps even the need to push themselves to travel a little farther, and a lot faster, than they otherwise would have.

Not that he believed mere beings were responsible for the fallen trees, however perfectly they had landed across the road. With how the trees still clung to their roots, they definitely hadn't fallen by way of an axe. It would've taken a lot of hefty folk to drag more than one to the ground.

Even if men had been capable, they weren't the biggest threat.

He hadn't a proper gauge for how far the spellster's magic could be felt by his fellow hounds. He'd been in the same town when he first felt Dylan approach, but passive power, however strongly it flowed off the man, was always trickier to pinpoint. Using it? For someone of his strength, he could've very well lit a beacon for any other nearby hounds.

The low pulse of power tugged at his senses, bringing Tracker back to his immediate surroundings. He cracked open an eye to the sight of Dylan standing behind Marin, his palms pressed to her shoulders, his magic imbuing the woman.

The hunter trotted off into the forest almost as soon as Dylan was done, her traps slung over her shoulder. Meanwhile, the spellster had moved on to grant a similar treatment to Katarina, finishing whatever he was doing far faster with the hedgewitch and leaving her to settle on the far side of the fire to attend their meal.

Dylan sat close to him. He arched his back in a mighty stretch, causing all manner of little clicks and pops.

The soft moan that followed had Tracker's thoughts drifting, unbidden, to when he had last heard similar sounds coming from the man. Albeit, with a far more carnal source. A part of him had hoped the spellster's visit might've repeated last night, if only so he could once again witness the hunger that so easily took Dylan's face.

Sadly, his tent had remained quiet and lonesome, with only the memory of Dylan beneath him—panting, desperate, *begging*—to keep him warm.

He had considered the merits of seeking out the man in his tent but, given everything Dylan had been through, he was stalwart in letting the spellster dictate when, and even *if*. He just hadn't expected a complete lack of acknowledgement of anything having happened. *Like after the tower.* He didn't think it was meant as a slight to himself, and definitely not to his performance, but that left precious few other reasons.

Something nudged his shoulder. A boot, if he wasn't mistaken. "You better not start snoring," Authril said. "Otherwise, I'll thump you."

He turned his surreptitious gaze from Dylan to find the woman standing over him, her hands planted firmly on her hips. "I do not snore," he curtly replied before rolling back. If he did, his bed partners certainly hadn't been bothered by it. "My dear man, I trust you are minding that you do not overexert yourself."

A small smile tweaked Dylan's lips. "Soothing a body of the day's aches doesn't take much. I'm just sorry I can't do the same for you."

Warmth suffused his chest. He was used to falling into his bed in all manner of states that he barely paid it any mind. For his comfort to cross someone else's thoughts wasn't something he had encountered for a long time. "The consideration is appreciated, but I will manage. *Although...*" he purred. His gaze swept over the spellster, taking in the gentle flex of anticipation that twitched through Dylan's posture. "If you are truly concerned, there is always the non-magical method, yes? I am sure your touch is more than skilled to give an adequate massage."

Tracker fought to keep his expression neutral as the man's ivory cheeks gained a subtle pink hue. Was Dylan considering how much he'd been avoiding Tracker after their previous passionate night? When he'd shown exactly how capable his fingers were when it came to Tracker's body.

"Trust you to pervert an innocent gesture," Authril growled, giving his shoulder a harder nudge with her boot than before. Not quite a kick, but as close as it could be without rousing suspicion. "But if massages are on offer as well, I wouldn't mind one." She shucked her thick armour padding before settling in front of Dylan. "Concentrate on my neck and lower back."

Frowning, Dylan dug his fingers in just below the warrior's neck. She groaned and squirmed for a brief moment, but uttered no word of complaint and soon started making softer noises.

Returning to lying on his back, Tracker closed his eyes and sought the peace he had attained before Authril's interruption. It wasn't a simple matter, not with the moans and murmurs of her pleasure assaulting his ears. At least the noises were low. He likely wouldn't have been able to halt his blade if he heard anything close to the sounds she used to make whilst bedding Dylan.

The acrid tang burning in the back of his throat chased away any hope of rest without seeking his bed. Sighing, he sat up and stretched the worst of the kinks from his body. He supposed that whatever Katarina warmed up atop the fire could be consumed when it was actually his turn on watch, but he had grown to enjoy sharing a meal again. Many of his evenings on the road prior to joining the others had been with Lullaby, and the warhorse had never been much of a conversationalist.

Guilt twisted his gut. He hadn't given the animal much thought over the past fortnight. Without a means to contact Toptower, there was little he could do beyond worry, wonder and hope. *I should be back with him by now.* At the very least, closer. A week's travel on foot to Oldmarsh, where a purchase of a horse would see him south within a handful of days.

Civilisation meant waiting until they'd reached Whitemeadow, which sat another week away. Maybe more if they encountered further natural disasters or another group of straggling Talfaltaners. But once there, the pigeons at the hound station would be more than enough to get word to Commander Rhiannon and, hopefully, Lullaby had stabilised enough to be moved from *The Blade and Blanket*.

What would he tell the commander? The answer depended on so much and he wouldn't be able to linger for a response.

Maybe speaking with Katarina about organising the animal's transport across the border into Dvärghem would be a more prudent step. Getting her alone wouldn't be difficult. The woman was habitually up with the dawn.

Of course, it would require trusting her with a portion of his plan to get Dylan out of the kingdom. She might not stop from attempting the act—he largely believed her to be an ally in that respect—but he couldn't be as certain when it came to her ability to keep secrets. He couldn't risk Authril knowing. *That* he had no doubts about.

"Is such effort necessary to mend her ailments?" Katarina asked, drawing Tracker back from his musing. She idly stirred the pot that contained the evening's meal, but her attention seemed more on Dylan and Authril.

Under the man's steady ministrations, the warrior sat like a puppet with its strings cut, flexing only to lean into Dylan's motions.

"Surely, the healing alone is enough to soothe all the aches," the hedgewitch continued. "*I* feel quite refreshed." She rolled her shoulders, twisting and stretching in a manner she hadn't been able to do a moment ago. "Or does the magic not work on simple matters like aching muscles for elves?"

"It does," the spellster replied distractedly.

Katarina hummed. "It is interesting seeing what effect your healing magic has in a less drastic situation and certainly useful. I've heard rumours of spellsters doing incredible feats with such magic."

Dylan's brows knitted together. "What feats? Healing is only capable of mending injuries. It can't do anything else."

The hedgewitch opened her mouth.

Tracker loudly cleared his throat, garnering the woman's attention. "You speak as if such information is yours to give freely." He had no idea what, but if the man didn't already know it, then the knowledge was something the Overseers had forbidden. "If Dylan was to arrive at Wintervale with abilities he could not have possibly gained with tower training, it could be detrimental to—"

A low rumble of enjoyment tugged at his ear.

His gaze swung to Authril, the corners of his mouth lowering. What had caught his attention was the purring emanating from her.

"Fascinating," Katarina breathed. "I've not heard her make that noise before." She snickered. "It's like listening to a giant cat." She stretched forward, her fingers hovering over Authril's head. "Makes me want to scratch behind your ears."

"I would not recommend it, dear woman," Tracker said as the warrior playfully batted away Katarina's hand. "Unless you plan to scratch an altogether different itch for her afterwards."

"Oh?" The hedgewitch withdrew her hand, her cheeks darkening. "Oh! Yes... uh... I mean to say that I forgot stimulating the area around an elf's ears provokes instant arousal."

"Instant?" he blurted, the word barely escaping the laughter that followed on its tail. He ran his fingers over his ear, feeling the cold metal of his earrings and the warm, harsh angles of flesh and cartilage. Even such a simple touch from himself stirred a small measure of heat through his blood. "I would hardly say *that*, but you certainly should not touch if you are not also looking for something more."

"Is that so?" Dylan murmured.

His gaze flicked from Katarina to the spellster, catching the small secretive smile curving his lips. Tracker had thought the man unaware of what he'd done to him during their tumble in the tower. Clearly, that wasn't so.

He couldn't even remember the last time he had permitted someone else to touch him so intimately before then. It had to have been years. Maybe even decades.

Others had tried. Even if he hadn't an array of earrings, he'd had far too many prospective bed partners attempting to prey on the fact for him to remain blissfully unaware. They'd been humans, mostly. Either looking to see the tavern rumours surrounding elves in action, or inexperienced fumblings that would've far more likely cooled his ardour than stoke it.

And Dylan? The spellster might've been lacking experience in much of what they'd done that night, but the way he had handled Tracker's ear wasn't one of them. The experience was enough to leave the memory of his touch still sharp even with it being weeks since.

The teasing tingles of him toying with Tracker's earrings, sending thrums of pleasure dancing just on the knife edge of pain right to his groin. The silken glide of his tongue along the upper ridge culminating with the jolt of his teeth grazing the very tip that had almost made him climax on the spot...

Tracker flashed the spellster a grin. "That is indeed so, my dear man," he purred. Even with Authril between them, he couldn't help but tease. "Were you looking to see it in action? I could be persuaded to show you."

Dylan's eyes widened, his cheeks steadily gaining a deep pink hue, before he ducked his head.

"He is *not* after anything from you," Authril snapped. Reaching back, she prodded Dylan's side with a forefinger. "I didn't say you could stop. And don't *you* even think about laying your hands on him in that capacity," she snarled in Tracker's direction.

Dylan resumed kneading along the warrior's back to the immediate return of her purring.

"I wonder," Katarina said, drawing Tracker's attention. "I've seen several of your kind with adornments in their ears. But if they are as sensitive as your people claim, then why do it? Don't they hurt?"

He bent forward, propping himself on his elbows. "They most certainly did when I first had them pierced. But now? I would think it is no different to humans and dwarves." He'd been on the cusp of fifteen when a human patron of *The Gilded Lily* had suggested it, offering to pay if he would let them watch. The brothel mistress had almost banned them from the premises for it. Whilst she didn't mind if patrons indulged in pain, she drew the line at blood, especially if it was one of her workers doing the bleeding.

"Then why do you have so many? Do they have a particular meaning?"

He shook his head, focusing on how the majority of his earrings swayed. After the first one, he had craved additions. If only for the catharsis he had found in the act of letting in more pain upon his person, dulling the immense ache that had been in his chest. "It is a simple matter of vanity, my dear woman. They are pleasing to the eye and I enjoy having them."

"I hear men amongst the elven nomads pierce themselves to impress a mate," Authril murmured, one side of her face squished by the upraised hand she rested her head upon. "The more piercings he has, the more virile he's meant to be."

Tracker frowned. This wasn't the first time she had mentioned the elven nomads. Had she encountered them whilst serving her mercenary company? Had they been part of a contract? Many didn't like having the wandering folk and their caravans around, regardless of who they belonged to. "I had not heard this."

She gave an affirmative hum that dipped into a brief purr. "I heard the really wealthy ones, those that own more than one caravan, have piercings in all sorts of places." Her gaze flicked down, seemingly indicating his groin.

He grimaced at the thought. Each piercing residing in his ears had been like a jab to the balls, he couldn't see himself actually allowing a needle anywhere near there. Not even his tattoos touched such an area. "I imagine they also have access to healing magic." He likely would think differently if the pain was temporary and easily mended.

Humming, Katarina rummaged in her belt pouch. She pulled out the slim wooden box he'd seen her use a multitude of times on their journey. It held a capped metal inkwell and a featherless metal quill. The small, leather-bound booklet he would often see her scribbling in late at night also surfaced from another pouch. She took up her quill and, after a precise dip into the ink, proceeded to write furiously across the page.

"Are you taking notes, Madam Hedgewitch?" Dylan asked, the cheeky tone and the quirk to his smile suggesting the man already knew the answer.

It wasn't hard to spot the difference from the woman merely detailing the day's travel and cataloguing something new to her. It was in the way her nose scrunched as she wrote, the tip twisting to one side whenever she sought more ink to carry on.

"Of course," she replied without lifting her gaze from the book. "I've never heard of this elven purring phenomenon and can only assume others back home have not either. It must be recorded."

"Truly?" Tracker stretched in an attempt to peer at the woman's booklet. He'd seen the hedgewitch's handwriting the once and hoped to make sense of her notes. Alas, even if he could've made out the spidery writing, it looked to be exclusively in Dvärg. He understood a little when it came to speech. The written word was a vastly different matter. "Whatever for?"

Dylan chuckled. "Because it's knowledge. No one hoards facts quite like the Dvärghem Coven." A bemused look crossed his face as he also watched Katarina write. "How is this new to you? All elves purr."

"We do *not*," Tracker curtly replied. The very thought of making such a sound like Authril was ridiculous. He wasn't some damn mouser. "I certainly never have."

Both Dylan and the warrior looked at him as though he had taken leave of his senses.

"I've been around elves all my life," Dylan said. "Several of my closest friends are—" As it always did whenever the man mentioned his companions in the tower, his face grew stiff. "*Were* elves." He remained silent for a heartbeat, then shook himself. "I know they purr. I know *you* do. I've *heard* you."

"You've what?" Authril growled. "When?"

Panic drained the last remaining scraps of colour from Dylan's cheeks. "In his sleep."

"When have you ever shared sleeping quarters close enough to hear him purr?" She frowned and seemed to consider the times. "Apart from the tower." Her eyes narrowed. "Did he have you sharing that cot we found all bloody?"

The man's mouth opened, but not even the puff of a breath

escaped his lips. The answer was, of course, a resounding yes, but Dylan clearly didn't want anyone else knowing they'd been intimate, especially not Authril.

"I would think it more likely to be Oldmarsh," Tracker offered. They hadn't exactly been all snuggled up in the same bed, at least not in the beginning, but they had definitely shared a small room after their stint in *The Gilded Lily*.

"Of course," Authril sneered, her little nose doing its best to wrinkle with some measure of her arrogance. Her features were far too delicate to make much of an impact. "Bet you were still all fogged up with that brothel's incense and your mind too focused on your dick's satisfaction."

He kept his mouth shut. She had taken her fair share of Treasure's time, later claiming the incense had clouded her better judgement and led her into the prostitute's bed. It sounded pretty, but he knew the incense used there was nothing more than aromatic herbs and resin. The stuff that swayed people into lingering and having fun was put into the drinks, where the staff could monitor dosage and consumption. And Authril had consumed none of it.

"So, he was purring in his sleep?" Katarina asked. Her gaze remained fixated on her writing, not even glancing up when no one responded. "You claim it happens to all elves? Say you were to give him the same treatment." She pointed the end of her quill at Tracker. "He would also purr?"

Authril drew herself up so far that any further would've required levitation to achieve. "You want Dylan to massage *his* back?"

"My dear woman," Tracker murmured before anyone else could respond. "We are only speaking of doing so for experimental purposes, yes? Are you saying you are against the furthering of knowledge?" He highly doubted any purring would happen—he truly didn't recall ever doing so elsewhere in his life—but if a massage was on offer, he wasn't about to refuse one. Especially when Dylan appeared to know what he was doing. "Did your cutthroat company not tell you hoarding for personal gain is bad manners?"

Her tanned features paled at the mention of the mercenary company she had lost during the army attack. "All elves purr," she snapped. "I do. You do. Even most half-elves are capable."

"You've truly never heard an elf purr before?" Dylan asked. "Not even yourself?"

"I have heard the sound from others," he admitted. "Elven and human alike." The latter didn't make quite the same noise as what came from the warrior, but it was close enough. "I always assumed it was completely voluntary. As for myself..." He shrugged. "I do not recall."

Dylan's lips twisted with pity. His whole expression had crumpled into something that bordered on mournful. "Elves purr when they're content. Are you saying you've never *once* been peacefully happy?"

With his face slowly warming, Tracker snorted. When was *he* supposed to have found such harmony in his life? "The King's Hounds are tasked with bringing peace to others. We do not partake in it."

The man's expression only deepened, forcing Tracker to avert his gaze or face the uncomfortable churning in his gut.

Authril clicked her tongue in mock sympathy. "That doesn't change the fact *he*—" She jerked a thumb towards Dylan. "—doesn't need to be giving any more massages."

"Naturally, I would not seek to abuse his generosity but, surely, *who* gets the privilege of our dear spellster's skilled hands is up to him." His gaze swung to Dylan as he spoke, just in time to see his blushing bloom once again.

The man wet his lips. His gaze grew distant, clearly running their conversation through his head. "I see no reason to refuse the request. Only if *you're* willing."

"Really?" Authril murmured. "I can think of several reasons."

"Such venom is hazardous to the soul, my dear." Tracker spread his arms wide, bowing before Dylan. "How would you have me?"

The pinkness in the man's cheeks deepened. "Right there is fine. I just need you to remove your armour."

Tracker bowed his head, marking the slight glint in Dylan's eye. "As you command." He made swift work of stripping to his undershirt as Authril had done. The chill breeze nipped through the thin linen, causing his skin to pebble before the spellster could place a single hand upon him.

But lay hands upon him, the man did. Dylan worked methodically, his palm sweeping all over Tracker's back, before setting to work on the most knotted muscles. "Gods," he grunted. "I think you needed this more than Authril."

Tracker could only groan his agreement. With all the old lash scarring on his back, there were patches where surface sensation was fuzzy at best, but the depth Dylan worked literally pushed past that barrier. He hung his head, dragging the majority of his braid over one shoulder to give Dylan better access.

The man's movements paused. Then the ghost of a touch traced the tattoo that adorned the nape of Tracker's neck.

He tensed before realising it, hastily masking the stiffness by flexing the muscles Dylan had just loosened. Having been tattooed there since childhood, he had forgotten the sword on his back reached so far up his spine. Only the hilt of the design was visible whilst clothed, or so he'd been told, the rest hidden beneath his shirt, but he wasn't in the mood to discuss it.

Dylan wordlessly continued his massage. He pressed deeper into Tracker's flesh, searching out every little knot, just as he'd done with the warrior.

Tracker found himself leaning into the touch. He'd had massages before—several workers at *The Gilded Lily* specialised in them and loved to practice on their fellow prostitutes—but the soothing motion coupled with the hum of the man's magic was definitely new.

His thoughts drifted to what else those hands were capable of. *Like the lightning*. Dylan hadn't used it last time, but he still remembered the power. The buzz in the air. The way it tingled along his skin. How every breath had left the tang of a storm in the back of his throat.

"Well now," Marin declared, her voice neatly cutting through his musing. "Wasn't expecting to find this when I got back."

Tracker opened his eyes to find the hunter standing on the edge of the clearing, a speckled bird about the size of her head dangling in her hand. How had she managed to down a pheasant at this hour? The birds had usually tucked themselves away for the night by now.

Behind him, Dylan stilled. He withdrew his glorious touch. "I—"

"It's just a little experiment," Katarina replied. She had taken up position on his left, her quill poised over the inkwell. "Dylan was just showing me the purring ability our elven companions possess. Although, so far, I've witnessed it from only one of them."

"You might as well stow your quill, my ever-curious hedgewitch. You are not going to hear me purr. I never have and I am not about..." His words tapered into a low moan as Dylan slid his hands up Tracker's back to curl around his shoulders before dropping back down. He drew in a breath, centring himself lest he revealed a less appropriate reaction.

Marin plopped herself down on the other side of Katarina, plonking the bird in her lap. "You didn't know they could do that?" she asked the dwarf. "Pretty much every elf I've met does at some stage. They'll growl, too." She leant over to poke Authril's nose. "Especially when you try to suggest saving a little pork for the journey."

The warrior batted away the other woman's outstretched arm, making an assortment of garbled words and sputtered utterances. "I did that *once*," she snarled. "And if you had grown up in the slums, you wouldn't give up good meat, either."

"I'm no stranger to not having a good meal," the hunter shot back. "My whole family went days with little in our bellies after our home was burnt to the ground. If I didn't hunt it down, I doubted we would've made it to the next farmhouse." She grabbed a fistful of the pheasant's feathers and plucked them from the carcass. "Let me tell you, it was no simple matter trying to keep Papa and my mama's parents fed whilst on the move with nothing but the clothes on our backs. Hell, keeping you lot fed is easier."

He tried to focus on the conversation, but his attention kept slipping to how the spellster's fingers danced along his back. Just one hand and no longer quite as vigorous. The movements were delicate, almost absent of thought, the man's nails scraping along Tracker's undershirt.

Tracker discreetly bit his lip to keep from moaning. He slowly twisted into a better angle for Dylan, wordlessly letting it be known that he welcomed the touch. Sitting comfortably cross-legged, his elbows resting on his knees and his head lolling forward, Tracker closed his eyes.

The pressure increased, subtly but noticeable. The thrum of healing magic ghosted along his skin like a cool breeze.

He silently arched a brow at Dylan, unsure if the man was even aware of what he was attempting. Dylan often spoke about his healing ability being something he couldn't control when it came to mending himself, but he seemed capable of commanding where it flowed in others. Even though the magic couldn't actually affect him, the impression of it still tingled. Not as much as the lightning had, but enough to be pleasant.

The man's apologetic grimace answered him well before Dylan murmured, "Sorry." His shoulders twitched. "Habit." If that were true, then it had to have been something he'd done in the tower. Tracker certainly hadn't witnessed the man being so close to any of the others.

"You should conserve your strength." Especially when it came to wasting it on himself. "But I do not mind the physical aspect."

One corner of his mouth twitched upwards. "I know," Dylan said, the words barely audible. His gaze flicked to the other side of the fire, where the women were engaged in a conversation Tracker had long stopped listening to, before returning their full focus to him. The ghostly impression of impishness twinkled in the dark depths of his eyes as he leant closer and whispered, "That's also how I know for certain you purr in your sleep."

"I see," he murmured. A gentle sideways lean was enough to have their shoulders touch. "You are seeking to repeat the act, yes?"

To his surprise, Dylan tilted away from him, removing his hand from Tracker's back in the process. Had he done—*said*—something wrong? Searching the man's face gave little in the way of clues beyond discomfort and...

Fear.

Dylan tried to hide it, but Tracker had seen such emotion grip the spellster before. Terror lurked along the edges of his eyes and quickened the rate of his breath. It peeked out with his tongue as the spellster wet his lips, and jerked in the subtle twitch of his jaw as he made small grinding adjustments. His magic quivered at his core, held at bay by a trembling gossamer thread.

Tracker reached out, seeking to reassure, stopping when those dark eyes only widened further. The man's gaze unmistakably darted back to the other side of the fire before returning to hold his, silently warning him back.

The sight reminded him of when he had tried to teach the man how to wield a sword. He hadn't been able to coax the full reason out of Dylan then or during the quiet times afterwards, only that he wasn't willing to let others know they had slept together in the tower. He had thought the man wouldn't come to his bed seeking sex as he'd done the other night if the idea of anyone knowing they'd been intimate was still an issue.

Clearly, he'd been wrong there.

"Easy, my dear man." He inched his hand across the ground, slowly closing the gap to rest his fingers atop Dylan's. "Today has left you exhausted, yes? I think the best recourse would be for you to seek your bed early."

The man's guarded uncertainty faded as Tracker spoke until all that remained was a weary smile. "Sleep does sound good." His gaze drifted once more, this time towards the tents, two of which Tracker had pitched alone. "Thank you, by the way. I don't think I could've faced anything more difficult than crawling under the blankets."

Biting back the old suggestion that they could've shared his tent, Tracker bowed his head. "You are most welcome." After Dylan's efforts, giving the man somewhere to sleep in peace was the least he could've done. "I trust—"

"*What?*" Authril screeched, the harsh tone of her incredulousness like a jab to the ear.

A shield stuttered to life around Dylan, then vanished just as quickly when he jerked his hand out from beneath Tracker's fingers.

Tracker snapped his head in the warrior's direction, prepared for whatever barrage of insults she chose to throw his way, only to find the woman's attention was squarely on Marin.

"Your family *traded* with Udyneans?" she continued, sounding no less sceptical. "But they're the enemy. *And* they would've been a bunch of spellsters."

"Well..." Marin shrugged. "*Yes*, I suppose that, technically, they were the enemy. But they never sought to harm us."

"Your entire home was ransacked though," Authril pressed. "By

Udyneans. Those merchants were probably spies tasked with seeking out an easy target."

"They were fishermen. Damn good ones, according to my father. Maybe some were spellsters, but I don't know. Maybe they didn't send the magical ones across the border. I know *I* wouldn't, if I knew what became of them." She peered at him out the corner of her eye.

Tracker kept quiet. He couldn't dispute the unspoken words hanging over the campfire. If a spellster was found unleashed in any settlement, a King's Hound was expected to escort or kill. It didn't matter where they'd come from.

His attention slid to Katarina. The woman appeared to be writing in her little book. He supposed news of destroyed hamlets in another country wasn't considered as worthy enough to share across the continent. It had barely made its way to his ears, and he'd been training in Wintervale at the time.

"But they still attacked," Authril said.

"No. Not them. Tanvi's Rest is full of elves. The people who..." She halted, frowning. When she spoke again, her words were devoid of emotion. "The people who destroyed Lynhold were human."

Tanvi's Rest. Tracker recalled seeing the place on maps. Nestled in a cove, from what he remembered. No one really spoke much about the village as it was beyond Demarn's southern border and, thus, outside of their concerns.

Not once would it have occurred to him that it was elven-ruled. He hadn't realised such places existed outside of Heimat. They certainly didn't in Demarn. There was the odd sector in the bigger villages and cities, usually the more rundown parts, but never a whole settlement. The closest the kingdom got was when nomadic caravans rolled through in their bi-annual journey and he'd only ever seen those from afar.

He had always assumed that venturing into the Udynea Empire as an elf would mean enslavement. If he had known there were alternatives, he might have tried running a great deal sooner. Maybe even years sooner.

Did that mean he was taking Dylan in the wrong direction? Even if they'd doubled back from the tower, they would've passed Oldmarsh by now and be on their way back to Toptower with no possible threats lingering in the nearby forest. Perhaps even as far back as the border town if he had procured horses. He could've reunited with Lullaby...

And be chased the whole way by Authril.

Tracker silently observed the warrior as she continued trying to convince Marin, in both direct and roundabout fashions, that the innocent childhood memories of her home were actually full of spies. The way she spoke about spellsters, the fanaticism she gave to all

Udyneans being monsters bent on conquering...

He had considered attempting to convince her that leashing Dylan, taking him back into war, was not the best path for either of them, but nothing he'd seen told him she would listen. She certainly wouldn't give up Dylan easily. And he couldn't permanently eliminate the threat she posed to his plans without risking losing the man's trust.

For now, he could only remain vigilant about her actions and hope Whitemeadow offered a palatable solution. Preferably one that had him leaving the woman behind.

It really couldn't come fast enough.

CHAPTER 13

Silence lingered over the camp as Marin and Authril both came to the conclusion that their bickering wouldn't sway the other. It grew less awkward as Katarina dished out the evening meal and people involved themselves in their food. It wasn't much, chunks of yesterday's hunting with a few root vegetables the hedgewitch had dug up from the side of the road whilst he sliced a path through the fallen tree trunks.

Dylan prodded at the meat, watching it submerge into the weak liquid that could laughably be called broth. Much of their meal had started as droplets he had drawn from the air to fill several of their water skins. Authril had objected to the act, ceding only once it was made clear that they'd no access to any other fresh water even with the sky threatening to douse them every morning.

She objected to a lot of what he did. He hadn't really given it much thought, but now he knew why she opted to become so close to him, he realised she protested him using his magic far more than the others did.

Katarina seemed to take it in stride, but then, she had spoken of being in Udynea before the ambush that led to their meeting. He would occasionally catch Tracker glancing his way, but if the hound sensed magic as strongly as he claimed, then using any of his power was likely akin to tweaking the man's nose.

Marin's blasé approach had been surprising, but after hearing her defend the Udyneans who had once visited the village of her birth, he was starting to understand why she'd never seen him as a threat. She was, naturally, curious about what he could do, but no warier of him than of the others. The camaraderie she offered reminded him of the friends he had lost.

He was going to miss it.

The realisation seized him and he clutched his bowl a little tighter, his stomach cramping. The evening suddenly seemed a lot cooler. He shuffled closer to the fire. It didn't help.

Since leaving the ruins of his home, he tried not to think about their destination, or the fate that awaited him at Wintervale. He would be leashed. He knew that. He had... *accepted* that, however much it made his skin crawl and the scar on his throat burn. But losing the others? That hadn't crossed his mind before now.

Realistically, Katarina would press on to Dvärghem, likely with a whole new contingent of well-armed guards to keep her safe. He might wind up in her dissertations, a paragraph or two about a leashed spellster who had managed to break free of his collar.

Tracker would return to his brethren, tell his superiors what had transpired in the tower and be on his way, back to roaming the kingdom in search of more spellsters once Dylan was leashed and sent to the battlefield.

Authril was insistent on returning to the army, of becoming his warden. He wouldn't lose that connection at least, as bittersweet as the thought was. He'd still be on his own most of the time. The fresh wave of soldiers no less wary of him than the last.

And Marin? Who knew where the hunter would disappear to? She had vacated her home, had travelled farther than she had needed to. For them. For *him*.

She had almost *died* because of him. And there was nothing, no reward or recompense, he could offer in return.

Maybe one of the others could convince someone in Wintervale to present the hunter with the means to start her life somewhere new. And maybe some of them would reunite in their travels. Hedgewitches ventured into the kingdom whenever a new site was discovered, whilst hounds and hunters were always on the move. He wouldn't be one of them. Even if he was able to mingle with Authril whilst in the army camps, soldiers could leave the site. Spellsters couldn't.

Dylan rubbed his throat, feeling the too-smooth patch of his scar. *Just a few more weeks*. A month, if they were delayed. That was all he had before he lost more than his magic. He was used to making the best from what he'd been given, but now...

It wasn't enough.

It didn't matter if reaching Wintervale took months or years, a decade. Even another lifetime. None of it would be long enough. He didn't want to return to the army's clutches. Except there were so few spellsters left. Tracker had suggested he could be the last one in Demarn and the hound could well be right. The kingdom needed him to defend against the savages of the Udynea Empire.

The same kingdom that let his home fall. He had seen enough charts and diagrams to know where the tower sat in relation to other settlements, had watched Tracker plot the course the Talfaltaners would've taken on his map. There'd been ample opportunities for the crown to turn them back.

But what else could he do except follow the destiny laid before him? His duty. The thing he was trained for.

Nothing.

Letting the army leash him wouldn't even guarantee he lived for long. They would throw him back on the front line, where he had barely escaped death the first time. Authril's words to the others made it clear that his path was a choice between being slaughtered here or in another ambush.

It was his fate to be leashed and used. Just a weapon they expected to fight until he was spent.

Something heavy softly bumped against his shoulder, their presence leaning persistently but not pushing.

He turned his head, expecting to find the hound's soothing gaze, only to meet Marin's soft brown eyes. He caught the gentle curve of her smile before noticing the concern furrowing her brow. It was the same look she had given after revealing Authril's true motives for bedding him, before she had almost lost her life.

Dylan returned the smile, feeling the corners of his mouth wavering the longer he tried to hold it. Raising his bowl to drink the broth helped conceal that weakness, although it gave him the new struggle of trying to swallow past the lump in his throat. He needed to eat, to replenish all that he had lost in slicing up those trees.

Tracker cleared his throat, drawing everyone's attention. "Given light of what we have found in our path so far, I think we should make some changes to the watch."

"What kind of changes?" Katarina asked. They hadn't come across any actual people since the attack that had almost taken Marin's life, but there'd been plenty of signs heavily suggesting more like them weren't as far away as they would've liked.

Authril scoffed. "Why tell us now? You already make plenty of changes without informing us. I've lost count of how many times I've found you out patrolling when Dylan should be."

Dylan was willing to bet several of those times would've been with himself curled up in Tracker's blankets. He put his bowl to one side with some measure of reluctance. His stomach offered up a faint grumble, but it churned far too much for him to trust swallowing another mouthful.

If Tracker had made the same connection, the man opted to remain silent.

"*And* there are the nights when no one wakes me at all," Authril continued, narrowing her eyes at the hound. "I'm aware you don't trust my judgement on... other matters." Her voice faltered as she glanced Dylan's way, then she seemed to rally herself. "But surely you can't think I would do something to endanger us?"

"Not at all," Tracker agreed, that sharp smile he often levelled at her on full display. "I am well aware of your instinct to survive this little trek of ours. But forgive me, I thought you might have been tired after your little night-time romps."

Her face flushed. Anger or embarrassment, either one seemed possible. Was she recalling the last time she tried to sleep with Dylan, the one where he had refused her advances? "What I get up to with him is none of your business."

"It becomes such if it starts to affect him, my dear warrior." He turned to Katarina, his smile shifting into something more pleasant. "My suggestion would merely be to double the number of people awake. It would mean stretching the length of time between each changeover, but I believe we can manage until Whitemeadow."

"And *after* Whitemeadow?" Authril pressed. "We'll be travelling downriver. Towards Wintervale?"

"What happens after depends on what we find there, yes? We currently have no way of knowing whether the horde that besieged the tower attacked elsewhere. I cannot imagine they went through Whitemeadow quietly—in the coming or the going—the city could very well be in a similar state to what we left behind, or worse."

"What could possibly be worse than the genocidal slaughterhouse they made of the tower?" the hedgewitch asked, the typically musical tone of her accent cracking.

"Few buildings in Whitemeadow are made entirely of stone," Authril answered. "It wouldn't take much for large sections of the city to burn. The bastards could murder hundreds and kill thousands."

"That would be unfortunate," Tracker said. "But it would be far worse, for the city and ourselves, for them to still be there."

"How is that worse?" Dylan snapped. If the people responsible for the destruction of the tower were still within reach, it just made the chance to avenge all those deaths far more possible.

"I know what you are thinking, but you are one man. An extremely powerful one, yet still singular. You would need an army at your back to support in the defence of the locals and grant you the means to tell friend from foe." He spread his hands. "The four of us are in no shape to assist in either endeavour."

In that final sentence, he agreed. It would be especially arrogant to expect the hedgewitch to involve herself in a matter that didn't concern her people. However... "I'm pretty sure I'll have no trouble picking Talfaltaners out of a crowd." Dealing with them whilst keeping civilians safe would be the trickier part, but still doable if he applied himself right.

The hound's eyes narrowed, disbelief plain upon his face. "And *how* would you manage that? Do not think it will be a matter of selecting anyone who dresses the same as those we have already encountered. Their garb is but simple attire. Many Demarners working the docks and ships wear similar."

On the edge of his vision, Dylan caught Authril nodding. He didn't think there'd ever be anything the two elves could agree on.

"What do you mean he's powerful?" Marin asked. "Did I miss him doing something when I was unconscious?"

"Not at all," Katarina replied. "The Nulled Ones' ability to sense magic isn't merely when it's in use. They can perceive latent ability and those who have spent time amongst varied spellsters are able to gauge strength based on it."

"And most spellsters sent to fight in the army are strong enough to level a village should the mood take them," Tracker added.

Dylan supposed there was a smidgeon of truth to the hound's words. The tower had sent her best, if not always her strongest. He doubted that any of those leashed over the generations would've sought to attack a village, even if they'd been ordered to. Spellsters who showed an inclination towards violence within the tower often vanished soon after.

"What of *him*?" Authril asked. Her gaze slid his way, uncertainty glinting in the sea-green depths.

His stomach flipped. She often showed hesitancy in being around him when he used his magic for anything other than fighting or healing—and she seemed a touch squeamish about the latter. He had thought it because she hadn't been introduced to the idea of non-lethal magic like the hedgewitch clearly had, but Marin hadn't either and was far more accepting on that front.

"Does it matter, my dear woman?" the hound replied. "Are you afraid your future charge will prove too much to handle? Has he not shown how gentle his power can be?"

"Of course I know his abilities can be focused on less destructive tasks." Authril tipped her nose into the air. "Did you think I didn't? He *has* used his healing touch on me for more than mending injuries. Even before you usurped our group."

"Only a little healing?" The way Tracker spoke, Dylan would've thought the man had advanced knowledge of the subject... if he hadn't witnessed the hound's awe at how seamlessly his innate healing had repaired the stab wound that should've taken his life in the tower. "I imagine there are a lot of uses to be had in bed."

Dylan turned an incredulous eye towards the hound, finding nothing but a thinly veiled smugness. He'd only used magic on Tracker the once during the two instances they'd had sex. That had been back in the tower, where he had supplemented his inexperienced strokes with a little lightning. *Briefly*.

"The Udyneans have several texts on the matter of magic and sex," Katarina added. "As well as, I believe, several pleasure tools that require it."

He eyed the woman. "I thought hedgewitches were celibate?" Why would they have any knowledge of such practices? And why was she able to recollect such information so readily?

"We are," the hedgewitch confirmed. "But it's still interesting to see the variation of acceptance and usage amongst the kingdoms. My personal favourite on the subject is the wide variety of... colourful names the Udyneans have for certain positions. They can get very inventive."

"Yes?" Tracker piped up. "You simply must regale me with them some time."

"*M-magic?*" Authril stammered. Her once flushed face had drained to its usual creamy pallor. "During... during *sex?*"

"You have never considered it, my dear warrior?" A wicked grin stretched the hound's face. "Are you not even a little bit curious?"

She wrinkled her nose and made a gagging sound. "I've no need to be reminded of what he's capable of. It'd be like having sex with a sword involved."

"Ah, so you have not even thought to grasp the idea of what he could do. Back in *The Gilded Lily*, temperature play was a common request. It is a means to gift control to another, but quite tame amongst other activities. You would be amazed how a little extra warmth, or coldness, adds to the act. Having someone capable of precisely altering the ratio could only heighten it." Tracker's gaze slid to Dylan, the smugness on his face growing more prevalent. "And only the gods know what he could do with a little spark of lightning if given the opportunity."

Authril's expression grew increasingly disgusted the more Tracker talked.

The thorny vine of shame knotted itself around Dylan's gut. He had already gathered she wouldn't be receptive to him using magic during sex, especially with how she objected to the use in other areas, and he was all right with that. But seeing her reject the hound's words so vehemently had him wondering how she expected to be his warden if she disliked magic that much.

"No," Tracker concluded. "None of this has crossed your mind even once, has it? Do you not wonder what you might have missed out on?"

Authril stood, chucking the rest of her meal on the fire. The flames hissed and popped. "I don't wonder because I already know, thank you. Magic is not some extension of himself. It's a tool. A weapon. No less so than a sword. If you're fine with the idea of having sex with a blade involved, it speaks more to your depravity than his skills."

The teasing joviality on the hound's face vanished, the skewed tilt of his lips flattening. His brows lowered. "You have slept with him—a great number of times, I must add—yet *I* am the depraved one?"

"I let him be a man, not some... magical toy."

"Oh, please," Tracker scoffed. Something twitched across the hound's face, wrinkling his nose and twisting his lips. Annoyance? Anger? Distaste? Hard to tell as the expression vanished almost as soon as it appeared. "I suppose the next thing you plan to say is how you would rather he was incapable of magic?"

Her head tipped back. She glared at the hound down her nose. "Yes, since you brought it up. I'd prefer he had no magic at all. As he well knows."

The hound leapt to his feet with frightening speed. He stalked around the fire until they were barely a handbreadth apart. "So you would rather it locked away? Suppressed? Tethered? Caged where it can do no harm?"

Authril pressed close enough for their noses to touch. "Contained until requested is precisely where it belongs. And if I am to become his warden, I could serve the crown better if I knew his limits."

Tracker glared at the warrior, his hands flexing as if he contemplated attacking her. A grin spread across his face. Something oddly disquieting lurked in that flash of teeth, an almost predatory gleam made even worse by the excessive sharpness of his canines. It was there for a moment, then gone. "He is strong enough, my dear woman. You need not know anything further about your glorified sword."

"That is *not* what I called him," Authril snapped.

"But that *is* what you *meant*," the hound shot back.

She glowered at Tracker. She uttered no denial, not even an attempt, before turning on her heel and stalking off towards the tent she shared with the others.

Tracker returned to settle at Dylan's left. He didn't speak a single word more, but his rage practically vibrated off him. He sat bent over, staring into the fire, clasping his hands before his mouth as if unlinking his fingers would invite violence.

The sight was oddly endearing. He'd only ever seen his guardian get that upset on his behalf.

But if Authril riled up the hound this easily, then perhaps it would be better to speed up their journey, even if he saw merit in the suggestion of slowing their pace to remain at their peak should they encounter any further danger.

There was an equal chance of them arriving at Whitemeadow one member short. He needed Authril alive to become his warden. To have anyone else take up the mantel wouldn't be a case of risking worse, it would be a definite.

He could only hope Tracker remembered that.

On his other side, Marin fidgeted and cleared her throat. "Well, then." One hand tapped on her thigh, whilst the other fussed with something in her belt pouch, pulling whatever she searched for free. "Strong or not, everyone could do with a little protection, so... uh... *here.*" Dylan barely saw the flash of an item before she draped it over his head. "I carved it for you. As thanks for saving my life."

"You didn't need to, but thank you." He examined the gift, a pendant made from a polished circle of wood, bound in some sort of a fibrous thread and hanging by a strip of leather. The carving in question adorned one side and was a single rune in the old Demarner language.

Marin beamed. "It's a—"

"Rune meaning protection." Before leaving the tower, he'd only ever seen the mark during his linguistic studies, yet it seemed to be in common enough usage across the kingdom. He had spied it etched upon the city walls and carved into entrances, like the inn they'd stayed at during their brief stint in Toptower. Even then, he had seen them as more of a longing than an actual warding against harm. "It doesn't actually grant that." No more than writing a similar wish in the modern-day script.

Looking at it closely, he was reminded of how similar the design was to the ancient symbol for a magical barrier. Here, there were extra details—dual lines cutting off the ones radiating from the centre—but everything else, the number of points, the outer circle, the inner one that connected like the beginnings of a spider's web... it all matched.

He recalled asking about it once, back when he first started learning the old language. He couldn't remember the given answer, only his guardian's fear.

"I appreciate the gesture, though," he added before she thought her gift unwelcomed. He settled the pendant beneath his clothes. For a bit of wood, the piece was surprisingly smooth.

"It's all right if it can't really do that. I can do the protecting for it." She tightened her grip on his head and smushed his cheek against her chest. It would've been a soft death, if not for the roughness of her leather overcoat.

He struggled against her grip. His efforts only served to have his nose squished against the leather, heavily reducing his air supply.

"Now, now," Marin chided, giving the top of his head a few deft pats. "Don't fuss. Let your big sister take care of you."

"Big sister?" he managed, unsure how well anyone heard him with his face so distorted. He swayed back as she abruptly released him, sucking air in one almighty gasp. "How old do you think I am?"

Marin peered at him for a moment, then shrugged. "Twenty... two?"

Laughter bubbled through his chest. "Add another seven more years to that."

"*No,*" she exclaimed. She knelt before him, her eyes narrowed to mere glimmers of brown beneath her lashes. "I refuse to believe you're a year my senior. Your skin is unblemished, practically not a wrinkle in sight and definitely no grey in this mop." She ruffled his hair as though he was a child. "I don't know anyone nearing thirty who doesn't have at least one of those."

"Ah, but you would know farmers and merchants, yes?" Tracker said. He seemed to have calmed himself enough to resume eating. "People who spend much of their day in the elements, not wandering dusty shelves, reading whatever tome took their fancy."

"I did more than read books," Dylan objected. Granted, he hadn't done much else. There hadn't *been* much else. He was terrible at gardening. He was too powerful to work with raw *infitialis.* Tricia had forbidden him from the sparring, which he only understood why now it was too late.

The hound eyed him over the top of his bowl whilst he sipped. There was a dark glint in his gaze that had Dylan's tongue sticking to the roof of his mouth. "You are correct. I saw scrolls, too. And a fair few tablets."

Books, scrolls, tablets and more. *All gone now.* Sacrificed to the flames. The tablets might've survived the initial heat, but not the crushing weight of the tower pummelling them into the earth.

Wasted. Like the lives that had been cut short within the same walls. Now, like him, there was but one survivor. The tome he had gifted to the hedgewitch.

"It's far more likely to be the healing," Katarina added. "I hear that those with the innate strength are known to have less visible signs of aging, with many living well past their hundredth year. Provided they aren't targeted in some assassination plot."

He hadn't thought about the passive effects his healing magic gave him, not since first acquiring the innate ability. That it might affect his aging certainly hadn't been discussed during his training. He also didn't recall any of the elderly amongst the tower also being healers, any more than he'd heard of any healer making it to a hundred years. Not that the tower had lacked spellsters old enough to have outlived their guardians. They'd been few in number, though. Very few.

"I would imagine his healing also mends the effect of being outside all day," the hedgewitch continued, smiling as Dylan nodded his agreement.

"I wondered how his pasty self wasn't getting any darker. Even she—" Marin jerked a thumb towards Authril, who had plonked herself near the tent entrance and was fussing with her armour. "—is tanning between her freckles. I'm actually surprised she didn't tan sooner," she added, needlessly raising her voice to address the warrior. "You weren't exactly sitting pretty in some building all day."

"I spent a great deal of my time with a helmet on," Authril replied.

Dylan vaguely remembered her fussing with various pieces of armour when they first met, but the sight of those sea-green eyes glowering at him after donning her helmet was etched into his mind. That had been not long after their meeting, back when they'd first set out from the army encampment. He didn't recall seeing the helmet since then, not on her head or amongst her gear. "What happened to it?"

"Lost it whilst you were dealing with that Udynean spellster way back when. One of his lackeys tried to cook my skull. Forced me to take it off." She shrugged. "Never found it afterwards."

Tracker snickered, drawing the woman's baleful glare. It had no effect, as the hound merely widened his grin. Like his laughter, the expression carried a nasty edge. "I see you learnt the hard way why we do not strap large pieces of metal to our person."

"That could actually affect you?" Marin asked.

Dylan held his breath, acutely aware he sat directly between them. *Could it?* Tracker hadn't been harmed by Dylan's shield or the lightning, not when the man dove through it to help Marin or when applied to very personal areas. However, he *had* admitted to feeling the charge such magic left in the air. There was no reason to believe the man couldn't sense extreme temperatures in a similar fashion.

The hound tilted his head to eye Marin around Dylan. He sat like that for what felt like an eternity before shrugging. "Why would it not? Heated metal is still hot regardless of the *how*." Turning back to Authril, he said, "You are lucky they did not turn their power to your breastplate."

Authril's answering smirk sent icy fingers down Dylan's spine. "That would've been hard to do with Kat's dagger in their kidneys."

"Fortunate then that you had our dear hedgewitch's assistance. Although, I am sure Marin is just as capable of watching your back at night, should the need arise."

Dylan frowned, not sure if he imagined the contemptuous overlay in Marin's exhalation. Perhaps he had. Neither of the elves reacted and Tracker definitely sat close enough to have heard something.

"And who would you have alongside Dylan?" Authril asked. "Yourself, I suppose?"

"I was thinking more along the lines of Katarina."

Nodding, Dylan caught the hedgewitch doing the same. It seemed she also understood the hound's reasoning. Marin was capable of holding back a force at a distance, as was he, but they were both humans with poorer eyesight than either elf or dwarf. Pairing them with someone who not only had close combat experience, but saw better in the dark, was the best way to distribute their fighting strengths.

That did leave one of them having to take their watch alone.

"What of *you?*" he asked of Tracker.

The hound waved aside the concern with a flap of his hand. "I am used to guarding my own back." He picked up the bowl Dylan had put aside. "Eat, my dear man. You need your strength. And do not worry about tonight's watch, I will take that. After today, it would be for the best if you got a full night's rest."

Authril snorted. "Such coddling. He wasn't the only one who worked himself to exhaustion."

"I am well aware. However, magic takes a lot from a spellster. And he used a great deal today, including on yourselves. You are all feeling refreshed, yes? His magic took away more than the aches from your tired body?"

She eyed the hound sourly. "So? He can heal himself, can't he?"

Not from exhaustion. His magic could push him a little further, stretch his endurance to help him reach safety, but it would eventually demand more from his body than he could give. Pushing occasionally, like he had done today, wasn't too bad as long as he rested.

"I doubt such an act would be beneficial," Tracker replied. "You cannot hope to refill a tub using only the dregs of water already within."

Whether or not Authril accepted the explanation, she returned to silently studying her armour.

"You know," Marin said, her voice gaining a light-hearted note that immediately made Dylan suspicious. She reached behind him to give Tracker a friendly shove. "The way you're fussing over him, I could almost imagine you two as a couple."

Dylan's chest tightened at the declaration. He shovelled a spoonful of his meal into his mouth, paying a lot of attention to chewing the chunks within to paste before he said something stupid. This was just her needling them. No different from the dozen or so other times. No chance she knew about the other night.

It wasn't as though he had walked to Tracker's tent and back in nothing but his smallclothes. He'd been in his undertunic, and could've reasonably come from relieving himself in an entirely neutral manner.

Nor had it been the first time he had made the journey. *Just never whilst she was on watch.* At least, not during the return to his bed. In the times he had sought Tracker's embrace after a nightmare, the man often let him sleep through his own watch.

If she did know, he had hoped she would remain silent on the matter.

Over by the tent, Authril made a gagging sound. "Please, I've just eaten."

Tracker eyed the two women, the usual warmth in his honey-coloured gaze cold and flat. "My dear hunter, even if that were so, it would be none of your business. More importantly, for a hound such as myself to fraternise with a spellster is considered an abomination. I would not put my life on the line for something I can get at a brothel risk-free." He made a show of examining Dylan as though they'd only just met. "And also where I could find someone with a little more meat on their bones."

Dylan glared at the man. He couldn't tell if the hound was lying, but such a statement still stung. "Ouch."

"Well, maybe you should consider eating more."

Increasing what he ate wouldn't make much of a difference. It had always been that way. He could stuff himself almost as much as an elf half his size and never gain much weight. Yes, using magic burnt through a great deal of energy, but refraining from even the smallest flame made no difference. That very fact helped him win a hearty bet nine years ago after abstaining from magic for a month and barely gaining a thing.

Even if he had wanted to... "*How* would I do that? *Where* would we get more food? You two—" He gestured to both the hound and Authril. "—ate a whole rabbit each the other day. *Each.* Meanwhile, I'm sharing the same amount with two others. Or are you suggesting Marin needs to get better at catching more food?"

"I would never complain about our dear hunter's skills." He grinned at the woman. "I would even go so far as to say they are laudable. Better than my own not-so-insignificant talents."

Marin hummed, pleased with the praise, before her cheeks fattened and a mischievous gleam took her eyes. "Nice try, but you just talked your way into setting up the traps for the next week."

Tracker hung his head, a soft curse wisping out his lips. "Very well. I will endeavour to keep us fed to your high standards, but do not expect the haul you have blessed us with so far." He got to his feet and bowed low before her. "And before you go complaining your bellies are tight, I do hope you will remember you chose this."

Chuckling, Marin also stood. "If you're done trying to convince me you're bad at hunting, come on." She gave the hound a hearty slap on his back. "I'll show you where I've laid tonight's traps."

Tracker hesitated and Dylan could've sworn the man's gaze darted between Authril and himself. A smile that didn't quite reach his eyes softly curved his lips. "Of course, my dear hunter. Lead on."

Dylan's stomach twisted as he watched the pair vanish into the forest. He didn't realise he had moved until he felt the edges of the pendant dig into his palm. *They'll be all right.* It had been almost a week since the encounter that nearly took Marin's life, and there'd been no sign of any other Talfaltaner stragglers. That didn't mean they weren't out there. It was the very basis for Tracker's suggestion to double the watch. *Tracker can hold his own.* And the hound wouldn't let Marin come to any harm.

Still, he pressed the carved surface of the pendant to his lips and murmured a little prayer into the wood. The symbol might not work the way people believed, but neither did his prayers. Perhaps together, the gods would grant them a sliver of mercy. *Keep them safe.* It didn't matter if he fell in the process. It was the destiny of every leashed spellster to fall in battle. That he had managed to unleash himself didn't change his fate.

Nothing could alter the road to his death.

CHAPTER 14

Dylan lay atop the bedding within his tent, idly toying with the carved gift of Marin's as he stared at the worn leather stretched above him. His time on watch had been over for hours, yet he still couldn't sleep. His thoughts refused to still and, when he dared to close his eyes, nightmares flooded the darkness.

Tracker was currently on watch, sitting by the campfire. Dylan hadn't witnessed that explicitly, given that the man would've taken over from Authril and Marin, but his ears caught the occasional sibilant glide of stone across steel. Whilst Authril tended to her sword routinely, it was typically before seeking her bed. He supposed the hound possessed the weaponry to arm himself thrice over, if not more. Enough that he could spare not having one blade in battle.

Just knowing the hound sat outside, guarding them—guarding *him*—was enough to have him grinning. He often caught himself in a similar state these past two days whenever the man crossed his mind. He couldn't stop it. Every time he thought about that cocky attitude or the brazen face the man showed the world, uncaring what anyone thought.

The way Tracker acted as though he genuinely cared. How it set a strange fluttering in Dylan's gut, more powerful than anything he'd ever experienced.

Almost as terrifying as the dreams.

They weren't all ground-sucking terrors that had him waking in a cold sweat. Nor was he always plagued by the endless winding through a maze brimming with fractured memories, dreams that always trapped him in sleep but left his body exhausted.

These new nightmares haunted him with another fear. One that had never beset him until now.

The hound laughing as Dylan explained he was an indecisive, of how much he longed for the man's company, only to have that openness be ultimately rejected, paraded before all to hear.

Cold nights in the dark, huddled and alone. His hope for even a sliver of happiness dwindling with each day. Knowing his only worth was as a weapon. A toy. A thing that no one actually wanted as much as he'd been led to believe.

He wiped his cheek, smearing the dampness across his skin, before sniffing back the rest of the tears that threatened to follow. *Fool.* He recognised the dreams for what they were, his own fears reflected back at him, uncertainty in the face of the unknown. Nothing he'd seen suggested the hound would be so cruel.

And yet, he'd never been this vulnerable before. Tracker may not laugh in his face, but there were other options beyond distancing himself, be it mentally or physically. He could use the knowledge as leverage, either as a stick to guide him to his doom or a carrot to lead him into a worse fate. Or he could not react at all, dismiss Dylan's fears as baseless.

But what was his alternative? To lie here and hope exhaustion took him before the nightmares? To continue acting as though nothing had happened between them beyond the tower? Either one would eventually take its toll, making him the very liability certain people believed.

Dylan had barely pushed aside the tent flap before a cool breeze hit him. Halting in the entrance, he closed his eyes and tipped his head back to let the night air caress his skin. He hadn't realised just how hot the tent's interior had been until now. Wasn't even sure if that was his doing.

"Trouble sleeping?" Tracker asked, the tone concerned but light.

Opening his eyes, he immediately spotted the man resting atop the log they'd staked the tents around. "Yes." After so many times of having Tracker wake him from his nightmares or seeking solace after rousing himself, there was little point in hiding that truth.

The glint of a small blade briefly flashed in the hound's grip, vanishing as he stowed the weapon. "I would advocate for rest, but if you cannot..." He patted the space beside him. "You are welcome to join me."

Dylan settled on the log, silently staring into the flames. Even this close to the fire, the air was cooler than within his tent. His hand found its way back to the pendant. He tightened his fingers, wishing the carved wood actually possessed any strength to draw upon.

Tracker said nothing. He simply plucked another of his many knives from its sheath and continued his task of inspecting the blades. The rhythmic glide of the whetstone along each edge filled the silence.

Dylan slowly let out a shuddering breath. *I should explain myself.* How? He hadn't needed to in the tower. Everyone already knew the rules long before they'd reached the appropriate age to engage in sexual activities. Those who flouted them, who risked being caught, often were. They paid the price, became another example. "Thank you, by the way, for yesterday." He glanced at Tracker and, upon seeing the bewilderment creasing the man's face, added, "For not telling the others about... you know. Us."

His elaboration only seemed to deepen the man's confusion. "Why would I? You are clearly hesitant—I dare say *fearful*—to share such knowledge. I admit, I do not understand why, but it is not my place to decide if and when people know. I am certain you will tell who you wish at a time that suits you. Not a word will leave my lips before then."

He clasped his hands before him in thanks.

"Besides," Tracker continued. "I should be apologising for permitting my mouth to run away with my good senses like that. She—" Sighing, the hound flicked his braid over his shoulder. "I simply cannot fathom lying with someone who demanded I lock away a part of myself."

Ah. There it was. The comparison. He was amazed it hadn't started sooner. "She never made any *demands* of me and I've never tried or broached the subject." Even in the tower, magic during sex wasn't always a given. A great deal of trust was needed, especially when a spellster with healing knowledge wasn't involved. And Authril was already wary of what he could do.

"But she *is* the reason you are somewhat less magical at times, yes?" Tracker asked as he added several more lengths of wood to the fire. The light flickered across his face and glinted sharply in his eyes. "I should have seen it sooner. You only act a certain way when our dear warrior is around. It is not right."

"I can twist reality, wrap it around my little finger and make it dance at my whim. It frightens her." After the way he'd seen other people react to his magic, it was about normal.

The hound's brows drew together. "And yet, she readily takes advantage of your ability to heal and fight as well as slept with you. How can she claim to be frightened and wish to become your warden? If she is so bothered by what you can do, she should reconsider her line of work. And *you* should be able to feel free to be all of yourself with those who share your bed."

Dylan shrugged. He'd never been entirely himself with anyone. There was always a piece kept aloof. It was the easiest way to not only keep himself from getting attached, but from keeping his magic under control. "Whatever happens once I'm leashed again will be between me and my warden, won't it?" Before learning the truth, he had thought it was just fun, nothing more serious than what he had with the hound.

To think she'd been using him. That he may have to let her use him again or risk a worse fate...

Tracker's generous lips narrowed. It was brief. Gone in a heartbeat. But when he spoke, it was with a strained, light-hearted tone. "Of course. It is not my place to judge how you conduct your affairs."

There was more to it, Dylan knew, but pushing the hound wasn't going to get him answers. He ran his tongue over his teeth, fighting the urge to dig further. "What you said to Marin, about your people frowning upon hounds and spellsters being intimate with each other? I remember you mentioning something similar back in the tower." They'd barely been travelling for a fortnight, but so much had happened since then that he had forgotten all about it until he'd been lying in the dark with nothing else for his mind to dwell on.

A small, sad smile tweaked one corner of Tracker's mouth. "What I told her was a half-truth of sorts. Hounds are discouraged from being intimate with anyone, but we are permitted the chance to have meaningless fun, providing it is unlikely to end in a child. When it comes to our spellster charges... it is forbidden."

He hadn't considered for some time how he was technically under the hound's command until they reached Wintervale. Tracker rarely gave him any order and even then, it was often in the same gentle manner that Dylan got from the others—most of them—if he tried to push himself. "So, we shouldn't have...?" He gestured vaguely. Not that it appeared to have stopped the man in the past, if the hound's recount of his exploits could be believed.

"Had sex? Not really, no." Tracker leant back on the log, bracing himself with a well-placed hand. "Our first night would have received some disapproving looks, but be ultimately forgiven. As for the other night..." Frowning, he tilted his head Dylan's way. "If I may ask, did I do something wrong?"

"When?"

The hound's gaze hardened a fraction, like a shard of amber amongst honey. "You know what I speak of."

Just the thought of that night set his face ablaze, enough to make his ears burn. He had conducted himself so poorly. And what had he been thinking, telling Tracker how the hound's dream self danced naked for Dylan in his dreams? "I'm sorry," he managed through the tightness in his chest.

"I understand you have been through a lot these past few weeks." A rough laugh barked out his mouth. "Hell, it has not quite been a month since we met and we have only bounced from one disaster to the next."

A month. Strange how it didn't seem like such a short amount of time. He'd met the others not that much beforehand, too. A week or so, he hadn't really been counting.

Yet, he felt like he'd known them all for years.

"I am trying to be understanding, but if practically ignoring the fact we were intimate for days afterwards is going to be the norm for you..." The hound sighed. He closed his eyes, resting his forehead upon his clasped hands. "Years have passed since secrecy was a requirement when it came to who I bedded. I would never ask you to reveal anything about your sex life to others, regardless of whether or not you were ready to. No one else need ever know the truth between us."

The weaving of discomfort and panic binding Dylan's chest relaxed a fraction.

"However..." Tracker tilted his head, the hot gleam of his gaze searing itself across Dylan's skin. "*I* need to know why you are so keen to keep it hidden. As willing as I am to repeat the other night— should you also wish it, of course—I think perhaps we should go no further until you are able to give me some measure of justification. Because honestly? Without it, I cannot say how long I can continue this charade of indifference."

"You're right." It was foolish to expect anything else. He *shouldn't* expect it. He *didn't.* "And you've been *more* than accommodating." If things had been reversed, if it had been Authril instead, she would've demanded everything on the first morning. "You deserve an explanation, but I..." His chest tightened again. This time, it forced the air from his lungs and set his heart to pounding.

A weary sigh slithered between his lips. Something inside him deflated. The truth was, he had no idea where to start.

He stared out into the darkness lurking beyond the flickering firelight. The words were out there, hiding in the shadows, just as afraid of being spoken aloud as he was to admit it to himself.

He could find them if he tried. He just needed a little more light to draw them out into the open and...

And then?

Hope his nightmares truly were just his fears trying to keep him hidden in the shadows, cloaked in the familiar lies and half-truths.

"Was it something I did?" Tracker asked. "Or perhaps did *not* do? Were my actions not to your satisfaction? Did you not enjoy it as you had hoped? You can be honest with me. I will not be offended if I am not to your tastes."

Realising he'd been silently shaking his head in disagreement with the man's words, he laughed. It was a small sound, half-shrill with dread. "It's not that. Gods, I..." He fisted his hair. "I was more than satisfied, I just—" His throat tightened on the unexpected hiccup of a sob.

After everything he'd been through, why did the prospect of sharing his fears seem the most harrowing?

He glanced towards the tent the others slept in. Hoping that something would happen to help him escape this mess he had made. Maybe he should've told Tracker first, let the hound decide whether he was worth the complications.

No movement came from within. It didn't stop the prickling down his back. Just as his second-guessing wasn't kept at bay from not having any accusations levelled at him every time one of the others glanced his way.

Tracker briefly mimicked his actions before twisting to gently wipe a thumb across Dylan's cheek, the pad of it coming away damp. "I am well aware you are afraid of them finding out, but I do not quite understand why. Is it retribution you fear? Condemnation? For what? That they would know about *us*? Or that they would know about *you*?"

Us? He had imagined the slight lingering hiss in the way the man spoke the word, hadn't he? "I don't know," he finally managed, pulling his head out of Tracker's grasp to scrub at his face. "Both?" It wasn't knowledge that could be mutually exclusive.

"If it is their condemnation that you fear... Well, I find it highly unlikely that Marin would look down on you for lying with a man when she prefers other women. Katarina does not strike me as the type to judge such attraction. And as for our dear warrior..." He shrugged. "I will not lie and tell you she would accept the fact with any grace. But the worst she can do is rant, which would be directed at *myself*."

"No. I mean, it is, but—" He took a deep breath, his heart seeming to flutter in the back of his throat. How could he explain the dread clinging to his chest to someone who had never hidden himself, never denied what he felt for others? Worse still, they were fears that no longer bore any actual threat without a tower to punish him. Logically, he had nothing to be concerned about.

No matter how he tried to think about it from a reasonable point of view, logic had little effect as of late.

He ran his thumb along the pendant, tracing the design. *Protection.* Sanctuary. "I don't know how to explain it," he confessed. "It isn't just them. It isn't that we had sex. You were a distraction the first time." The hound had offered himself as such. "But I enjoyed it." His tongue froze as the admission slipped out. It hung in the air between them.

"And you expected not to?"

"I don't know what I expected." A part of him had put down their night in the tower to being a fluke, something that could only feel good due to his high emotional state, but that night in Tracker's tent told him the truth. *Nights*, really. He might not have sought sex all the other times, but he couldn't deny the soft intimacy of waking up after several hours of peaceful slumber in the man's arms. "You were amazing. Better than anything I had dreamt."

Tracker remained silent, but Dylan couldn't help catch the smug tilt to his smile.

"Honestly? It was a relief. My dreams are so often full of things I don't want to relive. Sometimes, I think it would be better if I was so exhausted that I fell into a dreamless sleep."

"That would not be viable for long. Your body needs proper rest."

"I know." He'd heard similar words from his guardian during this youth. But he was also well aware what his body needed that night had been Tracker. Something real.

Something *safe*.

"If it is not the knowledge you are having sex that you fear them discovering, then it is because I am a hound and you are a spellster, yes?" The man's usual charming smile wavered at the corners. His posture vibrated with a desire to move, the subtle shift of limbs distancing themselves from Dylan not enough to sate the want. "You need not be so coy about it, especially if you are seeking to spare my feelings. I can understand your reluctance to accept you gave into the lure of the forbidden, as well as the regret that follows."

Dylan shook his head. When they'd been alone, all tangled in each other's arms, he completely forgot the man was one of the King's Hounds. "I don't regret it was you." At least, he didn't think that was the cause behind the sensation twisting up his insides. "If anything, I'm thankful. I had shackled myself to lies and half-truths for so long that I'd..." Hidden. Fled. Denied. "...convinced myself they were true. Until you." It hadn't even been the sex that had broken those self-forged chains. Just a kiss.

A terrifyingly innocent kiss.

Tracker stilled. His lips relaxed into what had to be the most genuine smile Dylan had seen from the hound. His whole face was soft and receptive.

He quietly considered the merits of bridging the already short distance between them to kiss the man. Just a small one. A peck that offered the lowest risk of being caught.

Then, all at once, Tracker cleared his throat and the look vanished. He shook his head, his breathy chuckle heating Dylan's shoulder. "You are welcome." His brows lowered, bemusement plain upon his face. "I take it things were different in the tower?"

Steeling himself, Dylan nodded.

"*How* different? Did they teach you sex is natural regardless of gender? I have been assuming they did," the man rambled. "But if they kept you less aware of such a fact, I can assure you that—"

He laid a hand atop the hound's, silencing him. "They taught us that. Amongst other things." The tower might have advocated celibacy and punished those who were caught in the act with lifelong close observation, but they weren't of the opinion that ignorance would keep them from exploration. The guardians had been thorough in teaching them what sex was. And, given that the tower had also housed a wide range of genders, their education covered them all.

Never mind that some, like the nulls, tended to stick together, whilst others had a more fluid mindset. Sadly, the latter were more likely to be ousted by those who despised their carefree attitude towards both gender and sexuality. Just like they did to confirmed indecisives.

One gender or none at all. That was how spellsters were supposed to handle sexual attraction. Indecisiveness was looked upon as an aberration, a product of a sick mind, a malady that needed to be treated or culled. Even those who had one lover, like Harriet, weren't immune to scorn.

Stepping out into the rest of the world had shown him a different outlook. Sure, he could've waved away what he'd seen in *The Gilded Lily*, dismissed the brothel and its workers as being abnormalities. But no one there acted as though they were ashamed. Not even Authril treated being indecisive as anything but natural.

Only him.

Why do you continue to deny your interest in men? Tracker's question drifted through his mind.

He hadn't been able to give the hound a satisfactory answer back in the tower. He hadn't even considered it as denial. The idea that *he* could be one had occurred to him before, but any thoughts of exploring those desires had been quashed by the tower's thinly veiled threats of being outed by his fellow spellsters until he no longer considered the possibility of numbering amongst their ranks. He couldn't even disagree with the extremes others took to out those who indiscriminately slept with various genders to the guardians without suspicion being piled upon himself.

Never left alone with anyone for long. To be watched and suspected no matter who he interacted with, to assume his every glance was him prowling for sex.

But out here? Where things were different, less defined. The more he thought on it, the less he could cling to his old beliefs. It made sense. Deep inside. Like a piece he had rejected—kept locked away out of fear—had suddenly been shoved into the light.

No, he couldn't call what he'd done as denying interest in men. He had deluded himself into believing he wasn't. Suppressed his feelings, convinced himself he was merely getting caught up in the overall tenseness of a situation and confusing friendliness for something else.

It had always been safer than facing the alternative.

The truth.

But had things really changed that much from being beyond the tower's constraints? He was still afraid, still restricted. Still unable to even think about the reasons behind why, never mind fully articulating them.

If he could just think of the right words. Why wasn't it easy? He spoke several languages, for gods' sake. At least one of them should offer what he needed.

Yet the longer he sat there, fully aware Tracker expected some sort of explanation, the fewer words he managed to gather.

He stood, brushing bits of bark off his robe as best as he could. "I should go," he mumbled. "Stop distracting you from, you know, all this." He waved his hands at their surroundings. "Let you resume your watch."

"Of course," Tracker said, bowing his head. Nevertheless, Dylan was certain he caught a hint of disappointment tugging at the man's lips. "Get as much rest as you can. If you find yourself unable to..." He shrugged. "Your presence here would be a welcomed one." The words came on a whisper. So quiet that Dylan briefly believed he had heard wrong.

His heart all but vaulted into his mouth. *Stay out here?* The man actually wanted him to remain nearby until morning? "I..." He could. There was no logical reason why not. It was warm by the fire, in a far more comforting way than the kiln he had created of his tent. "I can't," he managed, silently kicking himself. He couldn't even muster a weak excuse. He had walked to Tracker's tent in nothing but his undertunic, had made the journey back just as easily.

If he stayed up now, joined Tracker in guarding them through the rest of the night, what would the others think? They'd query it, certainly. Marin would definitely tease him, although ultimately in a good-natured fashion. But Authril? She would have questions.

He wasn't ready for even that level of scrutiny, her shadowing him like a guardian with an outed charge. It was a freedom he would have to eventually give up to his warden, but he clung to the days, the weeks, counting them down. He couldn't risk anything that could take that from him.

"Sleep well," Tracker called as Dylan parted the tent flap. "You know where to find me if you cannot."

He did. However, getting to Tracker's side when the man wasn't on watch had become practically impossible. Sneaking off anywhere with Authril awake would only put him in her sights.

Perhaps he should reconsider changing their sleeping arrangements. One less tent would mean sharing with the hound, but even if he hadn't already approached the man for sex, Tracker had already proven his word when it came to restraint. He didn't always keep his hands to himself, but the touches he offered were innocent— the stroke of Dylan's hair, the soothing caress of long fingers down his back or gliding over a shoulder—designed to settle and quieten rather than arouse.

Although, the lack of heat in each brush hadn't stopped other dreams from steadily taking the place of Dylan's nightmares, wicked images prominently featuring the hound in all his naked glory with his dream self having a great deal more confidence than he would ever claim. He wasn't certain what to do about those, apart from be fortunate they hadn't actually occurred whenever he slept alongside the man. Especially when waking up after one left him with a rather centralised effect.

If *that* started happening whilst sharing the man's tent?

He couldn't even think of the scenario without his gut tying itself into knots, but he knew precisely what would happen. He'd become the same flustered mess he had been in the tower and the hound would definitely take advantage of that, seducing him with that damned voice and touching him in ways that—

Already feeling himself warming, he dove into his tent, desperately trying to turn his mind to less stirring thoughts. The mundane tasks he would need to do in the morning. The dread of not knowing what dreams sleep would bring. The uncertainty of whether the night would also see another assertive visit from Authril.

The latter alone might be cause enough. Over the past five days since his initial refusal, she had attempted to wheedle her way back into his good graces just the once. Tracker's presence would definitely keep her from trying again.

But first, he needed to find the words to fully explain the reason why he feared others knowing he was indecisive.

CHAPTER 15

"Don't forget to leave some attention for your footing," Marin chided. She circled him, her focus seemingly entirely on himself, yet she avoided all the little obstacles in her path with almost as much grace as the hound.

Of all the fighting styles he had attempted, unarmed combat was the only one he showed any improvement in. Albeit, slowly. Once they were grown, the tower never concerned itself with ensuring their spellsters got any sort of physical activity. Even those who fought in the brawl would've been left to train themselves, including finding partners to spar against.

Dylan's current choices were limited, to say the least. With Tracker being responsible for hunting, his absence during the vestiges of daylight left Dylan with only Marin to hone his skills against.

It meant he could only train for as long as the hunter wished, but with the man not around to distract with his very presence, his lessons came with the additional bonus of not being thrown to the ground quite as much. It also gave him time to think, which he'd been doing a lot of over the past two days.

Whilst the words to explain the way indecisives were treated in the tower eluded him, he had reached somewhat of a decision on another matter: the idea of sharing a tent with the hound on a permanent basis. But whilst he had reached the conclusion easily, how to go about broaching the subject was a little more complicated.

He had tried several times. All the words he had carefully gathered whilst they walked scattered to the winds the moment they halted to make camp until the mere thought of announcing it to the others churned his gut. No matter how carefully he worded the choice, it wasn't going to go over easily with Authril.

He knew what would happen. She would argue that it was unnecessary, threaten the hound as she threw multiple accusations in the man's face. Just as she had done in the brothel.

The glare she'd given Tracker after the man had attempted to give

Dylan a simple kiss was still engraved in his mind. The fury. The *disgust.*

He didn't want to think what she might do upon learning they'd been intimate.

The other women didn't seem to be any the wiser about what had gone on between them. He would've known by now if Marin did. The hunter might not be as vehement as Authril, but she was vocal. Katarina, he wasn't so sure of but, even if hedgewitches weren't trained to mediate all types of scenarios, he trusted her to at least remain neutral.

Movement out in the forest caught his eye. An impression amongst the deepening shadows, moving silently through the trees. A deer? A person? A *threat?*

No, Authril would warn them if it was anything dangerous. She outright refused to train him in anything, but remained nearby, claiming that one of them needed to stay on alert whilst the hound vanished into the forest the very second they'd set camp.

She had done a lot of complaining about Tracker's movements over the past few evenings, barely veiled insinuations that he was somehow working against them.

Naturally, when it came to the fruits of the hound's labour, she'd no objection in consuming it. Especially when exiting their tents in the morning had them being greeted by the sight of the previous night's hunting haul already gutted, skinned and, often, cooked before even Katarina's early rising routine had her awake.

Marin whistled a brief tune. "Keep your eye on your opponent."

"I thought you said not to look where I'm aiming."

"Yes, but that's so you're not giving away your intentions. If you don't pay attention to your opponent, then you won't know where *they* plan to strike either. The trick is to do both." She wrinkled her nose. "Honestly, these are basic squabbling techniques I learnt on the farm. How don't you know them?"

"We're trained to attack from a distance." Those who knew how to fight up close came from beyond the tower walls and were encouraged to forget what the Overseers had labelled as crude combat routines. "And those in command of the leashed tend to remain within earshot." Not that it had saved his warden.

Marin frowned. "I understand that, but even archers carry swords. Or a dagger, at least." Her face darkening, the woman's attention drifted to where Authril busied herself in tending to tonight's fire. "The army doesn't really expect you to *die* serving them."

He shrugged. The wardens themselves had treated their spellster charges as disposable. And there was a measure of truth in that, as there'd been maybe a dozen leashed in the army, but hundreds more awaiting their turn in the tower. All eager to replace the fallen without fully knowing what it meant. "I'd live longer serving the army than if I ran."

"That's true," Authril said. "A rogue spellster *and* a deserter?" She shook her head. "It would be only a matter of time before a hound caught him. Just look how fast he was found the first time we stepped into civilisation. And considering we're travelling *with* a hound..." Shrugging, she went back to coaxing the meagre flames of their campfire, either ignoring or unaware of the fearsome glare the hunter flung her way.

Marin's nose wrinkled in disbelief. "Track wouldn't hurt him."

Dylan also didn't believe the hound would make the attempt should he try to venture anywhere but towards their destination. The man was far too gentle for someone who was just doing his job. His life would certainly be forfeit should they come across another hound.

He wished he could be as sure about Authril's reaction.

The warrior laughed. "You clearly haven't witnessed his bloodthirsty side." Frowning, she rubbed at her neck. "But then, you would've been fighting for your own life when he was trying to take mine."

"He tried to *kill* you?" Dylan queried, sure he had misunderstood her. Tracker didn't hide his poor opinion of the woman, but he also didn't seem the type to attack a member of their group without reason.

Authril nodded. "He had that purple dagger out and everything. He probably would have slit my throat had Katarina not stepped in."

For the hound to deliberately use the one weapon he knew Dylan couldn't heal injuries from sounded even less likely.

"And he did it without reason, I suppose?" Marin sneered. "I know you chafe at his leadership, but making up tales to undermine him is just—"

"*Tales?*" Authril screeched. "It's *true*, I swear. Tell them," she snapped over her shoulder.

Dylan followed her line of sight to where Katarina had been busy setting up the last of their tents. He had believed her not at all aware of their conversation.

"There is truth in it," Katarina confessed, the words almost inaudible after weathering the other two yelling. "Although, the recollection lacks context. He retaliated after she implied he had killed a hound for his position."

Authril scoffed. "His reaction was extreme for someone who has no guilt. *And* it turned out my assessment was correct." She frowned before admitting, "Sort of. He admitted to killing his own kind. I know you heard him." She waggled the charred end of a stick in the hedgewitch's direction. "For all we know, he's a rogue hound. Not to mention he's the *only* one we've encountered. Places as big as Oldmarsh have a hound permanently stationed there."

On the edge of his vision, he spied Marin nodding as though that fact was common knowledge.

"If they can sense magic," Authril continued, still facing the dwarf. "And if *he*—" She jabbed the stick towards him. "—is as powerful as Tracker claims. Then why didn't we have a hound knocking on our door when we were in the city? Why couldn't they?"

"Because there was no one there," Dylan replied. Tracker had admitted visiting the place to verify Treasure's rumours of an armed mass in the north, only to find the station empty. It had confused the man. Troubled him.

"So he says," the warrior continued. "But where else could they have gone? How do we know he didn't actually do away with them to stop anyone following us?"

"I think I can answer some of that," Marin replied. "The second night after leaving the tower, I..." She turned to Dylan, her brown eyes distant as they met his. "You remember I took Track into the forest and, when we came back, we had to move the camp elsewhere?"

Dylan nodded. His memories of the first few days on the road to Whitemeadow were hazy, but he remembered that much.

Authril shrugged. "I just assumed you found some wounded Talfaltaners who hadn't made it."

"Close. There were bodies, but they wore hound armour. Or at least the remains of it. They'd been there for almost a week, by my count, long enough for wild pigs to find." She wet her lips, the focus of her gaze drifting for a moment. "I think they might've been attempting to intercept the Talfaltaners and miscalculated their odds. It wasn't a fight. Whoever killed them made them march to where they'd fallen."

The guardians had always referred to the King's Hounds as an elite force. If Tracker's skills with a blade were typical of their training, then a group of them would've been formidable. To find they'd failed against a hoard large enough to take out the tower wasn't surprising.

"When I showed Track?" Marin continued. "It shook him. He was trying to hide it, but he definitely didn't expect to find them there."

"Why would they kill hounds?" he asked. Talfaltaners had the reputation of killing every spellster they encountered. Whilst he had recently learnt hounds were also born from a spellster parent, that obviously wasn't common knowledge.

Marin shook her head. "I don't know. Maybe Track does."

"I'm much more interested in another point," Authril growled as she got to her feet. "Why are you only telling us *now*?"

Shrugging, the other woman folded her arms. "Track said not to say a word. I figured, with the tower being so close, it was to not upset... everyone."

Dylan carefully kept his face neutral. He hadn't misjudged that flicker of her gaze falling on him. He would've been the first to admit his emotional state in the week after leaving the rubble of his home had not been a stable one, even with Tracker's soothing embrace helping chase away the nightmares as the others slept on unaware. He didn't know what he would've done if he had also learnt a handful of hounds were executed not so far from the tower.

Why had there been so many? Tracker admitted they didn't work together very often. Two probably would've been a normal occurrence. The same might even be said of a trio. But more? Maybe Marin was right in them being sent to intercept the Talfaltaners and how they misjudged the force they'd face. But for them to be there a week when the tower attack had been days before spoke of the hounds advancing towards the fore.

"I'll accept that, for now," Authril declared, her sharp voice dragging him back from his musings. He had lost track of their conversation to have any idea what she was alluding to. "It still doesn't answer why he permits Dylan to use his magic so freely or why he's allowing him to learn *any* sort of fighting."

"For defence," Marin replied before Dylan could.

The warrior spread her arms wide. "Against *what*? Bandits? I doubt there are any left between here and Whitemeadow to bother us. Or do you mean straggling Talfaltaners like the ones who almost took your life? Nothing you're teaching him could've stopped them from running you through."

Barely contained anger darkened Marin's face. "I don't expect it to. Are you really going to begrudge him for wanting to know other ways to protect himself?"

Authril drove the charred point of the stick into the ground, her whole body stiffening as though the other woman had uttered a challenge. "I am simply asking what all this wrestling training is supposed to help him protect himself *from*. Neither you nor the *hound*—" She spat Tracker's status as though it were a slur. "—have given me an adequate answer. Never mind how peculiar it is for someone like him to permit a spellster to learn something that could be used to overpower him."

Laughter erupted from Marin in a rough snort before she succumbed to open-mouthed cackling. *"Dylan?"* She clamped her hands onto his shoulders, her unsteady weight pulling him every which way. "I doubt this scrawny frame can grow to be much of a threat to Track in the time it takes to get to Wintervale."

Twisting in her grasp, Dylan swung his arm at her, intending to knock her back enough to regain his balance. His fist landed square in the middle of her abdomen. The impression of the stitches he had made to repair her clothes grazed his knuckles and set his skin to tingling with magic.

Marin stiffened, then doubled over. She staggered a few feet to one side, still hugging her stomach. Her face was hidden, but the low keening spoke of being hurt.

"I'm sorry, I didn't mean to—"

She waved him back and the sounds he had first mistaken as ones of pain became clearer. She was still *laughing*? "Was that supposed to be a *punch*?" she wheezed. "I've had piglets tickle me harder."

"How did that *not* hurt you?" He hadn't been trying to knock the breath from her, but he'd seen the soldiers on the front line scuffling with each other and one always came away bruised. He had certainly put in enough effort to make a solid connection. "That jarred me all the way to my shoulder." Even though his healing had already dealt with the ache, he shook his hand in emphasis.

Marin straightened, although the occasional tremor that took her shoulders spoke of her composure being tentative at best. "Do I need to teach you how to throw a punch as well?"

"What?" he shot back, grinning. "You don't know how?"

She waggled a forefinger at him. "Cheeky." She wiped at one corner of her eye before balling the same hand and giving it a kiss. "Got a few taverns in Toptower who can attest to how well I dish out a good old knuckle pie."

He didn't doubt it. She might not have actually involved herself in the fight that drunken man had picked with Tracker way back in Oldmarsh, but she had definitely been ready to jump in should the hound have fallen.

Without warning, she swung at him.

Dylan tensed, trying not to let his shield form as he waited for the arc that would see her land squarely on his shoulder. If she hit any type of barrier, she would break her hand. After a long day of trekking and training, he didn't have the energy to fix that properly.

Her fist halted an inch from his shoulder. Grinning, she gave him a little tap. "I wouldn't dare. You might shatter. Here." She took up his hand, curling his fingers until they made a solid fist. "It probably doesn't matter much to someone who can heal broken bones, but you want to keep your wrist straight, like this." She jabbed at the air, her movements too fast for him to properly follow.

He mimicked the move, albeit, a lot slower. Still, it garnered an encouraging smile.

"Yes, make sure you keep doing it like that. All right, hit me." She thumped her fist into the palm of her other hand before holding it up for him. "Right here."

Dylan tentatively aimed for the palm. His knuckles connected solidly enough. By the way Marin beamed, the slap of skin meeting skin hadn't been loud just to his ears.

"That's it!" Still grinning, she planted her legs a little firmer and hunkered down. "Posture could do with some work. You've got to put your hips into play if you want to do any damage." She twisted slightly, barely swinging her arm as she went. "That way, you can give it a little oomph!"

Such instruction was a little more familiar, akin to what Tracker had tried to teach during his sword training sessions. Without the added length of a blade to worry about, putting his whole body into the punch allowed him only to focus on his target.

This time, hitting Marin's palm elicited a surprised grunt from her. Looking no less pleased, she nodded for him to do it again.

He gladly complied and soon they were moving about the campsite, Marin alternating between hands as she continued to instruct. With every hit, he swore the smack of skin against skin was growing louder. His knuckles tingled constantly, shifting from pain to the buzz of healing. How was Marin able to weather this training without so much as a wince?

The daylight had slipped over the trees by the time Authril announced dinner was ready. His stomach confirmed that food was well overdue.

Marin halted, still grinning. "Not bad. You wouldn't knock out a seasoned brawler anytime soon, but..." She flailed her hands as though trying to shake them off her wrists. "We should probably look into some sort of padding if you want to add this to your training."

He took up one of her hands. The palm was rough from years of labour and warm against his skin. His magic flowed into the site, soothing the pummelled flesh in both palms. The smallest tug at his power spoke of a scratch near her shoulder. She must've gotten that during their earlier training.

She smiled back at him as he let go, examining her hands before balling one to give him a good-natured nudge. "You're going to make me soft. Body can't toughen up without a little roughing from time to time."

"I'm sure you'll have years more of roughing to make up for it. I doubt the odd healing over the course of a few weeks will make much of a difference."

Refusing to meet his gaze, Marin's cheerful expression faltered. Only for a moment, but it was hard to miss her full lips practically vanishing into her mouth. Before he could ask if she was all right, the smile returned, albeit, strained. "Hopefully, there won't be a need for you to do much healing." Her hand had drifted to the repaired section of her outfit, a forefinger idly running down the stitching.

Only a week had passed since the attack that should've taken her life. Barely any time at all when measured against coming to terms with how close she had been to death. He knew what went through her mind. Had been right where she was now after the army fell to the Udynean forces.

He had spent so many nights wondering what he could've done differently. Maybe if he had tried harder sooner, then the events of that day could've changed. But mostly, he wondered if the sparing of his life was worth the cost.

It was *that* question which he saw in her eyes.

For him, the cost for his life had been those of the entire scouting party. For her, it was a far simpler matter: his strength, sapped enough that it had taken days for him to regain in full. "I would've taken the same action given a million chances."

Genuine fondness creased her eyes. "I know." She bumped her shoulder against his. "Let's hope nothing as drastic as that happens again. To any of us. We wouldn't want you overexerting yourself trying to heal everyone."

Not everyone. He would try, especially if his magic was the only thing keeping them from death. But none of that would work for the hound. Tracker could bleed out in front of him and there was nothing he could do to stop it beyond the simple aid he learnt at the beginning of his healer training.

And the man was reckless with his life, charging into fights as though it had no worth, risking himself to protect Dylan as though the world needed another unleashed spellster more than it did a hound.

They settled beside the fire, collecting their portion of the night's meal, his being the leg off a pheasant Marin had been lucky enough to come upon during their early morning travels. He picked at the meat, his attention drifting to the forest edge where he'd last seen Tracker. He couldn't keep the imagery of the man in trouble out of his head.

He's fine. The hound rarely returned before sundown and he never emerged from the same undergrowth he vanished into. He was probably circling their little camp right now, checking for any signs in the waning light, his elven vision allowing him to see potential threats far before they'd spot him.

Except if they were also elven. Not the Talfaltaners, who were entirely human, but there could be bandits. Of course, that would mean they had somehow survived a horde of hundreds storming along the road. He didn't know how likely that was and he didn't want to ask, lest the others thought him paranoid.

Even without people to worry about, there was still the wildlife. They hadn't come across another boar since the one back near the border. He didn't know if there were any out here or how big they could be, but he remembered the animal's tusks and how Marin and Authril struggled with the weight. If something like that had attacked Tracker...

He knows what he's doing out there. The man had mentioned multiple times about travelling with only a horse for company—although Dylan didn't recall ever hearing what happened to the animal—so Tracker having the skills to keep himself alive was the only logical conclusion to how the hound had survived for this long.

That knowledge did little to untangle the knot in his stomach. Just the thought of Tracker being seriously injured was enough to have a strange weight settling on his chest as though the threat rode his shoulders, huffing its hot breath down his neck until his skin was clammy.

Shuddering, he tore his gaze from the darkening forest to his meal. The frayed strands of torn meat stared back at him. Whoever was responsible for cooking the bird had definitely overdone it. He stuffed the meat down nevertheless, hoping that his stomach would stop fussing once it was full.

And that Tracker would return to camp faster.

CHAPTER 16

The hound returned after the last vestiges of daylight had well and truly faded behind the treetops. By then, the rest of them had finished eating and merely remained around the fire in the spirit of keeping each other company.

"Not a good hunt tonight?" Marin asked the moment the man sat next to her.

Shrugging, Tracker retrieved his meal from Katarina's offering hands. It looked to be at least a third of the pheasant. "I would be more concerned if the traps started to come up empty in the morning and so far, we have been fortunate there."

Unable to take the calmness in the hound's voice, Dylan blurted, "Then what took you so long?"

The outburst garnered everyone's attention. From Katarina's mild surprise that likely came just from him speaking, to Authril's scowl that spoke of her trying to figure out the reason behind him asking.

He hunched his shoulders, trying to ignore how hot his face had become under their scrutiny. *I should've kept quiet.* He just couldn't help it. His insides had been tying themselves into ever-complicated knots over imaginary dangers the longer Tracker had taken in rejoining them. Seeing the hound looked no worse for wear, Dylan needed to know the reason behind the delay.

"My apologies." Even one of the hound's brows had risen in silent query. "It was never my intention to take as long as I did. I heard a spring whilst checking the perimeter. That way." He gestured in the direction he had emerged from the forest. "I had hoped the water would be clean enough to use. Unfortunately, getting to it proved quite challenging. It is protected by a rather thick bramble barrier."

Marin perked up at the announcement. "Something that big will be fruiting. The berries could even be ripe enough to harvest. You'll have to show us when it's light."

"It would be nice to have something other than meat for a change," Authril agreed. She grabbed another piece of wood to throw into the waning flames. Something familiar glinted from a crack in the bark, reminding Dylan of an old section on dwarven beliefs.

"Wait!" Without thinking, his magic snatched the wood from the air before it could touch the fire.

"Did you not like the look of that piece or...?" Tracker asked, his gaze bearing a wary edge as he eyed the chunk of wood now firmly in Dylan's grasp.

"I thought I saw a bark maiden." They were sacred to dwarves. If he'd been wrong, then no harm was done. But if he was right and let the fire claim it...

Gasping, Katarina clapped her hands over her mouth. Her gaze didn't waver from the wood.

The hound gave them a puzzled frown. "And that would be?"

"It's an insect." Dylan rotated the wood, carefully peeling back the bark. Sure enough, a bark maiden crawled out from beneath. It was about as long as his middle finger and as thick as his thumb. Her gold and dark brown striped body gleamed in the firelight.

"Such a blessing that you spotted her," Katarina said. She snatched up the wood, insect and all, murmuring prayers and apologies to the insect in her native tongue.

"This bark maiden is a stripy wood-burrowing hopper?" Tracker murmured, no less confused. "Why did you not just say that? Let me find a sharp stick."

The hound was halfway to his feet when Marin uttered the very words that crossed Dylan's mind. "Why would you need a stick? Do they bite? Are they poisonous?"

"They can," Tracker replied, talking slowly as if he believed the woman had lost her senses. "And no. But I want to *cook* it."

"What?" Katarina screeched, her indignance great enough to see her sputtering and growling in her native tongue. She thrust the wood back into Dylan's grasp. "No!" She batted at Tracker with both hands, tumbling the man onto his rear. "You do *not* eat the bark maidens!"

The hound shielded himself with his arms, deflecting any of the hedgewitch's blows aimed at his head. A strange sound emanated from him, one that raised the hair on Dylan's neck and arms.

It took a moment for him to realise the man was cackling.

"I have eaten dozens," Tracker managed through his wheezing. The words vibrated and skipped over one another, each syllable not quite finished before the next began. "They taste good, sort of nutty."

Dylan shivered. His training as a healer had taught him the truth behind some elves having twin voice boxes, and he was familiar with the stories of certain elves being capable of unsyncing their voice, but he'd never heard it first-hand. Not every elf had the ability, certainly not amongst those in the tower. Too many had human blood diluting the chance and the few who did weren't likely to perform at a whim.

Tracker flopped back, ceding to the hedgewitch by throwing his arms up in surrender. "Honestly, I have never seen such fuss over a *bug*." His laughter steadily grew more breathless until he was doubled over, coughing.

Katarina stepped back, her head tilted to one side. The crown of her braid had unravelled slightly, letting it slip with the movement. "Are you all right?"

Tracker waved her back, his breathing slowly returning to normal.

Authril snorted. "Figures you'd have nomadic blood in you."

The man's next bout of amusement came deeply, without a hint of the previous ethereal tremor. "My dear, I was born of the tower. The possibility of me having nomadic blood is the same as being descended from an Oracle. A good myth, but ultimately impossible."

"I wouldn't be too sure about that," Katarina said. "The nomads say Oracles were more akin to nobility than mythic figures."

Tracker's brow furrowed briefly before he shook his head. "Even so, I doubt you would have found any ancient noble lines in the tower."

"I'm surprised there were elves at all," Authril snipped. She didn't look to have believed a word the hound had said. "Given how much interbreeding they would've done."

"When me and my fellow hounds kept... let us say, adding fresh bloodlines into the mix?" The smile Tracker flashed her held little of his former mirth. "Not every elf chooses to lie with humans, you know."

Dylan laughed quietly to himself, remembering the last elven woman he had tried to proposition in the tower. *Kaprina*. Proud, regal, and with a scream that could burst a person's ears. "That's putting it mildly." There was a small group who preferred to keep to themselves, even when sharing the communal spaces. He hadn't interacted with them much beyond a friendly greeting or two, which was always coolly ignored. "Some of them barely spoke in a human's presence."

Tracker gestured in his direction. "Well, there you go."

Tower rumour claimed the group was formed by those who'd been ripped from homes and families outside the tower walls rather than willingly handed over. He had thought it some extension of stories surrounding the King's Hounds and how ruthless they were in their task until Sulin confirmed it. The group had tried to absorb his friend into their ranks during his first few months in the tower. They might've managed to, had they been less insistent. All they achieved was driving Sulin further from their grasp.

Why hadn't he thought to ask more of his friend about it? Why hadn't he ever considered there might be families who would wish to keep their children even with all the danger an untrained spellster posed? That there'd be parents willing to risk their lives like Tricia had for him?

The answer was simple. *I was blind.* Kept blissfully ignorant. Shielded from so much. Even when it came to the inner workings of his very home.

But not out here.

He peered at Authril. "You've never mentioned having contact with nomads before." The way she'd spoken about them, he assumed she merely recited rumours. The idea of nomads entering Demarn clashed with everything he had learnt about the elven Caravans during his history lessons. Why would they take the risk when they'd spellsters amongst their ranks?

She shrugged. "I wouldn't call it *contact*. Not really. Not for long, anyway. Danny had a contract that took us close to the Heimatian border. Contractor made it out to be some tinker's caravan, that they'd up and kidnapped his son. When we discovered it wasn't an ordinary caravan, we left the bastard broke and bloody. Danny never liked to deal with nomads on the account of the..." Her gaze slid to the hound. "...you know."

"I am certain all of us know," Tracker replied drily.

"They were *in* Demarn?" That sounded like a strange risk to take. He'd been told the elven nomad caravans weren't permitted into the kingdom, that the King's Hounds made sure of it. But then, he'd been taught a lot of things that weren't true. "Do the hounds ignore the presence of nomadic spellsters?"

"I can't imagine they sense them all that well near the wall separating Heimat from the world," Katarina replied before the man could.

"We cannot," Tracker confirmed. "The barrier radiates power for miles. Identifying a spellster near it is practically impossible. Thankfully, such knowledge was not widely known amongst rogue spellsters. Too many tended to flee north as it was."

"If they didn't know, then why would they run that way?" Marin asked.

"Because they believed themselves capable of reaching Dvärghem. Any spellster who crosses the border is beyond our reach."

Authril scoffed. "You mean the King's Hounds aren't permitted to follow a runaway into dwarven territory?"

"It's against our treaty," Katarina said.

The impossible dream. He'd known for years about such a clause in the treaty between Demarn and Dvärghem. He had found such knowledge whilst perusing old history texts on a completely different task. It was a cruel joke. Reaching the dwarven-ruled land would be a difficult journey for any spellster to make alone. With hounds trailing after them?

Trying had always been a death sentence.

Even now, with a hound escorting him to a place he should never be headed for, he was certain someone would stop him if he so much as glanced anywhere but east. Maybe not with lethal force, maybe not even the hound's hand, but his fate was clear. *The army*. Any other path meant death.

"Just to be clear," Tracker said to the hedgewitch. "You are *not* going to let me eat that?" He gestured to the wood and the insect Dylan still held. "It will not take me long to char it over the fire."

"No!" Katarina snatched up the chunk of wood. "They are sacred beings, not some evening snack." She stalked out into the forest, glancing over her shoulder as though daring Tracker to follow.

"I can't believe you eat *bugs*," Authril said, drawing his attention back to the rest of them.

Shrugging, Marin uttered a nonjudgmental squeak. "I've eaten a few grubs in leaner times." The woman rested her chin on an upraised fist, her face split wide by a grin, every ounce of glee directed at the hound. "I'm more interested in *your* reaction to seeing him magically lift that piece of wood. You looked like you saw a ghost."

The smile Tracker returned the hunter was small, with a hint of sharpness. "I was merely surprised by how proficient our dear spellster is in the art of levitation. From my understanding, it is..." That honey-coloured gaze slid Dylan's way, only for a moment, but enough to steal his breath. "...a *difficult* skill to master."

Shrill laughter burst from Dylan's lips before he could stop it. He clapped his hand over his mouth, muffling the noise. He'd been too wrapped up in ensuring the bark maiden didn't burn that he hadn't even considered *how* he had snatched the wood from the air.

I'm dead. Tracker was right about levitation being difficult, but it was more than that. It was *illegal*. He had known. And he'd done it anyway. A *hound* had witnessed him using power the tower had forbidden.

All to save an insect.

"I-I didn't mean to," he managed past his fingers. "I... I'm not—" Proficient? He was *far* from that. "It was a reflex. I can't do much with it." Lifting a single solid object wasn't much of a challenge, but that took little more than brute force. To manipulate something with less form? To have an object do anything beyond a direct path? He lacked the deftness. "I certainly haven't practised with such magic. I wasn't about to risk being thrown in isolation for a few tricks."

He flinched as Tracker laid a hand on his shoulder. Only the gentle curve of the hound's lips stopped him from recoiling completely.

"Be at ease, my dear man. You are in no danger and I have no intention to punish you for it. This is not the first time there have been levitated objects in my presence." Tracker's smile twisted slightly, mirroring the wry mirth in his eyes. "Although, *they* were using it to hurl sharp things in my direction. Protecting sacred bugs is a far more innocent use of the skill."

The hound spoke of rogue spellsters. It could be of nothing else. Which meant those others were also likely dead.

"And *why* would he expect you to punish him for levitating a piece of wood?" Marin asked. "He has done far more dangerous things."

Dylan's gaze remained steadfast on the hound, gaining confirmation in the flattening of the man's mouth before a word was said.

Since hearing that magic-heated metal could in fact harm a hound, the idle thought of how else a spellster might defend against them had meandered through his mind, feeding the scant hope that maybe a few spellsters had escaped the tower slaughter.

Any magic the hound interacted with didn't work. He'd seen that firsthand, had felt the sting when Tracker passed through his shield, had watched the way lightning flowed around his body like water.

But *something* had to. The man's armour was suspiciously the type to have a brief resistance to flame. And magically-created fire became the rather ordinary sort once it caught tangible fuel. No one was immune to that, not even other spellsters.

When he thought of what the tower had forbidden them to learn, of those who used magic that acted indirectly, lifting objects, the manipulation of things that they hadn't created…

People who persisted would be temporarily isolated or vanish completely. Such punishment didn't stop everyone from practising the ability, albeit they did it in secret, but he had always wondered why the Overseers wouldn't permit it.

"He expects punishment because it is possible to harm a hound with such magic," Tracker replied. "The Overseers and the guardians were charged with keeping spellsters ignorant of the truth behind our abilities. They cannot retaliate if they do not know how."

Dylan wasn't the most adept when it came to levitating objects, but there were many things he could affect that weren't magical in themselves. A rock didn't stop being a rock because his magic lifted it instead of his hand. Nor did a dagger. Or a spear.

"But what if they needed to?" Marin asked, her brow furrowing. "What if a King's Hound went rogue and they had to be stopped?"

Then it wouldn't be a spellster doing that stopping. *Unless...*

Unless it was someone like Nestria, who could manipulate multiple small objects with ease and speed. A hound facing off against her would likely find themselves being hit by something akin to a hailstorm of steel.

She could've taken out a sole Talfaltaner force with ease. He hadn't seen any evidence of her handiwork. Or of her.

Exactly the kind of spellster they'd try to purge in the name of safety.

"My dear woman, a rogue hound would not be one who kills spellsters indiscriminately."

"Then what *would* a rogue hound do?" Authril asked, baring her teeth in a smile. Her fangs weren't as long or as sharp as Tracker's, but the intensity with which she stared at the man more than made up for it. She hummed with expectation, as if one word would be enough to cut the hound and she was almost eager to slice him into ribbons. "Hypothetically speaking, of course."

Tracker eyed her with the same degree of suspicion Sulin had first given the tower's mousers. "They would ignore the creed. Ignore orders. Perhaps even permit an unleashed spellster to wander the land without being under the guardianship of others, be that fellow hounds or the tower."

The fervour in the warrior's sea-green gaze seemed to dim. She accepted Tracker's words with a grunt, almost disappointed with his response. What had she expected to hear? Some sort of confession? A mention of the dead hounds Marin found near the tower?

Dylan frowned at the fire. So many questions filled his mind. Like the flames, they flickered and sparked from one breath to the next, fading as more demanding ones took their place.

Why had those hounds been there? Why so many? What had they been up to? What had caught them? Who had killed them? Talfaltaners, Marin had said. An educated guess or not, she couldn't know the truth.

Did Tracker? Dylan was certain of the answer there.

But was it one he wished to hear?

CHAPTER 17

The forest remained undisturbed and dark. This late into the night, even most of the nocturnal animals had quietened, leaving only the crackle of the campfire as the loudest sound to reach Dylan's ears.

Even though he was technically supposed to be in his tent, Dylan felt better being out here, sharing the final watch with Tracker. Not that he hadn't tried sleep. Since his attempted apology four nights ago, any effort made towards sleeping had him just lying there with his thoughts gnawing away at all hope of peace.

They hadn't spoken much during those nights, either. Mostly, he just sat near the fire, staring at the shadows beneath the trees. Meanwhile, Tracker would circle the camp or settle nearby, humming what sounded like lullabies as he fussed with his weapons or cooked whatever he had hunted during his watch.

The man was clearly waiting for Dylan to speak first, but he hadn't the words, no matter how long his mind plumbed the well of his own darkness in search of them. He couldn't just jump into explaining how the tower saw indecisives and expect Tracker to understand his fears. Especially when, logically, he knew the tower couldn't do anything to him.

But there was still the army. Still Authril and her desire to be his warden. She knew what the actual wardens had done to the other spellsters in their care under the guise of keeping them in control. He didn't want to know what action she might take to maintain hers over him if she found out he liked laying with men as well.

He wasn't even sure that was the truth. Didn't know *how* to be sure. Yes, he had enjoyed his nights with the hound. And yes, he knew that it didn't have to mean all those times he had lain with a woman was a lie.

Or was *that* the truth he struggled to accept?

"When did you realise you were attracted to men alongside other genders?" He didn't even fully register what came out of his mouth until it was spoken. A single query plucked from the depths of his scrambled mind to drift timidly into the night.

Tracker's head whipped around in silent surprise, the dagger in his grasp almost tumbling into the dirt.

Dylan pressed his lips together lest another foolish word escaped them.

Then the hound grinned, a short blast of mirth hissing through his teeth. "That is quite the question. Well, for starters, my realisations came from another direction entirely, but I was quite young when the notion that my bunkmates could be used for fun occurred to me."

"You liked men first?" That wasn't uncommon, even in the tower. But the way the man had eagerly fallen into bed with his prostitute friend, Dylan had assumed otherwise.

The hound hummed his agreement, his brows briefly twitching upwards. He pressed closer. "What exactly are you seeking with this line of questioning? To find if I have a preference?" One brow arched knowingly. "Of what I *do* like? And, no doubt, whether you fit into those limits or whether I considered you as merely *convenient*."

Heat flooded his face. That hadn't been his intention at all. "That's really not fair, you know."

"And asking me such questions is?"

It wasn't. Any other time, he wouldn't have queried his good fortune to gain the attention of someone like Tracker. Now? "I don't know," he admitted. "There are a lot of things I thought I knew that were..." How the world worked. What he'd been sent to become. Why certain mercenaries had slept with him. "...wrong. I guess—" His voice cracked, forcing him to clear his throat before it closed completely. "I... I—" He fell silent as Tracker laid a hand on his back.

Soft, soothing murmurs slipped out of the hound's lips. "Steady breaths. Try to centre yourself before speaking."

He bowed his head, unable to get the words out whilst seeing Tracker's face. "Everywhere I go, people see me as just a thing to be used." A weapon. A potential toy to abuse. A step up to a more prestigious rank.

"My dear man," Tracker breathed. Those long fingers caressed Dylan's cheek, gently wiping away the dampness that'd settled on his skin. "This is what has been plaguing your mind this past week? That I am seeking to use you like *she* did?"

Dylan bit the inside of his lip in an effort to halt its quivering. "No." He understood why Tracker had reached that conclusion, but that hadn't been the point he was trying to make. Still, he couldn't avoid the one shred of truth behind the observation. "If anything, *I* am the one who used you."

Unexpected laughter snorted out the hound's nose. "*What?* When?" He squinted at Dylan, his expression equal parts mirth and confusion. "Did you come to me whilst I slept and had your way as I dreamt on?"

"Of course not!" Last time, he had barely gotten near the man before Tracker woke. Doing anything further? Even if he'd been predisposed to that sort of tasteless behaviour, he hadn't the dexterity. "I mean the night we were together. When we... when *I*... objectified you, then used your body to—"

Experiment. Tracker had called it such that night. Dylan had objected the idea, but it was the truth. No matter how hard he tried to conceal his thoughts, his intentions, the hound always managed to figure it out before him.

The hound stared at him, his head tilted slightly to one side and his lips pressed together. "I recall you entering my tent and expressing your desire to have sex with me, which we did." He shuffled closer. "I remember the taste of you on my tongue, the way you moaned and begged me to take you. How much your heart raced when I teased you." The gentle curve of his mouth broadened into a wicked grin. "Probably a little more than I should have given the time constraints, but that is only because I find you getting flustered so endearing."

Dylan diverted his gaze to the fire, hoping that watching the flames dance would cool the heat running through his veins.

"And I believe we reached mutual satisfaction rather well."

They had. Gods, never had he orgasmed quite like that before. It had sent his core quaking and left him with the ghost of the hound's blissful touch once again stalking his dreams.

"I do not recall being *used*."

Dylan tore his gaze from the flames to find those honey-coloured eyes still fixed firmly on him. "Not at all?"

A soft breath of amusement left the man's lips. "You were transparent in your desire for me and I agreed to sate your needs. It is not the first of such transactions for me. Or have we forgotten that I spent some years working in *The Gilded Lily*?"

He recalled others telling him about the man working there years ago, back before he had become a fully-fledged hound. "I don't want to think about that." Because if he did, then he couldn't help remembering Tracker telling him he acquired his hound status at eighteen.

"Does it bother you that I once sold my body for other's pleasure?" He grinned. "Of course, nowadays, my services are free and I am more... select with who I bed."

He shook his head. "Given that I've bartered myself for various reasons—" Goods and knowledge, for the most part. "—over the years, that would be hypocritical of me."

The man ghosted a forefinger along Dylan's jawline. "Then you understand it would take a great deal to make me feel used."

Attempting to shy from the unease gripping his chest, Dylan ducked his head. The act only served to press his cheek against the man's hand. "I said so many stupid things that night."

The gust of Tracker's gentle laughter warmed more than Dylan's ear. "I do not know about *stupid*. Honest, perhaps. And sweet." Those long fingers drew Dylan's head up, cradling his chin as though afraid he might shatter under a firmer touch. "I was flattered. Truly. It was *unexpected*, but no less welcomed."

Whatever thing that was responsible for squeezing his insides so viciously didn't manage to capture his heart. It bounced around his chest and thundered in his ears. The only reason it didn't flutter at the back of his throat was because of the death grip that unseen entity had on his neck.

The hound took up Dylan's hands, holding them tightly in his lap. "Truthfully, after your insistence that our night in the tower would not be repeated, I was under no assumptions of being called upon to further broaden your sexual experiences." His sombre expression gained a concerned edge. "But if you took my offer as more of an expectation on your part, that was never my intention. I have lain with hundreds over the years. The reason has always been for mutual enjoyment. *Fun*. There has never been another motive. I have never— *never*—used sex to control people, nor has the act ever been a condition of my protection."

Dylan flopped forward, his cheek awkwardly landing on the hound's shoulder. "I know," he mumbled against Tracker's neck, unsure if he could be heard or if it even mattered. Sometimes, darker thoughts would slip through his nightmares. He could always rationalise them away, but they lurked in the depths nevertheless, preying on scraps of fear. Of how ignorant he was of the world beyond the tower. How he still wouldn't have been any the wiser about Authril's motives if he hadn't been told.

The hound's arms wrapped around him, pulling them closer. "I am aware how much trust you must place in me, in all of us, to risk travelling so far unleashed. I would never seek to abuse it."

Wetness pricked at Dylan's eyes. He blinked frantically, trying not to think, not to *feel*. If he let his guard down for one moment, there'd be no stopping himself until he was a sodden mess drained of every last tear.

"Whatever you have been told in the past," Tracker continued. "You should not feel bad for what was said between us. And certainly never for what you have dreamt. Such things are beyond our control. Besides, you are not the only one to have such thoughts."

Breathing deeply, Dylan gathered what composure he had left and sat back. "I suppose you got a lot of people confessing similar things when you were at the brothel." He hadn't exactly been original.

Tracker hummed his agreement of the fact. "A little more honeyed and usually drunkenly slurred. Certainly not with such raw bluntness." He gave a small lopsided smile, the upper corner wavering as soft laughter escaped between his teeth. "But I was actually referring to myself. About *you*."

"Me?" The hound had erotic dreams? About *him*? Hadn't he said something about liking men with meat on their bones? "You told Marin I'm not your type."

Scoffing, Tracker rolled his eyes. "That was to shut her up. I did not think you would take it literally. Or do you truly believe our nights together would have happened even if I was *not* attracted to you?"

"I don't know." He had thought Authril was attracted to him. Now he knew the reason behind sleeping with him, he'd a lot of misgivings regarding her past words and actions. "It wouldn't be the first time."

The hound stared out into the surrounding darkness for some time, noisily sucked on his teeth, before speaking again, "I like a lot of things. That is to say, my preferences are broad enough that it would likely be easier to list what I did *not* find attractive. In a perfect world, I suppose you could say I would have no qualms in sleeping with whoever asked. I have standards, of course—and, before you ask, you rank highly there."

Dylan doubted the truth of that claim. They had crossed paths with many who were more attractive than himself—there'd been dozens in *The Gilded Lily* alone—and the hound had barely glanced their way. "And it's the same across all the genders?"

"For the most part, yes. It is..." The hound rubbed at his mouth, silently grumbling to himself. "It is like a tavern menu."

"A *what*?" He peered at the man. How had their talk found its way to taverns and menus? What did either have to do with sex?

"That is how it was explained to me as a boy. When it comes to intimacy and who you choose to lie with, the world is like a menu. Most people stick to one thing. A stew, perhaps. There are many kinds and people have their preferences as to what belongs in one, but it is still all stew. Others are the same with soup. Some might try the soup and decide it is not for them and some bounce between both, whilst others might prefer fish."

Dylan's stomach twisted at the final mention. "Did you have to drag fish into this analogy?"

"Fish is actually a good one. You would never eat it bad."

I'd never eat it at all. He grimaced at the mere thought.

Tracker chuckled. "Such a face! Not a meal you enjoy, I take it?"

That was putting it mildly. "No." He couldn't recall one time in his life when such a meal hadn't come straight back up.

"There are no rivers near the tower, none above ground, at least. You must have only eaten preserved fish, yes?"

"Smoked, yes. But I don't think eating it fresh would've mattered." He rubbed at his arm. Just talking about it had him itching. "It makes me break out in hives. Or rather, used to. Before I could heal." Now, it just taxed his energy whilst the latent healing repaired whatever damage had been caused. "So, this analogy? You learnt it amongst the other hounds?"

The man bowed his head in agreement.

He frowned, trying to wrap his mind around it. "If I understand you right, you'd prefer to try everything from the menu?"

"Until I found something I liked enough to... savour? Yes."

Fresh warmth slowly crept across Dylan's face. That honey-coloured gaze had definitely taken a long sweep of him. "Where do I fall on this menu of people? What food am I under?"

Tracker shook his head. "That is not how it works. It is a mere oversimplification, a way to explain to questioning children. You are not food."

Grinning, Dylan leant against the hound. "Then why do you keep trying to devour me?" They'd only been intimate twice, but each time, the hound had been more than willing to have Dylan in his mouth. Even whilst in the midst of other, equally pleasurable, activities.

Laughing softly, Tracker tipped his head to one side, just enough for its weight to kiss Dylan's temple. "You have me there."

He gave the man a little nudge with his shoulder. "You must have had *something* in mind when you started your little comparison. I promise I won't laugh. Much."

The hound hummed for a while before speaking, "Stew. The type that has been simmering for so long that the meat melts in your mouth."

Laughter snorted out of Dylan's nose as he tried to muffle it. He shoved the hound, catching the man's little self-satisfied smile as Tracker conceded to the push and flopped bonelessly onto the log. "That was terrible."

"*You* are the one insisting I compare you to food." Stretched out as he was put him in range to chuck another sorely needed log onto the fire. "Come, it is my turn now. What do you see me as on your great tavern menu?"

"Flat cakes." The words were out before he had considered them.

"You refer to those bland discs of cooked batter, yes?" The hound's nose scrunched as he gave Dylan a puzzled squint. "Just what were you doing in your tower to consider *me* as plain?"

Dylan bowed his head, warmth racing through his cheeks. Had he really implied such? Would it be too much to ask the gods to drag him into the next life at this moment? "They were never plain when I got them. My guardian used to give me a stack of them every year on my nameday." Tricia always pretended to be surprised the plate was there, or that it was so full. And every single time, he would stuff himself to the brink of nausea. "They were always covered in syrup and cream."

"I see. So, I am a rare treat, then?" Tracker's question broke Dylan's fond recollection.

He lifted his gaze to meet the hound's. The gentle flush in his cheeks turned to an overall inferno. There was perhaps a grain or two of truth to those words. He tried to speak, but all that came out was a small, hesitant groan. Where did he start? The familiarity? The sense of home? The warmth that always ran through him when he saw that plate?

"And I also... taste sweet?" A brief, low chuckle rumbled through Tracker's chest. He tipped his head to one side, his smile crooked. "But how could you possibly know if your lips have never ventured that far south?"

Dylan's gaze flicked to the man's crotch and back up. "Not like that." He'd heard rumours aplenty when it came to elves, though. And there was one he hadn't verified, wasn't sure if he'd ever be brave enough to.

"Then perhaps you should explain it to me in detail." The hound shuffled along the small space separating them until their thighs touched. "Or better yet," he breathed. "Show me."

Reflexively swallowing, he tried to think of anything beyond how Tracker's lips sat mere inches away. It would be so effortless to claim them, to just tip himself forward and...

"I can't," he whispered. "I... I won't be able to stop." Nor did he think he'd be able to relegate himself to that innocent act.

The hound's brows twitched in confusion. "Who said you would need to?"

Unbidden, he eyed the occupied tent. No one should emerge from within until morning, but there was always a chance. A risk.

"Do you truly believe any of them knowing would mean trouble?"

Yes. Because if one knew, it was only a matter of time before the others. Before... "Authril wouldn't be happy to learn we've been intimate."

A mirthless blast of laughter escaped the hound. "That is quite the understatement."

He was right. Authril would be furious, doubly so after Dylan had rejected her last advance.

With that simple truth out, something inside him snapped free. "I doubt it would even matter it was *you*." She seemed to hate the very idea of him sleeping with anyone else, even that prostitute friend of Tracker's who the warrior had gone and done the exact same thing with the very woman the hound had suggested. "And I don't think she'd be happy to hear I like men." There was no refuting he had enjoyed everything Tracker shared with him. And if one night, just one time, was enough to label him as indecisive, then the fact he had sought more only solidified it. "As well as women, I mean." Both things could be true at once. He only had to stop denying.

That was the harder task. He kept reaching for the lies, even when there was no need. It felt familiar. Comfortable. Like a ratty pair of smallclothes well past their prime. He knew he should discard them, but he couldn't quite bring himself to.

"I am quite fond of them, too," Tracker said, leaning close as though confessing a great secret. "And nulls. Those who are fluid…" The hound's gaze shifted to the heavens, one corner of his mouth lifting wistfully. "Potentially anyone, really." His attention snapped back to Dylan like a mouser catching sight of a loose thread, his brows knotting together. "But you speak as though it is a bad thing to sleep with a man and still find women attractive. Such interest is common throughout Demarn."

It had taken *The Gilded Lily* to realise the world beyond the tower was so utterly different. That even those who had a clear preference towards one gender didn't have the dread of being labelled something they were trying not to be. That people could just *be* with whoever they wanted.

He only wished the revelation had taken his fear with it.

"The tower had a name for people expressing that opinion." Although, now that he thought about it, the way they'd spoken the word was more akin to a slur. "They were considered indecisive. I—" His tongue stuck. His jaw threatened to seal itself for the rest of his days.

He balled his hands, fighting the rolling weight building up in his stomach. "*I* am indecisive."

Tracker cocked his head. He stared, blinking in silent bewilderment for several breaths. "Truthfully, you do not seem as such." He grinned, the flicker of teasing humour dancing in his eyes. "In fact, I would go so far as to say you were *very* decisive the other night."

Irritation flashed through Dylan's veins. Here he was trying to open up like Tracker wanted, only to have the man respond with a joke? "That's not—"

The hound held up his hands in surrender, his mouth twisted in an apologetic grimace. "I understand the meaning, although I do not believe it is used in such a fashion elsewhere. It is because we are considered unsure about what we want, yes?"

"Something like that," he muttered, only now realising the bubbling in his stomach had vanished, burnt away by the anger that still simmered in the depths.

Tracker shook his head. "Truth be told, gender does not typically factor into my decisions when it comes to who I bed. It is definitely not because I am uncertain of what I want. Rather, I am very aware of my desires and the people I chose happened to satisfy them."

He had already gathered. "I'd a friend who told me as much." His chest tightened at the memory of Harriet. She would've been working in the gardens during the attack. He hadn't seen her body amongst the carnage, but so many had been unidentifiable. Had she managed to escape through the secret entrance before it had blown apart? Had any of them?

"Did you think your friend lied to you?" the hound asked, drawing him back from his darker thoughts. They still lurked on the edges of his mind, deepening the shadows beneath the trees.

Dylan shook his head, trying to clear it. Even when he hadn't understood Harriet, he never thought she lied. "I just didn't really believe it applied to me. Hoped it didn't."

"Why?"

"Because it would've been a risk." A leap he hadn't the courage to take. One he still wasn't ready for.

Not that he hadn't faced his share of close calls during a rejection. The chance of avoiding those he clashed with or ones who made their dislike of him plain was easier when he didn't share a bathing chamber—or, the gods forbid, sleeping quarters—with them.

He'd vague memories of wondering in his teenage years what it was like to have the person of your affections always close by. Of the numerous couples who had shared genders, some were fortunate to share rooms. A mere handful of those relationships had imploded and led to one or both being outed. Sometimes, by the very one they'd been so close with.

The idea of having his affections rejected, be it by another man or not, stung a little. He'd been on the other end of such interaction to know he could've weathered it, even if their presence would remind him day after day.

If they chose to out him?

His guardian's constant vigilance would dog him everywhere he went. He'd seen it in his friends, in those he had studied alongside. Being with just one gender was safer. Easier to deny attraction to anything but women rather than risk losing the freedom to wander the tower unsupervised.

After a while, that ease led him to continue along the path he'd made, to rebuff men who were surer of themselves than he, to convince himself that what he felt in the presence of a man who caught his eye wasn't attraction.

He had built a comfortable barrier to keep from straying into riskier waters.

How did he even start to explain the tower's treatment of indecisives to someone who hadn't been put in that position? "When we first reached the tower..." His voice caught, tripping over the words.

Every time he thought of his home for too long, of the shell it had become, the same memory surfaced. It sat before him, as sharp as the day it was made. The drone of the flies on the wing still filled his ears. The stench of decay still clogged his nose. He recalled every bloated body, how they blocked doorways and collapsed in corridors.

And the blood. So much of it. Marking the walls in splatters and handprints, pooling on the floors in dark and congealing masses.

Exhaling a shuddering breath, the mist of it stark in the night air, he continued, "When you first found me? Do you remember me telling you about a man who died before I left the tower, the one who slit his throat?"

Tracker silently nodded.

"He was... like us. An indecisive."

Concern twitched the hound's brows together. Quiet unease glinted across his eyes. "And being such led to his death? I did not think the tower was so unforgiving in these matters."

Dylan sucked his teeth. "The tower was pretty intolerant of any relations." Not that there weren't plenty of couples who shunned the rules. It wasn't as if they were in Tirglas, there was no stigma in Demarn attached to the act of two people of the same gender being together. "But there was also an internal pressure amongst spellsters to pick a side when it came to sex and, most importantly, to stick with it." Even a casual admission of having the smallest attraction to someone of a different gender could be enough to bring suspicion upon a person.

The hound hummed thoughtfully. "There are five different genders, though. How is a man meant to settle on just one?"

"You just do." Which one didn't matter. Some chose based on a belief that they were making the best chance to lie with either sex, but the same could be true across all the genders. That Tracker was his first experience involving a penis other than his own was more due to chance than any actual avoidance on his part. "Otherwise, you risk being ostracised to the point where they set you up to be outed."

"Outed?" Tracker echoed. "Having everyone know was the worst that could have happened?"

"You know spellsters aren't supposed to have sex." The rule likely started as a means to keep them from breeding, but it had obviously extended over the centuries to include everyone. "Did anyone ever mention the punishment if we were caught in the act?"

"*That* they did not."

"When we're old enough to be moved into the adult accommodations, our guardians lessen their presence. They ensure we're doing our duties and keeping out of trouble, but they're not stationed nearby as they are with children. That is the extent of our freedoms until death." That was partially why the risk of being found out didn't lessen, no matter the age or gender. The chance of the guardians discovering people together increased with the slightest bit of carelessness, just that fraction too much familiarity.

Especially if the vindictive offered up information. A thing that was more likely to happen to those whose preference went beyond more than one gender.

"And if you are caught?"

He breathed deeply, trying to loosen the tightness in his chest. "Then the nature of your activities is revealed to the overseers. Your guardian becomes a second shadow." Whatever pressure banded his ribs squeezed at the thought. There'd been so many times with Nestria where he had come close to that fate. "You are put under constant supervision to the point where you can barely eat and shit in peace. Every single move is monitored. Close scrutiny with anyone who fits the profile of whatever gender you were found with. They share your quarters, your routine. The only time they're not nearby is when you're in the dining hall or using the bathing chamber." Never having a moment alone, of peace, every interaction with another is scrutinised for ulterior motives. He had heard of guardians going beyond that. There were always plenty of rumours feasting on the unpleasant, but he'd never caught wind of anything with proof.

Whilst Tracker remained silent, a scowl slowly darkened his features.

It only had Dylan remembering the anguish on William's face. The betrayal. All because his lover had objected to him sleeping with a woman. "It never happened to me, but I've seen what it does to people. It's worse than the isolation cells. At least they have an end, an eventual release. Being outed is forever. Some even sought death to escape it."

"Like the man you spoke of."

He nodded. *Like William.* But also... "It's not just one person.

Whoever they catch you with is also placed under the same restrictions. You could've done nothing more than be alone in the room with them." A rare few hadn't ever had sex, yet were forced to suffer the same punishment. "All that can happen if you're not marked as indecisive. It increases the risk, though. Double. Triple." Some were fortunate enough to get a warning and settled into chasing one gender or stopped altogether out of fear. Others, like his friend Harriet, fell in love. "I'd already gone down the path of sleeping with women, which meant I couldn't risk even thinking about—or glancing at—another gender for too long." Some people had been so fanatic about it that even a single night had carried too much of a risk to dare straying from the gender he had chosen.

"That... It must have been difficult for you."

"Not always." The ease of keeping himself distanced from another depended on the person he slept with. Knowing he shared a vast majority of the women's affections with someone else helped. Almost everyone in the tower seemed to be sharing their lovers, or claimed to. It made things difficult for the guardians to trace. "I do wonder, though. What it would've been like to live not fearing anything, like you."

He had spent almost every waking hour of the past week since last sharing Tracker's tent looking back on his life. He didn't like the answers such introspection found, but he couldn't shy from them either. Even if his denial of finding men attractive had gone deep enough to the point he believed it wholeheartedly, it would've been a lie to say only the recent months after his leashing were affected.

How much easier would things have been if it hadn't mattered who he chose? He likely would've taken up a number of those propositions several men had dangled before him. Tracker certainly wouldn't have been his first.

But now it didn't matter and the fear... the fear was still there. It lay balled in his chest like a tight bundle of yarn, set to unravel until it became a snarl of strings tangling his insides.

He knew it was foolish, knew the root behind his concerns no longer existed.

That knot in his chest remained all the same.

~ ~ ~

Tracker stared into the darkness. He had run so many conversations through his mind about what Dylan could possibly be afraid of. The truth behind the man's actions wasn't what he had expected. *Perjury from his peers.*

He had first-hand experience with that.

Beside him, Dylan fidgeted. His magic remained under his tight control, but it thrummed at the man's core like a hive ready to burst.

"That is why you seek to hide, to deny, your attraction? Why you kept that part of yourself buried? To avoid a punishment others would give their lives to escape." He slid closer. "It is not—"

"It's not the same out here," the man blurted. "I know." He sagged, clasping his head between his hands. "I keep telling myself how foolish and *stupid* I am to fear being outed when…" His shoulders bounced in a tearful little laugh. "There's no one to out me to, but I—" He fell silent as Tracker laid a hand on the man's shoulder.

"You are neither foolish nor stupid. This fear you have runs bone-deep." Literally decades in the making. It seemed irrational now, but it had been very real not that long ago. "Such things cannot be easily shaken. Certainly not within the span of a few weeks." He wasn't entirely sure that it wasn't still completely unfounded, but Dylan didn't need that possibility hovering over his head. "And I understand the fear of not wanting to be caught. I truly do." The need to conceal a relationship, knowing that if anyone found out, it would mean death.

Young him had been beyond foolish. He'd been so arrogant. *Reckless.*

He couldn't make the same mistake again. Couldn't be the reason another soul met their end.

An old chill gnawed at his bones. The night seemed darker than it had before. *The Pit.* Tracker rubbed at his left arm, the tattoo wrapping around his bicep burning like a brand. *Down into the deep, into the dark.* Into a hole where screams reverberated through the mind as much as they did in the cavern. Where blood stained the rocks in smears of rust red.

Where he should have died.

The look Dylan gave him spoke of disbelief. "You… you understand? How? You said that desires like ours are common."

Catching himself in a scowl, Tracker smoothed his features. "They are. But there are more places than your tower where sex as a whole is discouraged."

"The hounds?"

"Indeed. Although, truth be told, it goes further than that. We are dissuaded as children from forming any close bonds." The order was presented as a mercy. Far too many died in childhood. Keeping aloof was the only way many kept their sanity. "They are more lenient in the matter of friendship when we are full hounds, but intimate relationships are forbidden and many gain those ties through sex, so *that* is also technically frowned upon." They were permitted visits to brothels—some urges were better kept in check if satisfied—but a great deal of his fellow hounds chose celibacy.

"And if *you* were ever outed? What then? You mentioned something in the tower, but I don't remember."

He wasn't surprised. He had let it slip whilst still criticising himself for putting Dylan in a situation that almost got him killed. The man had asked about it, but Tracker had simply pretended he never heard. "Bad things happen if we are caught with someone we should not be with." How he hated the way the words rasped his throat.

"The deadly kind of bad?"

Tracker bowed his head in silent agreement. The memory of loss still rang sharply in his mind, Wynne's pleas for Hunk to stop, the crunch of Zinnala's slight body being used to bludgeon the mother of his child to death. Their child...

All gone because of him.

If they had only moved faster, left sooner, then they'd all be alive. *Free and safe.* Far beyond Demarn's reach. There would've been no hiding from the other hounds. No chasing dangerous spellsters through the kingdom. No arriving too late to stop tragedy.

No finding a terrified unleashed spellster who just wanted to help his people.

Was that why he had lived then? Because the gods wanted, needed, Dylan to survive? Who else would've let the man live? Fetcher, perhaps. Whisper, too. Few others. Not past the tower's demise.

"Track?"

He blinked, surprised to find Dylan's hand on his knee. Not the wisest move, but the sight warmed him nevertheless.

Ever the healer. A wry smile tweaked the corner of his mouth. If the gods truly had a plan, he hoped it wasn't to have the spellster fight any battles in their name. Dylan had the wrong kind of heart for that.

To think the man had ever been put in a situation where he could believe the slightest sign of affection carried a hidden agenda. That Tracker's advances could be considered as just another in a line of people looking to use the man for his own gain...

A frustrated growl rumbled in his throat.

"Are you all right?" Dylan asked. Those dark eyes held his own, seeking the truth. They radiated concern, and a touch of wariness, eclipsed by purpose.

The sight stirred a longing, a *craving*, he had thought long confined. A desire that could only bring pain.

He gently removed the man's hand from his knee, swallowing down the pang of regret in its absence and affected a casual smile. "I am fine." The old lie came easily enough.

"I'm sorry, I didn't mean to imp—"

"No."

Dylan fell silent. His brows pinched together. His eyes, so impossibly huge, looked to be on the brink of tears.

"Be still, my dear man." He caressed Dylan's cheek, his fingers gliding along the soft skin until they disappeared into the curls of black hair at his neck. "There is no need for you to apologise. I asked for an explanation and you provided. It is more than fair that you get one in kind, but not tonight." Or ever. Dylan had already witnessed multiple deaths, the slaughter of friends and strangers alike. He didn't need to hear about more senseless killing.

Dylan leant closer, their foreheads barely touched. It was enough for his latent power to hum against Tracker's skin.

They sat there for a breath or two before he reluctantly got to his feet. "I need to check the perimeter." He didn't—the low sounds of the surrounding wildlife were enough to make him reasonably certain the night would stay quiet—but he didn't trust himself to remain in Dylan's presence without seeking more than this gentle companionship. Neither of them was in the right mind for that in this moment, and he certainly wasn't about to use the man's body to chase off old demons. "Thank you, by the way, for entrusting me with this piece of you. I will keep it safe."

The man's answering smile almost unravelled Tracker's resolve. Dylan toyed with the pendant Marin had gifted him, his thumb tracing the lines carved upon its surface. "Be careful out there."

He bowed in a sweeping flourish, garnering a muffled chuckle as he asked, "Whenever am I *not* careful?" He made for the edge of the clearing, pausing only to ensure Dylan had retired to his tent.

He would ensure the spellster didn't regret confiding in him. *I will keep you safe.* From danger. From being leashed. From Authril. The whole kingdom, if necessary.

He would *not* allow another person in his care to die. Not again. *I promise.*

CHAPTER 18

The deer stood placidly amongst the trees and shrubbery. A doe, small, perhaps a year old at most. Definitely mature enough to give them a decent feed. The deer's tail bobbed, flashing the white underside to the forest even as the animal nibbled at a nearby bush and paused every so often to glance about.

It had taken a fair bit of tracking to find the animal after he had stumbled upon it whilst setting the first few traps. Having to return to camp and retrieve Marin's bow hadn't helped, but the hound mistress gave him the designation of tracker for a reason and, unlike some amongst the pack, his skills weren't honed solely on spellsters.

Steadying his breath, he adjusted his grip on the bow and drew the string taut. He had lost a lot of daylight circling to get upwind without the deer noticing, but it had also gifted him the added benefit of being uphill.

However, with the forest steadily growing dark, he would have one attempt at downing the animal. Two if he was quick. Not that he ever had been.

Like all hounds, he had trained with a vast variety of weapons in his youth. Archery had been one of the first, but unlike the sword, it had been a long time since he'd a bow in his hands. He had always preferred his throwing knives for distant targets. They were compact and hidden, easier to aim. Unfortunately, the edges were also tainted with remnants of poison.

He loosed the arrow.

Flinching, the deer bounded into the undergrowth. The sounds that followed its disappearance spoke of the animal stumbling directly into the foliage.

Tracker hastened down the hill. He had seen the point hit his target cleanly enough to know the deer wouldn't go far, but that didn't mean he was willing to risk losing it in the bushes.

By the time he reached where the deer had been, the animal was completely out of sight. Even the sounds of its passage through the forest were absent. That could only mean it had already succumbed.

Good. No matter whether his prey was animal or being, quick kills were always better.

Following the direction the deer had fled, he found it head down and staggering like a man too deep in his drink. The arrow jutted from its chest, both shaft and hide stained in bright red blood.

The deer lifted his head, its nostrils flaring. The long ears flicked as it eyed him. It bunched its haunches, preparing to either take flight once again or lash out.

He halted well out of striking distance. As small and unsteady as the animal was, those delicate legs still bore enough power to maim, if not kill, the unwary. He had no desire to become someone else's warning.

Then, issuing a breathless snort, the animal collapsed.

Tracker waited a moment longer to ensure the deer had indeed breathed its last, before kneeling at the animal's head. He withdrew the *infitialis* dagger and made a clean cut across its throat. The dagger would need to serve him in gutting, too. It wasn't the most suited to the task, the weapon not being as long or as heavy as Marin's hunting knife, but he couldn't retrieve that without risking losing the deer to the night and it would be vastly lighter to carry back to camp if gutted here.

It didn't help that he hadn't worked on anything bigger than a hare for some years. Travelling alone meant needing to sate the needs of his horse and himself.

Rolling the beast onto its back, he got to work. The dagger's sharpness was the one thing in its favour, allowing him to effortlessly slice open the animal's belly. Getting the innards out was a little trickier. A longer blade would've made cutting away certain sections easier, but beyond his sword, he couldn't be entirely definite his other dagger was free of any poison residue. Nor was he keen on gambling with their lives.

The task had left quite the mess with blood and offal splayed across the forest floor. He knew burying it was the best recourse to keep anything even vaguely carnivorous from sniffing around, but this wasn't some rabbit or bird. The share volume he had extracted from the deer required a hole he hadn't the tools to dig.

Nothing would stay for long. The soil was already greedily drinking deep of whatever liquid oozed from the innards, whilst the wildlife would make swift work of the rest. He just had to hope their presence at camp was enough of a deterrent should anything come closer.

Hoisting the animal onto his shoulders, he secured the legs and began the trudge back to camp. With luck, this haul would mean decent slabs of venison for a few days.

~ ~ ~

Dylan stared into the campfire, watching the flames lick the underside of the pot hanging above them. The water within wouldn't boil for a while yet. He could've changed that in an instant, but this way at least gave him something to do.

Minding the fire hadn't been his task for this early evening. That was typically Katarina's job. He should've still been sparring with Marin, as he had done for the past few days. He would have, had Tracker's abrupt return, and just as swift departure, not shattered his concentration.

With nothing else to do, he was relegated to this whilst Marin harvested and cleaned the wild mushrooms Authril had spotted.

He didn't even know what the hound was doing, only that he had vanished into the forest to lay out the traps as usual and returned shortly after to grab Marin's bow and quiver. No matter how he tried to put it out of his mind, it nagged in the background like a droning fly.

The fire popped, prompting him to offer up another small piece of wood to the flames.

"You look like your mind is out to sea," Katarina said.

Blinking away the afterimage of dancing flames, Dylan swivelled his attention to the hedgewitch as she sat beside him. Unsurprisingly, she held the tome he had gifted her back at the tower. She often settled quietly by the fire to read it after her portion of the camp tasks were done. She must've had the pages memorised by now.

"Sorry," he mumbled. "I was just…" He gestured at the pot, with its barely steaming water. "Waiting."

Her lips curved, the softness reminding him of his guardian. "If you're looking for something more productive, then perhaps you can help me with something." She opened the book, gently turning each page until she reached her destination. "This passage here." Wrinkling her nose, she tapped her nail on the offending text. "I'll admit, my ancient Demarner is a little rusty, but this refers to a site somewhere along the King's Winding, correct? Except, I don't recall such a site ever mentioned in our own records and I can't find anything about *where* it is, never mind what the area might've held."

Dylan took the book from her. Even this close, the scent of old parchment was almost lost to the stronger odour of burning wood, but he knew it well. Had spent years surrounded by it. With his vision watering, he ran a finger over the edge of the leather binding. This had to be the first of its kind, started after the treaty with Dvärghem. Yet, as ancient as it must've been, someone in the tower had taken care to keep it from cracking.

Having such an old tome nestled in his lap like a foraging journal felt almost sacrilegious. The back of his neck prickled as though the tower's bookkeepers breathed down it.

He leafed through the wrinkled pages. Each one was full of old records about even older dwarven sites found across Demarn. He had contributed to a similar work—one that was now little more than ash blowing about the tower remains.

Unlike the new books, the records within these pages were written haphazardly, the latter quarter shifting to the common script he'd been taught as a boy.

The hedgewitch was right. Before the mention, the pages spoke of towns far from the river, whereas the records after were of shore-facing caves near Stonebay.

"What even is the King's Winding?" Marin asked. She set the mushrooms near the fire. On their own, they wouldn't be much of a meal. Paired with the leftover rabbit and a few herbs plucked from the roadside would at least help make this night's meal a little more filling.

Katarina frowned at her. The expression scrunched her nose and warped the scar running across her face. "It's your kingdom's major river, the one Whitemeadow straddles."

The other woman shrugged. "Never been this far north. Or east, for that matter."

"Still beats me having never left the tower until—" *Three months.* Had it truly been so short a time? It didn't feel as though it was long enough. But yes, as he counted the time spent travelling. Three months and a little over one week since that alchemist had wrapped his neck in *infitialis*.

His fingers brushed against the smooth patch at his throat. So much had happened since then. Things he never would've imagined coming true in his wildest fantasies. Things he never wanted to see again.

"Well," he murmured. "Until they let me."

Marin leant against him, resting her cheek on his shoulder. Even though he couldn't see her face, the twitch of her jaw was unmistakable. "I wish there was somewhere else for you to go," she said softly. "Other than Wintervale." She hadn't been keen on the idea even back when their journey should've ended at the tower, but ever since the attack that had almost claimed her life, she seemed to take the idea of him returning to the army as an insult.

Dylan pressed closer until his temple touched the top of her head.

"I'll be fine." It was a lie, of course. He'd no way of predicting exactly what would become of him once they reached the capital, but it was all he had. Like a rudderless boat set adrift on the seas, he couldn't change the course fate had set for him. Nor could he hope for any option that wouldn't end with him being thrown on an early pyre.

"Do you actually *want* to return to the army?" she asked.

Authril cleared her throat, no doubt preparing to explain how he needed to return, regardless of his feelings. He twisted her way, waiting, only for her to give a silent grimace and return to patrolling. He'd no idea why she hadn't discarded her armour like normal, but she strode about as if expecting an attack.

"Given the choice?" Dylan smiled down at the book. If it was up to his decision, he would've spent his life seeing every single site detailed in those pages. "I never truly wanted to be in the army any more than I wanted to be leashed." It had been the only way to leave the tower, to escape the life that had held so little purpose. "I just thought..." His throat tightened. "I thought I could make a difference."

Another lie. *For the good of the kingdom.* Perpetuated by the Overseers, parroted by guardian and spellster alike. Protecting the people from the Udynea Empire was for the greater good of everyone.

Except us. The army had made it clear that the common belief was the only good a spellster ever did was dying in place of regular folk. Leashed, he was a weapon. Unleashed, he was a danger.

He couldn't disagree with any of it.

Marin sat back, eyeing first him, then Authril's passage across the campsite. She waited until the warrior was the farthest away before whispering, "You could run."

He sucked in a breath. Running was a thought he had tried so desperately to ignore. No one except them knew he was out here. "It's not that simple."

Katarina laid a consoling hand on his knee. Her expression was one of sombre understanding. It set his eyes to burning to the point he needed to blink back the tears or devolve into a blubbering mess.

He couldn't risk losing any of them. Despite the scar his broken collar had left at his throat, he'd only Katarina's word to back up being at the site of the ambush that took his warden's life. Furthermore, he'd only her and Authril's word that he had actively opposed Udynean forces. Without them, he was an unleashed spellster under a hound's guard. Without Tracker, he was a rogue spellster.

If Marin was willing to suggest running in the first place, she would obviously be agreeable to joining him. He might even be able to say the same about Katarina.

Authril was a different story. For all her talk about the hound not doing his job, she hadn't made any attempt on his life. She seemed content to let him march his way towards the new army, to where she would be elevated to the status of warden.

And Tracker?

Dylan returned his attention to the book, unwilling to think about what the hound might do if he ran. No matter how much he tried to focus on the words, his gaze kept sliding from the page to where he had last seen the man.

What was he doing out there? Why had the task required a bow? How long would it take?

When should they start to worry?

"I'm sure he's fine," Katarina murmured, her lips curving into a secretive little smile. Just like his guardian's would whenever his much-younger self thought he had successfully hidden the truth from her.

"I know that," he snapped. There hadn't been a challenge yet the hound hadn't come out the other side of unscathed. "I just don't understand what he'd need Marin's bow for." Tracker hadn't said a thing about it, nor had he asked for any of the others to follow.

"Maybe he came across a game trail," Marin suggested.

"Better be something decent," Authril grumbled. She paused for a moment, staring out into the forest with such intensity that he expected something to erupt from the undergrowth. After a short while, she returned to her pacing. "I don't like being the only one with an actual weapon at hand."

Marin scoffed. "You're not. Dylan is right here *and...*" she added, gesturing to her hunting knife. "I'm not entirely unarmed. Nor is Kat."

Although her words were clearly designed to soothe the warrior's nerves, they seemed only to aggravate them. "Neither of you have the armour for close-range combat. *Your* attire has already proven itself a poor defence against anything that tries to split you open and the hedgewitch's is just cloth." Again, something out in the forest divided her attention. "I won't have anyone else hurt, not over stupid decisions."

Dylan tilted his head in an attempt to figure out what she might have heard. Nothing reached him beyond the hum of insects, the trill of birdsong and the odd rustle of a leaf. All perfectly normal. If anything bigger than a rodent scurried about, it was far enough to not be an immediate concern.

Still, being alert and ready wasn't a bad thing. The reminder that he'd been unable to prevent Marin's near-death from happening— that it was *his* fault they'd been out there in the first place—already twisted his gut.

"I could put a shield over the camp," he offered. He would need to ensure the upper part of the dome was porous enough for the smoke to leave, but it was doable for a time. If he put enough focus into the act, it might even have Tracker return faster.

Authril halted, her face creasing as she considered it. "Not yet. But remain near the others in case it's needed."

"I'm sure it won't be necessary," Katarina said. "We would do better to spend the last portion of the day recouping rather than stressing over threats yet to be proven. Now..." She laid her hand atop the same one Dylan gripped the outer edge of the tome with. "I believe you were helping me?"

"I don't know what else to tell you that you haven't already figured out." He stared back down at the pages. The text offered nothing new. "This was written centuries ago, well before our great-grandparents were gleams in their ancestor's eyes. It *could* be an unsubstantiated record, but I can't even be sure of that."

The hedgewitch nodded. "We'd always get the occasional report. Some farmer stumbling upon ruins after chasing wayward stock through the forest, or their plough just happened to dig up remains in the same field they've tilled for generations. All for a glimmer of renown." Her gentle smile twisted wryly. "I suppose it would've been the same back then."

"We could try to look for whatever it is all the same," Marin suggested. She scrunched up against him, twisting her head to read over his shoulder. How much she understood was unclear. She'd obviously enough knowledge of a few ancient runes to carve the symbol on his pendant. "We'll be going down the same river, wouldn't we?"

"Walking alongside its banks, I would trust," Katarina replied, looking a little ill at the mention of travelling upon the river.

"Dwarves are infamous for their dislike of boats," he explained upon seeing Marin's confusion. "Every single one gets seasick." Not that *he* had any experience with such vessels beyond crafting miniatures out of ice as a child. For all he knew, he'd fair no better than the hedgewitch.

The woman in question shrugged as though he had stated the sun set every evening. "It isn't just vessels. Any deep water is enough, although I've never had the nerve to experience it for myself." Her gaze dropped to the tome. She fondly caressed the pages before relinquishing him of its weight. "As much as I would like to seek out the truth, I'm aware travelling on foot would slow your journey to Wintervale. Just as I'm sure you've no need of my word with both a hound *and* a prospective warden to vouch for you."

"You're not coming with us to the capital?" He knew that, eventually, they'd all go their own ways, but he didn't think their travelling together would stop once they reached Whitemeadow.

"You'd leave us? Just like that?" Marin spoke as though the very idea had personally injured her. "But—" She glanced over at Authril, who still paced around the camp. "They're supposed to be protecting you. *We* are supposed to protect you. How can we do that if you're travelling in a different direction?"

Ducking her head and issuing a soft giggle, Katarina tightened her grip on the tome until it was firmly pressed against her chest. "I am heartened by the concern, but it's not the first time I've needed to avail myself of the local officials to make it back to my homeland unscathed. I'm sure whatever government body is in charge of Whitemeadow is aware of the treaty your kingdom holds with mine, and they will be quite willing to help once informed."

The hunter's lips alternated between pouting and opening to further voice her opinion, the words never quite making it.

"You downed a *deer*?" Authril's shrill question blasted across the clearing, alerting them to Tracker's re-emergence.

True enough, the man bore a small doe upon his back, its head lolling over one shoulder.

"Luck," the hound replied, dumping the animal by the trees. "I practically tripped over it whilst following a game trail. Came back to get the bow and—" He gestured to the carcass at his feet.

"Wouldn't it have fled by then?"

"Yes." The smile he gave Authril was broad and reminded Dylan of the times Sulin would explain something painfully obvious about *infitialis* to him. "That is where I started *tracking* it." Kneeling, Tracker withdrew the purple dagger and began separating the hind leg from the rest of the animal.

He had barely finished the task before Marin started on the rest, her hunting knife carving through far faster. She bent close to the hound, uttering something Dylan couldn't make out, but garnered only a simple shake of the head from Tracker.

Leaving Marin to quietly work away at the rest of the animal, the hound knelt by the fire, the dripping haunch in hand. He said little whilst deftly slicing the meat into chunks fit for grilling, motioning only for Katarina to place the pan on the fire, into which he threw a few pieces to merrily sizzle away.

The smell of cooking venison quickly overtook the previous scent of wood smoke. Dylan's mouth watered. It felt like an age since he had eaten anything more substantial than a pheasant leg. A shame they hadn't any more of the berries plucked from the bramble bushes three days prior, but they'd consumed the last during the morning's breakfast. The foraged mushrooms would have to suffice.

Tracker glanced Authril's way, frowning briefly before returning to his task. "You look very on guard, my dear warrior."

"Someone has to be." She levelled her sword at him. "You left this camp short of not only yourself, but another weapon to defend our position."

"Did I?" Still on his knees, he twisted to take in the camp. "I see no sign of any hostility. Present company excluded," he added, giving her a smirk he had to know would only rile her further.

"That's not the point," Authril said through gritted teeth. She thrust her sword in the direction of the road. "We've perhaps a few more days of travel before we reach the outer farmlands. The very same lands my company had to run bandits off from just last summer."

"You think they would have returned? That they somehow avoided being routed by the Talfaltan force?"

"I don't know," she admitted. "But I'd rather not find out with *our* forces scattered."

"Then I would say it is fortunate that, thanks to this deer, we no longer have a need to venture into the forest for more than nature's necessities and a little firewood to combat the chill nights."

Grumbling, the warrior sheathed her sword and fussed with removing her shield. She kept up the barely audible mutters even as she stalked over to the women's tent and, dropping her shield on the ground with more force than was required, started unbuckling her armour.

Only once she had stripped everything to its lowest layer did she return to the fireside, planting herself firmly on the far side to glare at the hound over the flames. Her nostrils twitched more than any irate flaring could account for. No doubt the increasingly salivating aroma of venison steadily worked to unravel her resentment.

Marin's sigh drew his attention. He found her digging the waxed linen out of her pack. Travelling with the hunter had enabled Dylan to learn a lot about transporting meat, cooked and raw, and he'd seen her use that cloth many times for either use. It would keep the meat from spoiling for a few days, maybe even long enough for them to reach the farmlands that bordered Whitemeadow.

"Is something wrong?" he asked her.

She shook her head, but the solemn gleam in her gaze as she eyed the deer spoke differently. "Small as she is, that doe still has a fair bit of meat on her. I don't like leaving so much behind."

"We cannot carry *all* of it with us," Tracker said. "Even cooked, it will spoil before we get to finishing it. Better the remains serve to feed the local wildlife."

"If it's a simple matter of preserving for the road," Katarina replied. "We could jerk it. Like we did with that boar."

The hound raised a brow in a wordless query. He hadn't been there the last time they'd preserved meat in such a fashion. All of them had barely known each other for more than a few days when that animal attempted to charge through their campsite. The only time Dylan had ever seen a boar in the flesh.

"It would indeed solve the matter at hand," the man eventually conceded. "But it would also require spending several days in one place. I do not think that is wise, especially when lingering in one spot almost got one of us killed."

"And yet," Authril interjected. "*You* saw no problem in depriving that one, and us, of the only proper weapon she has whilst you gaily wandered off into gods' knows where to hunt the damn deer in the first place."

Tracker scoffed. "A few hours with a spellster to help defend you should something dangerous come across the camp is hardly the same as delaying reaching our destination whilst also having smoke announcing our presence to those who may mean harm. Or do you not see the difference?"

"*You're* the only reason we're still out here. If it wasn't for you insisting we slow our travelling, we could be in Whitemeadow by now."

"Or we could have found ourselves in greater danger with fewer resources to fall back on and an exhausted spellster to mind. You forget, the army never intended them to make any reasonable excursion beyond the initial one that brought them to the border."

Much of his travelling to the army encampment hadn't been under his own power. Whilst he had spent some of it on horseback, that moment only encompassed the trip from Toptower. From what he remembered of the journey, the parts that hadn't been full of heat and delirium from the sun, he had spent the time settled amongst the supplies in the back of a cart.

"Be as that may," Marin said, getting louder with each word. She glared at the two elves, unconcerned that it had her bouncing between them, before focusing fully on the hound. "We haven't come across any more trouble in almost a fortnight. I know lingering poses a risk, but I also doubt an extra day or two will bring trouble or even cause that much of a delay." She whipped around to fix Authril with another sharp look. "We could even travel faster afterwards, knowing we don't need to find more food every time we make camp."

"Three days," Tracker conceded. "After that, we leave whatever isn't cooked or jerked and move on."

"Deal!" Marin jumped up, her hunting knife already unsheathed.

"Come on," she said to Authril. "Let's get a rack set up. The sooner we start, the more we'll have on the road."

Groaning, the warrior lurched to her feet and followed.

CHAPTER 19

Faceless bodies in dark armour flit through the tower halls. They crouched like coiled snakes to strike out at the unsuspecting. Silver blades flashed in the shadows, growing ever darker with blood.

With their targets still crumpling, the attackers moved on. Some marched down the corridor leading to the gardens. Others darted up the stairs. Everywhere they went, screams followed. The sound filled the halls. Blood ran down the steps. Smoke poured in from the garden archway.

Groaning and only half aware that he slept, Dylan rolled from his back onto his side.

He tried to run after them, to halt this madness and demand answers. Demand all the whys that pounded the inside of his skull, desperate to be heard. Why them? And why—after all these decades, these centuries—why now?

His legs refused to obey any command. He sent wave after wave of magic at the monsters, hitting them with every spell he could conjure. Nothing stopped their mindless pursuit of death.

One of the slinking figures halted in its journey up the stairs, its faceless head turning towards him. Bronze skin and dark leather equally stained with blood. He knew that armour. Had seen it every day for the past two months.

Hound.

"Dylan?" a gentle voice called. "Dylan, wake up."

The features shifted, turning from a haze of colour into something more distinct. A mad grin twisted the elven hound's handsome face, their honey-coloured eyes dark with glee. He advanced, his dagger held low. The blade glinted purple in the torchlight.

No.

Finally, Dylan's legs moved, allowing him to back away. He stumbled a few steps, his bare feet growing damp and sticky, but didn't halt. He didn't dare blink, didn't dare look away from the hound for even a second. What was there to see? More death? A way out. Where? There was nowhere to run. There had never been a—

His heel came down on something slimy, throwing off his balance. He fell to the floor, his fall cushioned by another's lifeless body. More lay around him. They stared up at him with vacant, mournful eyes. Just another on the pile.

The shimmer of his shield flickered around him and died. What difference would using it make? His opponent was immune.

The hound's footsteps rang out in the silence. He lurched closer with every blink, each step jerking like a puppet.

Not wanting to die lying down, Dylan scrambled to right himself. Nothing gave him any purchase. His feet slid in the blood pooling on the stone and the glistening pinkish-grey tubes snaking through it. The lifeless limbs surrounding him clung to his clothes and tangled his legs.

The hound stood over him. With that manic grin still plastered across his face, he stabbed the dagger into Dylan's chest. Pain, hot and electrifying, jolted through him.

Over and over, the man continued his assault, cackling like a madman. He sliced great wounds, licking them as they spurted blood over his face.

He grabbed Dylan's face, the long fingers squeezing, digging into his cheeks. "Poor little soul," he hissed. He smiled. There were far too many teeth in that grin. "To think, you trusted me." The dagger came up, blood dripping from the curved blade like a fang.

That tip was the last thing he saw before it plunged into his eye.

Dylan sat up, panting. His pulse thudded through his head so heavily that he thought it might burst. *Death,* it roared. *That's all they've ever brought, all they ever will bring.*

He raked his fingers through his sweat-soaked hair, trying to shake the words free.

"Dylan?"

The hound's voice drew his gaze to the entrance. Tracker crouched there, wary as if approaching a stray cat.

Or a volatile spellster.

"What—" His voice broke. He cleared his throat and, pitching his voice deeper, tried again. "Why are you...?"

The air was warm. The scent of leather and linen perilously close to combustion filled his nose.

Dylan drew his blankets tight to his chest, his hands shaking as he focused on chilling the air. He had almost set fire to the tent. To himself. Almost endangered the others.

"We are fully awake, yes?"

Nodding, he sat up.

"You had another nightmare." It wasn't a question. The hound didn't need to ask, not with the evidence shimmering around them like a midsummer heat haze. "The worst you have experienced in some time."

Dylan bowed his head. He rubbed at his temples with thumb and forefinger, trying to banish the glaring images still bouncing around his mind. The man in it had borne a remarkable resemblance to the one before him.

Foolishness. They knew who was behind their attack. They'd all seen the Talfaltaner bodies strewn across the gardens, had encountered not only evidence of their passage across the land, but stumbled upon stragglers. Besides, the hounds wouldn't attack the tower.

They have in the past. He hadn't heard of it before Tracker's revelation and he certainly had no knowledge of the full reasoning behind such an act, only what the hound had claimed. *Done at the king's express order.* And culling only the spellsters, not slaughtering everyone.

What if the hounds *had* been involved? Everyone beyond the tower walls might've feared rogue spellsters—justified in a number of cases, if what Tracker had divulged was common—but everyone *within* the tower had feared the King's Hounds even without knowing they were immune to magic.

"Given the strength of your reaction," Tracker drawled. He subtly shifted the tent flap, aiding Dylan's efforts to cool the space. "This bad dream was another of your home."

Again, he could only respond with a nod. With how many times nightmares had him seeking solace in the hound's arms, he wasn't surprised the man knew which ones elicited the more visceral reactions.

His attention drifted to the world outside, attempting to judge the time of night. Was it worth trying to sleep further? With the last portion of the jerky hanging over the campfire, offering more smoke than illumination, much of the campsite itself was lit only through moonlight. "You should return to your watch."

Tracker wrinkled his nose. "It is a little early for that. Our dear warrior and hunter have only started their turn."

A chill that had nothing to do with his magic prickled along his spine. Others were wandering about outside and the hound knelt at the entrance to his tent. At least the man had the good sense not to venture further.

"You need not look so worried. Both are currently patrolling the perimeter and, considering how dense some of the bush is here, they could be some time doing it. I will not stay long, if that is your wish. I merely wanted to ensure you do not burst into flame the moment I return to my tent."

"I'll be fine." If the other two had only taken over, then how much sleep had he managed? Half an hour? Less?

The hound tipped his head to one side. "Would you feel better staying with me for the rest of the night?" The suggestion came so quietly that Dylan briefly thought he had heard wrong. "I would certainly sleep more soundly with you at my side. And I believe it is the same for you."

Tracker wasn't wrong about that. His slumber became infinitely improved whilst snuggled against the man.

Was it strange that he found comfort in the embrace of someone whose very life had been honed to hunt people like him? He no longer felt qualified to measure normalcy. Not out here, where the tower's views held little sway over the world. Every time he thought he had figured out the world beyond those walls, he was proven mistaken soon enough.

He would still stir in the middle of the night. Not to the haunting realisation that the tent had almost been set alight, but to the soothing hold of Tracker's arm draped over his side. Or the grounding presence of the man tucked against Dylan's back, their legs either tangled or neatly pressed together. Rarely, that pose came with an unmistakable hardness nestled against the cleft of his buttocks, constrained only by the soft linen of the hound's smallclothes. It had surprised him at first, no more than the arm holding him in that sleeping embrace, but it brought up a whole new issue when it came to the idea of sharing a tent with the man.

"I am not hearing a refusal," Tracker pointed out, melodic smugness tinkling through the words.

Dylan tilted his head to peer over the man's shoulder. No sign of movement amongst the shadows. He wet his lips, his thoughts frantically seeking words.

Smiling mirthlessly, the hound laid his hand on the blanket, gently patting it and the foot lying beneath. "Think on it." He rocked back onto his heels, further parting the tent flap. "If I do not see you later tonight, I will check on you when my time on watch comes. Just to be sure you are still well."

He reached out for the man's hand, falling short by several inches. "Don't leave. Please? I need you."

When the hound didn't move, Dylan summoned a dim globe of light.

Tracker squinted at the light as if it had somehow personally offended him. "If you are able to do that, then why not do it more often?"

"Our guardians discouraged the use of magic outside of sanctioned activities. And, honestly, when normal methods work well enough, sometimes using magic is just a waste of energy." He frowned, considering all the times a certain warrior had expressed her displeasure at Dylan's attempts to magically assist in camp matters. "But don't tell Authril I said that."

The hound chuckled. "I shall take that secret to my grave." He crawled further into the tent to kneel at Dylan's feet. Just close enough to be considered appropriate should anyone else enter. "You wish for me to linger. For how long?"

"A short while," he promised. "I just... Part of the reason I don't want—" He bit his lip. That wasn't quite true. It wasn't a matter of want. He might've started not desiring to share such intimate space with the hound, but that bird had well and truly flown the nest. "I mean, my hesitation in sharing a tent on a more permanent basis is because..." Heat flooded his face, turning his words to dust.

"You fear what the others will think," Tracker said, once again voicing the words he couldn't quite form properly. "What a *certain* one might do. I understand this, but I do not believe they would jump to the conclusion that we are having sex. People are capable of sharing a sleeping space without such activities. After all, the three of them have been sharing one tent since the tower—two of them since we met, in fact—I have never once believed they were screwing each other."

"I know, but..." He breathed deeply, trying to cool his thoughts. A difficult task now the tent flap was fully closed once more, trapping the crisp chill of his magic and the citrus-cinnamon scent rolling off Tracker's skin. Intoxicating as life itself, it made the very idea of thinking difficult.

No, that wasn't entirely true. He *could* think. In fact, his mind was very clear. Just not on what it needed to think about. And that was part of the problem. "I'm not sure how well I'd be able to keep my hands to myself." It wasn't that he hadn't been with anyone in days. In the tower, he would sometimes go without such intimacy for weeks on end. But there was something about the hound that made him feel like a horny teenager.

It wasn't because Tracker was an elf, or even a man. He'd been around plenty of elven men and never wanted them as badly as he desired Tracker. The feeling made it nigh impossible for him to remain in a confined space with the hound and not touch him.

"Oh?" A tiny smile—definitely smug, but also pleased—tugged at the corners of his mouth. "Truth be told," he breathed. That honey-coloured gaze slowly descended, visibly taking in everything in its path. "I also struggle a little with that. But I am certain we could..." His gaze flicked up, holding Dylan's. "...assist each other there."

How? The last time they had managed anything, they'd a completely different watch roster. Even then, he'd almost been caught by Marin. The only time they'd be alone together was when the one person he didn't want finding out was awake and alert.

Like now.

Authril was out there, somewhere. Patrolling with sword and shield in hand. No doubt ready to use either on anything she deemed a threat.

But the hound was right here. Warm. Solid. Irresistibly close.

Dylan grabbed the collar of Tracker's undershirt and dragged the man into kissing range, tipping forward enough to meet the hound's mouth halfway. *Just a taste.* Something to bring back the sweet dreams where Tracker danced for him.

Those soft, full lips swept over his, enthusiastically heeding his desire for more. Dylan slipped into Tracker's mouth to caress the man's tongue with his own.

The hound leant against him, the heave of their chests pressing them closer still. He deepened their kiss as one long-fingered hand slithered up Dylan's side and into his hair. With his other hand, Tracker tugged at the undertunic, seeking a way to lift it whilst the fabric was still pinned by Dylan's weight.

Without giving it another thought, Dylan raised his hips enough for the lower half to come free with the man's next tug, then broke their kiss to remove the undertunic entirely. Tracker followed suit, barely pausing to shed his undershirt, before launching himself at Dylan.

Bare skin hit bare skin. They tipped to the ground in a mess of tangled limbs, open kisses and breathless laughter.

Tracker straddled him, grinding their hips together. Even through the leather of the hound's trousers, his growing arousal was palpable. But rather than remove the impediment to something far more pleasurable, he opted to kiss and nibble his way along Dylan's neck.

Dylan tipped his head to one side, giving the man full access. The hound's pronounced fangs grazed his neck, pricking almost to the point of injury with each suck. His magic buzzed, the latent healing undoing the row of marks Tracker left along his skin almost as soon as they were made.

The hound reached the hollow in his throat and sucked.

Moaning, Dylan grabbed Tracker's rear, digging his fingers into the leather. His arms jerked of their own accord, trying to drag the hound closer.

There was a muffled grunt as Tracker's body slid up, then his head slipped past Dylan's ear to hit the ground. A soft hiss spoke of brief pain. Tracker sat back, rubbing his face. "Easy. I would prefer not coming away from this night with a broken nose."

"Sorry." Dylan ran a consoling hand up the hound's chest, pulling away when his fingers reached the man's sternum and Tracker flinched. "What happened?" He certainly couldn't be the cause of any injury there.

"This did." The hound lifted the small, rune-carved piece of wood dangling from Dylan's neck. Tilting his head to one side allowed a thin gleam of firelight coming through a crack in the tent flap to hit the pendant. "This rune, if I recall correctly, you said it was an ancient protection symbol." He rubbed his thumb over the carving, a wry smile skewing his lips. "A fitting want, I suppose, considering how we always manage to find trouble. Not that you need a protection charm."

He chuckled. "They don't actually work." If that had ever been the case, then Udynea could've been stopped years ago. "Besides, I have something far more reliable at hand than a piece of carved wood."

"You refer to your magic, yes? I am aware of how well it protects you."

"No," Dylan breathed, his gaze drifting to the hound's midsection. The inked designs flowed along his muscles, accentuating them, teasing the eye to look lower and discover what was hidden below his belt. No scars, though. He had felt them on the hound's back, but they were absent on the front. "I don't mean that at all." He propped himself up enough to caress the man's cheek. "I mean *you*."

The soft hitch of Tracker's breath was loud in the otherwise quiet of the tent. He ducked his head and the faintest hint of heat flushed the cheek still pressed to Dylan's palm. "Flatterer," he mumbled. The soft, wet brush of the man's lips alighted on the heel of Dylan's hand.

Dylan sat up, cupping the back of the hound's head as he reached up for a kiss. Their lips met, soft at first, but steadily returning to its original heat. Coaxing pressure on his shoulders had him being pushed back onto the blankets.

Tracker abandoned the kiss to plant more down Dylan's chest whilst the man's fingers picked at the tie holding Dylan's smallclothes fast. Loosened, Dylan aided the hound in stripping him of the last of his clothes.

Once Dylan was naked, the hound wasted little time in teasing. He enveloped Dylan's length with such speed and ferocity that it took all of Dylan's willpower not to cry out. Still, Tracker continued to greedily suck, moaning.

Then, just as Dylan was certain he would slip over the edge, Tracker let him fall free of his mouth.

Dylan waited, each of the man's shallow breaths upon his skin stoking the fire of anticipation burning in his gut.

And yet, Tracker remained unmoving.

He wasn't usually one to tease like this. What was he waiting for? Had he heard something?

Dylan held his breath to listen and heard nothing. He was well aware of how vastly superior elven hearing was to that of either human or dwarf, but he hadn't really put much thought into how well they could hear. "*Where* did you say Authril was?" he whispered.

Tracker laughed softly, warming Dylan's groin with his breath. "Far from here."

"Right, of course she is." The hound wouldn't just kneel there like a statue if Authril had returned. There was no telling what she would do upon finding Tracker bent over him like this, but it would likely involve blades.

Tracker sat back to run a considering eye over him. "Still afraid of being caught?"

"A little," he admitted. There was always a chance she hadn't heard them during the times he had slunk into Tracker's tent, especially when all but one had been merely to sleep. But with her awake, whilst they were in the tent he shared with no one? If she hadn't known before, it wouldn't take much for her to find out.

Disappointment flashed across his face, vanishing as the hound sucked at his teeth. "Perhaps it is for the best. This was…" His gaze slid over Dylan, carnal need darkening his eyes. "…ill-thought out. Another time, yes?"

Time. He was short on that. "When?"

The man's mirth exploded in a flash of fangs and a blast of barely contained laughter. "My, we *are* eager." He chuckled for a few breaths more before meeting Dylan's gaze. "And serious." All at once, the smile fell. He cleared his throat. "Forgive me if I broke the mood. That was not my intention. I—" He gave an irritated huff. "I suppose we could wait for her to fall asleep."

Whilst that sounded like a far better plan than doing anything here and now… "That's not what I meant. Exactly how many chances do I—do *we*—have left? How much time? How many days before Whitemeadow? Before Wintervale? Before…"

Before he wasn't able to choose anything. Not where he went. Not who he fought. Not who he shared a bed with.

Wordlessly clasping Dylan's fingers, Tracker closed his eyes as he lifted the same hand to his lips. He sat there for several breaths— warm, slow exhalations that heated more than Dylan's knuckles.

When he spoke again, it was soft, reluctant, lacking any of the passion Dylan had come to expect from the man. "It will be roughly a week before we reach Whitemeadow. I cannot be certain until we reach the outer farmlands. Wintervale is likely to take another half a month." He opened his eyes, their depths bearing a sadness that dug into Dylan's chest and stole the moisture from his mouth. "We have time."

Dylan ran his tongue across his lips, the abrupt dryness doing little. "Or we could be quick," he suggested light-heartedly. He was already naked. It wouldn't take much to get him back to where he'd been.

One side of Tracker's mouth twitched into the ghost of a smile. He gave Dylan's fingers a final kiss before relinquishing his hold. "Perhaps it is better if we do not tempt fate tonight. You would prefer for our dear warrior to not learn of us, and *I* have no desire to spend the rest of our travels squabbling with her if she did."

The hound already clashed with Authril enough for their bickering to be a daily expectation. He couldn't imagine it getting any worse without the verbal blows turning physical, and they both had to be aware that he needed them to get anywhere near Wintervale alive.

Yet, he couldn't deny the acerbic lilt to Tracker's words whenever he spoke with the warrior was growing more pronounced as of late.

"Are you jealous of her?" The question was out before he'd a chance to consider it. He sat there, silently cursing himself. *Of all the foolhardy things to ask.* But what else was there? Tracker definitely didn't like her and Dylan doubted the hound was afraid of her.

"Jealous?" The laughter that left the man's lips veered onto the softer side of nervous. "My dear man, I have never been jealous in my life. What is there to be jealous of? Her fighting prowess?" He sneered. "Mediocre at best."

"I was thinking more intimate reasons." The hound knew Dylan had been sleeping with Authril. That it had started well before their encounter in Toptower. He didn't recall Tracker giving any indication of caring about it, not until learning the truth behind her actions. He even seemed fine with Dylan covertly seeking his presence, at least, now that he knew the reason.

Had he misread the man?

The grin Tracker flashed carried the same sharpness it did when speaking with Authril. "After hearing how utterly you denied her?"

He had tried to push those moments from his mind. It might've been less than a fortnight since the last attempt, but he hadn't exactly been enthusiastic about her insistence in the nights prior. Even when those nights came before learning the real reasons behind her pursuit of him.

"You do not wish to pre-emptively change the nature of your relationship with her, do you? Perhaps solidify her place as your warden?" He rocked back onto his heels, a wisp of disgust tilting his lips. "If that is so, then we need not pursue this fun of ours any further."

Dylan's chest constricted as if he were back in his nightmares of being sucked underground. *Stupid.* It wasn't the first time he'd heard those words. He knew what this was. *Mindless fun.* Just as sex always had been. Tracker had said as much in the beginning. No point trying to attach anything bigger to it.

"But if returning to her side was your intention," the hound continued. "Then I do not see why you would choose to initiate anything between us now."

"I don't..." Whatever went on between her and him may have to start anew once they reached Wintervale, but he was far more aware that anything he had with the hound would stop at the same time. He didn't want to think about either prospect. Not now. Not ever. "I don't want her that way."

"I thought not," Tracker breathed. He slunk up Dylan's body, not quite touching as he coaxed Dylan to lie back. Their lips brushed together.

Dylan arched beneath the hound, relishing the warmth such contact gifted him. His breath hitched at the chilling bite of the man's belt buckle kissing his abdomen. He grasped Tracker's rear. There was no fumbling to find it, his hands simply knew where to land. Dylan rocked against the hound, groaning at the raw sensation of leather against his skin. It wasn't as good as the man's mouth, but if Tracker wasn't prepared to finish him another way, this would do.

Then, just as he was about to fully relinquish himself to mindless action, Tracker broke the kiss. "She is very possessive of you."

"I know," he gasped. His hips still moved of their own accord. Did the man not realise how close he was? Surely, they could talk after.

"Do you think she would still let you slink your way into my bed if she knew?"

Dylan chewed on his bottom lip. Thinking with half of his thoughts swamped in pleasure wasn't easy. He had already made up his mind about the tent—even if he wasn't yet sure how the others would react—but he hadn't voiced his intentions to the hound. *Now's as good as ever.* He took a deep breath. "Actually, I—"

The hurried crash of something barrelling through the undergrowth froze his tongue. The unmistakable clash of steel meeting shield echoed into the night.

"Bandits!" Authril roared. "To arms!"

The call was like being doused in icy water, with a similar

reaction. *You have got to be kidding me.* No chance of it being a joke. Not with the shadows of other people dancing around the fire.

Tracker dove for the tent flap. There was the flash of firelight, the grunt of someone dying just outside, then the hound was out into the fray.

Dylan scrambled to dress. He wrestled with his smallclothes, already drawing forth his power to unleash on the first unsuspecting foe.

The tear of canvas preceded the arrival of one such unfortunate man. The bandit careened into him, sending them both to the ground. The tent fell around them, burning as Dylan let forth with a blast of fire. A pulse of air in the man's direction had him flying across the clearing, still screaming from the burns.

He took in the rest of the fighting. It seemed to be a small group, likely thinking they could sneak up on the camp whilst everyone slept. *They couldn't have waited another minute?* Most of them had their hands full with the two elves. They wouldn't be any trouble for much longer.

One of the bandits abandoned his companions to run at him, his axe raised high.

Lightning streamed from Dylan's fingers. It hit his target square in the chest.

The bandit collapsed, still twitching.

He turned from the dead man in search of his next target. *Not even half a minute?*

A woman leapt from the bushes. Her feet barely touched the ground before he flung her into a tree. Gods, he'd been that close that five more *seconds* likely would've sufficed.

Pain lanced across his side. Crying out, he fell to his knees as an arrow flew over his head. He clutched the wound. It was healing but, by the gods, it burned. Dylan threw up a shield. *Idiot!* He should've realised there'd be more where that woman had come from.

He glanced up in time to see an arrow shatter on his shield. Another arrow, flying in the opposite direction, greeted its call. Marin had entered the fight.

"Dylan!" Tracker knelt before him. His hand passed through the small bubble of his shield, sending tiny pinprick shocks racing along Dylan's body. Long fingers lifted his head until he was staring into twin pools of concern. "Are you all right?"

"I'm fine," he managed through clenched teeth. "Help the others." He braced himself as the hound's arm slid out from the shield.

A handful of bandits bearing swords and axes poured from the bushes. Tracker rushed at them, the quarterstaff tucked behind him. He swung his arm as the bandits closed around him, sweeping one off their feet and clocking another in the head. He ducked one man's swing, driving the end of the pole into the bandit's neck, and picked up the man's fallen sword. The rest of them fell back pretty quickly after that.

"Mercy!" one of them screamed, throwing down their weapon and running for the undergrowth.

Like a giant mouser, the hound followed and the bandit fell with one swift strike.

Tracker returned to the middle of camp, his gaze running over the fallen. "A terribly ill-balanced weapon," he muttered, throwing the borrowed sword to one side. "That is all of them, yes?"

Dylan stood there, clutching his now-healed side, his mouth agape. He couldn't tear his eyes from Tracker's half-clothed form. His heart pounded from watching the man fight, but the way the hound's bare chest still heaved set his pulse on a completely different rhythm.

"Does anyone need healing?" he finally mumbled.

At the silence, he tore his gaze from the panting hound to the others.

They appeared frozen in place, the majority of them staring. Katarina cocked an eyebrow at him and was definitely smirking. Marin had covered her eyes whilst Authril looked like rage incarnate.

He turned to Tracker for some explanation to find the hound was picking through the remains of Dylan's tent. The man returned in a matter of moments, holding a bundle of cloth.

"There is no need to stare." He flapped the length of linen, unfurling what was definitely Dylan's undertunic and concealing Dylan in one smooth movement. "It is perfectly natural. Happens when emotions are high and nothing gets the blood pumping like a night-time ambush. The body merely does not know how to react." He flashed his teeth at Authril in what Dylan guessed was supposed to be a grin. "You were part of a mercenary company, surely, you noticed it amongst the novices, yes?"

Dylan snatched the garment from the man, suddenly painfully aware of how naked he was and... *Gods*... How swiftly the sight of a panting, half-naked man could arouse him. *No*. This wasn't how he wanted this to happen. *No, no, no*. He hadn't wanted any of this out in the open and now... *She knows*. They all knew. *Shit!*

Hunching his shoulders, Dylan closed his eyes and waited for their scorn.

"*You*," Authril growled.

Dylan risked a peek through his lashes to find her poisonous glare fixed on Tracker.

"I warned you not to touch him. You just couldn't help yourself, could you?"

A thin thread of relief eased the twisting in his gut. She was angry, rightfully so, but not at him? He hadn't exactly been an unwilling partner in his little horizontal dance with the hound.

Tracker spread his hands wide. "You misunderstand, my dear woman. What you saw was not what you believe."

"I *misunderstand*?" Authril echoed, her voice shrill. She stood before the hound, her mouth curved into an unnaturally wide smile. "Are you trying to tell me I *didn't* see your half-dressed form darting out of *his* tent? The *same* tent he was apparently naked in?"

"I make no such suggestions as to what you saw, only that my reason for being there was benign. I am dressed thusly because I was up relieving myself. I admit to being in his tent, but the reason behind that is equally as simple. He was having a nightmare. I merely sought to wake him before he burnt down the tent. Or would you have preferred returning from patrol to find him immolated by his own flames? Believe me, it was close."

The gaze Authril affixed upon the hound bordered on murderous.

Dylan turned from her, scarcely able to breathe whilst knowing she was judging his every movement, trying to tease out the truth.

As for the others...

His stomach dropped. *Shit.* He turned to Marin and Katarina, unable to look either in the face. Whilst the warrior was clearly more upset over *why* he was naked than him being that way, she had at least consented to seeing him in such a state in the past. "I am so sorry. I—"

"It's all right," Katarina said.

"I really mean it." He wasn't a prude. Quite a number of women had seen everything—and more men than he really cared to count—but this... *Gods*... This wasn't the bathing chamber or some intimate affair. He hadn't been looking to put everything on display, certainly not for those who weren't interested. All he'd been after was a few more moments with Tracker to...

Have fun.

Something in his core knotted. He wasn't sure if his heart was about to give out or he would merely vomit. Maybe both.

"It's more sausage than I was ever planning on seeing," Marin added, the strained note in her voice one of someone who spoke merely to fill the silence. "But you'd have to be some sort of elven Oracle to know we'd be attacked."

One piece of her rambling tweaked at his curiosity enough to keep himself from being sick. "Oracle?" She hadn't mentioned them much in the past. Only one person she would've heard anything definitive from. "Been listening to hedgewitch tales at night?"

"*What?*" Her eyes widened a fraction before darting towards the dwarf. "No! I just..." She dragged the tail of her hair over her shoulder, fussing with the tussled strands as though they were of greater interest. "You know... hear things."

Katarina's bell-like laughter only seemed to deepen the other woman's flustered state. "She has. They both have." She smiled fondly at the hunter. "Marin has been an especially enraptured audience."

Marin cleared her throat. "Enough about that! I'm sure he has more pressing matters. Like his tent." She gestured to the collapsed shelter.

Between the fighting and his wound, he'd completely forgotten what had become of the tent. He knelt amongst the remains, gathering his possessions. Thankfully, the initial blast of his fire hadn't caught on much beyond his target. His clothes were intact, as was the bedding, if a little scorched.

The same couldn't be said for the tent, not when there was a gaping hole in one side.

He glared at the bodies littering their campsite. *Bloody bandits.* If they had just stayed away, none of this would've happened. He would've been in his tent, with or without the hound. He'd still *have* a tent.

Maybe if they'd a pelt to patch the area. A big one. Marin had skinned the deer on the first day, but she'd shown no interest in keeping the hide. Did that mean they hadn't the means to tan it? He didn't even know what was required.

His fingers brushed against the soft linen of the hound's undershirt. He hurriedly tucked the article in the folds of his robe. No amount of talking would convince anyone of it being innocently discarded.

Tracker halted at his side, laying a consoling hand atop his shoulder. "Fortunate we lost nothing that coin cannot replace. Although..." Grimacing, he gestured to the tattered remains. "It would seem that our dear spellster shall be bunking with me until Whitemeadow."

Authril screwed up her nose and gave a loud sniff as she also examined the damage. "I don't see him putting up with you for long, even if it isn't too far." Her gaze flicked his way. She said nothing further, but disapproval radiated from her like the echoes of a distant gong.

Dylan buried his face in his hands, his cheeks burning against his palms. She would have questions for him. He knew it. There was no chance she believed Tracker's tale of half-truths either. *Shit.*

What would she demand of him? Insist they once more shared a tent whilst the hound slept elsewhere? Would she refuse to leave his side, trail his every move like a relentless shadow? Always watching. Suspecting the worst in the smallest of gestures.

He clapped a hand over his mouth, unsure whether his heart might burst from it if he didn't. His skin felt raked by dozens of fine needles, each one shocking him to the bone. He shook with every ragged breath sucked through his nose. *More.* He couldn't breathe. The very air was stifling.

The long fingers resting on his shoulder tightened their grip.

He glanced up at the hound, meeting that concerned gaze through the shimmering film of his shield.

Tracker withdrew his hand as he knelt, the prickling on Dylan's skin vanishing the instant his fingers exited the barrier. "Steady yourself," he whispered, patting his chest and exaggerating the act of breathing. "Slowly."

He closed his eyes and followed the hound's directions. Bit by bit, his body obeyed. The tremors stopped, the thundering in his chest gradually became a less frenzied rhythm, and the hectic pace of his breathing evened out.

Letting out one last shuddering breath, he dissipated his shield and once more faced Tracker.

Those honey-coloured eyes were still dark with the man's unease. "Better?"

Not really. He no longer felt like he would explode at any moment, but he did feel weaker than using his magic could account for. He couldn't even be sure he'd the means to stand right now.

Not willing to trust his voice wouldn't give the truth away, he settled on answering the man with a simple nod.

Tracker's worried frown deepened. He glanced over his shoulder, watching the others who had moved on to check the dead, before turning back and speaking in the same low voice, "You did nothing wrong."

A fresh flood of tears blurred his vision. He pressed his lips together, keeping them in place with his teeth. *Don't think about it.* If he did for a second longer, he would become a sobbing mess.

"You want to *leave*?" Marin's question cut through the torrent of his thoughts. She crouched beside one of the dead men, her hand closed on the shaft of the arrow jutting from his chest and her attention on Authril. "When the moon isn't even up yet?"

"That's the choice, isn't it?" the hedgewitch added whilst nudging the same dead man with her boot. "Break camp in the dark or risk the possibility of these bandits having equally dangerous friends who will look for them."

"I am all for breaking camp," Tracker replied, getting to his feet. "I would even go so far as to suggest we wipe all trace of our occupation before returning to the roadside."

"At night?" Dylan managed, his face growing hot as the words left in a wet croak.

The hound's smile carried a little too much sympathy for his tastes. "It is not the greatest option in itself, but do not fear we will be stumbling blind. Between Katarina, Authril and myself, we will see well enough under starlight to guide you and Marin."

"And what of the jerky?" Marin demanded. "A few pieces might be ready, but we'll be leaving so much."

"It cannot be helped, but we survived without such nourishment this far, we can continue for a little longer. Lingering would be a foolish move." The hound gently shook Dylan's shoulder. "Come, my dear man, you can finish getting dressed in my tent."

Nodding, Dylan tucked his clothes under his arm—concealing Tracker's undershirt amongst them—and made for the last bastion of privacy. At least with them on the move and remaining silent, he would have some time to figure out what he was going to say when Authril's inevitable questioning came. *This is going to be a long night.*

CHAPTER 20

Dylan lay on his side, blindly staring at the inner wall of Tracker's tent. Although, he supposed it was technically *their* tent, now. He hadn't bothered to undress, nor even seek out the blankets. Between the fighting, the sleepless night and the wandering through the cold… even removing his boots seemed too big of an ask for his body.

After uprooting the two intact tents, gathering what food they could and leaving the campsite for the road—a task that had taken far longer with the moon opting to remain hidden behind dark clouds—they set about putting distance between them and the dead bandits.

Even the sun failed to make a proper appearance by the time dawn rolled around, hiding behind clouds that threatened rain but never delivered. They had left their old campsite far behind by then, not enough to have found a suitable spot.

The consensus had been to continue on. Which led him to here.

Part of him knew he should be at least attempting some degree of sleep before taking over the watch. But now his body was still, his mind wouldn't stop racing long enough for him to settle.

They knew Tracker had been in his tent. Authril had seen him naked and erect just at the sight of the man's half-clothed form. *She doesn't know.* Not with any certainty. But even if she accepted the hound's innocent explanation, she *suspected*.

And if she found out the hound had *lied*? That could only lead to one place.

Supervision. Command. *Control.*

His heart leapt, its quickening pulse clogging his throat. He scrunched into a ball, drawing armfuls of the bedding into a pillow beneath his head. The hound's scent permeated the blankets. He buried his face into it and tried to steady his breath, letting the notes of cinnamon, citrus and natural musk swirl about his scenes.

It was all his fault. As much as a cowardly part of him would like to shift the full blame to Tracker, the guardians always said it took two to make a bed.

If he had dismissed Tracker's advances, kept himself nice and safe following the same rules he'd used within the tower. Then the hound's explanation wouldn't have been some half true and Authril...

She'd probably still be suspicious.

Finally gathering enough strength to lift his head, he sluggishly marked the absence of a certain hound. Tracker should've entered to sleep by now. What was taking the man so long? It wasn't his turn to be on watch. Just as, technically, Dylan shouldn't be seeking sleep. Authril had insisted on taking the first watch, leaving the rest of them to slumber, a choice that the other two women had immediately taken advantage of.

Had Tracker been held up by other reasons? The world beyond these canvas walls seemed silent, which omitted a heated discussion with Authril. Perhaps the hound also patrolled somewhere outside. *Probably checking no one followed us.* He had seemed intent on hiding their passage whilst leaving their last camp.

The tent flap stirred and a figure slipped through. There came the muted jingle of a belt being undone, followed by the rustle of discarded clothes. "I thought you would be asleep by now," Tracker murmured as he also settled atop the blankets.

"Couldn't," Dylan mumbled, surprised his voice sounded steady. But with the hound's familiar warmth soaking through his back and those long fingers idly caressing his hip, the tension in his body slowly melted.

He pressed against that solid presence, feeling his heart slow, his muscles relax. He closed his eyes, hoping that the familiarity would lull him to sleep as it had done on so many nights he had sought the man's platonic comfort.

No such luck.

The man's arm fell from Dylan's hip to wrap around his waist. Tracker lay still for some time, with only his harsh breath to let Dylan know the hound hadn't fallen asleep. "I am not sure if knowing helps, but..." The man took a deep breath that had Dylan immediately wishing the tent was light enough for him to make out the hound's expression. "You have managed the past day remarkably well."

Had he? It certainly hadn't felt like it.

Still, hearing such praise warmed him more than blankets ever could. A bubble of mirth popped out his mouth. "I thought my heart was going to explode."

"I was certain your magic would." His embrace tightened. "Just as I believed our dear warrior was looking to add another corpse to the pile."

That wasn't much of an exaggeration. Right now, she appeared to be only angry at Tracker, but soon enough, she would come to her senses and realise that her focus shouldn't be on the hound at all.

"She wasn't supposed to find out this way," Dylan mumbled. *I should've told her sooner.* Perhaps not directly after the tower, but certainly as soon as he started regularly sharing the man's tent, regardless of the innocent reasons behind it. He should've put a stop to sleeping with her sooner, too. That was what any normal person outside the tower would've done.

Tracker hummed, the vibration running through Dylan's chest. "I will admit to some confusion. I thought you were upset they saw you naked."

Dylan eyed the tent flap with some consternation. "That too. It's just…" He scratched at his forearm as the words died on his tongue. "I've never been that exposed before, not outside the bathing chamber, anyway." That he'd been at full mast hadn't exactly improved things. Clearing his throat, he let his hand fall to one side and thwack against the blankets. "I'm certain you'd prefer to sleep rather than listen to me whine."

"If it would help in pacifying your fears…"

"I don't know." He couldn't see how anything anyone did could possibly help. It wasn't as if he could avoid the others for the rest of the journey. He would simply have to weather everyone suspecting the truth of what he really got up to when he was meant to be sleeping.

Tracker shifted, his warmth vanishing from Dylan's side. In the gloom, Dylan made out the man's silhouette leaning over him. "But there is more to it than the nakedness, yes? You still fear she believes we lied."

He rolled over until he faced the man, drawing the hound into his arms. "We *did* lie." It didn't matter that he hadn't said a word. He had let the hound spout half-truths. "She's planning on becoming my warden." She was definitely acting more and more as though she already was. "When we get to the army, when I'm leashed…" He swallowed, sure he felt cold metal against his throat. "I'll have to rely on her for *everything* and I can't even trust her reaction to knowing the truth."

Sighing, Tracker resumed his previous position alongside Dylan, those long fingers linking with his. "If you would prefer, we could always go on ahead. Leave the others to make their own way once we reach Whitemeadow?"

He bit his lip. "I can't leave Authril behind." They'd already agreed that doing so wouldn't bode well for him upon reaching the capital, especially if Katarina was to part ways with them at Whitemeadow.

He needed the warrior's report to help confirm that he'd been one of the army's leashed spellsters and not a Udynean spy.

"Of course," Tracker muttered. "I simply wish there was more I could do. It has been such a trivial thing to me for so long and I... Well, I hate to see you like this. There is no reason for you to go through it alone."

Dylan pulled the hound closer, planting a kiss on the man's forehead. "Thank you," he whispered. "I think I'll be fine." Eventually. Swallowing the idea that they'd all seen him naked would leave him blushing for a few days. As for the rest...

He had wrapped his mind around the reality of finding men attractive. More-or-less. More around the man himself. Less so with others. But it couldn't be *that* big of a leap into accepting everyone else knew.

Could it?

"Besides," he said, trying to sound more light-hearted than he felt. "I think it's *you* that Authril wants to skewer right now."

Tracker's soft laughter shook them. "She will get over it, I am certain. We could always invite her to join us? She could keep a close eye on you, and I on her."

"Not unless you want to wake up dead."

The hound hummed. "Is that a challenge?"

"Track..."

Again, the man shook with laughter, this time silently. He lifted Dylan's hand, pressing his lips against the back. "I am joking. Why would I seek her favour when I already have you sleeping right here? And speaking of sleep—"

"I don't think I can." What sort of nightmares waited behind his eyes? Should he even bother when it would be his turn to take watch soon? How long had they been talking, anyway?

The barely felt brush of fingertips caressed Dylan's jaw. "My dear man," Tracker breathed. "Do you think I am blind? You have not slept well for some nights now and to use your magic in such a poor state..." Tracker wriggled out of Dylan's arms, wrapping his limbs around Dylan like a four-legged spider and tucking Dylan's head against the hound's chest. "All I ask is that you try," he whispered, stroking Dylan's hair. "Even if it is only for a little while. I will be right here when you wake."

Dylan wordlessly closed his eyes as the low hum of a lullaby vibrated through the man's chest. Maybe with Tracker right here, the nightmares wouldn't find him.

He didn't know how long he laid in Tracker's arms, drifting in and out of sleep, never falling deep enough for dreams to find him. A mixed blessing, given that it also meant he wouldn't get the rest his body sorely needed.

"Dylan?" a voice whispered.

He tried to sit up, only to find much of his body pinned beneath the hound's weight. Craning his neck allowed him to see the tent entrance. Moonlight illuminated a figure standing there. *Authril.*

She scratched at the canvas, seemingly hesitant to enter. "Tracker?"

Dylan slowly extracted himself from Tracker's grasp, carefully unwinding the hound's legs from his own.

Tracker stirred. His head lifted from where it was pillowed on his arm. "Dyl—?"

"Hush," Dylan whispered, his fingers absent-mindedly trailing along the man's shoulder. "Go back to sleep." When he was certain the hound wouldn't wake, he slunk out into the night air, rubbing at his arms.

It appeared to be just the two of them awake, the warrior likely falling back to the old watch schedule to give everyone more of a chance to sleep. Due to everyone's weariness, they hadn't originally set up a fire. Authril had amended that, although it was far smaller than the one they'd left behind.

He hunched over the pile of barely burning embers, giving the flames a little nudge into life. The fire flickered begrudgingly before obeying. His gaze slid to the forest. The underbrush didn't seem that thick here, but perhaps he could forage enough fallen wood to build up the fire for the next person's time on watch.

"So..." Authril said as she sat next to him, the soft creaks and jingles of her armour loud in the relative stillness.

Despite himself, Dylan winced. He had rather hoped she would seek her blankets and give him time to think.

"Is what he said true? He was just waking you from a nightmare?"

"Yes." As bitter as the lie was on his tongue, he couldn't help but lean on Tracker's words, to deny anything further had happened between him and the hound.

Her gaze slid to where the hound currently slumbered. "I guess the point is moot. We are down a tent and you can hardly squeeze in with the rest of us." She turned back to him. "But it doesn't answer *why* you were already naked. I know you don't sleep that way."

He shrugged, his mind working furiously to come up with a logical reason. "I honestly don't know what to say. When I awoke, the inside of the tent was sweltering." His bedding had also been thrown partially aside. "I must've undressed in my sleep in a bid to cool down."

"I don't recall you being that restless. Nor were you having nightmares when I shared your tent."

He chewed on his lip. If he wasn't careful, he would expose the full reality. "I was." Not with the same intensity, but there was a marked difference between witnessing his fellow soldiers dying and seeing his home turned into a slaughterhouse.

"You never mentioned it."

"I planned to, I swear, I just—" Sighing, he ran his fingers through his hair. "It never felt that important to bother anyone with."

Authril stared at him for some time, her gaze piercing even in the low light. "He isn't—" She froze, holding up a forefinger before glancing around. In a lower tone, she continued, "He's not forcing you to service him, is he?"

"We are *not* having sex," he hissed. They might've gotten that far if they hadn't been interrupted by bandits. "Didn't you hear him the other day? I'm not his type."

Her eyes narrowed, darkening the sea-green hue. "But you want to be?" He caught her wry smirk in the measly firelight. "You could've told me you preferred men. I guess that explains your ogling in the brothel and your declining interest in me during the weeks since." She raised a querying brow at him. "Or does him being an elf override what's in our smallclothes?"

Dylan gawped at her. *By the gods, not her as well.* Why did everyone think he cared whether or not the people he slept with had pointed ears? He knew some elven folk preferred to stick with their own, but he'd never heard of humans chasing them exclusively. Was that outlook universal to the kingdom? "Excuse me?"

She shrugged. "You wouldn't be the first to believe that just because he's elven, it doesn't count as being with a man."

"No, it's not—" He fumbled to find the right words whilst gabbling incoherently. Digging his fingers into his hair and tugging helped in remaining calm. "I-I've been with a great deal of humans, too, thank you." He listened to the words pouring out his mouth and groaned. "That came out wrong. I mean, the bigger percentage of women I've lain with, which is not a massive amount overall, have been human... And that wasn't much better, was it?" He flopped onto the ground, his arms spread. "Just bury me here, if you please. I think I've dug the hole deep enough." If he kept this up, he was going to hit bedrock.

"Is it *just* women you've lain with?"

"Yes." The word left his lips before he could stop to think. *Strange.* Not that, after all the years of deceiving himself, speaking the lie came so readily. Never before had it left a twinge of shame tugging at his core. Professing that he hadn't slept with Tracker was almost as bad as denying he found the hound attractive.

Dylan sat up. If only he could trust her reaction wouldn't be volatile. "I'm sorry."

Her nose scrunched in confusion. "What for?"

He ducked his head, hoping the light was dim enough to hide his burning cheeks. "You're taking the idea of him having done something remarkably easy." He thought she'd be rather more upset at him, even suspicious that he was hiding the truth as she clearly was about Tracker's words. "Considering we were... you know."

"What? Lovers?" She shook her head, a small laugh tweaking the corners of her mouth. "Tracker was right, we have no agreement that it'd be just us." A sneer trembled along her lips. "*But* as much as I want a reason to hurt the bastard after I told him not to touch you, I believe you that he hasn't attempted anything. If I ever find out he has, though, I..." Her rambling devolved into swearing and muttered threats. The words were hushed, but most definitely not ones to use in polite company.

Dylan remained silent. Everything he'd ever read suggested people beyond the tower took a dim view of the casual way intimacy was handled within the walls. The hound's actions had muddied that belief, but he realised that maybe Tracker had been the outlier in such matters rather than the norm.

Eventually, she calmed down. "Even then, I'm just a soldier and you're a spellster who's fated to be leashed." There was a coldness to the words. And sharpness, like a jagged piece of ice. "I enjoyed your company, but we are destined to be bound as warden and spellster."

He grunted. "I had hoped we could still remain friends." Even the hound considered him as such and he had already lost so many. People he had shared his life with. His fears. His secrets. All gone.

"Perhaps it would be best to keep things professional." Taking a deep breath, she got to her feet. "I'll leave you to your watch. Be sure to call out if you spot anything suspicious."

"Sleep well," he murmured, bowing his head.

He waited for some time after she had disappeared into the tent before beginning his check of the perimeter. His mind would not stop buzzing, dividing his focus between the task at hand and how he was going to deal with everyone knowing Tracker had been in his tent, that he now shared the hound's, that everyone had seen him *naked*.

His watch proved rather less eventful than Authril's. He spent much of it gathering bits of wood for the fire. When the time came to wake Katarina, he stuck his head into the tent the women shared, taking great pains to only disturb the hedgewitch.

Dylan paced outside the tent whilst he waited for her to emerge. He barely gave her time to be properly orientated to their surroundings before turning on his heel and scuttling back to Tracker's side. At least he knew the hound wouldn't have awkward questions for him.

~ ~ ~

The ending stretch of night remained peaceful. It always seemed that way to Tracker. Just as the sky felt the darkest before the sun made its presence known on the horizon, so too did those few hours always appear the quietest. The nightlife stilling to a hush as they sought slumber and the creatures dominating the day not yet stirring.

As had become the usual morning routine, Katarina was the first to appear. She stretched and mumbled words in her native tongue that he assumed were some sort of morning prayer to whatever deities the dwarves worshipped.

"My dear," he called out once she had finished her ritual, gesturing for her to join him by the forest's edge and far from the tents. "If I may speak with you before the others awaken."

She did as he asked, hugging herself as she halted beneath the bower of a pine. "Unlike Authril, I don't need any further explanations for last night. I'm well aware of the danger posed by a spellster having nightmares and that it is fortunate you were able to wake him before disaster beset us all."

He inclined his head. A thread of relief unravelled from around his chest. After promising to not speak a word about Dylan's sexual preference before the man was ready, he had feared his lack of control last night had broken that dam beyond repair. "This is more of a hedgewitch matter. I know your people take in those who have been abandoned, especially the young, and I was wondering if—" He fell silent as she held up a hand. Glancing towards the tents told him no one else had awoken, but he couldn't have much time.

"As much as I would like to," Katarina said. "I can't make any claim towards Dylan. Even if he wasn't past the cut-off age, we are still within Demarn's borders. And I'm certain Authril would object."

All this, he knew. However, hearing her regret at the situation gave him hope. Getting Dylan out of the kingdom would be easier with a hedgewitch on his side. "I actually wished to enquire about animals. Say... a warhorse? Mine, specifically."

Her face scrunched with her confusion. "You have a warhorse and opted not to bring it with you?"

"It was hardly a *choice*. He ran afoul of a Udynean spellster back at what remained of the army encampment, caught the brunt of the attack." He still wasn't certain whether Lullaby would've been better off if he hadn't been aboard. "He was alive when we left Toptower, but in no state to travel." With no way for those he had charged with caring for Lullaby to reliably maintain contact with them, he also had no chance of knowing whether the horse hadn't succumbed to his injuries.

"I see." She chewed on her lip, her gaze drifting off into the distance. "Having an animal cared for until its owner arrives to claim it isn't a typical ask, but if I sent a message, those at the border would do as requested. You would need to have someone bring him there. Although..." Her frown further creased her features, the scar slashed between her brows standing out like a path amongst the hills. "Why would you want him in Dvärghem?"

"Sentimental reasons," he confessed. "Even fully recovered, he would be no good for his original purpose, but I have had him for a very long time." Since Lullaby had been a gangly yearling that wouldn't have won any prizes in beauty or composition. The stable master had barely trained him to do more than follow on a lead line and had been practically ecstatic to be rid of a knock-kneed steed no one else wanted. Whilst the animal still wasn't the prettiest thing, the legs had straightened out and proven themselves powerful weapons. "I was hoping we could be reunited."

"*In* Dvärghem?" she repeated, a glint of suspicion coming to life in the hazel depths of her gaze. "Surely, you could return to Toptower without needing another reason. You know a King's Hound crossing the border, even if it wasn't to hunt, is against the treaty."

He did. The same could be said of a spellster, but he had sent plenty their way. "I had no intentions of entering your lands as a hound." Heading back to Toptower to reclaim Lullaby wouldn't have been a problem if all he had done was escort Dylan to the spellster tower. But now? If he got the man as far as the border, there was no guarantee he could return to Demarn without the pack hunting him. Even without another soul in tow, he doubted his ability to reach the town at the far end of the kingdom before being found out.

"Are you looking to retire in my homeland?"

Mirthless laughter bubbled in his throat. The only retirement for a hound was death. He might've been ready to accept that fate not too long ago, but his outlook on life had been reinvigorated as of late. "Not exactly."

Her eyes narrowed. "Then you plan to defect?"

Was he? "I..." He considered something along those lines before the army met their fate. Not as thoroughly as completely abandoning the land of his birth, but living out his years on the northern border where few spellsters were found came as close to retirement as he could get without breaking hound law or dwarven treaty.

His gaze drifted towards the tent he now shared with Dylan. His whole childhood had revolved around preparing him to hunt spellsters, to kill. To protect. Some hadn't given him an option to stay his blade, but there had always been a choice.

"The tower is gone. Our creed would dictate death as the only course of action to take when encountering a spellster, but most of them outside of the tower were children." He bowed his head. "I cannot obey such a law." There were already those amongst the pack who revelled in hunting down runaways and making their deaths as painful as possible. They'd likely have no qualms about taking the lives of the very children they escorted.

Just the thought of it made him sick.

Katarina grabbed his arm, pulling his attention back. "What of Dylan? If he arrives in Wintervale unleashed, what'll happen to him?"

Death. Maybe not at first, but it definitely would come far sooner than it should if he permitted the man to actually reach the capital. "Dylan is no rogue or foundling. He knows how to use his magic and has been trained to fight with it." Both things had led the man to being leashed the first time. "Once our dear would-be warden makes the army aware of that, they will want their weapon back."

He would not give them the chance to lay that claim.

CHAPTER 21

Dylan tucked the edges of his cloak tighter around him, peering through the screen of rain and low cloud. A pointless endeavour. There was no chance of seeing anything in this glaring light, not before the two elves walking at the head of their little group could spot it.

They had endured two days of this weather, although the pelting rain had subsided over the previous night. He almost wished it would return. This drizzling alternative they were forced to endure stuck to every surface rather than trickling off. No matter what he did, there was just no getting rid of it.

At least the nights weren't as cold as the last time he'd been caught in the rain. Having a full robe probably had something to do with that. Spending part of the night in Tracker's welcoming arms likely also helped keep the chill at bay. It was always so much warmer in the hound's tent than it had ever been in his own.

They still moved along with purpose despite the weather, largely thanks to the forest on the left side of the road having opened into farmland. *Civilisation.* The outer signs of it, at least. That meant there would be a farmhouse somewhere nearby, along with the prospect of shelter a little more robust than the canvas of Tracker's tent.

Whitemeadow itself was nowhere in sight.

He hadn't realised how far the tower was from everywhere else. They might've taken the journey from the tower slowly and halted their passage altogether for a few days, but it had still taken several weeks. A convoy of horse-drawn wagons bearing grain for the tower would've been no faster.

All the maps he'd seen made the distance between cities look so small, but the road seemed to stretch forever. Granted, the sudden deluge of rain had hindered them, making their usually brisk pace across a compacted dirt road into a trudge through mud.

He eyed the grassy fields, spying nothing out there, no people tending the land, no tilled ground ready for planting as he'd seen whilst passing other farms on their way to the tower. According to Tracker, Whitemeadow was still a handful of days away. What did these people grow so far from everything? Not the buckwheat that had served as the staple grain in the tower. He knew nothing about raising any animal beyond a mouser, but the stone fence sat mid-chest high at best. It didn't seem enough to keep anything in *or* out. Perhaps the ditch marking the edge of the road helped with the latter, but he still hadn't seen any sign of animals grazing.

Authril halted. She slapped the back of her hand against the hound's shoulder and pointed off to their left. Dylan peered in the indicated direction. A darker bulk sat in the murk, large and boxy. A building?

The elven duo halted on the roadside, waiting for them to catch up.

Tracker pulled down the scarf covering the bottom half of his face once they had. Even without the scarf, his face was well-hidden in shadow. Only the glint of his eyes could be made out. How the man managed to see anything with his head so thoroughly covered was rather beyond Dylan. The one thing that had united his elven friends had been their hatred of any cloth touching their ears. He supposed the hound considered woven wool the lesser evil when the alternative was frigid drops of water. "There is a barn none too far from here." He gestured to the shape in the gloom.

"I had hoped it was," Katarina said. "Do you think the owners will let us spend the night there?"

"Of course," Authril grumbled. "Because who wouldn't want an armed troop marching up after witnessing the horde that would've swept through here in the weeks prior? Not to mention one of them being an unleashed spellster."

She had a point. A farmer might have pity on any other group of sodden souls, but one harbouring a spellster? He could refrain from using magic easily enough. Maybe if he stayed at the back, kept his cloak closed to shield his army-issued attire.

Tracker's hooded head swung in the warrior's direction. "I am sure that, if given enough coin, they would be amenable towards overlooking certain traits. Come." The hound hopped the ditch and clambered over the fence.

Katarina stepped back into the middle of the road as the other two women nimbly followed Tracker's footsteps. "Is that wise? I don't think they'd look too kindly on us approaching from their fields."

Dylan halted on the other side of the ditch, his fingers digging into whatever purchase they could find amongst the wet, uneven stones.

"The other option is to wander the road in search of the normal way in," Tracker replied from his perch atop the fence. "Which I assume is pointed more in Whitemeadow's direction. You would like to get out of the rain sooner rather than later, yes?" He held out a hand to assist Dylan over.

Tossing his pack across the fence—an act made far easier thanks to the lack of a tent—Dylan reached for the hound's hand. He had barely gotten within range before the man neatly snaffled him around the waist to deposit him on the other side in one smooth motion.

Staunchly ignoring the heat blazing across his face, Dylan readjusted his robe. He had forgotten just how inconsequential the weight of his entire self seemed to be for the hound.

Behind him, Katarina had opted to follow, hitching up her skirts and leaping the ditch to clamber her own way over. "This is wrong," she mumbled.

"I will be sure to give them a little extra coin for our rudeness," the hound promised, laying a hand upon his chest.

They remained alert in their trudge across the fields towards the barn. Not only for other people, but on where they walked. Although there was no sign of any creatures, the field had housed them and evidence of their occupation remained.

Dylan absently lifted the hem of his robe to better see just where he was putting his feet, instantly regretting the action as the wet grass blades slapped against his boots and sent chill droplets of water flying up his legs.

Mercifully, the drizzling ebbed, turning to the occasional spot thudding against Dylan's cloak and vanishing completely by the time they reached a solid wooden fence separating the fields from the buildings. The grey clouds above still churned their threat of more, naught but empty promises for now. He hoped it stayed that way.

His gaze slid to the modest single-storey structure of the barn to the smaller farmhouse butting up against one side. None of it seemed occupied. The few windows showed no hints of light and, unlike the closed barn doors, the front door stood open to the weather.

Perhaps the people living here were out in the fields. Several of the spellsters who tended the tower garden had farming backgrounds and always said the weather had made little difference to their tasks.

Tracker slowed, his shoulders drooping for a moment before his entire posture grew square and stiff. "It would seem having our presence for a night is the least of their worries."

The others filed through a nearby gate, which had also been left wide open and likely explained the absence of any livestock. Dylan paused to peer at the barn. The people here had left every entrance swinging on its hinges, yet someone had gone to the trouble of securing the barn doors. "Do you think they abandoned this place?"

"Yes," Authril said. "And quickly."

"It would be more accurate to say they were driven out. See there?" Tracker pointed to a set of marks in the dirt. Rain had eroded the definition, but Dylan could make out bare and booted footprints. There were far more of the former, some haphazardly overlaid in places by hooves. "These markings are simply too many to belong to a handful of people, even if they were employing farmhands. An armed company visited these people."

Marin halted in the gateway to climb the railed fence. Perched on a post, she took in the ground around them. "Oh, shit."

"The Talfaltaners?" The words were out before Dylan could stop them. It wasn't really a question. What other armed company could've been out here? "How many? How long ago?"

"Several hundred, I would think," Tracker replied. "Quite recently." The hound's lips thinned as he arched a brow at Dylan, his pointed glare a warning to stay put.

Dylan shuffled on the spot. He wasn't about to go racing off alone, but if those people showed their faces, then he would ensure they joined their compatriots in whatever afterlife they believed in.

Marin walked up and down the fence, her focus entirely on the footprints. "I don't know about *recent*. Most of them look to have come from the road up north." She pointed to where the farm's main entrance, wide enough for a cart, joined up with the road they'd been travelling down. "Over a month ago, by the looks of things." She stared at the farmhouse's open door. "Doubt the people survived their arrival, the poor sods."

We're too late. Dylan bit his tongue to keep silent. It didn't matter that this household had likely been attacked weeks before the tower, being too late was becoming far too common an occurrence. Just once, he' would like to get somewhere in time to help, to stop more bloodshed.

Tracker wordlessly pointed out a patch of mud to the woman.

Marin hopped off the fence to crouch next to the group of markings. It appeared covered in footprints, just like the rest of the area. "*These* look fresher, a few days at most." She twisted, looking over her shoulder at the road, then out into the field. "Coming from the opposite way to all the others. Maybe even the same way we arrived."

The hound nodded, his hand closing around the hilt of his scimitar. "Even less uniform than the first attack. Not as numerous, though. I would say a good two dozen or so returned."

Dylan frowned. He thought he'd been imagining it, but the man's gaze kept drifting towards the barn. With the building's doors firmly closed, Dylan couldn't see anything that might draw the eye. Could Tracker hear something within? Or perhaps sense it in whatever way hounds did?

"Returned for what?" Marin queried. "They had the means and power to take everything the first time. If they left any food behind, it would've perished by now. The cattle were clearly driven elsewhere and probably filled their bellies on the first night." She returned to stare at the house, a little more critically. "I doubt they'd any valuables worth ransacking."

"We should move on," the hound murmured. Clearing his throat, in a much louder voice he added, "Staying here, even for the night, would be a bad idea."

"I agree," Marin said, clutching at her bow. She had unstrung the weapon at the first drop of rain. Now she fumbled in her belt pouch for the cord.

"Let's not get paranoid." Katarina held out her hands as if calming a group of children who had just witnessed one of them deliberately manifest magic. "You just said they ran these people out of their home, took off with their livestock and have vanished, which means they can't be here now. There is shelter—beds, if no one is truly here—right there. Are you seriously suggesting we walk away from all that?"

"That depends on how strong your desire to stay alive is, but yes," Tracker said.

The hedgewitch shook her head. "You are perhaps the most paranoid Nulled One I have ever travelled with."

The hound chuckled. "In my line of work, that is the only way you live to old age. Believe me, I would like nothing more than a comfortable bed to spend the night in, but this place has been compromised once already and I have no desire to be corralled by whoever could be near. If we stay, we risk being set upon by anyone who chooses to venture here."

"Then I will defer to your experience, but I still think it's foolish to walk away from perfectly good shelter."

"Can we wait long enough to rifle through their cupboards?" Authril asked. "There might be something left behind that could be useful."

The hound tipped his head to one side. "I doubt you will find anything of use, but if we are quick."

They entered the farmhouse somewhat hesitantly. Dylan expected to see carnage in the vein of what he had witnessed in the tower. Mercifully, the place was devoid of such a scene. Although the open door had allowed the rain to soak the dirt floor and wind-strewn debris piled anywhere it could. And it looked to have been that way for some time.

Much like the house itself, the doors to cupboards and wardrobes had been left swinging, much of their contents empty or broken. A few wicker baskets lay smashed where they had tumbled. A single chest lay on its back, the lid open and spilling its contents like a dead man's brain. There was no sign of beds or even bedding, although several gaps suggested where they might've been.

Only the woodbox near the fireplace seemed to stand where it belonged. And it, too, was bare.

So much for finding anything useful. Still, trying to remain optimistic, Dylan poked through some of the cupboards. Apart from an empty bottle that smelt strongly of whisky and little specks of evidence that spoke of mice, there was nothing. He closed the door in disgust. Perhaps they would have better luck searching the barn?

He had just opened his mouth to suggest such an act when Tracker froze in the middle of poking around a few cabinets near the entrance. Dylan tipped his head, trying to hear whatever had alerted the man despite knowing his senses were nowhere near as acute as the elf's. Nothing came. He risked a glance at Authril. She seemed engrossed in rifling through what appeared to be a chest of broken, assorted items.

The hound crept to the doorway and peeked out before flattening himself against the wall with startling speed. "Get back," he hissed, waving at them to go deeper into the house.

Dylan obeyed, huddling against the edge of a cupboard. Whatever the man had heard, it couldn't be good if hiding was his first option. Had the people who'd ransacked this place returned to pick at the bones?

"What is it?" Authril asked, the hound's frantic movements enough to draw her attention. She craned her neck to see around him.

Tracker placed an open palm on her breastplate and pushed her further from the doorway. "Have you always been this bad with obeying orders?" he muttered as, with the other hand, he slid a knife free from its sheath. "Get back and stay quiet."

A faint ruckus kicked up from outside, growing louder. Dylan rather doubted the noise was the family returning home.

The Talfaltaner army. They'd seen evidence of its passage along the roadside, but hadn't come across anyone beyond the bunch who had almost killed Marin. Their group couldn't have been that close on their tail before the rain slowed travelling to a crawl. But maybe the weather had done the same to the Talfaltaners.

He had a chance. *Just one.* One was all he needed. If the main body of the army had reached Whitemeadow already, he would never be able to avenge the tower. But if they were *here…*

He straightened slightly. A fine shield flickered to life around him, crackling with potential.

Tracker glanced over his shoulder at them. He held Dylan's gaze for longer than the others. The man shook his head and, pressing a forefinger to his lips, waved at him to resume hiding.

It went against every tingling instinct in his body, but he released his hold on the shield. *There's a reason.* Tracker wouldn't tell him to back down unless it was too dangerous for them to engage. That suggested a larger crowd than they could handle.

His gaze slid over the other two women. Unlike Authril, who still brazenly stood at the hound's side, they had tucked themselves into whatever nook would shield them from the direct sight of anyone outside. Neither of them wielded weapons suitable to face an army. Marin's archery prowess was enough to fend off bandits and she could probably hold her own for a while before being overwhelmed, but Katarina barely had a blade to defend herself.

He stepped back, flattening himself against the wall. He couldn't put Marin in that sort of danger again. Nor could he risk a hedgewitch's life.

Peeking around the end of the cupboard again revealed the hound had disappeared. Authril stood in the man's place beside the doorway, her sword drawn and her head tilted. A quick survey of the room led Dylan to believe Tracker was outside.

Voices—raised, jovial and foreign—drifted in from the doorway and cracks between the window shutters. The words were garbled and partially muffled by the walls, but he had heard enough of its quick and rhythmic tone when they'd threatened to skewer Marin.

It *was* the Talfaltaners. These men joked and caroused with each other as though they hadn't slaughtered thousands. He needed no proof they'd committed such an atrocity than what they were. The only reason they would be this far inland was because they'd come to kill—

My people. His home. His friends. His *family*. The monsters responsible for the tower slaughter stood just outside.

And the hound had cautioned him to stay put?

He couldn't. His blood roared for violence. His magic sang a cry of vengeance.

Snarling, he ran for the doorway, knocking Authril aside with a gust. His rage brought a flare of magic to life, lightning arcing off his fingers. He wasn't about to let those bastards just walk away. That stopped being an option the second he stepped through the tower gates.

A group of men stood near the barn entrance. They wore the same baggy shirts and trousers as the felled invaders in the tower, as the people who tried to kill Marin. A quick count revealed ten in all. Confused and bunched together like newly hatched chicks.

The lightning crackled erratically between his fingers, demanding to taste flesh.

He unleashed it on the group, watching it arc from one to the other, sharper than the sword that had run Marin through, quicker than the blades used to cut down every innocent life in the tower.

Their bodies contorted in ways none should. He couldn't tell if the high-pitched squealing they emitted came from their screams or was merely air escaping. Smoke and steam drifted off smouldering clothes and blistering skin. The man at the fore who bore the brunt had already become a grotesque thing dripping bits of himself.

"Enough!" Authril snapped. "They're dead."

He withdrew his magic. The lightning froze in the air for a blink, then was gone, leaving only a black impression on his vision. Rubbing his eyes did little to banish it, but he tried nevertheless.

The farmyard hadn't changed by the time his sight was clear. The men he'd slain lay in charred lumps, identifiable as people only through their outline. Thin tendrils of smoke wound their way to the sky.

Dylan took it all in, his very core numb. Should he not feel vindicated? These men had done so much evil, yet their deaths just left him strangely tired. It couldn't be the drain of his magic, could it? He'd used more in healing Marin without suffering this weariness.

Gathering himself, he turned back to the farmhouse. Authril stood in the doorway, her shield propped at her feet. The other two women were somewhere beyond sight, but safe. No sign of Tracker, though. Was the man's absence a cause for concern? He hadn't heard anything to suggest the hound was in trouble, but he'd always been nearby, or at least responsive, whenever Dylan used his power.

"We should—"

Authril snatched up her shield, her weapon already bared. "Look out!"

Pain lanced through his back at the same moment as her warning, the force of its arrival both knocking the breath out of him and also pitching him forwards. His head spun, blurring his vision and throwing him further off balance. His innate healing flooded the area where he'd been struck and also whatever was in his blood.

He stumbled towards the farmhouse, groping for the object embedded in his back with his right hand. Every move was like a hot knife carving through to his bones, but he kept trying. His fingertips brushed the shaft of an arrow. Reaching further was impossible. His left arm could barely move at all.

"Demon!" someone bellowed, the gravelly accent pulverising the word. "We have come to send you back to your murky realm!"

CHAPTER 22

With his vision blurred by tears and the searing fire in his back forcing him to take shallow breaths, Dylan slowly turned towards the speaker. The shimmering surface of his shield snapped around him at the sight of many snarling faces.

More of them? His head was too fuzzed by pain to count how many, but they were certainly better prepared to do violence than the first with their weapons already at hand—the vast majority of them being blades, either sword or dagger, but a few had bows.

Was this what Tracker had tried to warn him about? *The footprints.* How many had the hound said returned here? Dozens?

One of the men ran at him, his sword carried low in a move Dylan had seen the hound use during sparring.

Dylan spread his fingers, willing the lightning to return. It didn't need to be as long as last time. Didn't even need to hit all of them. Just one, then maybe—

The burning in his back grew greater, consuming his focus until even his shield stuttered. He staggered against the wall, screaming as the unconscious twist to brace himself only brought more pain.

Trying again to bring his magic to bear led to the same end. He needed someone to remove the arrow, let his body heal, before he could focus on anything harder than children's tricks. *Fire.* It lacked the finesse of lightning and could slip from his control all too easily, but it required very little from him.

He raised his right hand. Anything to aid him.

The charging man crumpled before he crossed the halfway point. Momentum tumbled him closer, red spraying from the throwing knife embedded in his neck.

As one, the Talfaltaners glanced in the direction the blade had come from.

Dylan followed their gaze to find Tracker perched atop the barn rooftop, another knife already in hand. The hound barked something at the men in their own tongue. An order? A threat?

In answer, one of the archers took aim and released their arrow.

Tracker rolled to one side and off the edge of the roof. He landed on the ground much like a cat. There was a flash of metal and the archer fell as swiftly as the first man. "I see you are *also* terrible at following orders," he grumbled just under his breath, his lips thin with displeasure and his gaze unwavering from the Talfaltaners.

Dylan shook his head. The man really expected him to cower in a corner when he knew the people responsible for his home's destruction were just outside. "What were *you* doing on the roof?"

"Dealing with their friends a little more discreetly than you." He finally turned his gaze Dylan's way, tilting to look behind him. A hardness took his features as he unsheathed his scimitar. "You are injured. Return to the farmhouse and let me finish this the hard way." The long dagger seemingly appeared in his other hand.

"I can remedy that if you take it out." Wrenching the arrow from his back might hurt more than some careful extraction, but he could heal from it.

Tracker pressed his lips together. "That will take too long." His focus returned to the enemy. He flung another knife at them, his target collapsing mid-stride. "Get back inside."

"Not happening." Gritting his teeth against the pain, Dylan squared his stance and focused on heating the air directly in front of him. The haze danced in the air, waiting to burst into a fireball.

Tracker sighed dramatically. "I suppose that would be a bit much to ask of you. Just be sure to keep your shield up." His head twitched to one side. "And you two better watch your flank. I cannot be certain of their arrows, but their blades will be poisoned."

Out the corner of his eye, Dylan spied Authril and Marin filing through the doorway. Of Katarina, there was no sign. He hoped that meant the hedgewitch had opted to stay indoors.

"Yeah, yeah," Authril muttered. "This isn't my first fight."

This new show of force seemed to give the Talfaltaners some pause. One of them came forward and rattled out what sounded to be several sentences at once.

At his side, Tracker spat back something in Talfantanese. Judging by the reaction, it had either been a curse or a refusal.

Brandishing their weapons, the men rushed them.

One fell swiftly to Marin's bow. Their second archer replied in kind, forcing the woman to duck back through the doorway as she unleashed another arrow or be skewered. Her shot nicked her target, causing a stream of swearing to erupt from the farmhouse. She swiftly followed the arrow with another.

The man collapsed as it struck his throat.

Authril rushed the remaining six head-on, following the hound.

Taking as deep a breath as he could, Dylan allowed the fireball to form. He sent it hurling towards the Talfaltaners, hoping to scatter them and aid the pair's attack.

Only then did he realise he had misjudged Tracker's speed.

The hound didn't even hesitate. He raced right into the fireball to carve his way through the group. The sight had Dylan's heart stopping for a good minute, but Tracker didn't slow. Despite the fire exploding around him, he danced amongst the Talfaltaners, his blade slashing great wounds in his wake and leaving only wounded for Authril to finish off.

Dylan used the chaos to sidle closer to the doorway, hoping to put his barrier between the men and Marin, as he searched for another opening.

There were far more of them than before. A swift reassessment of their attackers revealed the group had roughly tripled in size, with half of them already dead or dying. More still appeared from around the far side of the barn. Surely they hadn't stumbled into the tail of the main force.

Attacking a company large enough to destroy the entire tower would be suicide. Tracker's warning echoed through his head.

Dylan swung about, bellowing through the pain, searching if more were about to descend upon them from elsewhere.

Nothing, not even a hint. He sorely hoped it stayed that way. The alternative was knowing he had dragged them into a battle they couldn't win.

With fear dulling the pain grating in his back, he barrelled into the fray, flinging bouts of magic wherever he could. Blades bounced off his shield, the attack leaving them open for more controlled bursts of fire that sent them tumbling. Another stumbled back, screaming and clutching his burning face.

A swift pulse through the air left everyone staggering, all except Tracker, who took out two stumbling foes without even an acknowledgement of magic being wrought around him.

Authril wasn't as lucky, but she managed to right herself before her opponent.

There was the darting movement of a foe on his flank. He had already proven to be a difficult target, yet they still came, roaring obscenities he couldn't understand.

Dylan strengthened his shield and turned, flames already dancing around his fingers.

Tracker was suddenly between them.

The Talfaltaner's dagger struck. There was a gasp and the hound lurched back, passing through the barrier. Dylan reeled, his limbs barely able to hold himself upright as a swarm of tiny shocks rippled through his body.

The hound seemed less affected. Snarling, he lunged for the man who had struck him. His scimitar slashed, sending more shocks into Dylan as the hound's arm passed through the barrier.

The rest of Tracker followed and Dylan fell to his knees.

One of the other men cried out as the hound dispatched his opponent. He backed away from Tracker's advance, repeating a single word. He tripped over a comrade and scrambled to his feet. The rambling changed. A plea. A curse. A warning to the others.

"*Him!*" Tracker roared as he took out another of the Talfaltaners in his path. He pointed his blade in the direction of the deserter. "I want him alive!"

Dylan turned his focus to a narrow pulse. The air rippled, tearing across the space and smacking into the Talfaltaner. The man flipped, hit the ground and was still. Hopefully, through being unconscious and not dead.

The rest were far easier to pick off after that. Most of them heeded the man's words and tried to flee, the act leaving them open to Marin's arrows and the hound's knives.

Katarina appeared from the doorway after the last of them had fallen. She took in the pile of bodies, her lips pursed. "I've never seen so many Talfaltaners this far inland before, not even to chase spellsters. Whoever convinced them to must've had quite the glib tongue."

"It is certainly looking that way," the hound agreed. He wiped his scimitar on the shirt of a fallen man and sheathed it. Even in this simple act, he seemed to favour his arm.

"You're injured." If Dylan wasn't merely seeing things, the man's sleeve was wet where the enemy's blade had struck.

Tracker grinned. "I am fine. *You*, however..." He knelt at Dylan's side, his gaze definitely on the arrow. "This will hurt a lot more than the dagger did. Hold him," he commanded Katarina.

The hedgewitch did as instructed. Kneeling before Dylan, she drew him into her grasp, her arms wrapping around his shoulders.

Swallowing the abrupt lump in his throat, he closed his eyes.

"Steady now," Tracker's voice came from behind, its calm tone doing nothing for the churning in Dylan's gut. "On the count of four, yes? One..."

The arrow shaft shifted slightly as a hand closed around it.

Dylan felt his back tense. He gritted his teeth and willed himself to relax. It was going to hurt. He knew that. There was no getting past that. But his innate healing would fix it. He just needed the arrow gone. He could bear the pain until then.

"Remember to breathe, my dear man."

Fresh pain seared his flesh. That wasn't the arrow. It felt like something going *in*, not out. His magic flared around the new wound, seeking to heal it before the arrow and—was that a blade?—was out.

"Two..."

The usual tingling of his healing only increased the sensitivity. He shoved his face into Katarina's shoulder, his teeth clamping down on mouthfuls of cloth. It did little to distract him, but it muffled his whimpering. He fought the pull, trying to give the hound more time to do whatever it was he was doing. It got him nowhere. Nothing could stop this ability. It would kill him before it gave up.

"Three!"

White agony tore through his back. Screaming, he sagged into the hedgewitch's arms. His power rushed to close the site, leaving only an echo trembling through his body.

Katarina released her secure hold on him, but continued to keep him close, making soothing noises and whispering in her native tongue. "What happened to *four*?" she demanded of the hound.

The man shrugged. "He would have tensed further by then and *this*..." He held out the arrow. The broad tip looked to be some sort of bone, different in design to the narrower tips Marin used. This one also bore a serrated edge. Bits of flesh still clung to the saw-like points. "Sharks tear chunks off their prey. Their teeth are not designed to release their hold easily and Talfaltaners like to mimic this." He pointed to the lower corners. Unlike the rest of the tooth, these had distinctly carved notches. "Add how your healing mended the entry wound close to the shaft..." He grimaced. "Slicing a new path was the only way."

He stared at the arrow, still shaking even as the echo of pain vanished. *Sharks...* He knew they were predator fish, but everything else came only from the memories of Sulin's tales. The nights his roommate would awaken in a cold sweat, screaming about teeth and frothing blood.

Tracker laid a consoling hand on his shoulder. "Will you be all right?"

His gaze slid up the hound's arm. It hadn't been his imagination. The Talfaltaner's blade had managed to land a blow. Hadn't he said the blades were coated in poison? "You've been cut." Dylan nodded to the injured arm. He could rationalise that the man might not have felt it at the time, but surely it had begun to hurt by now.

"Hmm? You mean this?" He parted the tear in his sleeve to examine the wound and shrugged. "It is not the worst I have had."

Having had a decent look at some of the scars marking the man's skin, Dylan didn't doubt it.

Taking one final shuddering breath, he quietly got to his feet. Retrieving his pack from inside the farmhouse meant winding through the bodies littering the yard. There were a lot more than he had expected. At least three dozen.

He rifled through his pack for a length of cloth. Found, he marched back to the hound and went to bind the strip around the idiot's arm.

Tracker flinched as Dylan grabbed the man's elbow. The hound frowned at him, then the bandage. "What are you doing?"

Undeterred, he resumed his task of bandaging the wound as best as he could. He would see to it properly once they'd set up camp. "You should be more careful," he grumbled under his breath. What had the man been thinking, throwing himself between Dylan and the enemy?

The thin press of Tracker's lips lifted at one corner. "I promise, this scratch will not hinder us."

It's not us *I'm worried about.* That blow had been meant for *him.* He should've been the one to take it. His shield had been strong enough to absorb the hit, but even if it had failed...

Well, like the arrow, the blow would've hurt at first, but his magic would've also taken care of the injury. Whatever had made the hound do something so foolish?

Tracker's mouth curved into what Dylan supposed was meant to be a reassuring smile. "I will be fine, truly. What of you, though?" Those long fingers grasped Dylan as if he wasn't capable of standing on his own. He was twisted this way and that, the hound examining him like he was a clumsy child. "You are otherwise unharmed, yes?"

He nodded. The man was bleeding from a cut Dylan wasn't too sure didn't also have poison in it and he couldn't use his magic to heal. Tracker had to know that, yet he was concerned for Dylan? "The archer caught me off guard. I thought them all dealt with."

"Good." Tracker absently pulled Dylan closer and patted his shoulder. "Good." He sighed and gave Dylan one last pat before turning to the pile of bodies littering the farmyard. "I have not fought that many people at once in a while."

"It would be prudent to ensure they stay down," Authril said. She clutched her sword as if the mere suggestion would have the bodies rising up to attack again. A few of them still moaned or gave the occasional twitch, but they seemed incapable of causing any harm.

"It would indeed," Tracker replied, his gaze lifting from the dead and dying to the unconscious man lying apart from the others. "Then we shall see what our dear friend has to say."

Not wanting to watch the grisly task of Tracker picking through the Talfaltaners to ensure all bar one were completely dead, Dylan turned his attention to checking over the others. Authril's armour and shield had gained a few dents, but she was uninjured. Likely thanks to following in the wake of Tracker's whirlwind assault.

Marin had sustained only a few splinters from evading the

archer's initial attack. She waved him away—insisting that such injuries weren't worth bothering about—in favour of gathering her arrows and picking through the fallen archers for more to add to her quiver. She would pause every so often to also pick other things from pockets and packs.

Dylan looked around as the others picked through the mass. Weapons littered the ground at his feet. He scooped up one of the swords, testing its weight. It seemed lighter than either Tracker's scimitar or the warrior's blade. Shorter, too, and thinner. Perhaps if he could find a sheath to fit it, then Tracker could teach him more swordsmanship.

"For the sake of my heart," Tracker said. "Put that knitting needle down."

A flush of guilt heated his face. He spun, instinctively tucking the sword behind him as he turned.

The hound squatted not far from where he stood, one brow raised. The purple alchemist's dagger dangled between his fingers, the blade wet with use. Ever since Dylan told the man of its ability, Tracker rarely unsheathed the weapon. It seemed he was prepared to take no chances in ensuring the death of these men.

Dylan slowly withdrew the sword. "I just thought that maybe—"

"I know what you are thinking, but look around." Tracker stood, swinging his arms wide to indicate the mass of corpses surrounding them. "That sword did not exactly aid its previous owner in staying either mine or our dear warrior's blade. It is a fine weapon—do not mistake me there—*if* you are fighting aboard a ship. On land? Against heavily armed foes?" The hound shook his head.

Dylan nudged one of the shields. That probably explained why they were such small things, about as big around as a man's head. The front side bore the black and white symbol of a sun rising over the sea. *They aren't even hiding where they came from.*

Did the Talfaltaners want a war with Demarn? Or were they striking at what the Udynea Empire would deem as an asset before the empire could claim it? Not to mention that he still wasn't certain how ordinary men would've struck down people taught to fight, like Sophia and Fredrick.

He supposed that was also a question for the unconscious man to answer.

Dylan turned his gaze on the lone living Talfaltaner. If the man could.

"Well then," Tracker said, brushing his hands clean. "Shall we see to our dear friend and give him the news? I am certain he will be quite broken up over it."

"You heard what he said, then?" Katarina asked.

"The dead would have heard him. I take it you also understood him." The hound knelt next to the unconscious man.

Dylan halted beside the hound as the others gathered around. The Talfaltaner had landed face-down in the mud. He still breathed, albeit shallowly. "What was he saying?"

Tracker met his gaze. He remained silent for long enough for Dylan to see the indecision churning in the man's mind. "He… identified me as a hound." He grasped the mop of dark hair and lifted the man's head. "But *how* do you know that, hmm?" Grunting, the hound let the man flop back to the ground. "There will be rope in the barn. We should tie him up before he wakes. I think what he has to say will be most interesting."

Marin and Katarina hoisted the man up, carrying him between them, his legs dragging. The two elves went ahead, parting the barn doors and disappearing into the shadows before returning to beckon them onwards.

The barn stood empty. No one appeared to challenge their entrance, at least. The structure didn't look quite as hastily abandoned as the farmhouse. The barn interior was a single vaulted space except for a dark entrance to another room tucked behind a cart. Dylan guessed the space was for storage, much like the tower's glasshouse had an attached shed.

Tracker vanished into the room, returning swiftly enough with a length of rope that could do the job of binding the Talfaltaner's limbs thrice over and then some. "Here." He threw the rope down at the man's feet.

The hound paced whilst Authril and Marin busied themselves with securing the unconscious Talfaltaner, his expression grim. "Wake him," he growled.

"How much of the language do you know?" Dylan asked. The hound might've readily spewed what sounded like obscenities to the men earlier, but that didn't mean he had enough of a grasp on the language to converse civilly with their captive.

Tracker chuckled. "You seem to have forgotten I grew up in Wintervale. The docks are deep enough to permit Talfaltaner city ships to make port there. It does not take much for a curious boy to learn their language." The hound crouched by the man's body to pat his cheek. Gently at first, then harder.

Dylan wet his lips, fidgeting as each pat was met with no response. Perhaps he had been a little exuberant in stopping the man from fleeing.

The lack of response didn't seem to deter Tracker. He lifted one of the man's eyelids before pressing an ear to his chest. Sighing, the hound leant back. "My dear man, would you be so good as to heal him?"

He frowned at Tracker before turning to glare at the unconscious man. "Really?" The word fell flatly from his lips. What made this bastard worthy of such magic? There was no reason not to just leave him to die here.

"I cannot speak to him if he will not wake."

Dylan chewed on the inside of his lip, trying to see any flaws in that logic. The man could tell them where the rest of the company was, its size, how they managed to win against a tower of spellsters when thirty or so of them couldn't take out one.

All the information he'd need for when the time came to avenge the tower and her slain inhabitants.

"I need to know what really happened in the tower, Dylan," Tracker persisted. "We both do."

"But can we be entirely certain that the Talfaltaners orchestrated the attack?" Authril asked. "Seems a bit farfetched, if you ask me."

"Then it is fortunate no one did," the hound snapped back. "They were there. The crest on their shields does not belong to anyone within Demarn and their garb is all wrong."

"I'm not saying they didn't attack the place, just... What if they were merely hired? By the Udyneans, even?" She gestured to the unconscious man. "He might know nothing beyond where his people were meant to march, maybe even less. What then?"

Tracker remained silent, although his face grew cold. He glared at Authril, his eyes eerily flat.

"Then we do the only thing we can," Marin said, nudging the warrior aside until she stood in Tracker's line of sight instead. "We find out where his superiors are. They would have to know more, right?"

The hound nodded. He turned his head, peering at Dylan over his shoulder. "If you please?"

Dylan laid a hand on the Talfaltaner's shin and drew on his ability. Simple injuries whispered for his magic—a scrape on his shoulder from where he'd landed, a few crushed vertebrae in the lower neck, a broken nose... the list seemed endless. He gently aided their mending whilst searching out the cause for the man's unconsciousness. Nothing seemed serious enough to—

Oh. As the smaller injuries faded under his skill, Dylan found the root of their problem. There was too much fluid surrounding the man's brain.

He shifted his grip, clasping the man's head, and focused on the area beneath his palms. Slowly, the swelling that kept the fluid there went down, returning everything to normal.

"Is he salvageable?" Tracker asked once Dylan stepped back.

Dylan rubbed at his forehead. Healing the man on top of the fighting and mending his own wounds pinched his brain. "He'll wake," he replied. "Although, I'm not sure how much he'll remember. The blast hit him harder than I meant to." He hadn't been so sloppy since his first year in combat training. Perhaps Tracker would be agreeable to a little sparring session against his magic. It certainly wouldn't hurt to hone his skill.

The hound once more bent over the man to gently slap his cheeks. "Come now, wake up."

The man's eyes fluttered open. He struggled against his bonds until he seemed to realise their presence. That dark gaze silently swept over them, before settling on Tracker.

"I still don't think he actually knows anything," Authril said, crossing her arms. "Soldiers usually aren't told shit except what direction to march."

"In the army perhaps, but things work a little differently aboard a ship. He will know enough." Tracker nudged the man with his boot, earning him a faint sneer. "Is that not right, my friend?"

The man said nothing. He stared straight ahead, his face carefully blank.

"Oh, there is no need to be so coy." Tracker knelt before their prisoner. "I know you can understand me. So, tell me what it is you know about the tower."

The Talfaltaner continued his silence. His gaze flicked to Dylan and his lip quivered in a sneer. He muttered a single word.

Dylan folded his arms. Even without understanding the man, that word couldn't have been complimentary.

In one swift move, the purple dagger was in Tracker's hand, the flat of the blade lying against the man's cheek. "Do not look at him. It is *I* you must be more worried about. Where did you see hounds to identify me so readily?"

The man's jaw squared. The glare he shot Tracker suggested it was just as well that he was bound. He growled something and spat in the hound's face.

Tracker's arm came up far faster than Dylan expected it to. The back of his hand connected with the man, sending the Talfaltaner onto the ground. "So, it is going to be that way, yes?" The hound sighed as he stood. "The rest of you carry on to Whitemeadow. I will catch up once our dear friend decides he would prefer to talk."

A sick, sinking feeling took Dylan's gut as the others filed out of the barn. "Track..." At times, it was all too easy to forget the man was trained to hunt and kill spellsters. He probably knew plenty of painful ways to extract information. "Are you going to torture him?"

Tracker said nothing, merely glaring at the trussed man as though that alone would wreak unspeakable horrors. As he had been outside, the hound seemed distracted, constantly glancing at the entrance to the storage room.

Only now did Dylan realise Tracker had shut the door, sealing off whatever was within from an accidental glance. Just as he'd done in the tower.

Were there bodies on the other side? Was that what had become of the farmer and their family? The workers, too?

The Talfaltaner's eyes bulged. Through an extraordinary amount of wriggling, the man made his way across the barn floor to Dylan's feet. He uttered what sounded like a plea. His accent wasn't as grating as that of the other group they had encountered, almost a heavier, faster version of the coastal Demarn inflection Tracker's voice carried. If the man wasn't speaking a different language, Dylan could've seen himself thinking this one was a Demarner.

He took a step back, then hesitated. The others had already left the barn and gathered their gear from the farmhouse. If he stayed, he wouldn't understand a word of what the man had to say, but if he left…

Was he really going to leave the man alone with Tracker, knowing what the hound planned to do?

Grasping the man's shirt, Tracker hauled the Talfaltaner back to the post and, bending over the man, growled what was definitely a threat. He turned to pin Dylan in place with a single look. Those honey-coloured eyes had grown hard, like chips of flint. "*Go.*" The word came on a whisper, yet carried all the force of a war hammer.

Dylan's feet obeyed the command well before he thought to move them. Soon, he was running out of the barn after the women, who were readying to make their way down the path leading to the road. He stumbled as he crossed the farmyard to join them, the toe of his boot catching on the charred lump of an outstretched limb. Arm or leg? He could be certain of neither.

Righting himself, he lifted the skirts of his robe and wove around the carnage they'd caused. The screams of the dying, the inhuman shrieks of those he had electrocuted, filled his mind and chilled his blood. The sound continued to chase him as he caught up with the others, slowly fading to echoes only once he reached the road.

Glancing over his shoulder, he found the barn doors closed. The faint crack of light leaked where they didn't quite meet. A dozen nasty scenes sprang to mind. Did the hound cut him? Was he breaking the man's bones? Burning him?

He kept looking back until the barn was out of sight, vaguely hoping he would find Tracker right behind him and that this was just another nightmare. Maybe the hound would do the merciful thing and just kill them.

The man's a murderer. He had to remember that. The Talfaltaner hadn't looked terribly frightening whilst bound, but he wouldn't have shown mercy to the spellsters he cut down. Not to the children he slaughtered or the people whose only crime was living in the tower. They would've begged for their lives and gained nothing but an end to it.

That Talfaltaner deserved everything he got.

~ ~ ~

With Dylan and the rest out of sight, Tracker lit a lantern and secured the barn doors. It wouldn't keep the man's screams from escaping, but it would muffle them. "Shall we begin, my dear man?" he uttered in the Talfaltaner's native tongue. "Or do you wish to speak now and avoid the pain?"

"Torture me all you want," the man snarled back, his head held high. "I'll die before you get anything from me."

He circled the Talfaltaner, taking stock of their surroundings, the exits and viable cover within, solidifying his own belief that there was limited availability on both counts. "You are aware what a death far from the ocean will mean, yes? No giant sail birds to carry your name across the waves to the great fleet on the horizon."

Uncertainty flickered across the man's face. He had likely never met someone outside of their ships who knew their beliefs. "No..." he murmured, low enough that it had to have been to himself. Closing his eyes, he puffed out his chest. "The elders were clear. Our journey would take us far from the shores, but He-who-rides-the-waves would still know of our victory over the demons. We may never taste the sea spray, but our souls will see the horizon. We would be blessed, just as..."

Half-listening to the man spew a doctrine he had heard many time before, Tracker found himself staring at the closed door to the barn's storage. There'd been no openings within, no patches of light creeping through holes in the walls like there were in the rest of the barn. He hadn't needed them. His hound senses warned him of enough.

Magic had been in use here. The impression of it was faint against the beacon of Dylan's power and, just as it had been in the tower, already fading now the source was gone. His nose had spoken further of what became of that source. Spoiling blood. Flesh at the beginning stage of decay. A day old, maybe two.

Keeping one eye on his bound captive, Tracker cracked open the door. Lantern light spilled into the space, deepening the shadows in the corners. He originally thought only a single body had fallen here, but a closer look spoke of them having died protecting a far smaller form.

Knowing that whatever life had been here was now gone, he crouched next to the figure. Their small stature and slight form had him believing them to be elven, but as he propped up their bloodied torso, the lack of pointed ears told the truth there. *Human.* Likely barely old enough to mark their years in the teens.

A swaddled bundle tumbled from their lifeless hands. Tracker caught it on instinct. His senses already spoke of a distinct lack of active magic. His fingers confirmed the absence of life. Although, *how* that life had passed was less obvious.

And still, the Talfaltaner prattled on, reciting their litany of how spellsters were monsters from the deep waters in mortal forms, that their magic marked them as abhorrent, that cleansing both them and those who aided them from this world was *just.* As though the man hadn't a hand in slaughtering thousands of innocents, hadn't the blood of children irreparably staining his skin.

Dozens of men like him lay sprawled outside, drenched in their own blood. How many of them had pursued these two?

He gently lowered the little body back into the arms of the child before whispering a small prayer over them. With luck, the Seven Sisters would look kindly on their travel.

He shut the door, sealing off what was now their tomb.

His blood seethed as he faced his captive, red tingeing his vision. He grabbed the man's bound wrists, lifting them above their heads, and rammed the *infitialis* dagger into the man's palms.

The Talfaltaner's screams lent a fuzzy edge to the world. He thrashed, trying to free himself. With Tracker driving the dagger's point into the pole, the man's every movement only worsened the damage.

Tracker waited until the man had become accustomed to this new pain, then tore the dagger from its fleshy sheath. "Now that I have your attention..." He drew the flat of the blade along the Talfaltaner's sun-weathered cheek, smearing blood.

To his credit, the man didn't flinch. Although his reddened eyes widened.

He lowered the dagger, letting the razor tip gently glide along the arc made by the man's shirt collar. It wasn't hard enough to break skin, but it wouldn't take much. "You are going to tell me *everything* you know."

CHAPTER 23

Rather than pressing on down the road, they entered the forest blanketing the roadside opposite the farm entrance. A little poking through the undergrowth had them eventually coming across a clearing big enough to set up camp. Night wouldn't come for a little while, but they set about their routine anyway.

A fallen tree jutted into the clearing, its grey branches still supporting the vestiges of brown leaves. The wood was still damp, but he had ignited plenty of water-logged pieces during their journey.

The branches fell easily enough to a few swipes of magic, enabling Dylan to set up a fire as the others pitched the tents. No one made a move to stop him. They were well out of sight of the road. Even with the firelight, if anyone came upon them, it would be deliberate. And he needed to feel warm again. The screams still echoed in his mind.

A quick fireball set the wood to burning. He settled next to the blaze, his hands outstretched. Slowly, the warmth reached his extremities and burrowed into his core. How long would it take for the hound to get what he was after? Would he be able to look at Tracker the same way, knowing what the man had done?

Authril joined him at the fireside. She carefully removed her armour, fussing over the dents and blood splattered across the surface. Dylan followed the warrior's movements as she rubbed a cloth over the tarnished spots on her breastplate. Blood also stained the leather where the metal joined. He could probably draw it out if he focused hard enough.

Knowing better than to offer, he settled for poking the fire. They should probably cook some of the venison, but he wasn't sure he had the stomach to eat a single bite.

The solid *chonk* of a blade hitting wood drew his attention. He swivelled to find Marin hacking more branches off the fallen tree, her efforts steadily creating a pile that looked far drier than what he had taken.

By the tents, Katarina rifled through their packs, taking stock of supplies. She moved on to check all of their water skins, then called

Marin, who put aside her axe and pulled out the map they'd been following since Oldmarsh.

The hunter muttered and mumbled to herself. He caught hushed calculations, but before he could figure them out, she said, "We should reach Whitemeadow in roughly a half-week."

"We'll be out of water before then," Katarina added.

Authril nodded. "We should've checked the farm's well water before abandoning it." She shrugged as if resettling a thought. "Nothing for it, I suppose. We'll need to leave the road tomorrow and seek out a stream to refill them."

"Why?" Marin asked. Having returned the water skins, she joined them by the fire. "Can't Dylan just use his magic to do that ice trick he does every morning?" She wiggled her fingers as she spoke. Always did whenever she mentioned magic. He still wasn't sure why. To his knowledge, he didn't do such an excessive action.

"I'm not drinking magic water," Authril declared, nodding her head as if that put an end to their discussion.

Dylan straightened. "It's not mag—"

The warrior continued to talk right over the top of him. "And it wouldn't exactly be a smart use of his magic. What if more of those bastards show themselves? Do we really want to be without his aid because he exhausted himself? All because we didn't look for an alternate water source?"

A notable concern, if it actually took that much out of him. But in this damp environment, forming ice was a ridiculously easy feat. "It wouldn't— Look." Dylan dug into his pack, grabbed his cup and focused. Tiny crystals of frost formed, thickening until half the cup was full of ice. He pressed a finger against the frozen surface and slowly let a pulse of heat radiate through the digit. "See? It's just melted ice."

Authril eyed the cup as if it might savage her. "That you formed out of nothing."

"Not *nothing*. Out of the water in the air." He flung his arm wide, slopping water. "The same water that makes our rain, that fills lakes and the river."

She screwed up her nose. "I refuse to drink it."

"Leave her be," Marin said. Getting to her feet, she gave his shoulder an affectionate squeeze. "I don't see any difference, but since someone is feeling so very precious..." She pulled a face at the warrior, who rolled her eyes in response, before grabbing a couple of water skins. "I'll go back and fill them whilst we wait for Track."

Dylan leapt to his feet, the memory of her being skewered jumping to the forefront of his mind. He couldn't have her risking that again. "Are you sure that's wise? What if there are more?"

Smiling, she patted his arm. "Don't worry. You're in good hands with those two."

Unable to remain still, he silently buzzed about the camp, gathering up the cut wood, procuring the hedgewitch's little case of sewing supplies to go with the bottle of whisky he had spied in Marin's pack.

As the sky grew dark, Authril eventually sought her bed, whilst Katarina vanished into the forest to ensure their surroundings were safe.

His ears strained to pick up anything beyond the forest's natural sounds.

Surely, the hound was done with the man. Or had Tracker learnt something that changed his priorities? What could be more important to a hound than escorting a spellster?

Was it possible for a spellster to enter the capital without a hound at their side? Maybe if they were already leashed. But if that were still true, then Tracker never would've encountered them to begin with. Dylan likely would've fallen along those he had failed to protect.

His gaze fell upon the small pouch hanging on the outside of his pack. The two pieces of the collar sat within, separated from each other by a strip of cloth.

Who else would believe he survived its destruction?

Trying to shake the thought free, Dylan busied himself with sterilising a needle for when the pair returned. Despite Tracker's insistence that the injury he gained from foolishly diving between Dylan and that Talfaltaner was nothing to be concerned about, the cut would need stitches.

Night had well and truly claimed the sky by the time the pair arrived at their camp. Marin vanished into the tent she shared with the other women, whilst Tracker settled before the fire, munching on what looked to be a pasty. Dylan couldn't recall their group still being in possession of such food, which meant the man had taken it from the very people they'd slain.

He eyed the hound. Odd how there didn't seem to be anything different about the man. It was still just *him*.

Dylan thought the mantle of torturer would put another light on the hound, but that was perhaps the problem. What the man had done wasn't new. Tracker had always been capable of such deeds. He'd just never been so open about it.

Tracker cleared his throat, causing Dylan to jump, and stood. "Well, I guess I should get some rest and leave you to your watch. Unless you would care to tell me the reason you stare so intently?"

Was there a reason? His gaze dropped to the sewing case, ensuring it still resided in his lap as though it could scurry off on its own.

"Your arm," he managed. "Let me see to it."

"I am uncertain there is much you can do without your magic. It is mostly superficial anyway, nothing to worry about." He shrugged, seeming to grit his teeth. "It does not even hurt anymore."

Dylan patted the ground in front of him. "Superficial or not, I can sew it shut."

"Like you did with Marin's clothes?" Tracker tilted his head to one side. "You are aware flesh is different to cloth, yes?"

He nodded. "This won't be the first time I've stitched someone back together." Although it had been some time. "It was how I learnt to sew." No spellster was permitted to use their magic to heal without knowing the basics, and that only came with experience.

The hound's brow twitched enquiringly. "I did not think they would teach you such mundane healing techniques. They hardly measure up to your magic."

"It was required. The only way to learn how to repair a body through magic is by understanding how things work. It took years to learn everything, and that's before my tutors would even let me use magic to heal." He had hated the task, especially knowing how cleanly the alternative was in comparison. But he could, at least, be confident in the knowledge he'd never run the risk of sealing a vein or atrophying a muscle.

"The tower was hardly a dangerous place. There could not have been many patients to hone such skills on."

"Most were from the training grounds," he conceded. A small, homesick smile tweaked one corner of his mouth. "We don't exactly have blunt weapons to practice with. We're taught restraint, but those in the arenas always have to be vigilant in their attacks and mind their defences." He shrugged. "Sometimes, they weren't fast enough to block a hit."

"Or strong enough to hold off an attack, yes?"

The memory of the last time he hadn't held back enough bubbled to the surface. Dylan pushed it back down, its recession taking his smile, and gave the earth before him another pat. "Sit."

"As you like," Tracker murmured, bowing low. He positioned himself cross-legged on the ground.

Dylan slowly unravelled the bandage. Mercifully, the site no longer bled as profusely as before. Judging the wound's severity was a different matter. Congealed blood coated both the cut and much of the surrounding jerkin.

"Although, I cannot help wondering… what will I discover next?" Tracker continued, seemingly unconcerned with Dylan's examination. "Is it possible that you have been holding out on us and *can* actually cook?"

Unexpected mirth bubbled up his throat, feeling a little more comfortable with the hound's usual jibes. "You don't want to eat whatever I cook. People have been known to die. Unless you can find me some pig trotters." He might've only cooked them the once, and under Marin's careful instruction, but he was certain he could do it again. "Now, give me your arm. I'll help you disrobe."

Tracker gasped. "Out in the open?" He swayed back and forth, his head swivelling as he searched the area, before leaning close. "How very saucy of you."

He glared at the hound. The man had carved his way through a great deal of people, thrown himself between Dylan and his attacker and, to top it off, had just returned from torturing a man for information. And yet he still attempted to flirt?

It could've been the flickering shadows, but it seemed that his grin wavered at the corners. "What did I say to deserve such a fearsome look?"

"Top half only."

"Oh?" His bottom lip jutted out almost as far as the tip of his nose. "Does this mean no sympathy sex? Or perhaps a little thank you hand action? I *did* save you from getting struck, after all."

Dylan bit his tongue. He'd heard enough about Marin's sleeping habits to know the woman would be fast asleep the moment her head hit the ground. Katarina was still somewhere out in the forest. And although Authril had sought sleep some time back, he couldn't be certain she didn't hear the hound. If she did, hopefully, she would take it as Tracker's usual brash teasing. "You didn't save me because I didn't need saving," he pointed out. "You put yourself in harm's way when I had a shield up."

Tracker waved his uninjured arm as if Dylan had spoken of mere semantics. "I am meant to protect you. Your safety is my responsibility. And I definitely saved you from bearing the force of his swing."

"Well, excuse me if I don't swoon." Tracker might've been right about shielding him from weathering the blow, but he wasn't about to give the man even that when he'd been irrational enough to risk himself over something as inconsequential as Dylan's life. "Now, does my hero want to be stitching his own wound shut, or is he willing to stop being a smart arse and let me help in fixing this foolery?"

The hound wrinkled his nose. "Not if you are going to be that way about it." He unbuckled a few of the belts and struggled for a while with the others, grunting and huffing into the night air, until at last conceding and placing the injured limb in Dylan's hands.

Dylan aided him. Fresh blood welled as they withdrew the layers, running down the hound's arm. Blood darkened the leather in more places than the right sleeve. He tried not to think about why it was still sticky when the fighting had been hours ago. The man's quilted shirt and undershirt were in less of a state, the patch where they'd been sliced almost black in the low light. "It's a shame it happened to your sword arm."

"That is not so bad. I can fight left-handed if need be. It is not as elegant, but it will keep a blade from our necks. My arm will not, however, be able to support my weight for a few days."

He dabbed the spot with a clean cloth, trying to get a better idea of what he was dealing with. "Why would that be of concern?"

Tracker grinned. "I guess that depends on whether you plan on continuing our little nightly activities." Pressing close, he whispered conspiratorially, "I could just lie on my back if you cannot wait. I do not recall us doing it that way." One russet brow twitched upwards, mimicking the smug skew of his lips. "Yet."

Dylan rolled his eyes. Of course the hound would try to lead things back to that. "And who says I'd want anything to do with you when you're injured?" He carefully lifted the man's arm, trying to get a better look at the injury in the campfire's light. The wound sliced straight through the intricately woven band design encircling his bicep. "It doesn't look like too deep a cut." Enough to require stitches, though.

The hound also peered clinically at the wound. "Ah, a pity. I was rather fond of that one."

He examined the band. The ink was old, the lines bleeding and blurring the swirling design within. There seemed to be words amongst them. At least three. The wound cut a diagonal path through one. He twisted his head, trying to make out the letters. One clearly said *Hunk*. The others? "They look like names."

Tracker grunted. "They are."

"Do they have some sort of special meaning?" Were they family? Past lovers? Current ones?

A wry smile twisted the hound's mouth. "Not for some time." He fingered the wound, tracing the line to where it cut into one of the scrawls. "Had to be through that part," he mumbled. "Why could the bastard not have chosen a little more to the right?"

Dylan frowned. If it had, the cut would've bisected *Hunk*. "It wouldn't have happened at all if you hadn't jumped in front of me." The arrow in his back had sapped him of focus and power, but his shield had still been strong enough to repel a blade. The dagger wouldn't have gotten anywhere near as close to him as it had with the hound. "Frankly, you're lucky the blade wasn't poisoned."

"Oh, it was. The Talfaltaners always treat their weapons with such. Makes it easier to board ships if the crew's busy turning all sorts of interesting shades." His lips parted in a tooth-clenching grin. "But I have some variety of immunity, remember? It just stings like crazy."

Dylan uncorked the bottle of whisky. "I thought you said it didn't hurt?" He poured the liquid over the wound.

Tracker hissed. He closed his eyes, but otherwise remained still. The man relieved him of the bottle once Dylan was done and took a tentative sip of the contents, swiftly followed by several large swallows. "This is strong stuff. Where did you get it?"

"Marin had it stashed in her pack. I didn't ask where *she* got it."

The hound hummed questioningly around the bottle's neck. "Well, she is a resourceful woman. And I do recall her rummaging through the gear of those unfortunate souls we stumbled upon."

Dylan glanced up from threading the needle he'd already sterilised. If he hadn't known better, the man looked rather remorseful. "You think she took a dead man's drink?"

"Why not? He has no need of it." Tracker took another long swallow. "It is *very* good."

Dylan turned his full attention to the first stitch. Blood welled around the needle and dyed the thread. It'd been years since he'd done this, but it all came back so easily. "That man you planned on questioning? Did you—?"

"Get answers from him?" The smooth way Tracker quipped could only mean that the hound knew exactly what Dylan intended to ask him.

Dylan broke the thread with his teeth and rethreaded the needle for the next stitch. "That, yes. But did you *kill* him?"

"I did. What else was I meant to do? Leave him strung up to starve? Release him to tell his cohorts about us?"

Dylan paused in the middle of threading the needle for a third stitch. "You think there are more of them?" He had thought these men were stragglers, much like the bunch who had attacked him and Marin. He hadn't considered the possibility of being close enough to the main force.

He set the needle down. His hands shook too much to be of any use.

So many people. Both elves agreed the force required to topple the tower would've been immense. Measured in hundreds, if not thousands. A city ship's worth, the hound had said. Yes, some had fallen in the attack, but it clearly hadn't been enough to turn the tide.

Were they truly so near? Could they push a little harder, travel a little faster, and reach the Talfaltaners before Whitemeadow? To what end?

Revenge. Their lives for those they had stolen. Not just those of his fellow spellsters, but the servants and guardians who had no magic, yet were deemed tainted just by aiding in a spellster's survival. The alternative was to let the Talfaltaners leave. His blood seethed at the idea. He'd been promised justice.

His bones demanded more.

"Dylan?" The hound grabbed Dylan's arm. Tracker's free hand slid up to cup one side of Dylan's jaw, those long fingers warm against his skin. "My dear man, come back to me." The coarse pad of his thumb brushed across Dylan's cheek, disturbing the trail of tears that he hadn't been aware of crying. "Whatever those men back there did, whatever part they played in the tower's downfall, they have been punished."

"It doesn't make anyone less dead."

Tracker's brows drew up in the middle. "No, that it does not. But it is the best we mortals can do, yes?"

Nodding, Dylan took several deep breaths, steadying himself enough to pick up the needle and resume stitching the hound's wound shut. "What did *he* tell you?" He assumed their captive said something of note, especially if his gut feeling was correct and the hound had tortured the man.

A part of him hoped it had been nice and slow.

The hound grunted. "He told me a great many things."

"Anything useful?" The words fell like blocks of wood from his mouth, his mind elsewhere. *Excruciatingly slow.* Make the man wish he'd never set foot in Demarn. Never seen it. Never heard of it.

Tracker hummed, those full lips flattening and his brows knitting together. "There was his confession, of course. They always start with that. But he…" His frown deepened, wrinkling his nose. "He *had* seen other hounds. Recently."

"Do you believe him?" The Talfaltaner could've told the hound anything if he thought it would keep him alive.

"I would require another source to be sure, but we *do* send the occasional scout to monitor conditions around the tower from time to time, but I have found no sign of movement along the usual routes. It is likely he was mistaken." He waved a hand distractedly at the discarded jerkin. "This is a uniform, no different from the robe you wear. It is possible the man didn't see what he thought. Or someone was foolish enough to duplicate the look. Or…"

"Or the Talfaltaners are also responsible for the hounds Marin found in the forest."

Tracker's focus snapped to him like a mouser on his prey. "How much did she tell you?"

"Everything." Their placement. The number of bodies. The speculated length of time. "Authril said you don't hunt together."

His lips puckered as though he'd eaten something sour. "She is correct. We are trained to rely only upon ourselves, but assisting those who have found a particularly dangerous target is not unheard of. However, I have never seen so many together outside of Wintervale. I do not fully understand why they would be travelling together."

Dylan's mind leapt to the memory of charred outlines adorning the tower walls, the nightmare that had plagued him the night they lost the third tent.

When he had first thought the attack came from the Udynea Empire, he had believed they'd brought their own spellsters to deal with those in the tower. They'd done similar at the border to brutal effect.

He hadn't thought much about who would've combated the spellsters once there was no doubt every horrible thing had been the work of the Talfaltan people. But everything he had learnt about Talfaltaners and magic, how they slew every spellster they found. How they detested even those immune to it.

If it had never been the Udynea Empire. If Talfaltan didn't even allow Nulled Ones to live...

Then who was left?

Dylan remained silent as he finished the final knot in the suture. Then, breaking the thread with a snip of magic, he managed to find the words he wanted, "The hounds..." He wet his lips, unsure if he could voice the thought dominating his mind without vomiting. "Do you think they helped in the tower?" Did Tracker suspect it and thought to spare him the speculation? Had the man known before the deed was done?

"Helped?" the hound echoed, his confusion tugging at his brows. "In the tower's defence?" He chuckled. "We are better trained than the average soldier, certainly more so than the tower guards, but we have our limits."

"I meant in the attack." He hadn't witnessed the hound interact with his magic during a fight until now. He'd seen the horror on the enemy's faces. He could well imagine it on those of his friends, his peers, as they realised what bore down on them.

Worse still, it made sense to send in the people who were least likely to be harmed in a counterattack.

The man shot him an incredulous look. "Of course not. That would go against our creed, against everything we have been trained for." He shook his head in firm denial of the very idea. "No, if that man truly saw hounds, then it was likely someone sent to investigate the attack, not initiate it. Even if we had the numbers for such an assault, there is no reason to attack."

"They did once before."

"*Centuries* ago, yes. Our orders are to contain spellsters. They are not deemed a threat once within the tower."

"They?" Dylan mumbled, digging out a fresh bandage from his pack. "I'm one of them."

The hound snorted. "In terms of having the same power, perhaps, but I would not consider you as a threat, in *or* out of the tower. Not to me, not to these dear women, not to anyone who is not foolish enough to attempt harming you first. You are trained and in control of your abilities. You even limit your full strength without thinking." Gingerly flexing his arm, he finally looked down at the wound, taking in Dylan's work. "Very neat. Although, I should not be surprised. You have already proven yourself to have very sure hands when it comes to my personage."

Heat flooded Dylan's face. He hadn't been commended for his needlework since he started healer training. Clearing his throat, he began wrapping a bandage around the man's arm. "Don't ever do that again."

Tracker stiffened. He eyed Dylan as though he'd been slapped. "My apologies. My intentions were merely to relieve the tension with a dash of levity. You looked very serious stitching me back up."

Smiling, Dylan shook his head. "I don't mean just now. You didn't have to jump between me and that man."

"You were already injured and I have failed to protect you from a blade once already." The angle of his jaw gained a stubborn edge. "I refuse to repeat that mistake."

The hound meant the attack in the spellster tower, he had to. Even during the ambush when Marin had gotten hurt or the other scuffle that had claimed one of their tents, Dylan hadn't been struck.

"That was a different circumstance." He'd been half-asleep and exhausted—mentally and physically—unable to tell the difference between Tracker's form and the Talfaltaner who had stabbed him. "I had my shield up this time." Only a hound could've passed through and the only one nearby was on his side.

Tracker scoffed. "You cannot expect me to stand back when you are in harm's way."

"I do." And he hadn't been in any danger. None of the weapons those men possessed would've broken through his shield. "Even if my shield had fallen, I can heal whatever they do to me. What if that man had struck higher and sliced your neck open? Or your face? What if the blow had hit a major artery?"

The hound's expression turned stony. Falling silent, he stared off into the forest, slowly nodding.

In that quiet, Dylan focused only on securing the bandage.

When Tracker spoke again, it was in a solemn tone. "We both know there are several injuries *you* would not come back from."

That was true. But a strike to the heart or being beheaded was permanent for anyone. "I can still heal myself better than I'm able to heal *you*." The mere thought of having to stand helplessly on the wayside whilst the hound bled out twisted his insides. The idea that his actions might get the man killed made him nauseous.

The hound shrugged with his good shoulder. "Death comes to us all in the end."

"That doesn't mean you hasten its arrival by being careless. I'm not worth risking your life over."

Tracker chuckled, a half smile tilting his mouth. "If I choose to sacrifice my life in the pursuit of you keeping yours, you do not get a say in that. That is *my* choice."

"No."

"No?" he echoed. His smile widened a fraction. "Your denial of the truth does not negate it. As long as I am at your side, I will jump between you and danger."

"Because that's what every King's Hound would do, right?" He grabbed the hound's arm, pulling him close before Tracker's stark inhalation had him realising what limb he had tugged. Still, he kept his grip firm. "I know you see it as your duty to keep me safe, but promise me you won't put yourself in danger like that again. Not for the sake of saving my life."

His gaze met Dylan's for a fraction. Sighing, he shook his head as though any word he spoke wouldn't be enough. "I cannot give you that promise."

"I don't want you dying because of me." He had screwed up so many times. He wasn't worth the sacrifice of another.

"Dylan," Tracker breathed. Firelight caught in his eyes, giving his stare an unyielding edge. "If I die protecting you, it is not *because* of you. You understand that, yes?"

"But—"

The man laid a hand on Dylan's knee. "The only way to stop me from putting myself between you and danger is for you to not be in the position of requiring my aid." The hound's long fingers brushed his chin, lifting his head. "And, believe me," he whispered. "Your life is worth preserving."

Before he could think to speak further, Tracker's mouth was on his.

Their lips grazed each other, slow and as unrelenting as the ocean on the shore. Warmth washed over his body, pulling him under. Dylan let it carry him away, surfacing only to gulp down another breath of air. Sparks trembled along his spine, setting his head to spinning. His stomach fluttered so hard that his chest ached.

In too short a time, it was over.

He slowly opened his eyes. His lips still tingled. "Butterflies," he mumbled, a flush of heat infusing his cheeks. *That* was what this strangely familiar sensation was. He hadn't felt it in years.

The hound frowned. His gaze flicked to the campfire. "Not at night. Moths, perhaps. Stupid things are attracted to the light."

Dylan smiled. He wanted to laugh, to beat the man senseless for being so dense, to pin him to the ground and never stop kissing him. "No, I—" His voice squeaked. He cleared his throat and went to try again.

Tracker's long fingers found their way to Dylan's lips, gently tapping them to suggest he remain silent. "It is late, we have perhaps talked far longer than we should have—you indulge me far too much." The man gathered his clothes and stood. "I shall get some rest before you wake me for my turn on watch."

Dylan glanced up from packing away Katarina's sewing kit. The man couldn't be serious. "I'll take your watch tonight." He doubted he'd get much sleep and might as well have something to keep his mind busy.

"That—" The hound jerked his head around. "That is not necessary. I may be relegated to fighting left-handed for a little while, but I can still hold my own if someone attacks."

"You need rest more than I do right now. And give me your clothes. I'll wash and mend them whilst you sleep." With the aid of Tracker's soap, he should be able to scrub out a decent amount of the man's blood.

Tracker whined as he handed over the garment. "But if I leave now, then I miss out on seeing you dancing with them."

"Gods," Dylan moaned. He combed his fingers through his hair. "I thought you'd forgotten about that." He had certainly hoped.

The hound chuckled. "How could I possibly forget the sight of you twirling through the lavender in your undergarments?"

Shaking his head, Dylan shooed the man away. "Go rest, healer's orders."

He waited until the man had disappeared into his tent before turning his attention to the fire, encouraging the flames to grow hotter with a wisp of magic. The heat bathed his skin as he set about filling their little pot with ice that melted almost immediately.

Dunking the hound's undershirt into the pot to soak required more cramming than he had anticipated. Notes of citrus and cinnamon flooded his nostrils and clung to the back of his throat.

The rest of the hound's gear—the padded shirt that was far bulkier than mere linen, and the jerkin with its stiffer leather form and metal reinforcing—would require a different technique. Fortunately, his years of bathing in the tower had gifted him plenty of experience in funnelling hot water from small sources.

He scrubbed at the quilted shirt, seeking to break up the dried blood as well as work the water and soap deeply into the fibres. If he got the section wet enough, his magic might be able to draw most of the blood out along with the water. It wouldn't be perfect, he lacked the skill the tower servants had in keeping cloth clean, but he could fix that once they reached Whitemeadow.

With nothing else to focus on as the water boiled, his mind churned away. His gazed drifted to the tent they now shared. His lips still tingled with the memory of the hound's mouth.

Fool. He returned to the task at hand, scrubbing harder. He had let the hound kiss him plenty of times. And more. A *lot* more. A kiss shouldn't make his stomach bubble.

Except...

What they shared was purely physical. *Fun.* He was fine with that. Used to it. Such a term was expected back in the tower.

Except...

No one had even given him warm butterflies when they'd kissed.

Was this...?

Did he...?

But it hurt. The fluttering had turned into a dreadful ache in his chest, their every little flap feeding the swelling emotion that overflowed and spilled down his face.

"Are you all right?"

He jerked around at the sound of Katarina's voice. He had forgotten she was on watch with him. How long had she been standing there? Before the hound sought sleep? Had she heard the man prattle on as though the entire camp knew about them?

Had she *seen*?

"I'm fine." Snuffing back a wretched hiccupping sound, he wiped an arm across his cheek in an attempt to dry it. No matter how much he tried, more took its place. *Stupid.* He wasn't crying over a kiss. This reaction was nothing more than... "The soap's a bit intense close up, that's all."

Her expression remained unchanged as to whether she believed him or not. She settled next to him, taking the garment from his unresisting hands. "I'll work on this, you see to the pot."

Heat of a different kind warmed his face. They already asked so much of the woman in their day-to-day travels. What would his tutors say if they'd learnt he permitted a hedgewitch to take on such a mundane chore? "That's not necessary. I can manage." He reached out to reclaim the shirt, only for her to withdraw it from immediate reach.

"I insist. It's the least I can do. After all, without all of you, I never would've made it this far." Digging out a bowl, she smoothed the sleeve over the base. "I'll miss these quiet moments by the fire." She smiled at the flames as though they were dear companions.

He would, too. Leafing through the old tome of ancient dwarven ruins with her almost felt like he was back in the tower library.

"Unless..." Her gaze slid to him. "Would you consider joining me in Dvärghem?"

Yes. Ever since he had first studied the ancient dwarven runes, had aided a hedgewitch seeking answers, he had wanted to join them in the quest to uncover history.

"I can't. I belong to the army." If he diverted from rejoining their ranks, he'd be a deserter. Even with the tower gone, he was no less discardable once his usefulness had run out. Just a rare weapon.

And hadn't he proven himself a wonderful one, eradicating a dozen or so foes without even trying?

The ache in his chest was back, blurring his vision. He knew its source now. *Grief.* Not for what *had* happened, but for what couldn't. Dreams he couldn't have. Places he couldn't go.

Others he couldn't be with, couldn't dare think of in any greater term than carnal pleasure.

He was a weapon. A *thing* to be used. The lieutenant back at the army encampment had the right of that. He was good for nothing else. Nothing deeper.

People did not care for things, much less fall. It would be deluded to believe otherwise.

CHAPTER 24

The night mercifully remained absent of unwelcome visitors. Just as well, for Tracker's mind had only been partially on the task of keeping watch over the camp. He had spent the night with his scimitar in his left hand all the same, but his thoughts wandered far more than they should.

Hounds attacking the tower. Dylan's suggestion had come eerily close to his own thoughts after hearing the Talfaltaner's tale regaling him, between his screaming, of where he'd seen other hounds. It sounded like a conspiracy. One or two was plausible, and he had considered it.

But the way the Talfaltaner had spoken, the numbers he mentioned, suggested the majority of the pack, if not the whole. The only way that could possibly be was for the mistress to have ordered a culling.

And yet, the evidence was there. The ghostly outlines on the walls, Trapper's impaled body left to rot in that dungeon. He'd been generous in thinking that his fellow hound had been mistaken as the enemy.

Why? What possible reason could there be to set the pack on the tower? To destroy it so utterly that starting again was the only path. Was it because too many were escaping through that accursed secret entrance? But why use a Talfaltan force? The last culling hadn't required anyone beyond the King's Hounds.

Surely their mistress knew what the Talfaltaners would do to everyone within the tower. If they were attacking farmers as well— and not because they'd been hiding a child sheltering a baby—then who knew what they'd done to Whitemeadow.

None of it answered the mystery of why they'd killed eight of the pack, but knowing Whisper was amongst them, he'd a feeling the explanation was all too simple. *Bad dogs.* Put down for refusing to slaughter innocents.

To think he could've been amongst them...

The women's tent opened, permitting Katarina to exit. Rather than go about her usual morning routine, she stormed directly at him, wordlessly snatching up his uninjured arm and heading towards the shade of the forest with him in tow.

They travelled in silence, the dwarf's footsteps crossing the ground with delicate precision yet, also bearing the solid ferocity of an irritated tutor.

With the campsite no longer in view, she finally halted and released him. She stood facing the forest, her arms akimbo and her breath coming harshly. If he hadn't witnessed her multiple times outpacing the rest of them in terms of endurance, he would've thought her winded.

Tracker straightened his attire as he waited, his fingers unthinkingly moving along the new stitching adorning his sleeve. Each layer of his armour was in a similar state. He didn't know how long it had taken Dylan, only that he had awoken for his time on watch to find his clothes folded, all clean and mended, atop his pack.

Finally, she faced him. "You hypocritical bastard," she snarled.

Her vehemence rendered him incapable of a response for a breath. Rarely had he seen her angry and never in his direction.

He swiftly affected a carefree smile. "I am going to need an explanation for that statement. The hypocritical part, I mean. The latter is almost certainly an apt description of myself." Unless his mother had come from beyond the tower walls, she was unlikely to have had a spouse. And it was simpler to believe that than consider he might have a living parent. Or at least one he wasn't responsible for taking the life of.

"Dylan," Katarina grated, looking no less ready to tear out his throat. "You berated Authril for her manipulation of him, yet you're doing the same thing."

"Me? I assure you, things between our dear spellster and myself are purely professional."

"The kiss I saw you give him last night didn't look too professional to me."

He hadn't known she had joined Dylan in the first watch, although he should've realised one of the others was still wandering the camp. Once he spied her through the trees after kissing the spellster, he *had* hoped her dwarven senses weren't as keen as his own.

He had truly messed up. *Shit!* And after he had promised Dylan he wouldn't speak of them.

"Kiss?" He affected a suitably bemused laugh. "What kiss? We did not—" He fell silent as she held up a forefinger in warning. Her stern expression reminded him of the minders back when he was a boy and the beatings he got for stepping out of line.

"I *know* what I saw and I know you are aware of it. *Don't* pretend otherwise. And, given how Dylan reacted, it's not the first time you've done so."

"Not exactly," he admitted begrudgingly. He doubted it was surprising to her that he found the man attractive. Authril had been extremely vocal about her views on his attempt to seduce Dylan in *The Gilded Lily*.

Her hazel eyes narrowed. Close as she was, the look carried a sharpness that spoke of brooking no nonsense. "It is my understanding that your status as a hound puts you in a position of power over him. Is that not correct?"

"*Technically*," he ground out through clenched teeth. So was the hedgewitch. And Authril. A case could even be made that Marin also bore that description whilst the man remained unleashed.

The green patches surrounding the inner brown swathe of her iris gained a luminosity that shouldn't have been possible. "Yet you skulk about in the shadows to court him as though ashamed of the fact."

He focused on keeping his features pleasant. Or at least tried. He felt his smile fraying at the edges. "Not once have I ever been ashamed of who I choose to pursue." Those he'd been forced to entertain—clients he would've never have shared a room with, never mind a bed—was a different matter. "And believe me, what we are doing could not be defined as courting." His dear spellster would probably laugh at him if he tried.

"And that makes it better? If Authril were to do such a thing—"

"Do *not* compare me to her," he snapped. "There is a *vast* difference between what she did and what I do."

She stared him down, her arms folded before her. The hedgewitch wasn't as tall as Dylan, but it didn't change the fact she still towered over him. Or that she had a vastly more solid frame than the man. "Explain."

His impatience huffed out with the exhale. Did he really need to? "She did it in an attempt to control him. I have given a few harmless kisses. A handful at best." He paused, waiting to see if she believed that was as far as Dylan and himself had been intimate. He *had* promised not to speak a word of their activities, but he was definitely straining plausibility. "Does that make my intentions clear enough for you?"

Her expression remained stern. "How long has this been going on for?"

"The kissing? A few days before the tower." Barely a month ago and they'd done far more since. Yet, that night beside the campfire had emblazoned itself upon his memory. The gentle, hesitant, caress of Dylan's lips as the man made the first move. The soft hitch in his breath as Tracker replied in kind.

He'd been a child the last time he had shared a kiss anywhere near that innocent. He certainly hadn't expected it, not after Authril's intervention had him failing to garner similar a few nights prior.

The times since had mostly been hushed moments in the dark, be it his hands and mouth directly stimulating the man to completion or, far more commonly as of late, him grinding and rubbing their lengths together whilst he swallowed Dylan's every little moan and whimper.

He hadn't ever needed to slow down like that, not even with his previous loves.

She nodded, believing him. "What did you say to him before you left for your tent? I was too far away to hear."

His breath caught for a moment, the lush green world of the forest dimming into sooty corridors and rust-stained rock. He swore the jangle of chains vibrated from some distant cavernous place. "Why?"

"Because it was enough to leave him in a tearful mess."

Tracker had felt swirls of the man's magic whilst trying to rest. He assumed it little more than the spellster cleaning the very clothes he wore, as Dylan had insisted on doing. "I said nothing." Not anything of note, at least. "I simply told him there was no need to take my watch or launder my clothes, that *this*—" He indicated the cut sleeve and the bandaged wound beneath. "—did not render me incapable of doing either."

"You must have said something else."

He had said *plenty*. But not after they had kissed. He paced a few steps, tugging at an earring and biting his lip through the pain, as he considered what could've affected the man so. "You want our *entire* conversation?" He hadn't been interrogated for years, not since his false lover betrayed him and the others. Did Katarina expect everything word for word, as the hounds had demanded for every interaction he'd ever had with Wynne, Zinnala and their betrayer? "We discussed what our now-departed Talfaltaner friend said." The abridged version, at least. "He called me a fool for standing between him and the enemy and I..." There'd been more to it than a simple berating.

He fingered the new stitching. His right arm hurt far more than he was willing to admit, especially to Dylan. Just seeing the man's sombre reaction to hearing the wound stung had been bad enough. Hearing him demand Tracker not attempt such a thing again, even if it meant letting Dylan die, had been worse.

"I said he was worth protecting." He had meant it. Whatever lessons they had taught the man outside of harnessing his power, self-worth clearly hadn't been part of it. Or had it been a deliberate erosion? Even though he displayed quite the prowess in healing, Dylan seemed to think he was good for little beyond being used as a weapon.

Katarina remained silent for far longer than he was comfortable with.

"Is that all? Shall we return to our companions?" His skin itched to be... elsewhere. Anywhere. The where *didn't* matter. He just needed to be moving. To be gone from here.

He had taken one step back towards the camp when she finally spoke. "When are you going to tell him?"

"What do you believe I am holding back?" Besides plans to take the man far from the kingdom's grasp. But he didn't think the hedgewitch had figured that out.

"What you feel for him."

Nervous laughter hissed through his teeth before he could stop it. "I think he is more than aware, yes?"

"So you are also in denial of your deeper feelings, then?"

Tracker stiffened. "It is not like that!" he snapped, instantly regretting the raised tone. He marched off, intending to take one more circuit of their perimeter and maybe check a few of Marin's traps that he had spied along the way last night.

Katarina followed. A silent pressure at his back.

"Whatever you think, you are mistaken. It is nothing but harmless fun. Children's games." He had witnessed such a scene plenty of times on the streets. Boys chasing each other, trying to give a little peck on the cheek whilst shying away from another's. "At best, my feelings for our dear spellster are purely basic."

The look she gave spoke of disbelief. "I'm a hedgewitch, not a fool. We are trained in a great deal of topics, including marital."

"*Marital?*" he echoed, almost choking on his tongue. Or was that his heart? It thundered loud enough to be lodged in his throat.

Hounds were barely permitted to indulge in sex. An intimate relationship brought only death. Marriage? That was... inconceivable!

Well, not entirely. He had thought about it more than once, back when he was a child and had no idea what adults even did behind closed doors. The illusion of ever having such a life had died alongside Wynne, Zinnala and his daughter.

He gave the hedgewitch a teeth-clenching grin. "My dear, I think you underestimate my goal."

"Then what *is* your goal with him?"

"I—" He halted. His gaze flicked from the ground to the distant canopy of leaves and needles. Fantailed birds flit around them. A few chattered imperiously, demanding the giants move so they could feast on the disturbed insects. Not a one held the answer.

He didn't know.

There was the obvious target of getting Dylan far from here, from anything and anyone seeking to use the man. But beyond that? He hadn't thought that far. He hadn't assumed it would matter. Not for him.

"I think that sort of introspection is beyond the scope of a hedgewitch," he managed.

"Not really. A lot of people outside of Dvärghem focus only on our mission to unearth the past, but we also guide our people, which requires both training and experience. Especially when there is denial."

"I told you, I am not in denial of my feelings, there simply are no deeper feelings to deny." Yes, he cared about what happened to the man. How could he not? Dylan was alone, the only unleashed spellster still alive in the kingdom. "Maybe all the matters you are trained in help back in your homeland, but you cannot be aware of hound law. Or of the tales they tell about us." He slowed to an indulgent pace, tucking his thumbs under his belt. "Hounds are not ones to be tied down, be that easily or at all. We are said to have no souls, no ability to feel. Not regret. Not empathy." Not even love.

He had learnt that truth all too well. If one of the pack even caught wind of him ever being in Dylan's embrace, then it was the Pit for the both of them.

That place would not taste another drop of blood.

"You're right," Katarina said. "I know little about hound law. However, I *have* studied Nulled Ones. You are people born from spellster bloodlines only without the magic. You're not soulless. You can feel. And you know I'm right."

He shook his head. "What I do with him is purely for entertainment's sake until we reach our destination. He knows that." The man had confessed such an arrangement had been normal within the tower.

"What you *do* with him?" she echoed, her brows pinching together with her suspicion.

"Must I divulge everything?" Shrugging, he continued before she could answer, "We kiss. This, you know. We also snuggle. The latter helps him rest easy and keeps the nightmares at bay." At least that was moderately truthful.

"Authril suspects you're doing more than that."

"Of course she does." They could've done nothing and she would've thought it. "She has been accusing me of sleeping with him since Oldmarsh. Given the motives she has confessed, she can hardly point the finger even if I was to bend him over and—" He cut himself off before he could become a little too specific. *Steady breaths.* The truth of their dalliances wouldn't come from his lips without Dylan's consent. "The fact of the matter is, our dear warrior is set on becoming his warden. Absolute control over their charges is expected and Dylan? Well…" Chuckling, he gestured to his wound. "He clearly has a problem following orders." If the man had stayed hidden, Tracker could've picked off the Talfaltaners without them knowing until it was too late.

But then, he never would've been able to interrogate that final one.

Her brows lowered, heavy with the disquiet that darkened her eyes. "I'm aware of what Authril wants. She often speaks as if she was the only one to see everything burn, but I remember the ambush. All those flames. The way the heat warped the air." She ran a forefinger down the scar. "I might not have come away with broken bones, but I hardly came away unscathed."

"You were exceptionally fortunate to not have suffered worse." After reaching the main encampment, Tracker hadn't made any attempt to scope out the front line. Magic had radiated from that direction, but Dylan's power had pulled him towards the bushes.

Her hand dropped to rest on her breast. She stared at seemingly nothing. "Your kingdom's army wants to use Dylan until he drops. The people you're fighting…" Her brows twitched, briefly returning to their furrowed state. "I don't know if they'll return, but if they ever get their hands on him, they'll sell him on the slave markets." Her head jerked his way, eyeing him like a bird finding a seed. "I know why Authril is prepared to march him across the kingdom and back, even knowing he will suffer either fate. *You* though? You clearly disagree with her, but you have the same goal. Why are you so keen to see him return to that?"

He spread his hands wide. "Even a hound cannot always convince a spellster to follow our lead." And he definitely couldn't with Authril whispering guilt and command into the man's ear. "He is determined to avenge his home. I cannot fault him for that. For now, the only path with answers lies ahead of us and is likely to carry on past Wintervale. A spellster approaching that place without a hound at his side will find only a swift end. He is the last one I can keep from an undeserved death. I shall not be swayed from that duty."

"It's not fair. The Tirglasians treat their spellsters better than this."

They did. He'd only scraps of information from Tirglasian sailors, but he knew they didn't leash their spellsters, nor did they send them into war or even use their more destructive capabilities. They confined them, but the treatment was almost like they were monastic priests.

Tracker closed his eyes, doing his best to shut out the birdsong and insect chittering. No one else knew what he had planned. Could he entrust the hedgewitch with such knowledge?

Why not? He had already given her one secret. What was another?

"When we get to Whitemeadow, I intend to commission a boat to head upriver." He faced the hedgewitch to find her looking unwell. Given that dwarves didn't fare well in such vessels—every dwarf ship he'd ever come across had always been manned by dwarf-claimed humans and elves—they would likely part ways at the city.

"To reach Wintervale faster?"

He shook his head. "About halfway down the river is a fork that heads north. My intention is to go that way, to get him into Dvärghem." Travelling the northern roads from Whitemeadow would see them heading further from the capital and any potential threat his fellow hounds might carry, but he wouldn't even get a day's travel under their belt before Authril made trouble. He had far better opportunities to be rid of her via boat.

"You *are* defecting from the hounds. And you're taking him with you. *That's* the real reason you asked me about your warhorse."

"No, that question was genuine. This is a…" He waved his left hand about, gesturing abstractly in search of the right words. "…more recent complication. Things have changed and, to be frank, I am unwilling to take Dylan anywhere near Wintervale. I have reasons to suspect he would not be safe there, even with others to speak for him." He needed confirmation. Something other than a pair of dead spellsters and a tortured man's confession. Something solid.

Something that could dispel the unease creeping through his soul. To convince him his pack hadn't—*wouldn't*—collectively turn their back on a centuries' old creed.

"And these *reasons* are enough for you to risk breaking the terms of the treaty your kingdom made with us?"

He knew precisely what term she spoke of. Rogue spellsters weren't allowed to cross the border. At least, they weren't supposed to. "It would hardly be the first time I sent a spellster into Dvärghem."

That confession raised Katarina's brows.

"They were children," he swiftly added. "For the most part. No one dangerous, I promise." He could never be entirely certain if those he sent actually made it. A few were guaranteed, like the hound and spellster siblings he had set on a dwarven-run ship. The rest? He'd been unable to do more than give them coin and pray.

Those prayers had definitely gone unanswered with his last attempt.

He would not let the same fate befall Dylan.

"Does he know what you're planning?"

"No. And you will not breathe a word to him, either. I cannot risk our dear warrior learning of it." There was little she could do out here, but once they got to Whitemeadow, it would be all too easy to alert the other hounds. He could do without the threat of them snapping at their heels all the way.

"You'd rather keep him in the dark?"

"It is better this way." He'd rather not have Dylan at all than let the man think his freedom relied on him staying at Tracker's side. Allowing that to happen would make him no better than Authril.

And once they were in Dvärghem? Who knew?

CHAPTER 25

The road to Whitemeadow was lined with farmland. Fences of wood or stone acted like a funnel, subtly guiding people towards the city. Not that there were many people beyond them using it.

Unlike the first deserted farm, much of the land seemed laid out for crops with the earth tilled in neat lines, no doubt to grow the vast quantities of buckwheat the tower devoured. Just as, in the distance, the silhouettes of windmills turned over in the breeze to grind the same grain into flour.

Dylan's stomach rumbled at the thought of decent food. To think how often he used to moan about the soft, brown bread that'd been part of their daily breakfast. The scones with their stew in the winter and the plate of flat cakes, buried under a thick layer of honey syrup and cream, that his guardian would surprise him with to celebrate growing another year older.

His mouth watered at the bittersweet memory.

With fall breathing down their necks, he knew enough about buckwheat not to expect a sea of undulating white flowers, the very reason Whitemeadow was named such. But patches should've still dotted the land, stalks that were late in their blooming. He'd seen the cycle in books, knew this late harvesting.

But the stalks in the fields they passed were all black, as though a fire had ravaged the land. The work of the Talfaltaner force or the farmers ridding themselves of excess chaff? He wasn't sure he wanted to know.

People walked through the rows of blackened stalks. Most seemed intent on the plants, although they passed a couple struggling to repair a downed railing in their fence. After so long with just the five of them, seeing others who weren't hostile was almost surreal.

A brisk warning came from behind, almost lost to the thud of hooves upon the hard earth.

As one, their group vacated the road to walk along the ditch as a cart rattled past, its driver lifting a hand to the wide brim of her hat in thanks.

Dylan's gaze was drawn to the dark marks running along the side of her cart like charred scars. He almost didn't notice the cargo. *Sacks.* Not in the bulging shape grain or flour would give, but a more distinct form that could only be a person. He counted at least seven before sheer distance made it impossible.

Whitemeadow, their destination, lay ahead. It was a far bigger place than Dylan had expected. He had envisioned a town sprawling throughout the lowlands, like Oldmarsh, only at the riverside. Or perhaps a larger version of Toptower, which huddled around its namesake.

The reality was easily twice the size of either village or town. On a map, the river split the city down the middle with three bridges connecting the two halves. On foot, he saw only the river flowing out from either side. Everything within the city was shrouded by its buildings and remained such as they neared. Across the river, the hills were blanketed in more buckwheat, the dark brown fields speckled with patches of white that shimmered in the breeze.

For days, Tracker had spoken of travelling the rest of the way aboard a boat, but Dylan spied little in the way of water-going vessels. There was a single sailboat huddled near the north-western riverbank and a few smaller boats dotted the river downstream from the city, riding the current that would eventually lead them to Wintervale. *And the sea.*

It was the very direction the Talfaltaners would've taken.

Just the thought of them had Dylan's bones itching for another chance to avenge the fallen. But with the city close enough to reach by the afternoon, he doubted such an opportunity waited for him. The Talfaltaners were far more likely to be downriver by now, if not already back aboard their giant sea-going vessels. Either way, they were far beyond his reach.

At least they seemed to have left the city in one piece. After seeing what had become of simple farmers, he had almost dreaded finding Whitemeadow in a similar state.

The people were a different matter. They crowded the sides of the road the closer they got to the city. Many looked harried and altogether lost. Carts congested much of the way, not a single one heading out of the city. Their cargo varied. There were many bearing barrels and crates, a few had sacks in more traditional shapes, and one carried a fragrant pile of what could generously be described as fertiliser.

Unlike Toptower, there were no walls to indicate where the city started, the fields simply stopped and buildings took their place. First, alone and in single stories, then in several and abutting each other the deeper they went, until the buildings gradually threw the streets into shadow.

The lack of gates and guards also allowed the people to enter in a steady stream. It didn't stop the prickling of suspicious gazes falling upon him. Dylan tugged his cloak further around himself. The style of his army-issued robe was common amongst those in the tower, and he had seen a few men from the temples wearing similar attire, albeit in brighter tones than this dark green. Tracker had assured him that few would identify his attire, but he would rather not take any chances. It would only take one person to alert any hound stationed here.

As he'd done in Oldmarsh, Tracker led the way, heading ever closer to the river.

Dylan hadn't noticed it upon first entering the city, but the streets seemed to be on a riverward slope. In some places, the way was only made accessible by a flight of stairs. They traipsed several. Always down, if not always pointed north.

The buildings were largely uniform in style, stone composing much of the lower levels, some of them painted or covered in plaster. Wood took up anything above and even overhead. There were the ever-present lines of clothing and sheets flapping high in the breeze. Bridges, too. Albeit, the structures looked far sturdier than the ones in Oldmarsh's slums. They connected buildings all over the place, with some of them being completely covered and looking like a whole extra room had been erected above the street.

Slowly, the style changed from tightly packed residential units forming a larger structure to big buildings sitting apart from others. The streets steadily became a maze of carts. Some settled at the side of the road, whilst others travelled up or down.

Tracker continued to confidently lead them. They wove around crates and barrels, ducking through gaps in the traffic as the drivers were less cordial than those outside the city. People who Dylan assumed were workers in the various warehouses did naught but sit on their wares and watch them pass by.

The way forward was abruptly bottle-necked by an overturned cart. Broken barrels sprawled around the mess. It looked as though someone had made some effort to right the crates, stopping part way through to leave them piled near the side of the street.

The hound merely diverted their passage to a nearby alleyway narrow enough to force them into travelling single-file.

"I get the feeling this congestion isn't the city's usual state," Katarina said.

"It certainly wasn't this way when I last came through," Authril replied. She halted briefly, pressing herself against the brick wall that hemmed their left side as a cat scrambled to get out of their way.

The alleyway led them into another street, this one running right alongside the river and its row of empty piers. He knew the river was wide—supposedly five hundred feet at its widest—but he hadn't thought about just how *big* such a distance was. Its very presence sucked at him, tempting him to go closer.

He crept back into the shadow of the alley. Tracker expected him to travel via boat on *that*? What if he fell in? He knew the river had to be deep, but he couldn't even *see* the bottom.

They were asking him to drown. To sink right into the murk, where whatever creatures lived in that gloom would feast on him.

"That's not good," Authril said. She stood on the dock, shielding her eyes from the sun as she peered westward up the river. "Don't think I've ever seen the docks deserted. I don't think I've even *heard* of it."

Not moving any closer to the riverbank, Dylan followed her gaze. Two of the bridges arched across the water, their inner supports mere posts that would block only the broadest of ships. Looking the other way placed the third.

What he failed to spot were any more boats. Despite the obvious places where they would be, there seemed to be a distinct lack on this side. Even the few he had seen from afar earlier were moored on the far bank.

"Do you think it's the Talfaltaners' doing?" Authril continued. "They would've had to come through here. Although..." She turned on the spot, flinging her arms wide as though tipping over and falling in the water whilst wearing plate armour wouldn't mean certain death. "The city doesn't look like a huge armed company hit it. And they must've had their own boats to get up here."

"The absence of trade ships would suggest otherwise," Tracker replied. "Simply another thing to ask my contact. But for the moment..." The hound gestured for them to follow him along the riverbank.

The buildings were done in the same brick and timber style as the rest of the city, with a small difference of the brick portion extending to the next level. A couple were all brick in the walls, the only timber to be had being their wide doors and the beams of elaborate pulleys. Most of the structures were blocky, a handful having a smaller section jutting out higher up that was too enclosed to be a balcony.

They passed them all before Tracker halted outside a collection of three-storey buildings. A sign hung above the courtyard entrance, declaring it to be *The Sheppard's Axe*. "Perhaps I could interest all of you in lice-free beds and food we did not need to catch first?"

Marin hummed as she eyed the place. "A little bit of a downgrade from our last stay, isn't it?"

The man chuckled. "If you are looking for that kind of inn, you would be best to start travelling across the river. If you can get past the bridge guards on the other side, that is. The people in the southern half of Whitemeadow tend not to have much coin."

Raucous laughter caught his ear. People congregated outside one of the buildings further up the river. Someone had tied red ribbons around the columns, the ends danced on the breeze like hands beckoning them closer.

"You're not one of those people, though," Marin pointed out.

"That I am not. However, my contact lives and works on this side of the river. I will speak with him in the morning, but I do not wish to bribe the guards another time to let us pass simply for a few extra pillows on my bed."

"I could forgo the pillows altogether," Authril said, hoisting her pack further onto her shoulders. "But I wouldn't mind a decent bathhouse."

"Some amenities of civilisation would be welcomed," the hedgewitch added. "I can't recall the last time I felt properly clean."

"You need not go far," Tracker said. "There is one such place in that direction." He nodded towards the inn's stable. "Alan should be working nearby. Tell them I sent you and he should be most accommodating to your needs."

"Another friend of yours?" Authril asked.

The hound scoffed. "Dear woman, Whitemeadow is an important stop in this part of the kingdom for a lot of people. I prefer staying here to either of the hound stations. Is it wrong for me to be on good terms with those who work here?"

"Sorry I asked," the warrior muttered.

Tracker watched the women file off. When they had disappeared around the side of the stables, he turned to Dylan. "I guess it is just you and me left to procure rooms."

Dylan's stomach grumbled. With the city so close, they hadn't paused for a midday meal, opting to consume the meagre amount left to them on foot. He jerked his thumb at the tavern door, a heavy-looking thing bound with iron. "I wouldn't mind eating first."

A fond smile creased the man's eyes. "I thought you might." He pressed a small pouch into Dylan's hands. "This should be enough to get what you want and keep you out of trouble." His gaze flicked to the door. His brows furrowed and his nose gave the faintest twitch that spoke of an attempt to conceal his concern. "I will attempt to not be long. Although, I truly dislike the idea of leaving you alone."

Did the man think Dylan was going to saunter in there flinging magic everywhere? "What if I promise not to start anything?"

Tracker's lips flattened into a grim smile. "*That* is not my concern.

This place is visited by most of the dock workers. It can be a little rough for the uninitiated."

"Then I'll try to keep a low profile."

That honey-coloured gaze roamed across Dylan's figure. "I rather doubt you will be successful there. That lanky frame of yours is built to draw the eye. Just... be mindful? Please?" He laid a hand on his chest. "For the sake of my poor heart. I trust you to know the appropriate moments to use your magic and I would never ask you to not defend yourself, but..." The furrow between his brows deepened. "If someone goes to summon a hound, do not leave the room. Not even to find me. Not every hound is as willing to give someone the chance to talk as I am, but if you run, they will assume guilt and pursue a great deal harder."

I know. He had gotten lucky with Tracker. If the man hadn't let him speak that night in Toptower...

He didn't want to think about what could've happened. Nothing good. Not for him. "I thought you said you'd be quick. You sound like you're going to be a while."

Shrugging, the hound issued a creak of uncertainty. "That really depends on Madam Gwen's mood. She is quite the mercurial type, especially when it comes to her precious inn. The rooms here are often packed at this time of year and I am uncertain how much negotiating it will take to convince her to kick a few people out if need be."

"If we're going to be that much of a bother, wouldn't it be best to find somewhere else?" The last thing they needed was to draw attention.

"What about that place?" He gestured to the ribbon-bedecked building. The patrons seemed to be enjoying themselves.

Tracker did little more than glance the way Dylan indicated before chuckling. "I am sure they would gladly give us as many rooms as we desired," he answered, his grin widening. "But that is a brothel."

"Oh." It looked nothing like *The Gilded Lily*. No one seemed to be monitoring the entrance and, now that he really paid attention to the patrons, they were being awfully friendly with each other.

"We can go there later, if you truly wish. As for a place to sleep..." The hound shrugged. "The inns will be pretty much the same everywhere on this side of the river. And, given how things look out there..." He looked over his shoulder at the far bank. "I am hesitant to believe crossing to the other side will be an easy endeavour."

"You're a hound, though. Aren't you able to go anywhere you want?" If it was a simple matter of denying them entrance to a place, he knew of at least two dozen spellsters who wouldn't have been in the tower otherwise.

"That is only relevant when I am engaged in an active hunt and it technically only protects myself from trespass and assault charges. I cannot use my status to barge through whatever barrier I wish, certainly not for a night's accommodation."

"Maybe I should come with you, then." He could always wait until either Tracker or one of the women returned before venturing in search of food.

His stomach rumbled its own opinion on the thought.

Tracker chuckled. "Go." He patted Dylan's belly and turned them around until they faced the tavern door. "Feed this beast before it chews its way free. I will endeavour to be swift." Giving Dylan the gentlest of nudges towards the door, the man departed in the opposite direction, jogging up a flight of stone stairs.

Dylan bounced the coin purse in his hand. It shouldn't be too difficult to stay out of trouble, so long as he kept his head down and made no attempt to use his magic—a simple enough task in itself.

He pushed the door open and stepped into the tavern.

Compared to the bright sunlight, the room beyond was dingy. A fire glowed at one end. Lanterns and smoky candles lit up other parts, poorly. He stood in the doorway, waiting for his eyes to adjust.

Even in the mid-afternoon, the tavern had its patrons. Elven and human alike, they watched him with an air of suspicion as he crossed the room to the bar, the rushes beneath his boots rustling.

Whispers reached his ears. Rumours and tales. People were nervous about the soldiers who had poured through here—an unheard-of route for the army and the people didn't look like the king's men anyway—and wondered if they'd return. Some baker had been found dead in an alley not far from here and apparently deserved it. Most of the trade boats had been commandeered by the same soldiers under the king's orders and taken to Wintervale, for what purpose, no one knew. And there was a priest wearing strange colours striding through here like he owned the place.

Dylan smiled to himself. That last one had to be him. *So much for keeping a low profile.*

The bartender, an elven man and quite advanced in years judging by the heavy amount of grey in his hair, eyed Dylan. There was a certain familiar wariness to his ruddy, weathered face, as if he couldn't quite decide if Dylan was trouble, or at least the kind the man was worried about. "What'll it be?" He was missing a front tooth and the words whistled through the gap.

Dylan looked over the bottles and mugs decorating the shelves on the wall behind the man. His stomach rumbled another reminder of the scant meal and, even though he caught the faint scent of mould over the smoke and stale beer, the place didn't seem too bad. "Food would be nice."

"There'll be mutton stew later." The man scratched at his cheek with a thumb. "But I haven't got much on offer right now. Can get you pickled venison or fry you up some eel a mate caught off the dock this morning. Suppose there's some roasted trout bones you can pick at, can't guarantee it'll be the freshest."

Those were the only options? He'd had his fill of venison over the past few days, but the alternatives weren't exactly viable. "I…" Had the man said *pickled*? What sort of people pickled venison? His insides squirmed at the thought, his hunger waning. He swallowed the sudden abundance of saliva pooling in his mouth and slapped two coppers on the countertop. "I'll wait for the stew, thanks, but I'll take a pint of beer now." If Tracker was fast enough with securing rooms, then perhaps he would know of a better place to eat. Somewhere that didn't serve so much fish.

The elf's gaze lingered on the money, one brow giving an almost unnoticeable twitch. Had he not given the man enough? He was sure Authril paid that much in the last tavern.

Dylan silently fiddled with the rest of the coins in his pouch, counting what was left. A silver piece and five more coppers. If he put down much more, he wouldn't have enough left to buy a meal later. *One more copper should do it.*

The man's hand closed on the coins the instant Dylan added another piece. The money was whisked away and duly replaced with a mug almost full to the brim.

He settled at an empty table, dumping his pack at his feet. The regular patrons hadn't stopped watching him. They might've returned to their chatter and drinking, but he could feel their stares digging like arrows into his back. A group of men on his left seemed to be particularly interested in his presence. They jeered at him, then at each other, shoving their cohorts about.

Dylan kept his focus on the beer. Each sip was watery, a little on the sweet side and tasted like home. Was Whitemeadow also where the tower had gotten its beer? He had always assumed the servants made it. He savoured each mouthful.

The jeering group died down, evidently finding little amusement in his mundane actions and lack of response. That suited him just fine. He hated to think what the hound would've done had he heard some of their lewder comments. If the man's reaction in the last tavern was any indication, then Tracker would bring far more attention down on them than Dylan did right now.

The rattle of dice caught his ear. A disheartened groan followed soon after, not quite drowned out by a chorus of cheers.

He twisted in his seat, searching for the source, his gaze falling upon the jeering group. They circled a table upon which sat seven dice. One of the men picked up a single dice as another collected the other six. Both threw their dice at the same time. They clattered across the tabletop, halting to another loud outburst of approval from the group.

The game looked familiar. He'd seen it played in just about every tavern they set foot in. Even vaguely recalled a couple of alchemists, discovered somewhere near the northern border in their twenties, trying to teach it around the tower before the guardians found out.

One man caught him watching. He jerked his chin up in greeting and, scooping up the dice, rattled them in his hand. "Looking to play a few rounds of Aerona's gambit, your priestly-ness?"

Dylan lowered his mug, suddenly aware of how quiet the whole room had become. "It's a kind offer, but I wouldn't want to intrude on your fun." He turned his back on them.

"Not intruding if we're asking, is it?" The man's question got a chorus of agreement from his companions.

"I don't know how to play," he confessed, hoping that would be enough for them to leave him be.

If anything, his admission increased their interest. They abandoned their table to surround his, and him.

"It's really very simple," the man said, throwing his arm around Dylan's shoulder. "See this here?" He held up a single die. It looked to be made of wood, the pips crudely carved as if someone had hacked at it with a blunt knife. "This is Aerona. You priestly types must know all about her."

Only in the sense that her other name was The Executioner. The tower's sermons had been sparse when it came to the Seven Sisters and eternal punishments, but she was said to be the one who came for those who had failed to earn blessed Olwyn's forgiveness. That one blow from her axe left a soul dazed and drifting forever in the lightless tunnels of the afterlife.

And they'd made a game of chance in her name?

Something must've indicated to the man that he knew her enough, as his grin widened. "Well, you just give her a little toss and my friend, Willy—" He gestured to a towering chunk of muscle with a scruffy, bearded face standing across the table.

Willy smiled, the expression splitting the muddy-brown beard to reveal a set of yellowed teeth. Even from across the table, his breath carried the pungent aroma of whisky and halitosis wafted in the air at every exhale.

"—he'll throw down her sisters. If your number doesn't match one of them, you win! Praised be! If they does, you lose." The man's arm tightened around Dylan's shoulder as he shook him. "What could be simpler than that?"

A lot of things. He plucked the wooden die from the man's grasp, rolling it between his fingers. It had only six sides, as did the others. It felt uneven, as though the side weren't completely flat. "I don't have any money."

The man scoffed, bathing Dylan's face in the scent of soured ale. "Money only matters if you lose, doesn't it? Big high-up sort like yourself has got to have otherworldly connections, right? The Sisters wouldn't let one of their lot *lose*, would they? Go on," he urged, clearly fighting to keep the oiliness from his smile. "Give it a little toss."

Dylan flicked the die onto the table. Rather than roll uniformly like the six pale dice Willy also threw, his bounced and pinged across the surface. None of the men seemed to find this behaviour odd.

He slowly released a breath and, focusing on keeping his intentions discreet, sent a wisp of it skittering across the table. His magic wove around the other, already settled, dice to set the die spinning ever so slightly. It fought the motion, wanting to fall one way in particular.

Another knock tipped the die onto the opposite side.

As one, the men craned over the seven dice. Several of the numbers on the pale dice matched each other, but none did to the die Dylan had thrown. By their own rules, he had won.

Something heavy slammed onto the table.

Dylan jumped. A forearm, almost as thick as his leg, had thumped down not that far from where his elbow rested. He twisted in his seat whilst his gaze travelled up the bicep as big and round as his head to the bearded face looming over him.

Dread boiled in his stomach. He had only given the die a little nudge. Nothing anyone but a hound would notice.

"You cheated," Willy growled. There was a faint brogue to the words that suggested foreign birth—Tirglasian, perhaps.

"Beginner's luck?" Unless they knew the die was rigged, they couldn't possibly jump to the conclusion of cheating.

"Nae. I saw you rolling it around your wee fingers. You fiddled with it. Just like you do with everything else." The man grabbed the collar of Dylan's robe, twisting him around on the stool. "I've seen your sort coming across the bridge with your holy attitude, begging for our hard-earned cash so you can live in the lap of Lady Luxury. And the dumb folk pay, too. Isnae that nice of them? Think they're securing their toll down the river when all they're doing is lining your purses."

"I don't want any trouble," Dylan said, trying to keep his voice even. If the man didn't leave him alone soon, then there would be fighting. A tussle Dylan would most certainly lose to this hulk of a man without resorting to magic. "I only arrived here this afternoon. I've never even stepped into this city before now. I have no idea how the priests here conduct their practice, although I assure you, I'm not one of them."

The hulking man laughed. "Listen to mister la-di-dah here," he said to the room, jerking a dirt-stained, sausage-sized thumb at Dylan. "Come here to slum with us folk who have to do all the real work. Look at you." He poked Dylan's chest. "All soft and scrawny. Bet you have nae had to do a day's hard labour in your life."

Dylan fumbled with the pouch of coins. "Look, let me buy you, and your friends, a round and we can forget—"

"Oh ho!" The man slapped Dylan on the back. "Look who's none too shy about flashing the coin he swore he didn't have *now*." There was a nasty overtone to the man's words. The smile that split his beard didn't look all too friendly, either.

Dylan bit his bottom lip, trying not to show how much the blow had stung, even as his magic soothed his smarting skin. He eyed the man warily. Willy wasn't going to be placated by giving what he probably saw as a simple, hearty thump to the back.

Sure enough, the brute shoved Dylan back against the table and spat in his face. "That's what I think of your offer," he snarled. "You want to part with your coin?" The man cracked his knuckles. Each fist looked easily twice the size of Dylan's. "Well, I'd rather beat it out of you."

Dylan dragged a sleeve across his cheek. He glanced past the man, scanning the room. No sign of Tracker or the others. *Damn.* Talking his way out of this wasn't working and he hadn't enough faith in the unarmed combat Tracker had taught him to attempt going toe to toe with the man physically. All he had left was magic and there was precious little he could do that couldn't be interpreted as a threat.

"You could," he agreed, trying to stall for more time. Where *was* Tracker? *You said you'd be quick.* What could possibly be taking the man so long? "But that wouldn't be a wise idea."

"Oh, you think so? We'll see about that." He drew back his fist in an obvious display. "What do you reckon, lads? One punch ought to be enough to crack his wee skull?"

Praying his shield wouldn't form, Dylan squeezed his eyes shut. The blow would hurt but, as long as it didn't *kill* him, he could mend it. And alert every nearby hound that he was here.

What were the odds that another hound would be as willing as Tracker to listen? *Slim to none.* Yes, he still carried the remains of his collar, but the man was right in that the explosion that broke it should've been his end.

A sickening crunch reached his ears. The lack of pain had him peeking through his lashes.

Willy lay on the floor, howling obscenities—in both the Demarn tongue and Tirglasian—as he cradled his hand.

Between him and Dylan stood a woman almost rivalling the man in height and thickness. She glowered at Willy before turning to address the man's companions. "I think it's time you boys took your friend on home before he gets himself into more trouble." She whirled on the group, brandishing a bloody club. "Or does one of you lot want some, too?"

Another of the tavern patrons jeered at the group as if all this, including Willy's busted hand, was some sort of performance.

Dylan felt along his jaw, his skin clammy. The brokenness of that hand could've easily been his face.

"What I'm going to do," said one of Willy's companions, a dark-haired fellow who looked like he might've been related to the one with the oily grin. "Is report you to the guard. They'll handle you."

The woman—Dylan decided she had to be part of the tavern's security—grinned. "You do that, sunshine. And I'd suggest praying Madam Gwen doesn't find out you're running scams in her house." She closed the distance between them. "Got it?"

Red-faced, the man stared her down for all of a few heavy breaths before gesturing to his companions to help Willy off the floor. They left without another word. Or their dice.

"You all right, love?"

It took Dylan a moment to realise the woman was addressing him. Unable to get words out past the lump of fear in his throat, he nodded.

"Poor dear." She gave his shoulder a reassuring squeeze. "The fright's gone and washed all the colour from your pretty face." She paused, giving him a considering squint. "Or are you always that pale?"

Before he could think of an answer, a jangle of noise exploded outside. Raised voices clashing with each other, something solid being struck, then swearing.

The woman grimaced. "Sorry, love. Got to get back to work. Oi!" she bellowed whilst marching towards the door. "If you're looking to kill each other, take it elsewhere!"

Dylan edged towards the door, halting after a few steps. He couldn't help feeling every eye was on him. If he left now, maybe he could find the bathhouse and wait outside it until the others were ready.

Do not leave. Tracker's warning came sharply to mind.

Taking a deep breath, he turned his back on the entrance. He might be under scrutiny here, but he seemed to be safe and the scuffle outside definitely wasn't. Returning to the counter, he set down a few coppers. "I'll have that stew as soon as it's done." If he was stuck here, he might as well eat.

Unfazed, the man nodded and took the money.

CHAPTER 26

Things had quieted back down by the time Tracker entered the tavern. No hound had come to collect Dylan, not even a guard had dared to poke their nose in here. The other patrons who had watched everything barely turned an eye towards him as he ate. Slowly, the room began to stir with the hushed chatter of people.

Dylan was halfway into his second pint of beer—bought more through a desire to wash away the aftertaste of what could vaguely be described as stew than a need to drink further. He hadn't seen any sign of the women. It was possible they could still be enjoying the bathhouse or had even decided to dine somewhere less dubious. If the latter was so, he wished they'd come for him first.

Tracker shouted for a tankard of mead to be brought over as he settled in the seat next to Dylan. The faintest scent of perfume wafted from his clothes. "My apologies for the wait."

"She took some convincing, I take it," Dylan mumbled into his drink. Between the length of time the hound had taken and the smell, he was certain he knew what the payment had been.

A man, young of face and human, set Tracker's mead on the table. He gave the hound a rather warm smile as Tracker nodded his thanks. "The bathhouse is vacated and ready for you, sir." The man lingered, leaning on the table, his hips gently rocking from side to side. "And could I perhaps pique your interest in an evening special?" The way the man spoke those last two words, all hushed and oozing suggestion, left very little ambiguity to the question.

Dylan lifted the mug, using it as a shield for his face as he drank. Did the hound sleep with everyone he came across? And was Dylan about to witness the prelude to Tracker slinking off to engage in some mindless fun with the inn's staff? *Quite possibly.* There was no reason why the man shouldn't if he desired the company.

So, why did the thought of the hound doing just that bother him?

"No." Tracker smiled at the man. His gaze flicked Dylan's way and back. "Not tonight, I think." He took a swig of his drink, watching the man leave over the rim of the tankard. "I do hope you have not drunk too much alcohol."

Dylan blinked, laughing as he realised that statement was meant for him. "Are you joking?" He eyed the empty inner of his mug. When had he finished drinking it? "The alchemists can brew an ale that'll put you on your arse after a sip and leave you feeling light-headed for days." They weren't meant to make them so strong, but that didn't stop them. Sulin snuck a few such concoctions into their room when they were far younger. They had spent those nights seeing who would pass out first, although neither one of them could ever remember who won.

"Ah yes," the hound murmured, his focus seeming to shift to somewhere behind Dylan's back. A tiny frown tugged at his brows. "Your friend and his cider."

"Is something wrong?" He started to twist in his seat to see what the man had spotted.

"Not at all." Tracker grabbed his arm, gently coaxing him around. "I was just thinking... I am not sure I want to see a drunken spellster." One side of his mouth twitched into a half smile. "You are bad enough sober."

Dylan chuckled. "I promise not to drink too much." Their journey across the kingdom had been rough enough, he was in no rush to add a hangover to it. "I take it you're done with securing our rooms for the night?"

"I am. The women already have the key to their room, which leaves us with one all to ourselves." His gaze returned to the man who'd served his drink, watching him move about the room, the hunger in those honey-coloured eyes plain. "And since they have vacated the bathhouse, I plan to make use of it and I wondered..." He twisted in his seat, suddenly giving Dylan his full attention. "I thought you might like to accompany me?"

Dylan playfully thrust out his bottom lip. "Do I stink that much?" He'd been rather thorough in his daily bathing routine. This morning hadn't been any different.

Grinning, Tracker set his empty tankard on the table. "No more than can be expected after a day's trek. Still, soaking in some warm water certainly would not do you any harm." The hound stood, his brows lifting when Dylan didn't immediately follow. "Coming?"

The thought of finding a tub he didn't have to squeeze into flitted through his mind. That hadn't been possible since he was a kid. He snatched up his pack and followed Tracker across the room to the gloomy entrance of the courtyard. "So, we've just the two rooms?"

The hound nodded.

"You couldn't wheedle a third through your negotiations? Or use one of those fancy token things the crown gives you?"

Tracker smirked. "My utmost apologies in disappointing both you and Madam Gwen, but I am not about to use the royal sigils just so you have a spare room to assuage our dear warrior's suspicions."

"She wanted one of the sigils?" Money. Of course she'd been after that and not intimacy. Sex didn't pay her workers, buy food or maintain her inn.

The hound frowned. "Why else would I have been so long?"

"I thought..." Dylan let the sentence die before he stuck his foot in it. He shrugged. "You reek of perfume."

Tracker sniffed at his clothes as if the leather wasn't drenched in the scent. "I smell incense." He halted. "Wait... You thought I had been intimate with her? And it *bothered* you?" One brow arched at Dylan. "Is that not a little hypocritical?"

Dylan rubbed at the side of his neck. "I know," he mumbled. He couldn't help it, but every time he thought of someone else with the hound, his stomach knotted like a gnarled rose bush. He knew it was childish and possessive and, yes, hypocritical. It made him sick, but he didn't know how to stop feeling that way. "I didn't exactly get a warm welcome and you said you wouldn't be long."

Sighing, the hound patted Dylan's shoulder. "Sometimes I forget how little you have spent out of the tower and how much of that time has been in company. But, if you will indulge me, is that also the reason for your sudden desire of space between us?" His fingers snaked into Dylan's belt, coiling around the leather until it creaked. "Or are you perhaps missing the thrill of sneaking your way to visit me?"

"That... that's not why I suggested—"

Before he could finish talking, Tracker had him backing up and pinned against the inn wall. Their lips brushed together. Soft. Hesitant. Dylan leant into each touch, barely breathing between kisses. His insides quivered. His chest ached.

"You know," the hound breathed against Dylan's lips. "If your desire is to have me all to yourself for the night, you only have to ask. That *is* your wish, yes?"

Yes. His mind was too fogged to form the right words. Dropping his pack, Dylan dug his fingers into the man's outfit and tugged the hound hard against him. Their tongues entwined. Firm and insistent. It wasn't enough. The impious fire in his gut burned for them to be closer still, but there was already the unforgiving wood at the back and Tracker's warmth pressing against his chest. No purchase to obey the growing need blazing through his body.

"Track..." Dylan moaned into the man's mouth. His grip tightened, the leather and metal in his grasp biting into skin. If they didn't leave for somewhere private soon, he was going to undress the man right here.

Those honey-coloured eyes opened, mirroring Dylan's desire. The smirk Tracker gave was small. Teasing. "Perhaps we should retire early?" The question escaped his lips in a low rasp, thick and hot. "We have such a long day of travel ahead of us tomorrow."

Dylan tipped his head back, letting it hit the wall with a dull thud, and groaned. Accommodations were on the next floor and that meant stairs. He really couldn't face them at this moment. But what was the alternative? Snog and grope each other in some dark corner of the tavern like a pair of randy adolescents hoping nobody caught them? He was rather past the point where such an act would be enough. "There was talk of bathing, was there not?"

Tracker laughed, the sound rich and dark. He clasped Dylan's hand and silently led him across the courtyard. The cool early evening breeze kicked up as they strode past the stables, slapping his cheeks and dulling the fire running through his veins.

Soft rustles within the stalls spoke of their passage being tracked by lazily curious horses. There didn't seem to be any sign of a stableman or whatever they called the people who worked here.

They rounded the end of the stables and came to a halt outside a stone hut. "I do hope he remembered I like my water extra hot," Tracker murmured whilst unlocking the door.

The hot, acidic twinge of... distaste—if Dylan was entirely honest with himself, he would admit to it being jealousy—hit his stomach at the memory of the man back in the tavern. His gaze swept over the hound's back and an altogether spiky thread of possessiveness wove its way into his gut.

Dylan took a deep breath, having to actively work to quash the feeling. It was not his place to interfere with the hound's intimate habits. Who he slept with was entirely Tracker's choice and he had made it by refusing the man's advances. "Did you actually specify two baths or—?"

"Two?" The hound chuckled as he pushed the door open. Steam curled around the wooden panel, waving in the air like a sensual invitation. "You might want to take a look."

Dylan entered the steamy world of the bathhouse and took in the depression filling much of the floor space beyond the threshold. "It's enormous." He had expected wooden barrels like back in the tower, although wistfully bigger, but this stone monstrosity embedded in the floor was almost a small lake.

"Mhmm." Tracker pressed his cheek into Dylan's bicep. "A little more intimate than the pond we shared some time back. Warm without the aid of your magic, too. And you should be able to stretch out quite nicely, yes?"

I can. He let his gaze sweep over the room, just to be certain he saw correctly. Benches lined the walls. A few towels sat on the nearest slatted surface, along with a bar of soap. There seemed to be little else. "So, I guess we'll be sharing, then?"

"Just like the women did, no doubt." The man gently unburdened him of his pack and set their things on the bench ringing the wall.

Dylan frowned and gave a noncommittal grunt. He really wasn't in much of a mood to think about their companions. Whilst he could objectively state that Katarina and Marin were equally stunning women, knowing either one wouldn't be interested in him rather took the shine off picturing them unclothed. Yet, even the thought of Authril naked and wet seemed just as unappealing now he knew her motives.

His gaze fell on the man's arm. "Do you think it wise to bathe with your injury?"

Tracker waved the notion aside as if having his arm sliced open was nothing. "It will have healed over by now."

"I find that hard to believe." He had heard elves healed faster than dwarves or humans, but he'd only attempted this sort of healing on other humans. *It's only been four days.* A cut like what the hound had suffered should be still quite fresh. "Let me see."

Tracker grinned. "Fussy," he teased. "But as you like." He slowly stripped off the top layers of his clothing.

Dylan grabbed the hound's arm as soon as the limb was free of the man's undershirt. He unravelled the bandage. Although the area was still quite pink in the centre, the wound appeared to have knitted itself together.

"Another scar to add to my collection, yes?"

"I would say so." He ran his thumb over the new skin, watching the man's reaction. To his amazement, the hound barely flinched. "I could probably remove the stitches. Give me one of your knives." The slim hilt of one was pressed into his hand before he had finished speaking. He eyed the mass of cloth and leather that was the top half of the man's attire sitting on the nearby bench. Surely the hound couldn't reach it from here. "Exactly how many of these do you have?"

Tracker smiled. "You really should refrain from asking a hound those sorts of questions."

"Why?" He gently slid the blade tip beneath the first knot. The thread gave easily under the knife's sharp edge and he pulled the stitch through. "Do I run the risk of having you invite me to see the full array of your weaponry?"

A stifled chuckle huffed through the man's nose. "I believe you have seen the extent of it. Truly though, we are taught that you can never have enough knives in your possession. I find them rather handy in taking down fleeing targets without killing them."

He dared to glance up. The man seemed serious. "You've never thought of using arrows?"

Tracker grimaced. "It is true I have loosed more than a few in my time. And a hound's training is not complete until they know how to use a wide variety of weapons. But I find bows somewhat cumbersome and temperamental. There is *so* much maintenance to be had. You have to keep the string dry, unstring it when not in use and restring it whenever you *do* wish to use it. Plus, I am nowhere near as proficient with it as our dear hunter."

"You'd be better at it than me."

"*That* would not be difficult. I heard about Marin's attempts to train you." The hound clicked his tongue in mock disapproval.

Dylan halted midway through removing the final stitch to shoot the man a scathing look.

"Such a glare!" Tracker scoffed. "You really need to work on your bedside manner."

"That was the first time I'd ever handled a bow." He could hardly be blamed for being so inefficient with an unfamiliar weapon.

"Yes, and when I tried to teach you swordsmanship, it was the second time you had handled a sword." His expression gained a sly edge. "Or maybe the third, yes? You seemed to know your way around a hilt."

Shaking his head, he pulled the last of the stitches free. "Must every conversation we have lead to that?" He was pretty certain elves had the same libido as humans, or at least the women did, but he was beginning to wonder about the men. One in particular.

"Not *every* one. But I am standing here, half-naked, whilst you pull threads out of my arm. And you are so very serious in doing so." Tracker tipped his head to one side. "I like seeing you smile. It is gorgeous."

Dylan slowly handed back the man's knife. "Thank you," he mumbled, instantly glad the bathhouse's warm air had already flushed his face. *Gorgeous?* No one had ever called his smile that before. Smug, certainly, and often cheeky, but never gorgeous.

The hound's gaze fell to his arm. He twisted the limb back and forth, examining the fresh scar. "Do I now have your approval to bathe?"

Bowing low, he indicated the pool with a sweep of his hand. "Be my guest."

He watched in a daze as Tracker shed the rest of his clothing and saunter to the bath's edge. How hadn't he noticed before that the candlelight made the intricate tattoos along the man's skin dance with each little movement?

The hound settled on the edge, twisting on his perch to eye Dylan. "Are you joining me? Or perhaps you merely plan to watch me get all hot and wet?"

Dylan licked his lips, his mouth suddenly dry. He stripped before his mind had any time to reconsider, tossing his robe atop the hound's attire.

Padding over to the opposite side of the bath, he dipped a toe into the water. Blissful heat caressed his skin. He slithered over the edge. The bath wasn't all that deep, waist height at best, but there was a submerged seat following the tub's curve made of the same dark stone. Settling on it enabled him to sink lower still.

Sighing, he stretched out his legs. Having his whole body submerged in one act was such a rich sensation. He had dim memories of the feeling. Dylan rested his head on the edge and watched the hound slip deeper into the water.

Tracker was taking great pains to slowly lower his injured arm, and he grimaced as the wound sunk under the surface, but didn't seem to favour it as he'd done a few days back. Slowly, perhaps mindful that he was being watched, the man started to cleanse himself.

Although there was some distance between them, Dylan's skin tingled. This wasn't like the pond, with its open air and the possibility of being caught. He might have bathed amongst those of his own gender before, but never had he shared a bath with anyone. Strange how intimate the simple act of sitting naked in the same body of water could feel.

He looked about them for another bar of soap or even a cloth. It seemed the hound had possession of the only ones.

"So," Dylan drawled. His churning gut demanded something be said to break the silence. He latched onto the first thing his mind could coherently think of beyond the man's glistening skin. "Tomorrow we visit Reji."

Tracker leant back, his arms raised clear of the water as he scrubbed. "That is correct."

"The *blacksmith*," he said.

The hound chuckled. "You sound sceptical of his trade."

Dylan shrugged. Treasure he could understand, a prostitute of a high-end brothel must come across all manner of people and gossip, but he couldn't see a blacksmith having the same reach.

"Are we perhaps disappointed we will not be travelling to another whorehouse come tomorrow? If you desire, we could visit the nearby establishment. I would hesitate to call it anywhere near as luxurious as *The Gilded Lily*, but they are very eager to please if you want to—"

"I wouldn't want to put you out." Dylan was certain Tracker had turned down the man in the tavern for him, especially if he used their earlier kiss to judge the hound's eagerness. To then opt to spend the night at a brothel instead would hardly be polite.

Tracker's brows shot up. "Nonsense. If you desire some fun beyond our little group, I am not going to object. The place is just up the street. You could indulge in whomever. And, if the thought of me being all alone is what bothers you, I am content enough to watch. Or join in. Whichever you like."

He shook his head. Although, the image of Tracker watching him have sex with another the man no doubt knew like a close friend was a tempting one. Would the hound do as he had the last time they'd shared a room with a prostitute, holding Dylan's gaze as he slowly stroked himself? "I'm fine with staying right here."

The hound shrugged, water sloshing around him. "The offer stands."

"So tell me, how did a blacksmith become one of your contacts?"

The man grunted. "It is not much of a story, if I am entirely honest. Reji's very good at what he does, although I think he mostly deals in weaponry now. And he has a great deal of high-paying customers. Last I heard, he had taken on a third apprentice just to keep up with the usual blacksmithing demands. But, to answer your question, we first met when I commissioned my scimitar. My order intrigued him. Few elves—or humans, for that matter—can afford what I paid." A small smile twitched its way across his lips. "I think I may have inadvertently sponsored one of his anvils."

It had taken Dylan a little while to come to grips with the idea of money. He knew of it, but the tower, or at least their occupants, bartered amongst themselves for anything they couldn't outright ask the guardians for. He had originally assumed their food came via the same system. That some people had less than others was easier to comprehend. "He wasn't at all suspicious of where you got the money?"

Tracker laughed, genuine fondness creasing his eyes. "He actually thought I had stolen the gold at first. It quickly became a choice of coming clean about who I was or facing jail. It escalated from there." He tipped his head, the washcloth idly running over his neck as he eyed their pile of clothing. "It is a fine weapon, though. Worth every coin."

Dylan watched the hound struggle to bathe his back. The man had wrapped his braid around his neck and was attempting to keep it clear of the water by biting one end whilst flailing ineffectively with the washcloth.

Finally, Dylan couldn't watch any longer. He made his way to the man's side and took the cloth from the hound's unresisting fingers.

"Let me."

"Far be it for me to stop you." Tracker turned around. With his good arm, he reached back and lifted his braid higher up his neck until it sat well out of Dylan's path. Water dripped off his elbows as he leant on the edge of the bath, each drop loud in the sudden quiet.

Dylan ran the soaped-up cloth over Tracker's back, eliciting a small sigh from the man. Tattoos peeked out from between the suds. Dylan averted his eyes before he became lost in the designs that begged for him to follow their casual descent to places far more interesting than the hound's back. His gaze settled on Tracker's head, but even this wasn't as free from marks as he originally believed.

"What's this?" He brushed the tiny paw print tattoo adorning the skin just behind the man's right ear. Water trickled from his finger and down the hound's neck, the bronze skin pebbled beneath his touch.

"It is the symbol of the hounds," Tracker replied, his smooth, rolling accent growing gravelly. The usual trills and hisses Dylan had become accustomed to hearing took longer to pass the man's lips. Even without the pressure of the cloth on the hound's back, he remained in place. "All of us are marked with it, just not in the same place."

Finished with bathing the man's back, Dylan slowly tugged on the braid, looking to free it from the owner's grasp.

Tracker's grip tightened. "I would prefer you left that alone, if you please. It does not need to be any wetter than it already is." One hand toyed with the end of his braid. "Damn thing takes hours to dry."

Dylan recalled that morning in the pond. The man's hair had certainly looked damp for much of the day. "I can probably help with that, but I'm pretty sure it's been weeks since you last did anything with it."

Sighing, the hound relinquished his hold on the braid, having already removed the tie keeping it bound. "As you like, but if I end up sleeping with wet hair, I am confiscating your robes until Wintervale."

"You'd have me travel for weeks in my undertunic just for spending one night with damp hair?"

"You are quite right. I will confiscate that, too. And your boots."

Slowly, Dylan unravelled the braid. Free of its bindings, the strands sprang into loose coils. He tentatively ran his hand through it, searching for knots. It straightened under his fingers, only to bounce back once released. The texture was coarser than his own hair. Thicker, too.

When he was certain he wasn't about to turn the man's hair into one big mat, he slowly coaxed the hound back to gently scoop water onto Tracker's head. It seemed that, no matter how much he poured, it didn't look wet enough.

His small grumbles must have reached the hound's ears, for Tracker chuckled. "I warned you it is a sponge."

Finally conceding that the coils were more likely to drain the bath before getting to the same soggy state as his own hair, Dylan set about washing them. He lathered his hands with the soap and gently massaged the resulting suds into the man's scalp.

The hound's small, contented hum drifted through the space between them. "All right," he murmured, tipping his head back. "I will let you keep your boots."

"How magnanimous of you." His finger brushed the paw print behind the man's ear. A little mark to denote that this man owed his fealty, his very life, to the crown. *And here I thought Demarn had abolished slavery*. It had been one thing to keep spellsters locked away, but they were far more dangerous to the average man than a hound. "So," he murmured. "This mark is a brand?"

Tracker cleared his throat. "It is not so bad. It helps identify those within the pack."

"I would've thought, given your rarity, that you'd know everyone by sight alone."

"I do, for the most part, perhaps not the younger ones. It has been some time since I have familiarised myself with my fellow hounds and the royal line has been collecting us for several generations now. We are not exactly as numerous as spellsters. I think most of you seem to believe there is a great many more of us than there are."

"And how many are there?"

He hummed. "I would not be able to give you an exact number. We are often scattered about the kingdom. Although, I am certain there used to be more fully fledged hounds living beneath the castle when I was a boy. I would say, fifty or so? Who knows, we might even be pushing half that again by now, although I doubt it. It really depends on how many young ones are born and whether they all make it through their training."

Dylan withdrew his fingers from the man's scalp. "That's... that's enough for a small mercenary company." Fifty or so men and women capable of facing a spellster without fear of their magic.

"If we were all in one place, we would make a reasonable-sized troop, yes."

Certainly big enough to be a spearhead for the army against Udynea's spellsters. "So why doesn't the king send you to the front line alongside us?" One spellster could shield several hounds at once from mundane attacks. If they were all as stealthy as Tracker, then they would have no trouble slipping through the enemy's defences.

Udynea's army could be slain in its bed.

"I do not know." He pushed himself away from the edge and dunked his head, resurfacing in a great spray of warm water. "Perhaps it has not occurred to him," he continued as he combed his hair with his fingers. "Hounds generally work alone. They do not exactly train us to fight together."

And yet the man seemed to have no trouble incorporating having others to fight alongside.

Sighing, the hound bobbed along in the water, halting before Dylan. "You know, I suggested we come here because I thought it might help you relax." Those long fingers walked up Dylan's chest, sending droplets of tepid water trickling down his front. "Or at least be somewhere private where we could further our previous little exchange. But if this is not working, I fear I shall have to take more drastic measures to get the former."

A small mirthless chuckle passed his lips. What right did he have to relax when the culprits still roamed free? "I just feel so... hopeless." It shouldn't have been this way. He had done everything right and it hadn't been enough.

Tracker caressed Dylan's cheek, the thumb leaving a wet trail along his skin. "I know you do, my dear man." He coaxed Dylan's head down and kissed his forehead. "You really do not belong in the army."

"You don't think I'm dangerous enough to be a weapon?"

Those honey-coloured eyes peered at him, searching. "What I think is that you vastly prefer not being as dangerous as you could be, even in the midst of battle." The hound pressed closer. "You have no idea how rare it is to know someone like that," he breathed. "I almost..."

Dylan waited for the man to continue. "Almost what?"

A wry smile curved Tracker's lips. "I am rambling. Pay it no mind, it is unimportant." He walked his fingers up Dylan's chest, his other hand groping along the edge of the bath until it settled on the cloth. "But if you are not going to bathe yourself, I am quite willing to do it for you."

He tugged the cloth free of Tracker's grasp, knowing full well where it would lead if he gave the man the chance. "I'm more than capable of doing it myself, thank you." Not that he didn't want to go as far as Tracker was looking to go tonight, he just preferred to be clean of their travels before then.

He placed a finger beneath the hound's chin, tipping Tracker's head back. "If you can refrain from teasing me, I might let you wash my back."

Those glorious eyes widened. Tracker grinned, a low, rich laugh slipping between his teeth. "A promise, is it?" he purred. He slunk to the edge of the bath and sprawled out on the submerged seating. "If you think I will not hold you to that, my dear spellster, you are sadly mistaken."

Dylan smiled as he lathered himself in soap. "I'm counting on it."

CHAPTER 27

Dylan busied himself with removing the day's travel from himself in silence, his every move observed by the hound, who seemed content to lean against the bath edge. Just knowing Tracker watched him was enough to make his stomach bubble, but every time he looked up, he would catch that small, knowing smile curving one side of the man's mouth. And the way Tracker's gaze ran over him like invisible caresses…

It forced him to turn away before his legs gave.

Tracker shifted as Dylan went to wash his own back, closing the small distance between them to relieve him of the cloth. "I think I have been patient for long enough," he whispered. A hungry light leapt into those honey-coloured eyes, giving his grin a predatory gleam. "And I believe it is my turn now."

Dylan didn't bother wasting his breath arguing that he was more than capable of doing it himself. Instead, he knelt on the submerged seats, folding his arms upon the pool's edge, and let the man have his way.

The cloth ran over his back in gentle, but firm, circles.

Between the water's heat and Tracker's touch—methodically slipping lower as he took his scrubbing duties seriously—all the muscles in Dylan's body finally relaxed. He propped his chin on his arms and closed his eyes. He couldn't recall the last time he had felt this pampered. A pity that they'd be leaving such luxuries behind as early as tomorrow morning.

The cloth slid lower still, becoming far more personal than mere fabric had any right to be.

Jolted fully awake, Dylan jerked upright with enough force to have his stomach collide with the bath wall. "Th-that's not my back." The words erupted through his lips before he could stop them. Fresh warmth slunk its way across his face. Of all the stupid things to say. "You probably already know that."

The breath of Tracker's little chuckle wove its way up the nape of Dylan's neck, raising every hair on his body. "I was thinking," he purred. Those long fingers slid from Dylan's backside to his hip. "Seeing that we are now both clean and rather undressed, that you might be amenable to picking up where we left off?" The hound's fingers wrapped around Dylan's semi-erect length, drawing a quivering gasp from his lips.

Dylan swallowed. He very much wanted to do just that, but... "N-not here."

Tracker's grasp loosened, the hand returning to caress Dylan's hip. "And where would you prefer?" Tracker murmured, further heating Dylan's neck.

He twisted in the small space the hound had left him to glance over his shoulder. "A bed would be nice."

"Oh?" Tracker leant back. His lips curved in a small, playful smile. "Then a bed you shall have." He slid along the edge of the bath and slithered out. "Let us not waste any more time here."

"It's that easy?"

The hound twisted to sit on the edge, his legs gently swinging back and forth. "Should it be complicated?" His gaze brushed across Dylan's skin, the honey-like colour dark in the lantern light. "I thought you would prefer I lay off the teasing... for now."

Dylan joined the man outside of the bath, shivering as the cooler air fully embraced his bare form. Snatching up the towel Tracker tossed his way, he hastened to dry himself and dress, the former helped along by a quick application of magic.

Half-stifled growls and muffled curses from the hound caught Dylan's ear. He glanced Tracker's way to find the man kneeling at the bath's edge. Still very much naked, he appeared to be squeezing the water from his hair.

"Remind me why I let you talk me into washing this beast at this time of the day?" The hound gave his hair another twist, sending a small trickle into the bath. "It is going to end up completely unmanageable and sodden."

Dylan bit his lip to repress a snigger. "Talking you into it, as you put it, consisted of a few words and a promise. Which reminds me." He allowed the dense heat of a fireball to dance between his hands, not permitting it to burst into flame. He wasn't sure if he could draw the water out of the curls as he'd done with his own hair, but if hounds were susceptible to indirect magic, then this method should work. "Stand up."

The hound straightened at the command, the tilt of his shoulders suggesting he didn't entirely trust Dylan. To the hound's credit, Dylan probably wouldn't either if he was the one facing the pool. "Exactly what are you planning on doing?"

"Just this." He held his hands either side of the man's head, not letting his palms touch the damp coils, but instead radiate heat.

Tracker's breath hitched. He shivered, the skin on his torso visibly pebbling, and tipped his head back.

Dylan couldn't tell if the reaction was because of the heat itself or if his magic was somehow affecting the hound. "Is this all right?"

The hound offered up a drowsy hum, before coughing as though he had something tickling his throat. "Yes, I—" He tilted his head, his shoulders squaring. "Forgive me, I was—" Again, he cleared his throat. "Is it safe for you to be doing this indoors?"

"It's just a simple application of heat to evaporate the water." As long as he didn't let the heat actually ignite, it wasn't too different to how he warmed up his bathwater. "I used to do this all the time as a child." He shrugged. "Never set myself on fire."

"You mean—?" Tracker raised a hand into the sphere of heat. "This is not fire?"

He *had* impishly considered lobbing a fireball at the hound, but figured Tracker wouldn't find being used for target practice as humorous. "You can't tell the difference?" Was this what the man had felt when he ran through that fireball back at the abandoned farmhouse?

Would he have the same reaction if the temperature went the opposite way?

The hound turned to face him. "Is it truly so surprising? Or were you afraid it might catch?" He gently patted his hair. Even partially dry, the curls stuck out much farther than Dylan expected, enough to cover all but the tips of the man's ears. "I told you, direct magic does not touch us. That includes all parts. Even when we are dead."

Dylan switched his focus to the few final pieces around the man's ears. The thick strands really did act like a sponge. "Is that why you keep it at this length? It doesn't look like it's at all easy to keep under control."

"It *is* a beast to maintain at times, but it is mine." Chuckling, he toyed with the coils that had fallen across his shoulder, his smile wavering at the corners. "There have been so few things in my life that I can control. No one has ever managed to take this from me."

Stepping back, Dylan appraised his efforts. "That ought to do it."

Tracker ran his fingers through the curls before nodding his satisfaction. "Something else I should add to your ever-growing list of skills, it would seem."

"Hardly." He settled on the bench as the hound started dividing his hair in preparation to form the mass into its customary thick braid. He'd never seen the man do so before and assumed it was going to be a long process.

Watching the three sections become one was almost soothing.

Tracker's fingers moved swiftly, flipping between each section in a firm, practised rhythm.

His gaze dropped to take in the hound's unclothed form. He had felt that firm body against him more times than he'd seen it. The tattoos were no less hypnotic. They still coaxed his eye southward. Even with the hound's fullness not currently on display, the sight alone was enough to stir him.

Dylan wet his lips, remembering just what the hound had promised. *All mine.* No having to worry about being silent, about how far into the watch Authril and Marin were. Just them.

He repositioned himself, well aware that ignoring the growing interest in his smallclothes wasn't going to change its state without assistance. Gods, it wasn't fair how *needy* Tracker made him feel without even trying.

By the time Tracker moved on to slipping into his clothes, Dylan regretted not taking the man up on his offer for a little fun here. Maybe they didn't need to leave at all.

The hound turned as he picked up his sword belt, likely sensing Dylan's gaze. "Was there something you wished to say?" Those honey-coloured eyes lowered pointedly.

He followed the man's gaze, confirming that his robe was indeed not enough to hide his thoughts. "N-no," he stammered. "I just—" Clearing his throat, he groped along the bench for his pack.

"And this is, just to be clear, your reaction to me putting my clothes *on*." Chuckling, Tracker crossed the distance between them. He braced himself with one hand against the wall at Dylan's back, bending over him until their heads were level. "Whatever will become of you once I take them *off* again?"

In his current state? He would probably explode.

Hunger darkened the hound's eyes. The twitch of his lips suggested he planned to feast well. "Shall we retire to our room and find out?" he purred.

Dylan couldn't help the grin that took his face, although he was successful in stifling the giggle bubbling in his chest. "Please," he managed to squeak out.

Bowing, Tracker took up his hand and led the way out into the night. They followed a path around the buildings, which took them through dark passageways until they arrived at a wider, well-lit hall and a flight of stairs.

They staggered upwards, pausing at the switchback landing to reaffirm their desire with haphazard kisses and candid gropes. Tracker rubbed against him until Dylan was certain he would burst. He grasped at the man's jerkin, desperately wishing to rid Tracker of all vestments and let the man take him where they stood.

Tracker slowly guided them to the second half of the stairway, clutching Dylan just as tightly and seeming just as reluctant to abandon their kissing. The difference in their height constantly shifted as they climbed in small hesitant steps, evening out every so often as the hound continued up.

Dylan stumbled as his foot came down in search of a step that wasn't there. He pitched forward, grasping for the railing and finding nothing.

An unexpected extra squeal announced they had crashed into someone.

Panic hit him first as the thought of being caught by the others slapped the ardour from his loins. His face grew hot. *Stupid.* Why hadn't he waited until the world was securely locked away? He shouldn't have dropped his guard, shouldn't have succumbed to his need to feel Tracker against him *now*.

The deep tone of the grumbling reached his ears, setting them to burning even more than the rest.

"Well, I never..." the familiar-sounding man blustered, his protest falling into huffs as Tracker and Dylan started giggling like a pair of adolescents caught outside of curfew.

"Do excuse us, Alan." Still sniggering as he helped Dylan to his feet, Tracker asked, "Are you certain you are not a little bit drunk?"

Dylan snorted. "What sort of lightweight do you take me for?" He dusted off his robe, taking pains to avoid eye contact with the man they'd collided with. *Alan, huh?* It was darker in the corridor, but Dylan was certain this was the same man who had served the hound his drink in the tavern. And propositioned him.

The little thorny knot in his gut flared to life. He tightened his grip on Tracker.

Alan eyed them, his expression turning cold as his gaze settled on Dylan's face. "Can I help you sirs find your rooms?"

"No, no, my dear man." Tracker snaked an arm around Dylan's waist, pulling him close. "I know the way."

Alan cocked one blond brow at them. "Are you sure? I am quite willing to help you—and your friend, of course—settle in for the night. I could perhaps ensure your bed is warm enough for you?"

I bet you could. The possessive thread coiling through Dylan's gut twisted, seeking a way to break loose and strangle the cause. But if someone was leaving this hallway jealous, it wasn't about to be him.

Standing practically hip-to-hip with Tracker, the man's ear sat teasingly close. Dylan bent to flick his tongue across the tip.

The long fingers resting on Dylan's hip grasped a fistful of cloth. Tracker bit his lip and squeezed his eyes shut, but there was no masking the small moan that escaped.

Alan said nothing, but his eyes widened.

Some elves were particular about who touched their ears and, clearly, Tracker hadn't let the man get that close. *Good.* Now Alan knew he'd no chance of getting Dylan to step aside.

In one long inhalation, the hound regained his composure. "Excuse us. We must be off." He latched on to Dylan's hand, dragging the arm over his shoulder. "Long day tomorrow." The hound made his way down the corridor, encouraging Dylan to follow with a tug on his arm.

Dylan fought to conceal a smirk as he glanced over his shoulder at Alan. Daggers couldn't have been sharper than the glare the man gave him. *Tough.* He'd been promised a night in Tracker's warm cinnamon-scented embrace, he wasn't about to give that up for anything less than an attack on the city.

Tracker stopped towing Dylan as they rounded a corner. "You are a terrible man, teasing me like that." The hound released his grip, flattening himself against a door, his pack sliding off his shoulder to drop unceremoniously onto the floorboards. His breath rasped, thick with desire. "Or were you simply flaunting our intentions before poor Alan?"

Dylan hung his head. By the gods, what had he been thinking? He doubted Tracker appreciated being used in such a fashion. "Sorry. I don't know what came over me."

The hound's hand flashed out, those long fingers grasping the collar of Dylan's robe, and he found himself pulled closer to the man's greedy mouth.

He parted his lips, his skin already buzzing in anticipation. He pressed against the door, paying little heed to the creak of protest it gave to his added weight.

Dylan waited, but the kiss didn't come.

"I think I know," Tracker breathed. The faint touch of their lips brushed together as he spoke and tingled along Dylan's spine.

Before Dylan could enquire further, their lips met in earnest. The touch soft and restrained, but boiling with the desire for more. He slipped his tongue into the hound's mouth, grumbling to himself at how infuriatingly passive Tracker had become.

Perhaps if he backed off and forced the man to take the lead, he—

The harsh click of a lock broke his thoughts. The door opened, sending them all but tumbling through the doorway leading into a gloom-shrouded room.

Dylan caught the outline of a squat candle sitting on a table just inside the door. A flash of magic was all it took to ignite the wick, illuminating their lodgings.

Venturing inside, he took in the space. Roughly half the size of the room he shared with Sulin and seeming smaller still in the candle's dim light. This was where they were spending the night? He tossed his pack to one side, with Tracker mimicking him.

A bed took up much of the area, even with one side pressed against the wall. Beyond the table bearing the candle and a small stool, it was the sole piece of furniture to be had.

"That's too small for the both of us." Dylan gestured to the bed with a jerk of his chin, although there was barely enough of the furniture to call it such.

Grinning, the hound secured their sole exit with the turn of a key. "Only because you are looking at it all wrong. There's plenty of room, provided you let me sleep on top."

He cocked an eyebrow at the man as Tracker sauntered back to his side. "Top?"

Tracker drew him lower with a gentle tug of his robe collar. "Perhaps I should show you," he purred, his long fingers already descending to work on Dylan's belt. Undone, the strap was tossed to one side.

Needing no further encouragement, Dylan replied in kind, tugging and loosening the hound's armour. The man's sword belt hit the floor with relative ease to the dull rattle of sheathed weaponry, only to clatter further as Tracker kicked it aside.

He hadn't ever attempted removing the hound's armour before. There was so much to undo. Why did it have so many layers and ties? His finger got pricked on what was apparently a knife hidden just within one of the layers.

"Careful," Tracker whispered. "Some of the blades still have traces of poison on them."

Dylan withdrew the abused digit from the man's clothing to suck the tip whilst it healed. By the sting of it, that blade had been one of them. Something mild. "This is ridiculous," he mumbled as he returned to battle with a particularly troublesome buckle. How did the hound manage this every single day?

Smug, throaty laughter heated his neck. It was all well and good for him; the elf could undress Dylan in a matter of seconds if he so desired, which he had not. "If it is causing you grief," he murmured, his lips brushing Dylan's earlobe. "I am more than willing to strip for you."

He weighed the merits of such an offer before stubbornness gripped him. The strap came free with a rather satisfying jingle and Dylan slid off the first layer. The quilted shirt was far easier to get rid of. Feeling the man's warm flesh quiver beneath his fingers as he finally removed the undershirt was almost sinful.

Their mouths met in deep, open kisses. They took several clumsy steps towards the bed, their tongues entwined. So enthralled by the passion behind each gasping collision of mouths, he scarcely noticed the hound hauling up his robes until they were bunched beneath his arms. He reluctantly released the man's lips to remove his attire.

All but naked, Dylan tugged at the belt securing the man's trousers, distracted from his task by the hound kissing and nibbling at his neck and chest.

His earnest mission in undressing the man halted entirely as Tracker's hands wandered across his bare abdomen and continued down. Those long fingers glided over Dylan's length before the palm massaged him through his smallclothes.

He groaned, grinding against the touch.

Tracker's head sank, branding a trail of wet, open-mouthed kisses down Dylan's chest. The hot, tickling blast of the hound's breath tingled across his skin.

Dylan tipped his head back, lost in the sensation. A small whimper left his lips. Such a tame thing should not feel this good.

Kneeling, Tracker plucked at the laces holding Dylan's smallclothes fast, struggling as though unable to keep on task. The tie loosened, and those wicked fingers curled around the waistband, tugging them down. The hound's lips continued to brush Dylan's skin, working ever lower as the fabric fell.

With his legs shaking and threatening to dump him where he stood, Dylan stepped back to fully divest himself of his clothing. He blindly searched for something to keep him upright, his fingers latching onto a wooden bedpost. Another step had him bumping into the bed end, practically sitting on it. He went to move only to be halted by Tracker's fingers wrapping about his shaft, slowly moving up and down.

He stared at the far wall, concentrating on following the grain of the bare planks, trying to hold on so that his trembling legs didn't give completely.

Bliss chased him anyway, setting him to moaning as the man's hand was replaced with the warm wetness of his tongue. It slicked along the underside of his length, curling about the tip and back down.

A groan slid up the hound's throat in answer. The sound vibrated across Dylan's skin, bringing a fresh wave of pleasure.

He tipped his head back, brokenly pleading to the rafters for release.

The heavenly being at his waist answered his prayers, engulfing him to the hilt, draining him of everything he had and sending him soaring over the edge.

When the room came back into focus, he was still teetering on the bed end with the hound kneeling at his feet.

Tracker rocked back, one hand grasping the bedpost to keep from falling whilst the other wiped the corners of his mouth. "Has anyone told you how divine you taste?" Unlike Dylan, his breath came unlaboured.

He shook his head, unable to manage words between gulps of air.

"No?" Getting to his feet, Tracker draped himself against Dylan, pinning him to the end of the bed frame. "How about I show you?" He pressed close, his lips parted, waiting for acquiescence.

Dylan gave it.

He lost himself to the sweep of the hound's tongue and the slightly salty tang that lingered in the back of his throat. No longer needing to grip the bed so tightly, his hands roamed Tracker's body, revelling in the warm, taut skin beneath his fingertips, seeking a way beneath the leather and linen still encasing his true want.

It didn't help that the man rocked against him, grinding that very desire into his abdomen.

He whined into Tracker's mouth. The man was determined to drive him insane. He was sure of it.

Pulling back, that honey-coloured gaze—dark with hunger—locked with his, clearly searching but unsure what for. "Is something wrong?"

"Apart from your belt buckle being freezing?" The metal rested against his stomach, chill enough that he couldn't completely ignore it, but nowhere near cold enough to soothe the heat still burning merrily in his core.

A small, and very much amused, huff warmed Dylan's neck. "Would you like to remove it?"

"Actually." He gently guided the hound around until the man's legs touched the bed frame. "I was thinking more... I watch *you* do it." Stepping back, he heavily appraised Tracker's attire. Boots, trousers and undergarments weren't much, but he'd been teased by seeing the man remove far less.

Shrugging, Tracker kicked off his boots and set about unbuckling his belt. "As you like." The tone might've been nonchalant, but there was a definite eagerness in his eyes. He slowly shed his clothing, not even hiding how much of a show he was making in doing it.

Dylan balled his hands to keep them from temptation. *Soon.*

Sure he couldn't control himself if he watched for any longer, he averted his eyes. The man's low, rich chuckle reached his ears, heating his face with its triumphant vein.

His gaze fell on Tracker's already discarded clothes, the hound's pouch of vials amongst them. He would need oil if he was going to get the man relaxed enough for what he had planned. Gently unfolding the pouch, he rummaged through the little glass containers filled with various coloured fluids and powders, many no doubt poisonous.

At his back came the soft rustle of dried grass as Tracker settled onto the bed. "You know," he drawled. "It is generally considered unwise to make a habit of rifling amongst a hound's arsenal."

"Are you afraid I might pour the wrong liquid on you?" Dylan carefully selected a promising-looking vial filled with amber liquid. Sniffing the contents proved him right. "I know what it looks like." He had seen the oil vials often enough in the hound's possession as he tended to his knives.

He turned back to find Tracker stretched out atop the bedding, reclining on his side and propped on an arm. The tattoos on his abdomen seemed to move all on their own with each breath.

"Do you require instructions? I am quite willing to direct you."

I bet. He rolled the vial between his fingers, trying to tear his gaze from the man long enough to form coherent words. "No, I'm pretty sure I've got the gist of it." A little oil to lubricate things, a little teasing to keep the senses raw. He could fumble his way through the rest if need be.

"So," Tracker purred. The forefinger of his free hand slowly trailed up and down his body, stopping only to play with his glistening erect length. "How do you want me?"

All thought fled Dylan's mind in one swift moment. "Hhn?" His core quivered, the room growing a touch hotter.

The hum of his power stirring snapped him back into reality. He had expected the teasing, the caresses, but that inviting gaze almost had him vaulting onto the bed, fully prepared to let the man do whatever he wanted. *I am in control of this.* He swallowed thickly, not entirely sure he could accept those words as truth, much less have the hound believe it.

Tracker sat up, concern furrowing his brow. "Dylan?" Gone was the sultry tone that set his blood aflame. "Are you all right? Do I— Do *you* need me to slow down?"

"No, I'm fine. I just..." He absently wiped the corner of his mouth. By the gods, had he actually been drooling? "Give me a moment to think." He turned his shoulder to the man, letting his attention roam the wall. The bare surface left him with nothing else to consider but the hound's question.

Did he need to slow down? He didn't think so. What did he want, then? Sex, obviously. And so much more. There were tricks of his own he wanted to share. But if he tried any of them now, he wasn't sure how well he'd be able to control his magic.

Maybe Tracker was right. He needed to slow down, to get his racing heart under control before it thumped its last. But how to do that without also staunching his passion?

His gaze drifted to their discarded belts, then the bedposts. The wisp of an idea formed. "Get on your stomach."

Tracker obeyed, the swiftness with which he did so belying whatever meagre attempts the man made in hiding his enthusiasm towards discovering what Dylan had in mind.

He picked up their belts and snapped them a few times. They seemed strong enough for what he had planned.

The hound's gaze darted to the leather straps, wary. "I would like to point out that, if you plan on hitting me with those, I will object."

"I thought you didn't mind a bit of pain," Dylan murmured, carefully threading the belts through their buckles until they made a loop large enough to fit a hand.

Surprisingly, the hound's chuckle carried a somewhat uneasy edge. "Certain types. I had enough of being beaten in my training, thank you."

"I don't intend to hurt you." He secured each of the loops around Tracker's wrists. "Just... constrain for a while." He knotted the belts around each bedpost, kneeling next to the man as he ensured the hound was comfortably secured. His gaze drifted to where the fresh scar stood out against the man's banded arm. "Do you think your arm can handle that?"

"I believe so." Tracker tested the bindings and grunted. "I also assume I have a way out of this."

Dylan bent over the hound, his torso connecting with the man's warm back. After pouring a little oil onto the palm of his hand, he tucked the vial into Tracker's fist. "You want to stop," he whispered, his lips mere inches from the man's ear. "Just say the word."

"And just what do you plan to do with me?" He wriggled, lifting himself to grind his rear against Dylan's thigh.

Huffing, Dylan sat back and rubbed his hands together to smear the oil as he coaxed the warm, soothing power of his healing magic to flow through his palms. He wasn't certain if Tracker would feel it, but the hound would still enjoy the basic touch. "First," he murmured, moving the long braid out of the way. "I'm going to get you all loose and *then*..." He straddled the man's legs. "I'll show you a few of *my* tricks."

Tracker fell silent, his eyes narrowed as he clearly considered if Dylan's offer was worth being bound. "You have me intrigued and—" He gave the binds another tug. The belts creaked, but refused to give. "—rather at your mercy. Do as you like."

"I promise you'll enjoy it." He started in the most obvious place, rubbing small circles into the shoulder blades, grunting as he worked to relax the stiff muscles. It was a harder task than he had originally presumed. Dylan hadn't ever picked the hound to be one who worried about anything, but the amount of tension in the man's shoulders suggested otherwise.

Tracker groaned as his muscles slowly gave under Dylan's fingers. His head flopped into the pillow. Whispers spilt from his lips, the words too warped for Dylan to make out.

Encouraged, Dylan moved on to lightly glide his thumbs down the hound's spine, the bronze skin pebbling in his wake. He reached the point where the man's back turned into his rear and pulled away, grinning as Tracker arched in an attempt to follow his touch. "Be still," he breathed. There would be time for more later.

Dylan ran tiny circles up either side of the man's spine, concentrating on keeping the warmth of healing pulsing through his hands on the off chance the hound could feel more than a faint buzz of magic being used. Unlike the hound's front, scars crossed much of the area laid before him, smooth lines and ridges slashing apart the designs inked there. Some of the clearly older scars had even been tattooed over.

How much of it had been inflicted by the very people who raised him? He wasn't certain he wanted to know the answer.

He reached the base of Tracker's neck and curved his fingers over the man's shoulders. There was plenty of tension here, too. He dug his thumbs in, working small circles until the resistance vanished.

Still, he lingered. Many of the tattoos marking Tracker's back followed his natural musculature, the one starting at his neck did not. Dylan had seen it before, or at least part of it, the last time he massaged the man. "I have to ask, what's the meaning behind this one?" He traced the image adorning much of the hound's upper body. It was old. The ink faded, the lines no longer crisp, but it was definitely a sword. The hilt ran from the edge of the man's hair to the base of his neck, where the blade carried on halfway down his spine.

The flesh beneath Dylan's fingers shuddered. Tracker lifted his head and the sword danced, twisting as muscles and tendons shifted just beneath the skin.

"It..." The word was slurred, heavy with pleasure, but not quite content. "It was an aid for my trainers. Not every hound is proficient in the same weapon. They mark us so it is easier for them to know where we belong and who should be teaching us to fight."

Dylan frowned. *Beatings, no name, forced marking, torture of every kind...* The more he heard of what Tracker had gone through, the more he wished the hound hadn't been born of a spellster, that he'd been given the chance for a normal life.

He pressed on, determined to push aside all thoughts of the outside world. His well-oiled palms slid over the bronze skin. He was thorough, and a little self-indulgent, in oiling every inch of Tracker's back until the hound gleamed in the low candlelight. Flesh rippled in his hands, moulding at his touch like the finest clay.

When there were no more knotted muscles to be found on the man's torso, he shuffled further down the bed. The hound's legs parted at the barest of requests, allowing Dylan to kneel between them. Tracker tensed as Dylan placed his hands on the man's hips to steady himself. His back arched, tilting his rear into a more agreeable position.

He ran his palm in circles upon the small of the hound's back, soothing himself as much as he did Tracker. "Not yet." Not until he knew the man was completely relaxed.

Placing one hand atop the other, he gently pressed them into the pliable flesh and slid up Tracker's spine. Dylan reached the base of the man's neck and pulled away to repeat the process. He did it over and over, listening.

Tracker sagged, a sigh gusting out with every stroke. His name.

Dylan froze mid-stroke. That hadn't been what he expected. He'd done this many times in the tower and the elven patrons had usually started purring or groaning by now, not whispering his name. And never in such a breathy, gut-quiveringly intimate way.

He finished the stroke and shuffled down a little more, tracing the swirling designs etched into the man's hips and thighs. Determination moved his fingers as he sought the tension that lingered in each leg. He would see Tracker completely relaxed before he went any further, however long it took.

He had made it part way down a calf when a few small, steady purrs emanated from the hound.

Dylan smiled. *That* was what he had been aiming for. A purring elf was a deeply contented one. Finishing up with the legs, he returned his focus to the man's back. The hound's entire body was pliable now.

Now that he was truly listening to the purring, the sound was different from other elves. Rather than an unending groan that rasped in the throat, this low rumble started in the man's chest, softly vibrating his whole body.

He ran his hands up the man's back, kneading Tracker's shoulders. "You still with me?" Some of his partners had fallen asleep under his ministrations. He didn't mind, usually. But if the hound ranked amongst them, then he wouldn't get a chance to show the man what he could do.

A short, but nonetheless pleased, moan breaking through the low purring was Tracker's only response.

Dylan clicked his tongue in mock disapproval. "Have we forgotten how to speak?" His hands fell upon the man's rear. He continued his ministrations, marking how Tracker's breath hitched at each teasing sweep of his thumbs. "Did your purring steal the ability? Or are we simply all out of words?"

All at once, the purring halted. "Neither yet."

Dylan slid up the hound's body. "Good," he breathed into Tracker's ear. "Because I'm not done with you."

CHAPTER 28

Tracker lay in a daze. His chest buzzed, not only with the pleasures of Dylan's thorough massage or even the headiness of causing the man's orgasm prior to this bliss.

He had *purred*. An endless sound that vibrated through his throat with every breath, rumbling from somewhere in his core. Caressing depths he couldn't remember ever being touched.

The weight on the mattress shifted. There was a tug at the vial of oil he still clutched in his fist.

He lifted his head, forced his eyes to focus, and found the sensation was Dylan working the vial's cork free.

Tracker's other hand reflexively tightened its grip on the belt. His skin tingled with anticipation. The fire in his loins had dulled to a contented hum during the massage. Now, it flared to life. This was more like it. He had known there was something on offer beyond a simple rub down.

Dylan dipped a finger into the oil, then replaced the cork.

He frowned. If the man was planning what he thought, that little amount was nowhere near enough to make things comfortable. He gave the belts another tug, the bed creaking at the force. The leather bit into his skin, reaffirming the knots were well tied. The belts weren't undoing from the bed frame without assistance, but the part around his wrists was a simple sliding loop. He had released himself from similar before.

The spellster shifted out of immediate sight. The warmth of Dylan's tongue ran along the upper slope of his ear, sending a swelling interest straight to his groin.

Tracker buried his face into the pillow, his cheeks aflame as he moaned into the feather-stuffed cloth. Was this what the man planned? Tease him until he was a whimpering mess, begging for more as he rutted into the blankets in search of release?

Dylan pulled back and Tracker found himself holding his breath for longer with each inhalation just to catch a hint of the spellster's intentions.

When nothing else was forthcoming, a thin tendril of impatience dulled the edge of his yearning. "*Do something*," he growled. Even if it was releasing him.

"Patience," Dylan murmured, his voice rich with long-stoked desire. The low hum of his magic briefly solidified like the glint of lightning caught in a vial. The heady tang of it sang in the back of Tracker's throat.

He breathed deeply, savouring the sensation.

If the spellster noticed, he chose not to comment. "You were right, you know," the man continued as something glass-hard, and radiating a coldness greater than mere oil, slid down the nape of Tracker's neck. "Certain things are easier when you can control the nuances." The item—for it was broader and longer than a mere finger—ghosted across his body, tracing the sword tattooed along his spine. Where the oil had soaked into his skin, this left a trail of dampness in its wake. "Take ice for example." Dylan blew up the path he had made.

Tracker shivered, a small moan creaking up his throat. He had played with temperature during his time at *The Gilded Lily*. At the colder end, it had mostly been small ice cubes and a few metallic toys, the latter of which warmed up quickly enough once the initial shock was done.

No one had offered to give him a turn on the receiving end before.

That chill touch slid down his body, briefly dipping into the cleft between his buttocks before encircling each cheek. Whilst he felt the cold well enough, whatever the spellster used never actually touched skin for more than a moment.

Dylan coaxed him into widening his stance.

Tracker mentally braced himself as the shifting mattress spoke of Dylan settling between his ankles once again. After all the teasing, he wasn't sure how long he would last, but he was determined to at least let the man go first.

The spellster's hand slipped between Tracker's legs, an act that took little effort with the way he had spread himself. Warm fingers caressed under his thigh, then up. They glided over his balls and along the underside of his shaft, teasing for a few strokes.

Then, with only that crystalline glint as a warning, the warmth turned to radiating cold.

Rising onto his elbows, Tracker pushed against the sensation, briefly feeling the full chill length of the object Dylan had crafted in the breath between contact and his body resisting the magic vibrating through it. Dropping his head enabled him to glimpse the ice shaft before it was drawn back up to halt at his entrance.

He shuffled his weight, excitement quivering through his gut. It had been *years* since he had come across something new. Although no stranger to improvised aids, he hadn't ever allowed anyone to put anything like *this* inside him.

The icicle's smooth tip slowly pressed against him, its relentless cold radiating deeper than the object at hand. His skin prickled. He sucked down an involuntary gulp of air.

"Too cold?" Dylan asked, withdrawing before Tracker could answer.

"No. It—" In the icicle's absence, the mild night air felt hot. He let out a steadying breath, waiting for his body to readjust. "Not too cold," he assured the man. That was surprising in itself. Ice, as a rule, started to burn exposed skin if left for even a short time. This was different. No matter how long Dylan kept the icicle in one place, the temperature remained the same. "I can handle it." He tilted his hips, giving the spellster a better angle to work with. "Continue."

Dylan complied.

His body resisted at first, refusing entrance not to the object in question, but the magic through it. Then the tip was in, and sliding deeper, to the accompaniment of his breathless cry.

He expected the icicle to melt once surrounded with warmth, to run down his thighs and make a huge mess like the other times he'd had others this intimately involved with ice. But this wasn't some little cube designed to chill a patron's drink. The shaft remained slick, hard and deliciously cool.

Tracker ground against it, angling himself to ensure it hit the right spot again and again, unashamedly grunting into the blankets.

Just as he was nearing the edge, the cold vanished.

He halted, an objecting whine trembling on his lips. Why had Dylan stopped? He'd been so close.

Slowly, his body adjusted to a more familiar warmth as he made out the spellster's fingers inside him. They twisted, lining up in just the right place. For a man who had never done this to another, he found the spot easily enough.

A buzzing pulse flashed through him.

Tracker gasped, his hips bucking into the sensation. The bed jumped along with him. The belts creaked violently around his wrists, threatening to break his bones.

Dylan withdrew. "I'm sorry. I—"

He twisted to peer over his shoulder. "Did I say *stop*?" He was damn sure no such words came out of his mouth, but if the man was hearing things, he was prepared to set him straight on that front.

Dylan stared at him, radiating uncertainty, for some time before speaking. "You didn't. I just thought—" A hand caressed Tracker's rump as though he were some spooked calf. "Are you sure you're all right?"

"You remember me telling you I am not the type to break easily, yes?"

Emboldened, the man slipped a finger back inside him. "Is that a challenge?"

The buzzing returned before Tracker could manage anything more than a low groan.

Unlike with the cold, Dylan didn't remain still. He pumped his fingers inside Tracker, his power alternating in intensity, whilst his other hand roamed Tracker's body. He caressed and kneaded Tracker's thighs, his rear. He planted gentle kisses up his spine.

And slowly, inexorably, increased the power buzzing within him.

Tracker rocked against it. His insides quivered.

Fingertips danced down his thigh. The spellster fisted Tracker's shaft, stroking in time to his thrusts. "Shall I?" he whispered. Tiny forks of lightning buzzed in his grip, there for a heartbeat, then gone. "Or have you had enough?"

"More," he commanded. He hung his head, determined to watch, and caught the instant Dylan obeyed. It was quite the sight, seeing the arcs of lightning part around his length as the man's hand slid up and down.

He thrust into the sensation. Words fell from his lips without thought, whimpered obscenities and mindless pleas to the gods. Over and over, they came, growing ever faster and more breathless. His body trembled, teetering so close to bliss.

Then he was over the edge, emptying himself into the night.

His arms gave, sending him collapsing face-first into the pillow. He lay there, too busy revelling in the euphoria thrumming through his body to care how the position squished his face. He could still breathe well enough. Everything else could wait.

Warmth slid across his back. It took him a moment to register the sensation of Dylan's torso pressed to his, and that was definitely the spellster's engorged weight hanging between Tracker's buttocks.

Rubbing his rear against the latter garnered a profane whimper from the man.

"Give me a moment." Dylan fumbled with the belts, trying to undo them, cursing further as he fought the leather.

"You untie me and I will give you something," he muttered. The man was right in that keeping him bound like this had constrained him. His fingers ached to roam that pale skin, to slip through the dark hair adorning the man's chest. To squeeze the perfect mounds of Dylan's backside, moulding the flesh as he rubbed himself between them, lubricating the path with his own slick.

Engrossed in his fantasies, Tracker barely noticed the spellster redoubling his efforts to untie him until the tension on one of the belts loosened.

He rolled over in the small space beneath the kneeling man, further shortening his bindings. "Is that what you want? For me to take you?" His groin gave a soft twitch of interest at the idea. Arching his back got him close enough to touch the man's chin with the tip of his tongue. "I am prepared for you to have your way with me." In more ways than one.

Wetting his lips, Dylan exhaled a shaky breath. "I know." He sat back, his gaze sliding down Tracker's body. Hunger burned in those dark eyes. "But you said being submissive was something you played at, not something you were and I..."

"Would prefer that role for yourself, yes?" Whilst it was true that Tracker had taken command for the majority of the times they'd had penetrative sex, he hadn't realised that was the man's preference. Rather, he had assumed the position was one of necessity, letting Tracker's experience lead the way whilst they were on the road.

Dylan uttered not a word, but the gentle bloom of colour upon his face said multitudes. He nodded, hesitantly at first, then with a stirring confidence.

Tracker settled deeper into the bedding, unable to contain his grin. If that was what the man wanted, he was more than willing to provide. "Untie me then," he purred. "And I will give you everything you desire."

Giggling, Dylan returned to picking away at the knots. "Did they teach you that line in *The Gilded Lily*?" He beamed down at him and Tracker's chest tightened. "You don't have to play that game with me."

With one belt undone, he'd the freedom to move his hand wherever he pleased. He chose to caress Dylan's side, savouring the hitch in the man's breath.

Sitting up, he licked along that pale neck, stopping as his nose brushed the spellster's earlobe. "You are sweet," he whispered, delighting in how richly *pink* the man's ear became. "But I do it because you get so beautifully flushed and flustered."

As if trying to prove Tracker's point, the man's skin doubled its efforts, reddening all the way down his neck. Dylan buried his face into his hands, mumbling a few choice expletives.

Tracker finished the job of untying the last belt and freeing his other hand. He worked off one of the loops around his wrist and, hissing, rubbed at the discoloured skin. The spot would definitely be a little tender underneath his bracers in the morning. "Remind me to teach you some proper trussing techniques." At least his hands hadn't gone numb. Casting the belt aside, he set about working his other hand free. "I knew there was a wicked man hiding beneath those robes, but..." The words tapered off into a groan, his body still tingling. "You truly are wasted as a weapon."

Dark eyes peered at him through the man's fingers. Dylan lowered his hands, his face only a fraction less red. "I've a rather limited set of skills. What else do you recommend, if not blowing people to pieces? Whoring myself out?"

Tracker hummed as he removed the remaining belt. Places like *The Gilded Lily* would probably jump at the chance to have a spellster in their employ again, especially if people got a taste for Dylan's magic as they'd done with Matz. "I would not go *that* far." The man might have claimed a broader selection of lovers than the average citizen, but he'd also had a say in who he shared himself with. Prostitute work wasn't as forgiving. During his time in the brothel, Tracker's refusal of prospective clients could be counted on one hand. Even then, he had needed a sound reason and the madam's approval. Dylan hadn't the temperament for that.

"How far would you go, then?" Dylan enquired.

Whatever choice takes you from here. Turning his gaze from the man's, he searched for the vial of oil. It must've dropped from his hand during Dylan's magic display. "I am sure there are more options than army weapon or prostitute," Tracker mumbled, his attention split by his hunt. "But as for now..." Groping beneath the pillow, he found the vial wedged between the bed frame and the mattress. "If you want me inside you, my dear man, you will need this." He tumbled the vial between his fingers, the amber liquid glinting in the candlelight.

Dylan's gaze darted from the oil to Tracker's face and back. He plucked the vial from Tracker's grasp and opened it, swallowing as the cork squeaked.

Tracker retrieved the vial before the man could touch its contents. "As much as I would enjoy watching you prepare yourself, I think you should leave that to me tonight." He drew Dylan closer, capturing the man's mouth as his hands descended to caress his rear.

With the spellster well ahead of him in the game of arousal, Tracker focused less on teasing and more on getting the man ready to accept him.

Not that Dylan made it easy to resist teasing. He rocked against Tracker's fingers, wriggling in an attempt to push them deeper. Tracker permitted it for a few strokes, greedily consuming every note of the spellster's moans, before returning to his task.

When he was satisfied, he gestured for Dylan to settle in the same place he had, halting him as the man went to kneel. "On your back." With a little guidance, he coaxed Dylan around, pushing his shoulders until the man was fully reclining. His fingers slid across that smooth skin to linger on the scarring at the spellster's neck. "I want to make the most of the light." He wished they'd something better than a single candle illuminating the room, but it was more than he'd had for so many of their encounters.

The man's already fully flushed cheeks somehow managed to darken further. His tongue peeked out, barely enough to moisten skin.

Tracker ran the pad of his thumb over the spellster's bottom lip. Gods, what he wouldn't give to have that perfect mouth wrapped around his shaft. *In time, perhaps.* Dylan seemed uncertain about the idea rather than completely against it. The latter being a more common reaction, even amongst fellow elves. Tracker was willing to wait until the spellster had space to think about it.

His lips upon Dylan's would have to suffice for tonight.

Lowering himself atop the man, Tracker couldn't help chuckling as Dylan practically levitated off the bed in his eagerness, no magic required. Their mouths rejoined, chaotic and breathy at first, gaining a rhythm as he guided their little dance.

He pulled back only long enough to move the spellster's lanky legs into a more agreeable position. Then he was filling Dylan, watching him bare his throat to the ceiling. Revelling in how those dark eyes rolled all the way back before closing.

Tracker kissed his way up the side of Dylan's neck to the man's ear. He gently toyed and tugged at the lobe, tracing the outer curve with the tip of his tongue.

Dylan couldn't feel the exact pleasure an elf would, but he moaned all the same. Trembling fingers, soft from a life of gentle work, ran up the bottom slope of Tracker's ear.

He groaned, feeling his slickness increase inside Dylan. If there'd been any worry of him still needing to chase his end by the time the spellster reached his, that silken touch had obliterated it.

His hips picked up a frenzied pace, bucking and rolling. The sound of their movements came loud and fast thanks to the combination of sweat, oil and his own lubrication. His lips travelled down the spellster's neck, leaving small marks in his wake of an even lower prize.

He had barely made it to the middle of the man's chest when his descent was halted by Dylan grabbing the base of his braid.

"No," the spellster panted. Already, sweat ran down his face, plastering messy strands of dark hair to it. "Gods, no. I..." He swallowed, gasping for a few breaths, before seeming to rally. "I haven't the strength."

He didn't need to ask for what. The man's magic quivered at its core, already flaring with Tracker's every thrust.

Gods. The utter temptation to ram himself home, to hear his name being cried out as the man unravelled beneath him in an explosion of power.

Gritting his teeth, he slowed his rhythm, giving Dylan a chance to regain control. He couldn't risk the spellster losing his hold on that much potential magic.

Even as he did, he knew it wouldn't be enough. Already the man's power swirled around them in unformed wisps or in the occasional spark from the candle. He doubted even stopping completely would've helped.

"Hold on to me." With shaking hands, he aided Dylan in wrapping those long limbs around his torso, sweat and oil making it a challenge even with the man clawing at his back. Having the spellster wound around him also hindered his movements, but the last thing he needed was to move.

This close, Dylan's laboured panting became more evident. His heart thundered against Tracker's chest, far more frantic than the solid thud of his own.

His name fell from the spellster's lips, ragged and pleading. Whispered prayers and stifled whimpers tumbled after, the hot air of his breath gusting over Tracker's ear.

It became his undoing.

Tracker's hips moved without thought, thrusting him deep within the man. He emptied himself into Dylan, heard the man's soft moan, felt him shudder.

Dylan's cry as he followed Tracker into bliss distorted in his ears.

He swallowed, ignoring the alluring tang of lightning singing in the back of his throat. Unformed magic no longer danced about them. It swelled like an approaching wave. Icy heat flashed across his skin. A wind he couldn't feel whipped at the bedding. His nose assured him something wooden was burning, or singed at the very least, but he saw no immediate evidence.

Pain lanced through his shoulder, the suddenness drawing a surprised yelp out of him. He jerked back only to find Dylan's blunt teeth firmly fastened onto his flesh, the blast of the man's breath heating his skin.

Tracker lay motionless, marking how the spellster's magic had stilled even as the man himself trembled and whimpered around his mouthful. He couldn't tell if that was because to Dylan regaining control or because the man was too exhausted.

In the clarity following his orgasm, one sharp thought came to mind. *Fool.* If any hound within the city hadn't caught Dylan using magic before, they definitely would've felt *that.*

It seemed he would need to pay the southern hound station an earlier visit than he had planned on.

~ ~ ~

Dylan clung to the hound, his body quaking, his breath coming haphazardly. The room spun, speckled in twinkling spots of white and blue. Everything seemed so bright, yet he could focus on none of it.

All he could be sure of was Tracker's weight, his warmth, the steady press of his chest with each breath. He closed his eyes and focused on matching that rhythm, letting the man's presence ground him.

Eventually, his heart stopped hammering wildly and the world was still again.

He breathed in Tracker's scent. The citrusy sweetness of the man's musk mingled with the bitter tang of sweat, oil and his own saliva.

Had he *bitten* the hound?

Slowly, he removed his teeth from the man's shoulder. "Sorry," he mumbled.

Tracker lifted himself on outstretched arms. How he was able to hold his own weight after what they'd just experienced was beyond Dylan. He didn't stay that way for long, though, collapsing on his side to rub at the bite. "For future reference, I do not mind the teeth, so long as you are gentle."

His face was already too warm to get any hotter. It tried anyway. At least he hadn't bitten hard enough to break the skin. He drew the man back into his arms to kiss the rather angry-looking crescents. "I might have gotten a little carried away."

"I could tell." Utter smugness curled his lips. Had he felt Dylan's grasp on his power slipping? Was that why he had slowed down? Demanded Dylan hold him? "And I will take partial blame for forgetting you are quite the biter."

"*When* have I ever bitten you?" His gaze flicked back to Tracker's shoulder. Already, the skin around the marks was darkening. No chance the man could hide it amongst the surrounding tattoos. "Before now, I mean."

"Never," the hound conceded with a bow of his head. "But if my blankets could talk, they would most certainly scream with the way you punish them. I guess I should also be grateful your bite is not sharp." His smile twisted, the tip of one fang peeking between his lips.

"And *I* should consider myself lucky you didn't retaliate given that *these...*" He tapped the exposed tooth with a nail, earning him a playful snap at his finger. "...can likely puncture flesh."

The man's good-natured smile fell a fraction. "They can do far greater damage than that." His straightforward tone made Dylan want to press for details. The haze of old pain in his eyes warned him off the idea. Whatever Tracker had seen—*done?*—wasn't something he wanted to hear with the echoes of pleasure still running through his veins.

And, oh, how it ran.

Dylan's lips twitched into a manic grin as he returned to his sprawl upon the bed. His chest swelled, the delicate dance of butterflies fluttering about in force. He hadn't felt this satisfied in... ever. Even their night in the tower hadn't been so intense.

He'd never been able to let go, to be his full self with someone, without worrying about being caught or losing control over his power.

Although, judging by the smell of scorched wood, he had failed at the latter.

He peered at the walls. In the fading candlelight, he couldn't tell what patches were shadow and what could've been a smudge of soot. At least nothing was on fire. They certainly wouldn't be keeping a low profile if he set the inn alight.

A faint knocking on his left drew his attention back to the hound.

"We are looking for this, yes?" Tracker rapped his knuckles against the wall at his back where a black, branch-like pattern scarred the wood. "I am unsure what to tell Madam Gwen—certainly not that you are a spellster—but she will not be amused, regardless."

Dylan laid a hand upon his chest. He no longer felt like he would burst at any moment. His breathing had slowed, not quite back to normal, but close. His pulse no longer attempted to beat its way out through his temples, either.

He tried to brush away the strands of hair sticking to his face, grimacing upon realising he had just run fingers that were slick with oil across skin equally as sweaty. His whole chest was coated in oil, too, gotten in the brief contact with the hound's back. *Right.* He might've made this mess without much thought towards cleaning it, but he shouldn't leave it up to the hound to fix it.

Except, there wasn't much in the room beyond their possessions and the bedding they laid atop. "I don't suppose the inn servants would give us some clean sheets?" He could make a bed easily enough. Getting the oil out of the wool and linen was a task beyond his skills.

"The *staff*..." Tracker stressed the word, causing Dylan's cheeks to warm at the reminder of the appropriate terminology for the inn's workers. "...will see to them when we leave tomorrow. For now, we will make do with our own. Which means you have to get up." One brow twitched as his lips curved cheekily. "If you can."

He most certainly could. Although, getting his partially jellified legs to comply was trickier. In the end, he half-fell, half-rolled off the bed to the face-heating accompaniment of the hound's smug laughter.

Tracker followed, albeit with a lot more grace.

They stripped the bedding. A generous half of the top sheet was still clean. He started with Tracker, gently wiping the excess oil off the man's back and legs, before settling on the side of the bed to deal with himself.

He idly watched the man make his way across the room, gathering clothes as he went. A strange, and oddly possessive, surge of pride bubbled up at the sight of the hound's unsteadiness. It was rare he had such an effect on those he'd lain with.

"What—?" He let the oil-soaked cloth tumble out of his hand and onto the floor. "Are you...?" He hadn't been sure at first, but Tracker was picking up *his* clothes specifically. And dressing as though he couldn't be out of the room fast enough. "You're leaving?"

He paused, a hand halfway extended to gather his robe. That honey-coloured gaze looked Dylan over and he gave a wistful sigh. "Would that I was not." His morose expression fell further as he turned to the window. "There are things I need to confirm before tomorrow."

"What happened to giving me everything I desire?"

Laughter hissed out of the man. "Was that not enough?" His grin broadened. "If you are still of a mind when I return, I will consider it. Sadly, I must cut this short and depart whilst I am still capable of walking."

Scrambling to his feet, Dylan hastened to don his undertunic. "I'll come with you." His legs wobbled as he bent for his robe.

"No." Tracker drew up the hood of his cloak and opened the window. "It is better if you remain." He deftly hopped onto the ledge. "That way, I know you are safe."

Safe from what? There was very little he couldn't defend himself against if the need arose. With the hound at his side, a lot of those troubles would be covered. "Is there a reason you can't use the door?"

"I would prefer if they believed you are not alone."

"They?" With his robe dragging behind him, all but forgotten in his hand, he crossed to the window. No one in Whitemeadow knew who they were and anyone hostile they came across hadn't exactly been left with the capacity to say much. "They who?"

Tracker sighed. He dipped his head, throwing his face into shadow. "Just some locals loitering near the docks. They were lingering near the courtyard when we left to bathe. Seemed interested in you, and not in a good way."

"What of it?" The only men he had encountered had been run off by the tavern guard. The way she'd spoken, he doubted they'd be allowed back anytime soon.

"They were still outside when we came up here."

Dylan rubbed at the side of his neck. "You think they're looking to start some trouble? With *me*?" Why would they risk having the city guard set on them? He had done nothing except thwart their attempt to cheat him. He hadn't even attempted any magic beyond that since entering the city. Outside of Tracker's presence, at least. "They're probably just still bitter about me not falling for their scam."

"You—?" Tracker hung his head. "Dare I even enquire?"

"They started it." The childish response was out before he could stop it. Blushing, he gestured to the robe pooling at his feet. "They seemed bitter about the priesthood. Mistook me for one of them. They insisted I play a round of some dice game—I forget what they called it—and I sort of..." He hunched his shoulders. "*Maybe* used a little magic to win. Discreetly," he added as Tracker's brow rose.

"*That* is what I felt earlier? You using your magic to cheat at dice?" He dropped his head into his hand. "I would prefer not to have to spend every waking moment with you to ensure your safety, but if you are going to get yourself into trouble, I will have a hard time convincing my fellow hounds everything is under control."

Considering that no other hound had appeared after the men were evicted, he doubted another knew of his presence.

How could they be sure there even was one within the city? Oldmarsh had been oddly vacant. Tracker admitted to having visited the hound station there after seeing his prostitute friend. But the man had also claimed the lack of hounds in the village itself was a common occurrence, given that stationed hounds often patrolled the roads and fields.

Perhaps the king knew of the tower attack and had summoned them back to the capital. "It's not like I just blurted I was a spellster. I didn't even risk putting up a shield when he went to punch me."

"He—?" The man's wide eyes somehow bulged further. "He was trying to *hit* you?" He scrubbed at his face, much like Dylan's guardian had done in his youth. "Maybe I should stay. I could go at first light instead."

Dylan frowned. He wasn't quite sure what Tracker needed to do so badly, but waiting would only mean a protracted stay here and he would rather avoid lingering. "I can handle the thugs if they try anything."

Tracker twisted on the ledge. "Of *that*, I have no doubt." The fingers that patted Dylan's cheek were already cool from the night air. "It is perhaps for the best if you show your face as little as possible whilst we are here. I will be quick, just stay in the room unless—" His hand fell, trailing down Dylan's chest. "*Stay.*"

"And what are you going to do to me if I do otherwise? Put me over your knee and spank me?"

The hound's brows lowered, although the quirk of his lips did ruin the overall seriousness of his expression. "Dear man, if that is what you want, you need only ask."

That was about the answer he expected. "I'll pass, thanks." He couldn't really say the thought had ever appealed to him.

Grinning, the man slipped out the window and into the night.

Dylan leant over the windowsill, trying to follow the hound's descent along the rooftops, failing as the dark clothes blended into the shadows.

The warmth that'd previously infused his body vanished. Even without the possibility of people wanting to kill him, he was in no mood to be alone. He straightened, trying in vain to rub the chill from his arms. If he wasn't to leave here, then perhaps sleep would be a good option. He hadn't lain on anything higher than the ground since...

The tower. And the gods knew not much sleeping had gone on there.

His gaze fell on the bed with its dishevelled blankets. It didn't look as inviting without Tracker's presence to warm him. Perhaps he should wait for the man's return before settling in for the night. *He'll be quick.* An hour, maybe? Sleep could be postponed until then.

He dragged the stool over to the window and sat. Pillowing his head on his arms, he stared out at the sky. He hadn't stargazed since the times he and Nestria would sneak to the highest window available to them. Strange how what had once been a thrilling hobby of mapping constellations and tracking the stars' subtle rotation now seemed so peaceful.

That had been years ago, back before they'd learnt what else could be done with the night. He had vague memories of wild dreams, fantasies borne from a thirst for adventure. And his first kiss.

He couldn't recall the last time he looked up and truly saw the night sky.

Thousands of stars dotted the heavens, a great glittering arc of dust. The moon would rise in time, then this sight would become obscured by its glow. His gaze slid to the horizon, muddied by the rooftops, darker shapes against an indigo backdrop. People moved in the houses beneath, their passage around the buildings tracked by candlelight, the fitful sputtering of flames mirrored in the twinkling heavens.

The night air was crisp and carried the foreign sounds of the city. Dogs barked at whatever disturbed them. There was the occasional clatter of a cart creeping down the cluttered street. Closer still came the laughter and chatter of the people below.

Dylan watched as the multitude of lit windows slowly went dark. His eyes were half closed by the time the moon breached the horizon. It hovered there, seeming to balance on the roof of a distant building, reflected in the hints of river peeking through the rooftops.

His eyelids grew heavier. Each blink took longer and longer to complete.

And still no sign of the hound.

Snippets of the rumours he'd heard in the tavern surfaced. That cook had been murdered, he was certain of it. Perhaps those same people had come upon Tracker. What was he to do if something had gone wrong? Anything could happen. To an ordinary man, the hound was...

Well, a lot more skilled than the average city thug, if he was to be honest.

Yawning, Dylan rubbed at an eye. *He'll be fine.* If there was any reason Tracker hadn't returned, trouble wasn't the cause of it. Unless the man *was* the cause.

CHAPTER 29

The lights within the southern hound station were dark. The building was a single tower, standing alone near the riverbank, repurposed from a guardhouse back when Whitemeadow had been far smaller.

Most settlements this size didn't require two stations, but no other city in Demarn, beyond the capital, was split by a five-hundred-foot-wide river. If Gwen's information about the bridges being closed was accurate, getting to the northern side would've taken an invitation from the city mayor.

Tracker circled the tower, seeing no sign of any forced entry or exit. He craned his neck up, eyeing the slits staggered around the wall. They were the only openings to be had near ground level beyond the door. Too narrow to climb through and spaced too far apart to be of any use in scaling to the rooftop.

Turning his attention to the surrounding buildings, he sought for any sign that someone was watching this place. Nothing obvious caught his eye. He had walked by a great deal of shop fronts to get here, the lower levels dark as people sought the comforts of family life. Few would be looking to draw a hound's notice.

He halted his stroll around the tower base, sauntering up to the door as though it was just another day out hunting. A quick rattle of the handle confirmed the entrance's locked state, one that was swiftly changed with a little encouragement.

The door opened soundlessly to a staircase that not only wound up, but also down. He cocked his head, listening for anything that could suggest occupancy. Pigeons softly cooed from above. From below, there was only silence.

Tracker ascended the stairs slowly, keeping his steps light and one hand on the hilt of his dagger.

The top opened out to a single room, illuminated by the rising moonlight streaming through a dozen open windows. A circular desk occupied the centre. Cages and roosts surrounded much of the walls, a number of them open to the sky. No sound came from within them, save for the susurration of feathers and the rustle of tiny bodies shifting in their nests.

No one had attacked the place. He would've seen *some* evidence of disarray, whether that be through a scuffle or of looting. The crates and sacks of grain stored to the left of the stairs would've been split open or broken into. The shelves of scrolls and books would've likewise been ransacked.

This space looked as though the hound stationed here would return at any moment. *Just like in Oldmarsh*. Except that place had harboured a man pretending to be a hound.

A few pigeons cooed as he fully entered the space, his every footfall causing the floorboards to softly creak. Even more surveyed him as he found and ignited the candle sitting upon the desk, their tiny eyes glinting in the flickering shadows. Several bobbed closer to tap their beaks against the mesh separating him from them. A handful still had little messenger tubes.

He quietly relieved each bird of their burden, paying more attention to the animals than the messages they carried. Without a tower, any hound stationed here would have only one recourse, regardless of how dangerous a spellster truly was.

But there was *one* message he had promised to send once he knew.

Whisper. The man's lover waited at Oldmarsh for news of what had become of the older hound. The coops held more than free-roaming birds. Ones brought from afar were confined in cages named for their home station and Oldmarsh was amongst them.

The desk still held everything he needed. He laid out a curl of unused message strip, securing it in the holder, and dipped the quill. The old hound's dagger seemed to burn in its sheath. How he wished he could've returned it, but the message would need to be coldly brief as it was.

His hand froze as he went to write the hound's name. The nib trembled as it hovered over the parchment, dripping ink like black blood. He stared at the blotches, his hide tingling from old memories of being beaten for making less of a mess.

He didn't know what to tell the man. Whisper had been executed, yes. But by who? The Talfaltaners? Why would they do that with the tower so close? Unless Whisper and the others had been protecting a spellster.

That didn't feel right, either. There'd been no spellsters amongst the fallen and the only magic to be felt in the area had belonged to Dylan.

Like now. The man's power hummed in the air. He hadn't moved from the inn room, but it felt faint.

Tracker closed his eyes, focusing on the sensation. The oncoming storm rumbled in the distance, sitting just on the cusp of hearing. The man must have finally fallen asleep.

A smile tugged at the corners of his mouth. Dylan had definitely earned his slumber. Tracker's body still tingled with the night's exertions and he suspected it would for some time. He would relish sinking into an actual bed beside the man once he was done here.

He tossed the ink-stained message slip aside and reached for a clean one.

Approaching footsteps caught his ear. Steady. Slow. Someone confident of finding another where they shouldn't be.

Tracker slid the quill back into the inkwell and eased a throwing knife from its sheath. His gaze darted to the candle and the flame merrily dancing away.

The wooden landing creaked.

He spun at the sound. His knife flew, embedding itself into the wall where the intruder's head had been. Two more followed the dark-garbed figure as they dove behind the grain sacks, the third eliciting a pained hiss and a muffled curse. The blade would've been poisoned. Perhaps not enough to outright kill, but certainly to hinder.

Nevertheless, he approached the area with caution. If it was another hound, then they would likely have the same advantages he did when it came to poison. "Whoever you are, it is unwise to squat within a building belonging to the King's Hounds."

Breathless laughter drifted up from behind the sacks. "I should have known they would send you."

Tracker halted his advance. He knew that voice. *Five-nine-eighteen-sixty-five.* Known amongst their comrades as... "Fetcher." The one who would've escorted Dylan to the army encampment. The last he had seen of her had been at a tavern in Toptower after doing precisely that. He'd never seen her this far north. She only ever travelled between the border town and the spellster tower.

"Hunter sent you, yes?" The woman peered over the sacks at him. "I do not envy the amount of bile you must have swallowed to obey her command." Her eyes narrowed, their grey hue dark in the candlelight. "Although, I cannot remember seeing you during the march. Did you not heed the summons?"

Did she mean the call for his return to Wintervale? The very last missive sent to every hound messenger post in the kingdom. "I know of no summons," Tracker lied.

Come home, it had demanded of him. Such innocent words. The pack had twisted them just as they'd done to the creed. Slavering animals tearing through everything in sight like feral mutts.

To think he had almost guided Dylan right into their gaping maws.

"You did *not* return?" More of Fetcher's head appeared. Her face seemed gaunt, as though she hadn't eaten or drunk for days.

He shook his head. Even if she didn't believe him, she'd no proof. He had burnt the message and discarded the tube far enough from Toptower's station that no one would believe it had ever arrived.

She slid back down until only her huge eyes sat above the crates. "If you did not get the call, then you— The tower... the spellsters... you—" She disappeared from sight to the clatter of limbs colliding with the floor.

Tracker hastened around the other side, shoving several of the sacks out into the room. Grain spilled across the floor, startling the pigeons. Most of the flock fled through the open windows. Those trapped in their cages jumped about, grunting and bashing their wings against the bars.

Fetcher had wedged herself into a corner made by a crate abutting the tower wall. She hugged her knees, rocking like a child after their first reprimand. If she had any weapons—from memory, she wielded only a sword and dagger—they weren't in sight.

He put himself between her and the exit, idly taking in her unkempt state, the tears streaking down a face that had previous trails cut through the dirt and dust. "We saw the aftermath."

"We?" She looked his way, but didn't seem to actually see him. "*Him.*" Her eyes carried the glazed expression most hounds had when they were focused on distant magic. "*You* brought him here. *With* you." A dreadfully broken sound creaked from her that set his skin to crawling.

Was that *laughter*?

"We heard the reports on the way through here—the army massacred." She pressed her chin to her knees. "I did not expect any of them to survive."

Tracker knelt before her. "You remember him?"

"Not just him. All of them. Every single one I escorted to their doom. They were all so happy. To serve. To be free." She turned her head, those slate-grey eyes finally focusing on him, their depths haunted and incredulous in the same instant. "Did you unleash him?"

"That was not my doing." He wasn't too sure how Dylan had broken free of the collar, but the man had definitely unleashed himself.

"How did you find him?"

"In time," he promised. Once, not too long ago, he would've trusted her with every detail. Now, he wasn't sure if she trusted herself. "What did our mistress order you to do?"

"No," she whispered, seemingly dazed by the question. "No..." Keening, she shook her head. "No, no. Not mistress. *Master.*"

"She is dead, then?" That was the only reason the king's sister, their mistress, would leave them in the hands of her son. A man who sneered at every hound as though they were little more than boot scrapings.

Nodding, Fetcher clutched at her head. Her nails, caked in dirt, dug into her scalp. "Master orders, you obey. You disobey? You get a raggedy new smile." She drew a thumb across her neck, smearing the grime.

He could well imagine. The mistress' son was the same man who made them watch as he beat a leashed spellster to death just for looking his way.

"I am not a bad dog. Only *they* get put down, but—" She grabbed hold of her jerkin, wrenching as if one good pull would tear the leather. "The children. There were so *many*." She lunged for him, toppling onto her side as he lurched back. "Did you *know* there were so many? The screaming. I—" She thumped the side of her head against the floor. "I can still hear it! Get out!" She pounded her fist on the other temple. "Get *out!*"

He grabbed her head, holding her still as she thrashed about. "You *were* there." Just as Dylan had suggested. "You purged the tower."

"*Tower!*" she shrieked. "Yes! All gone. He made us. *Told* us. *Everyone*, he said. Every single one. But—" A creaking wail escaped her lips.

He rocked back on his heels, letting her slip from his grasp to curl up on the floor. Even after interrogating the Talfaltaner, after identifying the bodies in the barn as spellsters, hearing the truth from her seemed surreal. That wasn't what the hounds were for. Attacking the tower without cause went against their creed.

Tracker grabbed her by the shoulders, hoisting her upright, searching for the woman he had known since childhood. If any remnant remained, it was small. "*All* of you?" He might've been the only hound to refuse the summons, but others must've known what their new master ordered was wrong.

She cackled as though he had told the most uproarious joke.

He shook her, hoping to jolt something coherent from her lips. "Tell me the whole pack was not involved."

"Not the *whole* pack," she murmured. "The elders, they..." Blood ran from her temple, slowly making its way down the side of her face. She wiped trembling fingers along the line. "They were..." She tipped forward in his arms, whispering, "...bad dogs. So many. Too many."

That had to be Whisper and the other seven he'd been unable to identify from the gnawed-on pile left to rot in the forest beyond the tower. To think he had believed them overrun and executed by the Talfaltaners. But no, they'd been put down by the pack for refusing orders, for refusing to take innocent lives.

Fetcher prodded his chest with a bloody forefinger. "*You* are, too. Master whistled and you failed to come." Her lips peeled back as she snarled, "*Bad dog.*"

He ignored the taunt. "How many were put down?" Between the low ratio of more spellsters born than hounds and the survival rate of the trained pups reaching adulthood, their numbers hadn't been great to begin with.

"Eighteen."

So many. When the loss of one fully fledged member had always been considered a heavy burden for the pack. "What happened to the other ten?" Even if his count of the bodies in the forest had been off, it wouldn't have been by so many.

Fetcher frowned. However unstable her mind had become, it was still sharp enough to catch he knew of the executed hounds.

Why had Whisper and the others tried rebelling *then*? Had they thought to bring the pack back to their senses without their master looming over them? Perhaps a final attempt to save the tower? Being so close, the Talfaltaners would've attacked regardless, but without the King's Hounds to nullify the spellster threat, they would've been pushed back. Destroyed. Not without losses, but certainly without the tower's utter annihilation.

Did that mean Fetcher had no idea of Trapper's fate? Did she believe none of the pack had fallen during the slaughter? Would his fellow hounds leave the man's body skewered in the old dungeon if they'd known? They typically burnt those who fell at the hands of spellsters.

With the man's remains now buried beneath the rubble, alongside the spellsters he'd a hand in murdering, his death would forever remain a secret.

"The others fell." She mimed the act with a hand. "Tumbling into the sea."

He knew she spoke of no simple drowning. The hound base was a warren of the castle's old dungeon halls and natural tunnels. One of the latter led directly to a cliff that jutted over the sea. That was where all hounds went in the end, thrown into the water to feed the fish. His lovers had wound up there. His daughter, too.

He bowed his head. Their numbers didn't change fast. If ten had fallen in Wintervale and eight more were executed a day's march from the tower, that would've left thirty-two to breach the tower gates and herd a thousand terrified spellsters to their doom.

"Why did our master give the order?" It was the one thing she hadn't said. "What was his reasoning?"

"They were dangerous. We..." She clutched at his arms. "We had to. If you had been there, if you had seen—"

But he *had* seen. The little bodies huddled together as death stalked them. The even smaller ones who'd been too young to know what was happening before the blade fell. The guardians who threw their own lives between the hounds and those they'd sworn to protect.

"*Dangerous?*" he hissed. Had she not felt their fear? A terror strong enough to leave its mark in every stone. The primal dread that not only were the monsters real, that they were *here* and *hungry*. "Is that what you told yourself when you slaughtered the children? The *babies?*" Ones so young that they'd died in their cribs. "What threat did *they* pose?" he demanded, knowing full well what the answer was. "Tell me that!"

Fetcher hung her head. At least she'd the sense left to be ashamed. "The guardians were compromised. Untrustworthy. But without them to look after the children... Better a swift death by the blade than a slow one of neglect. You understand how fragile they are. You must. Your daughter—"

He leapt to his feet, flinging her off him. "Do not speak of her!" Being five years his senior, Fetcher had already been a fully fledged member of the King's Hounds by then. She hadn't witnessed the fighting within the Pit, but she would've heard the rumours. They had run rife in the years he was forced to serve the Oldmarsh brothel. Rumours of how he had seduced the others, had convinced Wynne to carry his child, had caused their daughter's death.

Few knew she'd been a spellster. Even less had the talent to feel the latent magic in a newborn.

"Was that slaughter what they trained us for?" he snarled, pacing the few steps allowed to him between the wall and the sacks of grain. "We are meant to protect, to bring them where they could be safe. We were to cut down the dangerous, yes, but not... not *that*. We were never trained for genocide. Better for the pack to have slit their own throats than to have used those blades on the innocent." He would've chosen death, *any* death, over taking those lives.

It seemed eighteen had agreed with him.

"We are trained to *obey*." Her head twisted, her gaze growing unfocused. She stared off in the direction where Dylan lay safely asleep. Oblivious. "Every unleashed spellster is to die. It is ordered. It must be done."

"You knew he was here." Without even using his magic, Dylan announced his presence for miles. "Why did you not hunt him down? Were we perhaps waiting for the dead of night? So you could creep into his room and ram your blade into his heart whilst he slept?" His chest tightened at the thought.

He couldn't—*wouldn't*—allow that.

"Does he not deserve a merciful death?" Fetcher grabbed the front of his jerkin, dragging him close to her face. "Half the pack travelled west to cull the fleeing. They will be back. They will come for him. There is no place you can hide that power. Let him die peacefully."

Hounds at our back. The Talfaltaner had said the same thing. He'd no definitive amount, but with Trapper dead and Fetcher before him, it left thirty unaccounted for. Far more than he liked. Knowing they were an indeterminate number of days away wasn't much better, but that point would be less of an issue once he got Dylan aboard a boat. Even on horseback, they would never catch up. And if they never knew the man had been here, they wouldn't come looking.

He drew Whisper's dagger. The ruby on the pommel glinted back at him. The blade wasn't as pretty as the *infitialis* dagger, but the edge was just as sharp.

Fetcher eyed the weapon. She smiled. "Not planning on leaving here with me alive? Prudent."

Even if he trusted her enough to keep Dylan's presence a secret... "You aided in the slaughter of thousands. You killed *children*." Such a crime deserved far worse than death.

He hadn't the power to grant more.

"They always were your weakness." She held his hand, angling the dagger so that a single thrust would drive up through her throat and into her skull. The curve of her lips gained a sombre edge. The woman he had known fondly for years flickered to life in her eyes. "You would have made a good father."

We will never know. He sure as hell wasn't putting himself in that position again.

Tracker pushed, the blade effortlessly slicing into flesh. It broken through bone with a crunch, the same sound that haunted his dreams.

Fetcher stiffened. Her mouth dropped open in a breathless gasp, any air left burbling through the blood gushing from her throat. She slid gracelessly to the floor, red pooling around her.

Having wiped the dagger clean on her clothes, he returned to the message slip and wrote one simple truth. *Whisper died well.* The man had stayed no blade except his own, but choosing to give up his life rather than take those of innocent people was a good death.

He hoped the gods agreed with him.

Taking a pigeon from a cage marked with the Oldmarsh insignia, he secured the message. "Fly well, little one," he whispered, releasing the bird into the sky.

He watched the pigeon disappear into the night. A lone creature in the dark, bearing only heartache.

A moment later, he released the others. Better a chance of life out on the city streets than a slow death cooped up here. With luck, they'd be identified, caught and used to send more mundane messages.

His gaze drifted in the direction of the inn. Too many buildings stood in the way for him to see it from here. He didn't need to. Dylan still slept on. Safe and unaware of what could've transpired tonight.

How am I going to tell him? He couldn't. Not until the dear man was safe. He had to convince the spellster to leave Demarn. They could head north from here with Katarina and then—

Dylan was not going to take this lightly.

He took a deep breath. They would both lose their lives if they went to Wintervale. Perhaps if Dylan was told, he would see the sense in leaving for the safety of the dwarven lands. And if the spellster chose the destructive path...?

Well, there were other ways to get the stubborn man there.

~ ~ ~

The presence of another drew Dylan's eyes open just enough to see. Having his view full of someone's face widened them further and also pulled a yell from his throat. He jerked away from the sight, jumping to his feet. The stool wobbled under him, tripping him up and dumping him onto the floor. All in a matter of seconds.

The hound lay half-draped out the windowsill, laughing.

"It's not funny!" Dylan moaned as he rubbed his backside, his magic tingling through the tender flesh. "First you tell me that there are people loitering around the building who might want me dead, then you leave, only to scare me half to death when you come back. And I—" He clicked his mouth shut, but the words continued on in his head. *I was worried.* What had taken the man so long?

"And then you fell asleep." Tracker smiled, although there seemed to be a shadow within his eyes. "Were we waiting up for me?"

"I... Yes? Sort of?" He absently kneaded the side of his neck. Sleeping hunched over like that had stiffened his muscles. His innate healing would eventually soothe the area, but a good massage helped it along. "Did you find out what you wanted?"

The man's smile melted as if Dylan had thrown a fireball at a block of ice. "Yes." He secured the window, then started unbuckling his sword belt and armour. "Every city and town has a hound stationed there. I went to check on the southern lodgings here and it is... not what I had imagined."

Other hounds. Of course, Tracker had gone seeking more of his pack. Dylan had been far too free with his magic. Even if his little trick in the tavern hadn't alerted them, the resulting blast of power during his last orgasm would have. Better for the hound to convince them everything was under control than to wait until they burst through the door. "In a bad way, I take it?"

Tracker stilled, his eyes distant. It was there for a moment, then he shook himself and resumed undressing. Unlike a mere few hours ago, the jerkin and quilted shirt fell with no ceremony or attempt to tease. The man moved as though he wasn't at all present.

The hound settled on the side of the bed, still garbed in his undershirt, trousers and boots. Sighing, he scrubbed at his face with both hands.

"Are you all right?" he asked, dreading the answer.

"No." Tracker patted the mattress, inviting him over. "Sit. Please? There is something I need to tell you." His gaze lifted, finally meeting Dylan's. Hollowness lurked within his eyes. "And I fear it must begin with you were right, hounds attacked the tower. It was... ordered."

CHAPTER 30

Dylan awoke to find his legs entwined with another's, the man's heat a welcome presence against the room's gnawing chill. He remembered climbing back into bed with Tracker, but he hadn't believed he would fall asleep.

Obviously, he had at some point. Deep enough to dream? He didn't recall any nightmares, but that wasn't always a reliable indicator.

Craning his neck, he surveyed the room. Tracker had drawn the curtains before settling into bed, but the murky light of dawn snuck through a few worn patches. The walls showed little evidence of his magic, save for the scorch mark just behind his shoulder.

His gaze drifted to the window. He recalled the sound of precipitation pattering against it sometime during the night. At least, his first thought had been rain, followed by something far more sinister as his sleep-fogged mind recalled another of the pack had been out there, so close to creeping in.

That other hound was gone now. *Dead.* Tracker hadn't said as much, but the quiet way he spoke, the soft assurance that they wouldn't be disturbed, had been enough.

He carefully untangled himself from the hound's grasp to shuffle back across the mattress until his spine touched the wall. Tracker slept on, oblivious both to his movements and the new day. He had insisted on lying between Dylan and the rest of the room. The world really. *For protection.*

The man snored, much to Dylan's amusement. Not occasionally like Sulin used to, but with every breath. A low sawing sound that was almost, but not quite, a purr.

He had never woken up beside the man like this before, not even when they'd shared an actual bed back at the tower. Most times, he would settle in the hound's arms, content and warm, only to wake hours later with Tracker on watch.

Lying here now, he wished there had been more chances.

His gaze idly ran over Tracker's features. Never before had he noticed the faint wrinkles that had etched themselves into the hound's face, the soft lines across his forehead and between his brows. There was also a hint of them collecting at the outer corners of his eyes. Such marks of age were never as obvious on elves as they were on humans. It wasn't as if they lived any longer than dwarves or humans, they just seemed to carry their years better than either.

Tracker's nose twitched. A springy coil of russet hair, having worked its way free of his braid during the night, dangled across his face and threatened to wake him.

Dylan tucked the lock behind one of the hound's ears, taking great pains not to further disturb the man. Part of him longed to trace the slightly curved angles of those ears, to play with the earrings and hear Tracker's slow purrs turn heavy with unfettered desire.

Alas, no matter how light his touch, that act would certainly wake the man. They might have to abandon this warm cocoon of a bed soon, but he would prefer not to just yet. To wake him would mean facing the world and the harsh truth Tracker had revealed last night.

Hounds attacked the tower. No matter how many times he repeated it, the reality felt warped. Tracker had sounded so sure the hounds wouldn't have been involved in the tower's destruction that Dylan had thought—hoped, *prayed*—his conclusion would turn out to be wrong.

But to hear irrevocable proof? To know, without a single doubt, that the death of everyone he had grown up alongside had been *ordered*?

To be finally given the target his soul craved...

He'd been trying to make peace with the idea that the chance for revenge had slipped from his grasp before he even knew about the tower's destruction. With the main Talfaltaner force far down the river—likely all the way out to sea—it had certainly looked that way.

But it was so much closer, just waiting for him in Wintervale.

The Master of the Hounds. Once a title belonging to the king's sister, it now fell to the king's nephew. According to Tracker, the man was a wretched, abusive being whose distaste of magic rivalled that of the Talfaltaners he had allied with.

It just sounded like another reason to ensure his command over the hounds was short-lived.

And he'd the aid of a hound to help get him there. If Tracker's venomous recounting of his new master's deeds was any indication of his feelings towards the man, then surely the hound would have no compunctions in assisting Dylan. Tracker had promised, after all.

He was under no delusions when it came to the possibility of living after he took out the Hound Master. The man would be in Wintervale, their very destination, alongside most of the pack. Dylan wasn't even sure he could get close enough. He still had to try.

And if his life was the sacrifice the gods demanded to see the tower's fallen avenged, then so be it.

Tracker stirred. He stretched, arching in such a way that his whole body pressed against Dylan's. A hand slid up Dylan's chest, slipping into his hair. The man's russet brows lowered into a puzzled frown. His eyes opened to reveal their gorgeous colour. They flicked over him, seemingly surprised to find him lying there.

An unbidden smile tugged at Dylan's lips. "Morning, sleepy." The hound had been awake well before him the last time they had shared an actual bed. Had he reacted the same then?

The man grimaced, turning his head as far from Dylan's as he could manage without rolling over. "That is quite the breath you have."

He laughed. "Yours isn't any better."

Giving a mortified gasp, one that Dylan rather doubted was real, the hound whipped his head back around. "What a despicable lie from such a gorgeous mouth. My breath is as fresh as a flower."

"Sure," Dylan quipped. "Like one of those in the jungles of Obuzan that attracts flies."

"Such slander," Tracker whispered. He ran a hand down Dylan's chest, gently as if the man expected Dylan to vanish at the slightest of touches. "Has anyone told you that you are quite an angelic sight in the morning?"

"Not lately," he mumbled, aware his face had to be bright red with the amount of heat flooding his cheeks. *Or ever.* Until Authril, the last time he'd ever woken up beside someone had been as a child.

The hound's brows furrowed. "Did last night happen the way I remember?"

A flush of pride seeped into his chest at the raw memory of Tracker wobbling his way across the room. "That depends entirely on what you recall."

"You..." Wriggling closer, he kissed along Dylan's throat. The tip of his nose brushed Dylan's chin as he worked his way up. Their lips skimmed against each other for the space of a few quickening heartbeats before Tracker drew back. He traced where his lips had fallen. "It would seem you are in need of a shave."

Grunting, Dylan ran his hand over his jaw. Tiny hairs scraped his fingertips. He hadn't bothered with shaving yesterday morning and this was his price. He clambered over the hound, ignoring the man's muffled protests, and gathered up his clothes. It seemed quite early in the morning. Perhaps if they didn't linger here, they could manage the luxury of buying breakfast rather than cooking it for once.

Dressed, he rifled through his pack, unearthing his shaving equipment. He needed light and a place to rest his mirror. His gaze fell on the little table. *Perfect.*

Tracker sat up as Dylan dragged the table to the window. His brows lowered in bewilderment and Dylan could sense a question brewing in the man's mind, but the hound remained silent.

Dylan set about his routine, filling the small bowl from his pack with a little ice before melting it. The faint whisper of bedding coming from behind him suggested Tracker had finally vacated the bed. The more familiar rustle of clothing told him the man was getting dressed.

Feeling watched, he tilted his mirror slightly until it caught the hound's reflection. Sure enough, Tracker was still staring at him, almost curious as Dylan stropped the razor. "Is something wrong?"

Tracker shook his head. "Not at all, I just... Well, I am not usually one to pay much attention to your personal grooming habits whilst in camp. But I cannot readily recall ever seeing anyone shave." He rubbed a hand over his hairless chin. "We elves have a marked lack of hair to be rid of. In the region of the lower face, at least."

Dylan grunted as he lathered his face. There had been plenty of elven males in the tower and there weren't enough bathing quarters to segregate on both gender *and* species. He was well aware of what hair men like Sulin and Henrie couldn't grow, although he supposed the latter would've still had a hard time growing a beard had he been human.

His hands shook as he readjusted the little mirror. He hadn't found either friend amongst the bodies littering the tower, but he couldn't imagine them lasting long against a hound. Had their deaths been quick? Or had they made it to the training grounds only to be obliterated by the rubble caused when the secret entrance exploded?

Taking a deep breath, he folded the razor closed and picked up a cloth to wipe the foam from his face. There was no chance he could shave without nicking himself. "How are you planning on telling the others about your master's order?"

"Do they need to know? Is our dear hedgewitch not parting ways with us?"

Dylan paused, the cloth hovering inches from his skin. *She is.* He had almost forgotten Katarina planned to head north from here. And Marin, too? She seemed fond of the dwarf and upset at the idea of them separating. Did that mean he would be travelling with just the hound and the warrior? Two people who clearly despised each other. "Authril should know." If only so she understood the urgency.

Understood that becoming his warden was no longer an option.

Tracker remained silent.

He swivelled on the stool to face the man. "How *do* you plan to get me to Wintervale without your pack killing me?" How could they even be certain that the leashed spellster the hounds used in training their pups was still alive?

Even without the possibility of other hounds attacking him the moment he neared the capital, getting there was still weeks away on foot. *Weeks*. Not even a month between now and joining those who had perished.

The thought of it should've terrified him, but he felt only a strange calmness.

What reason did he have to fear the inevitable? For centuries, the tower had taught them giving up the freedom of their magic to the kingdom's might was an honour. And the priests always claimed the gods looked favourably on those who fell defending the weak. Surely, giving up one life to rid the kingdom of a threat from within counted.

It was the only thing he had left to live for. The only death he could choose. Everything else—being leashed or killed simply for being a spellster—were ends others had selected for him.

Better his end served a purpose.

Tracker's gaze drifted to the window. His eyes turned distant for a breath or two before he shook himself. "My plan has not changed. We travel the rest of the way by boat."

"*What* boat? The ones on the other side of the river? Did you not hear the rumours floating about the tavern last night?" They had continued even after the conmen had been driven out. "The bridges are closed. No one can get to the northern bank, much less get downriver." The Talfaltaner force had commandeered every vessel they could under the king's orders. That was why an abundance of crates and barrels were stacked along the streets. With the cargo ships gone, the only way to move them was by wagon.

"I heard. But being a hound..." He trailed off, grimacing. "Safe to say, I have made many connections over the years."

Dylan didn't doubt it. He had seen the man talk his way through several encounters. "Would any of them be open to speaking with you?" The Talfaltaners had made their mark passing through the city. Practically every bit of gossip in the tavern had circled back to them. Casual eavesdropping hadn't permitted him to learn if the hounds made themselves known amongst the horde and, after the conmen incident, he hadn't wanted any further scrutiny upon himself that asking might've brought.

Tracker had confessed that no more than thirty of his pack could be alive. But with the Talfaltaners numbering in the hundreds, the hounds could've easily hidden in their midst even with the executed eight still amongst their ranks.

"I cannot be certain," Tracker said. "Reji will. Although, speaking with him would be but a start. If I could get to the other side, speak with the mayor..." He paced the room, muttering and growling his frustration. "All I can reasonably hope for is some answers reside with Reji, especially regarding what may lie ahead. I am averse to the idea of blindly heading towards danger."

With the Talfaltaners likely beyond Demarn's borders by now, any danger they encountered would be largely targeted at himself. At least they wouldn't have to worry about the hedgewitch's safety. As much as he would miss Katarina and the time on watch they'd spent discussing ancient dwarven history, she was better off in safer company.

He picked up his shaving razor. His hand still trembled slightly. Nevertheless, he brought the blade to his face, letting out a steadying breath. The shaking ebbed as he made the first stroke.

Silence fell over the room as Dylan shaved without the usual camp rush. He had almost forgotten how relaxing it could be. Stroke. Wipe. Stroke. Wipe. Then re-lather and start over. Each move done leisurely by necessity. It was almost trance-like.

He had fond memories of Tricia teaching him once puberty struck. *Slow, even strokes.* Almost two decades later, her voice still echoed in his head. Soft and soothing.

At last, he cleaned the blade one last time, wiping the foam on the cloth. He patted the excess from his jaw and stood to face the hound. "Better?"

Tracker reached up to kiss him. He nuzzled the smooth patch on Dylan's throat, his lips not quite touching any higher. "It would be better if you were a little lower."

"Kissing me is not a requirement, you know." He placed his hands on the man's hips, steadying them. Tracker was standing as tall as he could and yet he couldn't reach. He smiled, recalling all the times he'd been hauled down to the man's greedy mouth.

"Why are you grinning like that?" Tracker demanded, the frustration already in his voice gaining a hard edge. "What is it?"

"I just realised that, even if you stand on your toes, you still need me to lower my head to kiss me." It was an act he was so used to doing with most of his elven partners that it hadn't occurred to him the man was no different.

Tracker drew back, thumping down an inch as the heels of his boots returned to the floor. "This surprises you? Elves are not exactly known for their height."

He knew that, had become very well acquainted with such a fact years ago. It didn't help that he was on the taller side of average for a human. "It's still cute."

Those honey-coloured eyes narrowed. *"Cute?"*

Dylan nodded, his heart skipping several beats as he caught the quirk of Tracker's lips. The way the left corner of the man's mouth curled slightly more than the right suggested mischief.

Sure enough, the hound clamped his hands onto Dylan's shoulders and, in one deft move, hoisted himself up Dylan's body.

Dylan staggered back until his shoulders collided with the wall. The man wasn't overly heavy when lying on top of him, but in his arms, the hound was a lead weight.

Tracker wrapped his legs around Dylan's waist, pulling their bodies together. "You were saying?" he breathed into Dylan's ear.

"You cheat," he puffed.

"To get what I want? I most certainly do." Tracker nuzzled Dylan's neck before leaving tiny kisses along his jawline that set up a flutter in his gut and made his legs shake.

"Track?" he breathed. His arms trembled with the effort of keeping the man from slipping to the floorboards and possibly taking Dylan along with him. If the hound didn't get down soon, they were both going to wind up collapsing.

The man's satisfied little hum heated Dylan's skin. "To answer your question, this is much better."

Dylan tipped his head back. Maybe he should just let go and risk being dragged to the floor by the hound's descent. "We should meet up with the others." They *had* disappeared from the tavern before their companions could meet up with them.

"Or we could linger." The fluttering touch of Tracker's lips descended Dylan's throat.

He groaned. It was tempting, especially with the way the man ground against his stomach. "What if—?" He gasped as the hound's fingers dug into his back. "What if they come looking for us?" If they remained here too long, they might come to the conclusion that something was wrong.

Or worse, Authril could barge in under the same assumption she had made in Oldmarsh, that the hound was seducing him. Only this time, she'd be correct.

Sighing, Tracker unwound his legs and dropped to the floor. "You are right, we should find them and visit Reji as soon as possible." Those long fingers seemed to move absently as the man smoothed the rumples in Dylan's robe.

Dylan weathered the hound's fussing. It reminded him of Nestria in the moments before his first duel. Although, her touch hadn't lingered the way Tracker's did, as though the man was loath to release him.

"A pity we cannot acquire something less tattered for you." The man's touch alighted on the patch adorning the robe's side, the one Dylan had sewn during his only night in Marin's little hut. "This cannot be comfortable."

Dylan's gaze dropped to take in the army-issued robe. Sticking with it had been a choice of practicality. Besides having originally been long enough to reach his ankles, he would only be forced into a similar outfit once they reached Wintervale. The patched side was done with bits of fabric Marin had lying around her home. It wasn't a perfect job, but the alternative had been to continue travelling with a gaping hole in the side. "I've gotten used to it." He barely noticed the occasional pull as the stitches jerked the robe in conflicting angles.

"Even so, we could take a detour by a few tailors. They might possess something a little tidier."

Dylan shook his head. "I'm good." He could survive the rest of their journey with what he had. Any funds they possessed would be better put towards supplies.

His stomach issued a gentle growl at the mere thought of food.

Tracker snickered. "I suppose we should feed you before all else, especially after last night's exertion." He wrapped his arms around Dylan's waist, drawing them together. "All that magic last night must have worked up quite the appetite."

"A bit," he admitted. The physical portion had taken a lot more out of him.

"And yet you eat so little. It is a wonder you have any meat on your bones." He shouldered his pack. "Come, they should still be serving breakfast in the tavern."

"Do you think they make flat cakes?" Dylan asked as they left the room, a little wistful for the comfort of home. "With syrup and cream." His cheeks warmed as Tracker arched a brow in his direction.

"Your rare treat? We have something of a sweet tooth, yes?"

"Not particularly." But after the plainly serviceable food on the road and the poor excuse for a stew here, he craved something that didn't make eating seem more of a chore.

The hound's chuckle was almost lost in the thud of their boots down the stairs. "Well, fortunately for you, I am in an indulgent mood. I will see to it that they make whatever you desire."

"You don't have to do that. I'm fine with—"

Tracker snorted. "Nonsense. After everything you have been through, ordering a few flat cakes is hardly a great task." They'd only begun to cross the courtyard to the tavern entrance when the man halted, his head tilted as if listening. "On the other hand, perhaps we should find the women and another place to eat."

The distinct sound of a person crashing into a table hit Dylan's ears. Cries of pain and outrage fast followed.

He eyed the door, expecting it to burst open. The scuffle inside was definitely getting worse. "What if they're in there?"

"I am certain they would also seek another place rather than stick around to brawl." Tracker turned on his heel. "Perhaps they already wait for us out on the street." The man took a few steps and stopped. "Gods, do not tell me—"

Above the fighting, came Authril's cry, "Marin, stop!"

They're inside? Thoughts of the brute Willy having returned with similar hulking friends flashed through his mind. Dylan ran for the door with Tracker at his heels.

He burst into the tavern, ready to defend his companions, and froze in the doorway.

Tables were overturned or broken. Chairs scattered about. He had expected that. A man cowered against the bar, his face bloody. The sight he shrank from was an angered Marin brandishing what appeared to be a table leg.

The normally placid hunter had become rage incarnate, screaming obscenities at the man and trying to win herself free of Authril's grip. Dylan frantically searched for Katarina and found her crouched near the bar, her little dagger ready to fend off the two men advancing on her with pokers.

"Oh, for gods' sake," Tracker muttered as he squeezed under Dylan's arm. "I cannot spend one day, just *one* day, in a tavern without someone starting a fight?"

A figure from the nearby shadows lunged for them, their fist raised.

The hound grabbed the offending arm before Dylan could think to retaliate. With barely a pause, Tracker decked the poor sod. He hopped onto the bar counter and drew his scimitar, the blade glittering in the sputtering candlelight. "That is enough!"

People stilled, their attention immediately drawn to the man who had levelled his weapon at the whole room.

"I *will* have order," the hound growled, "and I will have it now. You two!" He pointed his blade at the thugs attempting to skewer the hedgewitch. "Drop your weapons and back away from my friend."

The men obeyed, hastily tossing aside the pokers and raising their hands. "We didn't mean anything by it, sir," one of them gabbled.

"Of course," Tracker said in a tone that was far too pleasant. "Because running someone through is all in good fun, yes?" He kept watching the pair, even when Dylan couldn't see how they could be a threat. "Now then, if someone could kindly tell me what is going on?"

"This man here," Katarina said, indicating the bloody-faced human at the foot of the bar who was now wobbling to his feet. "He insul—"

The man slapped his hand on the bar, growling incomprehensibly under his breath. He felt his face, wincing as his fingers touched his broken nose, and glared at Marin. "Gods thrice damn you, woman."

Marin lunged for the man, held back by Authril lifting the hunter's far taller frame off the floor. The woman thrashed in the warrior's grip. "Put me down!"

"Soddin' pointy-eared lovers, almost as bad as the real thing." The man spat onto the floor, staining the ground red. "Give them some fancy sword and they think they can push around us normal folk." His hand curled around the ankle of Tracker's boot. "Well, I ain't afraid of some whelp getting all high and mighty with me."

Sneering, the hound dealt the man a kick to the head. "Everyone will stay put." The words came softly, each rich syllable dripping the threat of violence and sending an oddly pleasant shiver up Dylan's back. "If anyone tries to move without my say-so, their throat will be the first I slit. *Have* I made myself entirely clear?"

"Indeed, Master Tracker."

Dylan turned to find a rather angry, fair-haired woman in the doorway. She carried a short length of leather-wrapped wood, which she slapped against her palm in a manner that suggested she knew how to use it.

The woman strode into the room, the keys on her belt jingling with every step. "I believe you've made yourself quite clear. Although I would prefer you don't resort to slitting throats, blood means clean straw and my customers get so squeamish at the sight."

The hound jumped down from the counter and sheathed his sword before addressing the woman. "I sincerely apologise for my friends' behaviour, Madam Gwen. Allow me to pay for the damages." He produced one of the royal sigils and placed it into the woman's already waiting palm. "We will, of course, be leaving. At once." The hound shot Marin a scathing look that would've withered the woman had he been a spellster.

Authril released the hunter, who stumbled a few steps before righting herself. Marin glared at the man Tracker had booted, sneering when he did little more than stare vacantly back. She straightened her attire, tugging at both leather and cloth with equal viciousness.

"Now, if you please, my dear women," Tracker growled, indicating the door with a sweep of his hand.

All three filed past Dylan and out of the tavern. Apart from the hunter, the looks they shot him were rather guilty. The hound swiftly followed, the man's expression reminding Dylan of the last time he had disappointed his guardian.

"What did you think you were doing?" Tracker demanded of Marin as they stepped onto the street. "This is not the back of nowhere. There are rules here."

"And apparently a marked lack of manners," she snapped. "We only went in there to eat and that sack of swine shit starts shouting at Authril."

"Diseased, pointy-eared tart was the most palatable of the things he called her," Katarina added.

Tracker sighed. "Seasonal dock workers are not the worst of the bunch. And that does not explain why *you* were the one so bent on attacking them, my dear hunter." He turned to side-eye Authril before continuing his conversation with Marin. "Or perhaps you thought our dear warrior was incapable of her own retaliation. It was dark and my eyes perhaps deceived me, but she looked to be holding you back, yes?"

Marin folded her arms and grumbled, "Only because I planned to shove that table leg up his arse."

"As much as you believe he deserved it, I doubt that would have accomplished anything beyond you being escorted to jail."

Dylan didn't agree. Done right, it would've ended the world of one less bigot. And they could've sorted the whole jail business. Even if Tracker couldn't be persuaded to use another of his royal sigils to secure Marin's release, Dylan was willing to bet the hound was probably more than capable of picking locks.

Marin threw her hands up and let forth with a frustrated scream, much to the shock of those in the crowd who looked on with alarmed concern. "This is precisely why I hate coming near cities. Bunch of—"

"Enough," Tracker said. "Your distaste has been noted, but we are already leaving here and I would like to be able to return someday, if at all possible. Let us not make our departure any worse than it already is. I have no desire to be kicked out of the city before I have had the chance to speak with Reji." The hound lengthened his stride as if that would serve to stem any chance of them running into another confrontation with the locals, leaving them all to quicken their pace or be left behind.

The hound led them away from the docks. The crowds grew thicker and noisier. Carts and wheelbarrows of all sizes filled the streets. The chatter of people blurred into fragments. Dylan picked out a few conversations—mundane words of a widower's day, the exorbitant price of another's wares.

He paused upon catching one mention of a boat. Alas, that was little more than talk of repairs.

A cart, bearing little pots of flowers, trundled down the street towards them. Bundles of lavender hung on the sides. Dylan slowed as they neared, breathing deeply. He hadn't come across the scent since the pond, a time that seemed like yesterday and years ago.

His hand strayed to the coin purse still in his possession. He'd a handful of coppers left. Surely, it wouldn't cost more than that for a few stalks.

"This way," Tracker said, turning down a side street and away from the cart.

The others dutifully filed behind the hound.

Giving one last wistful glance at the cart, Dylan trotted after them. Perhaps they would come across another wild crop during their travels. Although, with autumn bearing down on them, he knew better than to get his hopes up.

They rounded the corner where the side street emptied into a market square. Here, armoured men on horseback rode through the crowd like ducks on a pond. They glared at everyone in passing, occasionally bumping their horses into those who weren't fast enough to move out of their way.

One such jostled man carried a sack over his shoulder. He fell, spilling grain all over the road. Large sections of the crowd slowed to a crawl as some attempted to help the man back up, whilst others berated him.

The smell of baking bread tweaked Dylan's nose. He looked about and spied a young boy exiting a shop with a basket of dark brown loaves. His stomach grumbled at the reminder of food, and he was soon tugging at Tracker's sleeve. "I didn't get my promised breakfast, you know."

The hound ruefully smiled up at him. "Nor did I. And do not think I am incapable of hearing this beast." He gently poked Dylan's stomach. "Sadly, it is likely best if we deal with the matter of feeding you whilst we restock our supplies, lest some other foul-mouthed person offends our dear hunter's sensibilities."

"You didn't hear what they called her," Marin growled.

"The usual, I suspect," Tracker replied over his shoulder as they veered towards the bakery. "No one who possesses a pair of pointed ears is immune to the slander of the small-minded, my dear woman. Retaliating only makes it worse."

"Says the man who kicked the same bastard in the face," the hunter snapped back.

"He laid hands upon my person. Just look at this." He halted before the bakery doorway and lifted the foot the man back at the tavern had grabbed. "Completely soiled the leather with his grubby fingers. It will take some good cleaning to get those marks out."

Katarina grunted. She hadn't removed her hand from the hilt of her dagger since leaving *The Sheppard's Axe*. "Dvärghem doesn't tolerate such hatred."

Now, perhaps. Dylan remembered his history lessons on Dvärghem quite clearly. The country was only created through the concerted efforts of many dwarven tribes. They had lost a great deal during the initial human occupation, more than mere land and ancient knowledge could account for. More still had been stolen from them when the empires of Udynea and the long-destroyed Domian fought over the very land the former had laid claim to almost two millennia ago.

"That may be so, my dear hedgewitch," Tracker said. "But here is not there."

This close to the bakery, the pungent aroma of cinnamon hung thickly in the air. The smell mingled with the citrusy scent of a nearing fruit stall and set Dylan's skin to tingling. He had begun to make certain associations with that scent over the past few weeks and, with his face flushing, found he had to work harder than usual to suppress the stirring in his gut.

Get it together. Anyone would think him some randy adolescent the way he reacted. And yet... there was certainly something about the man that he found irresistible.

A brief foray into the bakery had them leaving with several loaves and a small pasty that Dylan had finished in a matter of minutes. They continued down the road, bouncing from stall to shop to procure supplies, much like in Oldmarsh. Much of what Tracker bought was food, but there were a few other items that seemed odd. The strangest being a small collection of herbs, including a pouch of small pale root-like bulbs.

"Planning on fancying up our meals?" Marin asked.

"Fancy?" The hound laughed. "I would hardly consider adding a few herbs and spices to the pot as being particularly imaginative. But we will be travelling alongside a river that holds a great deal of fish and—"

Dylan had been silently munching on an apple until the mention of fish. He screwed up his nose and made a small gagging noise.

"—as you can tell from our suddenly seven-year-old spellster," Tracker continued, albeit with a smirk as he indicated Dylan with the jerk of his thumb. "It is not an option he happens to be fond of."

"How did you even know he doesn't like fish?" Marin asked.

Dylan wordlessly resumed eating. He didn't remember mentioning fish during their talks. Or had he? *I did.* Back when the hound explained that tavern menu analogy. There'd also been that one time when their group had caught such a meal from a stream and he had opted to stick with the paltry remains of the pheasant Marin had trapped the day before, but he didn't realise the choice hadn't been noticed by the others.

"I am a very observant man," Tracker replied.

"So, you plan on pandering to his dislikes?" Authril asked.

"I would not deem being considerate towards my travelling companion's dietary preferences as pandering. I simply prefer to not have him starve before we reach Riverton."

"Bah," Marin grumped. "He'll eat raw rat if he's hungry enough."

"I do hope it does not come to that," Tracker said. "They taste terrible raw." There was far too much confidence in that statement, as though it was more fact than speculation.

Dylan chewed slowly as he eyed the man, trying to determine if Tracker was joking. *When* had the hound ever been in a situation that required him to eat rats?

"In this instance," the man continued. "Our dear spellster would become quite ill if he was forced to consume fish."

"And you know this because...?"

"He told me." Tracker gave the warrior a toothy smile. "You plan to be his warden and you did not know such a simple detail?" He clicked his tongue disapprovingly. "The more important matter at hand is getting adequate tools for catching bigger fish. The line I have is only good for little ones."

Marin screwed up her nose in thought. "A stronger line is always a good investment, but my gear should be able to handle anything this river has."

"I would not think to devoid you of your equipment," the hound said. "Or are you not planning on joining our dear hedgewitch in her northward travels?"

Biting her lip, Marin returned to silence. Her gaze darted between him and Katarina, who likewise seemed torn. Did any of them wish to part ways?

"We don't even know if crossing the bridge is doable for any of us," Dylan pointed out.

Tracker grunted his agreement. "Learning that shall be our next stop."

They left the huge market square and headed further east. The sun blinded them whenever it peeked over the top of the buildings, forcing Dylan to throw an arm across his brow. Marin joined him in this act, as did the dwarf from time to time. If either elf was affected, they showed no sign.

He heard the clanging of a smithy long before it was in sight. The sound brought his mind's eye back to the tower and the small wooden awning huddled in the shadows of the wall. There'd been a few inner buildings where the servants did the laundry and, tucked underneath that awning, sat the tower's forge. Its mouth was always glowing and heat-hazy. The space held a single anvil and, most days, the rhythmic ring of metal on metal encompassed the outside training grounds. On a good day, it could even be heard in the gardens on the opposite side of the tower.

Tracker halted. "Here we are."

Blinking off the after-effects of the sun's glare, Dylan looked into the building before them. He wasn't sure what he had expected when Tracker first spoke of the place. Anvils, certainly. Maybe a slightly bigger forge than the one back at the tower, but this?

The main building stood several stories tall, the top two levels suggesting that this was also a place of residence. There was a massive chimney poking from the roof, smoke pouring out of it. The ground floor seemed to be mostly smithy. With three brick walls and little light, it was akin to staring into the maw of a cave. One that was perhaps home to a fiery beast of legend.

Movement came from within. Stepping closer put Dylan in the building's shadow. Four people worked in the gloomy space, three men and a woman. They each worked at an anvil, their hammers leaving very little room for any other noises.

Completed works stood by a door that looked to hold more of the same. Tongs and hammers and other strange things encircled each anvil. More implements lined the walls, odd twists of metal and wood that really wouldn't look out of place in some dingy dungeon.

A plough horse stood off to one side. A man lingered near the massive animal, leaning against the wall the horse was hitched to.

Tracker waved his hand. "Reji!"

One of the men glanced up, his pointed ears framed by the light of the forge at his back. His hammer echoed Tracker's gesture before it came down on the glowing metal.

The hound leant on the stone wall. "Now we wait."

Dylan crunched on his apple, trying to determine what the blacksmiths were making. They all seemed to be on different tasks. The woman was almost done with what was definitely a horseshoe, whilst one of the men alternated a narrow length of metal between the forge and his anvil, and the second man hammered away at what looked to be a poker or spear point.

The woman strode over to the horse, tested the shoe and disappeared back into the shadows to give the steel another few taps. She fitted the animal with its new shoe and, after a brief exchange of words and coins, waved the owner away.

And still, they waited for someone to acknowledge them.

Eventually, the elf who had gestured came out, wiping the soot off his hands onto his apron. Dylan thought it'd been a trick of the shadows, but the man was perhaps the darkest he'd ever seen. He appeared quite bulky for an elf, too, with broad shoulders better suited to a man several feet taller.

"Tracker." The man who could only be Reji slapped his hand into Tracker's. Reji vigorously shook the hound's hand—and most of Tracker with it. "It's good to see you're still alive."

"You were expecting me to be dead?"

Reji grimaced. "After all the hounds here up and vanished? When we've word from other cities of the same? Yes." He indicated the scimitar sitting snugly in its sheath. "How has my girl been treating you?"

Smiling, Tracker caressed the weapon's pommel. "She is serving me quite well." He eyed Dylan and the rest of their company before clapping a hand on the man's back. "Come, my friend. There seems to be a matter we must discuss. Let us go somewhere private." The hound glanced over his shoulder at the rest of them. "Wait here. This will not take long."

The pair walked through a nearby doorway and a little ways into the shadows.

Dylan paced before the smithy. If he turned his head at just the right angle, he could see them. That they talked was certain, their mouths moving in obvious conversation, but any hope of hearing the words was drowned out by the clanging of hammers and the roar of the forge.

What was the man telling Tracker that couldn't be said in public?

"Hey," Marin blurted, nudging him in the ribs as he swung about to pace some more. "Cut that out, will you? You're making me tired just watching you."

"Sorry, I—"

"Want to go get something to eat?" Her gaze dropped to his half-eaten apple. "Something with a little more substance. I think I smelt pies just down the road."

Clearly, she had forgotten the pasty he devoured earlier. And, judging by the low rumble his stomach gave at the mention of more food, apparently so had it. "A pie would be nice."

"Come on, then." Chuckling, she waved him to follow her down the street. "Let's go flush out whoever's selling them."

Dylan hesitated as a set of long fingers latched onto his arm.

"Where do you think you're going with him?" Authril demanded. Her grip tightened as she pulled him closer, dragging him back several steps.

"To get food. We won't be long."

"What if you get lost?" the warrior countered.

Marin snorted. "What sort of hunter do you take me for? If I can navigate us through the forest to a village, I can certainly find my way back to a smithy."

He glanced over his shoulder. Already, the crowd obscured the smithy's front, and they had only crossed to the other side of the street. "Maybe I should stay." That Tracker was sure no other hounds would bother them last night didn't mean there wasn't a chance of stumbling upon one today. With how poor his luck had become since leaving the tower, losing the smithy—and Tracker's protection— would be just the sort of cruel joke he'd expect from the gods.

"We'll be *fine*." She grabbed his wrist and turned to Authril. "Wait here. We'll bring something back for you two. Something hot."

Authril said nothing further as she released him.

Finding the bakery was a matter of following their noses. It led them down a side street where a few shops cringed out of sight of the main market square. Even so, the place seemed to have no lack of customers.

They were returning from the bakery, each in the process of wolfing down a warm beef pie, with more carefully stowed in their packs for the others, when a multicoloured array of twinkling lights caught his eye. Dylan followed the rainbow glints, halting outside what looked to be a makeshift stall of knick-knacks.

He polished off the remainder of his impromptu meal as his gaze swung over the merchandise. A vast majority of the table was covered in an assortment of runes, stones and potions. Little dreamwebs dangled from a horizontal pole, their intricate designs fine enough to put a spider to shame.

The gleaming light that had drawn him came from a collection of necklaces set up on a rack sitting just on the inner edge of the table. The pendants were little more than stones and what looked to be bits of polished glass and metal. A few of them bore runes and some of the stones had strange carvings that appeared to be seashells.

"Can I help you?" asked the elderly trader. She grasped a handful of the necklaces. "Perhaps a trinket for your love?"

Dylan glanced in the direction the woman nodded. It seemed Marin had followed him on his little detour. "She isn't— We're just friends," he clarified.

"My apologies," the woman murmured, returning the cords to their hooks.

Marin smiled. She caressed a few of the dreamwebs and ran a considering eye over the necklaces. "Is there a law I missed that says friends can't buy jewellery for each other?"

"No," Dylan said. "But firstly, I don't have any money." Not now he had bought the pies. "Also, I don't think any of the others strike me as the glittery bauble type." Neither Marin nor Authril wore anything ostentatious. Katarina's jewellery was relegated to beadwork and the large brooches that were a symbol of her hedgewitch rank. The hound might wear a dozen earrings, but everything else was purely functional.

"I'm not," Marin admitted. "But..." She unhooked a necklace from its friends. "I have money and you have your eye on *this*." In one swift move, she slipped the string over Dylan's head.

He inspected the ashen-coloured pendant. The stone was oval and smooth. An Ancient Demarner rune had been scratched onto its surface. The same as the one Marin had carved into the small piece of wood he already wore.

"Lovely choice, that one," the trader said, nodding to herself. "Means good fortune and strength in the old tongue."

"No, it doesn't," Dylan mumbled. How could she be that wrong? There was a huge difference between this symbol and the one for good fortune, or even strength, for that matter.

The old woman scoffed. "What would you know?" she snapped. "If you're not buying, give it back." Her bony fingers clawed at him, trying to snatch the stone whilst the cord still hung around his neck.

He jerked back on instinct, just enough to stay out of her reach. "Hold on, I—"

"Guards!" the trader shrieked. "Thief! Thief!"

Dylan hastened his attempt to remove the necklace, his fingers fumbling with the cord upon spying people slowing at her cries. He glanced around the street, desperately looking for any sign of armoured men. If they found him wandering about without Tracker, they might choose to deal with him themselves.

"Now wait a moment," Marin said. She fumbled in her coin pouch—which looked rather on the lean side after their visit to the bakery—and withdrew a copper. "Here," she said, slapping the coin into the woman's outstretched hand.

The woman eyed her, a greedy light gleaming in her pale eyes. "Rogues," she squawked, somewhat more frantically than the last cry. "Swindlers. Out to beggar an old woman."

Grumbling under her breath, Marin produced another copper. "And that's all I'm prepared to offer for it."

The very second the coins clinked together, those bony fingers folded around the money like a claw trap. "Thank you muchly for your patronage, my dear."

Marin turned from the stall. She stalked towards the smithy, muttering obscenities.

"I was about to give the necklace back," Dylan said as he strode alongside her, tucking the pendant underneath his clothing. "We could've just walked away."

"And have her keep shrieking until the guards arrived to lock us up?" Marin tilted her upper body, peering over his shoulder as if expecting such a group to emerge from the cobblestones. She clapped him on the back. "Come on. Let's see if Track's finished chatting up that blacksmith."

"He's not—" Dylan snapped before catching himself. "I mean, he's attempting to find out what happened."

"And that requires him to be in a room with the guy? Alone?"

He eyed the woman and caught the faint curve of a smirk trying to twist her lips. Was she attempting to bait him? "Maybe Reji doesn't feel comfortable divulging information in public."

"Sure," Marin murmured. "Few people would make a habit of— What did you call it?—publicly divulging information."

Dylan ignored the poor attempt to turn his words into an innuendo. Instead, he fished an apple from his pack and silently munched on it. He had really used far too much magic last night.

By the time they'd reached the smithy, Tracker stood outside with the others, holding a slim length of wood. The hound frowned at their approach and, before Dylan could speak, he growled, "I clearly recall telling you to wait."

"I was hungry," Marin replied, already digging out the pies they'd bought and passing them to the other women.

"What's with the stick?" Dylan asked, indicating the object with a jerk of his chin.

"This quarterstaff," the hound amended, thrusting the pole

towards Dylan, "is for you. I understand it will take some training to use it properly, but at least the worst you could do in the meantime is knock yourself out."

"You bought me a... staff?" He eyed the length of wood. In all, it stood pretty close to his height. Metal capped the ends and there were several spiked bands a little further up the shaft. "How am I supposed to defend myself with this?"

Tracker wordlessly relieved Dylan of his half-eaten apple and threw it into the air. There was a blur of wood and the fruit exploded. "Quite well, once trained," he said, handing over the weapon.

Dylan fingered the quarterstaff, suddenly aware of just how many people were staring. And the cat-who-caught-the-pigeon smirk Marin wore. His chest tightened at the sight. *He bought me a weapon.* This wasn't at all like the cloak or even the little trinket that currently sat nestled against the one the hunter had given him. "You really didn't have to—"

"Nonsense," Tracker interrupted. "I am, of course, under no delusion that you will be allowed to continue practising in the army, but we should be able to cover the basics on our way to Wintervale. Especially seeing there is a high chance we will be relegated to the roads."

"So even a hound can't get us passage aboard a boat," Authril sneered as they turned from the smithy.

The hound shook his head. "According to Reji, the city's dockmasters are under orders to only let specific wares travel the waters until the full complement of boats can be rebuilt."

"Not returned?" the warrior queried. She trotted on the hound's other side, forced to squeeze her way through the crowd as they left the square for a street heading north.

"The majority of the boats here were sunk. Likely to keep anyone from giving chase."

"Did your man know how they got so far upriver without being noticed?" Katarina asked.

"Who said their presence went unnoticed? The locals knew they were coming for several days before the Talfaltaners docked here. People had concerns, of course, but they were largely allayed by the mayor, who had no reason to fear their approach due to..." He cleared his throat. "Well, due to them being led by the entirety of the King's Hounds."

As one, the women halted. They shared wordless looks, their faces varying degrees of puzzled.

The hedgewitch was the first to speak. "Are you saying the hounds are responsible for the attack?"

Nodding, Tracker gestured for them to follow. He led them into a nearby alleyway, looking around to ensure they were alone and speaking only once he was convinced. "It was ordered, yes."

Dylan flinched as someone grabbed his arm. He went to jerk free only to discover the culprit was Marin. She said nothing, but tightened her grip.

"I knew it!" Authril snarled. She pointed at the hound. "You—"

"No, you do not," the man snapped back. "Even our dear spellster merely suspected the involvement of a few. I learnt the truth last night whilst investigating the southern hound tower."

As the others gathered around him, Tracker retold the events of last night. He spoke of the hound with the fractured mind, who had been hiding in the hound station—the man still omitting just what had happened to his kin. How the summons he found in Oldmarsh hadn't been for that hound alone, but *all* of them. That it was all at the behest of a new master.

Dylan half-heartedly listened as he watched the man pace the width of the alley like a trapped mouser. It still didn't feel real. All those hounds had been trained to find spellsters before they became a threat, to bring them to the tower. Every year, the hounds brought in dozens from elsewhere in the kingdom.

He couldn't imagine doing that then turning around and slaughtering the same people because of an *order*.

His attention returned in full as Katarina asked, "Do you think your king knows his nephew allowed a foreign force to invade his land purely to attack the tower?"

Did he? At the time, Dylan hadn't cared why the Talfaltaners were so far inland. He had assumed them to be some zealous sect that knew Demarn's spellsters were isolated and relatively defenceless. Hearing from Tracker that the King's Hounds had marched alongside them definitely put a new light on their reasons and movements.

"What if they weren't originally part of your master's plan?" the hedgewitch continued. "What if they were meant to bolster your reinforcements against the Udynea Empire?"

Dylan gnawed at his lip. Was it possible? If they were meant for the border and travelled the same roads their group had taken north, then they would've kept heading south. And could a force that big decide to take a detour simply to purge the kingdom of magic? Or would that have mattered once they realised how close they were to those they saw as demons?

Tracker gave a small, considering hum. "An alliance is altogether possible. I doubt the Talfaltaners want a horde of unmonitored spellsters on their doorstep, especially unleashed ones. And everyone in Wintervale would have certainly been aware of such a large force moving upriver. Whether the king knew their intentions..." He frowned, staring in the direction of the river as if not a single building stood in the man's line of sight. "I cannot imagine what he was told, but this river is not how I would transport any ally I wished to aim at Udynea. You have walked the distance from here to Toptower. Marching hundreds of men across that route makes no sense. Not when there are several ports in the south deep enough to berth their ships."

"I agree," Authril muttered.

"So the tower's destruction was a term of the alliance?" Dylan asked. With the kingdom already mired in one war, they couldn't risk starting another. Especially when they weren't exactly winning the one they were in.

The hound's eyes narrowed. "Now *that* is certainly a question I would like to know the answer to. Although I do not see how we could possibly mount a defence against Udynea without spellsters of our own to counter the enemy's."

"We couldn't counter them even then," Authril said.

Dylan grunted his agreement. It would've taken the entire tower to hold back the Udynea Empire attacking in earnest. "It might be possible if the hounds were to get involved." If thirty of them were able to clear the tower of hundreds, then he could imagine they'd be an effective force against Udynea's magic.

The warrior squinted into the distance as she also considered the suggestion.

"We are not trained to fight in such a manner," Tracker said.

"That didn't stop your brethren from massacring the tower," Authril pointed out. "Hasn't stopped you from fighting alongside us."

If the man had been a spellster, the look he shot her would've certainly been to kill. "All it would take is for one spellster to learn how to counter us and the army would be right back to where you left it. With the bonus of there no longer being hounds to deal with the dangers *within* the kingdom. Or do you think the kingdom will stop producing spellsters now the tower is gone?"

No. He had wondered in his youth how hounds kept finding more spellsters if most were brought in as children. Knowing people like Tracker were born from spellsters had answered that old question.

Hounds could sense magic, but Tracker had confessed they couldn't sense an absence of it, meaning they could've walked right by a potential pup and never know. All it would take was for that someone to have children and—

Watch them die. Without a tower, the only recourse they would have on any spellsters they discovered was the ultimate one.

Maybe it would be better if the hounds were to suffer the same fate they'd given the tower. Have the slate be wiped clean on both sides.

"Now then," Tracker snarled, still pacing like a trapped mouser. If he had possessed a tail, Dylan was sure it would've been lashing the air with his annoyance. "If you have all quite finished attempting to debate the tactics of a madman, we could move along, yes? There is one other I must speak with, especially if we had any hope of getting our hedgewitch across the river."

Authril stormed before the hound, halting straight in front of Tracker so abruptly that he was left with the choice of stopping or barging into her. Fortunately for the both of them, the man chose the former. "Aren't you forgetting something?" She jerked a thumb at Dylan. "Like *him*?"

The hound looked Dylan over as if they'd never met. "What part am I forgetting exactly?"

"The part..." she yelled, before catching herself and hissing, "...where he is *unleashed*."

Tracker's brows lowered, although he continued to stare at Dylan. Something dark flickered in those honey-coloured eyes. "And what action do you suggest I take, my dear warrior? What was ordered? Have you given up your ambition to become the kingdom's last warden?"

Authril harrumphed and folded her arms. "What I've been doing is considering our goal. Marching an unleashed spellster into the capital when the hounds have been ordered to kill them seems the sort of thing a traitor would do."

A contemptuous sneer tugged at the hound's lips the longer Authril spoke. "You have already permitted him to wander unleashed at your side for two months now."

"I don't know about traitorous," Marin said. "But if your master has ordered the death of all spellsters, does that include the leashed one in Wintervale?"

Dylan sucked in a deep breath. With everything that had transpired between the tower and here, he had forgotten the true reason for entering the capital was because the hounds had a leashed spellster under their control for training pups. Without the thin hope of them still being alive, venturing near Wintervale could be a death sentence.

If Tracker truly had slain one of his own kin to keep him safe, as Dylan was beginning to suspect had occurred, then he trusted the man had given some thought to what may happen once they reached their destination.

The hound waved Marin's concerns aside. "That was our goal, yes. If she has fallen, there is little to be done about it. Besides, as our dear warrior has said many times before, Dylan belongs to the army."

Authril nodded, her brow furrowing as if she was surprised to find herself agreeing with the man.

"If they learn he survived the attack, they are likely to claim him even unleashed. However, the longer he's left in that state, the less of a chance he has of the army believing the truth about his collar, but that is precisely why I am trying to get us a boat."

"Which your contact told you is highly unlikely," Authril pointed out.

"But *not* improbable."

"And what if we encounter more of your pack?" she continued. "Could you guarantee that we'd remain unharmed for escorting an unleashed? Or that *he* would remain docile?"

Tracker's scowl deepened. "I could ask the same of you. As I have said, he is doing nothing dangerous, has threatened no more lives on our journey than any of us have." His gaze slid pointedly towards Marin. "Even less than some of us."

The hunter gave Tracker a flourishing bow.

"*I* would like to see if we can cross to the northern bank." He glanced over his shoulder and caught Dylan's gaze. For a brief moment, a bone-deep sadness shone brightly in his eyes. Then he shook himself and gave a small, reassuring smile. "Perhaps speak with a few people who may be able to get us closer to our goal."

"Let me guess," Authril said. "You've a contact who can get us across?"

His gaze returned to Dylan's before his eyes closed and a small sigh slipped out his mouth. "Not as such, but coin loosens a great many lips." Turning on his heel, he returned to the street and strode off in the direction of the river.

CHAPTER 32

The gatehouse guarding the entrance across the city's central bridge loomed in the distance. Tracker eyed his destination with a measure of reluctance. Hopefully, Will was on guard. Otherwise, he would be forced to take a more drastic passage across the river, one the rest couldn't follow. Certainly not Authril.

Suppressing a growl, Tracker picked up the pace until he was stalking down the street, the others following in silence. Just thinking about the warrior had his fingers itching to close around the hilt of a knife.

He needed a boat, needed some way to separate the spellster from her before the woman decided taking up his master's command would be the favourable route. He certainly couldn't have her still travelling with them once they reached Riverton. But beyond a boat, the only solution that came to mind was the ultimate one and that came with its own set of problems. He needed time to think.

The crowd grew thicker as they neared the central bridge. That was normal. The other two ways across the river were to ease the foot traffic, with the eastern bridge having a rather steep flight of stairs and the western unable to have carts travelling in more than one direction. Passage along them was also barred far more readily.

However, he'd never seen the gates on the central bridge closed before.

They were huge metal things with the garish city crest welded to the fore. Guards patrolled along its breadth. That wasn't a typical sight, either. None of the folk were guards he had met before. Not new recruits. The ease in their stance as they addressed citizens spoke of years' worth of experience on patrol.

The sight didn't deter people from approaching the guards, be it in singles or groups. Every single one got turned away with a few firm words and the shake of the head.

Tracker waited until most of them were occupied with others before sauntering up, watching their demeanour immediately shift to alertness.

The woman closest held up her hand. "That's close enough," she commanded. "I'm sure you've heard the bridge is closed by the mayor's decree and now you've seen it. No one and nothing crosses without a permit."

Just as Reji said. Given that a large portion of the blacksmith's wealthier clients came from the northern side, the man had been very vocal about the blockade. But to get the mayor's permission, Tracker needed to be on the same side of the river as her.

He schooled his features into a broad smile. "Of course, my friends and I are not looking to cross. I simply wish to speak with one of your fellow guards, Will." He would've preferred not to get the man involved, especially when it came to acts of a more dubious nature, but without crossing the bridge, he had no other way to access the boats.

The woman turned to confer with the rest of the guards before making her way into the gatehouse. Will strode out a moment later.

The man's grin fell as he neared. His gaze lingered a little too long on Dylan. No doubt, Will marked the spellster's shabby attire, the company kept, and the immense power humming through that lanky frame.

The guard was one of the rare few he knew of who possessed the ability of a hound whilst having evaded becoming part of the pack. Tracker discovered that the same day they'd met, during an attempt at sneaking a spellster northward through the city. The man had already reached adulthood by that stage, young though it had been. Too old to start training as a King's Hound.

"I need to speak with the mayor," he said, eschewing the usual pleasantries. "It is urgent."

"And I'm guessing you don't have a permit." Much like the other guards, Will shook his head. "I'm sorry." Even though he appeared to be trying not to, his gaze kept falling on Dylan. "No one makes it to the northern side without a permit. Can't take the risk."

Tracker tucked his thumbs beneath his belt. "Still surprising me, I see. And when we usually get along so well."

Will chuckled. "Any other time, I'd let you cross without a thought, but..." He gave a single-shoulder shrug. "Orders are orders."

"I understand." And once, he would've agreed. "Take care, my dear man." He turned back to the group. His hopes of getting across with them all on the first try hadn't been high. Still, he had thought his status might garner a little sway. *The hard way it is, then.* If the gates were closed on this end, it was safe to assume the guards on the other side would be lenient to any who'd made it onto the bridge.

"Now that you've confirmed getting to a boat is impossible," Authril said. "Can we get on with the journey to Wintervale? I think we've burnt enough of this day following your whims."

"No, there is one more thing I must do." Tracker shrugged off his pack, handing it to Marin. "But it would be for the best if I continue alone." He tossed his coin pouch to Katarina. "There is an inn not far from here." He pointed down the street directly opposite the bridge. "*The Golden Tiler*, I believe it is called." Having been satisfied with the hospitality of *The Sheppard's Axe*, he had never done more than walk by the place. After Marin's outburst that morning and Dylan scorching the wall the previous night, he doubted returning to his usual haunt would be a sound idea. "See if you cannot secure rooms for the night, this will take me some time."

"You're planning on staying *another* night here?" the warrior demanded. "We could've already been on the road by now, but you'd rather consume the day over the *chance* of a boat?"

"It is a worthwhile gamble." If he was successful in getting them passage aboard a boat, even as far as Riverton, they would reach their destination faster than any of them possibly could on foot. If he failed, then they could easily make up the lost time during their travels. "At the very least, the mayor's personal command will have information even the city guards lack."

"And you expect us to just loaf around an inn whilst you do gods' knows what?"

"If being idle bothers you so, then you have permission to peruse the city's wares further." His gaze drifted to Dylan's attire. It certainly did catch the eye, in all the bad ways. "Perhaps you might find something a little less battered to garb our dear spellster."

"That... that won't be necessary," the man argued, his face growing a deeper pink with each word. "I-I don't need—"

"I disagree," Marin confessed. "It *does* look like someone ran your robe through several bushes." She grinned and prodded the spellster in the side that bore the patched section. "Then maybe set it on fire."

"It *was* on fire," Dylan replied, deftly swatting her hand away. "I just happened to be *in* it at the time."

"All the more reason to see it replaced now you have the chance," Tracker said. "And speaking of opportunities, the longer we loiter here, the more any hope of a boat dwindles. Go." He shooed the group away from the gatehouse as though they were children. "I will meet up with you all at nightfall."

Authril opened her mouth as if to object further, closing it when the hedgewitch laid a hand on her shoulder. They turned from him, making their way down the street he had indicated.

Tracker lingered outside of the guardhouse, watching the group merge with the crowd. Although, spotting the spellster remained a simple matter, partially due to his own abilities and the man's height, which put him slightly above the majority.

When Dylan's head was completely out of sight, he turned back towards the river. He could swim it, even with his armour and weapons, but there were more pleasant options that didn't involve getting soaked.

Other buildings abutted the gatehouse, creating a small alleyway and giving him the perfect cover. He backed his way along it, monitoring the street and any who might've been curious about his movements. True to form, many of the citizens made no attempt to notice him. The few who did quickly turned a blind eye.

The alley led directly to the river where, like much of the riverbank, the earth had been artificially squared up with a retaining wall. On his right was little more than the blank brick and wood of a building. To his left, the bridge began its journey, the structure rising high enough over the river for boats to sail underneath, its stone arches supported by thick columns.

The foot of the bridge was no different. The first support jutted out into the river, the huge chunks of stone carrying not only its weight, but that of the gatehouse. From the street, it looked to be a solid wall, but a small inset section contained a hefty metal door.

There was another tucked under the first arch, a back entrance to the gatehouse. The only means of reaching it without unlocking the first door or having a boat was to get wet and hope the river was high enough to clamber onto the shelf.

Although, that didn't mean the entrance was left unguarded.

He craned his neck, searching for the lookouts higher up the guardhouse. Their posts weren't angled to spot people from where he currently stood, but he was willing to bet that at least one had an eye on their back door. If he was getting through, he would have to be quick in opening it.

He crouched, maintaining an eye on his surroundings as he slipped the lockpick from his boot. This would've been infinitely easier to do at night, but he hadn't the time.

Keeping close to the bridge wall, he maintained vigilance on the lookout posts. He was by no means in full sun, and his dark attire would certainly aid in masking his movements, but all it would take was a single glance down at the wrong moment.

No one sounded the alert as he reached the doorway, but he wasn't taking any chances. He tucked himself as far into the frame as possible with his back pressed firmly to the door.

The lockpick slid in effortlessly. Manipulating the lock took mere moments and he had access. The hinges squealed as he pushed the door open, but the sound would be lost in the street's bustle, and there were several solid walls between him and anyone within the gatehouse.

He waited nevertheless, listening for any sign that someone was coming through either doorway.

When no one did, he moved on to unlocking the other door. This one thankfully opened a lot quieter. The stairs leading up were dark and had him entering the storage room. The ceiling creaked with a guard's footsteps, the measured pace of the unhurried. *Good.* If they weren't concerned, then they didn't know he was here.

Tracker cracked open the door at the far end of the room to the sight of more stairs. The sound of the street drifted from the open archway above.

He darted up the stairs leading to the space between the two gates. Halting in the archway, he focused on keeping his breath soft and steady as he gauged the guards' positions.

Several still patrolled the streets outside. They were occupied in dealing with citizens who came to air their complaints. Will was the only one still at his post. He stood just on the other side of the first gate, his back squarely facing Tracker.

Keeping an eye on the man, Tracker crept towards the inner gate. No noisy chains barred his way, just a simple lock. It fell swiftly to his touch, the latch giving with a solid clang.

Tracker winced. Any guard worth their pay would've needed to be dead not to have heard that.

He turned at the same moment as Will.

The man stared at him, his expression shifting from confusion to alarm, and finally, suspicion. "You old dog, how in the gods' good names did you sneak past?"

Tracker leant back on the gate. At least the man wasn't calling for the others. Perhaps that meant he had a chance at convincing Will, especially now that the guard wasn't distracted by Dylan's presence. "My dear man, you cannot expect a hound to survive hunting spellsters for long without learning a trick or two."

"Hunting," Will echoed, amusement pressing his lips together. He unlocked a section within the gate standing between them, eliminating the barrier. "Explain to me how you ended up travelling with one instead. Again." He stabbed the air with a warning finger. "And don't try to deny this one. I sensed it the second he approached." He wrinkled his nose. "Can still smell his magic on you."

Tracker shrugged. "That is to be expected. We are travelling close."

The man's dry chuckle was almost lost to the clunk of the lock as Will secured the gate once more. "There's close and there's *close*." One side of his mouth hitched upwards. "His scent rolls off you like a bad perfume. That's not normal. Was..." He shuffled from one foot to the other. Clearly unsure of his question, or whether he truly wanted to know the answer. "Was it *him* I felt last night?" The guard's abilities didn't have much range. Close up, his knack for pinpointing the smallest crumb of magic rivalled Tracker's own.

"That *is* a possibility." Dylan's power was the strongest Tracker had encountered and the resulting blast during the man's orgasm had been concentrated. He wouldn't be surprised to find even someone with Will's limitations had sensed it.

Will glanced over his shoulder. His meagre abilities wouldn't be enough to trace where Dylan had gone. "You know I'll have to arrest you for this."

"You could *try*." Tracker edged towards the archway leading down into the storage room. He could descend them and be out into the river before an armoured guard could make the attempt. Not that they would hold him in a cell for more than a day, but he couldn't leave Dylan unguarded that long. "However, I believe you will feel differently about that once you learn something about the force that came through here."

The man matched him step for step until they were both in the archway, their backs to the frame. "And what would that be?"

"They besieged the spellster tower."

Will froze. "What? No, that's..." He shook his head. "You're stalling. That tower has stood for centuries. Mere men could not topple it."

He would've agreed not too long ago. Maybe it was still true, given more than mere men had a hand in it. "I speak the truth. They killed everyone. Guardians, servants, spellsters... all dead. Every last one."

"But you're travelling with a—"

He grabbed the guard's shoulders, forced the man to meet his eye. "Did you not hear me? *Every* last one, Will, including her."

The man fell silent as the words seemed to, at last, sink in. "Seren? But—" He clapped a hand over his mouth, grabbing his lips as if he didn't trust the words trying to escape. "No," he mumbled. Tears welled in his brown eyes, rolling down his cheeks in fat droplets. "She... she wasn't a danger to anyone. Why would they?" He squeezed his eyes shut like a child seeking to change the truth. The tears continued to flow.

"I am sorry." He hadn't been the one to find the man's younger sister. She would've been given over to the tower well before Tracker had become a full hound, but he knew much of the woman from her brother. "I wish I came with happier news."

Giving a sniff that echoed in the stairwell, Will bobbed his head in acceptance. "Is that why you need to see Her Grace?"

"No. I..." He peeked out of the archway, searching for anyone who looked suspicious, be it in closeness or action. The other guards still patrolled the street. No one else stood within earshot, human or elven. "I need a boat."

The guard scoffed. "You'll be hard-pressed to get that."

"So I have been told." Reji hadn't the reach within the northern half of Whitemeadow, but the blacksmith dealt with enough merchants and wandering traders to have an accurate read of the situation. "I would only need it as far as Riverton."

"Not back to the hound kennels?" Will peered at him, suspicious even through the tears. "You going rogue?"

"No." He was well past *going*. "But I would suggest you leave Whitemeadow immediately. Leave the kingdom entirely, if you can. At the very least, head as far north as you are able."

Worry wrinkled the man's forehead and flattened his mouth. His gaze darted about the stairwell, no less put at ease to find they were alone. "I'm going to need a lot more information on what's going on before I try to pack up Ceri and three young ones."

"You *sired* children?" The man had mentioned his spouse many times throughout the years, but never any offspring. Had no one warned him of the high chance of even one child being a spellster? And *three* of them? Will would have to be exceptionally fortunate for none of them to be magically inclined. "Do any of the other hounds know?"

Laughing mirthlessly, Will clapped both his hands on Tracker's shoulders. "Peace, my friend." The humour creasing his eyes faded, sorrow darkening their depths. "I remember my mother's grief when they took Seren from us." He shook his head, no doubt still berating himself for not stopping them. Tracker had assured him numerous times that any intervention would've only seen him imprisoned, if not dead. "They're adopted."

"How old?"

Even through the sadness, paternal pride twitched at one corner of his mouth. "The youngest is six months, little howler that she is. The other two are three and four years." He frowned. "What *is* this about? No one knows what the hell is going on. Even the guards on palatial duty are in the dark, and those bastards usually can't wait to rub our noses in it when they're in on things."

"The full complement of hounds was with that force, following orders to kill every unleashed spellster. Beyond that, I know perhaps less than you." He wished he knew the reason behind their new master's command. From what he remembered of the man, it was likely some whim during a fit of temper.

Will's gaze drifted over Tracker's shoulder. His thick brows drew together. "Then... shouldn't *he* be—?"

He grabbed the guard by the breastplate, slamming his back against the wall. "My dear, *dear* man," he growled. "I am trusting you with this information because we are friends. Do *not* make me regret that bond."

Will's eyes widened. "You *are* going rogue."

What was he supposed to do? Let Dylan die? Kill the spellster himself? They weren't viable options. Few of the choices left to them were. He just needed one to work, to keep the man alive. "I am going through that gate. Do not try to stop me." The guards at the other end wouldn't be checking his validity, not if they were keeping all but a few from crossing on this side.

"Were you there? Did you—? My sister—?"

Tracker slowly loosened his grip on the man. "I did not raise a blade against the tower. You have my word."

Will held his gaze for several breaths before nodding. "All right." He adjusted his attire. "I can't let you cross unescorted, though. And I doubt Her Grace will speak with you."

"Let me worry about that." There were far more ways into the governing palace than the main entrance. He only needed one.

~ ~ ~

The crowd swallowed their group as they ventured down the street Tracker had indicated. People paid them more notice than any other group, skirting them where they had been pushed closer by others. That likely had to do with how Authril stalked alongside him, just as furious as the hound had been after leaving Reji's smithy.

"I would suggest calming yourself," Katarina advised the warrior. "You're drawing unnecessary attention."

Knowing better than to speak when Authril was in this mood, Dylan couldn't stop himself from nodding his agreement. Not every person in the crowd eyed the warrior, but enough. Without Tracker at their side, they couldn't afford to catch the wrong sort of interest.

Authril flung the hedgewitch a scathing look. "He *dismissed* us," she snarled. "Like we were common lackeys. Told us to go *shopping*, of all things."

"Technically, our orders are to seek *The Golden Tiler* and procure rooms for the night," the hedgewitch corrected. She frowned at the pouch of coins Tracker had gifted her. "The other part was a suggestion."

"One we should definitely consider," Marin added, plucking the coin pouch from the hedgewitch's hands.

Dylan's grip tightened on the quarterstaff. "I was being serious

392

that garbing me in something else isn't necessary."

The hunter eyed him then, shrugging, tucked the coin pouch into her attire. "All I'm saying is, you wouldn't find me complaining if someone offered to purchase a whole new outfit for me."

Except, Tracker had done more than that. If the man had only offered to replace his attire, Dylan might've hesitated in accepting, but he wouldn't have minded. On top of the recent acquisition of a weapon, though?

His gaze slid to the sturdy length of wood. Tracker hadn't made a single mention of procuring its like before now and had seemed pretty adamant that Dylan take it.

He couldn't help but wonder about the actual reasoning behind the hound's gifts. Were they some sort of payment for the nights spent together? He wasn't a stranger to exchanging sexual favours for items when he hadn't anything else they wanted, but that sort of transaction was always hashed out before either spellster engaged in the physical. He hadn't expected a thing from Tracker.

The idea that the hound sought to pay for what Dylan had given freely stung a lot more than he would've ever expected.

"Getting new clothing isn't the point," Authril continued to grumble. "It's the waste of *time*. I know heading along a road already crowded with people trying to get their goods and animals to wherever might not sound like the most pleasant way to travel. I'm certainly not looking forward to it, but we shouldn't be delaying." She glanced at the surrounding crowd before wrapping an arm around Dylan's waist and pulling him closer to the other two women. "What if there are other hounds nearby?"

A valid concern. One that Tracker had likely already weighed in his choices.

"He already admitted to finding a fellow hound in the southern station," Dylan said, half-agreeing with the warrior.

"Which makes lingering here even less of a good idea. Is he hoping more find us?" Authril narrowed her eyes until only a sliver of their sea-green hue was visible. "Is he looking for reinforcements?"

Before Dylan could open his mouth, Katarina said, "I'm sure if ending Dylan's life was his goal, it would already be done."

"I still can't believe they're responsible," Marin said, shaking her head. "My father always told me they protected the people."

"And so they did," the warrior replied. She gave a curt bob of her head. "Shuffling spellsters all into one place never seemed like the logical choice to me. For them to be trained and in their *thousands*? Whoever gave the original order all those centuries back, I doubt they ever considered just how many there could be, or even intended for that to happen."

The warrior seemed distracted as she spoke, glancing over her shoulder in the direction they'd come.

Dylan followed her gaze but spotted just the same people and carts filling the way. Nothing that could've held the woman's interest. Not even the gatehouse was within view. "And the slaughter we found was the answer?" he asked of her. Since learning of her reasoning in bedding him, he hadn't queried many of her actions or views, not even when she aired how she truly felt about unleashed spellsters. Perhaps he should have. "I suppose they deserved it?"

She eyed him as though expecting his questions to be some sort of trap. "I would never suggest anyone die the way your people did, but I'm also against innocents suffering the fate those at the army encampment fell to."

Just as the tower held more than spellsters and their guardians, the army employed others to keep their soldiers fed and attired. Their lives hadn't been spared any more than the tower servants'. "Keeping people safe was also the tower's goal." And now there would be more anguish and distress as untrained spellsters ran unchecked. No place to learn control. No one to take them somewhere safe. Any spellster who made their powers known would find only panic and prejudice.

The perfect recipe to have a spellster strike out in fear.

Once that started, anyone who had an ounce of sympathy for any spellster would find themselves in an ever-decreasing minority. It would only take a generation before not a soul would dare do anything but call upon the King's Hounds to eradicate the threat. In several more generations and—who knew?—Demarn could become the same as Obuzan, a priestdom in the distant west that fanatically purged every spellster within their borders.

"Since you all seem to be in agreement about staying here another night," Authril said, toying with the straps holding her shield in place. "There are a few things *I* wouldn't mind getting done. Like maybe seeing if that Reji fellow can't knock a few dents out of this." She tilted her shield before her, the surface of which certainly had seen better days.

"So now you trust us alone with him?" Marin snipped.

Authril peered at the hunter. "I trust *Katarina* to keep an eye on him. I won't be long and I'll catch up at the inn, but if you try to go anywhere beyond that without me, you will be in trouble." She took a few steps back, her gaze unwavering until the other two women acknowledged her. Then she was off and up the street.

Dylan watched her passage. If Reji's forge was truly her destination, she was going the wrong way.

Turning back, he caught sight of a large pair of scissors hanging above the doorway to a shop. Unlike the rest of the buildings along the street, this one had several wide windows taking up the front, the glass bedecked with a crosshatch of black lines. It allowed a casual passerby to see into the room beyond and the array of dressed mannequins. One of them was a dark blue robe not too dissimilar in style to what he'd worn in the tower.

Clothes had never been a thing he thought about much, especially in terms of acquisition. In the tower, his clothes had been made by the same servants who kept everything else running smoothly. Realistically, the robes he'd worn there likely had been handed down from those who had outgrown them, especially during his childhood. They had fitted him well enough, even if there was a little more fabric wrapping around his body than most. The army-issued outfit he wore now was much the same.

"Come on," Marin said, nudging him towards the tailor's doorway. "Let's get you something a little less tattered."

"I do feel a little silly getting something new," he confessed. Still, he would've been lying if the idea of having clothing he knew without a doubt he was the first to wear didn't tweak his desires. "The army will only take it off me once I reach Wintervale."

"Maybe they'll reconsider that stance," Katarina said.

"I can't imagine why they would." Even as the last spellster in Demarn, he was hardly in a position to make demands.

The tinkle of a small bell announced their passage through the shop door. Dylan wasn't sure what he had expected to find within, certainly not the array of cabinets displaying various styles of embroidery. One wall seemed to be nothing but a rack to hold bolts of fabric.

A smartly dressed, grey-haired man glanced up from the counter at the far end of the room. He said nothing, not even the utterance of what could be construed as a pleasant greeting, but continued to silently watch them move about the shop. It reminded Dylan of the times he would sneak into the tower library when he was supposed to be in the training grounds.

But like then, he was technically not in the wrong place.

Willing his cheeks to stop burning, he walked around the mannequin he had spied from outside. The figure's shoulders stood at roughly the same height and the length of blue fabric fell to about mid-calf.

Now he could inspect the outfit closer, it wasn't quite the style he had believed, but it was near enough. It still appeared to wrap around the body and the lower half formed an encompassing skirt, and definitely not the style he saw most others wearing outside the tower. The neck was higher than he was used to, which would help to cover the scarring. The sleeves had a lot of extra layers near the shoulders, and would definitely fit loosely to the arm, but they were also tight at the cuff and that would be enough to keep his magic from scorching the fabric.

He ran a hand down the sleeve. The material wasn't a type he was familiar with. It was soft and supple, finer than anything he'd ever worn in the tower. "How much for this?" he asked the man standing by the counter.

The tailor gave him a condescending smile. "This is not a grocer, good sir. All goods on display are merely here until their owners collect. They're not for sale." His upper lip quivered as he ran a considering gaze down Dylan. "But if you wish for something like it, I could set a fitting appointment in a few days' time."

"I was hoping to replace this today." He spread the skirt of his robe, showing off the tattered ends.

The man scoffed. "Work of my calibre takes no less than a *week*. Perhaps one of the rag sellers might have something more fitting."

Dylan practically felt Marin's inhale on the back of his neck before she slid between him and the tailor. "Good sir," she said, poking the man's chest. "Why don't you and I have a little chat?"

Clapping an arm over the man's shoulders, she waved them back whilst guiding him towards the back room. She spoke in a low tone, too quiet for Dylan to make out more than the odd word, but it seemed to keep the tailor close.

The man's eyes darted from her to Dylan and back whilst she spoke. He tried to counter her several times, but was unable to.

Dylan edged closer to the door. What was she telling the man? That he was in the presence of a spellster? That she intended to get violent if he didn't comply?

He really wished Tracker was here. The hound seemed to know precisely how to speak to everyone.

Once Marin fell silent, the tailor practically blurted, "Madam! I simply cannot—"

She wordlessly produced the coin pouch Tracker had given them. Bouncing it in her hand, the metallic susurration within immediately silenced the tailor. "How long has it been sitting there? Truthfully? A month? More? Your client didn't pay in advance, did they?" Marin shook her head.

Surprisingly, the tailor mimicked her.

Seeming to catch himself, the man blustered nonsensically, waving his hands before him as though batting away flies. "I cannot just *sell* my client's clothes to another on the basis that—"

"Do you *really* think they're coming for it anytime soon? Or would you like to be paid *today*?" She gave the coin pouch a little jiggle. "My offer is right here and now. I'll even sweeten the deal with a little extra for some swift alterations."

The tailor stared at the pouch for a long time. His jaw moved from side to side as if the man sucked on his tongue, not even stopping as he eyed Dylan.

Then he closed his eyes and let out a long sigh. "Nia!" he yelled, turning on his heel to march into the back room. "Get mannequin seven disrobed and have the boys ready to re-hem. *You,*" he said, turning back to Dylan. "In you come." He jerked his head towards the archway as an equally tidily dressed elven man scuttled through.

Dylan hastened to follow the directions lest his sluggishness made the man change his mind.

CHAPTER 33

No matter how familiar the raucous of the tavern was—the collective chatter of patrons, the strumming of a lute, and the bustle of the staff—did little to soothe Tracker's temper. He hadn't intended on staying another night in Whitemeadow, but getting an audience with the mayor had taken longer than it should have and garnered him nothing but wasted time.

The others had arrived not long before him. Marin laying claim to this table with its high-backed bench seats that formed a horseshoe shape, whilst Katarina had secured rooms. He had spied both of them only thanks to the hunter's gesturing.

Dylan was upstairs, donning his new attire. Tracker didn't want to know how the group had managed to procure a whole new outfit in the span of an afternoon. Nor did he wish to know how expensive such a transaction had been. He supposed, as long as they'd enough for supplies at Riverton, he didn't mind if it had taken the majority of their funds.

For now, there wasn't much to do beyond wait for the man and Authril to join them so they could make plans, which would need a little adjusting if he was travelling with only Dylan and the warrior.

He chugged down a generous amount of his drink before setting the mug back on the table. "We will need to make our way to Riverton on foot come the morning." The bitterness on his tongue came not from the mead.

Katarina glanced up from the map she'd pulled out at the mention of the fishing village. She had spread it atop the table to measure off the distance, mumbling numbers under her breath. "It'll take at least a fortnight to reach there on foot."

"Indeed." Maybe even longer if the road east was as packed with carts carrying what would usually go by boat as Reji suggested. He frowned at the woman. "But you speak as though you plan to travel with us. The mayor has given you permission to cross." The woman hadn't been willing to lend Tracker a boat—even his hound status held no sway—but she'd no compunctions when it came to aiding a hedgewitch. All Katarina had to do was present herself at the gate and the guards would let her through. "Given how eager she was, I am certain she will be more than happy to have you stay at the governing palace until you are prepared to leave."

Her brow wrinkled. "But that offer is only for me."

"And the assistant travelling with you, of course," he added, gesturing to Marin with a flick of a hand. Passing the woman off as the hedgewitch's bodyguard might've made a better story, but with his hound status holding little sway, he didn't want to risk anything that might leave the hunter behind. Seeing Marin didn't wind up further entangled in their mess was the least he could do after the woman had already lost her home. "Dvärghem is closer from here than anywhere else our travels could take us. I thought you would choose to head northward."

Katarina tilted her head to one side. "Without an escort?"

"Of course, the issue of guiding you to your people's lands." Tracker hummed, his gaze drifting in the direction of the river. If the simple matter of requiring protection was all that held her back, then she should be fully aware that the mayor would give her everything she required, not only a cart or horses to make the journey easier. "But you are concerned about more than that, yes?"

Her gaze dropped to the map, then slid to the stairs leading up to the inn rooms.

Tracker couldn't help but smile. The hedgewitch so often had her thoughts, and emotions, emblazoned across her face. "You are worried about him."

The frown gracing her brow deepened. "Is it true that the army will take him unleashed?"

"My dear hedgewitch, I am not a man who habitually lies." He hadn't lied at all when he told Dylan his situation was unique. By all accounts, the man should have still been leashed. "He may be unleashed now, but he *was* prior to the order. Being inducted into the army makes him the king's property." He hated thinking about Dylan in such terms, but it could very well be all that saved the spellster from the rest of his pack.

"As long as people believe that."

"Track'll be there once we arrive at Wintervale," Marin pointed out. "Authril, too. Surely, they're more than capable of declaring Dylan's status."

The hedgewitch remained silent as she carefully folded the map before stowing it into her pack. "I have never heard of a spellster getting free of their own collar before. I doubt any of your hound kin have either. I might not have seen the unleashing, but I was the only one there when he awoke." She fixed Tracker with a blunt stare. "*You* barely believed us, even when we showed you the proof, and you'd been following him since the attack."

That was true. Before encountering the man in Toptower, he had been under the assumption that he was dealing with a Udynean spy. And the collar had some very suspicious marks on it. There had always been a possibility that the army generals would believe Dylan was a deserter, if not a runaway.

Katarina lifted her chin. "I can attest to the condition he was found in. And I alone have nothing to gain from declaring my findings. I cannot, in good conscience, leave Dylan's side when staying could prevent his life from ending abruptly."

He gave the woman a small smile. "It would seem your homeland will have to wait for your return for a while longer, my dear." Being the only person aware of his true plans, she had to know Dylan was in no danger from his pack. Although, she had also been privy to how Authril had goaded him into an attack all those weeks ago.

Did she fear the warrior would be the one to meet a sticky end if no one else was there to stop him?

"I'm sure the Coven will manage without me," the hedgewitch replied, one side of her mouth briefly hitching as she spoke.

And so it will. He glanced towards the stairs as a figure descended, disappointment souring his gut when that person revealed themselves to not be Dylan.

Marin's brow twitched upwards, along with one corner of her mouth. "You look awfully expectant. Waiting to see how *our dear spellster* looks in his new getup?"

One of his own brows had lifted at what he assumed was her attempt at an east-coastal accent. "I will admit to some mild curiosity in regards to what type of garments you procured for him to be taking so long in dressing." The women claimed Dylan was only changing. The man was definitely still somewhere above them. He couldn't be *that* far off.

Her smile came in full. "If Authril was here, she'd be suspecting him of every misdeed she could think of."

"I am surprised she has yet to make an appearance." The day was over, with barely a glow of the sunset on the horizon. "Perhaps I should go look for her." If getting her armour sorted was her goal, then there were only so many places she could be. He could work his way from there.

Snorting, Marin flapped her hand dismissively. "I wouldn't worry about it. She can take care of herself. But I've been wondering..." She leant against the bench's wooden backing. "I'm not knocking the favour you garnered for Kat, but *how* did you manage to reach the mayor? I thought all the bridges were off-limits."

He schooled his lips into an affable smile. "I asked."

"Asked?" she echoed. "Or *asked*?"

"What is with all the questions? Did I wander into some round of Truth be Told?" he enquired, chuckling.

Marin shrugged. "We can do it that way if you'd prefer."

"Are we suddenly children?" He hadn't played that game since he was a pup.

She spread her arms wide. "You got something better to do? Perhaps *someone*?" There was a mischievous glint in her eye as she spoke the latter. "Or is drinking away the hours your only entertainment?"

He tipped up his mug, draining the last of the mead, before slamming his dagger flat on the table and signalling a passing server for another drink. "First spin, my dear?" he offered Marin, smiling his thanks to the server who settled another full round for the whole table.

The server grinned back, winking. Her gaze drifted to his waist, the gleam in her eyes definitely not one that came from appreciating natural attributes.

He made a mental note to keep a closer eye on his weapons and coin pouch whilst within the establishment. He'd never been here, but stories travelled and this place had more than its fair share of shady tales. Given the choice, he would've preferred trying their luck on the other side, but if crossing the bridge with everyone had been an option, they wouldn't still be in the city.

"You really want to play?" Marin queried. She toyed with the dagger, twirling it around on its side.

He gestured for her to continue. She was right in there not being much else to do at this hour. There had been a minstrel when Tracker first arrived, but both the man and his instrument were currently quiet, leaving only the hum of talk, the aimless shuffle of people, and the gentle clink and clatter of dishes.

Marin wasted no time in setting the dagger spinning atop the table.

The blade's point came to rest facing the hedgewitch, who cocked her head in confusion. "I've not heard of this game. What are the rules?"

"Simple ones," Tracker replied. It was a children's game, after all. "You spin and whomever the dagger lands on gets to ask anyone a question. The questioned either answers or challenges you to go first. You can refuse, of course, but you give up your turn and the question cannot be asked again."

"Then the questioned gets to spin and become the asker," Marin added. "Which would be you this round."

"I think I understand it." Katarina stretched over the table to give the dagger a flick. It turned languidly before wobbling to a stop pointing at herself. She hummed for a moment, her brow furrowing in thought. "So, seeing that it has landed on me, I get to ask a question of anyone?" She grimaced. "Although, I just wasted my turn with that, didn't I?"

Marin chuckled. "Ordinarily, yes. Given this is your first time playing, I think we can ignore that you asked. And yes, if you spin and it lands on you again, that's another question you can ask."

"So, technically…" She flattened her palm atop the dagger's hilt. "And just to clarify, this is another not-question. Does that mean someone deft with their fingers could control the game by having it land on them every time?"

"You mean if they *cheated*?" Tracker replied, propping his chin upon the heel of his hand. "That is always a possibility. But I am certain we all intend to play fair."

"Then…" She wriggled in her seat, turning herself to face him square-on. "Knowing what we do about the attack, are you sure it's safe for Dylan to continue heading east?"

No. Certainly not all the way to Wintervale. Even journeying to Riverton was a risk he'd no choice but to make. *With Authril digging her claws in all the way.* How to get rid of her? He wished he'd an answer even to that.

Marin pulled a sour face. "Perhaps I should've made it clearer. The questions asked in this game aren't usually so heavy."

"Truthfully, I cannot say," Tracker confessed. All the plans he laid out had been blocked by the city guards. If he had a way to sneak Dylan across the river, but the only option there was to swim and he doubted the spellster would've been taught how. "I am sorry. I wish there was something else I could tell you."

Katarina looked as though she wished to say more. She merely bit her bottom lip and slowly nodded.

In the silence, he gave the dagger a twirl. The point completed three revolutions before coming to rest facing the other woman.

"Finally," Marin muttered before clearing her throat. "Let me show you how this game is supposed to go." The grin she affixed him was undeniably impish. "Tell me, what was your first kiss like?"

Thrown off guard by the absurdity of her query, he couldn't help but chuckle. Here they were, all of them aware Dylan could die if Tracker couldn't convince him to stray from that path, and Marin chose to make the most childlike and frivolous inquiry. He supposed they could do with a bit of levity, at least for the night. "I thought this was leading to prying questions." He hadn't believed her bold enough to begin at the first chance.

"Isn't the whole game about asking them?" she shot back. "And I would consider it a pretty innocent one, thank you."

Waggling his finger, he clicked his tongue in mock admonishment. "The rules are one question per spin, my dear hunter. It is my turn now, yes?"

"You didn't answer my first one!"

He sighed. She was right in the question being harmless enough, but he wasn't in the mood to concede easily. "You first, since you are so eager."

Marin wrinkled her nose, huffing and grumbling like someone ten years her junior. "*Fine.* It was with this farm hand, Gwen or Wynn or something like that. She used to help out near the kitchen, always had this aroma of baked bread about her." She flapped her hand. "It was nothing serious. Couldn't be. She was promised to the farm owner's second son." Her lips curved into a sombre smile. "Seemed pretty happy with the idea. Can't imagine why. He was kind enough, but more chaff between his ears than in a whole sack of horse feed. Liked them that way, I guess." She shrugged dismissively. "I told my truth. It's *your* turn now."

"Mine happened when I was nine years of age and he—"

"*He?*" Marin echoed, instantly more intrigued by his answer. "So, your first kiss was with a man? You are into them."

He picked up his drink and raised it to his lips. "I believe you have had more than your one question this round," he mumbled into the mug before taking a sip. Knowing she would only persist, he continued, "But he was a *boy*. One of my fellow would-be hounds, to be precise. The elders kept us segregated beyond training and temple visits. Elven boys are easier to come by when you are one." He hadn't possessed the type of stealth needed to sneak out until a few years later.

"Boy." Marin tilted her head one way, then the other. "Man. It *was* because you're attracted to your own gender, right?"

"Amongst others." As was the norm for the kingdom. Whilst he had tried to keep his interest in Dylan from being publically anything more than what a hound should—failing more than a handful of times as the urge to tease the man overrode his better judgement— his lack of letting their night-time activities be known shouldn't have been enough on their own to have her believing anything beyond the norm.

She sat back, infinitely pleased with herself. "Authril's not going to be happy to hear that."

Tracker raised a brow at her. He wasn't entirely sure the warrior had ever been happy. She certainly had opinions about things that weren't her concern.

"Between her saying your contact in the brothel was a woman and your lack of interest in Dylan, I was starting to believe her insistence that men weren't your thing."

"That is a peculiar way to gauge it. I like a lot of things."

"Including men," Marin added, grinning. "And that makes me two coppers richer."

He flicked the dagger, setting it spinning just enough that it would stop on himself. "Why would my preferences make you money?"

"I'd a bet with Authril on whether you actually liked men or were just seeing how much you can make Dylan blush."

"Why did you not simply ask?" He wasn't exactly keeping it a secret.

Marin shrugged. "More fun to speculate."

"And how were you planning to reach a conclusion before we parted ways?"

"Well, we're here." She flung her arms wide, trying to encompass the tavern in its entirety. "There's plenty of men around to chat up or snog. Unless..." A slyness widened her already mischievous smile. "You'd prefer to start with someone a little more familiar?"

He couldn't have been transparent about his interest in the man if the warrior was decrying Marin's claims, but the hunter was clearly keener than he'd have liked. "What makes you think our dear spellster would be at all receptive to such a move?"

Marin scoffed. "Are you joking? That man goes redder than a bad sunburn whenever he glances your way. But he has yet to make an appearance, so..." She spun the dagger once more, leaning a little further across the table. "Was your first-time snog with your elven boy any good?"

Laughter snorted out his nose. "*Dreadful*, actually. I had no clue what I was doing." It had taken several more years before he gained the level of talent he had now. "Nor did he." Tracker still remembered the boy's shaky smile, the uncertain touches.

The way his lifeless body had bounced along the rock face as it tumbled into the water.

His gaze slid along the crowd, taking in none of the revelry. The fondness of memory that'd curved his lips suddenly fell. "He has been dead for some time now." Where Tracker had continued to grow older, Nine-twelve-eighteen-sixty-seven hadn't even seen the end of his eleventh year.

"I..." Marin reached across the table to lay a hand atop his. "I didn't mean to—"

"It is all right." He gently slid his fingers out from under her touch. "You could not have known and, like I said, it was a long time ago."

"What happened, if you don't mind?" Katarina asked. The hedgewitch had been so silent that he had forgotten she still sat with them. "Accident? Illness?"

"Nothing like that. Our training starts young and certain goals must be met if we are to become a hound. He failed them, so he was put down." Spying the two women exchanging concerned glances, he forced a smile and shrugged. "It is the way things are. The king must only have the best and those trained with such knowledge as ours cannot be permitted to roam freely."

"I had no idea training to become a hound was so fraught with danger," Katarina said.

Marin muttered something, but his attention drifted to the stairs where he caught the almost nervous flutter of Dylan's magic approaching. It appeared the man was finally changed to his liking and ready to join them.

"—and *then* she—" Marin continued.

Tracker lost all focus on the woman's words as he finally caught sight of the spellster descending the stairs, fully garbed in his new attire, which was the colour of deep water.

The man had been forced to re-hem his old robe higher after it had been singed back at the army encampment. Whilst a practical solution to keep it from fraying, it left the impression of his clothes being too small. The skirts on this robe hung to the ankle and, with an array of discs of silver adorning his belt in a starkly visual cinch, it added a touch of elegance to his lankiness. The several distinct layers also altered his figure, especially the upper one, where the sleeves stopped a little above the elbow and gave his narrow frame a wider silhouette.

Marin waved her hand before him, interrupting the sight. She eyed him, then glanced over her shoulder. A knowing smirk took her lips.

Refusing to acknowledge her, Tracker stood as the man neared.

"Oh!" Katarina exclaimed as if she also hadn't seen Dylan clothed thusly before. Had the man not tried the clothes on before leaving with them? "The tailor did a fine job fitting all of it to you."

"You think so?" Blushing slightly, Dylan twirled before them, showing off the outfit in full. The panels making the upper skirt parted slightly as they flared. The layers beneath wrapped around Dylan's body, just as the army robe had. Even the collar sat high enough to conceal much of his scarred neck.

The neckline also clearly showed the garment beneath was of a harmonising colour to the rest of the outfit and a different cut to his original undertunic. Did it also wrap? Could he, theoretically, expose that swathe of unblemished skin by undoing a few ties?

Tracker took a steadying breath and shunted the thoughts back into the depths, lest his tongue blurted the wrong thing. "You do indeed look good in it." He gestured for the man to seat himself and whispered, in a tone just loud enough to carry, "I will refrain from asking about its cost."

Dylan cleared his throat, his cheeks briefly darkening. "I actually have no idea about that. Marin handled the negotiating."

He already knew that. With Authril having gone on her own mission and the hedgewitch being from another land, Marin would've been the only one capable of striking a favourable deal.

The spellster slipped by him to sit. The faintly floral scent of soap wafted in his passage. He clearly had also availed himself of a bath before changing. That revelation didn't help cool the wisp of heat stirring in Tracker's blood.

Dylan tucked himself into the bench's corner. The music returned as the man settled, accompanied by a minstrel's dulcet voice. Even without glancing the man's way, Tracker picked up the subtle trill in his voice that marked them as elven and quite talented.

The spellster jerked his chin at the dagger still lying atop the table. "What's this about?"

"Nothing of consequence," Tracker replied, sheathing the weapon.

"Just a few rounds of Truth be Told," Marin added, grinning. "You know of it?"

The man nodded. "What was the last question?"

"How old were you when you'd your first kiss?" the hunter replied, her grin widening as Dylan's cheeks gained colour. "And who with?"

"You do not have to answer," Tracker added as he resumed sitting.

Beyond their table, several folk had taken up dancing. Most were at least in step with their partner, if not to the melody's precise rhythm. A few did so with all the grace of a drunken rat and were likely just as pickled.

"That's all right. I was twelve—we both were, actually. As for *who*, it..." His gaze gained the distant glaze of remembrance. "It was Nestria. She's—she *was*—an old friend. We kind of grew up together."

"Aww," Marin cooed. "Your first kiss was a childhood friend? That's so cute." A good-natured smile curved the woman's mouth. "Any good?"

With mirth stretching his lips, Dylan shook his head. "We were too nervous about being caught and clumsy because we were nervous. And I..." He grinned, his cheeks growing redder. "I sort of wound up with my nose in her eye," he confessed. "A little."

The hunter rocked back in her seat, her cackling drawing the attention of a few nearby patrons.

Tracker wasn't sure what he had expected to hear, but it certainly hadn't been that. "I would have thought sneaking about the tower would have been quite the challenge at such an age." Although, perhaps not as tricky as leaving one of the segregated units where they housed pups.

The faintest bloom of pink adorned the man's cheeks as he grinned. "It wasn't *easy* by any means, but we managed between lessons."

A couple bumped into their table, sending the shorter of the duo sprawling atop the surface and spilling what was left of their drinks. "Sorry," they managed whilst also swatting and giggling at their dance partner, who was attempting to right them. "You oaf, I told you I should lead."

The man grimaced his own apology before hefting his clearly more inebriated partner back onto their feet. Then the duo was off into the dancing crowd.

Shaking her hands dry, Marin got to her feet. "I'll grab us a cloth and another round. Maybe something to snack on, too." She wove her way through the throng, deftly avoiding a man who tried his luck at snagging a dance. Fortunately, it came without violence. In this environment, a simple punch could all too easily grow into an all-out brawl.

He couldn't deny people wanting to join in. The rhythm was infectious, even if the instruments obscured much of the minstrel's song.

Standing, Tracker extended his hand to Dylan. Although he hadn't partaken in the activity himself, he recalled how joyous the man had been after dancing back in Oldmarsh. The steps here weren't as ordered, but Tracker was more than capable of keeping them from colliding with anyone else. "Care to join in the fun? There is little of it to be had on the road between here and Riverton."

Uncertainty flickered across the man's face as he scrunched himself further into the bench. "I'd prefer to stay here for now." His gaze dropped to the table. "If you don't mind?"

Asking for a simple dance was too far? Did the man fear what Authril might do if she spied them so close upon her return? A possibility, even if he didn't see how she could make anything of it.

Nevertheless, he bowed his head in acceptance of the refusal and turned to the sole other occupying the table. "How about you, Madam Hedgewitch?"

She gently shook her head. "Another time, perhaps."

"Ah!" Tracker laid a hand upon his chest. "To be wounded so with your cruel words." He sagged against the bench's backing as though he'd been struck. "Declined by two beauties so swiftly, it appears I am losing my touch. What a dreadful fate to have befallen me."

Whilst Dylan still didn't meet his gaze, the man's lips twitched into a small smile. That would have to do.

He spied the hunter returning, clutching four mugs brimming with foam. "Perhaps I will get lucky with my third request, yes?" he suggested to the pair, not really expecting an answer.

Marin did indeed wish to indulge him in a dance. They whirled about the room, keeping time to the beat as best as they could whilst avoiding others. They halted beside their table, where she, now breathless, slumped onto the bench and drained her mug dry.

Tracker mimicked the latter before bowing and seeking another dance partner. He cavorted amongst the crowd, bouncing from one person to the next until he lost count of how many, whoever wished a gambolling turn around the room. He paused between songs and only long enough to down another drink.

As the night matured to its zenith, the minstrel stopped his singing. The melody changed, still rambunctious, but less refined.

Having relinquished his current dance partner to the crowd, he came to a halt by the bar.

"Another drink?" the bartender asked, shrugging as he waved them away.

It was likely time they headed upstairs. He swivelled on the spot, looking for the others. He had lost track of Marin and Katarina's whereabouts. Neither were seated at the table, nor was—

Dylan. He stretched up onto his toes, seeking some hint of the man over the crowd. *Still close*. His senses told him that readily enough. He had spied the spellster dancing with the women earlier and had assumed the man would remain close to them. Authril clearly hadn't returned. He would've known.

Had Dylan gone to bed? As much as Tracker would've enjoyed a turn or two on the floor with the spellster—or possibly dragging him off into some dark corner for a very different type of dance—he couldn't fault the man for seeking rest. Especially when they would be leaving at first light.

A soft figure collided into him. Tracker steadied them before either they or he lost balance, grabbing onto the bar counter to aid him. "My apologies, I was not looking."

The woman in his arms looked to be part of the staff. At the very least, she wore the same simple tunic and apron the rest of the servers wore. She gave a harsh chuckle, keeping her hands clasped onto his arms. "You elves are a lot more solid than you look, aren't you?" Dark eyes looked him over. "Always wanted to have a little fun with one of your kind. Been watching you take the other patrons for a spin and if you can dance on your back half as well as you do upright, I reckon we'd have a real good time."

Giving her a polite smile, Tracker put some obvious distance between them. "My good madam, I—"

The woman frowned. "*Sir*," they said.

"Forgive me, my good sir. I will still have to decline." He glanced over the crowd, still not able to place Dylan's position other than close. "I... uh..."

"You guarding that lanky, dark-haired fellow?" said the bartender, nodding before Tracker could give an answer either way. "He went off upstairs with our minstrel trailing him none too long ago."

Tracker sucked down a breath, trying to ignore the prickliness in his gut. The insinuation was quite clear on what the bartender thought they were up to.

If the spellster wanted to share his body and gain experiences beyond himself, it wasn't *his* place to tell the man who with. At least with Authril not here, he didn't need to worry about fending off her intervention.

He grunted his thanks for the information.

A scoff on his left had him turning back to the jilted server. "At least someone's 'bout to find himself screwed. In more ways than one, I'd wager." Cackling, they nudged him as though he was in on the joke.

The bartender shot the still-chortling server a hard look before addressing Tracker. "Look, keeping him from making an arse of himself is probably above what they pay you, but he seems like a sweet boy, if a little out of his depths on this side of the bridge. As my friend here said, if Al gets his way, he'll take that boy for every penny he's got."

"Let him," declared the friend in question. "It's not as if the fancy boys don't have the coin to spare. Just like Boss says, they know what they're getting themselves into when they choose to slum 'round here."

Sighing, Tracker pushed himself away from the bar. Giving Dylan the space to explore his tastes without intervention was one thing. Standing by and letting anyone take advantage of another had never been his speciality.

CHAPTER 34

Dylan stumbled up the stairs leading to his room and the bed within. His head spun more than the hours of dancing with Marin and Katarina could account for, but the world's edges had turned soft long ago.

He didn't know how many drinks sloshed about his stomach, or exactly what some of them had been. He only knew that, as the night had gone by, more people flocked to Tracker's side, eager for a dance with the hound's skilled body.

Watching the hound twirl around with Marin had been fine, like having all his friends joke with each other. But seeing him doing the same with others—those who eagerly threw themselves at the man— only fed the bitterness inside him.

The longer Dylan had watched, the pricklier the bitterness in his gut became, not ebbing until thoroughly drowned by copious amounts of alcohol.

It was a foolish feeling. He wasn't the man's keeper. He didn't care how many others Tracker chose to entertain. Why should he care? He had already turned down the offer, his cowardice had seen to that. Even after gathering the nerve to dance along with the others, Tracker hadn't made another attempt.

And why would he? He'd already been given his answer.

He wiped his cheek, smearing the damp that had collected there. Not all of it was sweat.

Stupid. What was he crying for? Because he wasn't at the centre of the hound's attention? Who was he to demand that right? Tracker deserved to seek fun without him, even if it was only dancing. What else could he possibly get up to here? It wasn't as though they were in a brothel.

"Hello there, beautiful."

Dylan turned at the sultry words to find the elven minstrel who had been singing not that long ago standing at his elbow. He glanced about, making sure the man's attention was on himself and not someone who actually fit the descriptor.

The minstrel chuckled, the low sound tingling along Dylan's skin. "Yes, I meant you." He sidled closer, that dark gaze darting over him. "Call me Al. I couldn't help but catch you dancing to my music earlier. A man would be remiss if he didn't speak of your grace."

"My *grace*?" he echoed, unable to fully keep his amusement out of the words. He had become a little more surefooted since learning to fight with more than just his magic, but he'd never been graceful.

"Of course," the man continued, gesturing wildly with his hands. "It was a symphony in motion and *I* know music, my dear. I don't give such compliments lightly, but your every stride could outmatch the most delicate of notes. The sweetest trill of the voice could not possibly compare to the way you twirled."

Dylan relaxed against the banister. It might've been the drink or the tavern's heady atmosphere, but the praise was at least pretty. If untrue. "Go on."

Once again, the man appraised him. Slower. "I was wondering if I could…" His tongue slid along his bottom lip a moment before wetting a fang, leaving it gleaming in the candlelight. "…increase your enjoyment of the night."

Not really. What had Tracker said? *Join in the fun.* That was all well and good, but the one he wanted to engage in any fun with was—

Where?

Dylan glanced around the room, looking for the others. Marin and Katarina had moved to a more secluded table, engaged in conversation. Authril was still nowhere to be found and, whilst he was no longer dancing with his adoring public, the hound appeared preoccupied with the advances of another.

"Don't worry about your friends," the minstrel said. "All the servers know how to ensure people have a good time." The man's suggestive tone only had the thorniness in Dylan's gut return in full force.

He turned from the sight, storming up the stairs. If the hound wanted a good time, then he was welcome to find elsewhere to indulge. It wasn't as though they'd made promises to the contrary. Tracker certainly wasn't—

Mine.

Nothing was. Just a few personal effects gifted to him in puberty. Even his clothes technically belonged to others… The tower. The army. The hound.

"We needn't go far," the minstrel continued, keeping pace with Dylan by trotting at his side. "I have a room upstairs. We could retire there and…" His gaze snapped up from where he'd definitely been eyeing Dylan's groin. "…compose our own sonnet."

Shaking his head, he aimed for his door. If he could get into his room, then maybe the man would leave him alone to wallow in whatever abysmal mood he pleased until sleep claimed him.

The minstrel didn't take the hint. The man walked backwards ahead of him, trying to subtly veer them elsewhere even as they approached the door to Dylan's rented room for the evening, nattering the whole way about beauty and music. Dylan swore he caught a line or three of bad poetry amongst it all, too.

When Dylan finally reached his destination, he hastened to find the key that would let him enter and rid himself of the man. The more he fumbled in his belt pouch, the more it seemed to evade him.

Victory came to him all the same, if not swiftly enough.

The man laid a hand on the door handle as Dylan turned the lock. "Sweet wonder," he purred, effortlessly sliding between Dylan and his escape. "You cannot deny the allure between us." He grabbed Dylan's collar, dragging him down to crush their lips together.

Their meeting was no different to kissing Authril. There was no warmth. No butterflies. His stomach bubbled, drawing the world that little bit more into focus. The growing hum of a shield ready to form buzzed along his skin.

Dylan pushed the minstrel back, the door issuing a warning creak as the man collided with it. "I—" He went to put more distance between them, freezing as he realised the man had hold of his belt. The buzzing increased. Suppressing it made him nauseous, but he didn't trust himself not to slice the man in two if he permitted the barrier to form. "Let me go."

The minstrel's chuckle set Dylan's skin to squirming. "Everyone knows it takes more than the pluck of a single string to create a symphony in the blood." His fingers tightened on Dylan's belt, stopping him from leaving. "You must play the whole melody."

"I believe the only music you make tonight will be a solo affair," Tracker growled.

Dylan twisted in the minstrel's grip. When had the hound approached them? Had he been standing there the whole time? "I—"

"Ah." The minstrel finally released his hold on Dylan's belt. He smiled prettily, but there was a jaggedness to the edges. "And who might you be, my good man, to be so definitive in that assessment? His bodyguard?"

Tracker's answering grin was no sharper than the man's, but it whispered of far more danger. He halted before them, his arms folded. "Of a sort."

The man's dark eyes flicked between Tracker and Dylan. "And what is it that you guard tonight? His chastity?" He laughed. "Surely, you aren't cruel enough to deny..." His gaze dropped, clearly taking in the hound before sliding Dylan's way. "...him..." Fear bloomed in his eyes. All the guile and charm slid off his face like water down a sluice.

Dylan's stomach churned, threatening to expel the copious amounts he had drunk.

The minstrel eyed Dylan as though he'd been cornered in some dark alley. Then he visibly rallied and bowed low. "On reflection, who am I to interfere with *your* type of job?" He was walking back down the corridor before he even finished speaking, as though he couldn't excuse himself fast enough, but didn't dare to run.

Dylan watched the man depart. He'd been rebuffed before based on what he was in the past, but that had been because he was human, not because he had magic. Seeing the fear, the rejection where there had been desire only moments ago...

Maybe it was all the drink, but it stung a lot more than usual.

Tracker snorted. "Good riddance."

"So acerbic," Dylan teased. "Was that a touch of jealousy that I heard?"

The hound tensed. The motions were subtle. Controlled. The minute flex of a balled hand, the faint jerk that spoke of shoulders squaring. "I am not jealous," he whispered, the words audible only because of the surrounding quiet. "I am furious. There is a difference."

"Furious?" What did the hound have to be angry about? "With who? *Me?*" That the minstrel had dared to proposition Dylan? He hadn't led the man on or let him continue without any sign of stopping him. "I didn't— *He—*" The hound had to know all he could explain. He must've been standing there long enough to see.

"Not *you*. With myself." Sighing, he pinched the bridge of his nose. "I should have kept a better eye on you."

So he was only deemed trustworthy to be on his own when they were out in the middle of nowhere? Dylan bristled at the thought. He wasn't a child and besides... "I wasn't actually going to sleep with him."

"That was not my point, but I believe you were the only one who thought that."

That was more truth than he wanted to admit. For all the man's musical terms, he hadn't been willing to listen to Dylan's rejection. "You didn't need to scare him with your... you know." He mimicked Tracker's stance and expression.

"He scared himself."

Only because the man had identified Tracker's attire and figured out just what a hound would be guarding. "He didn't need to know." At least, with Tracker here, the minstrel was unlikely to go looking for another hound.

"That so?" The hound had to have seen them kissing, saw the

minstrel *groping* Dylan. Yet he was reacting so calmly. "Do you also withhold this information from others you intended on being intimate with?"

"No." He hadn't needed to. Everyone in the tower had known. Tracker obviously knew. Even Authril had been aware before she started seeking his company. "And I hadn't intended on anything. He—" His skin crawled just thinking about it. "Even if I had, I could've just not used magic in his presence." It wasn't difficult to restrain his power. He did it all the time. Even in the tower.

"And if you had reacted to him the way you did with me last night?" That voice… Still soft. Still calm.

And far too logical for the anger and embarrassment churning in his gut.

"What of it?" Dylan snapped. "Is that what you're really concerned about? That another might elicit the same reaction? Or do you think I can't reel in my power?" He had been very generous with its use last night, both intentionally and not. If it meant that the hound couldn't sleep with another without thinking of Dylan, then he was fine with that. With the tower gone, leaving one person haunted by their memories together was likely the only impression his existence would have on the world.

The hound leant closer, sniffing the air. "I see." The words were dry. Lacking any emotion. Dull like the mask that had fallen across his face. "You are drunk."

"Because I'm talking truths?"

"Because your breath could rival a brewery." Laying one hand on the small of Dylan's back, he gestured to the door. "Come, let us get you to bed and you can sleep it off."

Dylan jerked away from the touch. "What if I don't want to do that? What if I want to go somewhere else and get *ploughed* into oblivion? Would *that* be all right with you?" They only slept together to have mindless entertainment—no different from how it had been back in the tower—the hound had told him that plenty of times. "*You* were the one who suggested I have *fun*, after all. And my ability to choose what that entails is as good as dead once I reach the army." Be it Authril who took up the leash or someone even crueller, he'd be under their care. "I might as well get comfortable with people using my body how they see fit."

What did it matter who did the using?

Concern flashed across Tracker's features, alongside a sliver of hurt. The expression was brief, but sharp enough that Dylan immediately wanted to bridge the gap between them and recant.

No. He squared his shoulders and took a deep, steadying breath. If he let the man touch him, he would start crying. He knew it. He couldn't take back the words either. They hung between them now.

"I cannot say I recommend it," Tracker said, his tone guarded. "Especially with the type of people who would take you whilst in this state."

Cold laughter bubbled in Dylan's throat. "And who would that be? Not *him*. He couldn't have run off any faster than if I'd flogged him." All because he'd been labelled as a spellster. Correctly, but still... "Not *you*." If Tracker had any such intentions tonight, he doubted the hound would've spent so long dancing with others.

"Well, no. I prefer my bed partners to at least be sober enough to remember what we did."

Heat flooded his face. He was not *that* drunk. He stalked down the hallway, not caring where his feet took him. "Stop it!" he hissed. "Just... stop being..." He flailed his hands, gesturing to the hound in his entirety, his words a garbled mess as he failed to find the right one. "...*this* for just one second?" Did he not care about what had almost happened? "Be angry. Yell at me. Hit something."

Tracker closed his eyes, eliminating the light shimmering across their surfaces. Frustration whistled out his nose. He remained silent, but Dylan spied the subtle shift of his jaw. The man definitely had something to say, but was holding back.

That only infuriated Dylan more. He clenched his hands, struggling to ignore how hot his palms were or the surrounding hum of a shield ready to snap into existence. "Do you have any idea what I would've permitted if you had pushed?" he grated, struggling to keep any emotion from his voice. The words still wavered. "You could've crept into my tent every night, imposed your will on me, pounded my mind to *paste* in preparation for my fate. But *no*." Bitterness burned in the back of his throat, more than wine could've accounted for. He swallowed it down. "You had to be soft. *Gentle*." He couldn't stop the icy heat of unshed tears from pricking the corners of his eyes, further blurring the edges of the world. "Had to make me feel—"

Cared for.

Loved.

He squeezed his eyes together, fighting back tears. His chest ached, the sweet fluttering that had consumed him over the past few days now hammered at his ribcage like a dying bird. It was more fitting. He hadn't deserved the butterflies.

On the edge of his vision, he caught Tracker rubbing at his neck. "Dylan..."

He turned his head, refusing to acknowledge the man had said a word. It was childish, he knew that, but if he met Tracker's gaze, he didn't think it would take long before his voice broke further. "Why do you care what I do? Who I sleep with? You literally offered to take me to a brothel last night." After Dylan had made his intentions known of how much he had wanted Tracker. "Or was that a hollow gesture?"

The man's soft growl lifted the hairs along Dylan's arm.

When the hound spoke again, it was with composure. "It was by no means *hollow*. I thought, perhaps, you might desire the chance you didn't get to have at *The Gilded Lily*, to explore without a certain warrior breathing down your neck."

"Explore?" he echoed indignantly. Like he didn't know his way around a person? "Don't talk about me as if I'm some untested innocent. I've lain with *dozens*." Any and every one who would let him.

"Of women. I am aware."

"My experience with them still counts."

Tracker's brows lowered, the chink in his calm facade revealing itself. "That is not..." He took a blustering breath and waggled a cautioning finger at him. "Do not go putting words in my mouth."

Dylan bit his lip. He hadn't meant it that way.

"As for me caring about *what* and *who*..." He bowed his head and sighed. "It is less about such things and more I lack a desire to see you get hurt. Or used. I would never have intervened just now if I thought you were in a state capable of determining when someone wanted to screw you versus rob you blind. Letting you get into a position where the latter almost happened was my mistake."

Taken aback, all he could do was stare at the hound. "Rob?" Why would anyone try to rob him? He had nothing worth stealing.

"I have seen that money-hungry look at least a hundred times. With that outfit?" His gaze ran over Dylan, lingering in places the other man hadn't. "You look like you have plenty of coin to spare. He likely would have slept with you, had you permitted it, then taken off with *this*." He pressed something familiar into Dylan's palm.

Dylan stared at the belt pouch with its cut ties for some time before registering it was his. "How did you—?" He patted the space where it should've been. "I didn't—"

"Notice it missing? Obviously. He took it from you whilst you were kissing."

He leant back against the wall. His mind felt as if he'd been slapped. *All those glances.* Not at all like Tracker's, who took in the sight without a care about the monetary worth. The pretty words, the insistence...

It hadn't been about him, just what had been hanging from his belt.

He wrapped a hand around the battered leather pouch, feeling the contents within. Nothing more than an old mirror, a razor...

And the pendant he had wanted to give Tracker.

But if the minstrel had been after money, what were the odds that he would've stopped to check the pouch's contents? *Poor*. He would've simply grabbed and been off, taking with him the only remaining items Dylan had from the tower, all he had left of his guardian. And he never would've seen them again.

His legs folded, dumping him onto the floor. All the anger welling inside churned, seeking an outlet. It boiled through his blood, gnawed at his bones. A sliver tumbled about his stomach, threatening to expel his dinner, before the whole rushed out in a torrent of hot tears.

Tracker settled next to him. Still. Calm. "Dylan?"

Laughter bubbled up from his chest. He tipped his head back, blinking furiously to eliminate the watery sheen from the world. "What? No '*my dear*' to be had?" Did he really look that pathetic?

One corner of the hound's mouth twitched in a sympathetic smile. "I am sorry."

"For what?" he mumbled. "You didn't do anything." *He* had, though. *Gods...* He'd been but a moment from pouring out so much vitriol in some attempt to lever open the cracks he knew were lying beneath the hound's calm facade. Any pain would've done so long as the man felt *something. Like a damn child.* He had already said so many spiteful words. Things he hadn't meant. Things only designed to hurt. That Tracker didn't respond in kind didn't mean he hadn't been struck.

And over what?

Nothing. The minstrel hadn't wanted him, just what he presumably had. What the man could get out of him. Like everyone else.

"I feel like an idiot," he confessed.

"It will pass," Tracker assured. "What are we without our mistakes?"

If the tower's Overseers were to be believed, then the answer was a curt barely on par with the average citizen.

The hound nudged Dylan's hand, the one gripping the belt pouch like a lifeline. "I will show you how to properly stow this so it sits less accessible to others tomorrow."

"I'm sorry. Everything I said, I didn't mean any of it. I just—" Had purposely sought to make Tracker feel the same covetous pain he did.

He laid a hand on his chest. The fluttering had stilled, but it ached. Mourned.

A small, cheerless smile curved the hound's lips. "Sometimes, I forget there are certain experiences, beyond sex, that you lack. Others would suggest allowing you to have those encounters, but I cannot agree with that."

Dylan bit his cheek. The man's current expression had started since leaving the tower, but he was seeing it more and more. Something had clearly been gnawing at the man's mind since before they'd reached Whitemeadow. Was it Authril's behaviour? Marin did say the two elves argued over his fate.

"*And* I should have realised before tonight that you clearly have a type," the hound continued. "That it, coupled with your inexperience, would blind you."

"A type?" He arched a brow at the man. "What's that supposed to mean?"

Tracker gestured to himself. "Elves." A soft cheeky note threaded its way through the word, growing more pronounced as he added, "You are attracted to them."

Dylan's mouth dropped open. He wiped haphazardly at his tears. "Th-that's not a fair assessment." The minstrel not being human hadn't really factored into anything. Yes, there was Authril, but he had only considered her being an elf as one of the reasons behind her initial rejection of him.

"Is it not? The way I hear it, we are considered quite beautiful. And from where I am standing, you are four for four." He held up his hand and, with his thumb tucked against his palm, wriggled the appropriate number of fingers.

"*Where* did you get that number?" Although he had slept with far more of both human and elven than the hound could readily display on his fingers, he hadn't spoken much about his past flings. "You know of two, including yourself, who are elves that I happened to have been intimate with."

"Well, as you say, there is myself and our dear warrior," Tracker said, ticking off the names with a forefinger. "Then there is your childhood sweetheart—"

"My...?" he squeaked out. Clearing his throat, he hastily added, "It wasn't like *that*. We were friends." Old, close friends. "Nothing more."

Although, now he thought on it, she *had* been his first in a lot of things. Just as he'd been for her. Even after all these years, he wasn't sure who had made the first move, but if there was anything they wanted to experiment with, they were often the first person each other went to. That's how he had discovered the lightning trick Tracker seemed to enjoy so much; through Nestria using him as her plaything.

"—and there is the minstrel," the hound continued as though he hadn't heard Dylan's protests.

He twisted to face the hound, his throat making incoherent sounds before it could form words. "I... I wasn't intimate with him." The man had barely laid a hand on him.

Chuckling, Tracker shook his head. "What does that matter? You still felt attraction. Still…" He gestured abstractly with a single hand. "Let us say, *entertained* the idea."

"For all of two seconds," he conceded. "But him being an elf had nothing to do with it."

The grin that took Tracker's face was far more authentic and warm, the hound's mirth twinkling in his eyes. "You do know I am only teasing, yes? It is nothing to be ashamed of. Elf… Human…" He shrugged. "I have lost count of how many of either has shared my bed. Why would it bother me which you have preferred in the past?"

"I don't know." Tracker had admitted to being attracted to men far sooner than other genders, but swore he saw them all the same. It wasn't that great a leap to believe the species made no difference in the hound's mind. "It's not true for everyone, though. I've encountered plenty of people, those I've wished to become intimate with, who were bothered by it."

"Ah. Considering I know you have never been with another man—"

"Not that I hadn't thought of it before," he blurted. It might have been some time since the idea of being intimate with a gender beyond that of a woman had crossed his mind, but it hadn't been nonexistent. "I mean…" His thoughts floundered, searching for the right words. "If you hadn't initiated anything I probably wouldn't have—" He fell silent, only because Tracker placed a single quieting finger upon his lips.

"I know. Even without your flirting, the way you looked at the men back in *The Gilded Lily* told me as much. Still, I can surmise that these people you speak of were women. There is a certain advantage to us both being male, yes?"

"I've noticed," he mumbled past the pad of Tracker's digit. Especially in the week after their dalliance in the tower, when Authril routinely snuck into his tent. But then, quite a number of things seemed sharply different as of late, and it had nothing to do with the obvious.

"I am sure you did. Nevertheless, the nature of the women you have slept with does not concern me." He rubbed at his neck before bowing his head with a sigh. "For what it is worth, you are everything he said and more. If his intentions had been more honest, I would have…" His gaze became distant for a moment, sliding off into the dark. "I would have *not* interfered." The words came briskly, the calm mask he had donned earlier not quite returning in full.

He peered at the hound out of the corner of his eye. "But you wouldn't have liked it."

Tracker shook his head. "I already told you, I do not get jealous. I never have been one for it."

"You know that's not normal, right?" In the tower, he never agreed on exclusivity with anyone and still, from time to time, he would be overcome with bitter ire at the thought that the women he frequently had sex with would, in turn, be with other men. It was irrational and childish, and he would generally spend hours after the fact scolding himself over it, but the feelings still happened. "Everyone gets jealous."

The man's brows rose. "Do they? I suppose it requires an attachment to someone as well as a threat to such a bond. Since the first time I had sex, I have done so knowing that I share a bed partner's body with others. It is *my* normality and I am… used to it." The smile he offered was small, almost solemn. "Having you all to myself has been a novelty—one I have enjoyed immensely—but I am not about to insist we… that *you* remain exclusive. Especially when you have barely begun to expand your sexual repertoire."

Something stirred in his chest, the faintest little flutter. There were very few people he had lain with more than once. Half of them had been outside of the tower.

But Dylan remembered being told sex amongst hounds was harshly punished, that they could seek it outside the pack as long as they kept it physical. That didn't mean emotional bonds never happened. "You've never been close enough to someone that you wanted them all to yourself—"

Tracker waggled a finger at him. "That is possessiveness, not jealousy."

"—that you'd feel even the tiniest wisp of anger, of resentment, at the very thought of them being with another person? That you might even think about doing that other person harm?"

The hound's back straightened as though he'd been run through. "Harm someone my…?" A haunted look darkened those honey-coloured eyes. "No…" The look vanished so cleanly that Dylan wondered if it had ever been there. "I could never… It would not…"

He waited for the man to continue, prodding only once it was clear he would remain silent. "Track?"

Inhaling loudly, Tracker bounced to his feet. "You should return to our room. Maybe freshen up? Then, if you are still of a mind, I will help you find someone a little less predatory to have some fun with." He tilted his head to one side, the wide grin not quite settling on his face. "Yes?"

"No." He stood, following the hound down the hallway. "I-I don't want to do that. I didn't even want to do that with *him*." That admission was one of the few honest things he had said before lashing out like a child.

Tracker's smile melted, confusion taking its place. "Then what *do* you want?"

He halted a few feet from the man. *I don't know.* What was there left to want? Everything he had ever been trained for—had fought for, had loved—was gone.

Wasn't it?

Even knowing they stood in the middle of a hallway, Dylan swiftly closed the gap to pull the hound in close. He breathed deeply, taking in the scent of citrus and cinnamon, the subtle musk that was Tracker. *His* hound.

"You," he whispered, placing a kiss atop the man's forehead. "I want you."

"Dylan, I am not—"

He bent his head, the man's lips just the wisp of a breath away.

The sweetness of mead coated his tongue, bringing to mind the conversation they'd had weeks ago. The great tavern menu where he had compared the hound to a meal he only got once a year.

A rare treat. The hound had been teasing when he made the observation, but it was the truth.

Just another thing he would lose.

"I know I don't get to have you forever." He was well aware of the fate awaiting him at the end of their journey. Of what he would lose beyond control over his magic. "I don't want to share you. Not with some prostitute. Not with those... *people*—" He all but spat the word. "—downstairs."

One of the hound's brows lifted, rising further the more Dylan talked. The man might not have spoken a single word, but the thread of emotion weaving across his eyes whispered of increasing confusion and concern.

"Just—" Dylan pulled the man in close. His chest hurt to meet that gaze any longer. "Be mine," he whispered, his voice quavering as fresh tears poured down his face. "Until the capital, until they take me. Until—" If the other hounds didn't kill him outright, the army would see him bound, stripped of everything that made him *him.*

"Until Wintervale." Slowly, Tracker's arms wrapped around him. "I promise." His fingers dug into the robe, seeking to pull them closer together despite there being no space left between them. "Until then, I am yours to do as you please with."

CHAPTER 35

Tracker sat on the bed, leaning against the windowsill to stare at the world outside, as he waited for Dylan to awake. He had been sitting here for hours, long enough to watch the sun crest the horizon and splay its fingers of shimmering light down the street.

Last night, he had considered the window placement a matter of security and would've insisted on shifting the bed, had the room space to do so. Right now, he took advantage of how the pane let in just enough light to let him revel in the pale beauty sprawled on the bed next to him.

Perhaps it was the haze of his sleepless state colliding with the dregs of alcohol in his blood, but the golden glow shrouding Dylan had the man looking set to ascend to the heavens. The sight tightened his chest, the memory of last night flooding his thoughts.

Dylan had spoken as though he was dying.

With the spellster lying beside him, sleeping off the copious amounts he must've drunk, Tracker realised he hadn't once asked what leashing was like. He knew it from a purely academic point of view—that it cut them off from their magic unless sanctioned by their wardens—but from one who had experienced it?

All he knew was Dylan would prefer not to be. Which was expected.

But how it had *felt*? Was it like losing a limb? He had heard how that felt many times. The mind reaching for something, expecting its will to be obeyed, then the pang of realisation that it was gone. Was it a numbness in the soul? An ache that burned with a coldness that spread across the body.

Or something similar to what Tracker had experienced after losing his lovers and child? Pain so deep and hot that its passage had left a cavernous emptiness in his core.

Darkness. After his first escape into the tunnels to uncover his daughter, the mistress had ordered him confined to the same cells the hounds had imprisoned the four of them in.

Solitude. Even now, he never truly knew how long they had kept him locked away. Days? A week? Longer? Without windows or company, time had been measured by the discarded bowls of gruel.

Death. He had craved it. Willed it. Sought it. The cell held nothing to aid that pursuit. No sharp edges to fall upon. No chains or ropes to hang himself. They'd given him no utensils, not even a simple spoon. The bowls had been metal, but no matter how he tried, they refused all efforts to shape into a weapon.

Numb. His efforts to starve himself had left him too weak to fight back when they finally came for him. He couldn't stop them from dragging him into the infirmary, nor when they stuffed him with concoctions that fogged his mind and dulled his senses. It left a gap in his memories. A pit he could span only with assumptions and blurs.

By the time he came to, he was at The Gilded Lily. *Far from where he had wanted to be. Amongst people who knew nothing of who he was or what he'd done.*

Tracker rubbed at his temples. Tears burned his eyes, still refusing to shed after all these years. And why should they? Crying now wouldn't solve the problem before him any more than they'd helped him back then.

His head continued to pound. Between the nightmares and his racing thoughts, any sort of rest had eluded him. Even now, his thoughts refused to slow, skittering from one plan to another, seeking a solution that would see them heading north.

He could swim across the river if things came down to it. That wouldn't get Dylan across, though, and he doubted the spellster had such training. He couldn't sneak the man over the bridge, either. *Maybe as Katarina's apprentice.* That was a big maybe, requiring more luck than he could realistically ask of the gods. Certainly not with Authril in tow. And if the warrior couldn't swim, then she would definitely kick up enough fuss to make the guards suspicious.

Even if all that went smoothly, what then? The mayor had been clear on the boats being beyond his reach. Riverton was the only option. An uncertain one at that. *And so far.* They'd travelled farther than a mere week just getting here, but anything could happen in that time.

He idly glided his fingers through the thick, dark hair adorning Dylan's chest, seeking to soothe his nerves. He inhaled and focused on the feel of each curled strand beneath his fingertips as he slid up, exhaling at the sound of his nails lightly scraping the man's skin on the downward stroke.

Dylan's sleeping form stretched and sighed along with him. The man's eyes fluttered open, the morning light reflecting in their dark depths as he observed Tracker in silence. His fingers danced along the hand Tracker caressed him with before they walked up his forearm. Like last night, the touch was soft, hesitant. As though either of them might shatter.

The sensation squeezed his heart.

"Good morning." He tried to keep his tone light. There was no telling just how much Dylan recalled. "Or are we already regretting last night's choice regarding alcohol consumption?"

The man's answering smile was small and a smidgeon unsure. "Is it? What happened last night?"

"Do you not remember?" He didn't want to dredge it up, but he needed to know if Dylan was aware of everything he had said. Especially when they had days of travelling ahead of them before the next settlement. "You seem remarkably refreshed to have drunk too heavily." Was it a ploy? Was that lanky frame able to recover from so much?

Dylan gave a lazy grin as he ran a hand over his eyes. "Probably because healing deals with the worst of the effects. Last night wasn't the first time I've been blackout drunk." He smiled sadly, clearly reliving a far older memory. "As for what I recall..." A frown briefly tweaked his brows before he rocked his head from side to side on the pillow. "Not much past dancing." One corner of his mouth hitched a little higher. "It was fun." His gaze slid down, clearly taking in Tracker's nakedness. "And I'm guessing *we* had fun afterwards."

Tracker matched the man's smile. He wouldn't have classed last night as *fun*. He had entered this room with every intention of sleeping and had almost convinced a barely clothed Dylan to join him in that endeavour.

Right up until the moment the man had straddled his lap and, after some very direct grinding, started playing with his ears.

His body thrummed with the memory. The points still tingled. Any other time, he would've permitted it.

"We did not have sex." Even without going so far, it had been the strangest attempt he'd ever had. Soft. Almost mournful. Dylan had clung to him, desperate, needy... *grieving*.

Somehow, Dylan had managed release, reaching the height despite Tracker's lack of participation. Even afterwards, the man hadn't let him go until the alcohol finally caught up, leaving Tracker alone in the dark with his thoughts.

Dylan's hand glided up from Tracker's arm to his shoulder, then his neck, drawing him back into the now.

He tipped his head to one side, allowing the man's fingers to graze his earlobe, not seeking to hide the desire in his breath such contact drew from him.

A small, but nevertheless contented, smile tugged at Dylan's lips. Then, frowning, he lowered his hand enough to run its tickling touch down Tracker's chest. "Something happened last night, didn't it? Did I...?" He looked around the room, growing all the more confused. "Did I do something wrong?"

"Nothing wrong," he confirmed. If the man didn't remember what words had been spoken, it was probably better for Tracker to forget he'd ever heard them. "Nor did anything bad happen. However, an attempt was made to steal your belt pouch."

Dylan lurched into a sitting position. He stared at Tracker, eyes wide and full of panic. "An *attempt*?" he echoed. "Meaning we still have it?"

Tracker nodded, curious at the amount of relief his answer gave the man. He knew the pouch held Dylan's shaving equipment. He hadn't realised the blade and mirror held that much sentimental value. "The ties holding it to your belt have been cut, but we can work around that."

"And everything is inside?" He scrambled off the bed, stumbling as one foot became briefly entangled in the bedding.

"I believe so. I admit, I did not think to check." The minstrel wouldn't have had time to rifle through the pouch, and it had felt weighty enough when he retrieved it from the man.

Dylan picked through his clothes, coming away with the pouch. He dug through it as he returned to the bed, plucking some small trinket from its depths. "I thought I'd lost it." He settled before Tracker, his legs tucked beneath him. "I wanted to give this to you yesterday." The ghost of a smile briefly took control of his mouth, twitching at the corners. "I guess I was too drunk to remember." Coaxing him closer, Dylan secured a cord around Tracker's neck.

The weight of something cold and slightly heavy settled on his chest. A pendant fashioned from what appeared to be a simple river stone and etched on one side. No one had gifted him any sort of adornment since his days performing at *The Gilded Lily*.

Tracker turned the stone over in his fingers to examine the symbol. The lines were sharper, but it appeared similar to the one Marin had carved for Dylan. He examined the engraving, tracing the lines with his thumb. What did the symbol mean again? *Protection*. "I thought you said these held no power." It didn't vibrate like the *infitialis* dagger or even the melted chunks of the man's original collar.

"Just in case." Dylan reached out, his hand stopping a hairsbreadth from Tracker's bare chest. "I don't—" His hand dropped into his lap, along with his gaze. "You make me feel..." A small, self-deprecating chuckle shook his shoulders. He rubbed at his neck, his nails scraping the skin hard enough to hear. "I don't think I can put it into words."

He cradled Dylan's chin in his hand, stilling the man with the sweep of a thumb across his lips. He already had a fair idea of the feelings he stirred within the spellster. Lust clearly had a part in it. Uninhibited likely had a say somewhere, too.

"*That*," Dylan murmured. He grabbed Tracker's hand, drawing it away from his face, but keeping the curled fingers within his own grasp and close to his chest. "You make me feel safe."

Tracker rocked back. That hadn't been at all what he expected to hear. "Safe?" he echoed. *Him?*

"And last night I..." That dark gaze flicked up, briefly catching Tracker's, gauging—*hoping*—before once more looking away. "I realised I don't want to lose that," he whispered. "It sounds selfish, I know, but I—"

He fell silent as Tracker claimed his mouth. Other words tried to find freedom as Dylan tipped back onto the mattress, their insecure vibrations stilling entirely once Tracker had found more pleasing notes for Dylan's tongue to play.

Only when Tracker was certain there'd be no further degrading of self coming from the man's lips did he permit Dylan the full use of them.

Dylan stared up at him, confusion turning his gaze dark. But that speck of hope gleamed in the depths. It called out to him, begging for him to do whatever it took to keep fate's bloody claws off the man.

And he would.

Warmth wrapped its fingers around his heart and softened the edges of his smile. "You are too sweet for words," he murmured.

Even in the direct sunlight, the full blush taking over the man's face blazed into life. "Sweet? I've been called a lot of things, but never that."

"Well, there is a first for everything." He caressed Dylan's cheek with one hand whilst the other ran along the trinket dangling from his neck. No one had ever concerned themselves that deeply about his wellbeing. They cared he was functional, capable. Not *safe*. "It is a fine gift. Allow me to properly thank you for it." He pulled them closer, sweeping his lips across Dylan's, revelling in the soft noise it drew out of the man.

With one knee, he coaxed Dylan's legs to part, settling himself between them. No matter how eager the spellster had been last night, he'd been unwilling to take advantage of the man's inebriated state. His ear still tingled with the memory of Dylan's touch. The way his tongue wove between his earrings, the heat of his breath as he pleaded to be taken.

Now that the man's wits had returned, Tracker was prepared to do everything Dylan had asked for. After all, he had promised.

Until Wintervale.

With aching slowness, he withdrew enough to take in the man's flushed face. Dylan's breath rasped into the space between them. His heartbeat pounded against Tracker's chest. The soft fingers clasping Tracker's waist tightened with the man's insecurity.

I have to tell him. He needed to clear the air, to be frank about what he had planned that wouldn't see them going anywhere near the capital. Before this dalliance got serious. Before either of them could get hurt.

Before it was too late to take back his heart.

"Dylan, I—"

He barely caught the tread of a boot outside before the door into their room flew open. Marin's bulk took up much of the frame, her expression grim. "Authril's—" The woman froze for a moment, her eyes widening, before she whirled around. "Sorry! Gods, I am *so* sorry."

Dylan squirmed beneath him, his magic shimmering into a shield that wasn't solid enough to hide anything. "Out!" Even up close, the command was muffled by the hands covering his face.

"Leaving!" she screeched, almost banging into the doorframe in her haste. The door slammed shut behind her.

Tracker held his breath, cocking an ear towards the exit in an effort to hear the woman's departing footsteps. The only thing that reached him was the spellster's frantic breath. It rasped hotly against his skin, abolishing all sound.

"Easy, my dear man." He cupped Dylan's jaw, seeking to turn the man's attention from the intrusion. Unformed magic surged up and down the spellster's body, hunting for an outlet. Running his thumb along the jawline had Tracker feeling each minute movement as the muscles clenching and releasing. "I have you. You are safe, I promise." Drawing the man into his arms had the frenzied pace of Dylan's heartbeat become more apparent.

Tracker kept them close. He stroked Dylan's hair and softly hummed a lullaby.

After a while, Dylan gave a shuddering breath. The man's shield grew less prominent, then faded completely. "I'm being stupid again," he said, the words barely audible as his lips moved against Tracker's shoulder. "Aren't I?"

The smile that tugged at one corner of his mouth definitely carried a bittersweet note. "I did not say that." Marin's actions had thrown back the curtain on their affair. There was no hiding, no yarn of half-truths he could spin like last time. Like it or not, someone knew.

They could only be thankful it hadn't been Authril.

A cautious knock rattled the door, preceding Marin's questioning voice. "Are you coming out anytime soon?"

"Yes," Tracker snapped back, cursing to himself as Dylan stiffened against him. In a far calmer tone that still carried, he added, "Wait for me below. I will be there shortly."

This time, the room held enough silence for him to hear the steady rhythm of the hunter's boots fading away.

Reluctantly releasing his hold on the man, Tracker slid off the bed and began to dress. How unwise was it to leave the spellster whilst he was still in this distressed state? *Very.* Yet, Marin's tone had indicated a great deal of urgency. *Authril.* What had happened to the warrior that required them?

"Gods," Dylan moaned. He grabbed the blankets, throwing them over himself as though it would change the past few minutes. "I thought the door was locked."

It had been. "Apparently, there are other keys."

Dylan offered up a shaky groan. The ill-defined lump of his body shifted.

Tracker cleared his throat as he finished securing his trousers. "I know it is not the same, but I am not exactly thrilled to be walked in on." He'd had plenty of experience with it, though. *The Gilded Lily* didn't look too kindly to locked doors when it involved their workers being on the other side. "However, it is not precisely news to her."

"*What?*" Dylan sprung upright, sending the blankets tumbling into his lap. "She knew? Before now? About—? Why didn't you tell me she—?" He buried his fingers into his hair, clutching a fistful. "How long has she known? Do the others know? Gods, has she—?" He clapped a hand over his mouth. He looked ready to throw up at any moment.

Hooking the chamber pot out from beneath the bed with the flick of his boot, Tracker settled at the foot of the bed. "*Known* is perhaps the wrong word. I would say more suspected. And if she did indeed speak to the others about what she saw then, our dear warrior has yet to voice her opinion."

The man remained silent, staring at the far wall, as he seemed to think it over before nodding. "You're right. Authril would've come at you breathing fire if she had known."

Tracker exhaled his relief. If Dylan was able to accept that logic, then the man had to be calmer than he looked. "Besides, the only thing Marin caught back then was you sleeping in my tent the first time you crept your way over."

"But we... we weren't having sex then."

"And I told her as much." He shrugged. Sometimes, the truth

wasn't easy for people to believe. "But whilst I am mentioning things others have seen between us... our dear hedgewitch happened to catch me thanking you for stitching up my arm."

"What did you tell her?"

He spread his arms. "A little stretching of the truth." Outright denial hadn't been much of an option. "That we have shared a few innocent kisses."

Dylan gathered the blankets in his arms, clutching them as a child might their favoured soother. "All right. Could've done with knowing *that* sooner."

Tracker hunched his shoulders. He had fumbled there. "My apologies. I was not seeking to keep such knowledge from you, nor do I wish to make excuses, I..." Sighing, he hung his head. "Between the Talfaltaners attacking so close to Whitemeadow and learning the pack aided in destroying the tower, my focus was more on—"

"Things that were actually important?" Dylan finished, the self-deprecating smile returning to tweak his lips.

"More life-threatening than a hedgewitch knowing we kissed." And now there was some complication with Authril. What trouble had she tangled herself into?

The curve in the man's smile grew the faintest amount, but it now creased his eyes.

Scooping up the man's smallclothes along with his undershirt, Tracker offered the former up to their owner.

Dylan shuffled across the bed to take his undergarments, clutching the blankets to his torso. Casting a wary glance at the door, he hastened to garb himself as if doing so would change the past.

Rather than continuing to dress, Tracker busied himself with gathering the rest of the man's clothes. It wasn't as though he needed his full armour right now.

He helped Dylan into each of the three layers, keeping himself, and the expanses of cloth, between the man and the door. Any other time, he would've teased Dylan about the act. If it had been anyone else, he might've attempted to diffuse the whole situation with some quip.

With the outer layer draped over the man's shoulders, Tracker collected his undershirt from where he left it on the bed end. "I have to go see what is wrong. You do not need to join me," he swiftly assured. "But... will you be all right? I can send in Katarina." Perhaps her virtue of being a dwarf and not at all connected to this kingdom would help soothe the spellster's nerves.

Dylan paused in tying the upper layer of his robe closed. He was silent for a moment, not even a hint of a breath, before he exhaled wearily. "I'll need to face them eventually, won't I?"

"Eventually," he agreed, donning his undershirt. "But it can wait until I return." Whilst he didn't know the precise details of *what* had happened, that it involved the warrior and brought Marin running to them meant it must've been more complicated than anything that could transpire from a simple bar brawl.

"Meanwhile, I hole myself up in here?" The man shook his head, a curtain of dark hair obscuring half his face. "What's done is done and I can hardly spend our journey avoiding them." He audibly swallowed. "Send her in."

Bowing his head, Tracker exited the room.

Marin waited at the top of the stairs, the hedgewitch standing at the railing. The former eyed him, smugness twisting her lips.

He stalked down the hall towards them, a growl catching in his throat. If she dared to utter the words he believed were brewing in her mind…

"I knew it!" she crowed. "I *knew* you were screwing him." She peered at him, her lips pursed thoughtfully. The slight cheeky tilt to them giving away her thoughts before she spoke. "Or is he screwing *you?*"

"*Shut up!*" he snarled. "The gods know I should still be in there doing damage control, so if you cannot conduct yourself seriously, I will take my leave."

Marin held up her hands. "I understand you're angry. Hell, I'd be furious if someone caught me in a horizontal dance, but I didn't see anything. Not that I was *looking* for anything," she swiftly amended. "Because I definitely do not want to—" She fell silent as he held up a finger in warning.

"*I* do not care what you may or may not have seen." He had danced naked for dozens in *The Gilded Lily*. His most popular routine had even included fellating himself during the finale. But Dylan was another matter. "If you had any idea of how volatile a startled spellster could become, you would not go barging into locked rooms. Speaking of which…" He searched for any sign of the means she would've used to enter. "Where did you get another key?"

"Key?" Confusion scrunched her face. "I didn't use a key. The door wasn't locked."

That wasn't true. After discovering the minstrel was a thief, he had definitely ensured their door was secure. "So the locks here are worthless. Wonderful." He ran his fingers over his hair, absently trying to tuck away the stray coils. "What has happened that could not wait? I assume Authril is in trouble." It wasn't really a question. What else could be happening with the warrior that required his urgent intervention?

Marin nodded anyway. "She's been arrested."

"When? And under what charge?"

"Some time yesterday evening. The messenger couldn't say anything else."

"Except that the guards specifically asked for your presence at the southern barracks," Katarina added.

Of course they did. Authril had likely thrown both his name and status around in the hopes of securing her freedom. Had she also mentioned Dylan? Will already knew about the man, just as Tracker knew he would keep quiet. Having the rest of the guards on alert about a spellster within the city was a whole other problem Tracker didn't need.

"Stay with Dylan," Tracker ordered the hedgewitch. "And be gentle. The tower would have punished him for being found in bed with another."

Both women's brows twitched with their concern. To her credit, Marin opted to remain silent.

Katarina opened her mouth several times, seeking answers to questions that refused to be voiced. Finally, her lips pinched together and she made for the room Tracker had vacated.

He waited only until she was through the door before descending the stairs. *The guard barracks.* Like the hound stations, Whitemeadow had two main ones on either side of the river. Both sites boasted facilities to hold a substantial amount of detained citizens. He couldn't imagine what trouble the warrior caused to wind up in one of their cells, but he wanted to shake the hand of whoever had presented him with such an opportunity.

All he needed was a chance to lengthen her stay. If he knew her well enough, she was bound to serve him that fortune all on her own.

CHAPTER 36

Dylan had just finished repacking his belongings when someone gently knocked on the door. He hunched his shoulders. That had to be Katarina coming to check on him. *Shit*. How had she reached here so quickly? Had she been standing outside? Had she been standing within view and he just hadn't seen?

The hedgewitch poked her head around the door, silently surveying the room before entering. "If I may have a word?"

He closed his eyes. Right now, he could've done with having Henrie's knack of turning invisible. Hell, he could've done with the man himself. And Harriet. Either one would've been the preferable choice to discuss this with.

Steeling himself, he straightened to fully face her. At least she had shut the door. He didn't need an audience. "I know you're only looking to help, but I really don't want to talk to everyone about my..." His tongue moved silently as he fought to come up with a suitable word. "My—"

"Relationships?" she helpfully suggested.

His blood went cold upon hearing the word. That was perhaps the complete opposite end of what he had been thinking. His legs trembled, threatening to drop him where he stood if he didn't sit. "My sex life," he finally mumbled, slowly lowering himself back onto the bed.

Katarina settled beside him. "From what I understand, the tower would have punished you."

Surprised, he could only nod. Of course Tracker had told them that. He should've expected it.

"Marin said you two have been sharing a tent well before we lost the third one."

"She—?" he blurted before composing himself. "So my sleeping habits are the stuff of gossip?" Bad enough everything else had happened, now they were discussing it as if his actions were worthy of idle chatter? This was what he got for not dealing with it sooner.

"She's concerned about you. You wouldn't have been in the best emotional state back at the tower and for the hound to choose so soon after losing your home to initiate intimacy..." She trailed off, but he knew exactly what she was getting at.

And she had it very wrong.

"I know what it looks like," he muttered under his breath. "But just to be clear, what Marin saw back then was *not* what she thinks and exactly what Track told her." He couldn't believe the hunter had suspected something for so long and kept it to herself. "After the tower, I couldn't sleep. I could barely close my eyes without nightmares and..." Dylan fumbled for the words to explain why Tracker had been the one he had sought. He toyed with the pendant, his thumbnail digging at the carved symbol, deepening the lines. "Having him near helped. He could watch over me, make sure I wouldn't hurt anyone."

Katarina nodded gravely. Being a hedgewitch, she would've heard plenty of stories regarding the dangers of spellsters. "Doesn't explain the kissing, though."

"That's nothing new." His chest grew tight as the admission slipped out. It didn't feel right divulging this sort of information so freely. *There is no one to out me to.* He tightened his grip on the pendant. *I am safe.* "He's been attempting it practically since we met."

"That wasn't the impression I've been given, but—" Her sigh carried a rather unnerving amount of relief. "This morning was... a recent development, then?"

Heat crept into his cheeks. "No."

Her brows shot up. "So, when did *that* start?"

"In the tower." He squeezed his eyes shut. "I know what you're going to say." If she considered Tracker's pursuit of him a few days after discovering the tower unfavourable, then she undoubtedly thought worse about him doing so the night of. "It's not what you think, though. He kissed me and I—" He could've stopped, Tracker had given him the means and opportunity to multiple times throughout the night, he just... let it all happen. "I wanted it."

Frowning, she tilted her head to one side. She didn't look terribly convinced, but her gaze held no judgement.

He explained it all. His refusal of Authril after the warrior had returned to her habits. How he had propositioned Tracker. How he had crept willingly into the hound's tent, the man's bed.

Katarina remained silent through it all. Only the twitch of her brows suggested she heard him at all.

When he was done, he sat there, waiting for her to speak. His heart fluttered nervously, feeling dangerously close to the back of his throat, unsure if it would flee out his mouth entirely if he dared to utter another word.

And still, the hedgewitch kept to her silence.

The furrow between her brows deepened, twisting the top half of the scar on her face. "Tell me, what exactly do you call this thing between the two of you? Is it serious?"

"S-serious?" He swallowed. "It... it's not... We—"

Us. The way Tracker spoke the word echoed in his mind.

What *were* they? He didn't know. Friends? Tracker seemed to think of them as such. More? That was a dangerous thought he didn't want to consider.

Still, the fluttering in his chest stirred as he took in Katarina's smile and the knowing twinkle in her eyes. "What makes you think we're anywhere close to *serious*?"

"Well, ever since we started for Wintervale, he has been changing. He seems more at ease when you're near. I thought it was just because of what we found in the tower and him wanting to ensure your safety, but—"

"He's just concerned for my wellbeing," Dylan said in a breathless rush. He had noticed a few changes in the man's routine since they'd almost lost Marin to the Talfaltaners, a sort of enhanced interest in Dylan's safety, which he supposed had only grown since coming across the other group at the abandoned farmhouse. Tracker was likely unaware of what he did. "He's only doing what the creed demands of him. Keep me safe. Get me where I won't be a danger to others."

Katarina pressed a hand to her mouth, a muffled chuckle escaping from between her fingers. "Oh, I've no doubt of that, but I think there's rather more to it."

Marin had said similar not too long ago. *The way he looks at you.* Which was what? The same way everyone else did? Dylan certainly hadn't seen any difference there. He'd been checking ever since the hunter mentioned it.

What more could there possibly be? "You think he's...?" He let the sentence trail off, not daring to finish it. *Surely not.* She thought Tracker had *feelings* for him. Dylan shook his head. The hedgewitch was wrong on that front, misinterpreting the man's change in his demeanour towards Dylan for something deeper. If there was any such thing happening, it was because the hound had been getting practically nightly attention between the tower and Whitemeadow. "It's just some mindless fun," he mumbled. "That's what he said."

She gave a considering hum, tapping her lips with a forefinger. "Do you think he said it to convince you, or himself?"

Dylan opened his mouth, ready to explain, then shut it. Seeing the smug certainty on her face, he could almost believe she spoke the truth.

What if she did? The question meandered through his mind, scattering his thoughts like a mouser amongst its prey. His chest tightened.

Katarina clasped his arms. Concern creased her brow. "Are you all right? You've gone pale."

He wet his lips, trying to work the words up his throat. "Providing you're right. What would I do with such knowledge?" He hadn't ever given even the thought any contemplation before. Never had a reason to. What did people normally do when faced with the notion? "Go all out and profess my feelings for him?" He scoffed at the idea. *Utterly ridiculous.*

She smiled up at him and patted his arm. "You needn't do a thing, but I suppose it would depend entirely on what *your* feelings are."

"I don't—" His voice broke before he could stop it. He had meant the words in jest, but she seemed serious. Strange, the thought that someone believed a person feeling something so... intimate for him was a possibility. A little too surreal to be true. Spellsters and love didn't mix. Expressing any great level of affection towards friends had been risky if shown wrong. Being in love had always been dangerous. It led to mistakes, to pain. "I don't know."

Smiling softly, she gave his shoulder an affectionate pat. "Maybe you should think on it."

Dylan watched her disappear back into the hallway, his vision blurring. Whatever Katarina thought was going on between Tracker and him, she was wrong. *Just mindless fun.* He had to remember that. Neither of them could afford to let it become anything deeper.

Unlike much of Whitemeadow, the southern guard barracks matched the northern building in terms of space and defences. This was largely thanks to the walled compound once being the home of a wealthy merchant, a being who no longer claimed either title. Its outer walls stood several stories high and were thick enough to stave off all but the most dogged attacks.

Like most city guard barracks, the main gates stood open. A contingent stood by the entrance, their presence designed to deter loitering by anyone who had no business within and to interrogate those who did. Amongst those strangers, a familiar face caught his attention.

"Will?" he called out. The guard hadn't taken his advice and left the city already?

The man straightened as Tracker neared, his answering smile grim. He gestured for his fellow guards to let them pass without halting for the usual questions. "I thought our message had gotten lost."

Grunting, Tracker continued into the courtyard. He rather wished the messenger hadn't found them. Then no one in their group would've been any the wiser about her predicament. The others might have worried and fussed, maybe even suggested searching for her, but ultimately would have moved on for Dylan's sake.

Now, he had to deal with this when he should've still been at the spellster's side.

There were far more people milling about the yard than he expected. Sure, some were training and others hastened across to whatever task was required in the opposite building, but a great deal lingered, doing little of import. As if they awaited an order.

Will fell into step with him, albeit, his pace far removed from the relaxed gait more typical of the man. Back stiff, he kept a measured timing, his sword hand twitching as if ready to arm himself at a moment's notice.

Were they expecting an assault on the barracks? Just what had Authril told them?

He leant closer to Will and, pitching his voice for the man's ears alone, asked, "What is the reason behind her detaining?" There had to *be* a reason. This wasn't some far-flung village where the local guards would've used anything as an excuse to throw an armed elf behind bars. Whitemeadow city guard was unique in that half of them *were* elves, or at least had a measure of elven ancestry.

Will's lips flattened in disapproval before twisting sourly. Like Tracker, he continued to stare straight ahead. "We caught her trying to cross the bridge, using the same method through the back entrance you took."

She'd been following him? And close enough to spy him entering the locked gate tucked beneath the bridge? *Impressive.* He hadn't once spotted her. No doubt such stealth was a skill honed from a childhood working under the heavies in the Oldmarsh slums.

"You should know," Will continued. "She's been very vocal about being necessary in controlling your special travelling companion. It's why I sent for you." He glanced over his shoulder, his brows twitching. Had Dylan's earlier panic been enough for the man to sense? "Is he—?"

Tracker took a deep breath, trying not to bristle. She truly thought of herself as *necessary*? "I suppose she told you she is a warden. She holds less claim to that title than yourself." Even her goal of bringing Dylan to the army was but a mere aspiration. "As for my companion, he is elsewhere. In the care of those I trust."

The man's shoulders relaxed a fraction. "Follow me." He lengthened his stride, leading the way across the courtyard to where a solid door stood with guards posted on either side. With Will giving a curt nod to the guards gaining them entry, they descended into the barrack's holding cells.

Tracker didn't know if the place had been a private dungeon built by the building's previous owner or a more mundane area merely repurposed, but they walked by several cell doors. Figures stirred in the shadows, the residents curious but not enough to risk drawing attention.

Authril resided in the cell at the far end, the only one with a door pointing directly at the exit. Such special accommodations kept her separate from the others and were likely due to her throwing around his status. Not many guards sought to make themselves targets of the king's elite.

"Finally!" Authril snarled, getting to her feet. She'd been stripped of all but her undertunic and trousers. The absence of armour did little to abolish the raw strength years of living a mercenary regimen had done to her frame. "I've been waiting all night. Get your friend—" She spat the word, sending flecks of spittle flying. "—to release me and we can leave this city."

Tracker halted a few feet from the cell door, just enough to remain out of reach. Even with her unarmed, she could still be a danger to the inattentive if she got her hands on them. He had no intentions of meeting the cell bars head first. "No."

The warrior stiffened. "What? *No?*" She clutched at the bars as though she'd both the strength and the bull-headedness to force them to part. "What do you mean?"

He almost smiled. That he might deny her freedom clearly hadn't crossed her mind. "I am aware others rarely say it to you, but surely you have heard the word before."

Her grip tightened, draining the faintest hint of colour from her knuckles and sending it all to her face. "You need me to keep Dylan under control."

His jaw ached with the strain of keeping his expression neutral. "Dylan has no need of someone controlling his actions, especially not your way."

"Who else but his warden can—?"

"So that *is* what you told them," Tracker snarled through gritted teeth. "You lied about your status?" One that sounded pretty, almost logical, to those who knew little of spellsters and how they were treated.

"I did *not* lie," she snarled back. Her gaze darted to Will as the man adjusted his weight and she swiftly composed herself. "Once we reach Wintervale, I'll—"

"You will take command over our dear spellster," Tracker finished for her. "But only once you reach the capital." Until then, any claim she made upon Dylan's self was false.

And one that he would ensure never came to fruition.

A part of him, the little vindictive piece that lurked in the darkness of his mind, wanted to crow his intentions to never have Dylan go near Wintervale. It wanted to see the arrogance slide off her face as the realisation settled in. But letting anyone know the truth was dangerous and, right now, he trusted the man at his side more than the one who happened to be behind bars for the moment.

Besides, there were other ways to pop her conviction. "How long is her sentence?" he asked of Will. He hadn't cared to know earlier and suspected they'd told her nothing.

The man cleared his throat. "That's currently undecided. The mayor declared she would personally oversee the trial of any and all persons who attempted to cross the river without proper approval." His lips pursed briefly, no doubt thinking over yesterday's altercation and if Tracker's status truly absolved him. "It could be months before she's even seen."

Not the worst outcome. If she truly had tried following him, then her attempt at crossing the bridge would've involved trespassing through the gatehouse. That act alone should've, at minimum, got her thrown in the stocks. It wasn't as though she had anything to fear being confined here. At least, not whilst waiting for her trial. *Perhaps boredom*. Barely a nick compared to other punishments.

Providing she didn't try to escape, and a little good fortune, life back in Whitemeadow will have returned to normalcy by the time the mayor got to her trial and Authril would simply be released.

With even more luck, the rest of them would be gone from the kingdom entirely.

"*Months?*" Authril screeched. "You can't have an unleashed spellster wandering the city for that long."

"That is true." When it came to escorting a spellster as powerful as Dylan, staying in the same place for more than a handful of days would be tempting fate. "There is no cause for worry, though. I have no intentions of lingering whilst your punishment is being decided."

Her eyes, which had already narrowed at his agreement, widened to their utmost. "You're leaving me here?" She lunged for him, clawing at the air as the attempt failed to get him in her grasp. "You can't!"

Despite her flailing arm clearly nowhere within reach, Tracker stepped further away from the cell. "I can. The law rather expects me to." He tilted his head, a toothy smile tugging at his lips. "Or could it be, my dear warrior, you are suggesting I subvert the law? In front of the city guard, no less," he added, gesturing to Will.

Swearing, she strained through the bars to reach him. Her shoulder wedged itself between the metal. With her flesh bulging on either side, it had to hurt. Still, she struggled. "Without me at his side, they'll give his command to another. Someone who will hurt him. You *need* me with you."

He turned his back on her, ignoring any other attempts to regain his attention. Will followed, remaining just as silent.

Her swearing echoed up the corridor as she raged. Insults and threats spouted from her with equal vigour, some of the more colourful phrases definitely lifted from her time amongst her fellow mercenaries.

She quietened only briefly as they reached the dungeon entrance before bellowing, "You'll regret leaving me here! Just you watch!"

By mercy's grace, may that not be true. He could never be described as pious—the gods never seemed to intervene when he prayed—but hoped the gods weren't so cruel as to put Dylan through so much suffering and loss, only to then ask for the man's life. There was always a chance.

Returning to the courtyard, Tracker halted outside the door and took a steadying breath. *This is it.* Throughout their travels, he had concerned himself with keeping Authril ignorant of his true plans, worrying over how to stop her from notifying anyone once they veered from the path she had laid out. Finally, that weight was off his shoulders.

Mostly.

She had already put the guards here on alert by informing them of Dylan's presence. Leaving the city was the only way to fix that. But if Authril managed to escape in the meantime...

They couldn't risk having that kind of trouble at their backs.

He eyed Will as they crossed the yard, marking how the man now walked with a more casual step. "Tell your superiors I recommend transferring her into a stronger cell, one with thinner gaps between bars." He paused for a moment, considering whether she might bolt in the presence of her cell door opening. "Sedating her when you do so."

Will remained silent until they were almost at the main gates. "You're really leaving her behind?"

"Dylan cannot linger here." He fixed the man with a pointed stare. "*You* would also do well not staying." He didn't know what his new master had planned for the King's Hounds, but if he was so willing to execute the hounds who disobeyed him, then who knew what orders he'd issue once he learnt of people like Will.

"And where do you suggest we go?" The man shook his head. "Passage to anywhere is difficult enough without three young children to take care of. I won't ask that of my family."

"I understand." Halting in the maw of the entrance, Tracker clapped a sociable hand on the man's shoulder. "Stay safe, my friend."

"You as well. And..." His gaze swung in the direction of the inn. "May whatever you've got planned fare well."

"We can but hope." His plans were little more than rough drafts at this point. They might not be able to cross the river here, but they had time. Time to nudge Dylan away from Wintervale, to let him see that Authril's path of self-destruction wasn't the only choice.

Outside the gates, Tracker made his way through the busy streets. His fingers strayed to the pendant lying beneath his shirt, feeling the engraving through the soft linen. *Protection.* It offered no further protection than any other bauble. But it carried a prayer. A wish. A hope. Like the gleam in the man's dark eyes. The thrumming in Tracker's chest.

He had forgotten the warmth that came with such a look, of being considered worthy of protection, of feeling safe in their presence, of...

Love.

The mere thought banished the warmth in his veins like a flame in a blizzard. The breath-stealing fingers of truth wrapped around his neck. Icy shards slipped beneath his ribs.

He stumbled blindly down the street, struggling to breathe, his chest crushed beneath the memory of Hunk's dead weight. It tightened every muscle in his body. Blood blanketed his senses. The saltiness on his tongue. The coppery tang in the air, how it mingled with the dirt and the damp. Images of the day he lost everything obscured his vision.

A man he had once called beloved standing over the broken bodies of their lovers, his tan skin smeared with their blood. The insults that leapt from his tongue, poison-tipped blades designed to cut with the precision edge of truth.

He collided into a figure—stocky, human, male.

Tracker was halfway to unsheathing his dagger when the image became clearer. A mere citizen, one of many he shared the street with. No threat.

He released his hold on the blade, feeling its weight return to the sheath. He had been so close.

The man's mouth moved, his voice distorted by the pounding in

Tracker's ears.

With his hands trembling, he fled into an alleyway before someone called the guards. His feet tripped over discarded bits of wood and refuse as all manner of small feathered and furry animals fled his approach.

The alley curved around the tall building on his left. He pressed himself against the wall, letting the brickwork support him as well as cool his fevered skin. His heart hammered, the pulse of it beating in his temples. It squeezed his lungs, forcing him to fight for every mouthful of air.

He closed his eyes. *Steady breaths.* It was the same command he had given Dylan many times throughout their journey. His fingers sought the pendant. Having lain directly against his skin since the inn, the stone was no longer cold. He ran a thumb in unhurried circles over the smooth backside.

Slowly, the rest of his body obeyed. It left him sweating and wobbly, but once more in command.

Bastard. It had been an age since the memory of his betrayer had affected him so deeply. It wasn't fair that, even after all these years, it still had the power to bring him this low, but then, all that man had ever done was taint things. Their love had been a lie. All the sweet words of adoration? Spoken only to keep Tracker in place as the man took advantage of every hole he could.

He had heard similar declarations from his clients back in *The Gilded Lily*, often moaned alongside other equally nonsensical things as he worked them towards their climax. So many words of adoration, of *love*...

Since losing Wynne and Zinnala to the Pit, its every cry had rung hollow, drenched in lust or deceit.

Dylan was the first he hadn't heard such words from during their throes of passion. Not that the man stayed silent. But they were all base sounds. Noises that merely thinking about was enough to stir his blood.

Still, it was just sex. Nothing more than a moment of pleasure, some mindless fun to distract his thoughts from everything he had done and the tasks he had yet to do.

He tightened his hold on the pendant. Maybe Dylan hadn't intended his gift as anything more than a simple display of gratitude. It still meant he cared. Felt safe.

There was nothing safe about him. He was a King's Hound. His presence heralded trouble. He pulled families apart. Brought death and sadness to so many, even those he had loved.

Especially those he had loved.

And Dylan? He knew what Tracker was capable of, knew what

he'd done, knew precisely how dangerous he was, particularly to a spellster.

And yet...

That same man, whose caring nature and soft lips Tracker knew he didn't deserve, considered him as *safe*. Someone he had first pursued purely to tease. For mutual fun, because that was all he could ever offer anyone.

Safe.

Worse still, he wanted that gleaming hope of more, wanted to let his heart run away with his good senses. To take what he couldn't— shouldn't—have. Wanted that spark in those dark eyes to be real. True. *His*.

He screamed into the morning air. Nearby dogs bayed and howled along with him. Several windows and doors opened. A few demanded to know what was going on, whilst others hollered for silence.

He quietened only once his throat was raw, burning harsh and metallic with the tang of blood. Tears blurred his vision and ran, unhindered, down his face.

Fool! How long had these feelings been tumbling through his veins, running unchecked like wildfire? How could the gods let him fall? How could they be so cruel to dangle such feelings, the hope of it all, before him?

Only children fall in love. The words of his trainers echoed through his mind. It had always been a mantra, a warning. One he had ignored in his youth. He was no longer that reckless, infatuated fool. That person, that *child*, had died almost two decades ago.

Love means death. It had been a lesson reinforced by the hound mistress. One he learnt the hard way, with the blood of those he had cared for so dearly staining his skin.

He couldn't go through that again. He *couldn't*.

He slammed his fist against the brickwork, biting back a curse as the rough surface scraped his knuckles. "You do *not* feel this way about him," he growled against the wall.

His heart thundered anew. This time, in furious objection. It might've known what it wanted, but he knew he couldn't have it.

"You cannot." The only thing admitting any feelings could bring him was Dylan's demise.

The man deserved better.

"You *promised*." He refused to be the reason the Pit claimed another soul.

He had made another promise, too. A more recent one. To let Dylan have his body until they were forced to part ways at the capital. Except, with Authril unable to alert anyone of note to their whereabouts, there was no reason for them to continue heading east.

No reason except for the river blocking their passage, at least. With a lack of boats to ferry them across and the bridges closed to everyone who hadn't come from the northern side, the places where they could head north was limited.

To Riverton, then. With luck, the Talfaltaners wouldn't have been as interested in claiming the shallow fishing boats. They could head north with no one the wiser.

The eastern road was heavy with travellers, both those on foot and horseback. And wagons. Dylan had never seen so many. From when they'd first left Whitemeadow yesterday, the wagons took up most of the road. They travelled in groups, carrying cargo he guessed would've otherwise been delivered via ship. They trundled by in both directions, their sheer presence enough to force pedestrians into the ditches lining both sides of the road.

The sun shone mercilessly, not once seeking cover behind the scant few clouds daring the sky and growing hotter as the day drew on. The occasional breeze wound between the trees flanking the roadside, too brief to do more than tease the idea of its coolness.

He eyed one wagon as they briefly walked beside the sun-hardened road. The load seemed to be mostly sacks. How much would it cost to hitch a ride on one? Even for a short time? The hound likely had enough coin to pay the driver for the inconvenience.

Dylan scuffed his foot along the ground and watched as the wagon slowly outdistanced them. *Probably wouldn't take a spellster, anyway.*

By the time the afternoon reached its hottest, he was already damp with sweat, his pace reduced to a casual stroll. Katarina and Marin walked several cart lengths ahead. He had tried to keep up with them at first, but pushing himself to exhaustion would've only made the next day harder. The pair weren't too far and, as long as Tracker remained with him, they would meet up again when the time came to make camp.

Except he had thought the same about Authril and her decision to wander from their side. Tracker hadn't told them exactly what had happened for the warrior to be imprisoned, only that her trial wouldn't be for some time.

He didn't understand it. In the tower, spellsters were sent to the cells as punishment and released or never seen again. Imprisoning someone whilst they waited for their actual verdict felt unjust.

And not even a King's Hound had been able to set her free. Without Authril to take the position of his new warden, joining the army could see him placed under the command of someone far crueller. Someone like the man who had died in the ambush. Who had threatened him with—no, outright *stated*—the idea he'd be servicing them like a... a...

Slave.

Gulping down a breath, Dylan clasped his neck. His throat all but sealed itself shut at the thought. *No.* He refused. Absolutely. Emphatically. He would die before he permitted that.

He *would* die. No collar. No tower. Even Tracker would admit the hound creed demanded a spellster's death if the other options weren't viable. And if he was dying, he would at least make that end serve a purpose by avenging the lives stolen in the tower. That required getting close enough to ensure the new hound master fell with him.

The brush of another's hand across the back of his own jolted him from his thoughts. Tracker walked at his side, seemingly relaxed and uninterested in the world. Dylan knew better.

The man's finger stretched across the minuscule gap between them and a shock ran through Dylan's body.

Flinching from the contact, Dylan glanced down. He half expected to discover a bolt of lightning had flared between them. Nothing.

"Are you all right?" the hound asked, his voice pitched low even though the others were too far to possibly hear. "You seem a little jitterier than usual. You must have looked over your shoulder a good dozen times by now."

"I have not," he shot back, pointedly turning his gaze to the road ahead.

Tracker's smile suggested the man didn't believe him. "My apologies. I must be seeing things." They'd taken perhaps a handful more steps before he spoke again. "About yesterday."

His breath caught anew, his chest squeezed at the memory of being found in Tracker's arms. It was so hard, breaking the flow of panic that coursed through his veins. The cry to pull away, to not show too much affection. Maddening how it clashed with what he logically knew to be true, but it grew no weaker.

Dylan took a deep breath. *This isn't the tower.* He understood things outside the world he once lived in were different, but after having everything suddenly thrown into the light when he had only begun to accept it...

Exhaling slowly, he kicked a stone along the road. "I don't want to talk about it."

"Because you are still embarrassed, yes?"

"I'm not ashamed," he curtly replied. That wasn't entirely true. He had barely been able to look the other two in the eye this morning. Perhaps a little bit, but that wasn't what gnawed at him.

Dylan picked up the pace. If they caught up with the others, then perhaps Tracker would desist with attempting to dissect his feelings. If he knew what Dylan planned, he might never get near Wintervale.

Tracker lengthened his stride, not quite skipping at every other step, in order to keep up. He hummed in thought, his brows twitching together. "No, you are right. Ashamed is not how I would have described your face. Terrified, perhaps. More so than being in battle. What did you think was going to happen?"

Dylan slowed at the question.

Is it that they know about us? *Or that they know about* you? Questions the hound had spoken nights ago drifted through his thoughts.

'Both' had been his answer then, but that wasn't true. It was in the knowing, rather than that they knew. Having someone aware at all placed them in a position of power, of leverage, over others. All it took was one whisper in the wrong person's ear and—

"Dylan?"

He blinked, surprised to find Tracker stood before him, the man's brow creased with concern.

Dylan stepped back, attempting to distance himself, only to barely avoid colliding with the wheel of a carriage that he swore hadn't been there a moment ago. More hemmed them in, forcing them to dodge wheels as tall as a person and cattle belligerent from the heat. When had he stopped dead in the middle of the road?

The hound guided them through the throng to the roadside. There they stood, the hound silently waiting. Those honey-coloured eyes seeking some sort of response. How long had he been standing there?

Dylan wet his lips. "I'm fine," he managed. His chest was still tight, his voice even tighter.

A soft smile curved Tracker's lips. He caressed Dylan's cheek. "Any man who reacts like that from a mere question is far from fine." He clasped Dylan's hands, pressing them to his lips. "You are used to hiding how you feel, even from yourself. I understand that."

He glanced up at the man. Tracker had mentioned that before. But how could the hound possibly understand? By the man's own admittance, hounds engaging in sex was tolerated.

"But you must face your fears lest they consume you." The hound's thumbs ran over Dylan's knuckles as he talked. "Is someone coming to whisk you away? Of course not. Nor will our dear companions mock you." One corner of his mouth lifted in a wry smile. "No more than usual, anyway."

Dylan grunted. He knew Tracker was right. He had told himself the same things many times. The worst he had endured was Marin teasing them, and he had heard better taunts than that in the tower.

If her ribbing was all he would have to weather, then it was nothing at all.

If only that stopped the tightness in his chest.

"There are no guardians here," Tracker continued. "No one to chastise you or keep vigilance over your actions. Just me. And them." He twisted to look over his shoulder at the women that Dylan now noticed had stopped a short distance away. "You are safe with us." The hound raised their linked hands, pressing his lips to the back of Dylan's fingers. "I swear it," he whispered.

His chest grew tight again. This time, the swelling of butterflies joined in the knotting of his stomach. His breathing came harshly, but easier than it had a moment ago. "I—" Looking into Tracker's eyes, seeing the sincerity glimmering in their depths, he could almost believe Katarina was right. "Thank you."

"Hey, loverboys!" Marin called, cupping her hands around her mouth. "Are we moving or what?"

Dylan winced at the address. From the way the hound had stiffened in his grip, he was pretty sure Tracker hadn't been amused by it either. *One mistake.* It seemed that was all it took.

The hunter continued to bellow across the distance. "We aren't going to get to Riverton before our food runs out if you keep stopping to smooch every five seconds."

Tracker rolled his eyes. "Shut up," he yelled back. "We will be right there." Taking a firmer hold on Dylan's hand, he marched up to the rest of their group and swiftly passed them. "And will you stop with your insipid teasing? It is not like *that.*"

"Says the man who has a vice grip on his hands," Marin continued, falling into stride with them whilst Katarina silently trailed behind.

Tracker looked down at his hand as if surprised to find it full of Dylan's fingers. "That is only to keep him from running away from your dreadful needling, dear woman, but if you are prepared to desist." He released Dylan as one would a hot coal. "Come, we should keep an eye out for a suitable camping site. Preferably a little ways from the riverbank." He jerked his chin towards where the forest seemed to be thickest.

Once they'd left Whitemeadow's shadow, Dylan had barely seen any sign of the river. Their seemingly endless slog along the road went by without incident.

They walked along the road for several more hours before venturing into the woods. Finding a place to set up camp was relatively easy. The sun wobbled on the horizon as they finished pitching the tents. Seeing just two of them no longer felt strange, but knowing they would shelter only two each definitely did.

Tracker tapped him on the shoulder. "Come, there is a flat area under the trees." He jerked a thumb at a nearby stand of pines. "We can train there."

Dylan eyed the opposite end of the clearing. "Train?" The hound had suggested teaching him how to fight with the quarterstaff last night. He had refused then, preferring the privacy of their tent.

They hadn't done much training together since the hound had been wounded. Dylan had relished such times, not only because he very rarely wound up injuring himself, but also because it gave the man a reason to be close enough to touch without anyone caring.

But now? "Are you sure that's a good idea?"

Tracker frowned. "Is there a reason it would not be?"

"Because…" He scratched at the side of his neck. "You know?" His gaze flicked to where Katarina sat near the fire. *Just her?* A more thorough look confirmed it. Marin must have gone off to scout the surrounding area for any signs of danger, be it man or animal. She'd be a while, too, setting traps or trying her luck fishing in the river.

Sighing, the hound pinched the bridge of his nose. "Dylan, when you were sparring with Marin, were you seeking to sleep with her?"

He scoffed. "Of course not."

"Then surely you understand that weapons training is not an intimate act."

"Obviously, but—"

"If you are going to treat the knowledge of others being aware that we have been intimate as something to be feared, no one is going to be able to get past it. Especially you." He gave Dylan's arm a warm pat. "Training will do you some good. Focusing on attack and defence will give your mind something to do other than running in foolish circles."

Dylan dropped his gaze to the ground, settling on where the butt of the quarterstaff rested in the grass. "But I don't know how to use this."

"You have forgotten everything I taught you about swordsmanship so soon?" He swiped the quarterstaff from Dylan's hands. "Come, let us see if you can get reacquainted with the base techniques before the sun finishes setting."

Dylan followed the hound to where the ground flattened beneath the pines. Unlike the first time Tracker had tried to teach him how to wield a sword, they'd come across few precious spaces giving them the luxury of a private practice area. Thanks to the lack of an extra tent, their small clearing had enough space, but it also meant that the tents were pitched not all that far from where they trained.

The flickering light of the fire danced on the edge of his vision. Fortunately, the women were too occupied to lend their usual helpful quips. Katarina saw to the fire and, he hoped, to their dinner.

"Remember how I taught you to hold your weapon," Tracker said as he unsheathed his own and tossed the scabbard aside. It had been weeks since they'd attempted any training involving the scimitar, but the man clearly recalled how tangled in his own feet Dylan had been then and sought not to repeat the act. Although, he could've sworn all the unarmed training had helped him improve there.

Dylan slid his hands along the quarterstaff. *Hold it firmly, like you would clasp a lover*. His fingers tightened around the banded wood.

"Do you wish to go over the basics again? Or shall we jump right into it?"

Dylan thrust the end of the quarterstaff in the man's direction. "I'm not going to get better if we keep talking instead of doing." That was all the man would fully focus on yesterday.

Bowing his head in acceptance, Tracker assumed a ready stance and waited for Dylan's attack.

He rushed at the hound, aiming for the man's head as he swung the quarterstaff ahead of him.

Tracker jerked back, brushing the staff aside with the sweep of his blade.

The staff flew out of his grasp. It hit the ground end-on, spinning chaotically before coming to rest far from where he stood.

The hound's disapproving tsk-tsking seemed far louder than it had any right to be. "You are too stiff. And you are meant to be holding your lover firmly, not trying to squeeze the life from them." He chucked the quarterstaff into the air with one twitch of his foot. Catching the banded length of wood, he gave it an almost idle twirl before presenting Dylan with an end. "Let us try it again."

Dylan chewed on his bottom lip as he took up the staff. His gaze drifted to where Katarina had settled by the fireplace—the scent of dinner being almost ready tweaking his nose—then lifted his eyes to the sky. "The light's fading awfully fast." More than he had expected. "Maybe we should pick this up tomorrow?"

Tracker laughed. "So eager for the day to be over. Training first, my dear man, then you can eat." He waited until Dylan had finished adjusting his grip accordingly before continuing, "Would you prefer I played the role of the aggressor?"

"Aren't we meant to be replicating a battle scenario?" He couldn't imagine any time he would willingly engage an enemy with just a stick to fend them off. Once he was leashed again, perhaps.

There was a subtle change in the way the hound gripped his scimitar. Tracker attacked him, the curved weapon a blur.

Dylan countered each attack, oftentimes barely. His heart hammered harder with each singing swipe of the blade.

The scimitar's cool edge slid along his bare leg. Dylan gasped and braced himself for the pain. None came. That meant the man had turned the blunt edge to face him. So if he swung the butt of the quarterstaff to his left...

Dylan jerked the staff back between them, smacking into Tracker's forearm and knocking the blade aside. On the edge of his vision, he spied the hound flinch.

Grunting, Tracker switched the scimitar to his left hand. "Again."

He glowered at the man as they circled each other. If his swing had a little more strength behind it, he could've broken the man's arm. "You're letting me win," he growled through clenched teeth. To the detriment of his own wellbeing. "Stop going easy on me."

With a twitch of his brow, the hound sheathed his weapon and rushed at him.

Dylan attempted to evade, bringing the quarterstaff up to block. The hound grasped Dylan's wrist. The hint of the man's suspiciously neutral expression was all the warning he had before finding himself lying on the ground at Tracker's feet.

Dusting himself off, Dylan retrieved the staff and once again faced the hound. His eyes burned from trying to keep aware of Tracker's next move. The man seemed indifferent to his presence, but he had been fooled by that in the past. No way Dylan could afford to be so lax a second time. His smarting backside was a rather sharp reminder of what would happen.

Tracker feinted, but Dylan was ready for him this time. He darted to one side, trailing the quarterstaff. A quick jerk of his wrist had the length of wood snapping up in front of the man as he circled behind.

Dylan grasped the quarterstaff in both hands, drawing the weapon closer until the man's back was pinned against his chest. His breath skittered over the hound's shoulder and, if he wasn't mistaken, that hitch in Tracker's breathing wasn't because of the suddenness in which they'd collided.

Pure wickedness filled his thoughts. What would the hound do if Dylan licked along the bottom angle of his ear? What would the others say?

Dylan glanced over his shoulder at their camp. Katarina had her back to them, engrossed in the meal cooking over the fire. Marin was still somewhere out amongst the trees.

He felt the barely perceivable brush of another's foot wrapping behind his leg. Then he was on the ground with the hound standing over him.

Tracker clicked his tongue critically. He ran a finger behind the ear Dylan had inadvertently breathed upon. "You are letting yourself get distracted. There is no time for that during combat." He held out a hand to help Dylan to his feet. "Again."

His gaze dropped to the quarterstaff. It lay within easy reach. He stretched up for Tracker's hand, grabbing the staff. He swung the end at the hound, aiming to catch the man's booted feet, and tugged on Tracker's hand in the same motion.

Tracker tumbled, landing with a grunt on his stomach beside Dylan. Utter shock and indignance took his face as he spat out a mouthful of grass and dirt before rolling over to glare at him. "That was a dirty trick."

Already laughing, Dylan flopped back onto the grass. "All's fair on the battlefield, right? You said to make use of every advantage I have."

Tracker chuckled. "I did." He sat up, propping himself on outstretched arms. "But few enemies would allow you to keep your weapon, let alone permit you the time to make such a move."

He rolled onto his side, leaning on an elbow. It could've been his imagination or the ruddy light of dusk, but the man looked decidedly more flustered than he had a moment ago. "So you're saying *I* distracted *you* for a change?"

Tracker's gaze ran over him, taking its time mentally tracing every bit of his six-foot frame. He bit his lip, his hand straying to once again rub his ear. "For a moment," he admitted huskily.

The loud, and somewhat forced, blast of someone coughing drew his attention to the figure standing over them. Marin had returned. She stood with her arms akimbo and shook her head. A small smile touched her lips. "Boys, if you're going to tumble about in the dirt, at least do us the courtesy of doing it where we can't see."

Gods... Dylan buried his face into his hands. He had been so consumed in their sparring that he completely forgot they weren't alone. Who knew what the others thought about them lying upon the grass like a pair of children?

Naturally, Tracker took the woman's words in stride. "I am uncertain what you *think* you are seeing, my dear woman, but it is hardly scandalous. But perhaps you are looking to offer yourself up as a target, yes?"

"Why? Has he been giving you a *hard* time?" She barely got the words out before cackling uproariously.

Fresh heat flooded his cheeks. *Damn it.* If he'd just been able to keep it in his smallclothes.

There was something in the woman's laughter that had him risking a peek at her. *She suspected it weeks ago.* From before he had snuck off for the explicit reason of sex, even prior to him trying his hand at unarmed combat. All the teasing, the jokes, the knowing glances...

It was all reminiscent of the ribbing his friends used to do.

Emboldened by the familiarity, Dylan nudged the man's thigh with his boot and whispered conspiratorially, "I think she's asking to watch me fumble with my staff."

"Ugh." Marin rolled her eyes and stuck out her tongue in a mock gag. "Gods, no, that's the *last* thing I want to think about is your staff, especially not when I plan to eat soon."

"Are you certain?" Tracker asked, a lazy grin lifting one corner of his mouth. "It is my experience that all beings could benefit from learning how to handle a length of wood."

She eyed the hound for a moment, clearly unsure what part he was serious about, if any. "All right, common sense clearly won't prevail here." She threw up her hands in surrender. "I am leaving this conversation before either of you talk me into something I'll regret. Do as you like. Teach him, screw him. Whatever." She turned on her heel and headed for the tents, still grumbling over her shoulder, "Just don't be surprised if I aim a stone or two at your arses if you choose the latter."

The hound watched her departure, chuckling. "As tempting as either suggestion is, we should continue another day." He leapt to his feet and extended Dylan a helping hand. "Let us eat whilst there is still light to be had."

"Food sounds good." His stomach had been too tied up in knots to eat much last night, or the morning gone. He grasped the offered hand. There was a certain spark in the man's eyes that suggested further mischief, but the hound refrained from whatever scenario twinkled in those honey-coloured depths.

The other two already sat around the campfire, eating. As one, the pair glanced up as Dylan and Tracker neared before dropping their gazes back to their food.

Although his burning cheeks would've vastly preferred seeking the shelter of their tent, his grumbling stomach drove him onwards. He settled beside Katarina, his movements decidedly wooden.

The hedgewitch wordlessly handed him a thick cut of bread and a slab of cheese before spooning some sort of soup into his bowl.

Dylan frowned at the food. He didn't recall everything Tracker had bought from Whitemeadow, but perhaps one of the others had made their own purchases along the way. That also possibly explained the little bottle of brown liquid Marin was currently drinking.

A rather unwelcome quiet fell over the camp as they chewed. There were the normal sounds of the forest, the birds whistled their evening songs, the insects chirped and buzzed, the trees creaked...

But the only sound issuing from their camp came in the form of the occasional gulp. This awkwardness was his fault. If he had just been using his brain instead of thinking with other parts...

Well, he hadn't. And this was what he would be dealing with until they reached Wintervale. Or possibly Riverton. He might not be able to avoid travelling with Tracker, but they could go on without the others. He would just have to risk whether or not the army generals believed the truth without a hedgewitch's testimony that he was at least in the scouting party. What proof did they have that anyone would even believe her?

"I will take the entire watch tonight," Tracker said, finally breaking the silence. "All of you would do well to rest."

"Whilst you have none?" Katarina countered. "Unacceptable. *I* will take the latter half. *You* will get some sleep."

"Yes," Marin drawled, her lips curving wickedly against the rim of her bowl. "*That's* certainly what he'll get some of."

Dylan's cheeks burned their hardest. Grumbling under his breath, he distractedly picked at the bread until it was little more than a mess of doughy crumbs. After the scrounging they'd done on their way to Whitemeadow, the bread felt too fresh.

The hound's answering smile was a fraction too sharp. "If the thought of me slumbering in another's arms bothers you, I could always share *your* tent." There seemed to be an extra spark to his eyes as he spoke, a suggestion that pressing any further would cause more trouble than it was worth. "It would give our dear hedgewitch a little respite from your snoring, yes?"

Marin snorted in disbelief, her face darkening. "I don't know what you're talking about. I don't snore."

"You *do*," Dylan said. He'd heard her plenty of times during their travels. "Like a rusty bucksaw."

"It does *not* sound like that," Katarina retorted. She patted the hunter's knee. "Don't listen to them. It's a cute little snore and I don't mind it, I promise."

Just like when Dylan had needled her on knowing a little more about hedgewitch tales than she should, Marin's blush only deepened. She brought her bowl up to her face, practically tipping the contents into her mouth as she shovelled the food down as fast as she could swallow. She surfaced only long enough to clean the dish before seeking her bed.

Tracker cleared his throat as the hunter disappeared into the tent. "You two should follow her lead and get some rest. Especially you," he added, giving Dylan a pointed look. "Do not think your struggling to match a quick pace went unnoticed. Although, I am surprised you still lack the endurance after travelling for so long."

"It's the heat and lack of shade," he clarified. The northern roads heading to the tower, as well as the one pointing to Whitemeadow, had been shaded for much of the day. Their current path hadn't proven so generous.

"I see." The hound tore off a bite-size piece of bread, dipping it into his soup and popping it into his mouth. He seemed to chew it far more thoroughly than it really warranted before swallowing. "Well, we need only to follow the road. There is no law forbidding us from walking under the trees flanking it."

"Won't it slow us down?" Katarina asked.

"A little," he confessed. "Not enough to matter, but all the more reason to seek your beds now so we can leave at first light and make the most of the cooler hours."

Dylan didn't mind if it took them longer to reach their destination. There was only one outcome waiting for him once they arrived.

All he needed was to get close enough.

$$\sim \sim \sim$$

Tracker strolled around their little campsite, keeping his gaze moving from one shadow to the next. So close to the river, the typical lulling hum of wildlife was overpowered by frogs. He had forgotten how sharp their croaks were, buzzing like the little flashes of lightning did between Dylan's fingers. And loud. Not enough to make sleep impossible, but certainly carrying on the breeze.

The flicker of torchlight through the trees caught his eye. He took a step towards it, his hand drifting to his scimitar. *Another convoy?* He had spied a couple of them daring to travel in the dark. It was almost a comfort. Their swinging lights would make them a far more tempting target to any bandits who might be in the area.

He watched the light move on, not relaxing until the faintest glow had vanished, before returning to the centre of the campsite. He had smothered the campfire several hours back, opting to rely on the moonlight. A few embers still glowed in the depths.

He had barely crouched to shovel more dirt over them when the hedgewitch emerged from the tent she shared with Marin. She threw her cloak over her shoulders as she straightened, although he didn't think the night was cold enough for that, and silently strode his way.

Tracker turned back to his task. The hedgewitch saw in the dark just as well as he and would have no need of any light to keep a vigil over them. And, as much as he wanted to object to handing that responsibility over to her, she was right in him needing to get some sleep. Without Authril, the duty of protecting them was his alone.

She halted at his side, opting to remain standing.

"You've been quieter since we left Whitemeadow. Is everything all right?" Before he could dodge the act, she laid the inside of her wrist upon his forehead. "You don't seem ill."

Grumbling under his breath, he shook off the touch. "I am well." As much as he could be.

Katarina settled next to him. She stared out into the dark, her lips pursed as though she sucked on something unsavoury. "What was that you told me before Whitemeadow? That you two had shared a few harmless kisses?"

He shrugged. "They were." Was he to blame for not divulging the other activities alongside them? "You wished to take the latter half of the night's watch, yes? Should you not be checking on the perimeter?"

Her expression hardened. "In time." Whilst the words were clearly meant as an assurance, the tone in which she spoke them suggested that such time would be a while yet. "Dylan said you've been sleeping with him since the spellster tower."

"I was not aware he had confided such in you." That explained the woman's grim manner. "We did indeed engage in such activities." After keeping the fact a secret for so long, he struggled in letting the truth free so brazenly. "Not that sex had been my intention then," he swiftly added. Dylan had been in a fragile state, one that could've easily ended with the man destroying what was left of the tower with them in it. Tracker had been looking to distract the man and had, perhaps, offered more than he should have. "But it happened nevertheless."

With the hindsight of a month between them and the tower, he regretted a lot of things about that night. There were so many decisions he would've made differently. Taking it slow. Stopping at Dylan's first release. He might've lamented not feeling that unclothed body against him as they chased bliss in each other's grasps, but his own hand could've served well enough. And yet...

The longing in his eyes...

The need in his kisses...

The unabashed ecstasy in his moans...

Dylan had made it clear that Tracker's affection was welcomed, *wanted* even, and he hadn't the will to deny the man. "Every time has been his choice."

"So he said." She peered at him, her brows knitting together. "Which is why I find it curious that he still believes he's destined for the army. You need to tell him where we're actually going."

"I was about to," he snapped. "Then Marin barged in and Authril..." He sighed. "After all that, I can hardly march up to him and tell him—" What? There were so many words he couldn't permit, or speak.

"You can't just decide to change his fate without letting him know."

"It is better for him to remain ignorant."

"About everything? Does that include how you feel about sending him to the army? I *know* you care for him."

A metallic tang sat thickly on his tongue. "Of course." How could he not? The man had stirred a part of him he never believed he would ever feel again. He couldn't tell Dylan that. He couldn't let anyone know. Couldn't even think it. "As I must to keep him alive."

"More than that."

Swallowing, Tracker could've sworn his saliva was more viscous than normal. "I cannot," he replied, managing to sound less choked than he felt. They weren't safe, yet. They never could be until they were beyond the kingdom's borders, in some place where word of a spellster's presence wouldn't set city guards on edge.

"Why not? And don't try to give me that lie about Nulled Ones not having such emotions again. We both know it's not true."

He shook his head. "It is more complicated than that. People hounds care for too much wind up dying."

"Is that some sort of superstition or...?"

"No." How he wished it was something so fanciful. "Hounds are forced to kill what they care about." Whatever he felt, they were both better off if he didn't admit to feeling anything at all.

Katarina remained silent for a breath. "It must be hard, denying the truth."

Not when you know the price. Tracker closed his eyes. The rusty light of the Pit flicked behind his eyelids. Dampness hung in the air, hot and oppressing. And the blood... the taste, the smell, the cooling heat of it coating his hands.

He turned from her to survey the tent he shared with the spellster, the sight blurry. Dylan slept on, content and secure. Happy despite everything that had happened.

Telling him could only ruin that.

"Give me time." Even without Authril to flog him down the path towards Wintervale, Dylan could very well resist the idea of leaving the kingdom. "Until Riverton."

"If he makes no mention of it by the time we leave there, whether that is by road or boat..." She looked a little ill at the mention of the latter. "Then *I* will inform him before he takes a step towards either."

Grunting, he dusted off his hands and got to his feet. Of course that was her answer. "Be aware, convoys are still travelling the road. They may draw less savoury company." No one's plans would come to fruition if they died to a simple brigand's blade.

They walked through the forest in silence with Tracker picking their way carefully. Although, the lack of talk wasn't through any choice on Dylan's part. Whenever any of them opened their mouth to ask where they were headed, the hound would press a finger to his lips.

Eventually, a low hissing greeted Dylan's ears. The sound grew, putting him in the mind of a stream falling over a lip of rock in its path. Only on a far bigger scale. Had Tracker been listening for it?

Tracker picked up the pace, aiming for the sound.

The shimmer of light caught Dylan's eye. He thought little of it at first. There was often a multitude of fantailed birds flitting through the undergrowth at this time of day, especially when they disturbed the insects. Upon the fourth little gleam, Dylan gave in to his curiosity and pushed aside the low branch of a willow in his path.

A stream, shallow and translucent, trickled through the undergrowth. He halted at a spot where the water looked deep enough to refill their water skins. "Guess we can forget about fishing tonight."

It had only been four days since Whitemeadow and they had easily enough supplies to reach Riverton without the previous supplementing they were forced into, but neither Tracker nor Marin seemed willing to give up the opportunity to add fresh meat.

When his observation was greeted with no answer, Dylan glanced up to find the hound still walking upstream towards the unending hiss. "Track?"

The man merely gestured for them to keep up.

Dylan followed alongside the others, a little apprehensive as the sound drowned out the insects and the bird calls. In their absence, he realised he had rather grown used to them. "What is it?" he whispered to Marin in the hope that she knew what the hound had spotted. Was it something dangerous? Bandits? A boar? A *bear*?

No, it couldn't be a bear. Only the northern lands of Tirglas and Cezhory had those. He didn't think such animals would venture halfway across the continent, but with his luck...

Marin simply shrugged.

Chuckling, Tracker flashed a reassuring smile over his shoulder. "Do not look so frightened." He rounded a large fern, ducking under the leaves, and disappeared. "Come on."

The rest of them followed through the foliage. Trees and bushes opened up to reveal a cliff proudly rearing above them. From it streamed a waterfall several horse lengths wide, the resulting stream forming a pool that took up much of the clearing. Ferns and bushes crept up the cliff face, framing the cascading water in lush greenery.

Dylan halted at the water's edge. "It's beautiful." He had read about waterfalls, even seen a few sketches in the tower library, but no mere image could compare to the raw power flowing before him. The pool was wide enough that he was far from the fall's spray. A refreshing scent hung in the air, one that reminded him of the tower gardens after a summer shower. He breathed it in, almost loathing the exhalation.

Feeling watched, he turned from the sight to find the hound's gaze on him and the man's mouth softly curved. His heart skipped a beat, trying to imitate the giddy fluttering in his gut. Something delicate balanced on his tongue, a feeling he didn't know the words to describe.

Tracker jerked his head around the moment their eyes locked. Clearing his throat, he hastened to shrug off his pack and rummage in its depths. "Best if we get these set before the fish seek a night harbour." He handed Marin the heavy fishing line.

Dylan grimaced. They had fished a few days back, catching a pair of eels alongside other aquatic animals. His stomach hadn't outright objected to the meal, nowhere near as violently as it had done to fish, but the weakness that washed over him in the following hours left him wary about ever again trying any animal that originated from the water.

Shrugging, Marin unwound her own fishing line. "I don't think this place has anything big enough to bother catching, but who knows, we might get lucky." She strolled along the side of the pool where a tree branch overhung the water. There, she cast each line, securing them to the branch, then settled on the bank.

The rest of them picked their way around the water's edge until they came across a section flat enough to pitch the tents. With the task divided between the three of them, it was done swiftly, leaving Katarina to poke through the undergrowth in search of firewood, whilst Dylan cleared a spot for it.

Meanwhile, Tracker dumped the water skins near the edge and set about refilling them.

Dylan eyed the water and its gentle current. Like the stream they'd encountered, it was clear. Nothing seemed to lurk in it beyond small fish. Still… "Shouldn't we be wary of things in the water?"

The hound paused in stoppering the last water skin. "Do you fear the fish will leave their realm to nibble more than our bait?"

"Actually, I was thinking the water might hold something bigger. Reptilian, perhaps." There'd been several large volumes in the tower's library dictating the dangerous creatures that lurked within places just like this, the most notable being big lizards with sharp teeth that dragged hapless victims to a watery grave.

The hound shook his head. "If the land was further south, perhaps. There is nothing in Demarn waters but fish and eels. Maybe more crayfish if we are lucky. Maybe enough for you to try them, yes?"

His stomach did a flip at the memory of Tracker tearing apart one of the little invertebrates he had cooked atop the coals whilst Katarina tended to the eels. Even Marin had baulked at trying the white flesh. "I'll pass."

Shrugging, the hound returned to his task. "Sure we are not simply afraid of a little cold water?" He slapped the surface, sending up a frigid spray.

Dylan flinched, summoning a small shield to ward off the droplets.

"Cheat," Tracker teased. "I know you do not melt when wet."

Although true, that didn't mean he welcomed being in such a state needlessly. He turned his attention to the water. He hadn't ever manipulated anything this big, or done much beyond a few small funnels, but surely doing so couldn't be any harder than manipulating bathwater.

He pushed against the pool's flow. It was a gentle trickle, no doubt feeding the stream further back, but it fought him nevertheless. Still, he eventually coaxed a wavelet in their direction. A hump formed on the surface, leaving tiny ripples that could be mistaken for a large fish just under the surface. The water hump rushed towards where the hound was still squatting near the water's edge.

One final shove of his magic was all it took to have the hump rear out of the water and splash over the hound.

Dylan maintained the funnel for as long as he could before laughter got the better of him. He clutched at his sides. He had hoped to remain innocent-looking in the face of this, but witnessing the usually graceful man falling flat on his backside was too much.

Tracker jumped to his feet, spluttering and dripping, the very second that the water stopped. "Dylan!" he growled, whirling on him. His braid snapped around, smacking him in the arm and lessening the menace in his snarl. "That was a foolish waste of magic."

Up on the bank, Marin rolled on her back, cackling her head off.

"Fair's fair," Dylan replied. "You *did* try to splash me. Or are we afraid of a little cold water?"

The hound waved his hand about before he started to undo his belts. "That was more than a *little*, yes? And not exactly what I would call a *fair* retaliation, but if you wanted me to strip, you simply could have asked." His jerkin and quilted shirt hit the ground in successive slaps. The trickle of water upon the already sodden ground followed him pulling off his undershirt and wringing it out.

"Don't take any more off," Marin said, the word muffled with her face buried in her hands. "For gods' sake, please. I'm sure it's very impressive, if you go for that sort of thing, but I have already seen way too much sausage."

Still doubled over, his sides hurting, Dylan tilted his head to get a better look at the man through all his hair.

Tracker had abandoned the upper half of his sodden attire to wrestle with the laces of his trousers. "I assure you, I have no intentions of fully stripping in your presence." He toed off his boots and peeled the soaked leather off each leg. It still left him in his smallclothes, which were merely damp in comparison. And revealing enough to have Dylan's face warming. "You *will* be drying my clothes," he added, jabbing the air with a single finger as though he could prod Dylan from such a distance.

He started nodding in agreement when an altogether wickeder thought came to mind. "*Or* you could let them air dry?"

"I must say," Katarina said. She stood by the spot Dylan had cleared for their fire, an armful of wood at her feet. "Those tattoos do sort of lead the eye downwards, don't they?"

The hound grinned. It might have been Dylan's imagination, but there seemed to be a hint of wavering uncertainty in the corners of his mouth. Such doubt was eradicated by the confident timbre in the man's laugh. "It was never my original intention, but the overall effect is quite striking, yes?" He twirled, giving them all a full view.

"That it is," the hedgewitch agreed. "I would very much like to discuss the reasoning behind some of them, but at a later date. Why don't you bundle yourself in your cloak for now, *before* you catch a cold?"

"I will dress in time," the man promised. The hound wrung out his braid and threw it back over his shoulder. "Once our dear spellster has dried our clothes."

"*Our?*" Dylan echoed, taking a hesitant step backwards. Even after soaking the hound, he wasn't a bit damp. He turned to run for the tents.

It wasn't fast enough.

Tracker rushed at him. In one swift movement, the hound wrapped his arm, still clammy from the drenching, around Dylan's waist. "Where are you going?" he growled, hoisting Dylan over his shoulder. "Do not think you can dump a bath's worth of water over me and not get a dunking of your own."

"Wait! No, I—" He squirmed in the man's grip. "Don't! I can't sw—"

"Fair's fair." Tracker released him, although not in the manner Dylan had hoped.

He sailed backwards into the air, limbs and cloth already flailing. He caught but a glimpse of the hound standing on the water's edge, then his back hit the water and the world turned muffled and murky.

Dylan pawed for the surface. His lungs strained for air. The layers of his robe adhered to his legs, hampering him further. He broke through briefly, gasping and flailing, before he slipped back beneath the water.

Strong arms grabbed him. They hauled his face above the surface, manipulated him into an upright position and kept him from submerging again.

"Be still," Tracker said. He didn't know how many times the man had repeated that word before Dylan's waterlogged ears understood it.

He tried to remain still. Each time, the water tried to suck him down.

The hound's grip remained firm. Although Dylan couldn't fathom how he kept the both of them from sinking. "Do not panic. Thrashing around will only make you sink faster."

He spat out the river water. A slight grit covered his teeth.

"Do not speak. Just put your feet down and stand up."

Dylan obeyed. His knees hit silt first. He pushed off it and rose out of the water by a foot. "Oh."

"Do you truly think I would throw you into deep water?" the man asked as he assisted Dylan in getting to his feet. "I had already gathered swimming was never part of your training. Although, I could change that, if you wished."

He glanced over his shoulder at the pool. He might be safe from drowning near the water's edge, but the main body of it looked deeper than he was tall. Before their stint in the tavern bathhouse, the deepest body of water he had seen were the bathing tubs in the tower and those had been knee-deep since his adolescence. "Another time." He took a step closer to the shore, the mere act of lifting one foot an arduous task thanks to his waterlogged robes.

"What if you fall into the King's Winding?" Tracker pressed. "It would be better to know before then, yes?"

"You still plan to take a boat?" Katarina asked from the shore where she gathered up Tracker's clothes. At her back, the smoky trail of a new fire began its climb to the clouds. "You think Riverton will have them when Whitemeadow didn't?"

Tracker was silent as he swam the distance to shore, beaching himself on the pebbles near the edge, rather than wade. He lay on his back, staring out at the waterfall, his expression vacant. "I do. Riverton is a fishing village. Their little boats would be of no interest to men who are used to more robust sea-going vessels."

If that was the case, then why would the hound wish to use those same boats to head along the very route the Talfaltaners refused to take them?

"But for now, my reasoning is more recreational." He turned to Dylan and pointed at the waterfall. "See that dark patch under the jutting rock? Where the water falls straight down?"

Dylan halted at the water's edge to examine the waterfall, immediately identifying the piece the hound spoke of. Unlike the rest of the waterfall, which trickled down the cliff side in little steps, there was a portion that ran unimpeded.

"That's likely to be a cave," Tracker continued. "I was thinking we could investigate before it gets too dark." He shrugged. "If you do not mind trying, of course."

"You really think so?" And the man wanted to explore it like they were a pair of curious children? He grinned. "Sure *you* aren't using this as an excuse to have *me* strip?"

Tracker laughed, the sound light and merry, as he slid back out into the pool. "I need no excuse for *that*. You are already wet enough."

"Fine," Dylan muttered. "I'm coming in." He stripped himself to his smallclothes, leaving the robe in an oozing pile just beyond the water's edge. Returning to where the land gently sloped into the water, he dipped a foot in. Even wet as he was, the coolness still soaked his ankle.

He pressed on, shuffling his way along the ground. A muddy cloud grew in his wake.

Slowly, the water level grew deeper, running further up his skin. It hit his groin, the coldness tearing a gasp from his throat. He held his breath, waiting for his body to become acclimatised.

Eventually, he stood shoulder-deep in the pool.

The hound bobbed ahead of him, raw pride curving his lips.

Tracker crooked a single finger, beckoning Dylan onwards. "Come on." The man's feet, already not quite touching the bottom, moved in a lazy walking motion. "You are perfectly safe with me, but if you would prefer to only go this far, I understand."

He eyed the shadowy area. From this low angle, it definitely looked like there was space behind the curtain of water. "No, I…" He tried to scrub the itchy trickling of water running down his face, grimacing as the act only further wet him. "I want to try."

"Then I will begin teaching you how to swim." Warm hands alighted on his shoulders. "Which will first require you to float. I need to tip you on your back, all right?"

"I'm not sure that'll be a good—"

"You are scared." The hound's thumbs rubbed gentle circles into his skin. "It is natural, but you cannot let those fears command you or they will drag you under. Just remember, I will not let you come to any harm."

Dylan let himself go lax in the man's arms. Tracker moved him slowly, tipping his shoulders back. He squeezed his eyes shut and held his breath, prepared for the inevitable slip beneath the surface. His head sunk partially until water filled his ears and threw the world into a murky, echoing realm. Hips, chest, thighs, arms... they surfaced, balanced as the hound moved around Dylan, adjusting as he went.

Finally, Tracker's touch withdrew, leaving Dylan cradled by the water.

He'd only been taking shallow breaths. Now, he slowly let it all out in one long sigh. He drifted on the lazy current with Tracker bobbing at his side, helping whenever Dylan felt himself sinking. It took a few tries, but he eventually managed to stay afloat on his own.

Tracker swam a lap around him. He moved as if born to the water, his passage kicking up very little disturbance. "See?" His voice was muffled, the words just understandable. "Not so difficult once you get the hang of it."

Dylan lifted his head to watch the man, instantly regretting it as his backside sunk. "Where did you learn to swim?"

The hound halted at his side, gently guiding him back to being horizontal. "The sea. In my youth, I harboured fantasies of joining a Talfaltaner crew and sailing the ocean. Perhaps even becoming a pirate."

He frowned, imagining someone with a hound's abilities amongst the horde that had destroyed his home. "Did you ever try?"

"No." Even with the water in Dylan's ears, the word was harsh. "Now, seeing I cannot float you to the waterfall, try kicking your legs."

Dylan did. A few strokes and his lazy drifting travel suddenly became a little faster. A small smile tweaked his lips, quivering with more than a sliver of fear. He was swimming. Actually swimming. He kicked a little harder, flinging water everywhere but also increasing the speed in which he drifted.

His legs objected after a short while, forcing him to resume floating. He lifted his head, seeking the hound, and found the man bobbing in the water not too far away. "How's that?"

"A little inelegant," Tracker replied as he swam up to Dylan's side. "But I would certainly class it as a start. However, we cannot be about this for too long if we want to be back at camp before sunset." The hound slowly tipped him upright. "Let us try something a little more advanced."

Dylan shook his head to clear the water from his ears, then slicked his hair back from his face. He eyed the waterfall, his heart racing at the thought of venturing out into the deeper section of the pool. "I'm ready."

CHAPTER 39

Keeping his chin above the surface, Dylan splashed and kicked his way through the water. Whilst he'd been fine with Tracker holding his hands and gently tugging him forward as he kicked, swimming on his own was a lot harder than the hound made it look. The timing of his breathing was always that little bit off, leaving him to either swallow a mouthful of water or hold his breath until he exploded to the surface, gasping.

Eventually, he forwent putting his head under the surface and opted to attempt mimicking the same arm movements as the man, only to end up clawing across the pool. His feet kept kicking just beneath him and water sprayed everywhere, but he moved forward.

At his back, Tracker laughed. "What is this? I told you to keep your body flush with the surface. Not whatever you are doing." There was a flash of bronze as the man sped by, only to pop up closer to the waterfall. "You look like a dog."

"It works, doesn't it?" Dylan shot back, spitting out mouthfuls of water. "Do you want to show me this cave before sunset or not?"

Shaking his head, Tracker swam a little closer. "At the speed you are travelling, it will be night before you get there. Come." He clasped Dylan's hands and towed him. "Just keep kicking."

Biting back the flare of defiance welling in his gut, Dylan allowed the man to escort him across the pool. The closer they came to the waterfall, the harder it became to focus on staying afloat. A deafening roar filled his ears. The spray all but blinded him.

Tracker released his hold, leaving Dylan to tread water. "Wait here!" he yelled, his voice barely audible.

Dylan nodded. He threw up a dense shield and realised his folly as the current pushed him further from their destination. With a little extra attention, he turned the usually complete ball into a hemisphere. It was harder to hold, and he had to constantly adjust it whilst trying to stay in the same spot, but it kept much of the waterfall's chaos at bay.

Hardening the shield also slightly muffled the waterfall's roar.

The spray already coated the barrier, turning the view filmy. How did it look from the outside? Would anyone stumbling upon this place see a man floating in a strange bubble? Or was there enough water that they wouldn't even notice him?

Tracker bobbed up next to him. "So—"

Dylan jerked back, almost losing his hold on the shield as he flailed ineptly in the water. It wasn't long before the hound grabbed him, steadying him enough to right himself.

"Sorry," Tracker said. "Are you certain you can manage all right?"

Spitting out a mouthful of water, Dylan nodded. It wasn't as if they could come back another day, or even a little while later. If he was to see this cave, then it would have to be now.

"Very well. We are going this way." The hound cocked his head, indicating to the left of the waterfall, before once again taking up Dylan's hands and towing him. "There appears to be an entrance of sorts. And an old path. Submerged, of course, but—" Tracker's voice became lost to the roar of the waterfall as they neared.

The water rumbled. Although muffled by the shimmering barrier, the sound carried itself on a low frequency on par with a minor earthquake. Dylan dipped his head beneath the surface. Underwater, it sounded like a giant blowing bubbles. Coming up for air, he followed the churning water at the bottom of the fall all the way to the top. From this angle, the cascade seemed to come from the very heavens themselves.

As they swam closer to the cliff face, he spied what must have caught Tracker's eye. Where the rock jutting out beneath the waterfall left a natural gap between the water and the cliff. It was there that the hound aimed them.

The spray ran over the dense hemisphere of his shield in rivulets. He tightened his grip on Tracker's fingers, trusting the man to guide him.

His shield bumped against the cliff face, dislodging a few stones. This close to the rock, the water was shallow enough to let Dylan find his feet. He shuffled along the silt shifting atop what his toes said was solid rock whilst the hound continued to paddle ahead.

The gap was barely wide enough for the man's shoulders. Mimicking the way the hound kept close to the rocks, Dylan followed. He winced as he sidled past the waterfall, the force of it hammering upon the outer curve of his shield. He hadn't realised how strong such features were.

With great reluctance, he let the barrier drop. Spray immediately flew up in his face, stinging his eyes. Dylan screwed up his nose and felt his way along the rock.

His hand slapped the smooth, wet stone rearing before him. A little more groping revealed a lip above the water's edge. *The cave floor?* The waterfall roared even louder here, and it was far colder than he'd imagined, but the stone beneath his fingers didn't feel as wet. He risked a peek, expecting more water in his eyes. A fine mist hung in the air, clinging to his skin and collecting on his lashes, but no more.

Further shuffling along the silt-covered path led him to a dip in the ledge where he could haul himself out of the water. Huffing, Dylan flopped onto the clammy stone. He stared at the cave ceiling stretched before him. Bare rock.

He wasn't certain what he had expected. Stalactites, maybe. All the caves he had read about seemed to mention them. Perhaps a little moss. Not this.

Tracker stooped over him, obscuring his view. Water streamed from his braid. His mouth moved, the words drowned out by the echoing roar.

"What?" Dylan yelled back as he sat up. The cave floor was more to type, damp and glistening in the low light. A boulder sat at his right hip, its position sturdy enough to lean against. His hand had fallen into a shallow puddle and more dotted the entrance.

The hound shook his head and motioned Dylan to follow him deeper into the cave.

Crawling a little ways from the edge, Dylan got to his feet and finally took in the cave as a whole. The entrance wasn't overly wide, but the cave itself bulged. He glanced down, wondering how the hound picked his way across the cave floor so effortlessly, and saw the remains of what could only be a path made of wide flat stones winding through the rougher terrain.

He followed in the man's steps, quickly leaving behind both the noise and the cold spray of the falling water. The greying press of darkness swaddled them. After one too many stubbed toes, Dylan sent a little globe of light to bob ahead. It illuminated what looked to be the start of a very long tunnel.

Dylan eyed the tunnel walls. There was a slight unnaturalness to the way the rock flowed. Everything was too perfect and crisp. There was evidence of stalactites now they were deeper in the cave, quite a number of thin columns. Those bothered him even more than the tunnel. Or rather the discolouration of the stalagmites close to the path. Had other people ventured down here? "Is this what you wanted to show me?"

"No," Tracker murmured. "I have never been here before. Usually, there is a small hollow carved out by the water, but this?" He shook his head, flicking water everywhere. "I was not expecting to find a place that seemingly goes on forever."

"Where do you think it leads?" Like the walls, the path they'd followed had definitely not been natural, submerged though it might've been. "Some secret hideout, perhaps?" Was there treasure at the other end of the tunnel?

The hound's hand hooked into the crook of Dylan's arm, stopping him. "That does not matter. Actually, I will confess to having an ulterior motive for bringing you here."

Dylan turned from the lure of the tunnel to face the man. They might've stopped, but he couldn't help continuing to scrutinise the walls for some sign of what lay ahead. "Oh?" he asked, distractingly. There were markings on the wall near the tunnel entrance. Worn and faint in places, but certainly not a natural phenomenon.

Tracker continued talking, "There is something I need to tell you and I would prefer to say it where the others cannot overhear."

"Right," Dylan mumbled. *Runes.* The markings were dwarven runes, he was sure of it. What did they say? The little double-legged rune that looked like the profile of a table meant house, no... building. Or maybe a tunnel given the placing. The wavy lines underneath must be water. *Watertunnel?* That couldn't be it. The records stated the dwarves took water from open air sources. "What is it?"

The hound didn't seem to have noticed. They stood not that far from the wall and the man seemed more transfixed on Dylan than their surroundings. "I was thinking we really have no need to go as far as Wintervale. I am certain the king knows what became of the army camp by now. Likely the tower, too. And without Authril to insist, we could—"

"*Smedja!*" Dylan slapped his forehead. How could he be so stupid? There'd been such a record on that slab he'd translated three years back. The wavy lines symbolised flowing rock, not water.

Tracker jerked back as if he'd been struck. "*What?*"

"There are dwarven runes here." He pointed at the marks. How could an elf—someone who could see far better in low light than any human—not have noticed them? His gaze slid to where the darkness finally swallowed the meagre light. It seemed to go on forever. "This *is* a tunnel." The tome Katarina carried.

The old record she had shown him none too long ago, before they reached Whitemeadow. A dwarven site near the King's Winding.

It led to a dwarven forge. Abandoned. Rediscovered, then forgotten again. Untouched.

The hound followed his fingers, frowning at the symbols. "I thought dwarves lived above ground? In trees? That they always have."

"They do. And they did, sort of." The hedgewitches of Dvärghem swore their ancestors used to live with the land. Housing amongst the branches, but forging what they could out of ore. He grasped Tracker's shoulders. "We *have* to get Katarina." Alerting the hedgewitches of ancient sites was part of the alliance between their kingdoms. He couldn't *not* tell her.

Hesitance narrowed Tracker's eyes. "Does it have to be right now? We really need to tal—"

Dylan swung back the way they'd come. "She *needs* to see this." Katarina hadn't complained about travelling with them all the way to Wintervale, but this would certainly smooth over any chance of ruffled feathers back at the hedgewitch's Coven. If it truly was what he believed it to be, then it might make up for the chaos around the old structure his scouting party had been ambushed at—a time that seemed years ago rather than a scant few months.

"I understand that, but I am trying to tell—"

He glanced over his shoulder. The man hadn't moved from beside the tunnel. "Can it wait?"

Tracker rubbed at his arms. His gaze dropped and, if Dylan was to judge by the way his lips thinned, the hound sucked at his teeth. "I guess?"

"Then you can tell me later. Now come on, before it gets too dark."

Dylan found it hard to remain still as Katarina traced the worn symbols. What if he was wrong? What if he had upset Tracker and dragged the hedgewitch here for nothing? The markings were old, which suggested the tunnel had a similar age, if not more. Maybe he read it incorrectly and it was actually a warning.

Eventually, the hedgewitch stood back and sighed. There was a lot of promise in that one little exhalation.

"Well?" he pressed. His stomach twisted as if he'd been transported back into his seven-year-old self and waited on his tutors to inform him of his grading.

"You're right," Katarina said. "These are most definitely runes from ancient times." Her head turned towards him, although she still eyed the dark tunnel with visible interest. "I wonder if it's still down there." She took a few hesitant steps.

"I do not think venturing down there would be wise," Tracker said. The hound shuffled from foot to foot. "The tunnel could be unstable. The forge might not even be there anymore. This place is so remote. Surely, they must have taken it with them when they moved on."

Dylan grinned. "The ancient dwarves didn't build their forges like that. They moulded them from what was already there." Still, having an entire forge carted away was a feat he would've loved to have seen.

At his side, Katarina nodded. She was practically beaming like a babe presented with a sweet. "Do you know what they used for forges?"

Tracker rolled his eyes. "My dear hedgewitch, what makes you think I would know *that*?"

"Molten rock!" She bounced on the spot, grinning and jigging like a child. "Which means it could still be working, thousands of years later."

The hound stepped back from the tunnel. Fear flashed across his face. "Lava? Were your ancestors perhaps not entirely sane?"

"They were very hard to make," Katarina went on. "We haven't found a single one intact."

"Perhaps because they made them near unstable pockets of lava?" Tracker drily suggested. He continued to eye the tunnel opening as if he expected molten rock to spew forth at any moment.

"This could be our chance to discover the techniques of old. Reclaim that little bit more of my people's past." She marched up to the tunnel entrance. "It's my duty as a hedgewitch to discover what lies at the other end. I can't just walk away because it *might* be dangerous. Dylan? I'm going to need your light."

"Of course." He trotted up next to her. His stomach bubbled. That a forge sat at the other end of this was in no doubt, but whether they could access it was an entirely different matter.

"And I am expected to guard the entrance, yes?" the hound snapped.

"Nonsense," Katarina said over her shoulder before striding into the tunnel. "You're more than welcome to join us."

Dylan waited until the man had joined him before following the hedgewitch.

Tracker grabbed Dylan's hand as they entered the tunnel entrance, entwining their fingers. The grip was tight, a silent cry for reassurance.

"Are you scared of caves?" It was a silly thought, considering the man had first suggested venturing into the dark, but it seemed logical.

"Of caves? No, not specifically." The words came quickly, his voice pitched an octave or two higher. "And certainly not if they are shallow or have a big enough exit. Tunnels, though?" He cleared his throat. "Now, *those* I will admit to having a few issues with."

Dylan peered at the man. In the gloom, it was difficult to determine if he was serious. *Tunnels?* Not caves, but tunnels? "You can return to camp, you know."

The hound shook his head, his jaw taking on a determined edge. "And leave you to suffer the fate of drowning when you attempt to swim out of here? Perish the thought."

He squeezed the hound's hand. "I'll be at your side the whole time, all right?"

Tracker smiled. The curve of his lips was small, genuine and likely thought lost in the dim light. "That will be acceptable, thank you."

It was slow going, despite the smoothness of their journey. Katarina's hurried footsteps echoed. Even with just her silhouette to go on, he could tell she chafed to run down the tunnel's end and witness a piece of her people's history that had been lost for so long. He didn't blame her. In her place, he would've likely run the entire length with no regard for what dangers could await them.

Dylan had expected the tunnel to narrow as they pressed deeper, or at least drop in height. Neither happened. Instead, the tunnel meandered on, its natural curves kept in favour of ease. Even with his little ball of light floating ahead of them, the heavy darkness prickled the back of his neck.

He bent closer to the hound and, with his lips a mere inch from the man's ear, whispered, "How are you holding up?" He'd never been anywhere that'd led him to have tons of rock above him, but now, with the mere thought of the crushing weight fluttering in the forefront of his mind, he could almost see why the idea of venturing down here unnerved Tracker.

"I am fine." The words were small, tight. Little more than squeaks in the gloom. The grip on Dylan's hand tightened. "I would feel much better if we were leaving, but I can manage until then."

He drew the man closer and brushed his lips against Tracker's temple. "You're safe with me. I won't let you get trapped down here."

There was that smile again. "I know, my darl—" It was hard to tell with the ball of light throwing strange shadows, but Dylan swore he spied panic of a different nature dart across the man's face. "—dear spellster."

Dylan chewed on his bottom lip. He wanted to ask what the hound was going to say, but he didn't have the heart to push Tracker. Not when the man looked so uncomfortable. "You haven't called me by that one in a while." Not since they left Whitemeadow.

"My most sincerest of apologies. I was unaware you missed such a moniker."

He glanced at Katarina, ensuring the hedgewitch was more interested in the tunnel than them, before confessing in a breathless hush, "Only when you say it." Everything sounded good coming from the man's lips, not as delicious as Dylan's name, but close enough to warm his skin.

The hitch of Tracker's breath was almost lost in the gentle echo of their footsteps. "You cruel man," he admonished, the words barely loud enough to hear. "How can you tease me so at such a time?"

Because it distracts you. The hound's mind might still play with his fears, but if he were to judge by Tracker's slightly more relaxed stance, his thoughts didn't worry at the idea. Dylan couldn't tell the man that, of course. Instead, he smiled and lifted their entwined hands to kiss the back of the hound's fingers. "Is that a complaint I hear?"

"Not at all," Tracker quipped. "Do continue with your flattery, my dear man."

"I'm not very good at it." He turned his attention back to the hedgewitch as she faced them. Was something wrong? Had they hit a dead end? He squinted, trying to see past the light. There seemed to be a corner and a seething, dull orange glow.

Heat hit him as they caught up to Katarina, sweat instantly coating his barely dry skin. The woman all but bounced on the spot. She tugged on his free arm, urging him faster. Dylan obeyed, dragging the hound with him.

They took the last curve and halted in the entrance to a large, bulbous cavern. The orange glow emanated from a rivulet of molten rock. *The forge.* It poured from the far wall and meandered across a channel in the floor before disappearing down a well in the middle of the cave. Churning away as if millennia hadn't passed it by.

To look at, it was a pool of molten rock, nothing different to what could be found anywhere else within the world. But how many sported channels carved into the rock? Or the peculiar empty ring of stone behind it?

"It's really here," Katarina breathed. "This is…" She wiped her eyes. "I haven't the words." Both hands clutched at her chest, crushing her breasts. "I'd hoped, but I never believed."

Dylan tore his gaze from the hypnotic flow of the forge to their surroundings. The dwarves who first worked here had further curved the cave via stones and mortar, the latter baked to hardness in the forge's heat. Shelves decorated the lower portions of the walls.

Everywhere he dared to look, it seemed nothing had been disturbed since the last time dwarves had ventured down here. Dylan reverently traced one of the emblems carved into the stone near the entrance. "These markings look like the crest of the bear." The advancement of the centuries, along with some blatant vandalism, made it difficult to be sure. "See the curve?" He pointed to a spot where the sharp lines of spikes intersected with smoother, older, carvings.

"And made out to look like a dragon." The hedgewitch bounced on the spot. With her also only garbed in her undergarments, it caused a rather distracting amount of jiggling. "Oh, it must have happened during the third-century wars. And over there." She pointed to where someone's sooty hand had marred the wall. The faint impression of another mark had been carved just beneath. "The stamp of the smiths. I must take notes, lots of them." She grasped his arm, squeezing to the point of bruising. "You can help me!"

"Of course." He had dreamt of aiding the hedgewitches and their apprentices in documenting an ancient site such as this. The closest he had ever come would've been when the hedgewitches sought the tower's archives. "I'd be honoured."

Tracker's hand tightened its grip, all but crushing Dylan's fingers. "The light will be fading on the surface," he said before Dylan could think to open his mouth. "We should return to camp before dark."

"But we can come back tomorrow." Katarina turned her gaze on the hound, those hazel eyes pleading. "Can't we?"

The grip on Dylan's hand grew tighter.

"My dear woman, our goal is to reach Riverton. I know we do not have Authril's daily reminders, but it would be unwise to delay."

The fingers encircling Dylan's arm constricted the limb like tiny snakes. "But I need him. This sort of find must be documented. I need records, meticulous ones. That requires a small team." Katarina left their side to flit about the cavern, her hands hovering over markings with such reverence that anyone could be forgiven for thinking they'd stumbled upon a holy site. "There's so much here." She spun to face the hound. "Give me a day. Just enough to make a preliminary report."

Tracker stared at the hedgewitch for several long breaths before sighing. "I suppose lingering for so short a time will not change our goal."

"Yes! Thank you!" She flung her arms around the hound's shoulders, almost lifting him off the ground as she hugged him tightly. "I swear, I won't waste a moment of time."

"*We* won't," Dylan promised. As a hedgewitch, this discovery would be Katarina's to claim. But with only the two of them working to catalogue it all, there was the possibility she would mark him as, not an apprentice, but her assistant. Whatever happened in Wintervale, he could face it knowing his name, his existence, would live on in the dwarven records. Unable to be erased. Certainly not forgotten. The one mark he'd leave on the world that didn't hinge on him being a spellster.

He would make it count.

CHAPTER 40

Dawn had barely made its mark on the world by the time they entered the cave. Not that the weather mattered when most of them would be spending the majority of the day underground.

His stomach bubbled at the thought, nerves and excitement all tangled in a knot not even the cold water could break. And it had tried, nibbling at his extremities as they crossed the pool, streaming off his smallclothes as he clambered onto the ledge beneath the waterfall. He had banished much of the chill with a little magic, leaving behind only its ghostly breath across his bare skin.

Katarina knelt near the tunnel entrance, checking the contents of the pouch she had carefully carried into the cave were still dry. She had invited the sole absent member of their group, but Marin declined, opting to spend the day fishing and guarding the camp.

He turned to the hound. Tracker stood near the waterfall, rubbing his arms in an effort to warm up. Much like yesterday, he insisted on joining them. Although silent now they'd reached the mouth of the cavern, he had been chatty enough on their way across.

Dylan sidled up to the man whilst they waited for Katarina to finish inspecting her equipment. "Are you sure you're all right? You don't have to join us." It wasn't as though the tunnel or the forge held anything dangerous.

"Hmm?" Tracker jerked his head around. "Oh, I know. I will be fine. Utterly so, I swear. It is just—" He frowned, eyeing the tunnel entrance as if he expected the walls to sprout teeth. "You are quite invested in the whole..." He waved his hand about, flicking droplets off his splayed fingers, as he seemed to search for the words. "...cataloguing dwarven history, yes?"

"Is that condemnation I hear?" The man certainly hadn't seemed interested in the forge's contents yesterday.

The hound's brows lifted to their highest. "Not at all. I—" He scrubbed at his face, sighing. "Forgive me, it was an observation of how passionate you become in the presence of such an artefact as this. Not once have I witnessed such a reaction over a few objects and some scratchings on a rock."

"Then you haven't been in the presence of many hedgewitches." Every single one he had assisted within the tower had reacted to even the smallest scrap of knowledge as though it was the rarest sample in history.

Tracker chuckled, the tone slightly strained. "No. But I imagine the enthusiasm of our dear friend is typical to those with her station." He smiled at Katarina. "She would have us lingering for weeks if we permitted it."

"And then some," Dylan agreed. She was right in that there was typically a whole team sent to record a site. He wasn't sure how much the pair of them could manage in a single day, but he would attempt as much as the hours allowed. "You could go back to camp, you know." Marin hardly needed help in catching fish, but she might've enjoyed the company. And if anyone *did* come across them, two would make for a more intimidating force. "We will be hours cataloguing everything and—" His jaw snapped shut before the mention of the hound's select dislike of tunnels slipped out. "It'll be rather boring," he finished.

Like shooing a gnat, the hound brushed aside Dylan's words with a flick of his hand. "I do not mind a little monotonous lingering, as long as there is something interesting to keep me distracted." He slid closer. His warm, wet skin pressed against Dylan's chest. "Have I told you how positively ravishing you look?"

Dylan swallowed. He could feel himself pressing into the man's stomach with every breath. The cold water dripping off their sodden smallclothes did nothing to cool the heat radiating from the hound. He took a steadying breath, trying not to smell the faint aroma of cinnamon on the man's skin, and reminded himself that the hedgewitch sat none too far away. "Not lately." Or at all.

"Truly?" Tracker's hands wove behind Dylan's back, pulling them closer. "All those words spoken last night and not once did I use any to compliment you? How remiss of me."

Whilst the hound was right in that they'd done a lot of talking last night—had spent the time awake doing little else beyond conversing—*Dylan* had been the one who'd kept the hound awake with his nattering about their find. At least, until Tracker seemingly had enough and wound himself around Dylan before going to sleep. His restlessness must've bored the man half to death. "I take it you're not the least bit interested in the past," he said in an attempt to keep his own thoughts from delving elsewhere as well as the hound's.

Tracker sneered. "As everyone is so very fond of reminding us, elves do not hold the same historic ties to the land as humans and dwarves."

No. Dylan had witnessed ample evidence of what people thought of their pointed-eared brethren since leaving the tower. More than he'd ever wanted. Like the man tasked as his warden back in the army, most seemed to prefer the elves returned to wherever their ancestors came from.

But humans were also not native to these lands. At least, according to dwarven lore. *Sjöfolk*, the dwarven tongue named them. *Sea people.* Arriving to the continent via ships like the elves. But where the first elven people had come looking for sanctuary, the humans had come to conquer. "That doesn't answer my question, though."

"A hound's study of history is meant to be tied to the tower and our order. Delving into how the world was in millennia's past serves little purpose."

"*Track.*"

The man rolled his eyes. "Will it satisfy you if I admit to a passing curiosity from time to time? There are all these rumours of what the dwarves of old were capable of. Sometimes, I wonder how much is truth. The Udynea Empire was once at war with them, yes?"

"That was a very long time ago." Back when the empires were ravenous and clashing with each other just as much as they did with the dwarven tribes scattered across the continent. The realm of Dvärghem hadn't been a thought in anyone's mind then, much less a sanctuary for those who remained. "If you like, I could teach you a few things along the way."

"Another time, perhaps. You and our dear hedgewitch are here for a reason. Tutoring me would doubtlessly slow you down and I... would prefer not to linger more than is necessary."

Dylan gave what he hoped was a reassuring smile. "You'll be fine."

Tracker hummed thoughtfully. He rested the underside of his chin on Dylan's chest, staring up at him for some time before speaking. "Would you be happier as a hedgewitch?" The gust of his breath was prickly hot on Dylan's neck, but nowhere near as sharp as the question it carried.

He had considered of it, in the distant past. An apprentice's life was comfortably similar to the one he'd been living in the tower. Hours of recording, of compiling and translating scraps of text. Years of shifting his focus from the attentions of one hedgewitch's wishes to another's, getting glimpses of their work without the whole picture. Always at their call, never truly studying things for himself.

Not once had he ever believed he might miss those days.

Hedgewitches did more than wait for people's accounts of ruins. They scoured the land, hunting for all the places where an untouched piece of their history could be lurking. Aiding the occasional travelling hedgewitch in determining which part of a map would be the best area to start was as close as he'd ever gotten to it. The act had sated his hunger in the beginning. That had been some years ago.

Would travelling the world at a hedgewitch's side be enough? He had no chance of finding out. "This isn't Dvärghem," he mumbled. The gods had laid but a single path before him. To leave it would be no easier than scaling a cliff blindfolded, with as much chance of fatality.

"No, it is not," Tracker said. "But what if it was?"

"It's a little more complicated than that." Even if the king permitted him, the last spellster able to fight in the army, to leave the kingdom, there were other factors, personal ones, that made him unsuitable to become a fully fledged member of the Coven.

The man's russet brows lowered. His gaze flicked between Dylan and the hedgewitch. "Do they not permit human members to take such a status amongst its people? Or spellster ones?"

Dylan shook his head. He honestly didn't know the answer to that. "It wouldn't matter if they did. I would still have to become celibate. Without that, all they could offer me would be a lifetime of apprenticeship." He wasn't even sure if *that* was possible.

"Truly?" The hound tilted his body, peering around Dylan to address the woman, his face ashen. "None of you have sex? At all? But..." He clutched dramatically at his chest as though he was going to collapse. "The very thought makes me weak. How do you cope?"

The hedgewitch pressed her lips together, vainly trying to hide her amusement. She folded her arms. "It helps if you've no desire to in the first place, but it's a requirement of the coven that our lives be dedicated to preserving history, of learning from the little that remains of our ancestors and ensuring it does not fade further. Those who are willing to partake in the search of such knowledge are always welcome, but it must be done with the whole self. Having a lover or children is seen as a distraction. And speaking of such..." She prodded the hound's shoulder with the butt of the unlit torch she had crafted last night. "Don't go distracting my assistant, Master Tracker. He needs his mind on the task at hand."

Tracker thrust out his jaw, his bottom lip briefly quivering. "You truly know how to sap all the fun out of this little delay, my dear woman."

Katarina's brow twitched, causing the scar on her face to dance. Folding her arms, she glared down at the man.

The hound's nose wrinkled briefly, then he flashed the woman a wide smile. "But you parade him around like some delectable treat and I cannot have even the slightest nibble? What did I do to be subjected to such cruelty, my dear?"

A small chuckle curved her lips. "All I ask is for you to curb..." She indicated them with a twirl of her finger. "...whatever *this* is until later." She hoisted her supply of tools and writing equipment. "Shall we?"

Tracker's gaze silently slid his way. Those honey-coloured eyes swept over him, visibly drinking him in.

Dylan felt his face growing steadily warmer. He took up the unlit torch. The scrap of cloth wrapped around the end had gotten damp on the journey here. Drawing the water out was an easy enough task. As was igniting it.

The hound's focus snapped back to Katarina as Dylan handed the torch back. "By all means, my dear hedgewitch. Lead on."

The tunnel seemed shorter than yesterday's venture. Katarina held the torch high above her, the flames licking the ceiling, and she went ahead. It threw shadows of elongated bodies and twisted limbs, but the warm glow carried an odd comfort. Like the firm grip of Tracker's hand in his.

Even with foreknowledge of what awaited at the tunnel's end, Dylan still shivered when the forge's heat hit his face. He loosened his grip on the hound. There was no chance he could do any sort of work whilst the man clung so tightly.

Tracker's fingers briefly tightened their hold before he let go. "What would you have me do, dear woman?"

"Sit there." She pointed to the left side of the channel, where several hulking masses of solid metal squatted between the river of molten rock and the wall. "And stay quiet."

He gave the woman a low bow and, with a reluctant glance Dylan's way, silently departed from their side.

Katarina fished out her tools from her pouch. "Be sure to note down everything as you see it," she said, handing Dylan a handful of parchment leaves she had torn from her book. A thin, black stick wrapped in rope was also pushed into his hands.

Dylan examined the stick. It looked rather like the implements guardians gave the children who were first learning to write. From what he remembered of back then, it made for less mess than an overturned inkpot—and thus, less work for the laundry—but a lot of work scrubbing in the tub. Fortunate that they were forced to travel through the pool when they were done.

The hedgewitch pointed a stern finger at him. "Understand, I want *no* attempts at dissertations or theories. Try to copy the runes as they are, if you're capable. Trace over them if you can't. But I want a completely untouched view of this place."

From his perch on one of the metal chunks, Tracker laughed. "I do not fancy your chances of getting an unadulterated view on anything from him. There is quite the wicked mind hidden in that angelic body."

Dylan steadfastly refused to acknowledge the heat blazing across his face.

"Get off that!" Katarina snapped at the man. "Those anvils have been here longer than your ancestors. And I believe I told you not to say a word. Any more attempts to distract either of us and I will personally carry you back to camp."

Tracker hopped off the anvil and flashed a salute. "As you command, my dear hedgewitch. I will remain silent from now on."

Smiling, Dylan moved on to the first rune-etched wall. He positioned a little ball of light over his shoulder to see better and began sketching out the first line. The markings were curiously laid out. Some were fainter, like afterthoughts or suggestions. It would make quite the muddle to translate. That would be someone else's task once Katarina returned to Dvärghem. *A shame.* He would've loved trying to untangle the centuries.

"Ah, my dear woman," Tracker said. The man had moved to crouch beside the thick stone bench that ran the length of the back wall. "I do not mean to disturb you, but it appears one of your ancestors did not leave this place."

"Where?" Katarina demanded, hurrying to the hound's side. She gasped and clutched tighter to her torch.

Dylan tilted his body back, trying to line himself up with their gaze. From where he stood by the entrance, the anvils blocked the way. Rounding them gave him a clearer view of the bench.

In the shadows, tucked away in the far corner, sat the bony remnants of a person.

"Remains," the hedgewitch breathed. "We hardly ever find remains. And never this well preserved." She knelt by the skeleton, her torch deepening the shadows. In that light, the partial preservation of more than a few scraps of cloth became apparent. Skin, paper-dry and just as frail, clung equally to limbs and ribs. It had peeled from the skull's face, but a patch of dark hair still adorned one side.

"Who were you?" Katarina whispered.

The hollow sockets of a skull glared back at them. Wordless accusations seemed set to pour from the partially open jaws.

"Whoever they might have been," Tracker said. "They were also slain. Or at least gravely injured."

The hedgewitch nodded. Already, she was back to scribbling furiously in her book, glancing up from the page to the skeleton and back.

"You can tell that from a pile of bones?" Dylan asked.

The hound grinned. "True, the state is a little more advanced than how I usually find victims, but the clues are more or less the same. The way the spine is twisted, for instance. The hips are facing completely the wrong way to the ribs. And, of course, there is the fact of where they are. No one crawls beneath a bench to carve the walls for fun."

"You don't expect me to believe you deduced that from bones and fragments of cloth."

"Well, there is also the fact they have a chisel in their hand." The hound nodded at the skeleton's right side. The dried and cracked wooden handle of a chisel lay in the tattered remains of a leather glove.

"And the clothing suggests first century," Katarina added. "Or maybe just before the new era. There was a lot of infighting during that period. So many tribes with so little space."

The new era had been nineteen hundred years ago, marked by the elven arrival. *And of the wars between empires.* So many kingdoms spending centuries fighting for freedom against the Domian Empire. In the meantime, the hedgewitches had been captured. Eradicated. The dwarven tribes left leaderless.

Kneeling, Dylan turned his attention to the nearby wall. If he was going to die, what would *he* carve? Something important? Something worth his life's blood. Something only his kin would know?

There was a set of runes that had the look of being scratched into the stone with some urgency. Numbers had been carved beneath each word. *A formula?* But for what?

He traced the markings with a forefinger. *Svavel...* That one was easy. Brimstone. The next rune had a few cracks running through it, but he could make out *kol* at the end. A few possibilities there. The last one though...

"*Salpeter?*" he whispered under his breath, letting the word roll across his tongue. He'd never heard of it before. Had the dwarves also been experimenting in here?

He frowned at the name. *Sulin would know.* Alchemists were taught to handle more than just *infitialis*. They studied various formulas, especially if the outcome was unknown and, therefore, possibly dangerous, and attempted to replicate them. Sulin would've loved the chance to attempt something so old.

Grief squeezed his chest. He recalled aiding his friend with a strange recipe the hedgewitches had brought to the tower, which had turned out to be incomplete. *Never again.*

He searched the rest of the wall, looking for signs of similar hastily carved markings. Nothing near the dwarven remains suggested anything to do with this formula. "Does this have any meaning to you?" he asked Katarina, tapping the runes.

The hedgewitch squinted at the rock, frowning, before shaking her head. "I wish I did." She bowed her head. "Hopefully, someone in the Coven will."

"Whatever it means," Tracker said. "They clearly thought it of some import."

Nodding, Katarina got to her feet. "We can't afford to linger on this. There is a lot more to catalogue before the day's done."

They continued their work in silence, the hedgewitch returning to the far side of the cavern and he back to the entrance to resume his sketches.

The feeling of being watched crept up his spine. His gaze slid to where the skull continued to stare blankly at the world. Dylan shook his head. *Foolishness.* People didn't come back from the dead and bones certainly held nothing more than the chemicals they were comprised of. Even if they did, they were here to observe and catalogue, not disturb.

But the watched feeling didn't ebb.

He glanced over his shoulder, instinctively searching for Tracker, and found the man had returned to sit before one of the anvils with his head propped on a hand and his eyes trained on Dylan.

"Are you still all right?" Dylan asked.

A small smile, mirthless and watery, brushed the hound's lips. "I am fine." He flapped his free hand at Dylan. "Go back to helping our dear hedgewitch before she scolds you."

He returned his focus to the wall carvings. That watched sensation persisted, but it no longer carried a sinister air.

With no outside light reaching this deep, the time spent was impossible to tell. They travelled from one corner of a wall to the other, then began anew at the next, ensuring each section was thoroughly covered whilst also reaffirming each other's finds.

By the time Tracker suggested they leave, Dylan's stomach had already given the occasional query for food, its grumbling loud in the otherwise quiet.

He couldn't leave yet, though. There was one thing he wanted to do before they left this place in peace. Something he couldn't put into words. "You go," he insisted to the man. "I'll be along shortly." He settled against the wall near the tunnel, shuffling along the floor until he'd a decent view of the room.

He hummed softly to himself as he worked. The black nib of his writing stick glided over the parchment, creating the illusion of shadows and light where there had once been nothing but blankness. In swift strokes, he sketched the forge, the anvils, the bench and even the long-since-passed dwarf.

The faint puff of another's breath warmed his shoulder. "I had no idea you could draw," Tracker said, squatting next to him. "Why did you not tell me?"

Frowning, he continued to sketch. "Why would you have needed to know?" It wasn't magic or even a skill the tower taught beyond childhood, just the product of bored doodles refined by years of practice.

"Well, I suppose you have a point there. Still, I..." He fell silent.

Dylan lowered the page, turning around.

"No, no." The hound leapt to his feet, his hands raised before him. "Do not stop on my account. I will be waiting by the waterfall."

"Are you all right to travel through the tunnel on your own?" Every time they'd gone from one end to the other, the man had kept a vice-like grip on Dylan's hand.

"He'll be fine," Katarina said, holding her torch aloft. "I'll be with him." She threw an arm around the hound's shoulders and hugged him tight. "You'll be just as safe with me. Maybe you can tell me why you dislike tunnels so much whilst we wait for Dylan?"

"The reasons are rather personal," Tracker said as they started walking down the tunnel. "I would prefer not to."

"Fair enough." The hedgewitch's voice echoed the further they went and Dylan's ears strained to make out the words. "There are other things I'd like to discuss regarding..." Their conversation gradually became little more than garbled mutters, then faded completely.

He turned his full attention to the sketch, touching up the details until he could refine it no more with the tools at hand. Stashing it between two pieces of unused pages, he stood and gave the cavern one last look before trotting down the tunnel after the others.

Leaving the cave was far simpler than entering had been, especially on the fourth pass through the gap in the waterfall. Katarina went first, one hand holding the pouch stuffed with papers high above the surface of the water. Tracker was next, swimming backwards to help guide Dylan through, then closely at his side until they reached the shore.

Marin had caught more fish whilst the rest of them poked around the ancient forge. He knew that only by the smell of the catch cooking as they neared the fire, the aroma tempered by what he hoped was actually waterfowl.

His stomach gave a more demanding grumble about being empty.

Chuckling, Tracker gave his back a good-natured slap, the wet connection cracking across the pool. "Let us both get dry and dressed before we settle in for a well-earned meal, yes?"

With his cheeks still warming, he followed the hound into their tent. After spending the day in little but his smallclothes, he welcomed the idea of snuggling into the soft fabric of his robe.

They aided each other in drying off via the mundane method, although the cloth at hand wasn't anywhere near as effective as those Dylan was used to in the tower. Fortunately, the task was further helped along by the air inside the tent growing warmer as Dylan used a little magic to dry their undergarments.

Having flung on all but the outer layer of his clothes, Dylan exited the tent to find the hedgewitch had already settled by the fire. She rifled through their work, mumbling to herself whilst rearranging the loose pages.

Marin handed him a bowl as they joined the pair. "I downed this one not long after you all left, so it should be nice and tender." She offered another bowl to Tracker, but the hound refused, opting for one of the fish cooking atop the flames.

With brief thanks, Dylan fell upon his food, shovelling in spoonfuls of what his mouth told him was indeed duck amongst the greenery and cubes of mushroom. True to her word, the meat barely required chewing.

Once his belly was content, he took up the task of drying the hound's hair. Yesterday, Marin had teased him about it, suggesting he could set himself up in a barber's shop. He had no idea what she spoke of, but laughed along with her all the same.

Katarina reached his section of their records, pausing to admire his sketch of the cavern, before stowing everything back into the pouch. "This wasn't too big of a disaster."

Dylan glanced up from the mass of damp russet hair. "You thought it would be?"

She gave a small, uncertain chuckle. "A little," she confessed. "I've never worked with a non-Dvärg before. It's rare we find those outside of my homeland with such a respect for our people, but you've been most helpful. I'd almost suggest coming with me and taking up an apprenticeship. There are plenty of hedgewitches who would be eager to expand your rudimentary knowledge, except..." Her gaze drifted to Tracker. "Well—"

It would be illegal. To head anywhere except towards Wintervale wouldn't only be against the creed of the King's Hounds, it would affect the treaty.

Snuffing the heat radiating from his hands, Dylan withdrew his fingers from the hound's hair and let Tracker work on returning the thick curls to a single braid.

"But Dylan could become an apprentice of your Coven?" Marin asked. "Even though he isn't a dwarf?"

Katarina nodded. "For someone not trained under the Coven's order, he has so much knowledge."

He shrugged. Between helping the hedgewitches and spending much of his time in the library... "There wasn't much else to do but learn." Some preferred to while the hours out in the garden or tinker with individual overseer-approved tasks. "It kept me busy." Useful.

"If we were in Dvärghem, he'd already be on his way through an apprenticeship." She tugged at her belt ties, carefully avoiding the hound's gaze. "Even now, if given the right master, he could become such an asset to our studies. He could even attain full hedgewitch status if he forsook intimacy."

Tracker paused in braiding his hair, his fingers still tangled in the coils. He frowned as the women continued to chatter, but said nothing. Instead, his gaze drifted to the waterfall.

Dylan laid a hand on the man's shoulder. "Is something wrong?"

His gaze lifted from the water. "Not at all." He flipped the finished end of his braid back over his shoulder and stood, offering his hand. "Come, there is something I would like to show you."

CHAPTER 41

Tracker leant back on the grass, uncaring that his feet weren't far from the cliff edge. They sat near the top of the waterfall, far enough from the water that the mist wouldn't dampen their clothes. Up here, the largely northward passage of the stream feeding the waterfall was more pronounced, which meant it eventually met up with the King's Winding somewhere further downstream.

Dylan knelt next to him, currently invested in the view their high vantage point offered. When he had climbed up here last night, most of the river was sheathed in shadows. Now, the moonlight had it running through the darkness like a silver ribbon.

Tracker had found an old route leading to this spot whilst patrolling. Had he known of it sooner, he would've brought Dylan here instead of trying to speak with the man in the cavern beneath them.

Katarina and Marin remained below, tending to the fire. The pair appeared to be talking, most likely about the body they had uncovered in the forge. Whatever their conversation happened to be about, their voices were drowned out by distance and the constant hiss of the falls.

The same would be true of their ability to hear Dylan and himself up here.

With their perch peeking over all but the highest trees, the air was crisp enough to have him idly wishing for a little alcohol to help warm the senses. Although, given how Dylan reacted the last time such a substance touched the man's lips, it was perhaps for the best that they'd only water on hand.

Tracker frowned, thinking back to that night, of the broken tremor in Dylan's voice. The sheer dejected acceptance of a fate he thought immutable. Such a tone hadn't touched the man's lips since. Somehow, that made it worse.

The spellster abruptly tapped his arm and pointed into the distance. "What are those lights?"

He followed the man's finger. The glow of caravans moving in the dark lit up patches of the surrounding forest, easily spotted by human sight, yet what Dylan appeared to have singled out stood still. "*That is Riverton.*" He hadn't travelled this way for years, preferring to keep his distance from the capital, but it was the only settlement for miles around.

"It's so faint. How long will it take us to reach?"

"Not long." Less than a handful of days. Although, with the road so unusually crowded, it could take longer.

Humming thoughtfully, Dylan rested his chin upon Tracker's shoulder.

Strands of the man's loose hair tickled his ear, sending a pleasurable shiver straight to his groin. Biting his lip, Tracker repressed the groan threatening to tighten his throat.

If the man noticed, he made no move to rectify the touch. "Do you think they'll have any boats?"

Inhaling, Tracker managed a tight, "Perhaps." After Whitemeadow, he didn't dare put his hopes on finding a boat capable of making the crossing. He only needed one but, failing that, there was always the ford.

"And where's Wintervale? Are we close enough to see it?"

"See? No." Even with the castle cresting the cliff entrance of the river, he wouldn't have spotted the capital in good weather during the day. "But it is that way." He flapped a hand vaguely in the relevant direction. On foot, it would be at least another week.

Dylan turned his head, following the motion. The hot blast of the man's disappointed sigh ghosted along Tracker's ear.

He couldn't help the moan that broke through his lips.

"Sorry," Dylan murmured, not looking the least bit apologetic.

Tracker clicked his tongue reprovingly and the man's cheeks at least had the good grace to redden. Twisting to face Dylan, he cupped the man's jaw. Their lips met in slow, delicate brushes. He maintained that pace, relishing in each sweep and the soft noises it eked from the spellster.

Dylan toyed with Tracker's belt buckle, slowly undoing it.

He linked their fingers before the spellster could go any further. "My, my," he purred, grinning as the man's blush deepened. "We are certainly eager tonight." He brought Dylan's hand up to his lips, kissing the heel. "You know, sex was not the reason I brought you here." Besides, his vial pouch was still down at their camp, sitting alongside his scimitar and daggers. Although, there were other means to the same end that didn't require oil.

"I gathered." The man straddled Tracker's hips and, as Dylan sat back, Tracker felt himself responding to the weight quite a bit faster than expected. "It's just, lately, I get the feeling you're waiting for *me* to make the first move, to be more—I don't know—forward?"

That was partially true. Since the events in Whitemeadow, they hadn't engaged in anything more intimate than snuggling in search of warmth and as a shield against each other's bad dreams. "And I am to believe *this* is your move?" A sweetly innocent caress. Gentle and that little bit unsure, much like the first time they had kissed.

"Is it all right? You seemed to enjoy me taking command in Whitemeadow."

Chuckling, he walked his fingers up the spellster's chest. "I did." Why wouldn't he have? Watching Dylan confidently go after what he wanted had been a captivating sight. "However," he murmured, ghosting his hand up one side of the man's neck. "My dear sweet man, all I have ever desired is for you to just be you. If you wish to be more direct..." He softly traced the rounded outer curve of Dylan's ear, smiling as the spellster leant into the touch. "I am no stranger to heeding another's requests, nor am I averse to the idea."

Dylan shifted his hips. The fabric between them did little to hide the bulge in the man's trousers. "And yet, I don't see you getting any more naked."

Tracker wordlessly tugged at the man's belt, tucking his thumbs beneath the leather. When no objection was made, he slid to the buckle, undoing it, before roaming to the robe ties. Whilst the spellster hadn't fully dressed, two layers stood between him and bare skin.

He undid both, opening each one until they draped like wings on either side of the man. Pale skin greeted him, warm and responsive to his every touch. "I must admit," he purred, grinning as the flesh beneath his fingertips pebbled. "Today has been quite the exercise in restraint, especially with you teasing me all day."

"Me?" Dylan leant close, draping his arms atop Tracker's shoulders. "If I recall correctly," he breathed into Tracker's ear. "*You* were the one doing the teasing."

Groaning, he buried his face into Dylan's neck. Even after their swim across the pool, the spellster's skin still bore the hot metallic tang of the forge. The scent mingled with the man's storm-cloud aroma. "If you are not going to behave, I *will* find other uses for your mouth."

His ear was further warmed by Dylan's soft laughter.

Then the warm wetness of the man's tongue snaked between Tracker's earrings, adding to the pressing interest in his trousers.

Tracker trembled, barely able to keep his thoughts grounded. Digging his fingers into the robe's loose folds helped. Not by much.

He grabbed the spellster's rear. Each buttock fit nicely within his grasp, moulding as he rocked Dylan atop him. The fabric strained in his grip, threatening to rip right off the man's body.

Before too long, the spellster's hot breath turned to pants. He arched atop Tracker, his head tipping to one side and baring his scarred throat to the sky.

"Perhaps, restrain ourselves this time?" As ego-boosting as the man's reaction in Whitemeadow had been, the unfettered magic was far stronger than anything Dylan did knowingly and quite the beacon for those who could sense it. He didn't want to find out if any more of his former comrades were close.

Scoffing, Dylan shoved at his chest.

Tracker complied, flopping back onto the grass. With only his undershirt on, the individual blades made themselves known through the linen. He would've suffered ones of steel to bask in the vision above him.

The way the tautness in Dylan's body slowly melted as he rocked. The feral curl of his fingers gripping Tracker's clothes, willing to claw their way through flesh if it would sate their craving. The futile bite of his teeth that did nothing to muffle his pleasure.

His heart thrummed, desire and more mingling in a passionate beat.

He lifted himself up, bracing his weight with an arm. It left a single hand to roam, but he made it count by exploring every inch his mouth couldn't reach. With a little coaxing, he drew Dylan's lips close, their tongues duelling as their hips slowly found an agreeable rhythm.

Dylan pulled back for a beat, his brow creasing. "How did you get back up here?"

"You should know by now that I am very flexible." He ran a finger up Dylan's spine as he spoke, silently revelling in how well the man's body arched to gift him the perfect canvas to lay his lips upon. He ran kisses from clavicle to nipple with Dylan's rasping breath filling his ears.

His tongue had barely graced the taut nub of skin before it was drawn out of reach.

"You do not like it?"

"It feels…" Dylan bowed, his hair falling forward to cover his face. "…strange."

Tracker tilted his head, trying to see the spellster's expression. The combination of elven sight and moonlight helped him to see much more of the man than Dylan could of himself, but the shadows were no less harsh. "Given that you have used such a phrase to describe what you clearly now enjoy, I will need you to clarify further."

"It tickled."

A wisp of amusement tugged at his lips. Was that all? He drew

Dylan closer. "I can be firmer."

"I..." He went rigid in Tracker's grasp. It was for no more than a heartbeat, but that was long enough. "If that's what you—"

"Dylan," he purred. "If you do not desire it, you only have to say so." His free hand meandered from the man's rear to toy with the ties of his smallclothes. "I am certain I can find other places to rest my tongue."

"You can't actually reach further down sitting like this."

"It depends on how motivated I am." He didn't do it often in this particular position, but after the tricks Dylan had shown him back in Whitemeadow, he was extremely eager to repay that bliss. "And it would help immensely if you were fully naked. The question is..." He bent further, planting a kiss squarely in the middle of Dylan's abdomen. "Do you want me to?"

The skin beneath Tracker's lips shifted as Dylan laughed. "Is that a serious question?"

Tracker wordlessly lowered himself, using his teeth and tongue to undo the ties. With them loose, a little tugging on the waistband was all it took to release Dylan into the night air. Free, the man's erection swayed before him, already leaking. He lapped up every drop to the blissful sound that was Dylan's pleasure-soaked sigh.

"Track," Dylan moaned breathlessly, his shaking fingers alighting on Tracker's shoulder. His weight shifted in Tracker's grasp, tilting back.

Glancing up revealed the spellster's head tipping to one side, trying to watch. The shoulder supporting the man trembled, but he seemed stable enough.

He lowered his head, gently kissing the tip before taking the man into his mouth. Dylan's hips shifted, slowly at first, but soon he was down Tracker's throat.

Tracker let the spellster continue at his own speed, relishing both the soft grunts that came with each thrust and the breathless moans as he slid back out. Sounds he rarely heard when they shared a tent. His own erection strained against its confinement, steadily growing slicker the more Dylan shifted atop him.

Then, with a strangled curse, the man collapsed onto his back. One knee came up, grazing Tracker's chin before he could fully evade it, closing his jaw with a solid click.

"Sorry," Dylan blurted. "My arm gave. I didn't—"

Chuckling, Tracker rubbed at his jaw. "I am fine," he assured the man. "I promise." It hadn't hit hard, but it had been unexpected. Fortunately for the both of them, Dylan's inertia had him slipping free of Tracker's mouth before the man's knee connected.

Dylan clapped his hands over his face.

"However…" Tracker slid out from beneath the spellster, allowing Dylan to properly lie back. "I think it would be safer for everyone if you to remain on the ground." He fully stripped the man from the waist down, gifting him uninhibited access. "At least, for the moment." Sitting back, he paused to admire the figure sprawled before him.

This was the first time he had truly taken in the sight. During their night in the tower, he'd been far too involved with keeping the man distracted to savour. Even then, the torch had flooded the room in brassy light. There'd been the candlelit nights at Whitemeadow, but there'd been no moment to slow down. And the times they'd shared between were all hasty, almost shameful, fumbles in the gloom.

But the way the moonlight illuminated the man's skin, an ethereal glow that would've had him believe Dylan was a figure of stone if not for the man's heavy breaths. The wisps of unformed magic drifting around him, the thrum of need vibrating through his every muscle…

"You are so beautiful," he murmured, sliding his fingers into the dark hair running down the man's abdomen.

The flesh under his fingertips lurched as Dylan snorted. "Beautiful?" A soft, uncertain chuckle slipped out his lips.

"You do not think this is true?" How could the man remain completely ignorant of it?

The spellster shook his head. "I look average at best."

Tracker clicked his tongue in disapproval. "Whoever instilled that lie was doing you a great disservice. I have a lot of experience regarding beauty, you know?"

"Of course you do," Dylan quipped. "You're gorgeous."

So he had heard. "And *you* are a sculptor's dream."

Even the moonlight couldn't wash out the pink dusting itself upon the man's cheeks. "Wh-what?"

"The shape of your face." He traced the man's jaw with a forefinger. "The curve of your mouth." He ghosted the pad of his thumb over Dylan's lips, ignoring the twitch of interest from within his trousers. "Even your eyes match the proportions I have seen on many statues."

If he had thought Dylan had blushed before, it was nothing compared to the full bloom now adorning his face. That only added to the masterpiece. "But I'm naked and sweaty and—"

"True," he purred, letting his touch meander down the man's bare chest. Technically, Dylan still wore his robes, even if much of the fabric now lay beneath him. "But as the one who got you into such a state, do you think that matters?" His fingers wrapped around the spellster's shaft, stroking to the accompaniment of the man's moans.

"Please," Dylan breathed, tipping his head back. "Gods, *please*." The desire trembling through that final word almost became Tracker's undoing.

Tracker inhaled deeply of the night air, letting the coolness temper his inner fire as he stripped off his undershirt. If he didn't keep his wits about him, he'd wind up taking the man where he lay, oil or no.

Bending over the spellster, he continued his languid strokes as he whispered into the man's ear, "Am I going too slow for your liking?"

Dylan grabbed the waist of Tracker's trousers, seeking to drag them off. Even with the ties undone, they slid no further than a few inches. "These should be gone by now," he growled.

"In time," Tracker promised, tugging the waistband back up and repositioning himself. "But first, permit me to finish what I started." He took Dylan back into his mouth, angling to gift him the very view he had been attempting whilst in Tracker's lap.

The spellster's fingers slid along the nape of Tracker's neck before entwining themselves into his braid, their minute twitches guiding him. Vestiges of magic drifted off the digits, humming as they wove through his hair. He moaned as the ghostly passage of one such thread slid behind his ear.

Dylan's answering groan only added to the fire. Just like the man's pleas and prayers.

The impending pressure of a building storm was all the warning he had before Dylan cried out and emptied himself down Tracker's throat. He swallowed it all, adjusting his position so his tongue could work against the underside of the spellster's length to ensure he got every drop.

Only with the spellster spent, did Tracker finally release him.

"*That*," Dylan managed between pants, "wasn't fair."

"No?" He ran his tongue along the man's softening length. "Was a night ending in sex not your goal?"

"Well..." The man grinned. "Yes, obviously. I just thought you'd— I *wanted* you inside me."

Tracker smiled at hearing the spellster speak so frankly about his desires. He would've been a blushing, denying mess none too long ago.

"And I wouldn't class what we just did as sex."

"Oh?" He sat up and gestured to their half-naked states, mostly naked in the spellster's case. "What does your body tell you happened?"

Dylan giggled, the colour in his cheeks deepening. "That doesn't count."

"*Really?*" He had met some who considered oral as purely foreplay, but they all agreed it was a sexual act. All those times he'd been paid for doing precisely so with others. "So when I asked if I was your first phallic venture, you meant only in terms of penetration, yes?" Had the man always been on the receiving end, or had those lips taken others in? Had Tracker assumed inexperience where there'd been plenty?

"It doesn't mean that at all." Dylan's fingers worked at the waistband of Tracker's clothing as he talked, tugging down his trousers and undoing the ties to his smallclothes. "I simply don't see it as sex when the ending is one-sided." Having failed to further lower Tracker's clothing, the man settled on palming the erection through the layers.

"I see." He grasped Dylan's wrist and carefully withdrew the hand. "Having us both finish is not a requirement." It hadn't even been a constant state within *The Gilded Lily*. But then, they were expected to ensure their customers' needs were fulfilled before thinking about themselves, even if that meant actual restraints. He might not have been there for more than a few years, but holding back until all parties were satisfied had ingrained itself nevertheless.

"Don't I know it," Dylan grumbled. "I'd quite a number of attempts in the tower end that way more times than I would've liked, but that was because we were almost caught. I don't want it to be like that between us."

"If you are worried about leaving me unsatisfied, I am perfectly content." Still, the notion that it bothered the man stirred a fluttering warmth in his chest. So many of his previous bed partners—including many of those he had lain with outside of the brothel—had only been concerned with ensuring their own pleasure. He would always deliver. He aimed for it. Prided himself on it.

Dylan cupped the nape of Tracker's neck with his free hand, tilting him closer. "And if the roles were reversed, don't tell me you wouldn't insist." His hand slid higher, thumb and forefinger gliding up either side of Tracker's ear.

Tracker bowed his head, biting his lip to keep from moaning. His hips rocked ever so slightly, rubbing himself on Dylan's abdomen. Of course he wouldn't have left the man wanting, but that was different. "I take it," he managed, his voice husky, "this is *you* insisting?"

"Yes."

Grasping the man's forearm, Tracker slowly drawing those soft fingers away from his ear. He needed a moment to centre himself, to at least strip. His smallclothes were damp enough without adding to the problem.

Clambering off Dylan, he began divesting himself of his remaining attire.

"Track?" The man's voice came softly, a breath below a whisper.

Designed only for a close ear and no more.

He hummed a questioning note as he pulled off his trousers, curious as to what had caught Dylan's attention so thoroughly that he would seek out answers now.

"What you did when I was in your lap just now..." The man cleared his throat, his focus darting from the growing pile of discarded clothing back to Tracker's face. "You did something similar during our second time together. Was that one of the tricks you learnt in *The Gilded Lily?*"

Laughter bubbled up his throat. He should've known the man would eventually ask such questions. "It was certainly a favourite, but actually, that one I discovered before I was sent there."

"Discover?" the man echoed, disbelief thickly coating the word. "How does someone just *discover* they can do that?"

"I cannot say for others, but for me, it was a combination of horny adolescence and a lack of funds for a brothel visit." He peeled off his smallclothes and tossed them aside. "I paid for a session by dancing and fellating myself before their patrons." Unbeknown to that much younger self, that day would become one of many times such talent was called upon.

"You... you can do it to yourself?"

Tracker clicked his tongue in mock admonishment. "Do you not remember me saying I am flexible?" He straddled the man's waist. "Do you wish to see?"

Dylan's dark gaze flicked from his face to Tracker's groin, then back up. His tongue peeked out to run along those delectable lips. Was the man considering taking the position instead?

His erection twitched at the thought. He dragged his hand up his thigh, surprised to find Dylan already held both legs in a vice grip.

With a lack of an answer forthcoming either way, he lowered his head, slowly bringing his mouth down upon himself. Unlike with the spellster, no saltiness greeted his tongue, and all the teasing left him far slicker than normal. That only meant this would be a short exhibition.

The hold Dylan had on his thighs only tightened, balancing on the edge of pain. "Gods," he whispered.

Tracker closed his eyes and started in earnest, imagining the sensation wasn't his own mouth, but that of the spellster's. The rasp of his tongue, the rhythmic bob of his head, the soft vibration of his unabashed moans.

It was *not* his cleanest display. He'd never been this slick at the start. Combined with his saliva and the quickening fire racing through his blood, he was definitely leaving a puddle on the spellster's belly.

His orgasm hit and he emptied himself down his throat, straightening only once the final drop passed his lips. His now softening length unceremoniously flopped onto the pool he had created. He didn't care. His focus had been utterly stolen by the spellster's face.

Dylan stared up at him, his jaw hanging open to its fullest. Such absolute awe filled his eyes. "*Track...*" he rasped, his voice heavy.

With the taste of himself still thick on his tongue, he crawled up that pale body to claim the very lips that had begged and praised him not so long ago, swallowing the man's moans as he delved between them. He toyed with the spellster's tongue, exploring as they shared breath, softly coaxing Dylan to follow until the man was exploring *his* mouth.

After a moment that seemed far too soon, Tracker broke the kiss. He propped himself on an outstretched arm, breathless and grinning. "So," he purred, his free hand tracing the curve of Dylan's ear. "Do I taste as sweet as you envisioned?" The man had compared him to flat cakes, after all. Ones smothered in sticky sweet syrup.

Dylan frowned at him for a moment before his eyes widened in comprehension. "Gods," he groaned, slapping a hand over his face.

"I only ask because, if you do not mind the taste, I can think of a few things we can do to expand our fun." No doubt, Dylan also knew what they were.

Licking his lips, those dark eyes peered out from between his fingers. The thought was *definitely* running through his mind. "I refuse to answer."

"Then I should take your actions as acquiescence instead, yes?" Tracker murmured before slanting his mouth over Dylan's.

The man allowed him a moment before, laughing, he attempted to push Tracker back. "You're impossible."

Silently laughing, Tracker rolled to one side. "On the contrary," he breathed. "I think you are quite aware of how *easy* I am."

Dylan chuckled along with him briefly, then the mirth faded from his face. His brows knitted together in thought. "You said you performed it for the brothel patrons. Would you have done that for me if I had visited *The Gilded Lily* back then?"

He cocked his head, humming. "What ifs are dangerous questions to ask. I was a different man." Reckless and volatile. "But for the chance to take your virginity—"

The man sputtered and choked on several attempts at denial before coherent words left his mouth. "I was *not* a virgin the first time we had sex. I lost that years ago."

"*That?*" Tracker grinned, his mirth hissing through his teeth. "What is this? You think you only have the one to lose? You are a virgin for every new thing you try."

"That's just being inexperienced."

"Is that not what is meant by the word?" He laid a finger upon Dylan's lips to silence the man. "Come now, this is too heavy a topic for such an enchanting night."

"One more question," Dylan promised. "How did you end up there? You never actually said."

He hadn't. "Another time." He wasn't sure he could without picturing the spellster sharing the fate of those he had lost.

"It was part of your retraining, wasn't it." The words should've been a question. Instead, they were heavy with certainty. "They sent you there before you became a hound."

"Yes." It hadn't always been pleasant, and he considered himself fortunate to have prior experience with men before his first job, but the memories were far enough in his past that a haze had formed over his recollection of the time.

"Then the people who slept with you? They actually—"

Tracker cut him off. "They bought a moment of my time and skills." Not that he had ever seen a single coin of that money. He supposed it went into the mistress's coffer, be that the one who oversaw the hounds or she who managed the prostitutes.

"But the brothel sold what they had no right to."

A puff of understanding parted his lips before he could control his reaction. He could see where Dylan's line of thinking had gone. He hadn't expected the man to reach that conclusion. Yes, he had been forced into it with no option of leaving. The hound mistress had called it training the delusions out of him.

He was certain other people would've had a different name for it.

Still, Tracker grinned. "Do you think they would have cared? I was young and pretty." Very young. Too young. He didn't know what the hounds told the owners, but they had been furious upon finding out he'd been only fourteen. After that, his work in the rooms during the first year had consisted only of keeping them clean.

He had known what a brothel was like as a customer before being on the other side, but he'd given no thought to the day-to-day operation of such a business. Of how the prostitutes kept themselves fresh and clean. Or how they trained amongst each other in preparation for any request.

Perhaps they weren't all the same, but *The Gilded Lily* prided itself on having the best.

"I just..." Dylan sat upright. "I don't want you thinking I'm like them. I know you only slept with me in the tower because you were distracting me, but you don't have to say yes just because I ask. I have heard my share of nos."

Warmth wrapped its fingers around his heart and softened the edges of his smile. He truly was too sweet for words. "My dear man," he murmured, "the time when I had no say in who I shared my bed passed years ago. If I agree to your requests, it is because I want to. And why would I not? You are an attractive man."

A soft blast of denial escaped the spellster's lips as he ducked his head.

"I will not permit you to hide from this fact." Tracker cupped the man's cheek, marking the heat radiating from the pale skin. He drew Dylan's head back up. "You are smart." Academically, at least. He hadn't enough experience outside the tower to be streetwise or, Tracker guessed, had the chance to form relationships beyond friends. "Kind. Strong, in more ways than just your magic."

The cheek still resting against Tracker's palm grew hotter the more he spoke. Had no one paid the man a compliment before?

Those dark eyes surveyed him. Hooded by the night, Tracker could still imagine their gleam. Dylan drew him into a kiss.

The warmth in his core thrummed deeper, digging into his veins. *I love you.* It was all his heart could think to say, beating the same message endlessly.

No matter how his chest ached, the words shrank from his throat. Even thinking them brought up the last time they had passed his lips and the broken bodies such a phrase heralded. He tried to impose them on his tongue nevertheless, to somehow impress the words onto Dylan's.

He would make his intentions clear. If not with those words, then he would find others, offer all he could.

In Riverton.

CHAPTER 42

As reluctant as Katarina had been to leave the old forge without everything in it being properly catalogued, she led the way as they pushed on for Riverton. Not that they needed anyone to take the lead. Once they returned to the road, little changed from one day to the next. Carts and carriages continued to trundle on by. The amount of people they encountered on horseback or foot varied depending on how much they matched the others' pace.

The transport hadn't lessened the further east they'd walked, but Dylan had expected more to be travelling back by now—they had come across a handful, but nowhere near the amount that went east. He supposed even horses took a while to reach their destinations and who knew what they'd be required to lug back before passage along the river returned to normal.

With the village being so close, Dylan thought they'd encounter the same signs of a nearing settlement they had in approaching Whitemeadow and Oldmarsh. There was nothing. Not only a lack of outlying farms, but no guard posts or taverns for people to settle safely. He supposed there wasn't much call for the latter two when most things would've travelled down the river.

If it wasn't for the fact he had seen the lights whilst atop the waterfall, Dylan would've wondered if Riverton even existed.

But he'd a feeling they wouldn't be travelling for much longer. The current section of road seemed to veer northward, edging closer to the river, close enough to be cloaked in a mist that even the midmorning sun struggled to cut through.

Ahead of him, Katarina picked up the pace, drawing Marin along with her.

Dylan squinted, trying to will the haze ahead to dissipate. The hint of large shapes slowly formed the closer they got. They didn't look big enough to be buildings, but perhaps the mist played with the size as well as the distance. He hadn't expected to come across the fishing village so early in the day. They must've been almost on top of it last night.

The mist's thickness had lessened by the time they reached the village gates. It fell away like curtains, revealing a mass of tents surrounding the western side of Riverton. Almost enough to be another village in its own right.

Quite a number of carts and carriages sat amongst the temporary housing. He recognised a few from the previous days, carts he'd seen trundle ahead of them days ago. They all seemed to be collecting here as though they planned to stay permanently.

He lengthened his stride to catch up with the women, slowing only when it became clear that Tracker wasn't in any hurry. "What is it?" The man eyed their destination like the Seven Sisters awaited him.

"*That.*" He indicated the tents with a thrust of his chin. "If such a congregation signifies what I think it does, then we will have a hard time getting what we require today." He trotted towards the women. "Come, we best let them know."

Dylan's gaze lifted to the actual village. Although he had expected Riverton to take up less space along the river than the much bigger Whitemeadow, he hadn't expected the settlement to be perched on an island. Another river wound down from the north, creating a fork in the King's Winding directly opposite the village.

The other two had stopped on the edge of the tents, waiting for them. They remained silent as they strode by colourful pavilions and hastily made stalls. A great drone of noise filled his ears, the murmur of sales being made and hawkers calling out to potential customers.

Tracker urged them on. They moved with the crowd winding a path amongst the carts, pressing ever closer to the village.

Like the other settlements, entry was regulated via a gate. The open outer archway funnelled people across a bridge broad enough for a single cart. The bridge led visitors to a walled section of land where guards directed carts into curved bays for inspection, whilst the rest moved on.

A guardhouse straddled the only way into the village. The top of the archway bore the metal teeth of a portcullis. Other guards stood on either side of the entrance. They didn't stop anyone, but Dylan felt their gazes as their group entered Riverton.

The entrance poured everyone directly into the market square. Most of the buildings—many of them two and three stories—crowded around the spot. The exception was a gap that led to the docks. Small boats dotted the water. All of them seemed to be fishing vessels with their nets draped over the sides. No sign of anything bigger. Certainly not enough to warrant this many people camped on their doorstep.

Even without taking into account the dozens of people at their backs, the village looked far livelier than Tracker's stories had led him to believe. People milled around, hanging pennants and garlands around their stalls. There appeared to be some sort of platform closer to the river and several men were erecting an awning over it.

"What's all this?" Dylan asked, the words escaping his lips in a hushed tone. The people were clearly celebrating, but it wasn't the right time of the year for any of the festivities Dylan knew.

"I believe this is their founding festival," Tracker said, sighing. "I knew it was around this time, but I had hoped not to get caught up in it. Come." He jerked his head towards one of the few two-level buildings. There were no words on the sign hanging above the door, just a picture of a broken fishing rod. "I do not fancy our chances, but perhaps they will have room for us."

"Why do we need to rent a room?" Marin muttered, eyeing the stalls as though she suspected them to disappear. "It's still early enough. We could get supplies and be well away from here before sunset."

"A bed *would* be nice," Katarina said, a little wistful.

Dylan nodded in agreement. Especially if that bed also happened to have a certain man beneath its sheets.

"My dear," Tracker said. "The people of Riverton do not trade with outsiders during the founding festival. *The Broken Rod* is the exception. We will have to wait until tomorrow to gather supplies."

"What about the people outside?" Marin jerked a thumb in the direction of the tents.

The hound sneered. "I would not feed those vultures. They are here only to prey on the impatient. Our goal is not going anywhere. Staying for the night will not change much." He pushed open the inn door. Sickly-sweet smoke greeted them.

Dylan squinted as they stepped into the hazy room, the air causing his eyes to water. The area seemed to take up much of the lower floor. Tables and low stools dotted the room—a large percentage of them full, even at this early hour. Most of the patrons had their noses deep in their tankards. Were they perhaps revellers from the previous night?

Tracker wove through the haphazard layout of the tables, strutting up to the bar where a single human man served the livelier customers. "Greetings, my dear man."

The bartender eyed the hound before shifting his piggish gaze to the rest of them. He was big, but slender. Not overly old either, or at least his hair clung to his scalp well. The man sniffed long and loud, then spat into a bowl sitting at his elbow. "What do you want?" The words sounded as if they had to fight their way through the man's throat.

"Charming," Marin muttered, barely loud enough for Dylan to hear.

The hound's typically easily mustered smile faltered. "You have a cook out back, yes? They prepare the food, not you?"

"Maybe I do, maybe I don't." Again, the man spat into the little bowl. "What's it to you, elfy?"

Taking a deep breath, Tracker slammed a silver coin on the counter. "I will give you this, plus another after every meal, providing I have your word that you will not personally handle my food. Now, does someone else cook?"

The bartender's expression turned that little less sour at the show of money. Dylan didn't know what sort of coin the man usually saw, but if he was to judge by the current tavern occupants, it couldn't be much. The bartender shrugged. "My sister and her wife are out back." He tipped his head to where a little half-door divided the entrance to the kitchen. "They handle all the cooking."

Tracker moved the silver coin around the counter in small circles with his forefinger. "And the serving?"

The bartender spat into the bowl again. He scratched his chin, flakes of skin drifting on the air at each scrape, and nodded at the coin. "Master Elf, you give me that at every meal, and you can have my little girl as your personal server."

Wordlessly, Tracker slid the silver coin across the counter.

The man's massive paw of a hand snatched up the money. "Bronwyn!"

A small, rosy-cheeked girl of perhaps seven years trotted out from the kitchen. She scooted behind the bar, all but the top of her dark-haired head disappearing from sight. "Yes, Papa?"

The bartender's face seemed to soften in the girl's presence. "I want you to serve this elf here and his friends. I'll make sure your aunties know to give them exactly what they want." With that, the man strode off into the kitchen.

The top of Bronwyn's head bobbed out of sight. "Yes, Papa." She appeared around the end of the counter and halted at Tracker's feet. Big, dark eyes lifted to survey them before settling on the hound. Fisting her apron, she cleared her throat. "Good morning, sir." Her voice changed from the sweet tone she'd used with her father, growing deeper, more adult. "How may I be of service?"

"I must admit," Tracker said. "I was expecting a child."

At the man's words, Dylan re-evaluated the girl—or rather, the woman. Although her height and face were that of a far younger person, the rest was not.

"I get that a lot," Bronwyn replied, a tight smile flattening her mouth. "Now, what can I get you?"

The rest of them left the hound to speak with Bronwyn to find a table not currently harbouring a drunken patron.

Marin shook her head and muttered, "She is *his* daughter?"

Dylan held his breath and glanced over his shoulder, but the bartender seemed to still be in the kitchen. Nevertheless, Dylan casually stepped closer to Marin and elbowed the hunter in the ribs. "Shut up," he hissed.

They settled at a table near the stairs leading up to what Dylan assumed would be their rooms for the night.

"I'm just saying," Marin said as she took up a stool opposite Dylan. "A cute thing like her—" She pulled a face. "Are we sure she's not actually a dwarf? I mean, she has the stature."

Katarina sniffed, her mouth clearly fighting a frown. The woman had dragged a stool from a nearby table and now sat at the end opposite the bar. "It is true that our oldest reports state we were shorter folk in the beginning, that the addition of human bloodlines over the years has increased our height."

Marin stretched across the table to poke Dylan's shoulder. "Told you."

"*But*," Katarina continued, shooting a glare at the other woman. "As a people, we have never been that short. Even though my ancestors were perhaps no taller than elves are now, this human myth about our shortness seems perpetual. The height difference would be, for the most part, barely noticeable that I can't begin to understand why it started."

Tracker joined them at the table, settling on the stool directly opposite Dylan. "What are we talking about?" the man asked as Bronwyn trotted up with a tray of leather tankards. The woman dispensed them with obvious practised ease and, offering a curtsy, hastened off through the kitchen door.

Dylan took a swig of beer, ready for anything with a little flavour. A sweet malty tang washed over his tongue. He shuddered and took another swallow.

Marin jerked a thumb at the hedgewitch. "Just Kat chatting about her ancestors. Did you know they were as short as you in the beginning?"

The hound hummed around his tankard. "That would not be difficult to imagine."

Dylan snorted. "He doesn't count. He's on the taller side. But I know of a woman who only stood this high." He held his hand a little below halfway up his chest. "Knew," he amended. A bitter twinge hit his gut at the thought. *Launtil.* How cruel the gods were to have her survive the gruelling trek over the mountains between Demarn and the Udynea Empire, only to be slaughtered.

"Really?" Tracker replied. There was a cheeky note to the word. "*The Gilded Lily* has a man who can orally service a vast majority of his clients whilst still on his feet. I hear he is quite popular with the local lords. Charges a fortune, too."

"I take it you couldn't afford him, then?" Marin teased, giving the hound a nudge with her shoulder.

The hound laughed. "Such cynicism, my dear hunter. What makes you think I needed money to sleep with him?"

Before Marin could reply, Bronwyn arrived bearing a tray with simple bowls of what Dylan's nose told him involved a lot of fish. He should've expected that from a fishing village. Still, his stomach rolled at the scent. Maybe venturing back into the circle of tents would reveal more palatable options.

Their serving woman smiled at Tracker as the last of the bowls were laid out. Then, with her tray tucked under an arm, she turned to Dylan. "Yours will take a little longer to make, sir. I hope you don't mind."

"Not at all." Waiting for anything that wasn't fish wouldn't exactly be troublesome.

Dylan stretched his legs out underneath the table as the others ate in silence. No sooner than he did, his boot brushed up against the toe of another. Dylan went to pull back, an apology ready to leap from his tongue, only to find his leg had been neatly hooked by the other's foot. He glanced up from his tankard.

Tracker and Marin sat on the other side. Only one would've dared. Dylan gently bumped his foot against the other's ankle and was rewarded with a slight twitch of the hound's smile. The foot bumped back.

Something had changed between them. He had felt it atop the waterfall. He hadn't given it much thought then. Or whilst they travelled. But now he'd been given time to slow down, he couldn't stop wondering what it meant.

Katarina finished her meal first. She bounced in her chair as the rest ate, her gaze darting from them to the inn's entrance. Her fingers toyed with the ties to the pouch holding her writing implements.

As the others pushed their empty bowls away, she dug into her pouches and leapt to her feet. "I'll be outside documenting if anyone needs me."

"I'll come with," Marin said, casting a side-long glance at Tracker. "See if I can't talk a few of your so-called vultures down to some reasonable prices."

"You are welcome to try, my dear," the hound said. "I have had very little luck in the past, but perhaps the lack of boats to carry off their wares might temper their greed."

Grinning, the hunter cocked her head. "That might be because you look like you have coin. Whereas I don't." Marin twirled on the spot, opening her cloak to reveal the patched leather and linen of her attire. She turned to Katarina. "Couldn't convince you to join me, could I? Maybe having someone at my back might intimidate them."

"Or our dear hedgewitch could also perhaps hold you back when someone insults her, yes?" Tracker quipped.

Marin stuck out her tongue and blew a low, flatulence-like sound. "Still think that guy deserved it." She clapped her hand onto the other woman's shoulder. "Come on."

The duo left, with Katarina spearheading their departure. There was a flash of colour from the market square as they slipped outside. People and banners, for the most part. Before he could get a proper look, the door swung shut.

"Here we are, sir," Bronwyn suddenly announced, startling Dylan. She plonked down a plate before him. "Sorry about the wait. Will that be everything?" she asked of Tracker, who wordlessly inclined his head.

Dylan could barely tear his eyes from the plate, his mouth already watering. *Flat cakes?* Three of them, their surfaces a rich golden brown and steaming. Gods, there was even a small jug of syrup and a cup of whipped cream. How had they—?

"Just eat them already," Tracker urged, laughter colouring the words. "Before you start drooling all over them."

His gaze lifted to the man. "You're responsible for this, aren't you?"

The hound rested his cheek on an upraised fist. "Well, I *did* promise them in Whitemeadow. And I will admit to feeling a little guilty that I could not deliver on that."

A groan rumbled in Dylan's throat as he took a tentative bite. The flat cakes weren't quite like the ones Tricia would bring him, but they came close. He poured the syrup out in small doses, tasting every so often—it was tarter, and more reminiscent of pears than the tower's honey-based version—before upending the cup of whisked cream over everything.

Tracker stuck out his tongue and made a soft gagging sound. "I cannot believe you are capable of eating all that. So much sweetness would make me sick."

Dylan swallowed another mouthful and smiled. "Did you manage to get us a place to sleep?"

"I have, although it may not be to everyone's liking. They had but one room left."

The idle hope of spending time alone with the hound dwindled. "As long as there's a bed," he said around a mouthful of flat cake and cream.

The way Tracker's brow creased diminished Dylan's hopes even further. The best he could probably expect was a solid roof over his head.

Music started up as he finished the last few mouthfuls. Dylan glanced around the room. There was no sign of anyone playing. "Is that coming from outside?" He rose from his seat.

"We can linger a moment more," Tracker said, placing his hand atop Dylan's. "Believe me, the music will continue for some time, but right now, we need to talk."

The starkly serious look on the man's face had Dylan lowering himself back to his seat and draining the final drops of beer from his tankard. He couldn't remember the last time those words had ever led to something good. "All right," he managed around the thorny ball of sick dread tumbling about his stomach. "About what?"

"The last night we spent in Whitemeadow..." The words trailed off as a spark of hope lit up the hound's eyes. "Has any more of that evening come to light?"

Dylan's hand tightened on the tankard. The leather beneath his fingertips was far warmer than it should've been. "No," he admitted, shrugging.

"I figured as much." He fell quiet for a moment, his tongue softly clicking. "You said things that I can no longer ignore." The hound fidgeted on his stool. "You had me make promises that I fear I cannot—"

Marin slammed her hands down on the table, jolting both of them. "What are you two doing still tucked away in here? You've eaten, haven't you?" She barely waited for Dylan to give a bewildering nod before continuing, "You've got to come outside."

Tracker shot a death glare at the woman. "My dear," he hissed through clenched teeth. "We were *talking*. You better have a good reason for your interruption."

She raised a brow at him, the corners of her mouth flattening out. Shouldn't she have been longer in dealing with the merchants? Or had Katarina convinced her not to try? "Just about everyone in the village is dancing." She swung her attention back to Dylan. "You have to see it."

"Dancing?" he echoed, trying to keep his thoughts straight. He had danced alongside Marin and Katarina back at Whitemeadow. He recalled a desire to share one twirl with Tracker, but not much else, before waking up in bed with the hound. What promise had he made the man take?

He risked a glance at Tracker. The man's face had gone carefully neutral, those honey-coloured eyes trained on the inn entrance. Was he expecting Dylan to leap up and abandon him here?

"Later," he assured Marin. "As Track said, we were in the middle of a discussion."

The hound's gaze turned on him and, all at once, the neutrality melted into remorse. "It can wait. The festival, however..." One corner of his mouth lifted as he gave a sigh. "You should experience the day at its fullest." He pushed the chair back and stood in one smooth movement. "But why restrict ourselves to being mere spectators? I recall you being quite the dancer. We could join in."

Marin laughed. "Not unless you want to get trampled." She grabbed Dylan's hand and hauled him to his feet. "I promise this won't take too long."

Dylan grimaced an apology over his shoulder as Marin towed him towards the door. Despite Tracker's insistence, whatever the man wished to say clearly wasn't something to be put off for long. *Tonight.* Even if the conversation proved to be as unpleasant as he expected.

He came to a halt barely a few steps beyond *The Broken Rod's* entrance. Colour and music assaulted his senses. People twirled and pranced in the centre of the square. To one side, a small band of minstrels played their various instruments.

Children ran past, squealing and laughing. Some were entranced by a puppet show set up near the bakery. There was a half barrel nearby, filled with semi-submerged fruit. Children dipped their heads in it, sometimes coming up with an apple or a pear. Others danced off to the side of the adults or stuffed their faces with food.

"It's very hectic, isn't it?" Katarina asked. The hedgewitch sat atop a barrel near the inn's entrance, her little book open on her lap. "Almost like home."

"No," he whispered. This was nothing like home. The tower held no festivals. Not like this. There'd been several dances throughout the year, generally held in the arena where their guardians would keep a good eye on them. But no games, no puppet shows just for fun.

His gaze was drawn to those dancing in the middle of the square, his foot tapping to the beat. He knew the dance. Clearing his throat, Dylan held out his hand to the hedgewitch. "Care to join them?"

Katarina's cheeks darkened. She slid off the barrel and tucked her book and quill back into their pouches. "I'd love to," she said, taking his hand.

"What?" Marin whined. "What about me? I dragged you out here. I should get the first dance."

Dylan grinned over his shoulder at the woman. "I'll make sure to save you one," he promised.

It took a few tries before they could join the cavorting. When they did, the world became little but flashes of dyed linen as women kicked up their skirts and men twirled about. Laughter and scraps of singing filled his ears. His heart leapt to the rhythm of people's feet and their clapping. He followed along, dragging Katarina with him.

Then the music stopped and reality came crashing back into his limbs. They made their way back to *The Broken Rod's* doorway, where Marin leant against the barrel.

A new song started up and, even puffing as he was, Dylan made no objections to the hedgewitch dragging him back out.

The second dance was nowhere near as hectic. They were quickly pulled into a winding line that took them beyond the market square, towards the docks and back again before breaking into several twirling circles. He switched partners several times during the dance, always returning to Katarina. She stared up at him during those times, her face flushed to the tips of her ears and beaming.

By the time the second song had finished, Tracker had finally left the inn. He stood beside Marin, scowling. The woman spoke to him and he replied in turn, but whatever the hound said only seemed to deepen her frown.

With his heart still pounding, Dylan grabbed her hand and led the way into what seemed to be an endlessly growing throng. The dance was a less familiar one, but as they moved with the rest of the crowd, the steps came to him.

It wasn't until they'd completed a circuit of the square that he spied the hound dancing with Katarina. The man moved effortlessly, twirling the hedgewitch as if she weighed nothing. The pair talked as they danced, their chatter lasting for quite some time.

"Hey," Marin said. "I'd prefer if you kept your eyes off loverboy whilst you're dancing with me. I don't want your clumsy feet treading on mine."

"I happen to be a very good dancer, thank you." He ran the woman's words through his mind as she ducked under his arm. "And we're not lovers. He's—" What? Certainly nothing as extreme as she suggested. "We're just friends," he eventually settled. Couldn't that be enough?

"Right." She surfaced from beneath his arm, amusement plastered across her face. "A *friend* that you just, by chance, stare at as if you're a forlorn little puppy being ignored by his owner."

He scoffed. "I do not."

Marin gave a wicked chuckle that managed to raise little bumps across his arms. "It's all right. He does it, too."

"I find that hard to believe." Tracker was a great number of things, but Dylan rather doubted the man was the type to fawn over anyone.

"Of course you do. You're always looking the other way when he does it."

Had he been? Dylan's thoughts drifted to their strangely intimate time atop the waterfall. The soft expressions that vanished so swiftly and completely that he couldn't be certain they'd been there in the first place. The kiss before they had returned to camp that'd left a lingering sweetness on his tongue.

He shook his head. *It's just fun.* A bit of play between friends. He'd be a fool to search for any deeper meaning.

The music stopped and he allowed Marin to escort him back to where their companions already stood. He wasn't sure how long they'd been there, but the hedgewitch bore the sullen air of someone who had sat out the last dance.

He cleared his throat and squared his shoulders. Maybe if the next dance was a slow one and didn't take them on another trip around the entire village, he might be able to keep up with Katarina one last time.

Tracker grasped Dylan's hand as he walked by, halting him. "There is enough energy left in you for a final dance, yes?"

Dylan eyed the man, not entirely sure he'd heard right. "You want to dance with *me*?"

A bemused smile took the hound's lips. "That is why I asked. You have done so with both of these dear women, but I am starting to feel a little left out."

At his back, Marin snorted. "Don't you two do enough horizontal dancing?"

Tracker grinned and tilted his head to look past Dylan. "As pleasant as that is, I would very much like to indulge in a little of the dressed and vertical kind." He pressed the back of Dylan's fingers to his lips. Those gorgeous eyes peeked out from beneath long russet lashes. "What say you? You follow, I lead?"

His chest constricted at the sight, becoming so tight that tears pricked his eyes. *Don't start getting soppy now*, he chastised himself. "Sure." He followed Tracker out into the crowd.

New music started up. Slower. The shivering notes more intimate.

Before he could register what was happening, Tracker had swung him around to stand face-to-face.

The hound entwined the fingers of one hand with Dylan's. A small laugh slipped between his teeth. "Why the unsure look?" His free hand alighted on Dylan's waist. "I am quite willing to follow if you would prefer to lead."

"It's not that. I've never danced like this before." It had been deemed as too intimate for the overseers' liking. Standing here, with the pressure of Tracker's chest against his, he could see why.

"Not outside of your robe as a partner, yes?" Repressed laughter creased the man's eyes. "Dancing is not exactly required of a hound, but I have picked up a few things over the years. So do not worry, you are in good hands."

"I know." If he could trust the man when they were alone and intimate, then he could trust Tracker anywhere.

Something flickered over the hound's face. The corners of his mouth wavered. The hand on Dylan's waist moved, snaking around his back to press them tightly together. He ducked his head, a shuddering sigh slipping through his lips.

"Are you all right?" It sounded almost as if the man was about to cry.

The hound lifted his head. His smile had returned in full. It did nothing to abolish the glassy sheen in his eyes. "Of course. It is just—"

Someone bumped into them. They stumbled for a few steps to a chorus of curses and warnings, on the brink of falling several times before righting themselves.

Tracker regained his hold on Dylan's waist and hand. "I should probably get us moving before someone else collides into us."

A nervous chuckle slithered up Dylan's throat. *I can just see it now. Crushed by dancing villagers.* Not exactly the most heroic way to go. "You were about to say something?" he gently prodded.

The man's lips twisted into a rueful smile. "It can wait." He slowly swayed them to the music. Everyone else seemed to move much faster.

Dylan dipped his head, pressing his cheek against the man's forehead. Should his chest feel this tight? Maybe he shouldn't have tried so many dances in one sitting.

Or perhaps something else was to blame. What had Katarina said? Consider what he felt? He didn't need to think.

He *knew.*

"Track?" he breathed. "I—" The man's fingers pressed against Dylan's lips, halting the rest of the words crowding to escape.

"Hush," Tracker whispered as he slowly turned them. "This has been a pleasant day so far. I would not wish for your memory of it to be soiled." He tipped his head back. The smile he offered didn't reach his eyes. "Speak only if you are sure you will not regret it."

The tightness in Dylan's chest grew for a whole different reason. Did the hound not understand what he was trying to say? Or had he comprehended all too well and merely sought to spare them both a few awkward days of travel? "I wouldn't," Dylan murmured. "I won't."

"Still, let us not tempt fate, yes? There is still a talk we must have." Those long fingers caressed Dylan's cheek and Dylan pressed into the touch. "But not here. Later. You may speak then."

CHAPTER 43

The melody finished. Dylan stepped back, bowed to his partner and went to leave the middle of the square before another dance started up. A gentle tug on his arm halted him. He turned to find Tracker still holding his hand.

"Where do you think you are going?"

"The music's over." Even so, another group of minstrels were settling on the temporary platform beneath the awning. If he didn't leave by the time they were ready to play, he could wind up stuck out here until the dance was over. "I've been dancing half the day. Maybe we can find somewhere quiet to sit and watch them?" Or even peruse a few of the stalls ringing the square.

Tracker gnawed on his lip. "Just one more dance? I promise not to exert you too much." The hound pressed his cheek to Dylan's bicep. "Please?" Dylan wasn't certain how the man did it, but Tracker's eyes seemed to increase in size. What had Marin compared the look to? A forlorn puppy?

Dylan sighed his resignation. "One more, then I'm done."

They didn't have to wait long before the new minstrels started to play. The group was far livelier than the last and the rhythm they had chosen encouraged great bursts of energy. Dylan's pulse leapt at the beat and, even though his limbs were sluggish to respond, he couldn't help but follow along with the rest of the enthusiastic crowd.

He didn't know the dance, but Tracker's effortless movements helped him keep pace. They twirled and dipped between people's upraised hands, breaking from each other's side to form a tunnel, before falling back into the other's grasp.

At some point, the dance required one partner to lift the other. Dylan wordlessly threw his arms around Tracker's shoulders, his chest aglow with the soft warmth of the hound's answering smile. The beats in the music grew faster and his heart followed.

Tracker tightened his hold, lifting him and twirling about as if Dylan weighed nothing. The sensation—the sheer giddy force of being spun uncontrollably, coupled with the closeness of the hound's touch and scent—was a heady one.

Then his feet were back on the ground and he felt himself tipping back before he could do anything to stop it. Only when he didn't immediately fall did he notice Tracker's arms supporting both his rear and back. Dylan wrapped his arms around the man's shoulders. Uncertainty bubbled in his gut. What was the man up to?

Before a word could leave his lips, Tracker claimed them.

Dylan swallowed a gasp. Indecision froze his limbs. Pulling away would only result in landing on his backside. But if he stayed—

Tracker seemed to take his lack of objection as acceptance. He tightened his hold, pulling Dylan closer, and deepened the kiss.

Slowly, Dylan's lids fluttered shut. The music and cavorting of the village no longer seemed as loud. His hand slid from the nape of the man's neck to his hair, grasping to the sound of Tracker's delightfully rich moan. His tongue slid along the hound's, mirroring the man's actions.

They parted, both breathless. Then he was upright again.

All at once, Dylan felt every eye on him. He clutched at his chest and stomach, not sure whether he was going to vomit or have his heart give out.

Tracker's flushed smile melted into concern. He grasped Dylan's arms, supporting him. "Are you—?"

Dylan fled the square, pushing through the throng. Along the stalls he went, seeking a place to hide that would enable him to cool the heat burning in his bones and slow the hectic pounding in his chest.

His frantic wandering led him to a gap between the buildings. He nipped into the shadows, stumbling on uneven bricks and colliding with the remains of a barrel, before coming to a halt at the end of the alley.

Cool brickwork greeted his hands. He collapsed against it, pressing his cheek to the uneven surface. Never had he experienced the giddy, flushed sensation currently suffusing his body. Nor the frenzied pulsing of his heart, so strong that he thought he might collapse at any moment.

He kissed me. Yes, Tracker had done so a dozen times in the past and more, but not like this. Not in front of all those people. They'd seen. They *knew*. They—

He squeezed his eyes tight. *This isn't the tower.* The people here didn't know who, or what, he was. Without the army-issued attire, he looked no different to any other citizen walking the streets. Not a soul here could possibly know he was a spellster unless he announced it.

The tightness in his chest suggested otherwise. His heart continued to flutter like some enraged beetle. He wrapped an arm around his stomach, unsure exactly what part of him was shaking more.

Through it all, the memory of the hound's mouth tingled along his lips. The keening warmth. It had felt like...

Home.

Over his harsh breath, he caught the sound of approaching footsteps. He cracked an eye, peering through the blur of unshed tears. A figure loomed ever nearer.

"Dylan?" the hound softly called. "Are you all right?"

He shook his head.

Tracker squatted beside him. "I apologise, I did not think you would—" A small, mirthless chuckle stalled the words. The man rubbed at his forehead. "Well, that is the heart of the matter, yes? I simply did not *think*." Clearing his throat, he laid a hand upon Dylan's back, his fingers moving in slow, soothing circles. "This is all new to you, I know, and I..." He sighed. "I got caught up in the festivities, I suppose. It is no excuse, though. I pushed too hard."

"No," Dylan mumbled, speech difficult with half his face still pressed to the wall. "You didn't— I... I've never been kissed in public before." He still felt all those eyes watching them. They stuck to his skin like syrup. He could hear their whispers, he was certain of it. "Not like that." He might give his friends a little peck on the cheek for luck, but never anything that could be considered as intimate.

"If it is any consolation, no one paid us any mind."

The hound sounded so certain. He wished he could say the same, but the nagging watched feeling wouldn't fade. Running through the crowd like a madman probably hadn't helped matters.

Dylan hugged himself tighter. "I shouldn't still be like this," he mumbled into his forearm. "I'm scared of something that doesn't exist anymore." He knew that. So, shouldn't the fear have gone by now?

"Perhaps," Tracker murmured. He wrapped an arm around Dylan's shoulders, drawing him into a hug. "But such dread is not easily scrubbed from the mind." He stroked Dylan's hair as if comforting a child spooked by night terrors. "Not when its presence loomed over your life for so many years and its absence is recent. Even then, we all have a fear we cannot shake. Take me and tunnels, for example."

"That's not the same." Even if he didn't know why, or quite understand how, Tracker was afraid of tunnels, that didn't mean it wasn't a legitimate fear. If what the man feared was being trapped underground, there had still been that possibility, despite the chance of them remaining stuck for long being a slim one. "And you still went down that tunnel."

"Only because *you* were there," the hound whispered. "I would never have done it on my own, but you…" He pressed his lips to Dylan's temple. "There is nowhere I would not follow." The words came so softly that, had he not felt the man's breath against his skin, Dylan would've thought he had imagined Tracker speak at all.

He lifted his head. "I—" The concern that dominated the hound's eyes stilled his tongue for a moment. "There was something you wanted to talk about back at the inn. What were you going to say?"

A sombre smile curved Tracker's lips. He caressed Dylan's cheek, the back of his fingers disturbing the dampness Dylan hadn't noticed slicking his skin. "It can wait until we are settled at the inn." He stood, helping Dylan to his feet. "Do you think yourself capable of facing the world? Or departing to somewhere less fragrant?"

Chuckling, he did his best to dry off his face on his sleeve. He had been in no state to pay their surroundings much mind, but the air *did* have the distinct pungent aroma of spoilage. Thankfully, the wall he collapsed against bore little more than dirt and dry debris. "Give me a moment," he promised.

"Take as long as you need." Tracker took a few steps back towards the alley entrance, clearly reluctant to leave, but doing so all the same.

"Wait." He reached for the man's arm. "I don't—" He might not be able to face a crowd, but that didn't mean he wanted to be alone. "Stay? Please?"

The hound clasped Dylan's hands in both of his. "Of course."

"There you two are!" Katarina's voice boomed down the alley. The hedgewitch lingered at the entrance, seemingly not willing to come any closer. She glanced over her shoulder as if daring anyone to near. "Marin thinks we should seek our room, so we'll be heading there shortly. She doesn't trust the innkeeper not to sell it to someone else."

"Does she?" Tracker replied. "I suppose there is a measure of truth there. Tell her she need not worry, but I will be along soon."

The woman gave a curt nod and left the entrance for the fair.

He turned back to Dylan, shaking his head. A small, affectionate smile touched his lips. "I best go ensure someone does not dare to cast a sour word in our dear hunter's presence. I would like to keep the room I paid for tonight." He cocked his head, faint worry lifting his brows. "Will you also be joining us now? Or would you prefer to linger a while longer? You will be all right on your own? I can stay, if that is what you need."

A wisp of laughter passed through Dylan's lips. "Give me a chance to answer one of those."

Tracker's smile twisted wryly. "My apologies. You gave me quite the fright when you fled."

He squeezed the man's fingers, his heart jumping when the hound answered in kind. "I think you're right about not letting the others out of our sight for too long. We should join them."

The hound peered at him, those honey-coloured eyes seeming to burrow into Dylan's skull. "Are you sure?"

Dylan tightened his hold on the man's hands and nodded.

Lacing their fingers, Tracker led the way out of the alley and through the crowd. Most were focused on the dancing and the games or were busy buying wares. A few glanced their way, but their faces were of mild concern if not neutral interest. "They likely believe you had a little too much to drink," Tracker said after they passed the fifth such person.

"I could do with another one. Or three." The sun hung a full hand's width above the horizon. It'd set in another hour or two. Hard to believe he had danced most of the afternoon away. Or that the last time he consumed anything had been hours ago.

"And I would prefer you do not get drunk tonight, but I do share the sentiment. Perhaps alongside a little something to eat, yes?" He squinted at the sky. "There should be a few roasted ducks waiting for us by now."

The women lingered by a puppet show set up for the local children. Katarina sat amongst them, listening to the performers behind the curtain and writing in her book. Marin knelt at a nearby barrel, attempting to fish an apple from the water and failing spectacularly. Her antics had drawn a handful of the children, some of whom stood shaking their heads or outright laughing.

As a group, they made their way back to *The Broken Rod*, where dinner was indeed ready for their consumption. Whilst Dylan wasn't entirely sure the bird he ate was duck, it was still a far better alternative to the fish everyone else in the tavern seemed to be tucking into.

Dylan spun on his stool, leaning back on the table and listening to the music. A few minstrels had made their way inside as the daylight turned grey. They played softly, barely heard at times over the ruckus of a few nearby dicers, but the notes had been familiar. This new song was not.

A woman stood up near the minstrels and, as she plucked on a small lyre, Dylan heard Tracker humming a few bars. When the woman sang, so did the hound. Albeit, quietly.

Dylan listened to the song, twisting in his seat to hear Tracker better without the man knowing, and quickly realised why he had never heard it before.

The song spoke of an innkeeper's daughter who'd fallen in love with a rogue spellster. The man promised her a life where she would want for nothing, if only she would run off with him on the first night of the full moon.

Dylan clutched the side of the table. He'd a sick feeling of how the rest of the song went, of how many tales there were involving sacrifices, and was fully prepared to leave before such a conclusion. But there was something in Tracker's hushed voice, a wavering note of pain, that kept Dylan from getting to his feet.

The song spoke of another man, a young stable hand who listened in on the couple's plan and, when the hounds came sniffing, told them of the spellster's imminent return. So the hounds waited until the first night of the full moon. They trussed and gagged the maiden, placing her at the window facing the direction her spellster lover would come.

Dylan held his breath. Only then did he realise the rest of the room had fallen silent.

Tracker slowly got to his feet. "Perhaps you dear women would like to seek out our room? Dylan?" He softly cleared his throat. "Would you care to join me outside?"

Nodding, Dylan mimicked the other two in standing, but where they disappeared up a flight of stairs, he trailed behind the hound. His attention drifted back to the song. In it, the unnamed maiden struggled against her bonds, but the knots were tight and the rope bit her skin.

Whatever happened next was lost as they exited the building.

"How does it end?" he asked. Although Tracker had sung softly, the words had come confidently enough. Surely he knew the ending.

The hound sighed. "Typically. Her lover arrives at midnight to spirit her away. When she spots him in the square, she throws herself out the window to warn him and breaks her neck in the fall."

At their back came a cheer from the tavern patrons. The song was over, ending to their satisfaction.

Dylan swallowed, his throat far too tight. "I take it the spellster is blamed for her death." It seemed a logical conclusion.

Tracker screwed up his nose. "From what I recall, he flees, unaware the body is his lover's. He learns of her death from the hounds who were chasing him and is cut down when he attempts revenge."

The fate of every spellster brave enough to try for love. Even beyond the tower, such an attempt brought only sorrow.

They passed a group of children who couldn't be any older than six or seven years playing in the square. They had marked out two sections on the cobblestones with various bits of wood or fabric and ran between them, trying to capture the other in some elaborate game of *Get 'em*. The rules they played by seemed different to the ones he remembered.

Their laughter dominated the otherwise quiet evening, the sound tugging at the corners of his mouth. He hadn't believed such unfettered joy would ever again grace his ears.

He let out a shaky breath. The hound hadn't brought him out here to watch the locals. "There was something you wanted to tell me earlier." Something about their final night in Whitemeadow and a promise given.

"I did, but..." The man grimaced. "If I may enquire something first?" He waited for Dylan to nod before continuing, "I was wondering what your feelings about Wintervale are."

"What my—?" Dylan peered at the hound, trying to decipher the man's strangely neutral expression. "Why?"

Tracker waved the question aside. "Ah, pay it no mind. But if you wish to talk further, we can do so when we are alone."

Dylan took in the square. Besides the children, there were a few people making their way elsewhere. None paid them any attention. "Is this not private enough?" Perhaps not for most physical activities, but talking?

The hound shrugged. "More alone than this. I would prefer to not run the risk of being overheard."

"I see." He toyed with the collar of his robe. The fabric suddenly seemed far too constricting. There was only one type of talk he knew that would require such solitude. Had this whole day been a sort of last hurrah before the hound spouted out some confession that they should break off whatever it was they had between them? Those sorts of talks always happened in private and generally left a lingering bitterness in his soul that he could do without.

Gods. That's why the man had stopped him speaking when they were dancing. Why he'd wanted to speak back in the tavern. And why he had brushed it aside in the alley. Tracker had been trying to keep him from making this harder than it clearly already was.

"If you want to end this," Dylan whispered. "Just say it. I understand." That was the worst part. He did. Wintervale wasn't far from here, a week on foot at the most. Tracker would need to maintain a certain aloofness to him when they arrived. It was probably for the best if they started now. "I'm not going to make a scene." Sharing a tent might be a little awkward at first, but he would manage.

"I..." The hound's brow furrowed in confusion. "That was not something I planned to suggest." His shoulders straightened, all semblance of ease vanishing. Those honey-coloured eyes that had seemed so warm a moment ago were now dark. "Unless that is *your* wish?"

"No, I'm..." A tiny smile tugged at his lips. Stopping here wasn't what the hound wanted? Dylan exhaled in a small, tight sob. "I'm good with this." Strange, the way speaking those words infused his whole body in such pleasant warmth.

Tracker bowed his head and resumed his casual stroll along the market square. "I am truly glad to hear that. I rather enjoy what we have. It is good to know the feeling is mutual."

Dylan let his gaze drift over the village, the dark streets illuminated as the group of children scuttled about lighting torches. Being wrong had never felt this good. He still had Tracker at his side.

Until Wintervale.

His smile fled as the insidious thought stirred. "This—our fun?—will have to end once we reach the capital, won't it?" They'd a few more days before the final leg of their journey was complete. Then this freedom the gods let him taste would be taken once and for all.

The hound's silence drew Dylan's head back around.

Tracker stared ahead, his face strangely neutral. "Who says we have to end it as soon as *that?*"

Everyone. By the man's own admittance, they shouldn't be doing what they had been. "The army would see me leashed." After what had happened to the bulk of the army, there was no chance any remaining spellsters would be allowed anywhere near the meagre independence they used to have. They would be watched, hoarded jealously, until it was time to be used. "They'll frown on someone using such a rare weapon for anything as mundane as sex." At least, someone outside of the army. And only the gods knew how the other hounds would view Tracker's dallying.

Tracker halted, finally facing him, as they reached the edge of the square. "So, do not go." He gripped Dylan's sleeve. "No one knows you survived. Well, no one who is willing and capable of alerting the capital. All you would need to do is keep your magic hidden for a while and no one would suspect."

Dylan stepped back, pulling himself free of the man's fingers and keeping one hand stretched out to ward the hound from coming closer, even though Tracker made no such attempt. "I... can't." He couldn't even dare to entertain such an idea. Because if he did anything beyond travelling to Wintervale, then who would ensure the fallen back home got the revenge they deserved?

An uneasy smile twisted Tracker's lips. "If you are afraid the other hounds will come for you—"

"It's not that." Although, the hounds and their persistent nature in keeping the rest of Demarn free of unleashed spellsters was certainly not a thing to make light of. They would scour every inch of the kingdom to find a deserter. "I can't be that selfish."

Gone was the hound's careful neutrality. The stark concern that took its place wasn't any better. "I—" He bit his lip, clearly restraining any further words. His brows knitted together, those honey-coloured eyes lowering to scrutinise the cobblestones.

Dylan's throat tightened with each silent step Tracker took. *To leave Wintervale behind.* The hound's words were far more tempting than they'd any right to be. But to live like a normal man? *Selfish.* He couldn't do that.

No matter how much he wanted to.

~ ~ ~

Tracker lifted his gaze to the street. The docks beckoned at the far end, the rising moon giving the water an otherworldly glow. *So close.* The fork in the river sat within sight, a ribbon of moonlight that wended its way into the darkness.

Like in Whitemeadow, there were no boats taking passengers, but it was all right there, waiting just across the water. The promise of salvation. For Dylan. For him. *Us.*

It was a place he'd never reach without the spellster agreeing to leave all thoughts of Wintervale behind. He had known such an ask could be impossible, yet he had tried anyway, hoping. *Stubborn bastard.* Why did his heart always keen for the forbidden?

Dylan remained in the middle of the street, illuminated by the moonlight peeking over the rooftops. The man shuffled from one foot to the other, clearly uncomfortable. Over his shoulder, the glow from the inn.

Tracker strove for *The Broken Rod.* "We should head back. The others will worry if we are too long and we need rest. There is still plenty of travelling to be had between here and the capital."

"What?" Dylan squeaked. "Is that all you wanted to talk about before?"

No. There'd been so much more. He had spent days working up the courage to express those feelings, to plan out everything he wanted to say. Hell, he had even practised uttering *the* words. Wasted hours. "What point is there in talking further? Your mind has already been made up, yes?"

"As much as it can be when the choices are a death with meaning or..." His chin trembled for a breath before he regained composure. "...without."

He took a step towards the man. "Dylan..."

Clearing his throat, he continued, "You know, I thought everything along my path was all squared up and set. About life. About me." His lips curved, the wisp of a laugh escaping them.

"Especially about me. I thought I knew myself well before you."

"I cannot take all the credit." He had been doing his job—culling the dangerous, escorting the safe—uncaring if the unleashed spellster wandering through the town also meant his death. "But I hear the waver in your voice."

"I'm going to miss you."

Taken aback, Tracker could only stare at the man. "Miss me? I am not going anywhere." When had Dylan come to that conclusion? "I swear." Had he so utterly misinterpreted Dylan's drunken words back in Whitemeadow?

"You can't very well follow me."

"Back to the border?" In the past, that certainly would've turned a few heads. Hounds couldn't become wardens. A part of him wished it wasn't true. If Authril's knowledge of Dylan's abilities was enough to put her to the fore as a choice, then someone who felt the man's magic would be far better. But even before the tower's fate, the hounds were too few to have even a handful be confined to such a task.

Dylan smiled sadly. "It's all right. With you being a hound and me being *this*?" He gestured vaguely at himself. "I knew it couldn't be more. You told me at the start you were used to mindless fun."

He reached for Dylan's hand. "I did not mean to imply I—"

"There were plenty of people in the tower who slept together without it meaning anything deeper. Hell, I was one of them. I wouldn't have pursued anything beyond our first night if I wasn't all right with it just being about the sex."

"I see." Was that all Dylan thought they were? Bed friends?

Why would he not? He hadn't done anything to dispel that illusion. Until recently, he had chased away the very notion of deeper feelings.

Worse still, he could only blame himself. *He* was the sentimental fool, assuming Dylan sought more than the companionship he had been accustomed to. Hounds and spellsters were supposed to oppose each other. *Hunt until death.* Theirs or his.

The gods truly did like to laugh at his expense.

Dylan halted, peering at him quizzically. "You know I'm not completely innocent, right? You're only the first one to..." His cheeks grew dark, the confidence in his stature waning. He paced a few steps one way, then the next, combing his fingers through his hair as if messing the strands further helped. "I've slept with a lot of people." He paused mid-step, shock widening his eyes and slackening his jaw, before whirling to face Tracker. "That sounded worse than I intended. I'm not trying to boast."

"I did not take it as such." Between working at the brothel and his own exploits, he had lost count of how many had shared his bed. "You were making a point?"

"I...?" Confusion briefly moulded his face. "Yes! I miss them. I miss a *lot* of them. And I know I'm going to miss you. Not because of the sex. That was..." His gaze slid out into the square. If it wasn't for the torchlight, the man's face would've definitely been a gorgeous shade of red. "...literally been the best I've ever had," he confessed in a breathless rush.

Tracker couldn't help the brief chuckle that tightened his throat, a sound that threatened to turn into a far wetter emotion. His chest ached. He sucked on his teeth, hoping the act would banish the excess moisture from his eyes and work more into his mouth. "Why are you still intent on rejoining the army?"

"I—" Hanging his head, the man turned his back to Tracker. "Wintervale is my fate." They were words the man had said before.

Maybe it could still be changed.

Grabbing Dylan's wrist, he strode towards the docks before the man could object or ask further questions. He might not be able to offer wardenship, but he did have something better. He hoped Dylan felt the same way.

But if he was confessing anything tonight, it needed to be somewhere less public than in the middle of the village square.

CHAPTER 44

The docks were silent save for the steady flow of water and the oddly soothing creak of moored fishing boats. Dylan wasn't sure why the hound had brought them here, of all places. In terms of privacy, it was less confining than the square. But they also weren't surrounded by buildings and the ones at their back appeared to be more warehouses than homes.

The splash of something hefty hitting the water disturbed the quiet. A few vessels bobbed out where the river forked. He spied people aboard them, throwing splayed nets into the water. Another hit with a single splash, then all was silent once more.

Finally loosening his grip on Dylan's hand, Tracker leant on the railing to stare out at the river. There was a weariness to him that Dylan had never seen before.

He joined the hound at the railing. "Track?"

The man sighed. "Before we discuss anything else, you should know I never intended to take you to Wintervale." He pointed towards the divide in the river. "That flows from a lake far up north. Boats travel along it every day." His hand dropped, defeated. "Or rather, they did until the Talfaltaners seized most of the cargo and passenger boats. I *had* hoped to get you aboard one, to have you up the river and heading north. As far from the capital as I could before you realised."

"*What?*" *That* was what the man had been trying to tell him before Marin interrupted? "How long have you been planning to kidnap me?" Were the others aware? Had he been the only one kept in the dark?

"A while," he confessed, his gaze still on the river fork. "The Talfaltaners stealing every ship they could get their hands on scuppered my plans back in Whitemeadow, but without Authril, I had hoped you might come willingly."

"You promised you'd help me avenge my home, my *people*." Tracker had given his word back before they knew the hound master had ordered a culling, when the only thing they could be certain of was the monstrous deeds of the Talfaltaners, but it shouldn't matter. "You swore it."

"I did." He pushed off the railing, facing Dylan. "But you will never get close enough to the hound master. He wants to eradicate every unleashed spellster within Demarn and *you* are the last one. The others will not let you leave the capital alive. I am certain that the ones you are seeking revenge for would vastly prefer you live your life rather than give it up."

"You keep telling me how much of a horrible person he is. Why protect him?"

"I am not protecting *him*. I am protecting *you*! Entering Wintervale means death. They *will* kill you. Do you not understand that? Maybe not directly at the city gates, maybe not even within the castle walls, but definitely if you are handed over to the army." He clutched at the pendant Dylan had gifted him. "I cannot let that be your fate."

"I don't need that sort of protection."

Tracker's jaw twitched. Disagreement? Refusal to accept the truth? It was all the same. He closed his eyes. "Let us say, by some miracle, you *do* get near the hound master. What then?"

"Kill him." It was the least the man deserved.

"In the middle of the castle? Surrounded by those he commands?" He shook his head. "You so much as blink at him wrong and that day would be your last."

"I know." Coming to that sort of realisation only made him feel worse about asking Tracker to lead him there. But still... "As long as he goes with me, I don't care if I die."

"You—?" Tracker stared incredulously at him. His expression shifted from one breath to the other. Alarm. Horror. *Anger*. "You do not *care*?" Snarling, he stalked closer. "You stubborn, *selfish* prick." The moonlight illuminated his face and the starkness of his fury.

It had Dylan retreating at the same pace.

His back connected with a wall. He went to push off it, to continue putting distance between himself and the hound, but the man's fingers closed on the collar of his robe.

"How *dare* you," he growled through bared teeth, his fangs long and gleaming. "How dare you try to undo *everything* I have done to keep you alive. I have committed crimes short of treason and you seek to squander that effort in service to the ungrateful, as if losing your life would be a minor detail? As if no one would *care*?"

"I never asked that of—"

Before he could finish the words, his mouth was dragged down to Tracker's.

There was something familiar swimming in that rush. A warm spark, slightly prickly with the fear of being seen, tingled through his veins. The butterflies were back in force, too. Their giddy fluttering danced around his chest.

The call of home.

Despite himself, Dylan moaned. Against the screaming insistence ringing in his mind that he should push the hound away before they were caught, he grasped Tracker's waist and pulled them together, once again marvelling how well the man fitted against him, as smooth and precise as a blacksmith's puzzle.

Their mouths parted, reluctantly heeding the call for air, but the rest remained pressed against each other. "I admit," Tracker confessed between pants, his rage mollified for the moment. "My reasons for keeping you from him are not entirely altruistic. I—" His grip on Dylan's collar loosened, those long fingers gliding down the robe. "I... *care* far too much for you, for your wellbeing, to just stand aside and let you choose to throw yourself away in some martyr mission. Even if that means you end up hating me for it, I cannot—"

"Stop," Dylan rasped, silencing the man with a finger. "Please." His head still spun, barely catching the hound's words. Was it the lack of air? Had he been poisoned like the man claimed he could? Drugged so that the hound could drag him aboard a ship? Would he wake far from here?

Tracker gently removed the finger from his lips, but remained silent. His breath came in measured intervals, as though he was deliberately controlling each exhale. His eyes were huge, their depths almost glowing in the moonlight. They remained unwaveringly upon him, searching, *seeking*.

"You lied to me about your intentions."

At last, that piercing gaze dropped. Tracker bowed his head as though he already knew what the punishment would be and had accepted it. "Yes. At least, when it came to our destination." He stepped back out of reach. "You would never have agreed to such a thing whilst Authril was with us. With *her* whispering in your ear about duty and revenge, I saw no way to tell you and not have you thinking I was trying to manipulate you like she had." A wry smile tweaked his lips. He faced the docks, making the mere act of looking Dylan's way barely possible. "I could have. There are things I could do to you that would make you believe nothing in this world was ever real except for me."

Despite the wall, he tried to take a step back. The hound had done precisely that during their night in the tower. Making Dylan forget all about what he'd seen during that day.

Tracker nodded and softly laughed, seemingly to himself. "But that is not how affection, *proper* adoration, works. It certainly is *not* how I wish it to be between us. Any more than I wanted for you to believe freedom came with... certain conditions."

Us. There had been a slight change in the way Tracker uttered the word. A softness that spoke of longing, of...

Affection? Adoration? Wanting to flee elsewhere with him?

The way he looks at you. Marin's words came sharply to mind.

Dylan's throat tightened a little at the thought. *No.* It wasn't that. The man wasn't seeking him like prey.

And what *he* felt—this fuzzy, fluttering warmth buzzing through him—wasn't being hunted. Or real. *Just another bitter dream.* Wasn't it? He stood with uneven bricks digging into his back, the chill air nipping at his extremities, the stench of damp and fish invading his nostrils. Surely his mind could've conjured a far more pleasant place.

He swiftly turned his focus to what else the man had mentioned. Or rather, who. "Were *you* behind Authril's arrest?"

"No. At least, not deliberately. All that I told you there was true, she tried to follow me and got waylaid by the gate guards." He chuckled mirthlessly. "To think, I was wondering if more drastic means would be required once we reached here after my intention to take a ship in Whitemeadow and leave her behind was no longer an option."

"Was that why you left her imprisoned?" They had all long known the warrior would never have allowed him even the thought of doing anything beyond heading for Wintervale and the army forming there. "You could've gotten her free." Even if the hound couldn't use his status as leverage, Dylan had enough tales from the man to know he could've picked the locks holding her cell door closed.

"I could have," he admitted. "If I fancied joining her behind bars. Even if we managed to escape the city, and that would have been doubtful, why would I return anyone to a position where they could continue their abuse?"

"What abuse?" He hadn't heard of any mistreatment from either Marin or Katarina. "Who was she abusing?"

He took up Dylan's hand, entwining their fingers. His expression had become a twisted mixture of hope and anguish. "*You.*"

"No, she was just—" Always insisting, ordering. Their pace, their route. His night activities. Tracker was right, she had whispered and decreed.

Demanded he return to being a thing she could use.

He hadn't considered any of it as abuse—and even with her threats back in the tower, not once had she hurt him—but that was the truth. "Gods." Had he really accepted how she treated him that fast?

Tracker nodded solemnly. "It is true my motives for leaving her there were not without spite. I do not believe I could have travelled even this far without wanting to kill her. When I learnt what she had done, I took my chance to make her separation from the group more permanent without taking her life."

Dylan found his head bobbing along with the man's explanation. If he truly saw Authril as such a threat, it made sense he would take the gift of her imprisonment without question. "What of the days after?" There had been plenty of moments where they'd been alone. "You could've told me then."

Sighing, the hound released Dylan's hands and strode back towards the railing. "Those days have been... Let us call them *complicated*. You said things in Whitemeadow that I have been trying to rationalise as..." He inhaled heavily and released the breath in one deep sigh. "...*anything* else. I was not prepared to act on something you had no recollection of, but I fear I have failed that, too."

He still only remembered scraps of their last night in the city. How he had danced and drunk until his head spun. The jealousy bubbling in his gut whilst watching the hound garner so much attention.

The pain in Tracker's eyes.

He didn't know what he had said, what he'd *done*, to cause it. He had hoped such knowledge would come back to him in time, but it was truly swallowed by the drink. He had similarly lost other evenings, thanks to Sulin's brews. This was the first he regretted losing.

"At no point did you think that maybe you should've mentioned it sooner?" Whatever words they exchanged on that night, it had definitely ended in sex. *His* night had, at least. His body told him that much. He assumed it had been with Tracker. The man had given no indication of it being otherwise.

"I did." Tracker tugged at the dangling, dagger-shaped earring, hissing through the pain. He took a heavy breath and continued, "You were drunk. Very. And I have had many declarations flung my way, usually slurred and not at all true."

"And?"

The hound slowly crossed the space between them. "We are taught that affection is a weakness, that we cannot be true hounds if our heart beats for another. I have wanted to tell you for some time, but I sought to see you free first." Those long fingers clutched at Dylan's robes, holding them in a death grip. It might've been a trick of the moonlight, but he swore the man's shoulders shook.

Dylan bit his lip, unsure if Tracker expected a response or what he would even say. He hadn't ever seen the man so clearly exposed.

"I messed up," Tracker continued. "I will not deny that. I should have told you my plan earlier. I have no excuse beyond wanting to keep my intentions from Authril and then..." He hung his head. "I did not want you to think the choice was between being with me and being leashed."

With him? What did Tracker mean by that? They were already sharing a tent, a *bed*. "I don't follow." How much more together could they possibly be?

"Gods preserve me," Tracker muttered. "Is it so difficult to imagine that I..." He wet his lips. "...hold a deep... fondness for you?"

The twisting of his gut bubbled up his throat in a nervous giggle. "You speak as though you're planning to declare your love for me." That couldn't be right, could it? Never had he heard of people falling that quickly for another. Not that he'd many examples to pull from, certainly no personal experiences. All he'd ever done was run from the idea. And Tracker...

The man had said everything but that phrase. He circled and skated around it like it was a brand.

Tracker smiled out at the river. It was an oddly mournful expression, not something Dylan would've equated with love. "Those words sound so easy coming from your lips. They are not ones I have been able to utter for a very long time."

Blinking furiously, Dylan tipped his head back and glared at the sky. *Stupid cold wind.* Making his eyes water.

"My dear man." Those long fingers caressed Dylan's cheek, lowering his head. He met Dylan's gaze, just as sombre as the soft quirk lingering in the corners of his mouth. "My darling, it sounds the way you believe because that *is* precisely what I am trying to say." Again, his tongue peeked between his lips. "You arouse feelings that have not stirred for some time. Ones which make me want to be with you in ways that are forbidden, ways that would see the both of us dead."

Something warm and rich deep within Dylan's chest dared to try unfurling. *I want you, too.* The confession danced on the tip of his tongue. Dangerous words, right up on the list alongside four very similar ones.

He choked them down, their absence leaving a bitter taste in his throat. This wasn't a dream. This was a nightmare. Some punishment sent by the gods. It wasn't real. It couldn't be. Because if it was, then it meant he would lose so much more than he had originally thought. He wouldn't be able to handle knowing that now.

"There are many who believe I do not deserve you," Tracker continued. "There are times when I would have been one of those voices, but I am also a stubborn fool who often wants what I should not."

"And what you want is... *me?*" But the man thought he didn't deserve Dylan? "Why?" He was hardly some great prize.

"*Why?* What sort of—?" He silenced his indignant screech, glancing about them to see if he had garnered the attention of anyone who could be around at this late hour before continuing in a hushed tone, "What do you mean, *why*? You are a kind man. Gentle. Empathetic. I have not—" There was that haunted look in his eyes again. "I would be beyond foolish not to find those characteristics appealing."

Dylan stared at the hound, unsure what to say. His chest felt far too tight. This was real? Tracker...

Was shaking. The man's breath came unevenly and his throat constricted far too often. The longer Dylan remained silent, the more distress clouded those gorgeous eyes. His own slowly mimicked them, his vision blurring.

"You make me feel more alive than I have for years. I have been alone for so long and I did not expect to wind up fall—" Panic flickered across his face. He carefully extracted himself from Dylan's clothes and backed away. "—with this feeling." His voice was strained. The words hushed, as though he expected to be struck down if he dared speak any louder. "I would understand if you do not reciprocate. And if you—" He took a shuddering breath. "If you do not share the sentiment, then it is what it is. I would be no less willing to escort you somewhere safe."

"How can you say that?" he whispered, the words waterlogged with unshed tears.

Tracker stepped back, visibly confused.

Dylan grabbed the man's hands before he got out of reach. He squeezed the long fingers, now painfully aware of the source to the knot in his stomach. The reason why he dreaded the thought of Tracker leaving his side. "How can you stand there, open your heart to me, and think for one moment that I don't feel the same?"

Tracker remained silent, but hope flickered to life in his eyes.

"Of course, I do." Against every rational thought, he couldn't resist the butterflies that the man sent thundering through him. "I—" He lifted the man's hands to his lips, feeling his own smile against Tracker's fingers before the words blurted forth. "I love you." The phrase seemed almost sinful as it danced off his tongue, but it was so clear. Simple. *Right*. Tracker did more than fill his thoughts. The man filled his heart.

Warmth collected in the curve of the hound's lips and the fine creases around his eyes, but there was a hint of rueful melancholy wavering in the corners of his mouth. Was he mourning the answer?

"Have I told you that before?" Was that what he had meant by things being complicated? It would explain the man's actions over the past week.

"No." He grimaced. "At least, not with such clearly defined words." He drew Dylan closer, his fingers digging into the robe's folds as though any lesser grip would see them parted. "You expressed a fondness, but there are many ways to be fond of someone without—"

"—love?" he finished.

"—it having a deeper meaning," Tracker continued. "You also spoke of a desire for me to be yours until we reached the capital. In fact, you insisted I gave my word."

That had been the promise Tracker spoke of? *Gods*. His face was hot enough that he had to be glowing.

He tipped his head back, a wry chuckle parting his lips. The hound's words were like a key opening a door in what had once been a blank wall. "I think I remember that." Although, his recollection was of bitterly wishing he could have the hound all to himself, not actually *saying* it. "I was..."

"—drunk?" Tracker supplied. "I know. I am thankful for that night, nevertheless. It had me stepping back to evaluate my true feelings for you."

"And *you* want something a little more informal than..." He gestured vaguely between them, unable to find the right words to describe it. "...spellster and hound."

"I..." He froze, the hope in his gaze now tempered by caution. "I confess to wanting a longer liaison than our passage to Wintervale would have permitted." Again, each word snapped at the heels of the one before, as if Tracker expected an interruption at any moment. "The choice and nature of that relationship would be for *you* to decide."

"How?"

A small smile twitched along one side of the hound's mouth. "Let me take you far from here. A place where we could be something else."

"What *else*? Fighting for the army is what I was trained for. My sole purpose." His guardian might've delayed that fate, but it had always been his.

"And yet..." The hound pressed a hand to Dylan's chest. "The heart beating here is that of a healer."

"You think I can't kill unprovoked?" Maybe if he'd been more aggressive, then he would've reached the tower sooner.

"What I think is you are more than what they trained you for."

But being more meant crossing the border. They were practically on the capital's doorstep. Leaving now wouldn't be a matter of simple misdirection. It would be desertion. He would have to leave Demarn, find his way in a whole new country.

Dvärghem. Katarina had said he would make a fair enough apprentice. They could escort her home. *Live* amongst the dwarves and, as long as he didn't mind being at the beck of every hedgewitch in the Coven, they wouldn't have to give up this thing that had blossomed between them. There'd be no need to pretend nothing had happened.

His chest swelled at the thought.

Except, for a hound, stepping beyond the kingdom's borders made them more than a deserter. "Leaving would break your creed. They would hunt you." And strain the treaty the kingdom had with the dwarves.

Tracker shrugged. "They will hunt me if we stay."

He shook his head. The hound's life hadn't changed so drastically. "I couldn't ask you to live a life on the run for me." Maybe if it was just *his* life he risked in such an attempt, but not another's.

"Who said anything about needing to ask? I would gladly forge the way to wherever you wished to go, so long as I am at your side." He seemed so serious, so real.

Dylan wanted to believe. He couldn't see how leaving the kingdom could ever be that simple, but he wanted it to be.

And why hadn't he said something sooner? Why couldn't it have been somewhere more intimate? Somewhere they could actually be alone.

He thumped his head back against the wall, epiphany hitting him just as hard. "The cave." The hound *had* been trying to tell him earlier. How had he not seen it?

Tracker's lips curved in that affectionate, lopsided fashion that made Dylan's insides flutter. "It took you long enough to make that connection." Sorrow wavered at the corners of his mouth. "But I suppose your encounters with intimacy have been limited to the non-romantic kind."

"You've prior romantic experience?" The curiosity bubbling along his tongue wanted to ask what became of his past love. The dread hollowing out his stomach said he probably didn't want to know.

"From a very long time ago, yes." The hound's gaze refused to meet his as the man silently rubbed at his arm, directly atop the band holding the three names. "It is not something you easily forget." His gaze dropped as he whispered, "Nor want to give up. I was so sure I would never feel it again."

Dylan wrapped his arms around Tracker's shoulders. "How about a pact? We be honest with each other, truly honest. No secrets, no matter how painful the truth may be." He might not have any left for the man to eke out, but he was sure the hound already knew that.

Tracker squirmed against him, positioning himself so he could lift his head without clocking Dylan's chin. "That is quite the commitment to make, yes?" One brow lifted. "Almost serious?"

He tipped his head back, letting it brush the wall. Out on the water, the shimmering moonlight stretched northward as far as he could see. A glittering path to a promised freedom. Either pledge would require letting Tracker into the darkest parts of him, but if it kept that dreadfully troubled look from the man's eyes... "I'm willing to try if you are."

The hound laid his cheek on Dylan's chest. He was silent for a long time before speaking. "I am. And I do believe we will have a lot to talk about in the coming days. For now..." In one smooth movement, the man slipped free of Dylan's grasp and offered his hand. "Come. Let us find a more suitable place to discuss our future."

Our. Dylan clasped his lover's hand. Never had a word sounded so enchanting.

They walked along the dock. With the old wooden planks having left land some time back, their every footfall creaked. Dylan didn't care. Like the riverbanks with their shroud of fog, the rest of the world had fallen into a haze. Each step they took felt lighter than the last.

Only the subtle pressure of Tracker's fingers companionably linked with his held back the darker thoughts insisting this night was nothing beyond a hopeless dream. Not with that touch. The warmth and weight that kept him grounded and buoyant all at once.

They halted where the pier jutted further across the river and lingered at the railing separating them from a dunking. In the moonlight, the northern bank looked so close. The river so dark and deep.

His thoughts refused to be still. They tumbled over the days—the weeks, the *months*—since he had met the hound. All that time together, Tracker had given no indication that he was interested in more than sex.

Or had he? Dylan remembered the old fairytales the guardians used to read aloud to the children. He would be the first to admit he didn't know much about how love worked, although he knew enough to know love at first sight didn't exist. Surely people recognised when they'd fallen.

All those questions. They'd started innocently enough early on. But the latter ones? Clearly, Tracker had been doing more than just trying to distract him. "Exactly how long have you felt this way about me?"

Tracker sighed as he leant on the railing separating them from the water. "It feels like forever."

He settled next to the man. "Not when we first started travelling together, surely."

"No. Although I had gained a certain fondness for your presence before we reached Oldmarsh. And I know I teased you mercilessly." He rubbed at his forearm. "Then we reached the tower and—"

"If you tell me you fell for me after we first had sex, I'll thump you."

Tracker chuckled. "Nothing like that, no. You did not exactly seem open to the idea of continuing any sort of relationship. Truly, the question of when is one I have asked myself for days now. Was it when you kissed me? The night we shared a bed in Oldmarsh? The morning I found you dancing amongst the lavender?" His smile gained a warmer edge. "It is difficult to tell the moment when fondness evolves into more."

"We never shared a bed in Oldmarsh." A room, yes. But their sleeping arrangements had been in the form of two cots barely wide enough for one person.

His lover shrugged. "I did not sleep long in mine. I sought out the hound station once you were asleep. When I returned, you were restless, having nightmares. My presence seemed to calm you."

"You climbed into my bed whilst I slept?" Much of his memory from that night was scrambled. His innocent dancing at the inn, the far more lurid displays he had witnessed in the brothel. The hypnotic movement of Tracker's body as he danced with a blade. How his lips had tingled with the promise of a kiss.

How his dream self had gone after more.

"*Into?*" Tracker echoed. "Not at all. I remained clothed and atop the blankets." He glanced at Dylan out of the corner of his eye. "It was enough to soothe your magic."

That night in Oldmarsh felt so long ago. He thought they'd spend only a week longer together before parting at the tower. Yet here they were, about to become fugitives. "Are you really sure about this? Making a run for Dvärghem, I mean."

"Very. It has been on my mind for weeks now. All we need is to get across the river. We can do that at the ford." The certainty in his voice was almost enough to chase Dylan's doubts back into the dark.

Dylan stared out at the moonlit water standing between them and a whole uncertain life, a sombre smile tweaking his lips. "And if the hounds are alerted to our—*my*—presence?" Even without using his magic, he could still be found. Tracker had proven that the night they'd met. Without a reliable band of *infitialis*, there was nothing he could do to smother that beacon.

"It is unlikely we will encounter any, especially once we head north. If we do, they shall meet the same fate as the one in Whitemeadow. I will not suffer travelling with a weapon aimed at our backs."

"It would be that easy for you to spill kin blood? They're your fellow hounds. People you trained alongside." He couldn't imagine turning upon those he had lived beside with the intent to harm, let alone kill.

His lover remained silent for a long time. With the man's head bowed and his focus on the water directly below, Dylan didn't dare guess what thoughts ran through the hound's mind.

With a grunt, Tracker pushed off the railing. "Our trainers sought to instil ruthlessness over camaraderie," he muttered. "That goes double for those who are no longer of the pack. *They* stopped being anything more than feral dogs the moment they broke the creed."

Had they? "Or maybe they're still in line with its tenets." How else would their new master have turned the will of so many? "Maybe the one who stopped following it was *you*."

Tracker frowned. "No, I may have renounced my kinship before I knew about the order to cull the tower, but I still follow its creed."

"You renounced the hounds?" Why was *this* the first he had heard of it? "*When?*"

A smile borne of fond recollection creased his eyes. "Back amongst the lavender."

Warmth flooded his face. He remembered that morning. They had known each other for barely a few days. Dylan hadn't even expressed an interest in the man. Yet, Tracker had already considered him worth breaking his creed over?

Dylan draped an arm around the man's shoulders, tipping Tracker against him. A gentle fluttering in his chest accompanied the blaze in his cheeks. "I love you, too," he breathed against his lover's ear.

Tracker shuddered. "Darling," he growled, those long fingers digging into Dylan's robe. "Do not tease." He dragged him down to roughly seal their mouths together.

In reply, Dylan grasped the man's waistband and tugged his lover hard against him.

Tracker's body stiffened for a heartbeat before he sagged into Dylan's grasp, breaking the kiss. "Why must you be so tall?" the man murmured against Dylan's throat.

Dylan wordlessly spread his legs and braced his rear against the rail to sink the few inches needed to make their heads more-or-less level.

Tracker wasted no time in pressing against him.

Dylan grabbed his lover's backside and squeezed to the delightful sensation of Tracker's muffled moan humming against his lips. He dug his thumbs beneath the waist of the man's trousers and tugged the hound closer.

Their hips ground together. Tracker's hands were everywhere—his hair, his chest, his backside—seeking a way to be closer still. He moaned and whimpered into Dylan's mouth.

Just when Dylan was certain he wouldn't be able to take much more of the man rubbing against him, he caught the edge of a whistle piercing the night.

He twisted atop the railing, seeking the source of the sound. The fishing boat still sat out in the middle of the river. The figures aboard stood waving their arms and hollering. In the still night, their appreciation for the spectacle was clear.

Heat surged to his face, throbbing to the frantic beat of his heart. Unlike earlier, the panic was tempered by a hint of thrill. With the night cloaking them and the boat so far out, the fisherfolk couldn't possibly make out more than silhouettes.

Tracker's breathless chuckle warmed his neck. "We should probably stop." His lover's chest heaved with every inhalation.

The sight just made him want the man all the more.

Dylan leant back on the railing, a groan tightening his throat. He was so close. "Oh?" There had to be somewhere they could be fully alone. Even if only for a few minutes. "Such modesty from the one who, if memory serves, used to fellate himself before a crowd."

Amusement creased the man's eyes. "They were *paying clients*, not the general public. And that would still be less indecent than a little sharing of carnal knowledge right here on the docks."

He gasped, trying to sound scandalised even as his heart thumped a more familiar lust-fuelled beat. "As far as that?"

Tracker cupped Dylan's chin, brushing his thumb over Dylan's lips. "Believe me, I am quite tempted. Especially when bending you over this—" He tapped the railing, sending an oddly pleasant vibration through Dylan's backside. "—would put you at just the right height."

"Are you always this insatiable?" Dylan teased.

His lover's eyes glittered with mirth. "Not always." His hand slowly walked its way down Dylan's chest. "But you... Gods, there is so much I want to do with you, to you..." Those long fingers curled around Dylan's belt. A sharp tug on it had them fitting snugly against each other. "For you," Tracker breathed.

If his heart had stopped before, it now pounded a feverish tempo. He wet his lips. "We can't actually do it here." Even if there hadn't been the fisherfolk out on the river, all it took was for a single soul to round a corner or open a window and see them. But there was also no private room waiting for them back at the inn.

Tracker's answering chuckle was enough to increase the heat in Dylan's cheeks. "You were used to satisfying your desires in all sorts of places within the tower, yes?"

There'd been plenty of times he had gotten a moment of pleasure whilst tucked away in some corner of the library or an alcove somewhere. "Maybe," he squeaked.

"Maybe?" the hound echoed. His laughter deepened. "I hope you are not thinking of playing hard to get. Such a role is not one that fits you well."

Once more clasping Dylan's hand, Tracker led the way off the dock and back amongst the buildings. He paused at the entrance of a dead-end alleyway before gesturing his intentions with a jerk of his head.

Holding back a giggle, he followed his lover into the shadows. The thrill brought on by the fisherfolk hollering had only increased and his body practically vibrated with the desire to have Tracker in his arms. The street was still partially in view when Tracker flattened him against the wall and started undoing Dylan's robe, his belt undone before he had righted himself.

"Did I ever mention how much I am truly liking this new robe?" Tracker rasped as he undid the ties holding Dylan's attire together. "Especially how easily they let me do this." With all three layers undone, he parted them to lay a single kiss upon Dylan's chest.

With his giggling no longer able to be restrained, Dylan combed the hair back from his face. "I swear, I wasn't thinking about ease of access when I chose it."

Long fingers plucked at the knot securing his smallclothes, making fast work of the barrier. The undergarments fell, forgotten entirely as his lover wrapped his fingers around his shaft.

His legs wobbled the more Tracker stroked him. Combined with their stint by the docks, it wouldn't be long before he went off in the man's hands.

Dylan pushed against the wall, seeking strength in the bricks and plaster. Kicking out of his smallclothes, he laid his hands firmly upon his lover's hips and slowly turned them until Tracker's back was flush with the wall. His hand drifted to the man's belts. It didn't take much to undo both, the sword belt falling to the ground, whilst the other merely jingled his victory.

Getting his hand inside his lover's smallclothes was a greater challenge, one that offered the warm, slick length of Tracker's arousal as a reward. He wrapped his fingers around it, swallowing the man's moan, and let tiny sparks of lightning dance along his fingertips.

Tracker's grip on his robe tightened. He pulled Dylan closer, rubbing against him. With them both standing, the best he got was Dylan's thigh, but he didn't seem perturbed.

Breaking the kiss, Dylan withdrew his hand and, whilst those honey-coloured eyes followed his every movement, knelt before Tracker. He tugged at the man's clothes, releasing his lover's glistening erection into the night air.

The last time he had found himself in a similar position had been during their night in the tower. So much had changed since. He'd been so unsure of everything. His wants. The hound's motives. Never would he have thought it would end like this. The man he had been in the tower certainly wouldn't have considered he'd come to crave Tracker.

He wrapped his fingers around the base of Tracker's shaft, running his thumb up the underside and over the tip, eliciting a gentle huff from his lover's lips. Encouraged by that noise, he kept slowly stroking to the sound of the man's soft, appreciative murmur.

Dylan wet his lips. *I can do this.* He had seen past flings do the same thing to himself a dozen or so times over the years, had *felt* the hound's expertise many nights, had already tasted Tracker on the man's tongue. Even though he might not have all the tricks his lover did that left him keening for more, he could still do this.

"Darling." Tracker's voice trembled. Equally shaky fingers briefly rested atop Dylan's head, caressing his hair, before moving to his chin where a gentle pressure had him rocking back. "As much as I would like you to continue... not here. Not like this."

"I want to."

His lover laughed softly. "So eager. You could almost convince me, but *I* want to be able to see it when you do. Properly." The pad of his thumb brushed along Dylan's lips. "I want to take it slow, to savour you. I can do none of that here."

Standing back up, Dylan nuzzled at the hound's neck to the blissful sound of Tracker's appreciative murmurs and whimpers. He crept up one side, pausing only to leave a fluttering kiss on the man's jaw, before softly, slowly, curling his tongue around the small dagger-shaped earring dangling from the lobe.

Tracker's body shuddered against him. The warm flesh in Dylan's grasp twitched, its slickness increasing.

He toyed with the earring only briefly, paying far more attention to the lobe itself.

Tracker's breathing grew increasingly erratic, his name huskily leaving the man's lips. He grasped the underside of Dylan's thighs, his fingers digging into flesh.

Then, Dylan found his feet leaving the ground as his lover hoisted him up. He barely had enough time to wrap his arms around the man's shoulders to keep from falling back before Tracker spun them and his back connected with the wall once more.

With him off the ground and in his lover's grasp, their hips were level. Tracker wrapped his long fingers around both their shafts and started furiously pumping. Dylan joined in, adding a wisp of his magic to the sound of Tracker's rasping moan.

Tracker grappled for him, seeking a way to bring Dylan closer even with him already pinned to the wall. He sealed their mouths together as he continued to thrust into their combined grip. His moaning continued, the sound humming down Dylan's throat.

With them both being so close, it didn't take long before the act sent them over the edge. Warm, thick liquid hit Dylan's stomach. Still, he kept stroking until they both softened.

When Tracker didn't move to break their kiss, Dylan gently pushed the man's shoulders to part them. His lover's breath came in huge gasps. His arms trembled, even with the wall helping to support Dylan's weight. "Are you all right?"

Tracker huffed through a broad grin. "Yes." He tipped his head forward, the furnace-like heat of his temple grazing Dylan's shoulder. "Although, I confess to *not* thinking this one through."

Before he'd the chance to ask what, his lover's mouth had reclaimed his.

Tracker kissed as if he were reluctant for them to part even for a moment, stealing breaths between chaste pecks and languid sweeps of exploring tongues.

Dylan's stomach fluttered and he almost burst out laughing. By the gods, they'd just had sex. A kiss shouldn't give him butterflies. But it did, even if he could barely admit to himself how much he loved this light, giddy feeling brought on by the brush of their lips and the warmth of Tracker's breath in his lungs.

Tracker slowly relinquished his grip, permitting Dylan to find his feet. "Hold still. My mess, I clean." Before Dylan could fully regain his balance, his lover dropped to his knees.

Something hot and wet snaked across his stomach. It flexed along his skin, tickling with each stroke. Was that the man's... tongue? Glancing down quickly confirmed it.

Dylan bit his lip to keep from snickering as Tracker continued to lick along his abdomen. "Track?" he managed during a reprieve. "What are you doing?"

The man lifted his head. His brows rose. "Cleaning up?"

"A rag would've sufficed." A few minutes with a little warm water would've seen the job done. With less tickling, too.

"This is more efficient." Those long fingers latched onto Dylan's waist. "Now stop wriggling."

Dylan tried his best to remain still. It wasn't an easy task. Tracker seemed to be in no hurry and, if he was to judge by the feather-light brushes on parts of his skin that were most certainly not marked, the man was also deliberately seeking to make him squirm.

"Track..." he moaned, unable to stay still and silent in the same moment. If his lover kept up with his teasing, they would be right back at the beginning.

Tracker surfaced, apparently deciding on showing him mercy. His gaze ran over Dylan as his lips twitched in a very self-satisfied manner. "Is something wrong, my dear man?" Mischief danced in that honey-coloured gaze.

Swallowing in an attempt to wet his dry throat, Dylan shut his eyes tight. *Think of something else.* The battlefield. All those dead bodies. The charred stench of burnt hair and roasting flesh. The taste of—

Honey. Only now did he realise the hound's mouth was firmly pressed against his, that he had also unthinkingly parted his lips and allowed Tracker entry—a fact the man was using to his advantage.

Dylan slipped his fingers into his lover's hair, prepared to haul Tracker's head back. Now that he pushed against the man, Tracker's tongue moved slowly.

A smile twisted his lips as the fluttering in his chest returned. He wrapped his arms around the man's waist, pinning them together. The longer they stood there, the less inclined Dylan was to stop.

Tracker drew back, smirking. "I have no plans to leave your side, but we should make ourselves decent."

"In a bit." He adjusted his hold, drawing Tracker's mouth back to him. There was no use denying it. Like an infatuated adolescent, he had grown addicted to this lightness in his heart and there was nowhere he wouldn't follow it.

CHAPTER 46

The King's Winding had only widened since Whitemeadow.

Dylan sat by the bank, the armful of firewood he had collected momentarily discarded at his feet as he took in the sight. In the midday light, the river's depth looked no less ominous. He hadn't paid much attention to the water's passage since leaving the city, but now they were to cross it, the width gnawed at his thoughts.

Back in Riverton, they had agreed the ford would be the best place to attempt a crossing. The river bed would be higher there and the end of summer had the water level at its lowest. That still left a small piece to swim across. Precisely how wide that section would be was unknown. Neither Marin nor Katarina had ventured this far in the kingdom before and his lover hadn't travelled this close to Wintervale in years.

Nevertheless, Tracker swore the ford would make the distance negligible. Dylan wasn't so sure. Paddling about in the waterfall pool had been one thing, crossing something that flowed as strongly as the river did was another. It didn't matter that they planned to be tethered to each other during the attempt.

The rustle of another's passage through the grass alerted him to not being alone. Still seated, he twisted to spy Tracker standing just on the edge of the brush. Like it had for the past couple of days, just the sight of his lover brought a lightness to his chest.

"I thought you might be here," Tracker said. He left the shade of the trees to halt next to Dylan and stare out at the river. Having already stripped himself of his jerkin and quilted shirt, the breeze toyed with the lighter fabric of his undershirt. "It *is* quite beautiful."

He grunted, unable to disagree. As beautiful as the river could be, a deceptively swift current resided beneath its calm facade.

Tracker settled on the grass, crossing his legs before him. "Nervous about tomorrow?" The whole reason they were stopping to camp so early in the day and not forging directly across the river was to get plenty of rest for the task. None of them realistically knew how long it would take and letting the night fall with them still in the river, or worse, separated by its span, was something they all wanted to avoid.

"A little," he admitted, hoping that downplaying the churning in his gut would actually help convince himself that it wouldn't be so bad. It wasn't as though he'd be crossing the water alone.

His lover laid a hand atop Dylan's knee. "I will not let you come to any harm."

Dylan smiled as a soft fluttering danced gaily about his chest. He wished such lightness was enough to sweep up his nerves. "Are you sure that crossing the ford is the only way? That we can't risk crossing at Wintervale?" His recollection of the kingdom maps relied only on the crude one in Katarina's possession, but he remembered Authril describing mighty bridges spanning cliffs that flanked the river mouth. He didn't know how guarded any passage across them would be, but it couldn't be worse than Whitemeadow. "This—" He gestured to his robe. "—doesn't exactly make me look like I've escaped the army."

Sighing, Tracker leant back. "What you look like is a moot point when the other hounds will sense your approach before we reach the city gates."

He knew that. "How can you be so sure there even are any in Wintervale?" If there were the thirty-odd Tracker claimed and only one had been found in Whitemeadow, who was to say the rest hadn't scattered?

"I cannot," his lover confirmed. "It may be that none are currently stationed there, but it is still not a risk I am willing to take."

Nor perhaps one he should be asking with Marin and Katarina in tow. Although, in continuing to travel with the pair, they were also asking them to participate in the same dicey venture across the river.

Dylan returned to examining the water. As much as he would miss the two women, they could easily make their way east without him. The king would ensure any hedgewitch arriving at his castle would have everything they needed to be on their way in comfort.

Tracker cleared his throat. "You once asked how I wound up working at *The Gilded Lily*. Do you still wish to know?"

With his gaze still on the distant shore, Dylan nodded.

"It started because…" His strained, mirthless chuckle barely competed with the wind. "Well, you could say it is because I was young and foolish. Arrogant enough to think myself above hound law and creed. We all were."

"We?" The single word was enough to fully tear himself from any other musing.

"My past lovers." He ran a finger along the row of stitches Dylan had used to mend the undershirt's sleeve. "Wynne, Zinnala and—"

His lips curled in distaste. "—Six-one-eighteen-seventy. Although, we used to call him Hunk. He was a large man, even in childhood."

Dylan's thoughts turned to the band of ink marking Tracker's arm. The same area the Talfaltaner's blade had struck. He knew the designs had once been names, but he'd only managed to decipher one. "You were involved with all three at once?"

"We were all involved with each other. Mostly at the same time."

"I thought—" For so long, he had been under the impression that he understood how relationships worked beyond the tower walls. One partner. Such pairings had been common within the tower, but most had preferred the safety of drifting amongst many. "Is having multiple partners in a relationship common?"

"I would not say that. But it is also not uncommon enough to garner attention. The heart has the capacity to hold more than a single soul in reverence. For most, that means friends and family. For others, it can mean a little more. I know of several groups who make it work."

"I'm guessing yours wasn't one of them."

His lips twisted into a wry smile. "That is certainly one way to put it." He stared out across the river, his eyes misty with memories. "I met Wynne first, during our mutual stint in the infirmary. Me for breaking this." He slapped his left shin.

Dylan remembered seeing a faint scar on the limb whilst massaging Tracker back in Whitemeadow. He had assumed it earned fighting a rogue spellster or, like the scars crossing Tracker's back, an injury gained from a reprimand. "That must've been quite the feat." Elven bones were hardy, capable of withstanding forces that would see a human or dwarf crumble.

Tracker laughed. "Nothing that could not be accomplished by playing games in places that were off-limits. I fell through an unstable section and broke my fall in the tunnel below." His grin fell as that haunted look once more took over. "Wynne, however, was fresh from Stonebay, a prize gained in disbanding the underground slave market. Zinny was, too, but Wynne arrived half-starved. Took them weeks to get her strong enough to properly test."

"And for you to heal?" The increased healing rate elves possessed didn't stop at mere skin and flesh, but a broken shin would've still taken months to mend on its own.

The man shook his head. "I remained in the infirmary only long enough to shake off an infection. By the time I left, however, we had become friends. She introduced me to Zinnala, then *him*." Even without naming the man, Tracker's distaste was enough to sour Dylan's tongue. "Over the years, we grew to be more and things between us were good. We would sneak away from the minders during temple sessions to have fun, innocent and—" One corner of his mouth twitched upwards. "—well... not."

"That sounds dicey." Hadn't the man stressed intimate relationships were forbidden? "Why would you risk being caught?"

Tracker scoffed. "I told you, we were young and arrogant."

"How young?" Given that Hunk's numerical designation ended in the same eighteen-seventy as Tracker's, they'd obviously been of a similar age, but that only told him how old the man would be now.

Frowning, Tracker scratched at his cheek. "Wynne was twelve when we met. The rest of us were roughly a year younger."

At that age, Dylan had barely moved out of the children's dorms. His greatest challenge had been adjusting to sleeping alone, something he never really got the chance to after Sulin arrived. "What changed?"

Tracker pressed his lips together as if he planned not to speak anymore on the subject.

Dylan sat there, curious as to what had transpired that could make the man so reluctant to speak, but hesitant to press him any further.

"We were betrayed," Tracker whispered, the soft tone at odds with the words. He drew his arms around his midsection, hugging himself. "After three years together, you think I would have noticed his affection was different, but I was too focused on... other matters. We all were. When we sought to leave the pack, to leave the kingdom, we thought *he* wanted it too, but he—" He visibly fought to finish the sentence before falling silent.

Bad things happen if we are caught. Words the man had spoken in a time that felt like an age, but Dylan remembered that much. For a hound, being outed wasn't about constant supervision. It meant death.

He laid a hand atop his lover's fingers. "The other hounds killed them, didn't they?"

"No," Tracker said softly. "*I* did."

Dylan sat back, unsure he had heard right.

If Tracker noticed the withdrawal, he gave no indication. "There is this place. They call it the Pit." His voice cracked on the final word. "You are locked in, naked and unarmed, and you fight to the death. Either someone is victorious or no one is."

And yet here the man sat. "They threw you into a lethal brawl at *fourteen*?"

"And more, yes."

"*More?*" he echoed, before realising what had sparked this tale. "They sent you to a brothel after making you go through that?"

Tracker spread his arms wide, baring his throat to the sky. "My prize for coming out of the Pit alive." Settling back into a casual pose, he eyed Dylan, perhaps noticing the subtle distance between them, and smiled solemnly. "I will spare you the details, but know I slew him and him alone."

He didn't need details. The only way to truly disarm an elf was to pull out their fangs and Tracker's were still very prominent. "You said you killed *them*."

Tracker nodded, his head drooping as he rested his arms atop his knees. "I did." The haste in which he spoke did nothing to hide the fact his breathing had turned ragged. "*I* was the reason we got caught. *I* failed to stop him from butchering the others. *I* was the one who was too late to—" He abruptly bit his lip, his jaw trembling, his gaze elsewhere.

"Track?" Dylan reached out, hesitant to actually lay his hand upon his lover's shoulders lest the man was too deep in memories to know he wasn't another target. "What happened sounds horrible. To be put through all that... I... I haven't the words." He couldn't imagine trying to deal with the life or death choice they had thrown Tracker. "But it wasn't your fault."

The man's head snapped around. His eyes were huge and glittered with unshed tears in the dappled light.

"Love?" Had no one ever told him he wasn't to blame? Had *he* never told anyone else what the hounds had done to him? "Are you—?"

Tracker all but launched himself at Dylan, throwing his arms around Dylan's waist as they fell back onto the grass, his fingers grasping great handfuls of robe.

Dylan had barely recovered his breath when he caught a muffled sniff coming from his lover. Then what sounded very much like a sob.

He pressed a cheek against the man's crown. "Are you... crying?" He couldn't recall Tracker ever letting such emotion overcome him. Perhaps a few unshed tears, but never anything stronger.

A faint, watery hum of affirmation bubbled along Dylan's chest. He tried to pull away.

Dylan tightened his hold, wrapping his arms around his lover's shoulders, squeezing until he had no more strength. "It's all right," he whispered into Tracker's hair. He rubbed small circles into the man's back, trying to replicate the soothing motions Tracker went through during Dylan's rougher nights. "After all the times I've bawled on you, I'm hardly going to judge you for doing the same."

Tracker's shoulders shook anew. This time, the motion was briefly accompanied by a thin thread of laughter.

They lay there for a while, wordlessly holding each other. He had suspected something terrible had happened for Tracker to wind up at

The Gilded Lily. Not the torture the hounds put him through. Never would he have considered that.

"Thank you," he whispered, almost afraid to break the silence. "For sharing this with me." It put so many things into perspective.

"You know," Tracker said, his voice muffled by fabric. "I never thought I could... *feel* this way again, not after losing them. But you..." He squirmed out of Dylan's hold to sit once more, his head bowed. "You came along and I was not even aware of how attached I had grown to your company until I realised how much losing you would hurt." He glanced Dylan's way, his eyes red and the curve of his lips carrying a sombre edge. "I cannot risk them finding you."

"You won't have to, I promise." As nervous as he was in crossing the river, he could weather it far better than the haunting look in his lover's eyes. "Tomorrow, we'll be on our way north, right?"

Tracker hummed in agreement, the sound still a little teary.

Sitting up, he laid a kiss upon the man's temple. "Everything will be all right."

"There is more."

He didn't doubt it. His lover's life seemed fraught with misfortune. Small wonder the man worried about Dylan becoming another cautionary tale. "One sorrow at a time."

His lover leant against him for a breath before his posture grew rigid.

"What is it?" No sooner than the words had left his lips did an old dread creep upon him. The back of his neck prickled. Every nerve in his body screamed that they were being watched by more than the wildlife.

Tracker arched a brow, his head tilted slightly. "I felt..." His gaze slid to one side as if he could see behind him without turning. His hand strayed down to where Dylan knew the man kept a throwing knife. The blade slid free of its secret sheath.

Movement in the dappled undergrowth drew Dylan's eye. There for an instant, then gone. Light twinkled through the trees beyond. A section of the river? Had that shape been an animal or something a little more sinister?

"Wait," Dylan whispered, relieved when the word stalled his lover's actions.

"Can you see them?"

"No, I—" He squinted. It wasn't a trick of the light. Nor was it a figure, but the void of their passage through the brush.

Something stalked amongst the trees. Something bigger than a mere bird. Some *one*. Watching. Waiting.

Someone Tracker could sense.

Someone Dylan couldn't see.

Henrie? His heart stuttered. It couldn't be. He had prayed with all his heart for the slim chance anyone had escaped the slaughter in the tower. That optimism had dwindled with the distance. No spellster could've made it this far. Not alone.

But the alternatives were limited. It wasn't either Katarina or Marin. He must've been a while out hunting kindling for Tracker to come after him, but they would've made their presence known, the latter especially so. With Tracker already here, they weren't likely to come looking for him if they didn't immediately return. Marin would probably assume they were off having fun and likely be quick with a jest regardless of how she found them.

No, what he felt wasn't the casual ease of familiar company approaching. That could only mean trouble.

Dylan stood, his shield flickering to life around him, and abruptly halted as Tracker grabbed his arm. "Let me check it out." If it truly was another spellster, then he'd a better chance of keeping things calm.

Tracker loosened his hold, albeit his grasp lingered. His attention slid past Dylan, his eyes widening. Whoever it was, he could definitely see them.

"Don't move," he commanded. Now was not the time for the man to attempt heroics.

Reluctance might've lingered in the stubborn set of his lover's jaw, but Tracker conceded with a wordless bow of his head.

Dylan ventured towards where he had last seen the figure. His shield shimmered around him with each step. It was a drain to have it filmy enough near his legs to let the foliage through whilst keeping the top half strong, but he wasn't about to risk being injured by a startled spellster.

He reached the spot where he'd seen something moving through the undergrowth and waited for a similar sign.

Nothing.

Searching the ground gave him little in the way of clues. He had already traipsed over this area during his hunt for firewood. Even if he had been able to pick out individual footprints amongst the dirt and leaf litter, he wasn't sure if he would also be capable of distinguishing which ones belonged to whom.

A sigh ghosted through his lips as he dispersed his shield. Dylan turned to pick his way back to Tracker's side. Maybe his mind *was* playing tricks on him. The light, combined with the stresses of their journey, could've conjured all sorts of apparitions.

That didn't explain Tracker seeing something.

"Dylan?"

He whirled at the familiar voice. "Hen?" It couldn't be. Nothing could've survived what they had found in the tower. Was he losing his mind now?

The air before him shimmered, the outline of his friend appearing through the veil. It certainly looked like Henrie, if a little haggard and dishevelled. But he was *here.*

"You're—" He pulled the man into his arms, squeezing with everything he had in him. "You're alive." Someone *had* answered his prayers.

Henrie chuckled. "I am. And so are you." He tilted his head up, concern etched across his face. "We heard about the army encampment. Everyone thought you dead or worse. Then Ness swore she saw you dancing in the village. Tricia said she must've been seeing things, that you couldn't be this far east, but..." He crushed Dylan in a similar embrace. "Here you are!"

Dylan could barely focus on the words. He blinked back tears, trying to take in everything. Henrie was here. Nestria, too. And... "Did you say Tricia was with you?" His guardian lived.

His friend nodded. "Not just her. There's Harriet and Sulin. Tillie, too. A handful of others and some guardians. A group of us managed to get out some of the children and even a few younger ones." He pulled away, his eyes growing distant. "There used to be more. Other guardians. Other spellsters. Even some of the servants who'd been outside the walls when it happened. They wanted to split up, try their luck elsewhere, and then..." His gaze snapped back into focus. "You came the same way, right? Travelled the same roads from the tower? How did you avoid the hounds?"

Dylan tried to ignore the shiver running through his blood. "What hounds?"

"The ones who came for us, who sent those other bastards to hunt us down."

"You mean the Talfaltaners?" His thoughts turned to the raided farmhouse they'd encountered on their way to Whitemeadow. The men there had been searching for something. "We encountered some of them. I don't know if they were the same people who've been chasing you, but they're long dead now. As for hounds..." There had been the woman in the Whitemeadow station. She hadn't been much of a threat. "There was only one. She's dead, too."

"Good." He nodded curtly, a savage satisfaction gleaming in his eyes. "The only safe hound is a dead one. And I assume by we, you mean the elf I saw you with?" One side of his mouth hitched in a shrewd smile. "I already gathered you wouldn't have gotten so far without some help. Only the gods know how we would've managed without the guardians." He grabbed Dylan's hand and ploughed through the undergrowth. "Let's go get him. Everyone will want to see you straight away. They'll want to thank him, too."

"About that. He—"

"I can't believe you've been behind us this whole time. Imagine if you'd been able to catch up sooner."

With a hound in tow? He couldn't imagine that reunion going well. "I really don't think that would be a good idea. There's something I need to tell you about Tracker before—"

"So that's his name?" His friend gave a knowing chuckle. "Honestly, I didn't think you were interested in the muscular type. You always seemed more into, you know..." He mimed grabbing a handful of flesh. "...soft."

Panic gripped his chest, squeezing his heart until he thought it might pop. "Hen!" he croaked. "You know I'm not interested in—" His face warmed with the lie before it finished leaving his lips. "I mean—"

His friend bumped him with his shoulder. "It's all right. I think we're far enough from the tower that you can drop the act. Harry figured you were indecisive a long time ago."

"She had?" When *he* had barely come to the realisation? Had he been *that* bad at hiding it?

Henrie nodded. "Catching you two cosying by the river was also a dead giveaway." He waggled his eyebrows suggestively. "Trying a little something different, are we?"

The tightness in his chest eased somewhat. If he could've trusted anyone with such knowledge, it would've been Harriet. They hadn't moved in the same circles as children, but he knew her indecisive stance nearly had her being outed during their teens. That'd been back before her and Henrie became exclusive.

"Where did you find your Tracker?"

"He..." Dylan swallowed. "He sort of found me."

Henrie's brow twitched. He opened his mouth, a question clearly on his tongue, then sealed his lips. A strange glint formed in his eyes.

Their silence continued until they returned to where he had bid Tracker to wait.

His lover still sat beside the firewood Dylan had gathered. Although he already faced them, Tracker waited until they were near before standing. He tilted his head, clearly puzzled and a little surprised, his gaze darting from Henrie to Dylan and back.

Dylan halted between the two men. His stomach churned enough that he could probably make butter in it. Without his jerkin, Tracker didn't immediately look like a King's Hound. He still had to be careful or this could go wrong fast. "Track, this is—"

"Henrie," his friend interjected. In an unexpected display of brashness, he pushed past Dylan to clasp Tracker's hand in greeting. He seemed a little too transfixed on the hound's face. "I'm Henrie."

Tracker's brow twitched in the ghost of a frown.

Henrie jerked his hand free as though bitten. He eyed Tracker with the wary dread that came from knowing precisely what he faced. The same look bore a hardness promising he had no intentions of going down easily.

"It's all right," Dylan blurted, reaching for his friend. "He's safe."

"Safe?" Henrie growled, pulling away from him. "He's a *hound*. Didn't you see what they did to our home?"

"I saw, but—"

"Then how can you say he's *safe?*"

"I'll explain everything." He inched closer, readying himself to throw up a shield and contain the man lest he tried bolting. The last thing they needed was for Henrie to announce Tracker's presence to the others whilst he still considered the man a threat. "But I need you to remain calm."

His eyes widened. "You're *with* them, aren't you? Gods..."

"It's not what you think."

"Oh, it *isn't?*" He took another step back, smacking his palm to his temple. "Well then, please tell me what it *is*." That feral gleam returned to his eyes. "Tell me that one of my dearest friends didn't get dick for the first time in his life and decide to throw his lot in with the very people seeking to kill us. Go on, tell me *that!*"

"I didn't—" He glanced Tracker's way, rallying his courage. "*He* wasn't there when... it happened."

Henrie's brow rose in silent disbelief.

"I swear on my life, Hen, he—"

"No," his friend snapped. "Not yours. *His*." He jabbed a finger at Tracker. "The others know I'm out here. Ness will come for me if I don't return by sundown. She *will* kill him."

Dylan didn't doubt it. Nestria had a knack for levitation and a vengeful streak wider than the river at his back. "The only soul he harmed within the tower was a man trying to kill me." It had been an age since he had thought of that morning. The searing pain as the blade slid between his ribs. How it had punctured his lung and come so close to his heart. "*He* slew the hound we found in Whitemeadow."

Henrie's gaze flicked to Tracker and back, his eyes narrowing. "And you know this how?"

"Because he was with me. He has been at my side since the army fell." Like tending to a spooked cat, he reached out and gently lowered his friend's arm. "Listen, have either of us ever led the other astray?"

Uncertainty and fear twitched across Henrie's face, but Dylan saw what they both knew shining brightly in his friend's gaze. From the first night he had comforted the crying young boy on the other side of the wall, they had been there for each other.

"Take us to the others," he gently urged. He had considered first requesting they regroup with Marin and Katarina, but approaching a bunch of nervous spellsters with Tracker in tow was already going to upset things. He didn't want to make things worse by appearing with a group. "I'll explain everything."

CHAPTER 47

The sky began to drizzle as Henrie led the way to the rest of the spellsters and the air carried a clean, earthy scent he had learnt heralded heavier rain to come. The canopy of trees sheltered them from the worst, but the intermittent droplets that made it through the foliage seemed heavier for it, their soft splats filling the otherwise silence of their passage.

Dylan halted as they broke through to the clearing. The others Henrie had spoken of had set up a crude camp consisting of a single fire. His gaze was instantly drawn to the tiny figures huddled on the far side. *Children.* After the massacre they'd found at the top of the tower, he hadn't dared to hope that any of them might've been spared the fate of their kin.

And here they were. The younger were likely unaware of how close they'd come to death, whilst the older ones eyed their approach with a suspicion that broke his heart to see. He thought of the children they had encountered in their travels, the groups chasing each other through the streets, playing games without a care. How that same untroubled life had been stolen from their spellster counterparts. All because of the hound master's hatred.

"They managed to get other children out," Tracker murmured, the words choked with emotion.

"*Other?*" Dylan echoed. When had the man encountered spellster children outside of the tower? Why hadn't he mentioned it?

He had barely glanced in his lover's direction, seeking answers, when a more familiar sight crouching amongst the young caught his eye. *Tricia.* His guardian, the woman who had been his only reference for a parent. Henrie had said she was here, but seeing her in the flesh, knowing she was alive...

His vision blurred. He took a step towards her, the urge to fall into her arms driving him on. He longed to hear her voice, the soothing tone that would tell him she could fix it, that everything was finally going to be all right.

He halted as a small figure collided into him.

"Dylan!" Nestria's squeal obliterated all other thoughts. Delicate fingers tugged at his robe, pulling him down to her level with an amazing burst of strength.

Her mouth collided with his, hard and hungry. Her arms wound around his neck, holding him fast as she attempted to devour him. He had kissed these lips countless times. The sweep of them was just as soft, warm and...

Wrong.

He gently untangled himself from her grip. Once, not even that long ago, he would've enjoyed this, but now? Something about her had changed since the last time they had touched.

Nestria stared up at him, those big light brown eyes growing larger still with concern. "Dylan?"

"It's good to see you," he murmured. He lifted a hand to her rosy cheeks. Everything about her seemed exactly as he remembered.

It wasn't *her* who had done the changing.

Smiling, she nuzzled his fingers. "I missed you."

"I think he can figure that out, Ness," said a familiar lilting voice. The same one he had heard most mornings for the past decade or so.

Sulin.

Laughter, sounding dangerously close to sobs, bubbled up Dylan's throat. He whirled about and flung himself at the man, wrapping his arms around Sulin's shoulders and squeezing tight. Tears pricked his eyes. Weeks of believing they'd all been slaughtered...

The relief flooding his senses weakened his legs. He sagged against his old roommate, unsure if he could fully hold himself upright. "I thought you all dead."

"We almost were," Sulin replied, helping him to keep his feet. The jagged line of a scar marked the alchemist's cheek, a starkly lighter shade of brown than the rest of his face. Dylan couldn't recall the man having it when he left. Had he gotten that little souvenir in the tower attack?

He grabbed his friend's chin, examining the scar closely as his magic delved. The mark was surface level and still healing. If Sulin had gotten it at the tower, it would've finished by now. "Who attacked you?"

"I imagine it was bandits," Tracker replied. "Or perhaps an offshoot of the Talfaltaners we encountered outside Whitemeadow."

Sulin's eyes narrowed. He said nothing, likely waiting for an explanation as to the presence of this stranger.

Nestria wasn't so patient. "Who are *you?*"

Henrie darted between them as if Nestria's glare could've killed. "He's the one responsible for getting Dylan here."

"You mean he's his warden?" she demanded, her glower only

deepening.

Tracker's lips stretched into a waxy curve. "I am certainly not that. But *you* must be one of Dylan's closest friends, or so I assume from the way you greeted him."

"You knew about the men at Whitemeadow," Sulin mused. He eyed Tracker with less hostility than Nestria, but with the same level of suspicion. "You have travelled far with our friend, then?"

"Since Toptower," Tracker confessed.

The response seemed to be enough for Dylan's former roommate, who simply nodded.

"You're not looking to enter Wintervale, are you?" Dylan asked, hoping to pull the topic away from Tracker. They would learn soon enough, but he needed time to gently broach the subject.

"No," Sulin replied. "We are attempting to reach Dvärghem. Hans says they use spellsters to test any unknown recipes they uncover, so we figured they might at least let us pass through if not stay."

The name wasn't any more familiar than when Henrie mentioned it, but he silently thanked the gods his friends had such a person to guide them. "We're heading for Dvärghem, too." They could travel together, help protect each other. "I actually encountered a hedgewitch near the border. She's back at our camp."

"An actual hedgewitch?" Sulin echoed, laughing. "And they are still travelling with you? You must have talked their ears off by now."

He chuckled at hearing his friend's familiar jibes again, the threat of tears—or perhaps the light rain—collecting at the corners of his eyes. "Not quite." Katarina was more likely to do that to him than tire of answering anything he said or the questions he had about her people.

"I will need details on how you came to meet them," his old roommate continued. "I always thought the crown kept dwarves from going near the battlefield."

His grin wavered as he recalled the moments upon meeting Katarina. The ash hanging in the air. The smell of burnt wood and charred flesh. The hum of fading magic on his neck as his body healed. "It was a... unique circumstance." Demarn might not have permitted Katarina's presence, but Udynea had. And to ensure her safety, the empire had wiped out the threat, proving they'd only been toying with the kingdom before.

"We heard what the empire did to our forces," Nestria said, snaking between him and Sulin. "We all thought the worst. What happened to you? How did you escape? Your collar..." She felt his neck, his skin tingling at the feather-light touch of her fingertip gliding along the scarred skin. "How is it gone? I thought leashing was permanent."

"I'll explain later," he promised. His story would make sense once they saw what remained of his collar, but that was back at their camp. With Sulin here, he could finally get the answer to why the *infitialis* exploded. "I'm glad to see you're all safe, though. When we reached the tower, I..." He had questions about how they had managed it, but that tale could come once they were settled on the other side of the river. "I still can't believe it."

"It was terrible," she whispered. Her eyes widened, tears flowing down her cheeks in huge drops. "The hounds came and... and..." She fought to speak further, but the words disintegrated into sobs.

Dylan pulled her close, tucking her head beneath his chin. Seeing the aftermath had been enough, he didn't need to know precisely what happened.

"Most of us were in the gardens when the first wave struck," Sulin continued. "You know what they are like—" He fell silent for a breath, closing his eyes, before correcting himself. "What they *were* like at midmorning."

He did. During that time, it was often teeming with life. Alchemists pottered about with concoctions designed to improve plant growth, children learnt their way around the more dangerous talents whilst being watched over by their guardians, and there was always the occasional spellster who sought a bit of fresh air or, like Launtil, preferred to play with plants than magic.

He also had no trouble recalling the bodies they'd found strewn about the grounds. Guardian, servant, spellster. Friend, rival, enemy... All equal in death.

"We had no idea who they were," his old roommate continued. "Or what they wanted, beyond our deaths. But—" He cocked his head, peering at Tracker. "Talfaltaners, you said?" He nodded thoughtfully. "That would explain a great deal."

"I tried to stop them!" Nestria abruptly wailed. "I *tried*. I couldn't save everyone, but—" She clawed at Dylan's robe like a mouser. "*They* came and—"

"They?" Dylan grabbed her shoulders, holding her still before she ripped the clothes from his body. "You mean the hounds?"

Nestria shook her head, seemingly too lost in recalling the past to hear him. Tears fell down her reddened cheeks in a steady stream, dripping off her chin. "I couldn't defend against them." She tightened her hold on his robe. "My shield. It didn't work. It held back the first lot, but not the others. All those stories," she whispered. "They were real. Every single one. They're monsters, Dylan. *Demons*. They poured out of the tower, dripping blood and just *walked right through the shields*."

He slowly loosened his grip, letting Nestria slide to the ground before they both collapsed. She clutched at his legs, softly wailing and rocking. Laying a hand atop her head, he absently stroked her hair until she fell quiet.

His gaze slid to those sitting around the other side of the fire. They didn't huddle quite so much now, enabling him to pick out more individuals. Launtil sat near a child almost as big as herself. His own guardian crouched between a pair of smaller children, comforting them. Several figures in the same garb tended to a few of the others, one of the adults appeared to be missing a hand.

There weren't as many familiar faces as he had hoped.

Dylan bit his lip. When he first saw the aftermath, he had blamed himself for not reaching the tower sooner. Now he knew his presence likely would've spelt disaster, even if they had been able to make it out.

With his legs still bound in Nestria's grip, he twisted on the spot to find his other two friends. "How did you escape?" Unless there was a prodigy amongst the children, all they had to bear was a handful of adult spellsters. None of whom were strong enough to breach an army. There was only one entrance through the tower's outer walls and, with the Talfaltaners likely filling the gateway as they stormed through, his friends couldn't have fled that way.

"Our route was not something I recommend unless you are as desperate as we were," Sulin replied.

"I imagine keeping the wall from collapsing would have been quite the challenge," Tracker murmured. "And yet, here you are."

Dylan frowned. The man's observation carried too much confidence for his liking. Now he thought about it, Tracker didn't seem quite as surprised to see these people here as Dylan would have expected. "You knew spellsters had escaped?"

His lover winced. "*Knew?* No. I had *hoped*. I saw the damage their escape did to the tower's outer wall, but without investing in a proper hunt, it was just as likely they had died in the attempt."

"The outer wall?" He hadn't been paying much attention to the tower's structure at the time. "You mean the secret entrance?" Something had blown it open, but he didn't think anyone had made it through there alive.

"No," Sulin replied, directing his attention to Dylan. "Henrie herded us to the conduit at the back of the gardens when the hounds came. Did you know the bars were bloody dog metal?" He shook his head, incredulous. "Had to dig out a tunnel whilst we fought to hold them back. We got through as many as we could before we had to collapse the way." His mouth stretched in a humourless smile. "That seems to stop the bastards."

"It would." Tracker matched the alchemist's expression. "Nothing stops a man in his tracks like a ton of rock through his skull. But I do wonder…" His focus slid across the clearing before returning to Sulin in full. "Such a display would have alerted your attackers. I find it hard to believe you were not followed."

"I *did* say there were a lot more of us," Henrie gently reminded them. "We split up once outside the tower walls. And we've had our share of encounters. Not with hounds, but those… other folk you mentioned. They split our group again when we sought shelter at an old farmhouse outside of Whitemeadow."

"We encountered the same enemies," Tracker said, his expression grim. "They are dead now."

"*You*," Nestria snarled, drawing everyone's attention. With her malice crackling through the air and hissing through her teeth, she clambered to her feet. "I know where I've seen your face now. I know *what* you are. You were in Riverton. And *you!*" She swung to Henrie. "I told you not to go looking. I can't believe you'd bring a *hound* right to us!"

Hurried movement came from the other side of the fire. The flicker of a shield being thrown over them all barely glowed in the afternoon light. The flames of the campfire flared. Whimpers and hushed sobs broke the silence.

"Hold on," Dylan commanded. "I can ex—"

Nestria's glare switched to him and he flinched at the raw fury burning in her eyes. "I saw you. We were getting all the supplies we could afford and I saw… Eirian assured me I had to be seeing things. Your guardian agreed and I thought maybe they were right." Her gaze darted over Tracker, no doubt taking in the lack of armour or visible weapons. "I didn't recognise him without his full attire, but he's who I saw you with. One of *them*." Her eyes narrowed as she hissed the final word.

"It's not what you think," Dylan insisted, slowly putting himself between her and Tracker. He glanced at Henrie, seeking assistance. The man's focus was on speaking with Sulin, who seemed to be handling the news far better. Whilst his old roommate eyed Tracker warily, with his fingers firmly wrapped around the hilt of his dagger, he didn't appear as eager to claw out the hound's throat. "He's safe, I promise."

"*Safe?*" she shrieked. "How could you know what they did to us and consider him as *safe?*" She pawed at him, her nails scraping along his clothes. "I saw you dancing with the villagers and letting that… *thing*—" She thrust one finger at Tracker, who sneered ever so slightly. "—snog you in front of everyone like some simpering maiden."

Dylan opened his mouth to object, but the lie refused to come out.

"You don't deny it?" Nestria screeched. "You're not even going to try?"

"No," he admitted, the word leaving his lips far calmer than he felt. Why would he dare such a thing? It was true. Every word. He had danced with Tracker, let the man kiss him, and enjoyed every second of it.

His reply only further upset Nestria. "We're taking Dylan with us," she declared, pulling Dylan alongside her with a brisk tug at his sleeve. "And *you* won't follow." Snarling, she raised her arm. Already, fire flickered on her palm. "I mean it. Don't even take another step. I'm warning you."

Tracker narrowed his eyes at her. "That would be *Dylan's* decision to make, yes?"

"There's nothing to decide," she retorted, her back straightening in what seemed to be an effort to make herself taller. "He's amongst friends now. He doesn't need *you.*"

"Just stop it," Dylan snapped. "Ness, put the flame out before you hurt someone."

"Did you even know what that man was?" Nestria snarled back before raising her voice towards Tracker. "How many lives did your blade take, murderer?"

"Track wasn't at the tower," Dylan replied before Tracker could. He could see it in their eyes that they wouldn't have believed the man anyway, but maybe they'd listen to him. "That's what I've been trying to tell you."

"Is that what he said?" Sulin growled, his coastal accent—a slightly deeper one to Tracker's, now he heard the pair together— thickening with each word. Those dark eyes narrowed, promising murder if he even suspected Tracker was about to close. "You cannot trust a word he says."

"I know because he has been with me. You know, the group I've been travelling with?" he added, trying to nudge them into remembering the man had been with him since Toptower. "We couldn't have been more than a few days out from Oldmarsh when the attack happened. He didn't get there until everything was over. He couldn't have."

Sulin's gaze flicked in Dylan's direction. The hand that clutched tightly to his dagger wavered. He loosened his fingers, but kept the weapon within easy reach.

"Even if he wasn't there," Nestria said. "His kind *were.*"

Dylan clasped her shoulders. "Are you really going to condemn him over something he didn't do just because the rest of his pack did?"

Something flickered in the back of her eyes, an uncertainty that slowly thawed out the icy hardness.

"I swear," Tracker growled, earning Nestria's baleful glare. "What happened was an atrocity, but the whole pack was not responsible."

"And where were the ones who refused to slaughter us?" she retorted. "Why weren't *they* there to help us? Why didn't they *stop* it?"

"Because they were already dead!"

"Then maybe you should join them," Nestria snarled. Jerking out of Dylan's grip, she whirled towards Sulin. Their friend's dagger slid from the sheath, the metal emitting a terrible shriek as it spun in the air.

Dylan found his hand around her wrist before he could think to move. His leg swept behind hers, knocking her to the ground.

Time seemed to slow. The dagger hit the ground, blade first, sinking into the damp soil a few feet from his lover's position.

Nestria stared up at him, her brown eyes impossibly big, full of confusion and glistening with tears.

He released his hold to race across the clearing, stopping only when he connected with the shield he'd slammed around Tracker. Putting his back to the barrier, he bellowed, "No one is touching him!"

"What are you doing?" Nestria queried, still a touch breathless, as she got to her feet. "Why, in the name of the Seven Sisters, would you protect that thing?"

"Because I l—" He caught the word before it could leap from his tongue. That would be a bad thing to confess right now. Henrie might've darkly joked about sex, but all his friends could be sure of was Tracker had only gone as far as a kiss.

Sulin narrowed his eyes at him. "So you would attack us in his stead? Your friends? Your *people*?" He continued to hedge around Dylan, trying to get between him and Tracker.

He followed his friend step for step, slowly moulding his shield to form around himself as well. He didn't know what Sulin planned, but he wasn't about to give the man an opportunity to show him. "I'm certainly not going to stand here and let you kill an innocent man."

"*Innocent?*" Nestria echoed. "You didn't see what they did. Didn't see them slaughter—"

"I saw enough!" he snapped back. "You have no idea what I've witnessed since they leashed me." The memories of the ambush on the border came flooding back. The smell of burning flesh, the inhuman screams of the dying. He hadn't been able to stop it, had barely managed to save his own hide. "I have killed far too many who made foolish choices." Bandits. Desperate or greedy, it didn't matter. They were still dead. By *his* hand. "I don't want to fight you, but I won't let you harm what is mine."

"What's gotten into you?" she asked, softly pleading. "You were never like this. What do you mean... *yours?*"

"Is it not obvious?" Sulin replied. "This is clearly *his* hound."

"His *man*," Henrie amended.

Nestria made a retching noise. "Don't be disgusting. Dylan doesn't like men. He's not some indecisive."

Dylan's chest tightened at the declaration. His shield wobbled, exposing Tracker for a moment until he regained control. He had known that would be her reaction. His heart continued to thump wildly, nevertheless. *It cannot hurt you.* He swallowed through the prickling in his throat. *There is no one to out you to.* No overseers. Guardians, yes, but not even enough to attend to the children. *He* was not a priority.

"If you had seen how I found them," Henrie said, "you wouldn't be saying that, Ness."

Indignance sheared through the final thread of fear. "We were not doing *that*. And even if I hadn't slept with him, it wouldn't mean I'd stand aside and let you kill him." Groping blindly behind him, Dylan sought his lover's arm that, once found, he drew around his torso. "He has risked his life to keep me safe, to—"

"You *slept* with him?" Nestria's eyes widened in horror as she grabbed Sulin's arm. "That's not really true, is it?" she asked of their friend before facing Dylan once more. "You're not interested in men. You've never been interested."

"I—" He fell silent upon sensing Tracker's hand move, smiling as he realised his lover was merely seeking to link their fingers. "I am," he whispered. Clearing his throat, he continued in a louder tone, "I always have been. Some of you already knew that." He sought Harriet, finding she had come to stand at Henrie's side. "Or at least suspected it." He caught Sulin's gaze, holding it until he got a confirming nod from his former roommate.

That small movement wasn't missed by Nestria. She rolled her eyes. "Don't entertain the rot they've put in his head, Su. Next thing you'll tell me *you* are indecisive. It's not natural."

"Actually," piped up a familiar voice. "It's not as unusual, or as uncommon, as you've been led to believe."

Tillie. He had spotted Launtil helping with the young, but seeing her standing beside Sulin almost had Dylan in tears.

Nestria scoffed. "What do *you* know about natural? You were a slave. You still speak of your mistress as though she was a guardian."

Launtil ignored the other woman's outburst. Instead, she left Sulin's side with a squeeze of an arm to stand before Dylan. "Udynea isn't perfect by any means, but they do not judge on sexuality. The very people the tower calls indecisive are the most common."

"For gods' sake, Ness," Harriet growled. Even though she was technically shorter than the other woman, she still managed to tower over Nestria's slight elven frame. "I know you used to keep track of who Dylan was screwing back in the tower, but is that really your top priority here? You didn't care when Henrie and I became exclusive."

He had never outright confronted Nestria about her monitoring of his affairs, but there'd been enough signs without her admission. People who had once been friendly suddenly avoiding him, her letting slip knowledge she shouldn't have. It hadn't bothered him, then.

Nestria scoffed. "Of course not. You were both my friends. I was happy you'd found each other. Besides, your situation was different. You chose a side and—"

The crack of Harriet's hand connecting with the other woman's cheek echoed across the river and back. "I chose a *person*, thank you very much," she growled, shaking her hand. "You were always claiming you knew him better than anyone. I thought you knew it about him. That all your bluster was to keep others from guessing. I can understand speaking lies to keep our own safe, but I didn't think you *believed* it."

"It's not about belief," Nestria snarled through clenched teeth, the words further warped as she pressed a hand to her cheek. "None of us will be able to return to the tower if—"

"There is no tower!" Dylan roared. "I burnt it all. Every beam. Every book. Every bed. All that I could." His eyes watered at the memory. The heat kissing his skin. How the flames sought to suck the air from his lungs. "I would've gone up with it if not for *him*!" He jerked the thumb of his free hand over his shoulder at Tracker.

"Don't say that!" Nestria shrieked, clapping her hands over her ears.

The rest of his friends stood still, a perfect row of horrified expressions adorning their faces.

He hadn't meant to be so blunt, but it was out. They knew. Taking a steadying breath, he continued in a more level tone, "I thought you were all dead, thought myself the last. I just—" Fresh tears slid down his cheeks, each drop falling on the heels of the other. "I just wanted to be home again." He knew the truth, though. That even if the tower still stood, he had stopped belonging there the moment they wrapped *infitialis* around his neck.

His lover's arms slowly encircled his waist, drawing him closer.

Dashing the tears from his face, he leant into the touch.

"Look," Harriet said. "He's alive. We're together. They've been travelling together for months. If this man was at all a threat, neither of those things would be true. Isn't that enough proof he can be trusted?"

"Oh, it's proof of something," Nestria agreed, before sneering at

Tracker. "What sick thing did you do to him, hound?"

"Could you be a little more specific, my dear woman?" Tracker replied. "We have done quite a number of *things*."

Despite the wetness still smeared across his face, Dylan couldn't help the abrupt honk of laughter that parted his lips.

In an instant, the brief shock on Nestria's face hardened to rage. Screaming, she snatched Sulin's dagger off the ground and lunged towards them. Her momentum halted as she slammed into Dylan's shield.

She barely paused to evaluate the barrier separating Tracker and himself from the rest. The *infitialis* dagger came up and sliced into the surface.

Dylan doubled over, clutching at his head. He stumbled and strong hands grabbed him, keeping him from collapsing. He clutched at the figure, seeking strength in that hold.

His lover's grip tightened, keeping him upright.

"Get your hands off him!" Nestria screamed.

"Ness!" Henrie cried out, the word clanging in Dylan's ears. Both Henrie and Harriet stood between Nestria and the shield, trying to get her attention as Sulin sought to wrest his dagger from her grip. "Stop it! You're hurting him!"

"He's a *hound*. He could kill us all." Bowling her friends away with a blast of wind, she resumed hacking at the shield, putting all of her weight behind each strike.

"That is enough!" Tracker roared, the words reverberating as though two people spoke. He lunged through the shield to grab Nestria by the arm.

Dylan collapsed to his knees. The shocks of the man passing through the barrier might've been minute compared to the dagger's attack, but that didn't make it any more bearable.

Tracker wrenched the dagger from Nestria's hand, shoving her aside before stepping back through the barrier. The blade flashed in the afternoon light as he flung it to the ground at his feet.

Instantly, his friends fell into silence. They stared at the man with a mixture of confusion, shock and horror.

"Listen to you all," Tracker growled. "Squabbling like children over a toy. Do your guardians not have enough to worry over with the actual young that they must coddle you as well?" He gestured to the fire where the guardians and several older spellsters had their hands full calming the children.

"They're scared, Track," Dylan replied, slowly getting to his feet. "Most of them haven't ever been beyond the walls." He couldn't be sure about the guardians—they came from all over the kingdom, and sometimes beyond—but of the spellsters he recognised, only two had been raised elsewhere.

"Perhaps," his lover conceded. "But they should be focusing on truths."

"And what truths would they be, sir hound?" Tricia demanded. His guardian marched across the clearing, planting herself directly opposite the man.

Tracker held her gaze for some time, his whole body prepared to retaliate.

Standing at his lover's back, Dylan laid a hand on the man's shoulder. If there was one person he could depend on to keep a steady mind, it was his guardian.

Tracker glanced over his shoulder, one brow raised as he caught Dylan's gaze. Then, giving Dylan a curt nod, the man relaxed. "Truth?" he murmured. "Well, my dear guardian, let us start with the fact I am no longer a hound, nor have I been one for some time. I was not there when my former pack committed the unspeakable, and not a day goes by where I do not regret being unable to aid its occupants in escaping that atrocity."

Dylan fought to keep his expression neutral, even as he tightened his grip on his lover's shoulder. He hadn't considered Tracker might have similar feelings to himself on being too late to help, but the man had a definite soft spot for children and he must've brought dozens of young spellsters to the tower.

Tracker laid a hand atop Dylan's, gently patting his fingers. "I mean none of you any harm. We are merely trying to head north, same as you all. And if you are this far east in your pursuit, you must know there is only one way before you reach Wintervale."

Nestria growled.

"If you're heading north," Tricia said, laying a stilling hand on Nestria's upper arm. "Then why attempt a crossing here? We didn't dare enter Whitemeadow to cross the river, but *you* weren't being chased."

"We were not," Tracker agreed. "But the bridges were blocked, thanks to the same force that attacked the tower. They destroyed all but a handful of ships. You must have travelled alongside the river for some of the way. Did you not notice a lack of cargo vessels?" He pointed to the wide body of water at their backs. This close, the narrow part the man had called the ford didn't look as easy as he had claimed. "*That* has been our goal since the city."

"As it was ours." She glanced over her shoulder, following the direction he pointed. "However..."

"It is a lot of people, yes? Both the small and those who cannot swim. We can help."

"Yes," Dylan swiftly agreed. With the others here, they could cobble their shields together into a bridge, negating the need to swim across. "We could head north together." With children in tow, they'd be stuck travelling at a slower pace. *And with winter approaching.* But with Tracker and Katarina to guide them and Marin teaching the others how to survive, they were likely to get through it a lot easier.

Nestria scoffed. "Sure, let's just invite the hound into our embrace."

The others weren't as verbal in their aversion to the idea, but their expressions made it no less plain.

Frowning, Tricia pinched the bridge of her nose. "It's a lot to take in. And they have been through a lot."

"As have you," Tracker softly added.

His guardian said nothing further, but Dylan caught the faint flattening of her lips.

Sighing, Tracker turned to face him. "Perhaps it would be better if I left for now. Give your friends time to calm down, yes? I can head back to camp and let the others know you are here, whilst you—"

"Others?" Tricia interjected. "I heard mention of a hedgewitch. There are more? Are they also... former hounds?"

"No," Dylan replied, vehemently shaking his head. "They're just travelling companions I picked up before Track found me. And there's only two."

"A hedgewitch and her apprentice, then?"

He nodded. He had learnt during their travels down from Whitemeadow that Tracker had used such an excuse when trying to get the pair to the city's northern side. Marin would definitely make for a poor apprentice, but if having the hunter seen in such light kept her safe, then proper explanations could come when the atmosphere wasn't as tense.

"Are we really going to just let him wander away from our camp?" Nestria demanded of the others.

"What would you prefer, my dear woman?" Tracker countered, his smile stretching until it was broad and toothy. "That *I* stay put and Dylan brings our companions here? You wish to keep me in your watchful view?"

Nestria's eyes narrowed until they were little more than a gleam between her lashes. "I'll allow it," she finally replied. "*Only* if you're tied up."

"If it will make you feel safer and keep you from seeking my death..." Tracker spread his arms wide in surrender and walked out from beneath the shield's cover.

"No." Dylan grabbed the man's arm, stopping his lover from taking another step. "You're not actually suggesting this," he demanded of the others before turning back to Tracker. "You've done nothing wrong."

Smiling sadly, his lover gestured to Nestria, who bared her teeth at him. Even with the full length of her fangs on display, their points were practically nothing compared to Tracker's. "Your friend would disagree."

"But—" He fell silent as the man patted his chest.

"Peace, darling. If it helps them to see I mean no harm, I will allow it." Grinning, he added, "Besides, this is hardly the first time someone has tied me up."

Dylan turned back to his friends, seeking reassurance that they truly weren't going to follow Nestria's suggestion, only to find Sulin already held a length of rope.

His old roommate gestured for Tracker to kneel and bound the man with a precision Dylan wasn't aware Sulin possessed. "It is only until your return," he assured.

Tracker sat back, testing his new bindings, and nodded. "Go," he urged. "Everything will be fine."

CHAPTER 48

The sky continued its shift into a dreary grey as Dylan backtracked through the forest. The rain steadily grew heavier from its earlier drizzle, pattering the ground and the foliage. If it got any worse, then crossing the river could become even more dangerous.

Waiting until favourable weather presented itself would be ideal, especially when it came to getting the young across. But how long could they realistically linger before someone noticed them? It didn't even need to be a hound. Any person stumbling upon the group would pick them as refugees. Once word reached the pack, it wouldn't take much for them to piece together they were rogue spellsters.

The distant cry of an unfamiliar voice had him pause for a step. Creeping closer, he peered through the trees, straining both sight and hearing to determine what lay ahead. It definitely sounded like trouble. And, if he hadn't been turned around, their camp sat directly in its path.

The others. It had been so long since encountering any threat near the road that he had almost forgotten there could be. Tracker had mentioned bandits claimed large sections of the road between Riverton and the capital. Dylan assumed they would focus on the merchants, but also hadn't intended to be as long as they had been.

He picked up the pace, ignoring the sting of a branch slapping him in the face. If anything bad had happened to one of them, he would make that perpetrator wish they'd never heard of their current vocation.

He burst into the middle of their camp, his shield strong and his magic ready to do damage. "I'll give you one opportunity to leave us in peace." He scanned the site, spying the pair facing down a large group.

"Get out of here," Katarina ordered, swiping at her opponent with Dylan's quarterstaff. "They're—"

"*Run!*" Marin bellowed. "Now!"

He barely had time to recognise the armour before he realised the warning was for him. The figures—a dozen, at least—weren't just heeding his presence. They were encroaching on it. *No.* Any ordinary person would flee at the sight of a spellster ready to defend.

These weren't ordinary people.

He turned to run, halting as everything Tracker had ever mentioned about hounds flooded his thoughts. Where could he go to escape them? Nowhere. Even if he could outrun them, they would only follow his magic. Let him lead the way to his pyre. Or worse, a second slaughter if they found the others.

No. These monsters had already glutted themselves on enough spellster blood. He would see that savagery repaid in kind.

He tucked his shield into the back of his mind. The barrier might not keep *them* at bay, but it worked on projectiles well enough. What did he have at hand to combat them once they *were* within reach? Nothing. Which simply meant he couldn't let them get that chance.

Funnelling his control into the ground, he blasted the earth with a series of vibrations. The surrounding trees swayed and groaned. The crash of a fallen branch came from somewhere in the distance.

The hounds stilled their approach, unbalanced as the earth continued to undulate. It wouldn't hold them back forever. Already, a few were bracing themselves.

He breathed deeply, trying to keep his emotions steady. His usual attacks, the things he could do with ease, all relied on direct magic. He needed something that could harm them, something he could manipulate without relying on finesse. *Like the pond water.* He had never tried to move something that big, but the river was too far to make the attempt. If only it was closer so he could draw upon the water and try to—

The musical clink of heavy droplets rang atop his shield. He drew from the moisture, honing it into a sharp form even as it froze.

He aimed for the closest hound and let the icicle fly.

The man dodged, snarling as it nicked him.

Dylan drew more moisture, sending out a volley of shards at another. His second target wasn't so lucky.

The hounds hesitated. It was for a moment, but long enough for him to ring his shield with icy daggers and re-examine his surroundings. His opponents numbered more than the dozen he had originally counted, no doubt called back by his magic. Not the full pack of thirty, but definitely more than a third.

Over the shoulders of one hound, he spotted two more holding Marin and Katarina fast. Still alive. Unlike the Talfaltaners, they made no move on their lives.

"Come on!" he screamed.

They rushed at him.

He continued to spray them with ice shards. Faster, smaller, sharper.

His focus remained divided. Being surrounded forced him to whirl on the spot. He targeted those closest, but they dodged his attempts with an almost supernatural speed. If he put too much magic into the ice, they slipped by harmlessly. Too little and they lacked the force to slip between the metal plates hidden in the hounds' leather jerkins.

The shock of his shield being breached had him swivelling to confront a hound's sword. He grabbed the blade, gritting his teeth against the pain and pushing heat into the steel until it glowed. His blood sizzled along the edge. The stench of searing flesh invaded his nostrils.

With an enraged bellow, the woman on the other end relinquished the hilt. She staggered back, clutching her hand to her chest. Then she drew a dagger and rushed forward, impaling herself on her own sword.

Dylan released his hold on the weapon, letting it fall with its owner rather than try to reclaim the blade. Her approach had given him a break in the enclosing circle of death. He raced for the trees, flattening his back against the broad trunk of an oak.

The hounds followed, wary. Tracker said those of his former pack often expected to die in pursuit of their quarry and he had just twice-proven himself a tale of caution.

It just gave him time to recoup.

He thumped his chest, hoping they couldn't feel the strain warbling through his magic, the tug of him reaching the end of his endurance. He couldn't stop. Couldn't risk the hounds finding his friends. His guardian. The children. They were too close. He needed to soak this spot in enough magic that they couldn't sense anything else.

Having lost track of Marin and Katarina, he sought their presence amongst the tents, failing to spot them. His shield stuttered at the thought of them amongst the dead.

The flash of orange-red hair caught his attention, just as a familiar figure darted behind one of the tents. *Authril?* He shook his head. His exhaustion had to be playing tricks with his mind. The warrior was imprisoned back at Whitemeadow. She couldn't possibly—

The figure re-emerged. It *was* her. She was actually here.

With *them*.

Lightning crackled through his veins. The wind beyond his shield grew hectic, whipping up dust and debris. It obscured not only the tents and his companions, but also the hounds closing in on him.

He ringed his shield in ice shards. They wavered in the air, buffeted by the wind. If he flung them without aim, there was no telling who it might hit. Katarina and Marin were still out there.

"Halt!" someone roared from above.

Dylan snapped his head up. At the same moment, a figure dropped on top of him.

They both tumbled to the ground. His chest slammed into an exposed tree root, a definite crack of a rib preceding his breath rushing out of his lungs.

He lay still, struggling to breathe as his magic rushed to heal the break. His shield failed, as did the ice shards. Wind briefly lashed at him before that, too, died.

"How nice of you to come back on your own," the woman hissed in his ear. "But all alone?" She lifted her head a fraction, surveying the surrounding forest. "Cutter," she ordered. "Backtrack his trail."

No! Still fighting for air, he thrashed every ounce of weight he possessed. He couldn't let them leave here. His shield flashed around him, gone in the instant it appeared.

"Be still," growled a second voice. Deeper and angrier than the one ordering her pack about, but less menacing.

"Scout. Archer," the woman continued. "Check our flank. Be mindful of every branch and the shadows. We do *not* want him sneaking up on us."

His face was further ground into the dirt. Stones and sharp twigs scraped along his cheek. His magic, having finished repairing the broken rib, sought to heal this new injury. His face tingled with power he couldn't bring to bear. At least he could breathe.

"I said be still!" The hound slammed their fist into Dylan's gut, expelling all the air he had just regained.

He lay gasping anew, unable to explain that he couldn't help what his innate healing did.

"Easy, Seeker," the woman purred as she rolled Dylan onto his side. "Our little warden said he could heal himself." Rough fingers caressed his cheek. "I can see why she was so eager to reclaim you. Such a pity." She grabbed his hair, hauling back his head.

The cold edge of a blade kissed his neck.

"Wait!" Authril demanded. "You promised he was mine. He's no use to me, or the army, if he's dead."

Dylan rolled his eyes, trying to find the warrior. Tears stung his vision. His scalp prickled, itching as the pain had his magic flooding the area to constantly heal. *That* was why she travelled with these monsters after everything they'd done? She had brokered a deal with them to let her have him?

"*You* promised us a traitor," the woman snarled. Nevertheless, the blade left his neck untouched. "If you lied to us—"

"He's here," Authril insisted. "He'll come to Dylan's aid. I've seen it."

The hound released Dylan's head, letting his face slam back into the dirt. "So you say."

He lay still, trying to recoup both his breath and his power. Maybe he could stall. Tracker had to have felt his attacks. The man had to know something was wrong.

As though soothing a spooked cat, the hound caressed his shoulder. "Let us see if we cannot call upon him a little faster."

"Wait," he croaked. "Plea—"

Pain lanced itself through his side, tearing a scream from him. Magic flooded the site, knitting together skin and flesh until only a sticky dampness remained on the surface.

Dylan pushed off the ground only to find another set of arms grappling him back onto his side. He fought them to no avail. In the midst of his thrashes, he caught sight of a bloodied blade.

"Hold him still," the woman calmly ordered as she once more brought her knife down.

~ ~ ~

The ropes were bound tighter than Tracker had expected, especially compared to Dylan's shabby work with the belts back in Whitemeadow.

Sulin, the man responsible for such bonds, squatted before him. Those dark eyes—their colour and shape reminiscent of one Tracker had lost so long ago—alternated between watching his every movement and that of Nestria, who marched restlessly around the clearing, clutching the alchemist's dagger.

The more Tracker focused on the man, the greater such uneasy familiarity became. It was more than the eyes. It lurked in his face, the gentle curve of his jaw and the way his ears twisted just a fraction at the tip. He had only ever met one other elf who had that trait. And Zinnala had been dead for a long time.

"You know," Sulin said, his tone casual as though Tracker wasn't bound. "I never told anyone, but I always knew there had to be something special with you hounds."

"A wise choice," he replied, trying to sound just as relaxed. He recalled Dylan saying the man had been born elsewhere, had been brought to the tower as a young adolescent. Years of living in the tower had altered the man's accent too much for Tracker to pinpoint *where* he came from, but Sulin had definitely started life somewhere along the kingdom's coast. "They would not have permitted you to live had you made it known you were aware of our immunity to magic."

The man shook his head. "Immunity never crossed my mind. Thought it some sort of refined spellster ability, that you were all just capable of sensing magic like my sister. When they found us in that godsforsaken slave market, your pack took her away and I knew." He tipped forward, his eyes unblinking. "Whatever *you* are, she was the same."

A chill settled into Tracker's gut. His throat tightened. The hounds only ever uncovered one slave market within Demarn's borders, likely because there had been a spellster using their infinitesimal amount of magic. *This* spellster.

He swallowed. "You came from Stonebay?" The same place his fallen lovers had originated from. Whilst the man could've claimed a sibling bond with a human like Wynne, Sulin's resemblance to the elven woman was undeniable. "Then you are Zinnala's brother."

Eyes that were the same hue as hers blinked slowly at him. How long had it been since the man heard another speak the woman's name? "You know Zinny? I guess that means they turned her into one of you."

"No." They had tried. Zinnala was often reprimanded for how vocal she'd been when it came to what the pack deemed as a dangerous spellster. She had never mentioned having a sibling, though. "She..." The last he'd seen of her had been in the Pit.

The wet crunch of breaking bone drifted on a memory. He could practically feel the stickiness of her fractured limb in his grasp, just as it had been when he jammed the splintered end into Hunk's eye. An act he had been praised over the ingenuity of.

He turned his face from Sulin. He couldn't tell the man his sibling had been choked to death, then used to bludgeon another until they were both broken and bloody. But still, after everything the man had been through, he deserved at least a thread of truth. "She—"

Dylan's magic flared in the distance, a roiling ocean caught in a seaward gale, rumbling with the echo of a quake. What possible reason could he have to—?

The ground trembled.

"Release me," Tracker ordered.

Sulin moved to obey, halting as Nestria levelled the man's own dagger at him.

"No," she commanded. "Not until Dylan returns." She turned her gaze on Tracker, her eyes narrowing. "Maybe not even then."

"Dylan is in danger." There was no other reason for his lover to be using so much magic. "If you do not untie me now, he may not return at all." Or worse, Dylan could be forced to lead whoever was responsible right to these people.

His lover's power continued to roil, a churning mass of flesh-prickling energy with spikes and flares piling on top of each other. He knew that magic, although he had never felt it colliding like this. Dylan was healing. Over and over, as though a new injury was being made before the old could be fixed.

Someone was toying with the man's magic and there was only one way they could possibly know how. "Now!"

The woman scoffed.

Tracker fought his bindings. The ropes bit into his skin. His shoulders objected to the strain. He jerked harder, gaining more pain with no hint of release. "I swear," he snarled at the woman. "If he dies because you kept me bound, I will hunt you down. Your last breaths will be as his."

"You see what kind of monsters they are?" Nestria demanded of the others. She pointed the *infitialis* dagger at him. "Look at how he's practically rabid. Hear how he can't help but threaten harm even as he lies to convince us to free him."

"I wasn't exactly calm when Harry was in trouble," Henrie said, tightening his hold on the human woman at his side. "Nor were you."

Sulin stood. "He speaks the truth."

"You don't know that," Nestria insisted. "This could be just another ploy. A means to keep us divided."

"And if it is not?" the man countered. "You would risk Dylan's safety?"

Her mouth moved, clearly seeking an answer. Nothing further escaped. She lowered her head, shaking it.

Sulin reclaimed his dagger from her unresisting hand. "I know that look, Ness. I saw it on Zinny's face for years. If you cannot trust his words, trust in mine."

Nestria's expression remained sceptical, but she stayed silent and made no effort to do more than hug herself as Sulin used his dagger to slice through the rope.

Tracker took stock of his weaponry as he shook off the binds. His scimitar and daggers were back at their camp, along with a great deal of the throwing knives concealed in his jerkin. He still had a handful, but that meant little until he knew what he was up against.

He turned to the guardians, many of whom were busy soothing the young. They'd few blades amongst them. None that he felt right in seizing. "Take your charges and go," he ordered. "Get across the river."

"When we've dusk approaching?" the one-handed man countered. "Crossing the Winding with this lot will be difficult enough during the day."

"I understand." Attempting any deep water with children in tow had its risks, especially for those too young to stand on their own. "And I cannot force you, but know staying could very well mean death."

The man's eyes narrowed. "It's your pack, isn't it?"

He nodded grimly.

"Hounds?" Nestria growled. She stalked towards the undergrowth. "We should go after them. Eradicate the threat."

"No." He hastened to put himself between her and the edge of the clearing, hoping she'd reason to listen before racing off into the forest.

The crackle and lash of power begging to be used snapped the immediate air around her. "If my friend truly is in danger, I will not run and cower."

"Your readiness is commendable, my dear woman, but you would so brazenly march towards a force trained to kill you without knowing their numbers?" Only the foolish or the brave dared such a move. And he'd a feeling she might be both.

"Why not? I'm responsible for plenty of deaths in your pack. More than you."

Such a claim was equally doubtful, but he hadn't the time to argue over it. "And if you lose this fight? You would leave *them* unprotected?" He gestured to the children. "Do you think Dylan would thank you if helping him got them killed?"

Her brows lowered further, her gaze darting as she considered the options. "They'll come for us anyway. Better to take the offensive."

"They do not even know you are here." Just the mere presence of Dylan's being was enough to leave a trail but, as much as he hated thinking it, the current flow of the man's power blanketed any hound from sensing usage elsewhere. "Stay and protect your kin," he ordered Nestria. "Leave mine to me."

Her lips tightened into an unflattering line. He thought she might waste more time by arguing further, but the subsiding of her magic spoke otherwise, even before she could sourly nod and step back.

Tracker risked only the barest glances towards the others, ensuring no one else had attempted to follow. Not a soul had made such a move.

He turned and raced towards their camp. *Please*, he prayed to whatever would listen. *Do not let me be too late.* He had sworn he wouldn't permit his kin to take Dylan. That was one promise he couldn't break.

CHAPTER 49

Tracker was no more than halfway to their camp when he caught sight of someone walking amongst the bushes. He ducked behind a tree, peering around it only once he could be certain they hadn't spotted him.

The being wore a dark attire that had them melting into the shadows. They strode through the undergrowth in the quiet, deliberate movements of someone not only on the hunt, but after something equally dangerous as themselves.

He followed the figure for a short distance, looking for any sign they weren't alone and creeping closer when he was certain of the fact. Without his poison vials to give the blade a recoating, he couldn't rely on his knives killing quietly from a distance.

He had a hand clapped over their mouth before they knew he was there. His knife bit into their neck as they turned, aiding in tearing open their own neck. Tracker stepped back as they fell to the ground. They clutched at the ragged hole, gurgling and wheezing as they fought to stop their life from further soaking the wet earth.

Before too long, they lay still in a puddle of their own blood.

Tracker kicked the body over, rifling through his kin's gear. The man hadn't much beyond a simple arming sword and dagger, the same sort of weapons they outfitted every newly made hound. The man didn't look old enough to have reached his second decade. Likely freshly named. *Just in time for the slaughter.*

He slid the sword free of its scabbard, testing its heft. The short blade hadn't the finesse of his scimitar, but it was sharp and well-balanced. That was all he needed. He sheathed the blade and unbuckled the man's belt to secure it around his own waist.

With a quick scan of his surroundings to ensure no more of his former kin were nearby, Tracker moved on.

The sound of horses caught his ear as he neared the site of their camp. He crept closer to the noise, circling the area through the undergrowth. A good dozen or so of the animals milled about on the western side. They stomped their forehooves and snapped at each other, as belligerent as their riders and impatient to be on their way now the spellster threat had been nullified.

Edging away from the sight, Tracker sought a sturdy tree to clamber up. So many horses meant at least as many hounds. Facing them without a plan would only end badly.

Up in the branches, he hopped from one solid limb to the other until he sat near the edge of the clearing. Peering through the foliage swaying in the breeze, he made out their tents. Marin and Katarina knelt amongst them, both bound and with blades pressed to their throats. Although they were captives, at least they lived. And with another hound keeping watch over them, it put three of them at a disadvantage.

On the far side of the clearing, Hunter and another of the hounds knelt over Dylan. Red stained the surrounding earth, but his senses told him the man lived, and was still healing despite being extremely weak.

Standing over the trio was an orange-haired figure he hadn't expected to ever see again. *Authril.* He rolled his tongue, swallowing the growl rumbling in his throat. He should have properly dealt with the warrior when he had the chance. She seemed to be boldly arguing with Hunter, knowingly or otherwise, affording Dylan a reprieve.

His lover struggled, though. Tracker had felt it as he closed, the sluggishness in response to each new injury. As powerful as the man was, his strength wasn't infinite.

Finally gesturing for Authril to be silent, Hunter raised her knife, preparing to resume her torture.

Tracker hesitated, torn between keeping the element of surprise and stopping her from hurting the man further, then flung one of his knives at her.

The man holding Dylan down lifted his head at the wrong moment and bore the full force of the throw right through his ear.

Hunter jerked back as her fellow hound slumped over. She surveyed the surrounding trees, smirking. "So nice of you to finally join us, One-four."

Tracker remained still. Being human, she might not see him amongst the leaves, but there were others down there besides Authril who were also of elven descent. Although he spied only a couple of his former kin with bows nocked and ready to draw, most of the pack had some form of ranged weaponry.

"There!" yelled Hawker, his gravelly voice one Tracker hadn't heard in a long time. He wouldn't have marked the man as willing to slaughter innocent people, either.

An arrow flew by his head, the breeze of its travel ghosting along his ear. He answered the attempt on his life with a knife to the man's throat.

Knowing he'd been caught and would only find himself bailed into a corner if he remained in one place, he hopped a tree over. The branches creaked ever so slightly as he moved amongst them. Arrows followed his passage, catching on the leaves and branches. He would deal with them soon enough. Right now, he needed to give Dylan a chance to finish healing and regain even a sliver of strength. If he could stall until sunset, all the better.

~ ~ ~

Pain.

It was all Dylan's mind could focus on. He had screamed his throat raw, even his magic couldn't take away the prickling hotness. His chest ached with every breath. His clothes stuck to his skin, tacky with sweat and worse.

Blood filled his senses. He smelt the metallic tang on the air, tasted it in the back of his throat.

Between his panting and the blinding agony, he became aware of no longer being pinned to the ground. A figure lay beside him, a throwing knife embedded in the side of their skull. Their glassy gaze stared back, shock still plastered on their face.

Track? A dead hound had to mean the man was here.

Dylan risked pushing himself upright, refusing to acknowledge the sticky dampness of the earth. Everything still ached. Both magic and body all but wrung of strength in keeping him alive. The breeze was too cold, too bitter. He shook through to his core.

Over the drum of his heartbeat pounding in his ears, he caught the soft sound of something darting through the air, followed by a body collapsing.

The woman who had so viciously sliced at him crouched nearby, her attention on the tree canopy. "Cowering in the treetops like a dwarf, One-four? How very unlike you." She cocked her head, listening.

If she expected an answer, none was forthcoming.

Clicking her tongue like a disapproving guardian, she gestured to a couple of her fellow hounds, who saluted and disappeared into the forest. "Perhaps starting on one of your other companions will stir you into action."

"No," Dylan pleaded. He groped along the ground, seeking the woman's boot. Without his healing, they would die.

She merely kicked his hand aside.

There was a rustle in the tree canopy. Like everyone else, Dylan peered up at the thick foliage, trying to spot the man. A few hounds loosed arrows into the leaves. Not a one of them hit.

"Halt!" the woman roared. "Do not waste your advantage on shadows."

Tracker dropped from high above, rolling across the ground as he landed. His sword flashed before he stood, the clang of it striking away a throwing knife echoing through the clearing. One of the man's knives sailed back in answer, barely missing slamming into his target's eye.

Dylan sought to put a shield around his lover. It formed thinly, crumbling seconds after an arrow shattered against the surface. The chill gnawing at his bones dug its fangs into his chest.

The woman whirled to face him, her hand swinging before she had finished turning. The back of it hit Dylan's cheek, throwing him onto the ground. "You will stay down, or you will be dead."

Dylan did as commanded. He had no choice. His latent healing sucked at his remaining strength, soothing his stinging cheek as the cold inched itself further into his core. If he used much more, then the hounds wouldn't need to concern themselves with doing him in.

A pain-soaked scream had his attention snapping to where Tracker fought his kin. Like mousers encountering an unknown in the courtyard, the hounds had piled onto Tracker. And he fought them with everything he had.

But now, the hounds reeled back. One of them clutched at the side of his neck. Red spurted between his fingers. "He has gone feral," the man declared.

Tracker stood in the middle of the throng. Blood dripped down his lover's chin as, withdrawing his dagger, he bared his teeth at the others and gestured for them to come closer. Two hounds lay at his feet, one with their head barely attached, whilst the other was impaled on a sword.

The man he had bitten stumbled even further back. He tripped over his own feet and fell onto his side, still fumbling to keep the wound from leaking his life all over the forest floor.

The remaining four who faced Tracker hedged around him, none of them willing to risk becoming the next corpse.

One of the pair overseeing Marin and Katarina raised her bow. She loosed the arrow.

Tracker snatched it from the air.

A whip lashed around the limb, the man at the other end holding it tight. One of the human men, a being easily twice Tracker's bulk, tackled him. They rolled across the ground, exchanging blows. The rest of the hounds fell upon Tracker. He fought as much as he could, but was ultimately overpowered and bound.

The man who had tackled him delivered several blows to his pinned opponent, one striking him across the jaw.

The pale, frizzy-haired human man of the group snorted as his comrade stepped back. "Almost seems a shame to knock in that pretty face."

Tracker laughed. It was a low, dark sound, one that left Dylan's neck feeling oddly exposed. "You aim to flatter me, Seeker?" The grin he flashed the other man was a touch manic. The way he spoke, the hushed threatening note rolling through the words, sent a far too pleasant shiver down Dylan's back. The blood coating his teeth didn't help. "I will take the compliment, but you are not my type."

A snigger came from a nearby elven woman. She nudged Seeker in the ribs with her elbow and cupped her fingers over her mouth as if she was about to whisper, but her words came loud enough. "As if that would stop our little whore."

Seeker examined Dylan, his dark eyes piggish and a sickly yellow where they should've been white. "This one has the look of being brought in on your dick. Or did you let this one pound you sore, too?" The man leered at Tracker. "That *is* how you hunt, yes? By allowing everything under the sun to crawl up where it does not shine?"

Tracker wrinkled his nose as if the duo had wriggled out of a midden heap. "You are merely jealous that no one wishes to sleep with that ugly mug. Or was that meant to be an insult? Sniffer taught you better than that, yes?"

"That sad sack of manure?" spat the man with the whip. "He was the first one to back out of our orders. Fell on his own sword to keep us from having the pleasure."

"You should have done the world a favour and followed suit," Tracker sneered.

"Pretty words from a dead man," purred the woman who had tortured Dylan. "I mean really?" Her lips curved into a small, and decidedly unpleasant, smile. "All this over a spellster?"

Growling, Tracker bared his teeth.

With everyone's attention on the man, Dylan fought to stand. He didn't know what he could possibly do against so many with his magic consumed from healing him. He knew only that he couldn't just lay here.

Authril grabbed him the second he got to his knees, forcing him back onto all fours. He struggled, but it only served to have her hold tighten. "I have to stop them," he pleaded with her. He knew the warrior didn't get on with Tracker, but surely she wasn't about to let him die.

"Keep out of this, spellster," the hound growled, momentarily turning her cool gaze on him. "Or the next stab you get will be your heart."

He bit the inside of his cheek, craning his neck to watch her approach Tracker.

She halted a few feet from him. "I thought you, of all people, would not dare risk this again. Was your last lesson not enough, One-four?"

"My name is *Tracker*," his lover snarled. "You know this well enough."

The woman sneered. "You are a disgrace to the name you were given. You would spill the blood of your kin to keep *this* safe?" She levelled her blade in Dylan's direction, the edge still dripping red. "You choose that wretch over the pack?"

"Better spilling the blood of murderers than that of the innocent."

"They were *spellsters*. They had not an innocent bone in their bodies."

Tracker laughed. "If *that* is not the knife calling the dagger sharp. We all know how much you like your prey to suffer. Tell me, my dear Hunter." He spat on the ground before her boots, the resulting gob far too red for Dylan's liking. Hopefully, none of it was the man's. "Do you enjoy sitting at the foot of your new master? Enough to lavish in murdering children? Infants?"

The woman halted before Tracker. She grabbed a fistful of the man's hair, craning his neck back. The knife in her other hand flashed to Tracker's throat, the edge stopping short of slicing. "I *did*." The dagger tip pressed against his neck, drawing a thin line across the bronze skin. "Just like I will enjoy taking you apart."

Tracker's smile broadened. "I know you are inexperienced in it, my dear Hunter, but there are easier ways to access my throat without slitting it open."

"When I am done, you will beg for a simple slit throat." With her fingers still entwined in his hair, Hunter forced the man's body to one side. "Disobedient dogs like you always got off far too easily."

"I assure you," Tracker snarled, wrenching himself free of her grasp. "There is no chance of you getting me off in the slightest." He spat in her face.

She straightened, wiping the spit from her cheek, and laughed. The sound lifted the hairs on the nape of Dylan's neck.

With no change of expression, Hunter slammed her fist into Tracker's stomach, watching as he crumpled in the men's grip, gasping.

Tracker was hauled upright. One of the hounds holding him muttered something to the man, the words too quiet for Dylan to make out. It didn't seem to make much difference as his lover slid to the ground.

"You are so wet," Hunter said as she bent over Tracker. She shook her head, the tail of her blonde hair flicking over her shoulder. The woman drew her dagger and grabbed Tracker's braid. "Hold him steady."

She needn't have given the order. Tracker remained on his side, silent, barely moving. Shock froze his face. He stared straight ahead, not even blinking away the huge droplets falling from his open eyes.

The hilt of a knife jutted from his gut. Fresh red spread across his undershirt.

No! Magic surged through Dylan's body. It crackled through his blood, rumbled deep within his bones. The cold in his core ploughed along his veins, seeking every scrap he had left to give.

The world abruptly turned dim.

He clutched at his neck. The icy-cold touch of metal seeped into his skin. His fingers brushed up against a chain. He didn't need to see the colour. The numbness seeping into his bones told him all he needed to know.

Dylan struggled to get a grip on his power. He clawed at the chain, his fingers hooking behind the metal, desperately seeking further purchase. Nothing. Tracker swore he could remove the collars, so there had to be a way to part the links. Some sort of trick.

"Be still and do as I say," Authril hissed into his ear. She fiddled with the back of the chain, tugging it as she worked. "That's the only way any of us make it out of this."

Not all. His gaze slid to Marin and Katarina. Like Tracker's inert form, they remained bound. But despite Hunter's threats, they were in no worse a state than they'd been when he arrived.

Authril was right. Putting down a rogue hound was expected of the pack. If he challenged it, they might turn on the pair, use them as tools to humble him as they'd done with Tracker.

He turned his tearful gaze back to where his lover's body lay in time to see Hunter step back. The full length of Tracker's braided russet hair dangled from her hand.

And still, the man lay unresponsive at her feet.

"Why are you just standing there?" Hunter demanded of the remaining hounds. "Ready the horses. I want to be far from here before the sun sets."

The rest of the hounds jumped into action. They brought several horses forward, draping Marin and Katarina across the saddles, the former fighting the manhandling all the way.

The whole time, Dylan stared unblinkingly at his lover, willing with all his might for a sign—a twitch, *anything*—that the man still lived.

Only when his sight began to blur and burn did he concede Tracker wasn't getting back up. He sagged against Authril, unable to muster the smallest spark of resistance when the time came for him to be hoisted upon a mount. They had been so close. The ford, their path to freedom, had been within reach.

His friends, his guardian, were still there, waiting for his return. He had only just found them. He couldn't lose them again, couldn't risk the hounds catching their scent.

There was but one path left for him, the one Authril's presence afforded. He felt the chain around his neck, inching along the links. It wasn't a proper collar, which meant they would need to remove it if Authril ever wanted to make use of him in the army.

He would bide his time, obey their orders. And when they finally unleashed him, he'd set the whole damn place ablaze. He would avenge the tower. His friends. His family.

And reunite with his love.

CHAPTER 50

Searing cold blazed through Tracker's veins. His lungs screamed, straining for air. He danced on the edge of darkness, struggling to stay awake. His eyes refused to open, but he was pretty sure he lay face down in the mud. He might as well have been trying to breathe underwater.

Silence surrounded him. He didn't know how long he'd been lying here, only that he had been left to face death alone. The iciness radiating from the stab wound told him what his fate would be. Its numbing touch edged across his flesh, an emptiness that gave the paralytic its name.

The void.

Of all the poisons he had been schooled on, never had he used this one. It was slow, practically torture. Victims often suffocated long before their hearts seized in their chests. He'd an antidote, a catch-all elixir that would flush the toxin from his blood. It sat in the same pouch as his poisons and oils.

He also knew he'd never reach it. Extremities were the first thing to freeze and, already, his limbs refused to obey.

And Dylan? Like his failing body, he couldn't feel his lover anymore. The impression of magic was all around, but stale. Dead. *Forgive me, darling.*

His breathing grew shallower. The darkness closing in on his mind steadily engulfed his thoughts. It promised emptiness. An end to pain, to sorrow.

Air finally hit his lungs, uninhibited, blissful and sweet. He fought for every gulp, his body struggling against the numbness binding it.

Voices buzzed around him, indecipherable murmurs. Magic bloomed to life, a pinpoint of focus in the mist. Flickering light gleamed on the other side of his eyelids. He clawed his way towards it, fighting to speak. Just enough to let them know his vials were nearby.

His own body refused to heed him. Words were beyond him. He struggled to breathe. He couldn't even open his eyes to let them know he lived.

Exacerbated by his attempts, the poison's icy touch crept up his chest.

Panic gripped his throat. His heart thundered. Each laboured breath had his stomach dropping into the encroaching void. He couldn't let it take him. Not here.

Darkness sucked at his mind, a suffocating sludge that obliterated even the smallest of thoughts.

He drifted. The world around him was nothing but inky blackness, but he knew the rocking, buoyant sensation of being cradled by water. Warm wavelets sloshed against his face, the current pulling him ever further along.

I must be dead. The priests spoke of an afterlife like this, the river through the tunnels, where he would be judged and move on or given an eternal sentence. The idea of floating through the endless black had sounded terrifying as a child, but the silence was oddly peaceful. He closed his eyes, or at least attempted it.

Something brushed against his arm. He jerked back on instinct.

"You forgot us," a voice hissed accusingly in the dark. One he hadn't heard outside of his nightmares for years.

Zinny... If this was the afterlife, if she had ever passed through, she would've been long gone, not stuck waiting in the dark for him.

"You abandoned us," whispered another—Wynne, he was sure of it—their chill breath dancing along his ear.

"No. No, I did n—"

Hands grabbed hold of him, dragging him beneath the surface. They clung like seaweed. He flailed his arms, clawing at the water to keep his head above the waves. Their grip tightened, pulling him down until he sank into the cold depths of oblivion.

He resurfaced to the thrum of rain atop stretched canvas and the distant chatter of young voices. The icy heat scorching through his body had subsided, although the ache in his blood persisted, along with a sharper pain in his side that bit deeper with every breath.

Muted light danced across his eyelids. He cracked an eye, idly observing his surroundings. This was the inside of a tent. *His* tent, specifically. *Not dead, then.*

"Welcome back."

He blinked slowly, taking in the figure kneeling at his side. Dylan's guardian. The last he saw of the woman, he had ordered her to cross the river. "I see where he got his stubbornness from."

"Feeling well enough to crack jokes already?" She pressed something cool against his side. "You lot truly do heal at a remarkable rate."

Steeling himself, he uttered the question his heart desperately needed the answer to. "Where is Dylan?" His hound senses told him there was ample magic around them. None of it was the stormy aroma he had grown accustomed to being nearby. That lack meant his lover was taken or dead. Either way, he had failed.

Her lips gave the smallest grim twitch, dashing his hopes before a word could pass them. "They took him."

Not dead. The tightness in his chest didn't let up. The pack letting the man live meant they'd a use for him.

He sat up, clenching his teeth against the pain. His hair swung forward as he bent upon himself, tickling his ears and pebbling his skin. Carefully gathering the curls at the nape of his neck, he became aware of a distinct lack of weight. *My hair...*

Tears welled in his eyes as he felt for the braid and found nothing. It was gone, sheared off just below his shoulders. *All that length.* The decades of growth and careful maintenance, they'd just... hacked it off. The only part of his body he'd ever had control over and they *took* it! Claimed it like a damn trophy!

Hunter. She was the only one who had the sick practice of collecting souvenirs from her targets and an unhealthy obsession with his hair. He would repay her for the violation, amongst other things.

Dylan. He was in her presence, his life hinged entirely on her mood.

He dried his face. There was nothing he could do about his hair except start again. He couldn't let it affect him. Not now. Not when they'd taken something far more precious, and utterly irreplaceable. "How long was I unconscious?"

"A day. Which is why you should be still and let yourself mend."

And let Dylan slip further from his grasp in the meantime? Shaking his head, he flung the blankets aside to discover he was mostly naked. At least those tending to his injuries had permitted him his smallclothes. "You should be across the river by now." He would've believed only Tricia had chosen to stay behind, if there weren't far too many voices and magic beyond the canvas walls to suggest otherwise.

"If we had followed that order, you'd be dead."

"Perhaps," he conceded. He didn't know if the woman was aware of precisely what that blade had been coated in, but someone had known it to be deadly. "But in staying put, you risked far more lives. You are fortunate Dylan's magic cloaked their presence from the pack." Even now, he felt the distant dregs of the man's frenzied healing thrumming over the latent power milling around him.

Growling, he rummaged around the tent for a scrap of leather to bind what was left of his hair. With the curls out of the way, Tracker hauled on his trousers and boots before pushing the tent flap aside.

He halted just outside. Both tents had been moved to the spellsters' little river-side camp. The one Marin had made of hides was now splayed out to protect as many as it could reasonably shelter, mostly the children. Those beneath it watched him warily, their gaze lacking the outright terror such looks bore only yesterday.

Of the older folk, most of them—spellsters and guardians both— milled near the river where they were building some sort of structure. Precisely what they aimed to build eluded him, but they'd already gathered a number of logs.

A single horse stood tied up beneath the trees. It looked more akin to one a messenger might ride than any of the King's Hounds, suited to get a person somewhere fast rather than be solid enough to fight alongside its rider. Yet the saddle, with its thick straps draping at the flank, suggested it was meant to carry some big loads.

He said nothing about either people or animal, merely permitting his senses to draw him back to the site of his failure.

In due time, another set of footsteps hastened to follow him across the sodden ground. He glanced back to find Tricia shadowing him. Her expression set into one that suggested he dare not argue about the company, so he merely turned his back on her and continued on.

The scent of old ash hit him long before he saw what remained of the pyre. He halted before it, his skin prickling. A charred skull, half-buried amongst the ash, stared accusingly at him. Despite what the guardian had said, his stomach still dropped at the sight. Even dead, Dylan's remains would carry traces of his power and the pyre was soaked in magic.

The guardian's footsteps stopped a few feet behind him.

"Are you sure they took him?" he asked of the woman. All his life, he'd been taught that burial wasn't an option for spellsters. Having witnessed some come back from the brink of death, he understood the reason behind such precautions.

"He wasn't amongst the dead. We made sure of that before we burnt them."

That partially answered a few other questions buzzing about his mind. "We were travelling with two others." Dylan had mentioned returning to their camp for Marin and Katarina, but he hadn't seen either woman amongst the spellsters. "A hedgewitch—"

"—and her apprentice," Tricia finished, nodding. "We found belongings in the other tent that must've been theirs—a book and findings of a forge, I believe—but not them."

Tracker nodded, recalling seeing the tome from the tower whilst hunting for a leather thong. He hadn't noticed the forge papers, but he supposed they'd been with the book. The lack of bodies suggested they still lived. Given that Katarina wouldn't leave her work behind without coercion, they were likely being used as hostages or leverage to keep Dylan compliant.

He gestured to the pyre. "How many?" There'd been the one whose sword he had stolen out in the undergrowth, and the two who had fallen to Dylan's rage before Tracker reached their camp, as well as Slayer's unfortunate luck in lifting his head in the same moment Tracker aimed for Hunter. He had taken out Hawker swiftly enough and landed several blows before being subdued, but that didn't mean his every hit had been fatal.

"What?" Tricia asked.

"You helped put them on the pyre, yes?" His count yesterday had picked out a rough handful of guardians and he couldn't imagine them asking for the spellsters to assist beyond starting the fire. "How many hounds did you burn?"

She shrugged. "Five? Six? Maybe more. We weren't exactly focused on counting them. What does it matter?"

"Before our unfortunate collision, there were only thirty left." Fetcher had said half the pack went to chase spellsters eastward. This group could've been them, especially if they'd been on horseback. If he was going to free Dylan, he needed to know what sort of odds he could be facing.

Falling to his knees, Tracker pawed through the debris. Pieces of familiar armour—hound armour—surfaced, buckles warped by heat and metal panels that would've once been hidden inside leather.

He burrowed deeper, upending blackened bones, sending skulls tumbling to the bottom of the pile. The tightness in his chest remained until he knew not a single bone held even a whiff of magic.

Dusting the soot from his hands, he carefully lined up the skulls. *Eight.* All but one of them were human. The other was a half-elf, judging by the length of their fangs.

That still left twenty-one of his former kin to face if they reached the capital.

He lurched to his feet, stumbling as his body objected. Backtracking to where he had fallen told him nothing new. The surrounding footprints were a mess, the rain having smoothed out their edges. The spot where Dylan had lain beneath the oak tree, soaked in his blood, held a little more promise.

Amongst the residue of the man's magic sat several pairs of footsteps showing signs of something heavy being carried to where the horses once stood. A living person or a corpse, it was all the same.

"Was he leashed?"

She shook her head. "By the time we came, they were gone. All I know is there were only hounds amongst the dead."

He laid a hand on the area as though doing so would help him piece together what had happened. He'd been near the edge of consciousness. Dylan had called out. His magic had been bright and vengeful, roiling like the sea.

Then gone. Snuffed.

There was only one thing beyond death that could end a spellster's tirade before it could begin. *Infitialis.*

Whatever they had done couldn't have been a proper leashing. That required an alchemist or, at the very least, a spellster with the expertise of keeping the metal from exploding. He felt no remnants of another's magic and knew Hunter well enough to know she wouldn't tow around such a spellster on the off chance of needing them.

But a chain, a simple band not fully wrought, would hold even Dylan's might. And if he was being contained, then perhaps Authril had managed to convince the other hounds to hand the man's fate over to her. Permitting the kingdom's last spellster to die in service to the army sounded like something Hunter would delight in.

Which meant he had time. To find Dylan. To *free* him. More importantly, he'd a place to start looking.

He stalked back towards the spellster camp. He'd need to travel light, essentials only. And perhaps the hedgewitch's records. He would miss the tent, but he could bundle himself in his cloak easily enough.

Making any sort of approach without weapons was a different matter and one that could too easily end with his former comrades finishing the job of killing him. But if the guardians had collected enough from the camp to have the hedgewitch's notes, then his scimitar and daggers were likely amongst their gear.

Some of the older children had stepped beyond the tent cover by the time Tricia and himself returned. They froze upon seeing him, hesitating in their actions. The shield of one stuttered around the poor boy.

Tracker waved for them to carry on with their tasks. He wouldn't be long here, he couldn't.

He made his way to the structure. Closer, he recognised the array of logs as the base for a wall, or a crude raft. People swarmed over it like wasps, adjusting the position of the logs, propping one end up to lash it to another piece.

Nestria worked amongst the group, as did the rest of Dylan's friends. She stood as he neared, holding his gaze. The hardness in her eyes remained, although the angle of her brows suggested a measure of uncertainty. Her lips parted.

Tracker squared his shoulders, ready for a repeat of yesterday's accusations. The act twinged his side, and he reflexively put a hand to the wound.

Pink bloomed across her pale face. She bit her lip, swallowing whatever words lingered on her tongue, and turned back to the raft.

On the far side, tucked beneath a bowing branch, Sulin sat hunched over a pile of weapons. With Dylan so close, the man's magic might as well have been nonexistent, but the haze of iron and the tang of smelted metal hung around him. He spoke with one of the guardians, nodding as the woman talked.

The alchemist selected a sword from the pile as Tracker neared. The length of steel sagged in his grip, moulding into a saw, complete with a handhold that didn't look too comfortable to grip without some sort of padding.

Sulin wordlessly handed over the newly made saw to the guardian, who nodded and strode over to a selection of smaller logs resting near the raft.

Tracker nudged the rest of the weapons with the toe of his boot. For the most part, the pile was comprised of swords and daggers. One of the former had been scorched with immense heat and sang of Dylan's magic. His scimitar was easy enough to pick out from the pile and Tracker swiftly reclaimed it before it fell into Sulin's hands.

A razor whip also sat amongst the blades. That would've belonged to Lasher, who was only slightly less cruel than Hunter when it came to dispatching his targets. That put a name to the half-elven skull. He didn't recall fighting the man. He must've been one that Dylan had dispatched.

The quarterstaff he had bought back in Whitemeadow caught his eye. He pulled it from the pile. Being mostly wood, there didn't seem like much the alchemist could do with it. "Do any of you know how to use this?" he asked the group surrounding the raft.

"I do," replied the one-handed man, lowering the axe he'd been swinging to hew the notches. "Although, that was some time, and two hands, ago."

Tracker eyed the man. His accent was more in line with the nomadic elves than any Demarner he had met, even those on the northern border. His garb also wasn't the same as most of the guardians. "You are far from your home."

The man frowned. "The tower was my home, until the overseers took away my reason to obey their laws. Then, it became my prison." His eyes hardened as he snatched the staff from Tracker's grasp and tested its weight. "I can do some damage with this."

A little more rummaging brought up his sword belt. Two of the daggers—both his own and the jewel-tipped one of Whisper's—still sat in their sheaths. The *infitialis* blade was nowhere to be found. "Where is the other?" he enquired of Sulin, tapping the empty spot.

The alchemist side-eyed him as though Tracker had committed some personal offence. His hand drifted to his own belt, where two daggers nestled against the leather. "This blade was not yours to have."

"As I explained to your friend, the original owner attempted to kill me with it."

"Why do you want it back? I assume you plan to head after them. It is only a simple dagger against your kind."

He nodded his agreement. The blade hummed enough that he had already gathered the same magic that let the collars work was used to give the daggers their infamous edge. "That may be true, but the one who sent my former kin to your door is an ordinary man." He may be the king's nephew, but that didn't make him any less human. "And I promised Dylan I would help avenge your people."

Sulin's gaze remained unwavering for several breaths. Then, he withdrew the second *infitialis* dagger. "Let it drink deep," he said, handing the weapon over.

"I intend to."

Fully kitted, he returned to his tent and busied himself with packing as little as he could get away with. He stashed the tome at the bottom, along with the papers on the hidden dwarven forge, in the chance he encountered Katarina. Or one of the merchant ships headed for Dvärghem.

With his pack the lightest it had ever been, he made his way to the horse. He'd been of a mind to try his luck in negotiating passage with a merchant convoy, but seeing the guardians planned to ferry their charges across the river via raft, he had fewer reservations about taking the animal for his own needs.

The horse nickered good-naturedly as he neared, blowing its grassy breath into his face. The scent brought on a pang of longing for his old warhorse. This animal was no Lullaby, but it would hopefully be as steadfast.

He secured his pack to the saddle and tested the gear. As aged as it looked, the leather was still in good shape. Someone had given it a lot of care. The same could be said of the horse. Just where had the hounds gotten the extra mount? Had they paid for it? Or had it been the sole survivor of some unfortunate rider?

Sighing, he bent to check the animal's hooves. How the horse came to be here didn't matter. He'd no way of finding out who owned it, nor was he willing to waste time in doing so.

"What are you doing?" Tricia demanded.

"I must leave." The hounds had travelled on horseback and he was already a day behind. If he left now, pushed the horse to travel faster and for longer than a group could logically manage, he might catch up to them before they entered Wintervale.

"You are in no state to travel, especially not via horseback." Tricia grabbed his arm and attempted to guide him back to the tent. "What you must do is rest."

Growling, he jerked out of her grasp, gritting his teeth against the twinge in his side. "They have Dylan. I do not have *time* to rest."

"You don't even know where he is."

"I do." It was a place he hadn't been in fourteen years. A place where his last attempt to save his beloveds had ended in failure.

Not again. He would snatch Dylan from their claws, avenge the tower and flee this kingdom with his lover in tow. He *would*.

I am coming for you, darling. And he'd destroy anything that tried to stand in his way.

About the Author

Aldrea Alien is a bisexual, New Zealand author of romantic speculative fiction of varying heat levels.

She grew up on a small farm out the back blocks of a place known as Wainuiomata alongside a menagerie of animals, who are all convinced they're just as human as the next person (especially the cats). She spent a great deal of her childhood riding horses, whilst the rest of her time was consumed with reading every fantasy book she could get her hands on and concocting ideas about a little planet known as Thardrandia. This would prove to be the start of The Rogue King Saga as, come her twelfth year, she discovered there was a book inside her.

Aldrea now lives in Upper Hutt, on yet another small farm with a less hectic, but still egotistical, group of animals (cats will be cats), and published the first of The Rogue King Saga in 2014. One thing she hasn't yet found is an off switch to give her an ounce of peace from the characters plaguing her mind, a list that grows bigger every year with all of them clamouring for her to tell their story first. It's a lot of people for one head.

aldreaalien.com